Y0-BRR-463

CRIPPLED SPLENDOUR

CRIPPLED SPLENDOUR

A Novel by

EVAN JOHN

1938

E. P. DUTTON & CO., INC.

NEW YORK

PRINTED IN U. S. A.

FIRST PRINTING . . . SEPTEMBER, 1938
SECOND PRINTING . . SEPTEMBER, 1938
THIRD PRINTING . . . SEPTEMBER, 1938
FOURTH PRINTING . . SEPTEMBER, 1938
FIFTH PRINTING . . . SEPTEMBER, 1938
SIXTH PRINTING . . . SEPTEMBER, 1938
SEVENTH PRINTING . . SEPTEMBER, 1938
EIGHTH PRINTING . . SEPTEMBER, 1938
NINTH PRINTING . . . SEPTEMBER, 1938

DEDICATED TO THE MEMORY OF JAMES STEWART
FIRST OF THAT NAME TO RULE IN SCOTLAND
COMPANION-IN-ARMS TO HENRY THE FIFTH
PRISONER POET MUSICIAN SOLDIER
LAW-GIVER LOVER AND KING
OF WHOSE STRANGE LIFE
AND TERRIBLE DEATH
THE TALE IS HERE
RE-TOLD

Author's Note

OF THE CHARACTERS in this book, those to whom no name is given are mostly imaginary. But all those who are mentioned by name represent actual, historical persons, who either might have been—or actually were—present on the occasions described. Of some, little or nothing is known beyond the names. Others occupy a large place in the somewhat scanty records of their times, and to these (though their motives and characters must remain largely a matter of conjecture) I have tried to avoid imputing any major action for which I cannot find warrant in contemporary State Papers or the chroniclers of the fifteenth and early sixteenth century. Where their actual words (or poems) are on record, I have taken the liberty of translating them, from Latin, French, or Mediaeval English, into a more modern idiom.

Contents

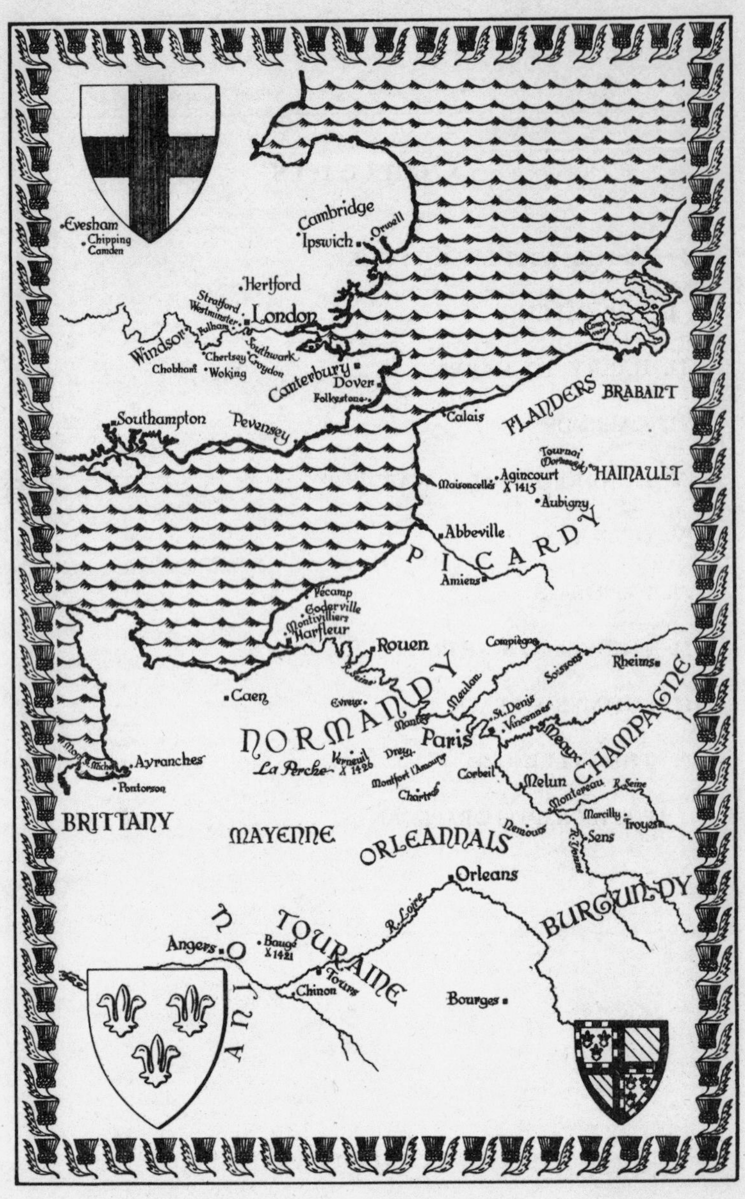
Evesham
Chipping Camden
Cambridge
Ipswich
Orwell
Hertford
Stratford
Westminster
London
Windsor
Fulham
Southwark
Chertsey
Croydon
Chobham
Woking
Canterbury
Dover
Folkestone
Southampton
Pevensey
Calais
FLANDERS
BRABANT
HAINAULT
Agincourt X 1415
Maisoncelles
Aubigny
Abbeville
PICARDY
Amiens
Fecamp
Goderville
Montivilliers
Harfleur
Rouen
Compiègne
Rheims
Soissons
R. Seine
NORMANDY
Caen
Evreux
Meulan
Mantes
St. Denis
Vincennes
Paris
Meaux
CHAMPAGNE
Verneuil X 1426
La Perche
Dreux
Montfort l'Amaury
Chartres
Corbeil
Melun
Montereau
R. Seine
Avranches
Pontorson
BRITTANY
MAYENNE
ORLEANNAIS
Nemours
Marcilly
Troyes
Sens
Orleans
BURGUNDY
R. Loire
ANJOU
TOURAINE
Angers
Baugé X 1421
Tours
Chinon
Bourges

Cape Wrath
Freswick
STRATHNAVER
CAITHNESS
LEWIS
Stornoway
SUTHERLAND
Dornoch
Tain
ROSS
Dingwall
The Black Isle
Elgin
Pluscarden
Nairn
Cawdor
Inverness
BUCHAN
Bennachie
LOCHABER
Dundreggan
Daviot
Moy
Lochindorb
The Highland Line
Harlaw
X 1411
Aberdeen
SKYE
The Great Glen
Loch Ness
Abertarff
Cullachy
BADENOCH
R. Spey
Clan Chattan
Kingussie
Ben Screel
Dalwhinnie
KINCARDINE
Clan
Inverlochy
Cameron
ARDNAMURCHAN
Brechin
Dunkeld
ANGUS
Lunan Bay
R. Tay
Loch Tay
Killin
Scone
Perth
Tyndrum
IONA
MULL
Crianlarich
Ardvorlich
Crieff
STRATHEARN
Lindores
St. Andrews
Cameron
Callender
Falkland
Ochil Hills
Lomond Hills
COLONSAY
LORNE
Loch Awe
Dunblane
FIFE
Dunfermline
Kirkcaldy
Stirling
Falkirk
Fintry
Inchcolm
Bass Rock
Dumbarton
Leith
White Kirk
Linlithgow
Dalmeny
Edinburgh
Dunbar
Coldingham
JURA
ISLAY
Paisley
Glasgow
Largs
X1263
Pentland Hills
Dalkeith
Berwick
Coldstream
LOTHIAN
Kintyre
LANARK
Kelso
ARRAN
Goat Fell
Dundonald
R. Tweed
Crookham
Flodden
X 1513
Melrose
Piperden
X 1435
Roxburgh
Homildon
X 1402
The Cheviot
Ayr
Douglas
Crawick
CARRICK
Otterburn
X 1388
IRELAND
DUMFRIES
Caerlaverock
GALLOWAY
Newcastle
Carlisle
Durham
ANTRIM

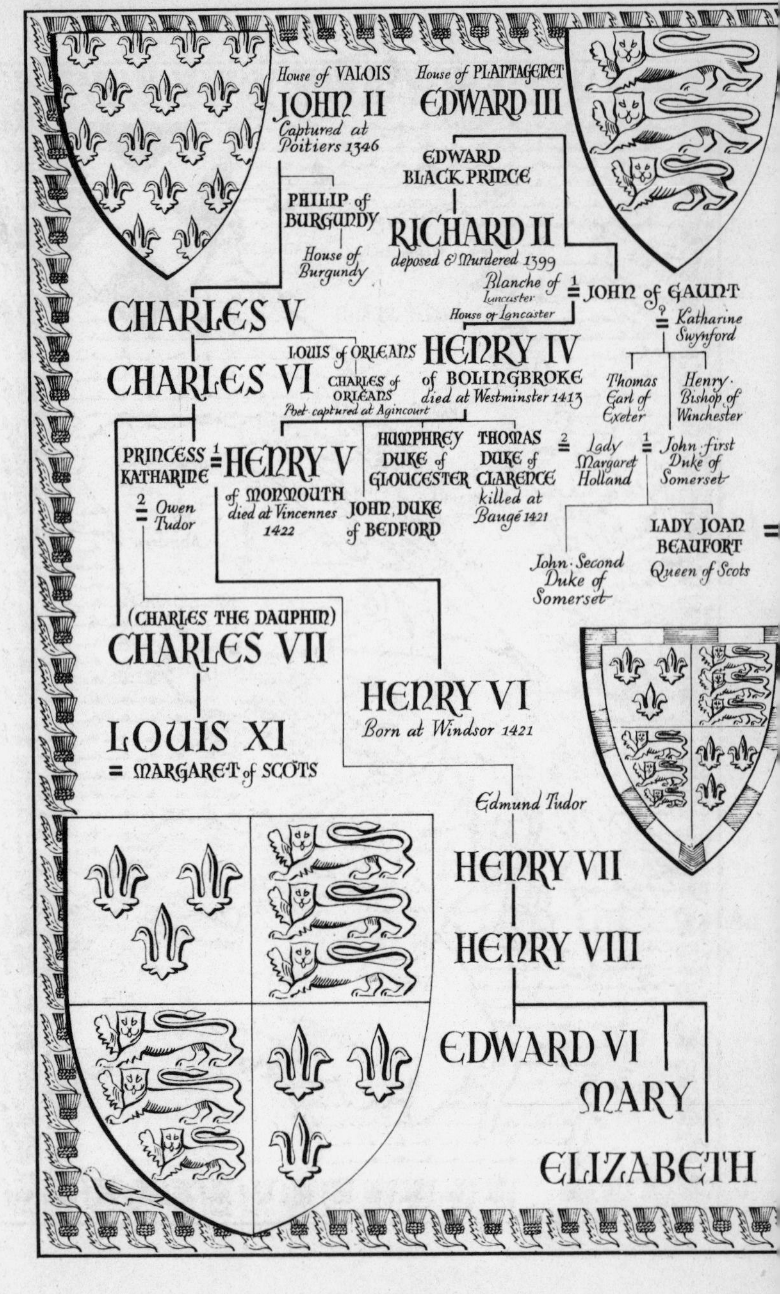
House of VALOIS
JOHN II
Captured at Poitiers 1346
House of PLANTAGENET
EDWARD III
EDWARD BLACK PRINCE
PHILIP of BURGUNDY
House of Burgundy
RICHARD II
deposed & Murdered 1399
Blanche of Lancaster
House of Lancaster
1
JOHN of GAUNT
2
Katharine Swynford
CHARLES V
LOUIS of ORLEANS
HENRY IV
of BOLINGBROKE
died at Westminster 1413
CHARLES VI
CHARLES of ORLEANS
Poet captured at Agincourt
Thomas Earl of Exeter
Henry. Bishop of Winchester
PRINCESS KATHARINE
1
HENRY V
of MONMOUTH
died at Vincennes 1422
2
Owen Tudor
HUMPHREY DUKE of GLOUCESTER
THOMAS DUKE of CLARENCE
killed at Baugé 1421
JOHN, DUKE of BEDFORD
2
Lady Margaret Holland
1
John first Duke of Somerset
LADY JOAN BEAUFORT
Queen of Scots
John. Second Duke of Somerset
(CHARLES THE DAUPHIN)
CHARLES VII
HENRY VI
Born at Windsor 1421
LOUIS XI
= MARGARET of SCOTS
Edmund Tudor
HENRY VII
HENRY VIII
EDWARD VI
MARY
ELIZABETH

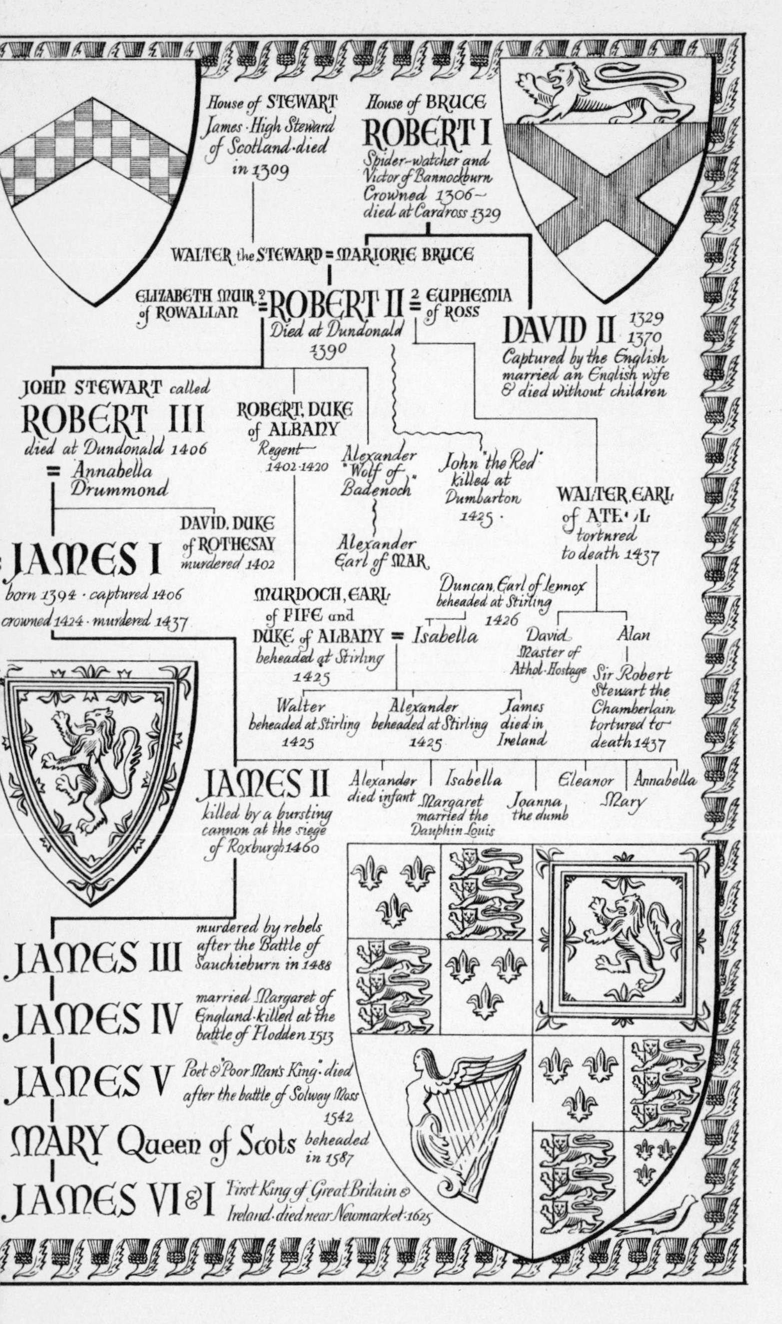

House of STEWART
James · High Steward of Scotland · died in 1309
House of BRUCE
ROBERT I
Spider-watcher and Victor of Bannockburn Crowned 1306 – died at Cardross 1329
WALTER the STEWARD = MARJORIE BRUCE
ELIZABETH MUIR of ROWALLAN 2 = ROBERT II 2 = EUPHEMIA of ROSS
Died at Dundonald 1390
DAVID II 1329 1370
Captured by the English married an English wife & died without children
JOHN STEWART called
ROBERT III
died at Dundonald 1406
= Annabella Drummond
ROBERT, DUKE of ALBANY
Regent 1402-1420
Alexander "Wolf of Badenoch"
Alexander Earl of MAR
John "the Red" killed at Dumbarton 1425
WALTER, EARL of ATE L
tortured to death 1437
DAVID, DUKE of ROTHESAY
murdered 1402
JAMES I
born 1394 · captured 1406
crowned 1424 · murdered 1437
MURDOCH, EARL of FIFE and DUKE of ALBANY = Isabella
beheaded at Stirling 1425
Duncan, Earl of Lennox
beheaded at Stirling 1426
David Master of Athol · Hostage
Alan
Sir Robert Stewart the Chamberlain tortured to death 1437
Walter beheaded at Stirling 1425
Alexander beheaded at Stirling 1425
James died in Ireland
JAMES II
killed by a bursting cannon at the siege of Roxburgh 1460
Alexander died infant
Isabella
Margaret married the Dauphin Louis
Joanna the dumb
Eleanor
Mary
Annabella
JAMES III
murdered by rebels after the Battle of Sauchieburn in 1488
JAMES IV
married Margaret of England · killed at the battle of Flodden 1513
JAMES V
Poet & "Poor Man's King" · died after the battle of Solway Moss 1542
MARY Queen of Scots
beheaded in 1587
JAMES VI & I
First King of Great Britain & Ireland · died near Newmarket · 1625

PROLOGUE

The Withered Stock

True, Love finally is great,
Greater than all,—but large the hate,
Far larger than Man can ever estimate.

W. H. AUDEN, *The Ascent of F.6.*

PROLOGUE

The Withered Stock

April 4th 1406

In a small stone-walled room in the castle of Dundonald, a large man lay sprawling on the matted heather of the floor.

It was broad day, but he was still asleep. The morning was cold, despite the April sunshine outside, but he iay without a blanket to cover his huge and hairy legs. He was surprisingly ugly, but his left arm pillowed and was imprisoned by a young girl's neck.

She had been awake now for the better part of an hour, lying with her eyes fixed on the groined ceiling above her. She was wondering just how foolish she had been to surrender to her mother's insistence and tie her life up with that of the unappetizing creature who lay wheezing at her side.

The problem was not an acute, still less a painful one. An unusual sense of physical well-being pervaded her. It was Sunday—Palm Sunday, she remembered; she had spent Saturday evening in consuming large quantities of ale, capped by a pint of strange French wine. One woke up next morning. One knew that doubts and worries would be returning soon. Meanwhile the important thing was to lie scrupulously still, avoiding any little movement that might break the pleasing torpor in the limbs. The mind could be let wander over the situation in a vague, impersonal way, as if it were some other girl who had gone to church one Saturday with the Doorward of Dundonald Castle and then, aiming for bed, settled down for the night upon the heather-strewn floor.

She was glad, on the whole, that she had gone to church

first. The priests were for ever dinning it into poor folk that the ceremony was of vast importance, in the next world if not in this. They were naturally less strident in their advice to the rich: the rich did as they liked—possibly to the peril of their souls. If it came to that, the king himself had been born out of wedlock and legitimized, long after, by the Pope: he had twenty-one brothers and sisters, by this mother or that, and there were eight of them that not even a Pope would care to rescue from bastardy. There was even an old woman in the town of Ayr, of whom the neighbours told stories unknown at Court. . . .

The girl's thoughts rambled down pleasant and forbidden lanes. One could afford to indulge them, now that one was a married woman. All the same, she had to admit that things were different nowadays, even at Court. The king had not followed his father's ways, nor encouraged others to ape them. He was an old man now, but one sometimes doubted if he had ever had the vitality to make a good sinner.

She looked at the man beside her, her newly-married husband; he certainly did not lack vitality. If he moved slowly, it was with the slowness of some lazy but inevitable beast. He brushed aside cleverer and more scrupulous men, jockeyed them out of their places, and sank comfortably into the vacancy. When it came to actual war, he could show a surprising energy. Perhaps his inner, most slothful self recognized that some effort was necessary in this unsatisfactory world, and that a raid conscientiously conducted, a battle fought to the end, was often prelude to weeks of ale and ease.

Faintly, through narrow windows, came the sound of trotting horses—the dull rhythm on the sods, the sharp and sudden cry where a hoof struck stone.

The man stirred and grunted on the floor. It seemed as if he were about to wake; then, as though thinking better of it, he fell into deeper gulfs of sleep. Some dreamy instinct reassured him that no one could be coming to the castle that day: no one, at least, to whom the doors need be opened. The king had ridden away, three days ago, to cross the water to Bute, hear his Mass at Kilmichael, and spend Holy Week among his farms on the far side of the island. He could be counted on to linger, as long as possible, at Kilmichael or Ettrick Bay; there was nothing and no one to call him back. The Doorward of Dundonald, if he chose to do so, could slumber for a week beside his new-found bride.

For it was a king's officer that the girl had married, it was in a royal castle that she lay gazing at the ceiling. Her mother had not let her forget the fact during the last few weeks, and, no doubt, was still repeating it to her neighbours in Ayr. The old man who pottered round his outlying farms in Bute, was, in name at least, the King of Scots. He was great-grandson to the Bruce, who had saved Scotland from the English. They had taken him to Scone and set the Bruce's crown on his head, while some of them thought of Jacob's stone in Westminster Abbey, and cursed England for a nest of thieves.

It had not taken them long to discover that there was nothing kingly about him except his majestic appearance—the melancholy grandeur that sobered them all in his presence, and set them laughing behind his back. Even in Ayr, folk talked of him as they would of a local laird, and decided that he was well disposed towards the poor but a feckless sort of body when it came to protecting them against lords or prelates. As for his kingdom, it was sometimes governed by his brother Albany, sometimes by a committee of barons, and sometimes not governed at all. The Border lords planned inroads into England without consulting him. The Regent Albany wrote to France or Norway in his name and did not trouble to show him the letters. And in the glens and islands of the north-west, clansmen in saffron shirts slew and maimed each other as their chiefs directed, and hardly knew that there was a King of Scots in the Lowlands.

All this was common gossip in Ayr; the girl had heard it a hundred times; and, to judge by last night's talk, tongues wagged just as freely in the royal castle of Dundonald.

She sat up. There were voices outside, demanding admission in the king's name. She could distinguish the words, recognize the urgency of their demand: the gates must be opened immediately. She could also recognize (or imagine) a hint of half-heartedness in their tone—a suggestion that, with so indulgent a master, it mattered little how promptly the summons was obeyed. Thus they cried in the king's name, but there was no sound of the king's voice.

She woke the man beside her. He sat up, ground his fists, resentfully, into his eyes, and scowled round. Then he remembered what had happened last night, and smiled at his chosen mate in a dull, heavy fashion.

"They're back," she said, "they've come back from Kilmichael."

"Blethers," said her husband.

He scowled at her again. Then he looked at the thin slits of window, saw how high the sun had climbed, and heard from outside the repeated clamour of the horsemen. He rose to his feet, galling the girl's side with his foot. He wiped his nose with his fingers, and stood still for a moment, hardly sure yet of his balance. He had not even the dignity of his inches.

"What way did ye not waken me before?" he said, and lumbered out of the room.

The rest of the household had been long awake, in spite of last night's junketings. Some of the boys, returning from Mass, had even peeped in through the curtains to see how the Doorward fared with the woman he had brought out from Ayr. Now the gatesmen, waiting his word to unbar, were already sending up to rouse him from slumber. Their messenger nearly ran into his legs on the steep spiral of the stair. Surprised at escaping the expected kick, he turned and fled downwards again.

The Doorward paused to peer through the unglazed

oblong of the stairway window, and make sure that it was indeed the king. Framed in stone, a dozen men sat their horses beneath him. In their midst was an old man on a white mare.

His dress was barely richer than theirs, but royalty was stamped unmistakably upon his face and bearing, on the white hair and smooth, broad brow. Nothing belied the impression except, on nearer view, the eyes. One searched them in vain for any possibility of disdain or righteous wrath. They were clouded with self-reproach. They seemed lost in perpetual admiration for other men—men who could make what they would of a world that baffled and defeated their king. The questing beast that was locked behind those eyes had little in common with the wolf that lurked in most men, these ravenous days. It was something more shy, more tender, more inquisitive. Since it had first looked forth from its earthly prison, seventy years ago, it had sought in vain for some refuge, some way to dodge the sickening blows of circumstance. It had grown a little warier in the dodging, yet never once dreamt that a blow can be returned.

The sight of the king's face, long since familiar to the man at the staircase window, made him turn and shout down an order. As he descended himself, he heard the gate-hinges groan in the thickness of the wall, the courtyard rattle with horse-hooves. By the time he reached the ground and emerged into cold sunshine, the riders had already dismounted, to gather round the king. They were about to help him from his horse when they saw that he was trying to speak. He inflected his words like a question, though he knew the answer better than his listeners.

"It was here my father died?" he asked sadly.

The king's eyes strayed up to the stone roofs of Dundonald and then down to his ungainly Doorward, still blinking at the foot of the stairs. The man had little intuition where his master was concerned—less, perhaps, than the white mare that stood there so patiently, throning the Majesty of Scotland. But even he could see that the king was sick to death, that he had encountered some final blow at Kilmichael, and that sentiment or superstition had urged him to hurry home, to die where his father had died. His strength, one saw, had barely sufficed for the journey: in a few hours from now, a new king would be reigning in Scotland, while Dundonald made its simple preparations for a royal funeral. And perhaps it was hardly a matter of hours.

They helped the old man off his mare, and supported him as he shuffled to the stairway door. The Doorward, standing aside for them, heard him muttering to himself as he passed.

"Taken at sea," said the king; and then again, "The English!" So he passed out of sight, the men bunching behind him in the doorway.

For many years he had been a cripple: one of Dalkeith's horses had kicked him lame, before ever he came to be king. Now he was seventy, and in mortal sickness, and none of the men knew how they were to get him up the narrow stair. At last an Arran man, bolder than the rest, crouched down before him, drew the king's arms over his own sturdy shoulders, and hoisted him into an ignoble pick-a-back.

The girl in the upper room had begun to clear away the ale-mugs when she heard them enter. The Arran man elbowed the curtain aside and marched in—the king's white beard spraying over his shoulders, the king's eyes staring dumbly above his crouched head. The girl turned to see them and she, too, caught the nearness of death. She suddenly remembered that she was now the Doorward's wife, the only woman in the castle. There would be need of a bed and sheets, of towels and water. She crossed to the door and pushed her way out through the crowd of men-at-arms. Behind her their leader was setting down his royal burden.

The king tottered to a bench.

The nightmare of his journey was over, the jogging horses, the smell of the sea, the heaving sky above him. He had come home. He need never leave shelter again, never even move from this room. They would bring in a bed, so that he could lie quietly and wait for the end.

He would have preferred the western room, with its wide window overlooking the sea; he would have liked to see Arran and the vast snow-piled mass of Goat Fell. He had pictured himself looking out from his deathbed upon some wide expanse of the Scotland he had loved so well and governed so pitiably. But perhaps he had better not trouble them to move him again. He must be content with these narrow slits in the stone-work, the glimpse of green trees, the distant hint of the Lanark hills.

They had brought the bed. They lifted him onto it with clumsy tenderness. He recognized the faces, as though in a mist: the men-at-arms and their captain: that gross fellow whom they had made him appoint as Doorward. Only one was unfamiliar—a girl's face, not uncomely. He wondered who she was, and how she came to be in the castle. Not that it mattered. Nothing mattered now, except that he need never move again. Never, never again.

It had ceased to trouble him that the windows were small, the room pent in from spacious views. He had even forgotten what evil thing it was that had brought him back from Kilmichael, and set death's seal upon him. Some bad news, no doubt. He would remember soon. Meanwhile he had come home and now lay content—or almost content.

Happiness he had not known, not for forty years. He would have forgotten the savour of it, but for the momentary reminders that had been granted him, as respites from the accustomed desolation. There was a Christmas spent at Linlithgow, when the Frenchmen came on embassy, bringing their wives to his Court. There was that strange and lovely day at Fintry, when he had risen at dawn and heard the Little People piping up in the hills. And then there had been that unbelievable summer, before the queen's death, when, for some reason he had never fathomed, the cloud lifted from his brain, and for a month and more, the world had seemed new and gay and splendid. Apart from such blessed moments, he had little to look back on, except the grind and pressure of the daily round—the mountain of things that he ought to be doing, the inability to do one of them as it should be done. He could barely remember the days before that torment had started. The pressure had eased a little now; if there was no glory, no meaning in the things around him, at least they had ceased to mock him as he had known them do.

The girl he could not recognize was offering him a cup of wine. He smiled gently, in refusal. Wine had never meant anything to him, save as a drug. He did not need it now; if pain should return, he had pride enough to reject the anodyne.

Pride—few men suspected him of that; most of them blamed him for having so poor a stock. He was not proud of the crown that had descended to him: there was no merit in being the recipient of such a gift from Fortune. He had not even been crowned in his own name of John. King Johns, they told him, were unlucky: John Lackland of evil memory: John of Balliol, whom the English had tried to foist on Scotland: John of France, captured at Poitiers. They had crowned him as Robert the Third, in memory of the Bruce; they had hoped to trick fortune with a false name. As Robert the Third he had ruled Scotland for sixteen years, or presided over her misrule. And all the time John Stewart had looked on, miserably enough yet cherishing his secret pride.

For there was one precious thing he had brought into the world, and he had suffered neither time nor accident to obliterate it. They had called him weak because he would not gain his ends by injustice, and by the trickery that ruffians mistook for kingship: he himself knew that it was not weakness, but conscience. He would rather fail in everything than succeed as others succeeded, as he had watched his own brothers succeed. Was it success to be called Wolf of Badenoch, as Alexander was called, and justify the name by slaughter, devastation and sacrilege?

Was it success to become Regent, as Albany had done, and perpetuate his power by intrigue, by truckling to the sins and sloth of others, and at last by secret murder? Among the common people, men were not admired for cheating and killing their neighbours. Why should kings and princes be judged by different laws? Why should whole nations be led into tricking and ravaging each other, as if they were bands of heathen brigands? No man asked these questions, for no man could face the answer. The world conspired to trample them away. But he, John Stewart, misnamed King Robert the Third, had seen what was hidden from the worldly-wise, and had clung to his vision, unseduced by failure.

He liked to think that some of his poorer subjects knew what it was that he had stood for. He was certain that Posterity would do him justice. One day, across the wrack of evil, all nations would learn that Force and Cunning must in the long run defeat themselves, and that there is no statecraft except Simplicity and Truth. Then they would look back to him, and salute him as one born out of his time, one who had seen the light amid a dark and savage world.

He looked up and saw that they were bringing him a priest.

It was not the old man from Dundonald village. It was a wandering Irishman, returning from the western isles: young, clear-eyed, upright. The stranger looked round him as he entered, almost in disdain. He did not like the Scots. He told himself that King Robert was probably no better than his subjects. But duty had sent him to this uncongenial country, and duty certainly despatched him to any deathbed where a soul was in peril of passing unshriven. Nor was it every priest who could say that he had once given extreme unction to a king.

Seeing the Irishman advance, the Doorward shambled forward and took his wife by the shoulders to displace her from the bedside. She rose, setting down the cup of wine.

For a moment all three stood motionless, gazing at the king's broad brow, the stately calm upon his features, the wealth of silvered hair.

It was the first time that the Irishman had seen the king's face—or any face that resembled it in the least. "What is this now?" he asked himself, "is it a saint I am called in to shrive?"

"He is a king indeed," thought the girl, "the folk in Ayr belie him."

Her husband had coarser standards, and knew better the story of the sick man's reign. "How long will it be," he wondered, "before that old fool dies?"

The last judgment was perhaps the best. Yet none of the three who stood there was very near the truth, nor guessed for an instant what was passing behind that majestic mask. For King Robert of Scotland was hardly a saint, and not very kingly, and not altogether a fool.

The shriving was soon done, for the king's powers were swiftly failing. He confessed to sins many but unspecified, in a tired, thin voice. He had not been covetous, or bloodthirsty. Compared with his father, he was unspotted from women. He hoped for mercy. He faltered unbroken adhesion to the Creed.

It irritated the Irishman that he must listen and answer with others in the room. They were more or less out of earshot, for the king's voice was barely audible at the bedside. Still, it would have shown more reverence if they had gone outside. When he told them to do so, they had merely stared. They had other things to think of. One of them was even showing another, in covert fashion, a pack of pasteboard cards: no doubt it was the trumpery game from the Continent, still a novelty to be gaped at in these northern lands. The young priest was glad to think that before the month was out, he would be working among Irishmen again. Meanwhile he had a duty. His prayers were needed, though the dying man could no longer hear his voice.

The king was alone now. No message could reach him from the living, no harshness break into the brittle fabric of his dreamings. For the first time in his life, he could give free rein to the fancies which had prompted his most inexplicable actions—the actions that had most stirred the contempt and laughter of his subjects.

One of the thoughts that comforted him had always been beyond their ken; he and his father were founders of a dynasty; from them sprang a royal line that was destined to unimaginable splendours. Throughout Christendom, and even in heathen lands, men felt that there was a mystery and a sanctity in kingship. The Stewarts of Scotland would one day give shape to that half-formed legend, unfurl that yet unwoven banner. Men would suffer and die in unreasoning loyalty to his descendants, and their sacrifice would bring nearer the Kingdom of Heaven. Men would look back to him as to an origin. If he had missed being great in his own lifetime, he had at least sired greatness.

His eldest son had been murdered. Albany and the Douglas had starved him to death in Falkland Castle, and huddled his body into an obscure tomb among the monks of Lindores. When he, the king, demanded enquiry into the crime, Parliament had been too obsequiously terrified of the murderers—strong in their vast wealth and unscrupulous retinues—to pluck aside the curtain from the evidence of their guilt. Young Rothesay, they sheepishly enacted, had died "by Divine Providence, and from no other cause." King Robert had raged in impotence against that cowardly lie. He still believed it cowardly, but he had come to see that it conveyed an unintended truth. Providence had indeed removed young Rothesay, the gay and gracious sinner, as one unworthy to carry on the great line of the Stewarts. Thus, and thus only, could Providence make way for Jamie. Jamie, the child of his old age, was barely twelve yet, but very soon, perhaps in a few minutes' time, he would be King of Scots. He had been born on St. James's day, christened after the Apostle. No one could say that there was ill-luck in his being crowned in his own name: there had never been a King James before, except in distant Aragon. James of Scotland would bless the name by his example.

For they could not murder Jamie, nor contaminate him with their filthy politics, their cruel Reason of State. He, Robert, weakling and simpleton, had for once outwitted the cunning schemers. He had had Jamie conveyed in secret to the Bass Rock, kept him in hiding, and then sent the Earl of Orkney, in a ship of Leith, to escort him overseas to France. Jamie would be brought up in France, learning knighthood and virtue and the true wisdom of kings. France had already seen a canonized saint, the great St. Louis, on her throne. Within living memory, another French king, the very John whom all despised, had done a deed that should have put them to shame. Captured at Poitiers, he had left a son as hostage and gone home to raise his ransom: when that son broke parole and fled, he had returned, like Regulus of old, to die in an English prison rather than accept dishonour.

In God's good time, Jamie would come back from France to rule his own kingdom. Regent Albany had pretended to smile at his escape, had seemed glad to see the last of the boy. He had not seen the last. Jamie would return to put an end to regencies and restore to Scotland her golden age. He would make her prosperous again, more prosperous than she had been before English armies had begun their brutal inroads. He would foster the arts to which Scotland was still blind and still contemptuous. He would purge the Church and repress heresy. He would avenge Rothesay by reigning better than Rothesay's murderers. He would curb the powerful, and bring gladness to the poor man's hearth. France would watch her pupil in proud wonder: the Pope would send his blessing: the distant Turk would tremble, hearing that Christendom could breed such princes. Even the English, hardest-hearted and most treacherous of nations, would yield to Jamie's spell. They would repent of their pointless ravagings, their lying claims to the Scottish crown, their recurrent breaches of faith and honour. They would spew out the upstart, Henry of Bolingbroke, whom they had allowed to murder King Richard and usurp his throne. Even the English. . . .

With the repetition of that name a sudden pain smote him, dull at first, growing rapidly in precision and enormity. Piece by piece, the scaffolding of his hopes began to collapse, precipitating him into the nothingness of Despair. He felt again the anguish which had come upon him as he sat at meat in Kilmichael and turned to hear the news. The white face of the messenger was again before him. He had risen and called for the horses, rushed back in bewilderment, his first instinct to smother the wound until he had reached home. Now the agony returned, doubled and redoubled. He fought hopelessly for the one thing that might have been saved from the universal disaster of his life, the one gain that could have made good all his losses. He struggled still, knowing that the struggle was in vain. His last worldly desire, deep-rooted in his soul, was torn violently from him, and with the sharpness of that wrench, King Robert had finished with the world.

"Dead," said the priest, and fell to prayer again.

"Dead?" said the Doorward, looking unmoved at the ruins of his master; the face was more peaceful than ever: there was no sign of the tumult of his passing.

"Well," added the Doorward, by way of epitaph, "he must have been close on seventy."

His eyes began to appraize the rings on the dead man's fingers. Then he saw his wife go up behind the priest and stand for a moment, as though in prayer. She turned away, taking from the king's side the untasted cup of wine.

The Doorward suddenly knew that his mouth was a sandy desert of dryness. He took the cup from her reluctant hands.

"I am thinking," he said, putting a bold face on it, "that maybe we ought to drink a health to King James. Here's to him, and long may he reign!"

He drank alone, though the remnants of last night's carousal still stood at the end of the room. Nor would the men accept the cup after him. He felt a certain resentment in their stillness. But he noticed that one of them, sitting in the corner, had begun a game with his cards.

"It may be a long time," said their captain, "before King James begins his reign. Have you not heard the news?"

The Doorward was finishing his cup. His wife answered for him.

"What news is that?" she said, "we've heard nothing."

"It followed us up to Kilmichael," said the captain, "it's a wonder it did not come your way. The English have captured the prince. Sailed out by Flamborough and captured him in truce-time, like the bloody pirates they are. It must have been that that killed the king."

"Nine of diamonds," said the man in the corner. The Doorward muttered something about people who were mighty easy to kill.

"What'll the English do to the prince?" asked the girl.

"Who knows?" the captain answered. "Take him to London, to begin with. He'll make a fine Easter present for King Harry."

"And then—they won't kill him, will they?"

"Don't be a fool, lass," cut in the Doorward. "It'd

never pay them to do that. They'll just keep him locked up so long as it suits them to see Scotland without a king." He swilled his cup round and emptied the dregs down his throat. "And that," he added, "is likely to be for ever. That's politics."

The card-player looked up from his game. "D'you know the English?" he asked, "have you been in England?"

"I have not. There's no need to have been there."

"Well, I have, and I know them. They're too fond of money to hold him long. They'll be selling him back to us for the ransom. The English'd sell anything—even their wives."

"They might that," said the Doorward, seeing a chance to regain the upper hand, "but what's making you think we'll buy? Do you see Regent Albany raising all that silver, just for the pleasure of ending his own regency?"

The captain felt himself called on to interpose. He had no head for politics, but it was his duty to discourage talk against the regent.

"I expect," he said, lamely, "that we shall manage to buy him back in the end."

The Doorward squinted at him contemptuously, and then handed the empty cup to his wife.

"You may be right," he said, "but I'm thinking it'll be a gey long time."

The Sapling

I tell you naught for your comfort,
Yea, naught for your desire,
Save that the sky grows darker yet,
And the sea rises higher.

G. K. CHESTERTON.

CHAPTER ONE

The Sapling

November 1408

I

UP AND DOWN, round and round, the boy paced the limits of his narrow room. The black mood was upon him again.

He knew that it would pass soon, that this restless walking was a kind of remedy, helping to hasten its passing. So much he had learnt from experience, though he was over-young for the knowledge. Few boys of fourteen had felt the bitterness of two years' captivity. Fewer still would have practised the cure with such determination. Up and down: round and round.

To reach the window, one marched to left of the table: to return to the shadowy end of the room, where were book-shelves and the door, one ranged down the other wall, though the table and fireplace were too close to admit of easy passage. Books and a harp, lying on the floor, made minor obstacles, easily avoided. Up and down: round and round.

They had done much, perhaps all that was possible, to help him forget that he was a prisoner. They were a strange people, these English, simple and straightforward in their friendships, inscrutable to those whom chance made their enemies. Dungeons and ill-treatment one could understand; ransom and release would have been comprehensible. But this denial of liberty, coupled with care, kindness and even deference, was a riddle beyond a boy's unravelling.

There had been a certain mystery about the incident from which the whole business had begun. He had sailed in secrecy from the Bass Rock, and even in Scotland few men knew of his departure. Yet when the strange sails had closed round him, looming up through the fog, they had seemed curiously purposeful, as though the English shipmen had learnt already that they were capturing a prince. The Earl of Orkney, in charge of his escort, had been red with shame and anger at the failure to slip past England; when they were brought before King Henry, Orkney as good as taunted him with treachery. Henry, fourth of that name to reign in England, sat irritatingly unmoved, though with a hint of uneasy conscience behind the bluff manner that he affected. He asked why King Robert was so eager to send James to France: he himself, a gentleman by birth and once a continental traveller by compulsion, could teach James French; and in all other matters, as everyone knew, an English education was the finest in the world. Orkney had raged at the smugness of King Harry, sitting there in the security of possession.

All the same, one had to admit that the king had kept his promise. James was beginning to speak French with tolerable fluency, even if his accent would hardly pass muster on the Loire. He had skilful teachers to ground him in Latin and rhetoric and theology. He was grasping the principles on which English musicians built their prim little tunes, so strange after the wild airs of Scotland. His tutors had even fired him with admiration for English poetry, which surpassed, in power as well as sweetness, any that the Scots had yet produced. Nor was there any lack of instructors to teach him the tricks of horsemanship and war—greybeards who had once followed the Black Prince into Spain, cheerful youngsters with most of their real fighting ahead of them.

James knew too—they did not scruple to remind him of it—that he was safer in English prisons than he had been in Scotland. He could remember the day, just before his eighth birthday, when news came that his elder brother, the reckless, winsome, adulterous Rothesay, had been starved to death in one of Albany's castles. It was dangerous to possess anything that other men coveted, and doubly dangerous to be royal, or heir to royalty. Here, in English prisons, he was at least safe from murder. He was learning things that would help him to rule Scotland when he was permitted to return. The Abbot of Evesham, his present warden and tutor, was for ever preaching patience and gratitude, and, to some extent, circumstances seemed to justify the argument.

But there came times when nothing seemed so unattainable as patience, when James felt as desperate as if they had clamped fetters on every limb; exercise in the tiltyard or the meadows might occupy the day, but at night the harp lay powerless to tempt his fingers, and Chaucer and Gower, instead of holding the keys of fairyland, were merely Englishmen like his gaolers.

The fit was passing at last. As if to redeem a cheerless day, the winter sun had put the clouds of evening to temporary rout. It was shining into the room. The boy halted in his prowlings, climbed into the window-seat and sat at gaze. There would be frost tonight: the mists would soon be creeping up from the river. But for the moment Evesham's roofs were rosy with sunset, the orchards flaunted brave leaves in the face of advancing winter, and peace came flooding back into his heart.

A slight noise made him screw himself round upon the window-seat. Giffard had returned from the Abbey. In the pale golden sunlight he looked handsomer than usual, but, as always, over-solemn for a young man of twenty.

Giffard was a Lothian man, and James's chief link with the past. He had been on the Bass Rock, and sailed southward as the prince's esquire. He was so abominably sea-sick by the time they were captured that his patriotic indignation was much impaired by relief at finding the voyage cut short: the English were hereditary, and treacherous, enemies, but England provided something solid to stand on. For that matter, Giffard had always cherished secret doubts about James being sent to France; he had seen some French knights at Edinburgh and was not impressed. When one came to know the English, they were no worse than other foreigners. They at least talked an intelligible language. French was Greek to Giffard.

The first year, at London, had been weary enough. After the great rock of Edinburgh, the Tower seemed a feeble parody of a citadel: and the City itself was cramping as well as hostile. When they were transferred to Nottingham, Giffard's spirits rose. Evesham was better still. Here they were in the abbot's custody, though not lodged in the abbey itself. They and their guards occupied a new stone house, standing on abbey property, in the High Street. Giffard had James to himself here, and the boyish figure twisted up in the window-seat was beginning to mean more to him than he would have cared to admit.

"Well, what's it to be tonight?" asked James, "chess or mathematics?"

"No time for either, your Majesty. It's clothes and a visitor. I've brought Badby." Giffard knelt and began to pick up the books.

"Oh," said James, scrambling down from the window, "is the green suit finished? What does it look like? Has Badby done it well?"

"As well as he can, I expect, with such a heathenish colour. You'll see in a minute or two."

"Well, bring him in! There's no need to set the room to rights, just for a tailor."

"I told your Majesty," said Giffard, frowning, "that there was a visitor. And the room's like a bear-pit."

"Who is it? Not another bishop?"

"No," said Giffard, still tidying, "and nothing like a bishop. Your Majesty will break this harp one day, if you leave it about on the floor. And harps cost money."

"William Giffard!" said James, "I charge you, upon your allegiance, to tell me who is coming." He folded his arms, striking an attitude. "As King of Scotland," he added, belatedly.

"Quack, quack!" said Giffard, and hung the harp up on its peg.

James took up another book from the table, and threw it onto the floor.

"Here's Badby," said Giffard, stooping reproachfully. "He's bringing your suit up."

"Donkerton told me yesterday that we oughtn't to have employed Badby. He's got something against him."

"Donkerton is a priest," said Giffard. "I believe the priests would like to make tailoring a branch of theology. But I can't see why a heretic shouldn't cut as good clothes as the godly—even if you do make him do it in green."

"But Badby isn't a heret——" began James.

"Ssh!" said Giffard. "Here he is."

The door swung open: in marched a plump little tradesman with a worried, conscientious face; he held a bundle before him with almost sacerdotal reverence. He bowed awkwardly, and then, nonplussed at meeting no response, decided to bow again.

"Your new suit, your Majesty," he said apologetically. "We were up late with it last night, long after dark. Breaking the Guild rules, I'm afraid. And the last button wasn't on till an hour ago. I think your Majesty will be pleased. I admire your Majesty's choice of colour."

He placed his burden on the table, and, unwrapping its cloth covering, exposed a neat pile of emerald green. He glanced nervously at the boy's dim figure, immobile against the window.

"Badby?"

"Yes, your Majesty?"

"Giffard says you're a heretic. Is that true?"

A sudden terror, like that of a cornered rat, seemed to spring into the tailor's eyes.

"No, no, sir! God forbid! That is——." He looked round him as though at any moment he might make a rush for the door. Then he half pulled himself together and returned—miserably, but with a certain dignity—to the clothes on the table.

"If your Majesty would allow me to help him out of his tunic," he said, "we could try this on. I've cut a wide bag-sleeve. And this is the best fur I could procure in the time. This gentleman said you had company tonight, and wanted the work done quickly."

"You haven't answered my question," said James.

Giffard made a movement of protest, but the tailor had now recovered his poise.

"No, your Majesty," he said. "That is, yes. I did answer it. . . . This gentleman said that your visitor was from the Continent. I hope he will notice that we are not behind the times at Evesham. I copied the bag-sleeve from a foreign gentleman I saw at Gloucester. Very full at the elbow."

"It's Mar," said Giffard to distract the boy's attention. "I didn't tell your Majesty."

"What's Mar?" asked James.

"Our visitor. The Earl of Mar. He is returning from the Low Countries, and they have given him a safe-conduct to come through England and pay his respects to your Majesty."

"Oh?" said James, beginning to peel off his tunic, "I never knew my cousin was so affectionate."

"Cousin" was something of a courtesy title. Mar was the son of James's uncle, but no one quite knew who his mother had been: the Wolf of Badenoch had a number of doxies in the Highlands. Mar had now managed to conceal his bastardy under a title, but his method of acquiring it did not reflect great credit on the family.

Giffard smiled rather sourly.

"It might not be just affection," he said, "that'd bring a man to visit his future king. . . . Here, give that to me."

He relieved Badby of James's tunic, leaving him free to fit his own handiwork on the boy.

"Future?" protested James, putting his hands into the

stiff new arm-holes. "May I remind you, William Giffard, Esquire, that I have been your king, and Mar's, for a matter of two years?"

"It'd not be the first time," grumbled Giffard, "that you've reminded me of that. And may I repeat that no one's more than half king till he's been crowned? I doubt it'll be another two years and more before either of us see Scone."

"Well, you're wrong," said James, as Badby fussed and patted round him. "A little bird has been bringing me news. King Henry's decided to release me this winter, as soon as my uncle Albany can collect the ransom. You told me yourself that Albany's embassy is on the way. I expect Mar will be coming to tell me that they've succeeded in arranging my release."

He fastened the high collar round his throat.

"H'm," said Giffard, "your wee bird seems to have brought a mouthful of news. I'll believe him when he comes with the ransom money in his beak."

"I hope your Majesty is pleased?" said Badby, popping up from behind James's back. "I think my efforts have been successful. Our efforts, I should say. I had to get two journeymen in."

"My Majesty would be better pleased when my squire brings me a mirror to show me what I look like—instead of standing there trying to damp my hopes."

Giffard only replied with a wry face as he went to fetch the mirror. It was the tailor—unexpectedly enough—who took up the challenge. "If your Majesty will allow me to say so," he ventured, "we've an old saw in these parts about Hope souring the apples if you keep it too long in the loft. We always say it's better to expect things when you see them."

The next moment professional pride ousted all other thoughts. "I'm noted for my sleeves," he said, smoothing James's arm. "As far off as Exeter, people talk of Badby's sleeves."

"Well," said James, as Giffard angled the glass up and

down him, "they may be talking of them in Dunfermline soon, in spite of your croakings."

He frowned at his reflection, more pleased that it seemed dignified to admit. It would show more knowledge of the world to find some small fault with the cut, and Badby, whatever his private thought, would probably accept criticism meekly.

The next moment he was upbraiding himself for the notion of taking so unfair an advantage. "You have done well," he said.

"I do my best, your Majesty." Badby beamed gratefully; but the craftsman's eye was not quite satisfied.

"If your Majesty would wear it tonight," he said thoughtfully, "I think I could come in tomorrow and make a small improvement in the epaulette. That's what we call this piece on the shoulder, your Majesty."

"Ah, yes. The epaulette." The boy knitted his brows in connoisseur fashion. "I was thinking it was a trifle too . . . a trifle——." He fingered his shoulder, wondering how to finish the sentence with credit. Perhaps he would be safer to leave it unfinished.

"It wouldn't take me long, your Majesty."

"Very well. Tomorrow. Take the work home with you, if you like. I shall be out riding all day."

"And there's no hurry," put in Giffard, "so you needn't hire journeymen." The English were paying for everything, but there was no need to have extra labour on the bill.

The tailor bowed, wondering if he were expected to take leave. A final glance at the green-clad boy refreshed his sense of pride.

"And meanwhile," said James patronizingly, "I hope my cousin Mar will not notice that there is anything amiss with the . . . with the shoulder-piece."

"Indeed I hope not," said Badby. He looked up apologetically, but with a hint of the tradesman's cunning in his eyes. "I wonder," he said, "if your Majesty will be so kind as to mention my name to him."

"Pouf!" exploded Giffard in the background.

"I beg pardon," said Badby, turning nervously.

"Nothing," said Giffard. "But I don't think it is much good your trying to work up a connection in Badenoch. My Lord Mar's neighbours run about in yellow shirts—when they aren't naked to the waist."

"Oh," said Badby, wondering if his leg was being pulled. One could never tell. One had heard such strange things, in the old days, about the Scotch savages. Badby had believed them as faithfully as his neighbours, until this extremely civilized young prince had been brought to Evesham, to upset Evesham's most flourishing convictions. Now there was no knowing what to believe.

"Master Badby would soon change that," said James, "he'd get Mar's Highlandmen into houppelandes and bag-sleeves. Would you like to come with me, Badby, when I go back to Scotland this winter? We need good tailors, and we aren't afraid of Lollardry. We don't burn heretics in Scotland."

There was no mistaking it this time, the sudden terror that leapt into Badby's eyes. But now there was something beside terror—an obscure resentment, almost a defiance, such as princes do not expect to meet in the eyes of a tailor. For a moment they stood thus, the hunted quarry with his back to a tree, the flippant hunter, already uncomfortable at the implied tragedy which he had suddenly encountered. Then Badby turned away, defenceless, pathetically *bourgeois*, but not without a certain dignity. He began to smooth out the wrapping-cloth on the table. King and squire watched him in silence as he folded it into four with mathematical trimness, and then into two again, before tucking it under his arm.

He swallowed to recover his speech, his eyes still fixed on the floor.

"It is kind of your Majesty to suggest it," he said at last, "but I think I am better in Evesham. I was born at Evesham. May I wish your Majesty a good night?"

He bowed himself out of the rapidly darkening room.

"And now," said James, "for cousin Mar. Does he eat with me, or do I receive him after supper?"

"As your Majesty pleases," said Giffard absently, his eye still on the door.

"Well, bring him in, if there's enough food. The lamb shall feed with the wolf; drink, too, if I know cousin Mar. A good long toast for the King's Return."

Giffard walked thoughtfully to the door, opened it, and paused on the threshold. Faintly from below came the sound of a door closing: Badby was hurrying home to his family.

"Your Majesty?"

"M-m?" James was standing at the table, turning over the leaves of a book.

"That man's only a tailor, and he may be a heretic, but he said something that struck me as good sense."

"Oh? What was that?" James picked up the book, took it towards all that was left of the daylight, and began to curl himself up on the window-seat.

"Something about apples going sour, about hope being an ill thing to keep too long in your loft."

"Is this another lecture?"

"No, your Majesty. But I'm feared for you."

Giffard paused, looking at the dark shape in the window, the boyish profile bent over the book.

"It may be a long time," he said, "before either of us see Scone. A very long time."

"Quack, quack," murmured King James.

November 1408

II

"Envoys?" said Mar, spitting into the fire. "Och, they were not in London yet when I left it." He kicked the logs with his boot. "I'd say your uncle Albany had sent a pack of noodles to do your business for you. Brechin and Lennox are a pair of slow-moving old stots that wouldn't start before they need. He should have sent soldiers, men that have seen war. I remember at Lüttich. . . ."

Mar always managed to get back to the same subject, his recent campaign in the Low Countries, and generally to the pleasing theme of his own prowess and the incompetence of others. James had long ago despaired of interrupting him; he sat resigned to boredom, watching this uncouth cousin of his without affection.

The worst thing about Mar—so James decided—was the way he showed his huge and discoloured teeth. No, almost worse were the sudden gaps in them, the two dark caves in that double rank of yellow tombstones. Even the rosy fire-light, playing charitably on Mar's ugly face, could not detract from the ogreish coarseness of the open mouth. It was better to talk to him—or rather listen—with eyes averted.

Supper had seemed to the boy to last for interminable hours. Mar had eaten slowly and enormously, and, now that he had at last finished and turned his chair to the fire, he was still swallowing great gulps of wine in the intervals of his boasting. James, watching, wondered how much it must cost to keep this animal in food and drink for a month; a year's reckoning was beyond the scope of after-dinner arithmetic; and Mar (though he looked older still) had been eating and drinking for close on thirty-five years.

James waited for a respite in the flow of reminiscence. "I was afraid," he said, determined to bring the conversation round again, "that Lennox and the Bishop would take their time. I was hoping that your lordship would have an opportunity, when you were in London, of putting a boot behind them."

James was rather proud of that; it sounded manly, and was quite in Mar's own vein. He was surprised to see Mar looking almost shocked. He had forgotten that no one can be so careful of the proprieties as your reformed bandit.

"That'll not be the way," said Mar sententiously, "to be talking of your nobility. We'll not like it mentioned that we can be kicked."

By "we" Mar meant the land-holding circle into which he had forced himself by somewhat unorthodox means. For he was merely a bastard of one of King Robert's brothers, and had spent his youth as a scapegrace leader of his father's Highland caterans. He had learnt much thereby, for the work was varied; one raid had even ended in the reduction of Elgin Cathedral to a heap of cinders; most had no further aim than pressure to be put on a rich neighbour by burning his crops and lifting his cattle; and at times there was only the harrying of a village that refused to pay blackmail, or the rape of some local beauty. His father had been the king's lieutenant for the North, nominally responsible for enforcing the king's peace; he had thought more of the opportunities his position gave him than of the responsibilities it should have entailed; he was flattered when men nicknamed him "Wolf of Badenoch," and had taught his son how to laugh at such jokes.

James, watching Mar in irritation across the fireside, remembered how the man had profited by his father's teaching. It was an incredible story, though a true one: doubly incredible when one looked at Mar's unpalatable grin. For he had risen by means of a lady—one whose personal attractions were indeed negligible, but one who was daughter to the Douglas, and Countess of Mar in her own right. She was married to a Drummond—a nobody but for being the queen's brother: when the queen died he was more than ever a nobody, and could be safely murdered. Then Kildrummy Castle was rushed by a party of yelling Highlanders, and the widow terrorized into signing away her hand in marriage and a share in her title. But Mar—as he now called himself—had had to keep his bride against Albany and the poor old king combined, to say nothing of the vast menace of the Douglas. He had done it by working on her passions, getting her to declare that she accepted him, violence forgotten, as her lawful husband. Mar was safely Mar, and thought it no bad thing when the lady died soon after. That had enabled him to accept, recently, a Dutch bride—as substantial as his other rewards—from the master he had been fighting for at Liege. He was talking about her now, though without enthusiasm. "I've sent her round by sea," he told James. "I prefer a horse for myself." He was bringing home some fine Hungarian horses to breed from, and did not want them to get seasick on a long voyage. No, he did not know where Hungaria was, but he'd seldom seen the like of these horses.

"I hope," said James, "that you'll be sending me a horse soon—to carry me back to Scotland."

"Ay. Maybe." Mar finished picking his teeth. "And maybe you'll have to wait till these ones' foals are full-grown."

"D'you think Lennox will botch the business?" asked James. "I'll know the reason why if he does."

Mar stared at him. Mar had come to Evesham to take a look at King Robert's second brat, and see if he were any improvement on that young limb Rothesay. He was not so handsome; a good thing, for women had been Rothesay's ruin. He was short, stocky, and would be fat before he was forty. Now Mar was beginning to wonder if James would ever see forty. He seemed the kind of young fool that would get himself into trouble in Scotland. They might have to send him the same way as Rothesay, if he started interfering, and find some one more comfortable as their king, someone more like old Robert.

James, returning his stare, had no clue to Mar's thoughts. He was merely wondering when Mar was going to take his leave and allow him to go to bed. He could not quite summon up the courage to dismiss his cousin, and he felt sure that the most heavy-handed hint would never batter its way into that primeval skull.

In the end, Mar was dislodged by the failure of the fire. He asked for more fuel to mend it, and James pretended that it was too late to get any, as everyone would be in bed. The lie was palpable, for the house was far from quiet: it could only make Mar despise him for a timid fool. But anything was better than allowing the man to warm himself into a renewal of his pointless small-talk.

Mar sat on a little, growing chilly in the backward parts. At long last he rose, took leave and expressed clumsy thanks for his entertainment.

"I'll be riding tomorrow," he said, "I'll not be seeing you again."

"You'll be seeing me at Scone before next winter. Even Albany's envoys cannot spin things out much longer."

Mar looked pensive. "Ay, man," he said, "but you must remember that it's not as easy as that. Albany's own son is in an English prison. Has been ever since that fool business at Homildon . . . standing there and waiting for the archers to tumble 'em over and capture 'em! That's six years ago, and Albany's not managed to get the English to ransom Murdoch yet. His own son, mind you."

"I should have thought," said James, "that his king had first claim."

"Och, ay," said Mar. "But he's fond of Murdoch." He gazed stupidly at the fire, and then turned as if to go at last. Then slowly a new thought seemed to strike him. "I'll not be seeing your uncle much," he said. "I'll be in the North. They say there's trouble coming. That's why I'm for home."

"Trouble? From the Highlandmen?"

"Ay. Who else'd make trouble?" Mar launched into a stream of obscenities against that section of mankind (hardly, one gathered, to be classed as Scotsmen) who spoke nothing but Gaelic and went fighting-mad in their cups—instead of drinking themselves sleepy like other Christians. Mar's own tenants knew little English, and were hardly less excitable than the barbarians he was denouncing; a Lothian man would have found great difficulty in distinguishing one from the other; but Mar spoke as if a few miles north or west from Lochindorb made all the difference between civilization and outer darkness.

"I had a Highland man to visit me here a month ago," said James. "He said nothing of trouble."

"Maybe he did not. They're cunning enough. And maybe there'll be no trouble. You can never tell, with that pack of sheep-stealers. Sometimes it's two thousand of 'em with no word of warning: and sometimes you get ready for 'em weeks ahead and nothing happens at all." He lumbered towards the door. "Any way," he said, "it'll not do to meet trouble halfway."

They repeated their farewells, and Mar was gone at last. James, hoping for news of release, had seen a dreary evening peter out to its uninteresting end. He heard his visitor cursing the sleepy servants below, the guards unlocking the door, the footsteps rattling up the frosty High Street and down Vine Street to the Abbey. Mar was staying the night at the monastery. A queer lodging for Mar.

There was food for thought in all that had passed, but James was too young, as well as too sleepy. He knew Mar's record, but he had no experience to teach him what such a record implied. He could see the savage face and frame, cased in inappropriately rich garments; he could not picture the man's past, with its trail of charred fields, and bleeding limbs, and broken hearts. The kingly thought was not yet astir in him, the resolve to prevent the Mars from having their own way in Scotland. Still farther off was the bitterer, more complex realization that a king might have to govern by means of such men, pardon and even reward their crime ; they might be too strong to be broken, and, evil though they were, might prove a barrier against more urgent peril.

But the boy's mind was not on Mar at all, still less on the problems of a king. After a brief interval of sleepy prayer, it was principally occupied with two comforting thoughts

—the prospect of his next visitors bringing better news from London, and the indubitable satisfaction of possessing a new green suit.

March 1409

III

"*Deployez les banniers!*"

Sir Thomas Burdet reined up his horse beside a drab little wood on the Chipping Campden road, and treated his pupils as always, to a taste of his best tournament French. He had two boys before whom to show off, his own son, Nicholas, and the young King of Scots. The Abbot of Evesham, who was responsible for the latter's education, happened to owe Sir Thomas a considerable sum of money and was glad to do him a service. Sir Thomas rather fancied himself as a tutor-in-arms, was certainly glad of the fee which King Henry had sanctioned, and liked young Nick to have a sparring-partner. A most satisfactory arrangement for all concerned.

It was a grey and cheerless day, and James had only half a mind for his exercises. After months of waiting, he had just heard that Albany's envoys had finished their business in London, and were returning by way of Evesham in order to report success. Any day now might see the old Bishop of Brechin and handsome, ineffective old Lennox ride into the town with the news of impending ransom. For it had hardly occurred to James that they might be coming less to report success than to disguise the lack of it.

He trotted beside Nick up the gentle slope of the woodside field. Giffard sat his horse with Sir Thomas at the road-edge. Giffard was resigned to the elder man's position as tutor, though not beyond jealousy and the open eye for his pedantry and inexperience of any but bookish wars. Behind them, two armed guards were dismounting; neither Giffard nor James had more than a hazy notion of the road from Gloucestershire to Scotland, but England was not risking the possible escape of a valuable captive.

A few yards away stood the quintain, the object of the morning's excursion. Nicholas had spent a happy hour or two painting it to look like a Saracen. He was a poor artist: his notions of Turkish physiognomy were vague: and, in any case, the next day's practice had knocked most of the colour off. The quintain resembled a wooden scarecrow, and the slightest blow made it creak like a soul in torment.

One trotted one's horse to the top end of the field; one turned, cantered down towards the road, and finally charged with levelled spear; one endeavoured to strike the Saracen full between his misbelieving eyes. Other parts of the face scored less, and to hit shield or body was to set the whole contrivance twisting round on its rusty spindle till it dealt its assailant a smart blow with the sandbag in its preposterously long arm.

After a few creditable rounds, Sir Thomas stopped proceedings in order to impress on the boys the importance of reining up quickly and neatly, after hitting the quintain, in the twenty muddy yards that separated it from the road. Great battles, he explained, had often been lost by knights who broke an enemy's line at the first charge and then found their horses out of control. In the background, one of the men-at-arms gave the other a wink; his father had been a bowman at Cressy and the family tradition allowed small place to mounted knights in the winning or losing of battles.

"And now," said Sir Thomas, returning to his usual jargon, "*Laçez heaulmes!*"

"We haven't any helmets," grumbled Nicholas, as they trotted up the field again. "I wish father would talk English."

James said nothing. They reached the top, and wheeled about. The group of which they had been part two minutes ago looked curiously distant and puppet-like. Sir Thomas, apparently scolding Giffard, was wagging his head in a ridiculous way. The two retainers were trying to trip each other in a half-hearted wrestling-match: the tethered horses stood watching them in puzzlement, brightly outlined against the wintry trees.

"There's someone coming along the road," said Nicholas. "Quite a big party. You can see them through the wood. I wonder——"

He was interrupted by a shout of "*Laissez aller!*" from his father, and spurred down the slope. James checked his horse's attempt to follow, watching, as he did so, the fitful glint of colours through the tree-trunks.

He saw Nicholas strike the quintain—presumably on the chin, for Giffard cried "One!" He heard Sir Thomas call out testily, "Less spur, Nick! You're mangling that horse!" Then his own signal came.

He plunged forward. He saw that the travellers were already emerging from behind the wood. He could not help looking at them; there was something familiar in their appearance. There was a bishop among them: two other Churchmen: a man carrying a pennon: the device on it was one he ought to know. He remembered——.

"Eye on the target!" yelled Nicholas, though it was none of his business. Too late, James pulled himself together and tried to set his spear at the right aim. He struck the quintain on the shield, cross-wise at that. The Saracen gave a rusty shriek and swung his sandbag round. The next thing James knew was that he had lost his spear and that his horse, frightened at the unaccustomed clumsiness, was quite beyond control. He was close on the road before he could check its career, and then the sudden sight of the travellers made it swerve sideways and spill James head over heels into the mud.

He sat up, speechless with bruises and anger. He heard the bishop say, "It's his Majesty!" in the tone of one who witnesses a grave social error. He found himself staring up into the face of a grey-bearded Scottish Earl—it was Lennox, and the old fool was smiling at him. It was mere nervousness that made Lennox smile, but James, in anger, imagined himself derided.

They tried to save James's face by forced witticisms. Burdet, seeing the badges on the servants' coats and knowing the heraldry of half Europe, welcomed Lennox and the Bishop of Brechin by name: then he turned and called facetiously, "*A logis! Ployez les banniers!*" to no one in particular. "Oh," said the bishop, "is this a tourney? I'm not supposed to attend tourneys." He tried to look whimsical, and quoted a Papal Decree against the " brawls and wild-beast-shows vulgarly called tournaments." Nick joined in, assuring the bishop that the game was *à plaisance*, not *à outrance*, and that the Saracen survived to fight next day. The bishop, bewildered and unable to recognize the quintain for an enemy of the Faith, conjured up an unconvincing laugh. And James, rising to scrape off the mud, wondered which of the four he hated most.

Lennox, he decided, as he recovered his horse from Giffard. Lennox had actually laughed at him. He'd regret it one day.

James swung himself into the saddle. "My lords," he said, half conscious that he was behaving like a boor, "I take it we shall meet in Evesham." Then he cantered off along the soft road, leaving his gaolers and uncle Albany's envoys to follow as best they might.

March 1409

IV

It was arranged that the formal meeting should take place that evening at the Abbey. James, pretending to shut himself up with his books, spent the interval in brooding over the afternoon's mischance, and imagining the obsequious laughter at the Abbey as the Scottish bishop and the intolerable Lennox repeated the story to their hosts. He ended by working himself up into a conviction that it was his duty to abandon all hope of ruling Scotland, to beg leave of King Harry and, departing incognito for the Crusades, to die in some obscure skirmish on the Syrian coasts. He decided to tell Giffard about it. Giffard would have to come with him, survive the expedition, and return home with the sad but glorious tidings. It must be repeated that James was not yet fifteen.

His picture of merriment at the Abbey was quaintly wide of the mark. The monks were not given to gossiping with strangers, even if their visitors had had any inclination to tell them about a young boy falling off a horse. Mar's recent visit had taken the edge off monkish curiosity about Scotsmen, and his grudging notion of the appropriate parting-gift had not assured a cordial reception for further visitors from the North. Nor did Abbey routine give much opportunity for social intercourse until the creditable supper, on which the abbot insisted, was served to guests and hosts.

Even then, conversation was at first limited to requests for salt or more bread. The Rule prescribed a Reader at meal-times, and broth was despatched to the accompaniment of a chapter from Leviticus. Then the Abbey Chronicle was opened and the Reader turned to one of its later pages which he had himself copied out a few months before. He immediately launched into an account of the many buildings with which the present abbot, Zatton by name, had enriched the town of Evesham during his thirty years of governance. The community was proud of its abbot, despite the usual frictions; it was also proud of possessing a chronicle of its own, written in what it took to be elegant Latin.

Zatton listened complacently for a while, and then administered a gentle reproof which sent the Reader scurrying back to an earlier page and to the edifying exploits of Anglo-Saxon saints. The Scottish bishop murmured in a deprecating way and old Lennox, who had forgotten his Latin, opined that it was all very interesting. Most of their retinue was preoccupied with food and drink, and too pleased with what they were given to take notice of the intellectual refreshment. Only Master Robert Lanyne, provost of a little chapel in St. Andrews, munched in silent anger as his hungry eyes appraised the spacious architecture of the refectory, the rich plate and linen, the primly fluent Reader. If Abbot Zatton could have divined the unchristian envy in the Scotsman's heart, he would have felt even better pleased with himself than he did.

Supper was finished, and the guests were already gathered in the abbot's parlour when James and Giffard were admitted.

James had ceased to think of Crusades, he had contrived to forget his accident. He was telling himself that he was on the threshold of his kingdom and that his first act must match the prosperous reign which, with God's help, was about to begin. He made straight for the largest, most throne-like chair. He motioned Giffard to place it at the heavy table and to stand behind him. With no other retinue, he sat facing the circle of his countrymen and subjects, some twice, some thrice, and Lennox four times his age.

"My lords," he said, "I understand that you have come to tell me what terms you have arranged for my ransom with my cousin of England. I shall be glad to receive your report."

Giffard looked down in some surprise at the boyish head beneath him: there would be sparks flying soon—and no harm in that. If only one were not sure of the long years of waiting that lay ahead, enough to quench the liveliest of sparks.

The bishop, no less surprised, began to talk of the progress, the considerable progress, that had been made. The difficulties of negotiating a permanent peace between the two nations had proved insuperable, but an important truce was in sight. When a few details had been arranged with the Wardens of the Marches——.

"There was a truce already," interrupted James. "I was captured in time of truce."

"The English dispute that, your Majesty. They——"

"Naturally! But it's true."

"It would have expired this year," said Lennox, "but for our efforts. We should be at war with England."

"England has too much on her hands to want another war. I cannot imagine that any extraordinary efforts were needed."

Better and better, thought Giffard: tumbling off a horse had sharpened the boy's tongue: and a scolding would do the old mummers no harm.

Lennox was staring round as if wondering who might have put the boy up to this. The bishop tried to look cunning and diplomatic. "I hope your Majesty will credit us," he said, "with taking full advantage of the embarrassments of England."

"And my ransom?" asked James. "My release?"

The bishop swallowed audibly and opened floodgates of vagueness and verbosity. It was impossible, he said, to bargain with Englishmen: King Henry had wasted three whole weeks in refusing to accord Albany his proper title: when he had at length consented to style him *Regent of Scotland* instead of *So-called Regent*, he had begun to name utterly impossible figures for the ransom. Albany could hardly make both ends meet in Scotland as it was. He was administering the royal estates for James, but with so many calls on him, so many public servants to pay or reward, he was quite out of pocket over the regency. He only continued it (one gathered) in pure self-sacrifice. He certainly could not find vast sums to satisfy King Henry's unreasonable greed.

"He could raise a tax," said James.

More rivers of rhetoric, mixed with indulgent patronage of a young boy's ignorance. Taxes were quite out of the question. The regent—already ruining himself for Scotland's benefit—could not be expected to court the crushing unpopularity that a tax would entail. The country expected a king or regent to pay for all accidents of government out of the royal estates, to "live of his own" as the phrase went. And Scotland was poor, far too poor to pay taxes: her life had been one long struggle against penury for a century and more—ever since the succession to the throne had fallen into dispute and King Edward's English armies had entered, to drown her Golden Age in blood.

"Thank you," said James, detecting an attempt to obscure the issue. "I know the history of my country."

He ceased to listen. The bishop was preaching patience, a boy's duty to trust his elders, the gratitude due for the excellent education that England was providing. Lennox backed him up with further praises of Albany and Albany's wise governance of Scotland. "And if your Majesty," he says, "doubts that we have done all that lies in us to ransom him, I can assure you that it is only King Henry that is to blame. My son-in-law, Albany's dear son Murdoch, has been in the Tower six years. You can be sure we both want him home, but we cannot persuade King Henry to let him go."

The two old men ended in a sort of chorus, from which one could only gather that James was likely to stay prisoner so long as Henry the Fourth was King of England.

James could well believe that. He sat gazing past them, drumming on the abbot's table with restless fingers. He saw a vision of Henry and uncle Albany smiling at each other across the four hundred miles that divided Stirling from Westminster. Outwardly at enmity, they had secretly combined to put him in prison and keep him there. They had much in common. Both were usurpers. Albany, no doubt, contemplated founding a new dynasty, over Rothesay's dead body, and James's imprisonment—as Henry had founded one upon King Richard's murder. Murdoch, having served his purpose as agent in London, link between the two accomplices, would be sent back to reign in Scotland, while James still languished in gaol. Henry and Albany were chief plotters in that vast conspiracy of the middle-aged and the secure, which derided Ardour, and had forgotten Justice, and was only busy in riveting fetters on the limbs of Youth.

It was possible that the two old fools that had been sent him were dupes rather than partners in the wrong. He should have known, when he heard their names, that the embassy would accomplish nothing, was meant to accomplish nothing. Brechin was a cypher, and Lennox had married his daughter to Albany's son. If honest Orkney had been sent again, or Bishop Wardlaw, James's old tutor from St. Andrews. If——.

Wardlaw's name suddenly reminded him of another envoy—Robert Lanyne from St. Andrews, the bishop's friend and possibly agent. They were pushing him forward now—hoping, perhaps, to create a diversion. Lanyne's official mission was to report on the new University that Wardlaw was hoping to found, the first in Scotland. Wardlaw, having had the money—and the enterprise—to get his degrees abroad, was good enough Christian to champion poor Scotsmen who could never reach hostile Oxford or distant, foreign-speaking Paris. Such an enterprise—already receiving the Pope's sanction—might well kindle Master Robert Lanyne's enthusiasm. But James, looking desperately round for allies, for some link with those in Scotland who had not forgotten their captive king, fancied that the bright, almost fanatical light in Lanyne's eyes must burn for something more than learning.

As Lanyne spoke, James, self-persuaded, found it easier every moment to believe that he brought some secret message of loyalty and hope. If that were so, and if it could be got past Albany's henchmen, here was a possibility that might overweigh all the humiliations and disappointments of the day.

It almost seemed as if Albany's henchmen were on the

watch: it might not be only professional jealousy of a subordinate—or of a rival diocese—that was making the Bishop of Brechin interrupt Lanyne so often in his report. He was suggesting now—to James's amusement—that other prelates beside Wardlaw had had a hand in the originating of the scheme for a University. Lanyne was on the defensive at once: the stiff hair round his tonsure seemed to bristle, his little terrier's eyes to flash fire.

"Come, come, man!" said the bishop, "when did my lord of St. Andrews first set the scheme on foot? Some three or four years ago, after the Synod at——"

"Six years ago!" barked Lanyne, and then added more quickly. "When his lordship was first consecrated, the year after my lord of Rothesay's death."

James detected—or imagined—a slight shiver of embarrassment, particularly in Lennox. The signal from Lanyne seemed clear. There had been no need whatever to mention Rothesay's name: to do so, in such company, was to imply that the speaker believed Rothesay to have been murdered, and by Albany. Lanyne, looking at James as he spoke of James's dead brother, was trying to make it clear that there were Scotsmen—perhaps a considerable party of them though necessarily a wary one—that detested Albany and all his works. They had commissioned Lanyne to tell James that they were only waiting his word to smash the filthy web of the regency, to demand their king from England, pay for him if need be, and be true Scotsmen again.

Lanyne had finished his report without further interruption; he was laying a written document on the table, an outline for the new University's curriculum and teaching-staff. Even that would have to be searched, in private, for hidden messages. Meanwhile James could dismiss the embassy for the night; there might be many more formalities, signatures and so forth; they could wait till a second meeting, tomorrow; he must strike on hot iron.

He bid them good-night, watched Lennox motioning the

bishop to precede him through the door—one old sheep courteously offering another to the gap in the hedge. When they were almost gone, he suddenly beckoned to Lanyne, deceiving Lennox's backward glance by picking up the document from the table as though wanting some detail in it explained. Then he waited till the door was closed, the room empty of all save Giffard and Lanyne.

"Why did you mention my lord of Rothesay?" he asked, in a low conspiratorial voice, his eyes fixed hungrily on the priest. "Why did you mention my brother?"

The eagerness, the intelligence, seemed to fade from Lanyne's face. He stood nonplussed, fidgeted with the rough cord that belted his gown, blushed and stammered like a girl.

"I am sorry," he said, "if I . . . if I offended your Majesty. I was just meaning. . . . I did not mean. . . ."

"You did not offend me," said the boy. "Far from it! I only wished to know why you mentioned that name."

No answer. Lanyne merely shuffled, clearly at a dead loss. James looked up at the door again but none of the others had returned or could be in earshot. He made a last attempt.

"You brought no private message from Bishop Wardlaw? Nor from anyone else in Scotland?"

No. Lanyne knew of no private message. He was obviously concealing nothing, was obviously incapable of deceiving James. He had come to talk about the new University, being interested, fanatically, in that, and interested in little else. It was only James who had deceived himself.

Lanyne was looking helplessly at the report on the table, shuffling its familiar pages with nervous fingers. James saw no way to be rid of the man, except by telling a lie.

"You may not have known," he said, "that my brother, too, was interested in this scheme for a University. He visited St. Andrews shortly before his death."

A vague, half-incredulous comprehension stole back into

Lanyne's face. He had never heard of young Rothesay being interested in anything except women. Still, one never knew. Princes were always slandered.

"We will talk of that tomorrow," said James, determined to do no such thing. "And now, Master Lanyne, I will wish you a good night."

Lanyne bowed and withdrew, his thoughts, temporarily distracted, escaping back to their accustomed channels: the lecturers, the buildings, the courses: the great *Trivium*—Grammar, Rhetoric, Logic: the riches which would at last be within the grasp of the poorest Scot who could carry a sack of oatmeal from his father's cottage to St. Andrews. Lanyne hoped, tomorrow, that his Majesty would be less enigmatic, more thorough in his scrutiny of the scheme. It was a sign of James's capacity for kingship that, tomorrow, Master Robert Lanyne would not be disappointed.

Tomorrow. The immediate problem, for James, was how to get through tonight. He was alone, in spite of Giffard at his elbow, more utterly alone than the imagination of fourteen years could quite grasp: without allies, matched against Albany and King Henry, and the two great kingdoms that toadied to them. Without hope, save in their deaths, and his own persevering courage. Meanwhile there was nothing for it but watchfulness, the lone hand skilfully played in the face of grinding frustration—and the patience that the old fool from Brechin had recommended.

He suddenly realized that he was dog-weary, aching for bed. He would have given much for a litter to carry him there, save him from the walk through the dark streets. He would have given more, given everything, in a sudden, unnerving fit of anguish, to find his mother awaiting him in that gaunt stone house in the High Street. It was seven years since she had smoothed a pillow for him, whispered the comforting nonsense into his drowsy ear. Seven years since they had laid her to rest in her eternal bed.

"The men are waiting, your Majesty. Shall we be going home?"

Giffard was speaking, a rather awed Giffard: unable to digest all he had witnessed, unable to recognize his young charge in the boy who had behaved, through a long evening, in a way not unfitting to a king.

James rose, surprised to find himself stiff as well as weary. There was a hot feeling behind his eyes, a catch in his throat. He wanted, suddenly, to bury himself in Giffard's arms, sob out his anger and loneliness and despair.

Then he looked at Giffard, his elder, but deferential and slightly bewildered. His subject and servant.

"You must be tired, Giffard," he said. "You have been standing a long time."

Then he turned and marched out of the room, remembering, above all things, to hold his head high.

1409-1412

V

Three years passed by and there was no sign of change. James was taken from one place to another, still learning all that the English could teach him, still treated with respectful kindness, and still a prisoner. King Henry was sick—in mind no less than body. King Henry (so whispered Prince Hal and his friends) was growing incapable of government and ought to resign kingship to his son. But he gave no sign whatever of relaxing his grip on the captive James.

Meanwhile as the three years passed heavily over, Europe, largely unmindful of a young Prince's sorrows, played three more rounds of her ancient and discreditable game.

Europe had long seen two rival Popes, ruling from Rome and Avignon, each denouncing the other as unlawfully elected, as anti-Pope and anti-Christ. She was at last moved to desultory action; a General Council of Christendom met at Pisa to remove this schism; it deposed the rivals in order to raise its own candidate to indubitable Popedom. The result was discouraging, for in place of two Vicars of Christ, warring for the allegiance of the faithful, there were now three. Mediaeval civilization, whose essence was spiritual unity, was already showing upon itself the marks of death.

As if scenting the threat of dismemberment, barely a century ahead, Christendom roused itself to the feverish cruelty of the doomed. The blood of heretics began to hiss in a thousand banked-up fires. Princes and prelates agreed that there was no other way to keep untorn the seamless robe of Christ. England, for the first time in her history, called up primeval savagery to preserve her Faith. Her first victim was from Norfolk, her second John Badby, the Evesham tailor. Badby, haled to Westminster, maintained his convictions against the assembled lords and bishops. Prince Hal, whose reputation for loose-living seemed no bar to his zeal for religion, was asked to preside at the wretched man's execution. When the flames had begun to mount, he suddenly ordered the faggots to be scattered; approaching the stake himself, he begged Badby to recant, offered him life, freedom, and even a pension from his own purse. Badby, white with terror, found strength to resist the bribe. The fire was re-kindled, the ceremony completed. The little tailor departed to plead his cause before a higher tribunal.

In every country, men felt the foundations rock, and strange happenings nourished their alarm. The King of France had met a madman in a wood, and run mad himself; his powerful kinsmen, careless of their country's hard-won unity, were plotting civil war, hiring cut-throats to kill each other in the streets; his good city of Paris saw its Guild of Butchers and Flayers reorganized for the butchery of men. The Germans trembled to hear that heathen hordes had crushed the champions of Prussia in the great fight at Tannenburg. And if, at one end of Europe the menace of Islam was evaporating in the filthy intrigues of the Seville harems, at the other the Grand Turk carried all before him. Freed from fear by Tamerlane's death, he was dining with his pashas and plotting to turn back and blot out Byzantium, round tables built up of Serbian corpses.

Amidst so much that was momentous, Albany strove to keep Scotland's annals innocent of event. His inglorious aim could be attained by not badgering King Henry too importunately, by bribing the discontented at home with large slices of Crown land and revenue. But the peace he preserved was within an ace of being overwhelmed in an unexpected avalanche.

Only Mar had foreseen it, and, by the time it reached Mar's country, it had taken the form of ten thousand Highland men in full war paint; at their head came Donald McIan, chieftain of the vast clan of Macdonald and heir to the Viking kinglets who had once ruled from Stornoway to Man. As they poured round Bennachie, Mar stopped their way with a few steel-clad knights and such burghers of Aberdeen as had had the money to buy themselves armour. When the sun set he was still alive, still panting through discoloured teeth; but most of his men lay dead on the slopes of Harlaw, with uncounted Highlanders to keep them company. Macdonald hesitated, took stock, and then —after the manner of the Gael—suddenly decided to go home to Skye or Islay, acknowledging defeat. Scotland breathed again, and settled back to its business; but it was a sad winter for the widows and orphans of Aberdeen.

Albany had cause to congratulate himself upon his policy. Aristocratic discontent, well-bribed for years, had shown no sign of allying itself with Highland invasion; Mar had had no armoured Lowland knights to beat back at Harlaw. The discreet bribery had better continue, if necessary by a wholesale alienation of King James's lands and revenues. The nobles must be kept in good humour, even if the process entailed a certain winking at the oppression and robbery of the poor. It could not last for ever, since royal property was limited and the proud greed of nobles illimitable. But, Albany reflected, it would probably last his time.

Meanwhile he presided over a reasonably peaceful Scotland. He hoped, one day, to ransom his son, and perhaps hand on to him the regency. He was undeniably popular with such of his subjects as thought it safe to express an opinion. He, too, had burnt a heretic, and enjoyed the support of Holy Kirk. He was acknowledged and respected by the chief princes of Europe. It was surely a hard thing if more were expected from a man who had already passed his seventieth year.

Harry to Harry

My little finger shall be thicker than my father's loins.

2 Chron. x. 10.

CHAPTER TWO

Harry to Harry

August 1412

I

"HIS MAJESTY WILL receive you in a few moments. He regrets that you have been kept waiting."

It was an hour since James had first heard these same words, and now, at the fourth repetition, he was beginning to resent them.

He was more than weary of fidgeting around the sultry room in Fulham Palace, without even a book to pass the time for him. The windows, opening on a side alley, seemed to admit air more oppressive than that which already stagnated inside. In the far corner two dogs slumbered, waking every now and then to turn over and grumble at the heat. Men passed from one door to another on mysterious errands. Most of them slackened pace to stare at James. A captive king is always something to gossip about. And—since they were Englishmen—there was a further spur to their curiosity in James's athletic reputation. It is customary to exaggerate the personal achievements of princes; but in the guildhalls and alehouses where such weighty topics were discussed, it was understood that the Scotch lad's feats of running and wrestling stood in no need of exaggeration. King Henry's men, passing from door to door of the ante-room, were glad of the opportunity to appraise his short, thick-set figure, fingering his muscles with their impertinent stare.

James, misunderstanding their curiosity, could only imagine that they were eyeing his clothes. He was unpleasantly aware that, for a reigning king, he was disgracefully poor, worse dressed than most country squires.

"His Majesty regrets——"

James turned to see which of the servants had brought the message this time. He was surprised to find himself facing a Churchman, and a bishop at that. London seemed to swarm with clerics. He was staying with the monks of Stratford-at-Bowe. He was soon to be transferred to the care of Archbishop Arundel at Croydon. And here was another prelate, doing lackey's service at Fulham.

Not that he resembled a lackey in the least. He looked overfed to begin with; hardly one's ideal of a Christian priest: the full lips and sagging cheeks mocked the thought of asceticism. He was short, even shorter than James. A little turkey-cock, red and pompous. But no fool. The face suggested unusual ability, pride, irritated ambition. If he is not a great power in England, thought James, he'll never rest till he becomes one. He'll never let anything or anyone stand in the way of that. I wonder who it can be.

The bishop seemed to divine the question.

"Henry of Beaufort," he said, with a polite smile, "at your Majesty's service."

James knew the name well enough. The Beauforts were, in a somewhat dim way, half-brothers of the king. They had been legitimized, all three of them—Somerset, now dead: Exeter, the admiral and soldier: and this little prelate, made Bishop of Winchester and Chancellor, but now somewhat out of favour. One wondered why he was at Fulham. But he was reputed to be enormously rich, and might at any moment be a power again. James could not afford to alienate anyone who might influence England's policy towards her neighbours and her captives.

"My lord of Winchester," he said, "I am glad of the meeting."

"Very kind of your Majesty," replied the bishop, "very kind indeed." His voice was thick and slow, an odd contrast with the restless little eyes which pried and probed at James's face.

"Extremely trying weather," he continued. "I hope your Majesty is not incommoded by the heat." Beaufort himself lapped in fat and episcopal robes, was sweating like a pig.

"Has your lordship come from the king?" asked James.

Beaufort looked vexed.

"No. Not exactly," he said. "The Chamberlain asked me to tell you——. His Majesty has not honoured me with an interview today."

"Were you seeking one?" asked James, yielding to malicious impulse.

"We all wait on his Majesty's pleasure," answered Beaufort. "When his Majesty is free, I have, er, representations to make to him, from his Highness the Prince of Wales." He accompanied the name with a piercing look at James, as if to make sure that he was duly impressed. "But it is not urgent, not at all urgent. His Majesty nowadays. . . ."

His voice trailed away into nothing. James remembered that this man had hitched his waggon, long ago, to the back of Prince Hal's chariot. Another reason for keeping on good terms. King Henry was not yet fifty, but one could not tell when a new reign might not be starting.

One of the dogs had woken and was scratching itself vigorously, without thought of decorum. The bishop turned on it, as though in anger, and then checked. He could not conceal his irritation.

"This man will be in torment," thought James, "until he's in power again. And then he'll want more power. He'll never rest till he's Grand Cham in England, and Pope into the bargain."

"Here!" he called out, "stop scratching, Beauty!"

The dog looked up, puzzled and aggrieved. Then it decided it was too hot to dispute the matter and relapsed into whining slumber. The bishop recovered composure.

"Your Majesty sleeps at Stratford Abbey tonight?" he asked with an ingratiating smile.

"I do—unless your king has other plans for me."

The bishop hesitated, glanced round, as if weighing risks, and took the plunge.

"Your Majesty must be hoping," he said, "for the day when he can sleep in Dunfermline again. I can only assure your Majesty that, when I was Chancellor, my voice was invariably for release—and without ransom."

He had screwed his face up into an earnestness that almost persuaded one of his sincerity. "Friendship with Scotland," he continued, "and mutual assistance among princes; that is the cause I have always recommended. Naturally, I had opponents on the Council—I name no names—and I am afraid their views prevailed. But a change will come, I feel sure a change will come."

James had no difficulty in seeing through Beaufort. He was clearly a man who would seek allies in every political byway—and drop them again as soon as they seemed unprofitable. As he looked at the red, greasy face, straining to re-assume a long-lost candour, he felt a kind of nausea stealing over his senses. He broke abruptly away, and walked to the window, leaving Beaufort at a loss.

He was more than ever impatient to be admitted to the king. Henry might be a bully and a robber, but would prove better company than this fawning bishop. James tried to recall his memories of Henry at their interview six years ago, when the king had been so unseasonably jaunty over his capture at sea. He remembered a man of mature and powerful body, with an irritating bluffness of manner and (unless James had imagined this) a certain trace of guilty conscience such as might well beset a usurper. If that were so, he must be hardened by now; it was twelve years since Richard had been dethroned and murdered, and Henry had used them to beat down every enemy, even to rid himself of the accomplices who had put him on the throne. Archbishop Scrope had perished on the scaffold: Hotspur slept soundly under Shrewsbury turf: Glendower was a hunted fugitive. Henry was secure, beyond the shaking of reaction or revolt; if not loved in England, he was feared: rumour said that he was planning to spread fear in France, to lead an army there and revive his youthful renown as a tough fighter. He could perhaps afford to let his captive go, restore to Scotland her absent king. James wondered how to put his case to this unscrupulous, successful upstart. Perhaps it would be best to see first what manner of man he had become, and then trust to inspiration.

"If your Majesty would come this way——"

An usher stood beside the open doorway. James strode out: his time had come. As he went, he heard the bishop, still faintly disconcerted, murmuring good wishes, hopes for his success.

He passed down a long passage, attendants bowing him on his way. A turn to the right brought him into a kind of lobby, where stood an oak chest. The sun poured down upon it, through stained glass, in many-coloured splendour. Opposite, a sallow, foreign-looking man stood holding aside a curtain, revealing a doorway. James marched in. The curtain dropped behind him. He found himself in total darkness.

He supposed himself still dazzled with the sun. In a moment he would be able to see his way on. He had better stand still.

The air was heavy with strange, sickly smells, as of burning, of medicines, of decay. He put out a hand and encountered heavy velvet hangings, slimily soft. Even in the dark he could have sworn they were not clean.

"Bingley? Is that Bingley?"

The sudden voice, husky but querulous, made James start like a frightened girl. It seemed to come from below him, not very far away. There was silence a moment, then rustlings, like those of an injured animal in a thicket.

"Who is it? I sent for Bingley!"

The voice was more petulant than ever. James, growing a little more accustomed to the gloom, began to descry something that might be a face. Its owner seemed to be lying on a bed, or litter, set directly athwart his path. Limbs stirred upon it, displacing sombre coverings, and sending out a new wave of those intolerable smells.

"Where am I?" demanded James, "I came to see the king."

"Oh, it's you," said the unknown voice. "Of course. The Scotch lad. Well, you've found the king—all there is of him. Didn't they tell you I was ill?"

For a moment James felt an unreasoning instinct to turn back, to push into the sunlight, to quit, at any cost, this incredible presence. But the king's voice, whining again from the shadows, held him in place.

"I sent for you, didn't I?" it said. "So many things to do, before—in case anything happens to me. I get no peace nowadays. I wanted to tell you—— Something I want to do for you, if they'd only let me. They're all against me, you know; every one of them. Even Hal. I'm not sure he's not the worst of them. You were a good son to your father, weren't you? They told me you were a good son."

James said nothing. It was still difficult to believe that it was a human being that was speaking, impossible to imagine that it was King Henry.

"Of course, your father's dead. Died when we captured you. So much blood on my soul! And you were quite young—too young to be up to Hal's tricks. I suppose you've heard of that business at the Vintry; everyone's heard of it by now. What's the fellow's name that keeps it? John, that's it, Lewis John. Brings Welsh girls up to London—for the stews, you know. Fine place for the heir of England to be supping! And by midnight they were fighting all over Eastcheap; lucky they weren't arrested. He has been, you know. Gascoigne had him committed once, just for an hour or two. Tried to slap Gascoigne's face. Why don't you say something?"

James opened dry lips. His tongue seemed to stick in his mouth and no words came. The king had begun to cough in the darkness.

"Wait, wait," he said hoarsely. "Do something for me, James. Your name's James, isn't it? I wanted——."

There was a scratching sound as the sick man fumbled with a tinder-box. His clumsy fingers seemed unequal to the task, but the few sparks he managed to strike illumined an array of cups and bottles on a stool beside the litter.

"There it is," muttered the king. "Needn't trouble you. He's poured me out a dose."

He gulped the medicine, sighed, grumbled a moment and lay still. James was incapable of movement: for the sparks had thrown their light upon the sick man's features and shown, in a few seconds of lurid vision, the ruin that had once been King Harry.

He was still in the forties, but the face was that of an old, old man. To premature senility were added the horrors of disease. From its black centre between the brows, decay had crawled and spread like a fungus over the flesh. If the strong chin was still untouched, it hung loose, as though the jaw-muscles had already begun to rot.

Christendom spoke of Henry Bolingbroke as a good knight who had forfeited honour and stolen his master's crown: God punished such treasons, here or hereafter: seldom so swiftly or so signally as this.

James stared in fascination, though returning gloom hid all but a grey shadow of that ghastly face. He found himself thinking of a story that had once reached him from gossip's tongue. He had heard how Henry had returned from pilgrimage at Jerusalem by way of Italy and Milan: how the little Visconti girl, the Duke's fifteen-year-old niece, had lost her heart to the bluff stranger from distant England: how, years later, when they found her a great German lord for husband, she had stormed and wept and sworn to wear no wedding-garment for any bridegroom but her wonderful Enrico. She was dead now, sleeping in marble beside the husband they had forced upon her. Providence had been kind to shield her from the knowledge of what her lover could become.

"Useless," mumbled King Henry in the darkness, "the medicine's useless. They're all bunglers. They think I'm going to die, you know; that's why I sent for you."

He coughed again, twisting about upon the litter.

"I made my will yesterday," he continued, "just in case they're right. Not that I believe them. There's something I must do yet, something reserved for me. But I take every precaution. I've so much I must make amends for. I wanted to make amends to you. I can't release you myself, I can't go back on all I said to Albany. But I've told Hal he must let you go, as soon as he's king. A fine king he'll be! It'll be the end of England. But his one chance is to start clean: he can begin by releasing you. I've twice his powers, you know, and I've always known how to control myself. It's only my sins that have ruined me. They give me no peace. I've done all I can, except give up the crown. I couldn't do that, now Richard's dead and buried. They wouldn't let me, anyway; Hal wouldn't let me. Wants to be king himself, God forgive him. He's not a bad lad, you know, but he's cold, as well as wild. He can't understand."

James stirred in the darkness, half stepping towards the door. Embarrassment, added to physical disgust, was fast making his situation unbearable. He had heard all he needed to hear: the end of this creature's reign was to be the end of his captivity: he could not have long to wait: perhaps autumn would see him speeding up the Great North Road, perhaps the sun would still be warm as he rode over the Border, to Melrose and Edinburgh and Scone. Albany would have to cloak his annoyance and vanish into insignificance. A new age would dawn in Scotland. There would be no need to give another thought to the mass of corruption that the English would be burying, in lead and sculptured stone, beneath the nave of Canterbury.

"But they're wrong, you know," the querulous voice broke out again. "I'm going to recover. I'm going to be strong again. Shall I tell you how I know? I've never told anyone yet. Come closer, James, and I'll whisper it to you. I don't want anyone else to hear. . . . No, no. Closer. I'm not going to hurt you."

James mastered his repugnance and approached the litter.

"You saw that man at the door? That's Henry. I always call him Henry."

The king sniggered.

"He's a Saracen, you know. I brought him back from Syria, had him baptized. I keep him by me, to remind me I've been there. Been to Jerusalem. That wipes out a great many sins. And—listen, Jamie, listen—I'm going there again. A Welshwoman told me, a prophetess. I'm going to die in Jerusalem. I'll take you with me to the Holy Land, as soon as I'm well. You'd like to come, wouldn't you? It's good to have been a Crusader. And you'll like seeing it all: sun and little white houses, and the village where God was born. We'll conquer it, hold it for Christendom. They've a saying there that it's the English who'll conquer the Holy Land. We'll make it come true. Nothing can stop us, once I'm well again. Think of it, Jamie, think! You and I together!"

His hands were clawing at James's body, his foul breath in James's face. If his grasp was clumsy, it had a kind of desperate strength. The boy felt himself dragged down, suffocated and poisoned. He could find no words to cry out at the thing, half king, half monster, that had clipped him in its unclean embrace. He seized the sick man's wrists, set his knee against the litter, and wrenched himself away. The stool crashed over, cups and medicines rolling to the floor. The king whimpered with pain, and then let out a cracked shriek.

"Henry! Henry!" he called.

The curtain lifted, the Turk slipped into the room.

"Your Majesty?"

"Take him away! Take him away, I tell you! They're all against me, every one of them. They want to kill me."

"Your Majesty has the fever again. I will find his medicine."

The man spoke with a strange, thick accent, but soothingly as a nurse to a sick child.

"The medicine's useless," whined the king, "take that boy away."

"Master Bingley is waiting, with the music," said the Turk, "I'll light the lamp and bring him in."

"No, no, no! I won't have light in here. I don't want any music. I want to be left alone."

James was fumbling for the curtained door. He found it at last, blundered through and stood blinking in the coloured sunlight. He looked round as if awakened from a dream.

He saw that he was not alone. Opposite him, on the oak chest, sat one of the silliest creatures he had ever seen. His legs, clothed in two different colours, were as thin as spear-shafts, and much less shapely. His eyebrows were shaved or plucked, his eyes pale green. Two whisps of colourless beard hardly concealed a total absence of chin.

As James appeared, he hastily pocketed a little mirror in which he had been studying his unattractive features. He took up a little painted, beribboned lute.

"Is his Majesty ready to receive me?" he asked.

The voice was so low and melodious, so utterly out of keeping with the preposterous face, that James looked round to see if anyone else could be speaking. Then he turned to go.

"My name is Bingley," said the musician, and it was still a pleasure to hear him. "Bingley of Beckenham. The king requested my attendance."

"Mine is James," said the prince, in a sudden, unreasoned anger, "James of Scotland. And I wish you joy of your king!"

He marched away down the passage, thinking with relief of the ride that lay before him—the sun-soaked fields, the distant glimpse of London. If Beaufort was still waiting in the ante-room, he would ignore Beaufort and all his ready-made compliments. Sun: open air: a horse.

From behind his back, muffled by the thick curtain, came the high cackle of hysteria. King Henry and his Saracen were in train for a bad night.

January 1413

II

"Ay, I can lend ye some paper. I can lend ye that. When'll I see it back?"

"When your father sends me more of my own money, I suppose. Will that do?"

"I doubt it'll have to."

Murdoch, Earl of Fife and heir of Albany, sat upright in the great oak chair in Stratford Abbey and gazed stupidly at his ample fire. The monks treated him well, more for the sake of the money that reached him from Scotland than for his personal attractions—though he was an extremely handsome man. An outsider might have guessed that of the two cousins, it was Murdoch that was the exiled king; he was royal in appearance and mode of living, if somewhat after the manner of the majestic King Log.

James had the energy for King Stork, though hardly the inches. He was certainly impatient now. "Where do you keep your paper?" he said.

Murdoch began to rise and then decided to trust his impecunious cousin. "In the chest," he said. "Under that window."

James followed the slow jerk of Murdoch's bearded chin and made to help himself. "I'll have a morsel of wax, too," he said, "if you're sure you can spare it."

It was something of a farce sealing his letters to Scotland: he felt sure they were generally unsealed and read before they reached their destination in the country where Albany was regent. It was perhaps useless to write at all, when he hardly dared to say half of what he meant—if only for fear of getting good friends into trouble.

"You'll be putting back what you're not using?" said Murdoch over his shoulder.

"I will."

Murdoch seemed a little doubtful. "Maybe you could write your letters in here," he said. "There's a table and pens."

James smiled. The man deserved to be robbed. But he had a good fire in his room, and James's own quarters were poorly warmed, this cold January. James was still resisting his first temptation to be more of a parasite than necessary, when his search for sealing-wax revealed something that seemed to suggest a second. It was like Murdoch to leave his secret seal in an unlocked chest. He picked it up, and found that it was indeed what he had supposed, a solid piece of silver-work with the arms of Fife in intaglio. Here was the one key that might open a number of doors to secrecy in Scotland. One disliked using it, but it was not James that had started the game in which secrecy was so imperative—and, up to now, so one-sided. He would certainly write his letters in Murdoch's room, with Murdoch's seal in his left fist, while he decided whether or no he could quiet his scruples and use it.

He settled down at the table. Murdoch, to all appearances, was going to sleep. One could not be sure: Murdoch awake was so somnolent that it was easy to be mistaken. He was within sight of forty, had been captured at Homildon Hill some ten years back and still took imprisonment in such a spirit that James could not help wondering whether his manner, as of a slightly bewildered sheep, did not cover some more sinister purpose.

James nibbled his pen. He would write to Albany for form's sake. He would write to friends who were less in kinship and more in kindness. He would not tell them all, even covertly, but he would say a great deal more than he generally dared.

He would not even hint at the scene in that evil-smelling, darkened sickroom, nor at his subsequent sight of King Henry, here at Stratford, looking more sickly than ever. He smiled to himself, finding a formula.

'*I found his Majesty so gracious,*' he wrote, '*that there is nothing about him which I would have otherwise.*'

Neither, thought James, his desire to make amends to a captive, nor his approaching death.

Meanwhile his friend should know a little of the indignation that consumed him. He must certainly use Murdoch's seal, if they were to know, in safety, of the principal reason for his exile.

'*The delay in my homecoming stands only in them who should be most busy to forward it.*'

Let Albany intercept that and read it! It was almost worth the risk.

He grew bolder, turned back to a letter he had begun to Albany himself. He would tell him, with a straight pen, to bestir himself more thoroughly for his king's release, lest '*in your failure, I find cause to seek my deliverance, in future, from some other quarter.*'

It was an hour or more before all the letters were finished. Murdoch had not moved. He was still staring into the fire.

James rose at last, folded the sheets, and brought a candle to the fire to light it.

"I'll be putting the rest of the paper back," he said.

"Ay," said Murdoch. "But there'll be little left, the time you've been writing."

James returned to the table and began to seal, his fingers covering the silver work of the stolen bauble. Six letters, no bad batch for a Sunday evening. He had even written one to the Douglas, though the Douglas had for so long put his vast strength behind the inertia of Albany's rule that there was little hope of detaching him by a few sharp words. The wax sputtered, burning his fingers.

"It'll be cold in Scotland," said Murdoch unexpectedly. "I was thinking there'd be snow in Fife. Snow on the Lomonds."

"There'll be that," said James, "and in the west, too. It's January."

There was silence a moment, both gazing at the fire.

"I was thinking," said Murdoch, "of the last time I saw snow on the Lomonds. We killed a stag at Drumain, up by the burn."

"I remember one January," said James, "when my father took me up Campsie Glen to Inchmahome. There was ice on the lake, and the monks got their food across by sleigh."

He gathered up his letters mechanically, his mind four hundred miles away. Murdoch stroked his brown beard, gazing sleepily at the glowing logs.

"I wonder," said James, looking down at his letters, "I wonder which of us will be the first to see snow in Scotland again."

March 1413

III

King Henry never recovered. No one except himself had imagined that he would. It was whispered that the crown he had stolen was weighing him down to his death. It was whispered again—and more especially in monasteries and cathedral chapter-houses—that his affliction, which some called scurvy and others leprosy, had struck him between the brows upon the very day when he had ordered an archbishop to execution. God had avenged His own.

Henry had begun to haunt churches towards the end, to talk only of penitence and reparation. If he hoped to wring from Heaven a permit for longer sojourn on earth, a putting-off of his final audit, he failed in his purpose. Seven months after his summer visit to Fulham, he was seized with a fainting-fit as he knelt at the Abbey altar, and carried into Westminster Palace. There he died—as if to ridicule the human prophecies on which he had relied—in the chamber nicknamed Jerusalem.

He had been calmer towards the end, recapturing some of the manliness which had marked the beginning of his strange and dubious career. He died in reconciliation with his son Hal, with the Church, and perhaps with his own conscience. He kept faith with James, including among his last instructions an earnest recommendation that the King of Scots be sent back to Scotland.

James was at Croydon, under the guardianship of old Archbishop Arundel, when the news of the king's death came.

It was the last week of March and he had been flying his hawks along the downs above Oxted. He came home at midday with an appetite like a razor, and found that dinner was not yet laid. His Grace, he was told, was closeted with secretaries above. The ground-floor of the Palace seemed to be in complete disorganization. James went upstairs, sending Giffard to forage in the Buttery. As he ran up the last flight, a door opened and Arundel stepped onto the threshold. He saw James and hesitated, as if forgetful of his own errand. He looked even older than his age, tired and a little lonely.

"Your Majesty has heard the news?" he asked.

His Majesty had heard the news. For the moment it seemed less important than wet boots and the clamour of an empty stomach.

"I am resigning from the Chancery," said the archbishop. "A new reign demands new ministers. There is little left for me now, except to say prayers for his late Majesty."

"I can only hope," said James, "that my lord of Winchester will not succeed you as Chancellor."

"Who can tell?" said Arundel, "who can tell? The new king——"

He checked himself, and then sighed, as though Bishop

Beaufort's return to the Chancery would spell ruin for England. Indeed the England he knew, the England he had helped to make, was crumbling faster than the scarce-cold corpse at Westminster.

"I fear," he said, "that this may mean the end of your time with me."

"I am hoping," said James, "that it may mean the end of my captivity."

Arundel looked at him as if the few yards that separated them were unmeasurable distance.

"Ah, yes," he said, "I suppose that has been in your mind. One forgets, you know. Other men's troubles. . . . Life goes on, my son, and one notices it less. You too will be old one day."

His mind was clearly busy with its own affairs. James felt something like pity for the old man, standing so forlornly in the doorway. His story was almost told now. He had played some strange games in his time, as must anyone who had helped to hand old Henry up to the throne and helped to keep him there. Time had softened, almost justified, the ignobilities of the past, and one preferred this relic of slipping grandeur to the Hals and Beauforts of the new era. Still, there was no object in catching a cold for the sake of providing audience for Arundel's self-centred moralizings.

"I will come down to dinner at once," said James, and pointed to his boots. "Your Grace will excuse me while I change these."

Arundel hardly seemed to hear. His eyes did not follow the boy who ran past him and out of sight.

It was raining again next day, and James offered to keep his host company in the afternoon. He was working on a new tune and would have liked to try it on outside ears. But Arundel suggested reading aloud, and began to hunt round the room for some book whose title he had forgotten. James went to fetch his own Chaucer—a parting present from Evesham.

He had hardly returned, the Archbishop had only just settled into the right posture of tolerant disapproval, when the reading was interrupted. There was a bustle outside, a sharp *crescendo* of discussion between servants and some newcomer to the Palace. Then the door was thrown open to admit two damp pursuivants, bearing the king's badge. The younger of them bent a perfunctory knee to the Archbishop and presented a royal warrant. James rose and walked tactfully to the window. The rain outside seemed to be abating a little.

The old man crackled the paper open and began to read. He whispered complainingly to its bearer, darting embarrassed glances towards the figure at the window. His scruples, apparently, met with scant response. The pursuivant saw no need for a hushed voice, nor for beating about the bush.

"Today," he said, "and immediately. His things can be sent on after."

Arundel beckoned his guest to him and held out the paper in silence. It was an order, signed at the first Council of the new reign, ordering James to closer confinement in the Tower of London. Henry the Fifth was king.

As they rode through the drizzle, over Herne Hill and down to the river at Southwark, James tried to discover from his new guardians what the new reign held for him, and what this sudden order portended. When he got no answer but evasions, he persuaded himself that Henry was summoning him to London in order to prepare for his release.

He managed to preserve his conviction through the dull weeks that followed, with only books and music to solace his closer confinement. He shut his ears to the persistent gossip that Hal showed every sign of running counter to all the old king's wishes. He could not blame him for dismissing most of his father's ministers, even if that meant that Arundel must give way to Beaufort; Arundel was a sentimental dotard whose work was done. It was less pleasing to hear that Henry had missed an opportunity for being generous and dismissed Gascoigne from the Bench: for it was only after Agincourt that England fabricated the story of Henry renewing the commission of a judge who had had the courage to arrest him. But James, letting wishes be father to his thoughts, still believed obstinately in the ultimate goodness of the inscrutable young man that had climbed on to England's throne.

He had difficulty in maintaining his faith on the day of the coronation. The Tower was buzzing with activity, for fifty candidates for knighthood came to take their ceremonial bath there and watch their arms through a long night in the Chapel. James was not among them, nor was he permitted to see them receive the accolade. From his distant cell, he heard the clatter of hopeful youth, as they mounted to ride beside Henry to the Abbey. He could only set his teeth and tell the unresponsive Giffard that he would soon be knighting as many Scotsmen beneath the trees of Scone.

August 1st 1413

IV

It was midsummer before anything happened. James awoke one morning to hear his gaoler in the bedroom, announcing that King Henry, after a busy week or two out of London, had been seen near the Tower. "And you can strike me flat," he said, "if I'd have known our Hal."

James, still abed, was far too sleepy to strike anyone flat. He wondered who the turnkey was addressing. He wished the man would go away. For the first time in his life, he was beginning to enjoy lying in bed of a morning; there was so cursedly little to look forward to, when one did get up.

A voice through the door of his outer room soon resolved one doubt. "You wouldn't have known your own wife and daughter," it said, "the state you were in last night!" The rattle of plates announced that the gaoler's wife was laying breakfast. Her husband, already approaching the bed, turned back to shout at her. "I was not speaking of last night," he called, "he was in the streets at daybreak this morning."

"Not for the first time!" came the prompt reply. "When he gets to Eastcheap, and Lewis John's fancy-house, it's generally daybreak before he's away home! And looking like the day after yesterday, too."

The gaoler seemed to think this sufficient warrant for close quarters. He moved back to the door, and began scolding through it. "I tell you," he said, "that the king was coming up from Westminster early, as spick as a judge and three times as solemn. Eastcheap's lost her Hal; England's lost her Hal: and the Virgin only knows what's come in the place of him. They say he's taken an oath on St. Teddy's bones not to touch another woman till he marries."

"Well, all I can say is that the sooner he marries the better for everyone. You'd better buy our girl a new ribbon or two and put her up in the window. Hal has funny tastes, by all accounts, and he might do worse than her."

James felt it was time to indicate to the pair that he was awake and listening. He felt curiously disinclined to hear possible indiscretions about his turnkey's daughter. Not that she was a distasteful subject for contemplation as one lay in bed on a summer morning; rather the reverse, for she was decidedly pretty in her English, milk-and-strawberry way. James was always glad when business or laziness kept her parents below and they sent her up with a tray of food or a letter. But he had to own to feeling vaguely disturbed at hearing her dragged into the particular conversation that was proceeding at the moment. He sat up in bed.

He was anticipated by the sound of Giffard's voice, barking the couple and their gossip out of the rooms. Giffard was angry, knowing himself late and at fault: Giffard was also in a state of permanent irritation with them—and even with their daughter, of whom he was as jealous as an old maid. He had once warned James that the girl was setting her cap at him, and James had replied flippantly that he hoped she was. There was, he had to own to himself, a minute grain of truth in the jest. He felt an undeniable lightening of the spirit when she came up on some errand that should have taken her five minutes and often managed to take her half an hour. Preposterous, of course, but a fact. And then there was the afternoon when Giffard had come in to find his Majesty of Scotland pretending to admire a cheap copper ring that the girl had bought in Mincing Lane the night before; and since she was wearing the ring at the time, he had had to hold her hand for the purpose.

Still, Giffard should have been the last to throw a stone. He was at least free to prowl the streets and exchange a word or two with London girls. And though he professed to find them poor company, with no bite to them like the lassies of Edinburgh, James guessed that there were warm evenings in the City which Giffard contrived to forget next day.

James was barely up and at the breakfast table when the turnkey reappeared with a letter. It proved to be a summons —an invitation, as James preferred to call it—to appear that afternoon at Westminster, where King Henry would be holding Council.

James, certain that Henry was about to fulfil his father's dying wishes, spent the morning singing his praises to a glum and sceptical Giffard. He insisted on discussing the purchase of horses—rumours of a new French war were sending up their prices. He painted imaginary pictures of

Albany's face on hearing that England was sending his nephew home.

It was early August and a sweltering season; for years to come men would be talking of the summer of '13. Inside the cool walls of the Tower one had not noticed the heat; but as soon as James left his stairs to cross the courtyard to the Water-gate, the midday sun struck him with a vivid surprise. He thought of that queer expression in the Psalms *All my bones rejoice*, and found it apt. He revelled in the warmth, in the dazzling light on roofs and sky, in the gay little ships' flags that peered at him over the wall. He was like an invalid recovered and released from months of the sickroom. Everything was new and interesting, everything was worth looking at.

It was too hot for many people to be about. In the middle of the courtyard a little girl stood watching them with the intense gravity of three years old. As they drew nearer she moved aside, still gazing, stumbled on the edge of a flagstone and fell headlong. After a moment's reflection, she decided to start screaming like a lost soul. Disconcerted pigeons clapped and wheeled overhead. A soldier's wife left her wash-tub in the shadow of an archway and hurried up to coax away the clamour. James fumbled in his pocket and, disregarding Giffard's frown, tossed the child a small coin. She immediately set up another howl, and this time her mother came bustling out, in fine fettle for a quarrel with the woman who had dared to anticipate her. James with liberty and a kingdom awaiting him up-river, was sorry he could not stay to see the comedy played out.

It was cool and dark under the low arch of the Water-gate: green reflections danced up the dank stairway. On the bottom step, one twisted foot in the water, stood the Tower cripple. He was nearer seventy than sixty, and he had a face like a Barbary ape. He had never walked straight since one of the Black Prince's waggons, loaded with Spanish plunder, had crushed his ankle in the streets of Bordeaux, on the very day that King Richard was being born. No one knew how he had come to be established at the Tower, or even where he slept at night. But, for forty years and more, daylight had always found him holding horses at the Main Gate, or boats by the water-side—conjuring unofficial tips out of prisoners or insulting their guards with jests that would get a Court Fool whipped for impertinence.

"I'm here to wish you good luck," he said to James, extending a paw.

James took no notice; he was watching the men manœuvre a long boat with scarlet thwarts, easing her in till she rode alongside the steps.

"There's many a man," persisted the cripple, "that's lost his head for want of my good wishes. I bring luck, and God's blessing on prisoners."

"Beelzebub's more likely," said one of the guards, elbowing him out of the way. In the broken, greenish twilight the creature did certainly resemble the demons one saw painted on a church wall.

"I shan't need either," answered James, "if your king is the man I take him for."

"Oho, oho!" crowed the cripple, "and is it hot Hal you're visiting? If you get more than you give in that quarter, I'll eat my hood. You'd do better to stay snug in the Tower and spend the evening with your morsel of skirt."

James looked up sharply, wished he hadn't, and began to blush. That was foolish. The man had only drawn his bow at a venture.

"It's very hot," he said, as off-handedly as he could, and drew his hand across a flushed face. "And since when have you learnt to call kings by their nicknames?"

He stepped dryshod into the boat.

"I began it before ever there was a Jamie in Scotland,"

said the cripple, extending a palm again. "And no one's struck me for it yet," he added, as Giffard doubled indignant fists.

"Well, I'm not paying you for it either," said James, "though I'd wager you a half-noble that you're wrong about your king."

The boat was shoved off, the cripple contributing a perfunctory and symbolical hand-push.

"I'll take you!" he called out. "And no paying in old Harry's shortweights, that he struck to rob his poor subjects. I shall want a half-Edward."

It was next door to treason to impugn the late king's coinage. But there was a safe gap widening between him and the boat, and it was too hot for royal officers to bother themselves about a waterside beggar. The oars struck in. The Tower began to slide past, Water-gate and bastions and the sweating sentinel on the curtain-wall.

The tide was with them as they shot under London Bridge. Ferry-boats and even a Stralsund cog had to make way for the royal badge. High above all shimmered the great spire of St. Paul's, too high to see steadily against the burning sky. They were soon past Baynard's Castle and the Temple: then, as they swung south round the river bend, they were abreast of the ruined Savoy and of the bishops' houses which fronted the Strand and unrolled long gardens behind them to reach the banks of Thames. They hugged the Surrey side, with its mown fields, until the Abbey came into sight, houses huddled round the towers. Then they began to cut across the main stream: the whiff of hay was lost: a new batch of street smells assailed them, and they drew in smartly to Westminster wharf.

The first excitement of being free of prison was beginning to wear off. James's appetite for all the sights and sounds of life had lost its edge. He was all impatience to reach the Palace, to confront King Henry and his Council. He sprang ashore and briskly demanded guidance from the jaded loungers at King Henry's gate.

He was soon to learn that there was no occasion for haste. It was barely two when he had left the Tower, and the journey had been a swift one. But Westminster clock was striking six before he finished cooling his heels and received a summons to the Council chamber. He marched in with the chimes still hanging on the air.

The room was long and narrow, stretching away to left and right of the door by which he entered. Down it, and across his path, stood a great table, almost as long as the room. A dozen councillors were sitting at it, mostly along the opposite side: the majority rose as he entered. James ran his eye along the line, searching for Arundel or for some other face that he knew.

The first thing he encountered was Bishop Beaufort's smile. It was less fawning than it had been a year ago, and there was a hint of patronage in it; Beaufort was Chancellor of England now, and his prince was king. One could not help grudging Beaufort his success, but one had to admit that he would probably improve with growing power and growing scope for his undoubted abilities. The pompous statesman would be preferable to the hungry spaniel of last year.

Having caught James's eye, Beaufort bowed courteously. The secretary beside him bowed. Beyond them was a dark handsome man with shifty eyes—probably Scrope of Masham. At the far end sat an old lord from the country, staring at nothing with an air of well-fed stupidity. He woke suddenly, said "Oh? Has he come?" and rose ponderously, like a reluctant cow.

The king's brothers sat as far from Beaufort as could be arranged. The younger, Humphrey of Gloucester, was smiling at the sudden rustic voice. He had a reputation as a scholar, a *dilettante* manner, and huge melancholy eyes like a woman's. Beside him Clarence, newly returned from turbulent Guienne, looked all soldier. Neither had troubled to rise, though clerics and councillors were bobbing beyond. And above them, on a dais set back from the table, sat King Henry of England.

James hardly knew what he had expected of the king, whom, at a distance, he was prepared to trust and even admire. He had a chance now to make up his mind. Henry, turned a little sideways in order to listen to a whispering usher, was unconscious of being inspected. But it was no easy matter to decide, from so partial a view, what manner of man King Henry the Fifth might be.

The most obvious thing was a white furrow along the cheek where an arrow had scored him, almost in boyhood, at Shrewsbury fight. At twenty-six, Henry was already a soldier of ten years' standing. If his winters in London had been as riotous as some people liked to think, he had at least earned his pleasures by yearly campaigns on the Welsh March. 'He'll be coming north,' thought James, 'he'll be giving us trouble in Scotland—unless the French keep him busy.'

The usher backed away. King Henry turned and James saw his face. It was an unexpected one, ruddy in complexion, the features overlarge, though regular: a long nose: heavy lips: ugly, protruding ears. There was much to suggest a farmer's son, even a labourer's, rather than a prince. The English would like that in their king. But there was real kingliness in the iron control. As he gazed at James, his mind imposed on mobile features the rigidity of wax. Even the eyes, after one flicker of human recognition, went hard and cold. There was a hint of priestliness, of self-satisfaction in the expression. Henry might have been born impulsive, generous, friendly. But he had evidently decided that a king, except at carefully calculated moments, could afford to be none of these things.

Henry glanced towards Beaufort, who had been waiting to catch his eye. The bishop cleared his throat and began to speak. He was soon launched on a sea of formalities, empty compliments, long strings of titles. The stupid lord beyond him yawned audibly and settled down into coma. Humphrey of Gloucester looked at Beaufort with distaste, and then began to smile to himself, obviously thinking of something quite irrelevant. Clarence sat inscrutable. The voice droned on.

James, waiting for something important to happen, had almost ceased to listen, when a phrase caught his attention. Beaufort, reading from a document, had referred to King Henry's predecessors as "from ancient times the overlords of Scotland." It was the old lie, the old injustice. Too much blood had dried and rusted upon it for the English to renounce it now. But James felt that it should not have passed unchallenged. He must be more attentive.

His chance came in a moment. Beaufort was speaking of him as "prisoner of war in realm of England."

"Not of war," interrupted James. "I would remind your lordship that I was captured in time of truce."

There was a faint stir at the Council Board.

"Hardly so," said Clarence, "the Scots had already broken the truce by raiding Northumberland."

"Not before an English fleet had ravaged my father's lands in Arran. The raid was merely a reprisal."

Beaufort looked uncomfortable.

"The first breach——" he began, but the king cut him short.

"We need not discuss that," said King Henry. "There was no truce at the time. You may proceed, my lord."

Beaufort bowed, smiling. "Your Majesty is quite right," he said. "And in any case, the question hardly arises. We are not here to debate his Majesty's capture, but his release."

He pointed the word at James, as if to imply that it was through his own efforts that the prison doors were to open.

"Release?" James shot it back in the direction of King Henry, sitting impassively above him.

"That is the decision," said Beaufort. "We all hope that it will lay the foundations of a lasting friendship between the two nations. It should do so, provided that the Scots are willing. Christian princes——" He proceeded to quote Scripture, inaccurately and hardly to the point. Beaufort was no theologian.

He was interrupted by Clarence, who was turning the pages of a freshly engrossed document on the table.

"There is one point here," he said, "that had better be cleared up to begin with. This foolish business with Warde must be put an end to. No one in his senses believes in the man, but his ridiculous claim might make trouble in England. There's nothing that can't be used by sedition-mongers."

"Warde?" said James. "And who is Warde?"

"His Highness refers to Thomas Warde," explained Beaufort, "the wretched fool who has been pretending that he is King Richard—or is it King Richard's ghost?"

James remembered the affair. Warde was a wandering beggar from Trumpington, near Cambridge, whom someone had discovered in (of all places!) the island of Skye. He had been brought to Stirling, reluctant and protesting, and because of some resemblance to the murdered Richard, forced to accept royal honours. At Albany's dictation, he was still playing out the sorry farce of claiming the English crown. The whole business had had little purpose except to annoy King Henry the Fourth: and Henry had decided that he could afford to smile.

"I do not think we need anticipate difficulties there," said James. "I thought the man was dead."

"Nothing of the sort," replied Clarence crossly. "Albany is still supporting his ridiculous pretensions. And there are fools and traitors in England who look to him for their excuse."

"I would remind your Highness," said James, "that I am not responsible for the Duke of Albany's policy."

"Of course not, of course not," said Clarence. "But we shall need an assurance that you will put an end to the unseemly business, and hand the man back to us."

"I intend," said James, "to put an end to a great number of things that the Duke of Albany keeps afoot."

"Good," said Beaufort, impatient for progress, "then we can proceed to the main conditions."

Things seemed to be going a little too easily: James felt sure that there was something in the background.

"And my ransom?" he asked.

It was more than likely that the money would make a fatal hitch in the negotiations. The English might be tantalizing him with the hope of freedom, merely to destroy it by fixing a price far beyond the resources of his impoverished kingdom.

"There is to be no ransom," said Bishop Beaufort.

The pronouncement was followed by an uncomfortable silence, most of the councillors looking self-consciously at the table. King Henry had not moved a muscle.

Clarence cleared his throat.

"Our only demand," he began, "is for the repayment of our expenses in keeping and educating your Majesty in England. There is a clause in the agreement, a clause. . . ."

He was fumbling with the document before him.

"Page three," said Duke Humphrey, curtly.

"Yes, yes," said Clarence testily, resenting his brother's assistance. He turned to the page in question.

"My allowance," said James, "has been six and eightpence a day. It has not been paid with any approach to regularity."

"How long has he been here?" mumbled a new voice from the corner. The stupid country lord had awoken from slumber.

"Seven years," said Beaufort, with constrained courtesy.

The questioner knitted puzzled brows and began to scribble figures on a paper before him. Beaufort mastered his irritation, and decided to be jocose.

"I was always slow with my mathematics," he announced pompously, "and I cannot do the sum in my head. Your Majesty will find that there are a few additional items."

He pushed a copy of the draft agreement towards James, putting a short square thumb on the clause under discussion.

James noted the total. It was higher than his entertainment in England could warrant, but vastly less than a royal ransom. A short lien on the customs of Perth and Edinburgh would see the business through. Even Albany would not find excuses for refusing the bargain.

"I will take the draft away with me," he said, "while your lordships proceed to other business. I can let you have my answer tonight or tomorrow."

Beaufort seemed to hesitate. The councillors glanced at one another, or up to King Henry.

"We would like to get the business settled," said Clarence. "I do not think there can be any difficulty, so long as Scotland gives good pledges for the money. And there is pen and ink on the table."

"I had better read it through before I sign," said James.

"Of course, of course."

James was unwilling to endanger any chance of hastening his release. He smoothed out the document on the table—the seven-years prisoner with an order for discharge in his hands. He skipped rapidly over the preamble, the decorative *In Nomine Dei* and its attendant rigmarole. He was soon deep in the second page of long-winded Latinity. He hardly heard a slight stir round the table, Humphrey of Gloucester asking, in slightly bored accents, what came next on the agenda, and a new voice starting to describe the illegal detention of two London merchants in Genoa. A secretary passed behind him and round the table, handed a report to King Henry and returned. James read on.

The bulk of the agreement referred to the stable peace which (by God's grace) was to replace the uneasy truces and recurrent warfare which had divided English and Scots for a century and more. There were clauses about hostages, clauses about the settlement of the Border, clauses about the Church. Then came the matter of money: more hostages (England being England) as surety for its payment. Then—James's excitement grew as he read—the provision for the actual release, the commissioners to be appointed by both sides, the suggested date for their meeting at Durham. Freedom was sweet; these details made it seem unbelievably near. Before winter came, he would be crossing the Border, no longer a prisoner, but a king. He turned over to the last page and, without raising his eyes, stretched and groped for the pen.

Had his attention been less absorbed in the reading, he might have noticed that the Council had ceased to discuss Genoa, that they had all turned to watch him—Duke Humphrey half-cynical, Beaufort with a nervous smile, the king from hooded eyes that still pretended to be fixed on the report in his hand. There was dead silence round the table, except where the stupid lord at the end sighed and scratched over a mess of figures that was now beyond his control.

"*And whereas*," read James, "*the Kings of England, predecessors and progenitors of the said Henry, have been from ancient times, by right of suzeraignty and direct dominion, Lords of the Realm of Scotland, of the Scottish kings and of all their temporal possessions, it is hereby agreed and concluded that the said James doth covenant not to quit the said realm of England until he hath rendered liege-homage and an oath of service to the said Henry (as him behoveth) thereby acknowledging that the said realm of Scotland is and hath ever been subject to the kings of England, and binding his heirs and successors for all time to pay like homage to——*"

James sprang to his feet and looked round him at the circle of watching faces. For a moment he felt like laughing at them, at their startled solemnity, as it dawned upon them that he was going to refuse their bait. They had really imagined that he would repudiate all that his ancestors had done for Scotland, in return for permission to reign, fettered, over a race he had enslaved.

A great wave of disgust and anger swept up within him. These men, who were acting like a pack of schoolboys, had his whole life in their hands. They could hold him prisoner for ever, kill him, even, as they had killed their own King Richard. There was nothing Englishmen would not do, nothing for which they lacked a plausible and probably a pious excuse. But whatever the danger, they had made a mistake in counting on a Scotsman's surrender.

Beaufort was clearing his throat, but one blaze from James's eyes reduced him to silence. The secretary, seeing only James's back, reached forward to pull the ink-bottle a trifle nearer. James had a savage impulse to take and throw it in their faces, to hurl it at King Henry on his throne.

Then he mastered his anger, clenched his lips to keep back the useless words, and strode out of the door.

There was a momentary silence in the room he had left, everyone waiting for his neighbour to make the first comment. Then Beaufort gave tongue.

"I was afraid of it," he said, with an air of deprecating wisdom. "A most unmanageable young person. Your lordships will remember that I never thought we should get him to pay the homage."

"King Edward got it from the Bruce's cub," said Clarence. "At least, I always understood so."

"No, not exactly," hesitated Beaufort, "I think your Highness has been misinformed."

"In any case," said Humphrey of Gloucester, "it's quite clear that we are not dealing with a David Bruce. This young man is a problem on his own."

"My dear brother," said Clarence, after a preliminary snort, "you'll be telling us next you admire the young donkey for his obstinacy."

Humphrey seemed hardly to hear. He was staring at the door through which James had vanished.

"Did you notice his clothes?" he said. "I suppose Albany never sends him money for any new ones."

"If I may suggest——" began Beaufort, but the king cut him short.

"My lords," said King Henry, "I think we are wasting our time. May I remind your lordships that I am supposed to be in Surrey tonight?"

He glanced at the paper in his hand.

"What is our present trade with Genoa?" he asked. "And can we afford a rupture?"

August 1413

V

The evening sun still shone on London's spires when the red boat curved in again to the Tower. But under the Water-gate it was dark and eerie; the cripple still haunted the steps. A look at James's face was enough to tell him that he had won his bet; but it also warned to keep his riotous tongue quiet, at least for the moment. He loved money too well to risk losing a half-noble by unseasonable insistence. He could wait. He contented himself with gibes at James's escort, Rabelaisian surmises about the way they had spent their afternoon in Westminster.

James climbed the steps and crossed the courtyard in a daze. The cooler hour had now brought loiterers to every doorway, but he passed them with unseeing eyes. The only face he noticed was that of the girl in his own turnkey's lodging, peering out as he passed, at the ground-floor window. In the gutter below, a spavined cat looked up for a moment and then returned to the grimy fishbone between its paws.

He was soon back in his own room—the room that might now hold him for ten, twenty, forty years. He dismissed Giffard, and threw himself down on the bed.

He had one hope, though it was a poor one. King Henry had taken little part in the scene in the Council Chamber; he had only spoken once, and his words had been quite non-committal. James found it possible to believe that the whole business had been staged by one of the councillors, Beaufort, probably, or smug Clarence. Henry had allowed them to try their dishonourable experiment: he might even now be rating them for its failure.

It would mean delay. Even if he had disapproved of the manœuvre, Henry could hardly change policy at once and insist on another arrangement for release. It might be months, years even, before anything was done. Henry had plenty to occupy him, and Scotland must be the least urgent of his problems.

And it was possible that James was mistaken. Maybe the demand for homage had been made with Henry's approval; maybe it would be repeated, year after year, in the hope of wearing down the captive and extorting consent from his misery. A foolish hope, indeed, but one which the English might easily cherish.

If he was to be a perpetual prisoner, cut off from life as well as from his heritage, he would have to find some pursuit, some aim, to keep off the corrosion of despair. He might become a master of music, better still a scholar and a writer of books. Monks, mewed up in narrower cells than his, had earned immortality and altered the fortunes of the world. The thought fired him but little. He would lay it aside, to return to it when the wound of anger and frustration had had more time to heal. He craved, not for new aspirations, but for an anodyne.

If only he could feel a horse between his knees! A gallop across open fields, and then another and another, until speed and the wind had cured his mind of thinking: the bruises and buffetings of an informal tourney: the excitement of riding down a deer, or watching his falcon stoop and pounce upon a heron. It would be a charity, even, if they would let him mix with the London crowds for a short summer evening, see the faces of the laughing girls, forget everything in the stuffy uproar of a drinking-shop. But he was cut off from all remedies for his pain. He could only lie on his bed and wonder how long the coming night would seem.

There was a footstep on the stairs. James sat up, swinging his legs off the bed: he expected Giffard's premature return, and was prepared to resent it. The door of the outer room opened, and no one entered. Then there was a chinking of plates, and the sound of wheezing breath. The gaoler's wife appeared with his supper.

She was plump, blowsy, and middle-aged. Her hair escaped in streaks from under a grimy wimple. She foolishly attempted elegance in her nether extremities: a pair of scarlet stockings encased shapeless ankles, bulging hideously over shoes too tight for her feet. Above, she had daubed paint on a muddy complexion with distressing results. James wondered if she really imagined that all this helped to prevent her husband from running after other women.

She smiled at him through the door, in a good-natured, half-sly manner.

"Shall I call your Majesty's gentleman?" she asked. "He always likes to lay the table for you."

"No, he's out," said James, lying back on the bed. "You can lay it yourself. And I'm not wanting supper, anyway."

"Oh, come, come," said the woman, "we've all got to eat, even in this weather. You must keep up your strength."

She began to spread the cloth, stopping to twitch the hair out of her eyes.

"Well, bring me a cup of wine to begin with," said James, "and I expect I shall want a second bottle before the night's out."

"That's as may be," said the woman, beginning to pour. "I don't know that we've another bottle to spare. And it's getting late to send out."

She brought in the cup and stood over him as he drank, his head propped on a bent arm.

"What beautiful strong legs your Majesty has," she remarked irrelevantly.

James was amused in spite of himself—faintly pleased even. The wine was beginning to do its work.

"That's the air of Scotland," he said. "All Scottish children grow up with stout legs."

"Well, I never heard that before," said the woman.

Then she giggled, hesitated, and reluctantly left James's bedside to return to the table.

"Not that I ever think of *you* as a foreigner," she said suddenly. "You're as good as English, the time you've been here. And better than half these London lads. We're from Ipswich, you know. I never could fancy a London man."

James sat up. A new thought was taking rapid shape in his head. It had a dreadful fascination: if only he knew how to put it into words! Something was happening to him, something that had never happened before. He had no idea how other men dealt with such situations. He had little experience of the common people, less still of women. He was still cudgelling his brains when the laying of supper was finished.

"Will your Majesty be wanting anything else?" asked the woman, coming back to the doorway.

James sat silent, pretending he had not heard. He knew quite well what he wanted: he knew that he could only get it by means of this coarse creature who stood fawning at him from the door. But he could not summon up the audacity to ask her in plain words, and he had no experience to teach him a line of oblique approach.

The woman repeated her question. James still hesitated, loath to let her go.

"No, I think not," he said at last, "unless——"

"Yes?"

James could not follow up. The woman turned in the doorway.

"Well," she said, "you'll not be seeing me again. If anything's wanted, I'll send my daughter up."

James suddenly felt his heart beginning to thump in the most uncontrollable fashion. He hoped he was not blushing again. He wondered how men of the world attained their desires—and how they managed to keep so calm about it.

"Yes," he said, "send her by all means. Your daughter, I mean."

The woman smiled at him. "Just as you say," she answered.

She fidgeted where she stood, obviously without any intention of going.

"That second bottle you wanted," she said, "I'll send her up with that—if I can find one."

There was no mistaking the leer this time. She stood half-inside, half-outside the door, her shoulder leant against the door-jamb, the forefinger of her other hand tracing patterns on the rough stone.

"You don't happen," she said, "to be short of money again?"

"No," said James. "Why?"

The woman looked mildly disconcerted, as though she had played a recognized gambit and been answered with the wrong move. She was not accustomed to such inexperienced beginners as James.

"It was only," she began, searching for a way out, "—only that the cripple down there was saying you owed him a half-noble. I'd pay him for you, if you'll give me the money." She smiled again, enjoying her own diplomacy. "It's a pity," she added needlessly, "to be in that creature's bad books. We all say he has the evil eye."

She scratched her cheek, displacing streaks of hair; it must have been auburn once, as bright and fresh as her daughter's. It was now the colour of nondescript grease.

James swung himself off the bed and pushed past her to find some money in the outer room. "Here are two nobles," he said, "one for him and one for you." He knew perfectly well where both coins would go, but this was no time for cheese-paring. He felt that he was learning the game rapidly.

She took the money and stowed it away in some curious recess of her untidy person. Then she looked at the table. "You'd better have supper first," she said.

She retired outside the door, half-closed it, as if for safety, and spoke again through the gap.

"I've just thought of something," she said. "I can't send my daughter up. Not tonight, anyway. My husband's taken her off to the City, to a guild-supper there. The Lord knows how late they'll be, and no one's allowed up these stairs, not after the guard's changed for the night."

She began to fiddle with the keys at her belt, choosing one to put into the lock. James had not moved.

"Maybe some other night," she said. "I expect you'll be with us some time yet."

One would have thought that she would go as soon as possible, leaving James to face his desolate night. But she still lingered, looking almost wistfully towards the boy.

"It's a funny thing," she said, making conversation, "it's a funny thing about that cripple. I've heard it said his mother was a Frenchwoman, married to one of Sir John Chandos's archers—and used to carry on with a horse-dealer in Bordeaux, when her husband was away fighting. He has a wonderful way with horses, that cripple has. You should see him at the Main Gate, with a dozen and more to hold. They say those Frenchwomen have no shame. Not that I've been to France myself, nor wanted to, though England's dull at times——"

A step sounded on the stairs. The woman broke off to swing the door wider and slouch aside to admit Giffard.

The squire marched in, caught sight of James, and presented him with a letter.

"It has just come for your Majesty," he said, "from Westminster."

Then he looked round the room, and his eye fell disapprovingly on the ready-laid supper.

"Did you do this?" he asked the woman.

"I did," she said. "If there's anything wrong, it's *mea culpa*, as they say in church."

"You should have summoned me," said Giffard severely, "I was down below."

"Do you know what's in this?" interrupted James.

"The man said, your Majesty, that it was an order for

our removal. The king signed it before Council was dismissed."

"I am to leave tomorrow—for Windsor."

"Tomorrow?" said Giffard; "the usual discourtesy! I shall barely have time to get your Majesty's things together."

"Tomorrow?" echoed the woman. "They do do things suddenly nowadays. "It's been one long hustle since the old king died."

She turned to go, giving James a last look.

"I'm sure we'll all be sorry to lose you," she said. "But there you are! And I expect there are plenty of pretty girls at Windsor."

Giffard wheeled upon her, his own conscience not as clear as he could have wished it. Then he remembered himself, and decided to ignore the imputation.

"Is Your Majesty informed," he asked, pointing to the letter, "at what hour we shall be expected to start?"

"We?" said James. "It seems you are not to come. They'll probably send you back to Scotland."

"Well, I'll wish your Majesty a good night," said the woman from the doorway. "And I'm sure I'm grateful for the money."

1413–15

VI

They took King James to Windsor. They took him to Pevensey, whence, on clear days, he could descry a hazy France along the skyline. From there he went back to Windsor, then to the Tower again, though to new quarters. His life became an apparently aimless succession of guarded journeys and new prisons.

He was glad of the journeys, if only for variety. Many of his warders were strict, monotonously insisting on the importance of book-learning and looking askance at exercises in the field. Deprived of Giffard's services, he was attended mostly by Englishmen. He scented an attempt to make him forget his country, and, determined to defeat it, turned more and more inwards upon himself. He had been born serious-minded; captivity was making him introspective.

The Wheel of Fortune—that fancy so dear to the poets and moralists of his time—turned and turned again upon its eternal axis. Across the Channel it seemed to revolve with fearful rapidity, pitching peers of France to gaol or the scaffold, sweeping up the butchers and shopkeepers of Paris to its glorious but unstable crest. It had already begun to twist the three rival Popes into impotence and obscurity, raising a fourth into their place, to command the allegiance of a reunited Christendom. In Italy a King of Naples was spun down to death—murdered by the poison that enemies had smeared upon the body of his mistress; in Germany a Hohenzollern was hoisted into the lordship of Brandenburg and of the lands around Berlin. But still James Stewart, heir to the Bruce and rightful King of Scotland, waited in vain for the wheel to carry him up to his father's throne.

King Henry, balanced on the summit, seemed none too secure. The Lollards made a midnight rendezvous to kidnap —some said to assassinate—the king. They failed or were betrayed: many of them swung from the gallows of St. Giles. England was filled with stories of the wickednesses they were said to be contemplating. It was a small matter that one was captured in Windsor Park, equipped with ropes and a map of the road to Edinburgh, evidently intent on releasing the royal captive in hopes that Scotland might aid sedition. It was all of a piece, said the priests, that a heretic should look for support to the national enemy. Heresy, they tried to persuade England, was well mated with Regicide and Treason.

Escaped from one danger, King Henry headed straight for a greater one.

His claim to the throne was not quite unchallenged, though his father had done Richard to death and reigned twelve years in the dead man's shoes. There were some who whispered that Richard had bequeathed his crown to cousins with a better right than the Lancastrian Henries, cousins whose claim had descended to the great house of York. The red rose and the white were not yet plucked in the Temple Gardens, but there was ugly talk to be heard. Henry, thinking distraction the best remedy, decided to turn England's eyes abroad.

France offered a promising field for the unscrupulous. Henry's predecessors had claimed her crown, winning glory and causing untold suffering in the attempt to enforce the claim. He could revive their rancid pretensions. He could ignore the fact that the old arguments against the French king's right pointed less to himself than to a third candidate: he could suppress the awkward truth that, pressed to their logical conclusion, they endangered his claim to the English throne. Henry wanted war, not logic. The French might have legality, and even justice, on their side, but that would avail them little, now that they were rent asunder with domestic feuds. Paris was at odds with the provinces, Burgundy made war on Orleans. Henry expected an easy task.

He was soon disappointed. Hearing of his preparations, France desisted from civil strife. Henry had intrigued with Burgundians and Orleanists in turn, lying to both while they lied to him and to each other. The threat of his invasion drew them temporarily together. The Dauphin derided Henry's soldiership by a gift of tennis-balls. He had the unqualified support of young Orleans, a warrior as well as a wit and poet. Burgundy might march with them or, if that were too much to ask, would certainly stay at home rather than assist the foreigner.

At Southampton Henry detected a new conspiracy to assassinate him, part Lollard, part Yorkist. England was duly horrified. England, fired by King Henry's trumpetings, was in a fever of excitement. King Henry had aroused something terribly potent in her, though only a blasphemer could call it patriotism. Here was no love of home or kin, no ardour to defend what is dear and in danger, but only the outward projection of domestic greed and arrogance. Even the bishops had caught the infection, and, preferring their nation's folly to the sanity of Christ, sent a blessing with Henry's unhallowed enterprise.

He was late in starting, for the summer was far gone. He landed in Normandy and spent five precious weeks besieging the first town he came to, with ten thousand men. Autumn found him master of a second-rate French port, and poorer by the loss of seven thousand Englishmen, through wounds or desertion or dysentery. He could do nothing, said the men that knew war, except put a good face on it and go home.

Henry refused to go. Perhaps he doubted his welcome in England. He mustered the remnants of his army and the reinforcements that had reached him, and led them off for a reckless march, through two hundred miles of rain and mud, in the hope of reaching Calais. The two hundred miles lengthened into three hundred, as the French blockaded the fords and broke the bridges before him. Vast armies converged to crush him. The mad old king of France had recovered his wits and taken the sacred *oriflamme* from St. Denis. The Dauphin led the royal army northward, backed by the King of Sicily, the Dukes of Berri, Alençon and Bar. Orleans had left his young wife and his poetry to call up his men for war. If Burgundy held back himself, his brother was coming with a host of Burgundian knights. On a Thursday night in late October, six thousand Englishmen, tired, hungry and astray in hostile country, lay down to rest in the wet fields by Maisoncelles, with fifty thousand Frenchmen within sight or earshot. Two and a half years had passed since Henry had ridden into London to be crowned, and it would have been a bold man that wagered on his ever seeing London again.

He sent to ask terms from the enemy. He offered to restore the captured town and pay an indemnity for the damage he had inflicted upon Normandy. He asked nothing in return, except permission to lead his bedraggled little army into Calais. He was trapped, and he knew it. When the French refused to listen, another man might have yielded to despair; but Nature, which had let loose the destructive force called King Harry, had also endowed it with unalterable courage.

Friday dawned and the French shook out their pennons for battle. They waited to see whether the English would advance, or stay where they were and starve. The English advanced; the French moved to meet them. And then the arrows began to fly.

They flew, with intervals of hand-to-hand scuffling, for a matter of three hours. When the last sound of them had died away—the mournful sighing on the wind, the horrible thump of the impact—there were close on ten thousand French corpses between Maisoncelles and Agincourt, and all hope of peace or happiness had vanished from France for thirty years.

The slaughter was increased by an untoward incident. Many French had surrendered, the rest were dead or in flight, when Burgundy's brother arrived late on the battlefield. He borrowed his servant's armour, tore the flag off a trumpet and put his head through a hole in the middle to make a surcoat: thus accoutred, he rushed full tilt at the English. He and his few followers looked to Henry like a new and undefeated army, which the English could not risk meeting while encumbered with so great a host of prisoners. Henry ordered his men to butcher the lot, only reserving a few great ones from whom heavy ransoms might be expected. When they hesitated, he threatened to hang those who held back from the work. Kindly men from England's peaceful villages found themselves slitting the throats of struggling Frenchmen or bashing in their defenceless heads. Some of the prisoners lay wounded in the neighbouring cottages, and to these the archers set fire. Such things happen in war, even in an Age of Chivalry.

Henry, bound for London, marched on down the Calais road.

All that winter the French king was mad again, crying that he was made of glass and would fall to pieces unless they strapped him round with horse-collars. His son lay dying of fever and debauchery in the Hôtel Bourbon. The evil German woman whom the king had married fell sick also, but recovered, to France's bane. Paris, forgetting that next season might bring a new horde of English upon her, started arming her citizens to resist Burgundy and murder each other in the streets. It seemed as if the God to whom Henry was for ever appealing had indeed turned away His face from England's enemies and England's victims.

London held high revel. There were bishops and abbots to welcome the king, wives or harlots to make merry with his men. The school-children sang, the mayor and alderman read addresses at the conqueror. All the bells of St. Paul's thundered a paean, and the wineshops rang with money that had once clothed French nobles in fur and silk, or lain hidden in a stocking to guard the children in Normandy cottages from the daily threat of starvation.

[illegible]

who then came from the [illegible]. Rightly [illegible] from England
[illegible] others feared themselves [illegible] the [illegible]
[illegible] had been of England [illegible] their [illegible].
Some of the [illegible] the [illegible]
[illegible] that [illegible] in [illegible] those
happenings [illegible] of Charles.

Henry, bound for London, [illegible] of [illegible] the
road.

All that winter the French king was mad again, crying
that he was made of glass and would [illegible] pieces unless
they [illegible] him round with [illegible] collars. [illegible]
dying of [illegible] and [illegible] in the Hôtel [illegible]. The
evil German woman whom the king had married [illegible]
[illegible] of France [illegible]. Paris [illegible]
[illegible] might [illegible] of [illegible]
[illegible] woman [illegible]
[illegible] in the streets. [illegible]
Henry was [illegible] and [illegible]
[illegible] England's [illegible] and England's [illegible].

London held high revel. [illegible]
[illegible] the [illegible]
[illegible] and [illegible] the [illegible]
[illegible] of the [illegible]. [illegible]
[illegible]
[illegible] French [illegible]
[illegible]
[illegible] from the [illegible]

Kalends

For of your blisse the kalendis are begonne!

THE KING'S QUAIR.

CHAPTER THREE

Kalends

January 1416

I

James wondered where he was. The room was unfamiliar, the tapestries on its walls were strange, depicting scenes of surprising indecency; they seemed to shift and alter as one looked at them. But all that could be investigated later. Of more immediate importance was the presence of his mother, standing by the window and delivering a long lecture, not to him, but to his brother, Rothesay, who sat fondling a little black dog on his knees. Rothesay was not taking the slightest notice of the queen: he was putting the fingers of his right hand into the dog's mouth, and letting the dog bite them off, one after the other. Rothesay did not seem to mind. He was even caressing the animal's ears with his other hand. It was not exactly a dog, it was more like a monkey. James realized, with a thrill of horror, that Rothesay was deeply in love with it. That, of course, was the trouble that had oppressed them for so many years—his brother's guilty passion for a monkey. They had naturally concealed it from his uncles: it would never do for Albany to discover the secret. But, now that James knew, he must warn Rothesay, beg him to break off the whole affair. If only he could move, or even speak! But he was dumb as well as rooted to the floor. He could not even tell his mother that it was useless to go on preaching at Rothesay about wantonness and adultery and the duty of princes. She was making no impression at all. She could hardly hope to, dressed as she was. James noticed that she had nothing on but a French head-dress, absurdly tall, and a long white nightgown. Besides, he remembered, she was dead. She had died months before Rothesay was taken to prison. If it came to that, Rothesay was dead too, starved to death in Falkland Castle. There was something wrong here, something agonizingly wrong. It would be worse when Albany came into the room. James knew that Albany was coming, that he was already half-way up the stairs. The horror of it reached a climax in his desperate mind, and then, as if emerging from Hell to Paradise, he awoke from his dream.

He was in the chapel of the Tower. The sermon had just ended, and the priest, in a long white robe, was descending from the pulpit. James slipped on to his knees for the prayers.

He must be more watchful. Some dreams, he had been told, were sent by God. Of such must be the happy, picturesque absurdities in which he saw the heroes of his romances and poems of chivalry, lords and ladies courteously leading him through impossible gardens of bird-song and fountain music. He had tried to write poems in that vein himself, but his blundering attempts came nowhere near recapturing the magic of the dreams. On the other hand, there were times like the present, when he awoke from dreaming with an ugly taste in the mouth and a general feeling that Satan had had his way with him. It seemed worse that such a thing should happen during Mass. It increased his sense of personal guilt.

"*Deus, qui humanae substantiae dignitatem mirabiliter condidisti. . . .*"

That was it. Such dreams were an attack on the dignity of the human mind. He must be careful, in future, not to let the enemy slip so easily past his defences. All the same, it was difficult to blame himself for falling asleep while that old Augustinian was mumbling in the pulpit. He was tired to begin with. He had ridden all Saturday, coming up from Pevensey, and then, instead of going early to bed, had sat up, long after midnight, reading Chaucer's tale about Cressida and the fall of Troy. It had captured him completely. He had read and re-read that amazing opening, and the lines wherein Troilus, despising Love and its devotees, suddenly falls a slave to Cressida's beauty.

"*For caught is proud and caught is debonnair.*"

One read on, more fascinated than delighted. For Chaucer, as he unrolled the whole sorry tale, made one realize that a poet might reach the sky and yet have his feet not so much on earth as in the dung. James plumed himself on appreciating, even at his age, the darker tints in the poem as well as its heavenly dawn.

"*Motuum meorum tam carnalium quam spiritualium, perfecta quietatio.*"

His mind had been wandering again: the Office was drawing to a close. The priests might be right in condemning poetry, at least in so far as it distracted young minds from religious thoughts. Perhaps it was priestly influence as well as a national stiffness, that prevented these English from taking more pride in their poets. At Windsor, James remembered with a smile, Chaucer was spoken of as old King Edward's Clerk of Works, a painstaking and popular official: his writings were mentioned in an almost apologetic whisper, as though it was slightly derogatory in an Englishman to have written great poetry.

"*Per Jesum Christum dominum nostrum.*"

The Office reached its end, the congregation clattered out. The clergy melted away, more decorously, through their own doors. James was alone, except for the whispering and shuffling of the acolytes as they extinguished candles and discussed the prospects of dinner.

It was unreasonable, he reflected, to be too hard on himself; after all, what was there for him to do except dream? God, to whom the Conqueror had built the Tower Chapel, in whose glory the priests chanted their glib Latin, had given him no work worth the doing, no office but idleness in the midst of a busy world. His kingly title was a mockery, his growing strength and skill would never be used in any cause that mattered. He was twenty-one now, with the sap of youth turning sour in his veins. He had been born to rule and denied his kingdom: he had been trained to fight, and would never see a battle: he had been taught the lore of worshipful love, and so huddled away from women of his own kind that he hardly dared speak to them. At best he could only hope to awaken pity, and it was not pity that he wanted.

He was still brooding as he left the chapel, and crossed the courtyard towards his lodging. It was January, and searchingly cold. A bitter wind swept long-dead leaves against his ankles; even the Tower ravens seemed to have gone to shelter. He pulled his cap over his brow and quickened his stride, comforting himself with the thought of warm food.

There was a stir at the Inner Gate, men's cries and the jingle of harness. James waited to let them emerge and then saw that they were dismounting under the archway. There was some confused talking and a man strode out of the crowd. James recognized King Henry.

He was ruddier than ever, and more tanned than three years ago. He was, too, a human being, not a waxen figure throned above the Council Board. He was chatting genially to the unimportant people who followed in his wake. He stopped on seeing James, looked puzzled, and then smiled in recognition.

"The proper weather for a Scot!" he called out, and waited for James to come nearer. "Unless," he added, "we've made an Englishman of you."

James advanced.

"I hope I shall always be a Scot," he said. "Would your Majesty have me otherwise?"

A momentary shadow flitted across Henry's brow.

"No," he said. "No, I suppose not. You are right, cousin. What have you been doing since I saw you last? Studying, I hope; there's nothing like it."

James summoned up his courage.

"I do not neglect my books," he said, "but they leave me time in which to wonder when I am going to see Scotland again."

Henry looked dipleased.

"We can think of that," he said, "when your education is finished." It might have been a schoolmaster talking, and a man of fifty at that. James remembered the tales of a young prince who had been the pride of Eastcheap taverns a few years back. It was wonderful what a few years could do.

"There are other ways of learning," he said, "as your Majesty knows."

"Does that mean that you want to come to France with me? Fighting's a quick school, but a rough one."

"I want to go to France," said James boldly, "though I'm not sure on which side I'd rather do my fighting."

There was an uncomfortable fidgeting among the attendants.

"I hope you'd fight for France," said Henry. "The true France—not the Orleanist faction. More than half the French are on my side. I am their rightful king."

James smiled to himself. A little exaggeration was to be expected in war-time.

"Some of my Scottish subjects think otherwise," he said.

"Yes, yes, I know," said King Henry. "A few irresponsible Scots are assisting the Orleanist rebellion." He shot a glance at his embarrassed followers. "You must stop that, if you go back to Scotland. Or perhaps—if you were to sail with me . . ."

His voice died away. He was obviously thinking out some new idea that had struck him. Then he seemed to put it aside, and looked up with a friendly, half-patronizing smile.

"Well," he said, "I hope they are treating you well meantime. This isn't quite the place for a boy of your age. Can't let you loose—with London so near. I must think where to send you—until we can arrange about your release."

He paused as if to let the magic word have its due effect.

"Well, well," he continued, "I must go on. It's cold, isn't it?"

He slapped James on the shoulder, making him feel more like a schoolboy than ever.

"Well, gentlemen," he said, "we mustn't wait here. They will be wondering what has happened to us."

He gave James another smile, as if clinching a bargain, and then strode quickly away. He had the bow-legged gait of a man who has walked in armour from early youth. James blew on his finger-nails and went off to his Sunday dinner. He would be alone. He could read while he ate, propping Chaucer against the salt-boat. Or he could leave Troy for the moment and think over this interview with the king. He must be careful not to indulge too many false hopes again, but King Henry had certainly implied a promise, and might well fulfil it before the year was out.

For four months there was no sign that Henry remembered his captive's existence. Then came an order, disappointing in itself, to transfer him temporarily back to Windsor. There was no talk of ransom, nor of James going to France. He decided, charitably, that Henry was too busy with other things at the moment, and had temporarily forgotten the suggestion that the young King of Scots might accompany him on his next campaign.

But James had misjudged his man. King Henry never forgot anything or anyone that might be of assistance to his career.

May 1416

II

"Fine morning, your Majesty. Glad to have you with us again."

It was James's second day at Windsor and he was returning from his morning ride. The man on the noon guard saluted him cheerfully as he passed in through the Great Gate.

James had made himself mildly popular in the castle last autumn, if only by contrast with the other Scots: William Douglas, soured by long captivity: Murdoch of Fife, a great lout who looked at one as though there was nobody there. Burdock Fish-face, the soldiers called him, and thought themselves wonderfully witty.

It was May, but a dilatory spring was only just beginning. The sun came as quite a surprise—as though everyone had forgotten how warmly it could shine. In the little garden under James's quarters in the Devil Tower, the flowers were hurrying into bloom, intent on retrieving lost time.

The whole castle was far more alive than it had been while King Henry was away at the war. As James crossed the Upper Ward, making for his lodging, he noticed signs of occupation in the royal rooms. The windows were open, there was a glimpse of rich hangings on the walls inside, and there was a sound of many voices talking in French. On a balcony above the courtyard, a man with sleek black hair, fashionably dressed, was sitting at a small table covered with papers. He seemed to listen, half in irritation, half in sarcastic amusement, to the muddled report of a clerk or steward, who kept finding places on a parchment roll and then losing them in the excitement of his own explanations. The more the servant talked, the less the master seemed to listen; he had begun to scribble something, evidently unconnected with the matter in hand, on a set of tablets that he held at his knee. He looked round him and down to the courtyard. James pursued his way towards the Devil Tower. He was expecting letters from Scotland, hoping, as always, for a consignment of money. It was more than time that he had some new clothes.

"*Hé! Vous, le petit! Venez à notre aide!*"

James swung on his heel, inclined to resent the summons. He was conscious of being a little below normal height, though his breadth and muscle should be ample compensation. He disliked being reminded of his disadvantage, especially by a stranger. He looked up in anger, and was greeted by a sulky smile, curiously difficult to resist.

"*Vous êtes chevalier? Vous parlez Français?*"

"*Mais certes, mon sieur.*"

James, young and proud of his accent, half hoped he might be taken for a Frenchman.

"*Eh bien, mon petit. Prêtez-moi votre aide. Je suis étranger, prisonnier.*"

"*Moi aussi.*"

"*Vous? Vous êtes Allemand—Espagnol?*"

"*Non, monsieur. Écossais.*"

"*Mais chevalier?*"

"*Pas encore.*"

"*Écuyer peut-être.* You . . . are . . . squire?"

"*Non, mon sieur. Roi.*"

The man's face clouded for a moment. One guessed that he fancied himself as a wit, and was unaccustomed to humour in others. But he decided to accept the joke.

"*Eh bien, mon petit roi. Montez à moi. J'implore l'aide de votre Majesté.*"

James was half in mind to turn back again and go on to his rooms. But distractions were few and hard to come by, and this man looked as if he would be good company. He pocketed his annoyance and mounted the wooden stairway that led up to the balcony.

It was a simple matter for which his help was required —the translation of some clumsy phrases in a letter from an English harbour-master, who, it appeared, had stopped some imported luxuries on their way from France to Windsor. The difficulty was soon cleared up, and the steward sat down to compose a sharp reply, while his master ordered wine and seemed disposed to chat.

It was a little time before he realized that he had indeed fished up a king from the courtyard to be his interpreter. When he was convinced, his manner hardly altered. He had introduced himself as Charles, Duke of Orleans, and the title implied lands broader and richer than the kingdom of Scotland.

He had been sole ruler of them for some years—ever since his father had been butchered in the *Rue Vielle Temple* by Burgundy's assassins. He was the axis of one of the two great wheels that were rolling over France, trying to break each other and crushing her in the process. He had been married twice, the first time to the widow of King Richard of England. He had fought and been captured at Agincourt. In every way it was hard to believe that he was only three years older than James.

It was not he that mentioned the battle but his steward, replying to some enquiry about dates.

"In December," the man said, "two months after your Grace's misfortune at Agincourt."

"You were always a pessimist, Cousinot. You should have said—after my merciful preservation."

The duke's voice was as grave as a priest's, but there was a twinkle in his eye. James, hoping to share grievances against the English, said something about their slaughtering the prisoners during the battle.

"Not those of us," said Orleans, "with large ransoms attached. Henry is . . . hasty, but he has business instincts."

He sipped his wine, amused at James's frown.

"And," he added, "I was not exactly a prisoner at the time. They tell me I was lying face downwards, with four country squires from Berri on my back—all in full armour. I could well believe it when I woke up in an English baggage-waggon and felt my bruises."

"I've heard it said," observed James, doggedly, "that the English used witchcraft at Agincourt."

"It's a mistake to believe all that one hears said," answered Orleans. "If you'd watched us getting ready for war, you'd know that they needed no witchcraft to give us a thrashing. I suppose we shall learn the tricks one day, but meanwhile we have the misfortune to be gentlemen and are chiefly preoccupied in cutting each other's throats. The English are incurably *bourgeois* and they only cut foreigners'. Remember that, my friend, about the English being *bourgeois*; it accounts for so much. Though, of course, nothing could account for their cooking, could it, Cousinot?"

Cousinot gathered that his Grace was being witty and gave the official smirk.

"As for their climate," continued Orleans, "that is best accounted for by supposing that the Almighty, like so many worthy folk, is prejudiced against England. We're well into May, and this is the first day that I've been able to sit out of doors."

"I would not mind their climate," said James, "if it wasn't for the English themselves. Does anybody like them?"

"Not many Scots, I suppose. Nor many of my own countrymen. It's so difficult to appreciate the better side of one's neighbour when one only sees him through a helmet-slit. And, for us two, prison-bars distort the vision still worse. Our own fault; one shouldn't lose battles—or go on sea-voyages."

His voice trailed away. His mind was partly occupied with a rhyme he had been scribbling on his tablets before James came up; partly, too, with memories of a certain road in France, dusty, edged with poplars, and leading to a sun-baked farm where he had spent some months of his boyhood.

"They offered to release me last year," said James, "on condition I did homage for Scotland. Homage!"

Orleans recalled his wandering thoughts.

"What's that?" he asked. "Who did?"

"The English. The King's Council. I'm sure it wasn't Henry himself. He wouldn't do a thing like that."

There was a momentary silence.

"You may be right," said Orleans. "Henry has his faults, but he's no fool."

James felt flattered.

"No," he said, "only a fool could have made me such a proposal."

"You mean," said Orleans, with a slightly puzzled air, "that he'd have had no hold on you, once he'd let you go. By the way, I observe that he hasn't done so yet."

"Of course not."

"But you said they offered——?"

"Yes, and I refused."

"You—what?"

"I refused to do homage for Scotland."

Again there was silence for a moment.

"And how long," asked Orleans, "do you expect to be in prison?"

"I can't tell. I think Henry intends to release me this year or next. But there are difficulties."

Charles looked at him with a quizzical eye. Then he picked up his tablets and began to scribble in desultory fashion.

"You aren't," he asked, ". . . you aren't in love by any chance?"

"No. Why do you ask?"

"I just wondered."

"My lord," began James hotly, "I see that you do not appreciate the position. In Scotland, this question of the English homage——!"

"I've heard you are old-fashioned in Scotland," interrupted Charles. "Things, you know, aren't quite what they used to be. One can . . . repudiate. And without fear of thunder-bolts. Still, it's none of my business."

"My father," James replied angrily, "used to say that Frenchmen were the most honourable in Christendom. I see that he was wrong!"

"That is the kind of thing that fathers are apt to say. Especially when they have not been to France. Illusions grow on one, as one gets older. You must learn to check them."

"There are some illusions," answered James, "that I shall endeavour to preserve."

He rose and stood at the balcony railing, gazing up at the Round Tower with angry, unseeing eyes.

"It's a pity," said Charles, "that your father did not succeed in getting you to France for your education. He might have been surprised at the results, but that's neither here nor there. Have some more wine. It's from my own vineyards in Touraine."

"No more, thank you." James's back was obstinately turned.

The steward, scenting unpleasantness, chose the moment to interrupt.

"Your Grace will pardon me," he said, "but is that the letter from Blois in your Grace's hand?"

"No, Cousinot. It is not. It is a poem I was endeavouring to write."

"A poem!" said James, putting all the bitterness he could muster into his voice.

"Well, call it a rhyme," answered Orleans, scratching out and beginning again. "I was hoping to make a rondel of it. Stay to dinner and we'll talk about poetry. I can guarantee the food. I get things sent over from France, and I have my own cooks now."

"I thank your Grace," said James, with bare courtesy, "some other day, perhaps."

He clattered down the wooden steps and was gone. Cousinot finished the letter he was writing, and brought it to the duke for signature. Charles waved him aside for the moment, and tried a new opening for his rondel.

Le monde est ennuyé de moi
Et moi pareillement de lui. . . .

He stopped and took the letter from his steward.

"I feel sure," he said, "that I shall be able to get five rhymes to that. . . . Cousinot, I find myself liking that young man. But it's a pity that he doesn't know on which side his . . . er, bannocks are buttered."

Cousinot smiled mechanically. He was wondering whether he dared express what was on the tip of his tongue.

"I have heard it said," he ventured, "that King Henry may propose similar conditions to your Grace; I mean, that he may refuse to discuss the question of ransom, unless your Grace pays homage to him as rightful King of France."

"Possibly, possibly. Henry seems to be a man of limited ideas. What of it, Cousinot?"

"May I presume that your Grace will not consent?"

"There is no knowing what my Grace will do. But in this matter, I think you are probably right."

"Even though the alternative was many years of captivity?"

"Possibly, Cousinot. One must take life as it comes. I shall pass the time endeavouring to learn English."

"I am glad to have your Grace's assurance," said Cousinot returning to his seat.

"What's the matter with you, man? You are being extremely heavy-handed. What has all this to do with the young man from Scotland?"

"I beg pardon, your Grace. I only thought there was a certain similarity between your case and his."

"A superficial one, perhaps," said Charles, "purely superficial. . . . I suppose it's no good asking you what rhymes with 'world'?"

"I am afraid not, your Grace. No good at all."

"I thought not. Well, get on with those letters.

"*The world is bored with me,*
And I'm just as bored with the world."

Cousinot bent over the table. He was glad that he had spoken. But he could not help wishing, for the honour of Frenchmen, that the young King of Scots had stayed to hear the end of the conversation.

May 1416

III

James was reading Boethius. It is perhaps a mistake to read philosophy when one is barely twenty-two. A young man can devour romances, poetry or history, and picture himself doing deeds of incredible valour and devotion, without any great harm. He may even benefit from having been, in imagination, a momentary Hector or Galahad or Charlemagne. But to be Plato or St. Simeon before one has ever had a love-affair or been properly drunk is an unhealthy indulgence of the craving for day-dreams. Boethius, that strange meeting-place where the ancient river of pagan stoicism ran into the stream of Christian grace, was popular, fashionable even, among literary and theological connoisseurs. And fashion, undiscriminating as ever, decreed that the book must be a good one for children and adolescents.

'*Then said I thus,*' read James, '*Thou knowest well that desire for mortal things had never lordship over me.*'

That was the secret. To despise mortal things, and the folly of wishing to possess them. To watch other men—charitably, of course, and with pity rather than contempt—as they wasted their short lives in the pursuit of shadows. King Henry, hungry for fame: Beaufort, ceaselessly scrambling after the worldly consequence that ill became a priest:

Charles of Orleans, whose sneers could hardly conceal his desperate anxiety to be thought witty and disillusioned: what was it except shadows that they desired? Here, behind prison bars, in lonely poverty, he was teaching himself a better wisdom. A few books, music for relaxation, the view of a garden beneath the window—he was fortunate to have these and no more. If he was allowed to ride out, nominally to hunt or hawk, he could use the opportunity to watch, untempted, the meaningless illusions that filled the world's busy and futile life.

He was glad to have attained this mood before his captivity ended. By all accounts, the negotiations for his release would soon be complete. It might be good to go free after hankering so many years for freedom; it was still better to do so now that he had learnt to despise it, to despise, even, the imminent splendour of a crown. He saw clearly now that his imprisonment had been prolonged until he knew how to accept it gladly, as a boon—not rail at it as he had so foolishly done. Release was coming now because he had deserved it. His apprenticeship was finished and life could begin.

He dropped his book on the window-sill and sat gazing out into the soft twilight. The great mound of the Round Tower blocked distant views, but above it the sky was a deep peacock blue and, below, the rosebuds and the quaintly-curved paths of the garden made a fairy pattern in the dusk. The birds were settling themselves for sleep: here and there one of them chattered quietly among hidden leaves. From far away came the slow creaking of a farmer's cart, the voices of young girls, and the clattering of their pails on courtyard stones. The stars were coming out. It was time for bed.

His mood deepened as he made his simple preparations. He was very conscious of spring and approaching summer, conscious, too, of his own youth. But the desires that accompany youth and spring were unaccountably lulled into a peaceful, half-melancholy loveliness. Nature was providing her cure for the restless fevers of a captive, smoothing his path to the self-conquest and self-abnegation that religion and philosophy enjoined.

He was very young. It did not occur to him that Nature enforces rest when she is about to overtax her children's ardours, that her truces are often preludes to the strongest and most surprising assaults.

May 1416

IV

He rose early next morning, more from habit than from eagerness to be doing anything. He had finished dressing before he was properly awake. He had forgotten last night and hardly noticed the still-open book on the window-sill.

He had a slight headache and an indefinable sense of oppression. He recognized, as if at second-hand, that the air from the garden outside was smelling like the first morning in Paradise, and that every bird in the garden was shouting at the top of its little voice, as though there were no purpose in life except to drown the voice of every other bird. But all this seemed irrelevant, alien, even hostile. He would probably be confined to his quarters all day, forbidden the taste of the open air. The birds, singing their gratitude for life and liberty, merely mocked his imprisonment. He had vague memories of finding comfort and courage last night in some bookish abstraction about the folly and hollowness of desire: he had even presumed to pity other men. Life was still foolish and hollow, but he no longer felt comforted nor courageous in face of it. He had pity for no one except himself. If a man were to pass beneath his window that morning, he would look down on him with bitterness and envy. He was a victim of life's cruellest trickery, a wronged prisoner, without advocate or champion, useless to himself and a burden to the world. His sufferings had brought him to breaking point, and yet years of purposeless self-torment might still await him. There was no place for him anywhere, no prospect of happiness or even contentment. He would be better in the grave.

And then someone laughed.

It was out in the garden, though still beyond his view. It was a girl, and—since nothing is so snobbish as our primary instincts—a lady. She was coming nearer. In another moment she would be in sight. If King Henry and his Council had been standing behind him offering unconditional release, freedom and a crown, James could not have turned from the window to listen to what they said.

Three young women came suddenly into view, following a path between the rose-bushes.

It must have been their leader that had laughed—the one who walked a pace ahead of her companions. She was still smiling, a smile from some other and better world. Indeed there seemed nothing in her face or bearing that resembled those of any human being that James had ever known: she came from, or rather, brought with her, some realm of unimaginable purity, unmatchable splendour. Eagerly he scanned her features as though searching for a taint or flaw in her perfection—and yet ecstatically confident that there was none to be found.

She was dressed in white, as befitted the heaven-born. She wore jewels on her hair and on her breast, but her beauty owed nothing to their aid. From her flowed health and bliss and illimitable inspiration, yet none of these things began to express the secret essence of her being. James was content to leave it unexpressed. His imagination was far beyond the boundaries of mere words, galloping across a country of whose existence he had never dreamt. He felt all the blood in his veins run suddenly backward, pressing upon his heart. Life—the life that had patiently grown up in him during twenty-two years—seemed to vanish in a single instant, giving place to something incredibly wider and deeper, pregnant with multitudinous meaning.

She was passing beneath him now, her two companions in her wake. She halted for a moment and seemed about to raise her eyes towards his window. In a fluster of self-effacement, he stepped back from the sill, his eyes still burning towards her.

She passed on. She had not looked up. He was almost glad she had not, as if his innermost self, sated with joy, preferred postponement to the risk of a present excess. He became conscious, again, that the birds were still filling the morning with their triumphant song. Now a little dog, delayed, no doubt, by some important business, came bounding into sight, and rushed past his mistress down the path. She quickened her pace as though to share in its gambols. She would be out of sight soon, unless he called to her. And he knew that he was incapable of making any sound.

She turned half back and he saw her face again. It seemed more overpowering than ever in its sweetness. 'Beauty,' he found himself saying, as though he had never before known the meaning of the word. Then a sentence began to form itself in his head, a line of poetry, remembered, or created, that moment:

Beauty enough to make a world to dote.

She was speaking to one of her companions. He could not hear her voice. She seemed suddenly grave, playfulness giving way to a serious thought. As he watched her, a great awe settled upon him. It was not only delight that wracked him, but an effort of will, a decision of unending import. The shiver that shook him marked its passing. He had given a promise, sealed a compact that must govern his whole life and perhaps what lay beyond. He had chosen.

His eyes had never left her face. She was smiling again now. She turned, called ahead of her to her dog and passed out of sight. He craned out to see her, but she was gone.

He stepped back, felt his knees uncertain beneath him, and sank down on a stool.

He had heard enough and to spare of the worshipfulness of womankind. Courtly literature had explored the theme with monotonous thoroughness: it had been embroidered with a dozen different orthodoxies and a host of heresies: poets sang of little else. Words, words, words. How flat and inadequate they seemed now, in face of the reality! He had admired them once, thinking that he had learnt from them all that there was to know about the mystery they pretended to fathom. He had not guessed the elements of it, nor seen, as he now saw, that it was the axis upon which all life must for ever turn. Only experience could reveal its full possibilities, or teach the due measure of wonder and reverence.

He was content, for the moment, to sit in contemplation. Time enough, later, to do what must be done. There would be ways and means to be considered. He would have to discover who this ethereal creature might be, and under what name she walked the earth. She was presumably English, and he a stranger: she was doubtless free, and he a captive. There would be barriers to break or climb. But her appearance was a summons to him to use all his skill and strength and manhood until nothing kept him from the further converse with her which was, as he now knew, the reason of his existence. Endurance would have a purpose now, and effort a goal; there could be no question of doubt or dalliance. The world had been born anew and he would be worthy of its primal splendour. He still sat facing the window, listened still to the triumphant songs of spring.

Nature had once more worked her recurrent miracle—the miracle which even she, in her blind loyalty to routine, can hardly find stale or hackneyed. A young man had fallen in love. It was, perhaps, beside the point that he was a king, titular ruler of some small corner of the material earth. It was a little more relevant that he had in him the makings of a musician notable in his own generation, and of a poet whose writings would be able to command attention and delight across centuries of human noise. But these things did little to increase the significance of the central fact—that one more soul had entered upon its earthly heritage, and that the bounds of the world must expand to make room for what was in that moment created.

May 1416

V

He was still rapt when they brought him his meal, and he ate it without coming to earth. He had forgotten what time it was, and, when they spoke of riding out for the morning, he assented in a dream. As he went out to the horses, mounted, and rode through the gate, his eye searched every window of the walls, every cranny of the courtyard. To the surprise of his guards, he rode furiously by road or meadow, but never far from sight of the castle. They grew tired of his unconscionable twistings and wheelings and began to suspect that he was trying to give them the slip. They insisted on turning back early. James hardly cared. He sang aloud on the return journey, and a woman in Windsor High Street, soured by envy and rheumatism, cursed him for a noisy young jackanapes: it was like the rich, she told her meek husband, to flaunt their happiness in poor folks' faces. If James could have heard her, he would probably have tossed her money—though she was prosperous enough—and sung a little louder.

He returned to his room in undiminished excitement and made straight for the window. There was nothing to be seen. He was still too happy to be vexed at a temporary disappointment. Dinner, eaten with one eye on the garden, tasted better than he had ever known it. A meal now had something of a sacrament about it. As soon as he had finished, he ensconced himself on the sill, harp on knee, and began to sing again. He sang tunes he had learnt in England, at Evesham and Pevensey. He sang songs that recalled his childhood and the sharp tang of the North, artless airs that had been old when the Bruce was born—*By Yon Woodside* and *Late, Late on Evenings*. He felt glad to be a Scot.

When he had exhausted his remembered stock he tried singing fragments of Chaucer's *Troilus*, propping the book in front of him and devising a tune as he went along. He had made some difficult progress before he decided that the words were intractable and unsatisfactory. Loath to abandon his half-finished tune, he cast about him for some other poem in Rhyme Royal and, failing, wondered why he should not write one himself. He had tried before, generally giving up for lack of an inspiring theme. There was no such lack now.

The birds sang more quietly, the afternoon was hot and heavy. But their early morning chorus was still echoing in his head. He felt kinship with them as with every living thing. It would be amusing to put their spring-song into human rhyme. The harp slid to the floor, the window-sill became a writing-desk. There was a false start, a check and much chewing of the pen. Then the lines began to flow.

Worship—all ye that lovers be—this May.

If that was not what birds sang in the morning, then it ought to be. He laughed from sheer happiness, and then knitted his brows again to complete the stanza.

Worship, all ye that lovers be, this May,
For of your bliss the Kalends are begun
And sing with us, "Away, Winter, away!
Come, Summer, come, sweet season, with the sun!"
Let each in amorous joy lift up his face;
Thank Love that deigns to call you to his grace.

The last couplet was poor: he could improve it later. He must go ahead now, not stop to correct, while the impulse to creation was hot within him. The chance might never recur. Like every poet in the world's history, James was in fear that the precious gift came from a mere caprice of fortune, and that his first poem might be his last.

Night found him still scribbling. Graver thoughts had succeeded the first lyrical outburst. The serious side of his mind, which was the most genuine and enduring part of him, began to impress itself on his writing. If there was, here and there, a touch of downright morbidity, that was no more than the fashionable conventions demanded: self-pity was the mark of the true lover. And James, even without sanction from the courtly versifiers who prescribed rules for their day, had years of misery and disappointment to exorcise.

The poem failed to take shape. James knew vaguely that the right thing was an allegory. An imaginary lover must be pictured holding converse with Moral Abstractions: his encounters with Virtues and Vices must be arranged into a pattern which should also be a story, illustrating the progress of every man's love through joys and sorrows, hopes and rebuffs. The well-worn scheme had delighted James, often enough, in other men's writings, but he was now finding it impossible to impose it on his own. As his molten thoughts poured out and hardened into verse, he saw less and less prospect of re-moulding them into any approved shape. If at any time he saw a chance of doing so, it was soon spoilt by the pressure of new conceptions welling up to demand their place. The poem must remain a rhapsody—or at least demand a life-time of tinkering before it could ever please the fastidious with its pattern. For the moment this did not matter. Nothing mattered except that he was writing poetry. He wrote on.

Dazzled with Beauty, he never doubted that its only source was the heavenly creature who had so suddenly walked into his world. He could hardly have grasped the truth, that love—particularly the love of one unknown and unencountered—can be nothing but a mirror reflecting into consciousness whatever is unconsciously splendid or innocent or divine in the lover's own soul. He wrote in worship of a fellow creature, and did not know that he was forging a monument to his own youth and integrity: he attributed all the glory to her who, as he hoped, was now sleeping under the same roof, though ignorant, perhaps, of his very existence.

It was past midnight before the tide of creation began to ebb, and tired nature re-asserted her claims. Even so he would hardly have consented to rest but for the thought that he must wake early next morning and be at the window as soon as it was light. He made ready for bed with nothing in mind but the great moment when he would leap out of it again in the hope of a repetition of yesterday's miracle.

Sleep, he told himself, was quite out of the question: but for once he would not read in bed: he had thoughts for company which made books seem duller than the dust: he would just lie and think, resting his cramped limbs and delighting his mind by going over and over the ground which was so recent and yet so gloriously familiar. It would soon be dawn again: he would soon be springing up, refreshed, for another day of exhilaration. It was better not to try any more verse-making in his head. He could lie and think. To think of her was more restful than sleeping.

In ten minutes he was more soundly asleep than he had ever been in his life: and the sun stood high over Windsor Castle when they knocked upon his door and found him still blissfully dreaming.

May 1416

VI

"No, Cousinot, I object on principle. I know I am in the royal wing, and I do not mind surrendering my rooms if King Henry needs them. But I object to being turned out to make way for a German."

Cousinot, knowing his master, received the tirade from

Orleans in silence. He merely tried to indicate by expression and attitude that captives of war, even captive dukes, cannot always be choosers.

Orleans was not the only man with a grievance at Windsor Castle. Even the canons of St. George were being ejected—barely content with King Henry's promise that it should never happen again—from their comfortable quarters in the Lower Ward. They emerged to find the whole castle in a buzz of worldly activity. Men pulled and pushed and hammered, grumbled, planned and swore. Girls, according to their rank, chose new dresses, ordered provisions, or scrubbed floors. Everyone, except the prisoners, had something engrossing to do and no time to do it in.

The expected visitor who was causing so much activity was the strangest anomaly in Europe. He was a German, and claimed heirship to the despots of ancient Rome. He called himself *Augustus*, *Imperator*, *Rex Romanorum*, and ruled—in a vague fashion—over that Germany which the legions had never conquered. The gibe against the Holy Roman Empire—that it was neither Holy nor Roman nor an Empire—had not yet been born: but the thing itself was already verging on a joke. The Swiss had recently taken a large chip out of it and the Italians laughed at the idea of its extending to their busy cities. Sigismund, its present ruler and Henry's guest, was hardly the man to bring either to book. He had once managed to get together an army of cosmopolitan adventurers, and the Turks had promptly butchered it in the Balkans. Inside his undoubted territories, the principal vassals obeyed him only when it was convenient. He was treated with great deference in such parts of Germany as had a hankering for a long-dead past. But deference was a poor substitute for power, and he liked to forget his pompous helplessness at home by visiting foreign lands. He had honoured France with his presence, and now it was England's turn.

Humphrey of Gloucester, being a classical scholar, had met him at Dover in an odd fashion. Humphrey had waded out into the surf, drawn sword in hand, and refused to let Sigismund land until he renounced any claim the Caesars might have had to Britain. After these theatrical preliminaries, Sigismund was welcomed with due courtesy; his hard-drinking *knechts* and *ritters* were invited to live at free quarters on English inns and have the bills sent in to King Henry. The exchequer groaned under the double weight of war with France and hospitality to Germans, but Henry turned a smiling face to his imperial guest. He invited him to Windsor, suggesting that Sigismund might honour the Knights of the Garter by filling a vacancy in their ranks. Sigismund reached Windsor on the last Friday of May, was treated to his ceremonial bath next morning and installed on Sunday in the Chapel of St. George. He had brought with him, as a present from Germany, the alleged and desiccated heart of that improbable saint.

The ceremony concerned the Knights of the Garter only: the social event was the subsequent banquet in the hall. All England and its wife wanted to be there, and Henry was eager to collect every guest that might do honour to the occasion. Even prisoners might reflect a little glory on their captor: it was not everyone who could show a king, even so unimportant a king as the Scottish one, among his enforced guests.

When the day came, the Great Hall was fuller than its original designer could ever have intended. The tables, set in complicated pattern, solved, or evaded, a hundred difficulties of etiquette and international precedence. They must accommodate Germans and English, heiresses and celibate priests, warriors and ambassadors of peace. There was row after row of shining lords and ladies whose sonorous titles proclaimed that they had been born to determine, by the whim of word or gesture, how thousands, millions even, of the poor and humble must live.

The minstrels, working their best, failed to drown the clash of plates, the rising hubbub of compliments and jests Servants, deaf to everything but their stewards' commands, hurried anxiously out of the blazing kitchen, and steered vast dishes through the maze of high-peaked hats and undulating veils. The tables steamed with incredible viands: minced veal in custard, peacock painted with saffron and stuffed with ginger—any indigestible kickshaw that the ingenuity of a perverse generation could suggest.

James ate his fill, wondering whether he really preferred the fare to his simpler everyday meals. He decided, on the whole, that he did. He was to meet the emperor when the four hours' banquet was over. Meanwhile, in grudging deference to his rank, he had been placed at the head of a small table. On one side of him was a Bohemian countess who smiled nervously at regular intervals, but could speak neither English nor French; on the other a massive knight from Kent seemed determined not to talk in any language until eating was finished. James had ample leisure to prosecute, cautiously, the only search that mattered.

He felt sure that she was in the hall. She had probably come to Windsor, he argued, to attend the festival in the train of some great lady. In the six days that had passed since he saw her in the garden, he had come no nearer to discovering who she was. The code of his times and his class, hallowing First Love as the clearest intrusion of the divine into mortal life, prescribed reverence above all else, and the most rigid secrecy; the lover must not endanger its sanctity by indiscreet research among the outside world. James could only look round him and hope.

He was at one side of the hall, and his back was to the royal dais. Three-quarters of the company were in view, but she did not seem to be among them. She must be somewhere behind him, but it was not easy to think of excuses for continually turning round.

When he did look back, it was to see Sigismund and Henry at the high table. Bishop Beaufort was there, as prelate to the Garter knights, and the king's three brothers, Bedford, Clarence, and Humphrey of Gloucester. James wondered how Clarence was relishing Beaufort's proximity: the two were known to be at odds: Clarence had married the widow of a Beaufort, and quarrelled, ever since, with his episcopal brother-in-law over the matter of her jointure. Perhaps King Henry had ordered the present arrangement in the hope of teaching them to be friends. James noticed that Beaufort was frowning, and Clarence leant as far from him as possible, calling across to an ample, good-looking matron —no doubt his duchess whose dowry was the bone of contention—who sat at a smaller table, half out of view.

The lady from Bohemia gave her shy smile and ventured something unintelligible. James smiled back. The Kentish gentleman snorted, cleared his throat, and buttonholed a passing servant. Having made his wants clear, he turned to James and informed him, in a combative manner, that it was a fine day. A sporadic conversation followed, equally uninteresting to both. James's attempts to see what lay behind him were increasingly circumscribed.

He was no nearer his object when the feast drew to a close and he received his summons to the high table. An usher came to whisper an ornate message into his ear: his imperial Majesty would soon be pleased to be ready to receive his Majesty of Scotland: would his Majesty be pleased to be prepared?

James rose stiffly, smiling his apologies to the tongue-tied foreigner beside him. As he did so, he knew suddenly that the thing was about to happen. He was going to see *her* again. There was an odd pricking at the back of his head, and his heart had begun to thump. He turned to face the dais. His eyes travelled along the table where Clarence's duchess presided. The girl of the garden, the lady of his supernal dreams, was sitting there, twenty paces from where James stood. She was looking straight at James.

He began to move towards her, unconscious of obstacles, yet instinctively avoiding them. He did not take his eyes from her, could not have done so if all the world had been watching, greedy for gossip. All the world—or so much of it as was gathered in Windsor Hall—was fortunately intent on its own affairs. Young lords and ladies chattered about trifles, their minds occupied with love, or what passed for love in their circle of ideas. Others were more engrossed with thoughts of worldly advancement, congratulating themselves on making an acquaintance that might prove useful, or wondering why my Lord So-and-So seemed so unresponsive to their painstaking cultivation. Here a priest speculated on the vanity of feastings, tingeing his speculations with draughts of expensive wine. There a maid-of-honour came to the satisfactory conclusion that her silks were palpably better chosen than those of the girl opposite her. And beside her a Yorkshire knight sat thinking doggedly about money. None noticed the young man who threaded his way through their midst, or guessed that he was making his way towards the woman he desired, and had chosen, and could never on this earth forget.

A dozen choices were being made around him, seeming equally permanent in the imagination of their choosers, as they looked into bright eyes which were happy with wine and jollity and the pride of the flesh. Few would remember them in a month or two, most would be looking elsewhere after the next campaign or a new Court gathering. The air they breathed was no encouragement to constancy. Their poets extolled Love, but warned them of its impermanency. Their parents hinted that it must not be allowed to impinge on duty. One loved by chance, and there was an end of it. One married elsewhere, as policy dictated, as money or influence beckoned. Young men might worship woman in the abstract and even dream grand dreams about other men's wives; it was good form, too, to treat one's own wife with deference in company, even if one neglected or beat her at home. A mad world, but it was not they that had made it: and it had its compensations, especially where wine flowed free. James, wading through the noisy crowd towards his chosen bride, was an anomaly, a freak of Nature. Had he proclaimed his intentions instead of cloaking them even from himself, he would have been a butt for wry-faced ridicule: nor could the mockers have imagined that posterity might accept his story as natural and right, their laughter as distasteful, and possibly unclean.

He pressed on, deaf to the surrounding babble.

"Who is that little fellow? He trod on your heel, didn't he?"

"One of the Scottish prisoners—probably drunk. Father says they all get drunk as soon as they see decent liquor."

Laughter, and a toast. The little fellow is immediately forgotten.

"Forgive me, I didn't hear. That young man jolted me in the back. What were you saying, *mein Herr*?"

A pause and a guttural whisper.

"Well, it's a good thing you didn't say so aloud. I expect it will come to nothing. And you know the Garter motto: *Honi soit qui mal y pense*."

Laughter again. No one is daring to be serious, even about scandal. James heard nothing: he was nearing his goal.

It was the girl who first dropped her eyes, in confusion or in warning. James, losing the dazzling light, began to steer a steadier course. He turned through a gap between two tables, reached the wall and began to coast along it. In a moment or two he would be behind her, thrillingly near.

There was a knife on the floor, not too far from her to make a passable excuse. He stooped, picked it up, and approached the presence. He looked down on her golden hair, her white shoulders: everything about her seemed remote and yet already familiar. He summoned up his voice.

"My lady," he said, a little huskily, "is this your knife on the floor?"

She looked up, almost too quickly: one would have said she was expecting someone to address her from behind. She was smiling before her head had turned.

"I thank you, sir," she said. "How foolish of me to drop it."

Her voice, his first sound of it, came as a surprise. However he had imagined it, the reality was better, more coolly delicious. He ought to pass on now, or tongues might begin to wag: he must go and pay his respects at the high table. But it was still more necessary to hear her speak again. She was smiling up at him, laughing with her eyes. The emperor could wait.

"It was lying there," he began. "On the floor. I thought——" He could get no further.

"Yes, sir," she said, "it is mine."

She wiped the knife on a little hunk of bread, frowning prettily. The young man at her side, thinking that the interruption was ended, cleared his throat to address her again. He had straight, flaxen hair, and a scar at the corner of his eye. A silly face, thought James: and I'd wager that it's only a tournament scar: he's never seen a battle. The girl was ignoring him, turning back to James. She expected James to speak again.

"I hope we may meet," he said, "while we are both at Windsor."

"I hope so," she said, blushed and then laughed again. The young man with the scar made a movement of irritation.

"I was just telling you," he said, "about the French way of charging. We had some remarkable experiences, even before Agincourt."

The girl turned back to her companion: she had to, in mere politeness. He did not matter. In forty years' time, James felt, he would still be recounting his remarkable experiences at Agincourt to a yawning wife. But James knew himself an intruder: he also knew that King Henry's eye was on him, and that further delay might be unwise. He walked on, reluctant.

As he passed the table, the Duchess of Clarence leant towards the side he had quitted.

"Joan," he heard her say, "do you know what my lord was telling me? We are to go to Woking on Tuesday. It's only a few miles, and it is time we paid your aunt a visit."

James did not hear the last words clearly. He was already mounting the end of the dais in order to skirt the high table and reach King Henry. Bishop Beaufort looked up, attempting to catch James's eye and smile patronage and encouragement. The emperor had pushed back his chair and was stroking his long beard. He had looked impressive enough from a distance, and the nearer view was not altogether a disappointment. What was disconcerting, now that one was close to him, was the way he was dressed. His clothes, whatever their past, were now the seediest in the room.

It is fortunate for emperors when their beards grow long. It makes them feel like Charlemagne—however much they may lack Charlemagne's power and wealth, to say nothing of his character. Sigismund liked thinking of himself as picturesque and majestic. He had few other pleasures nowadays, what with Bohemian heretics threatening rebellion, the Turkish armies never far from the frontiers, and the abominable, incurable shortage of cash. But he was glad to meet James. He was a German, with a full share of the romanticism that afflicts and comforts his race. He found James romantic: James was King of Scotland, and Sigismund liked thinking of Scotland—*Ultima Thule* as he pictured it—full of mist-crowned mountains lit by a watery sun. He had a taste for travelling and would have visited Scotland, as he was visiting Windsor, if there had been the least chance of Albany paying his travelling expenses.

Sigismund looked at James's broad shoulders and grave, distant eyes. He began to say polite and patronizing things, hoping to make James like him at first sight. He was full of good-nature—except where heretics were concerned—and he always wanted to be liked. He began with a jovial banter that often succeeded with his own subjects. He felt sure he could win this young man.

James was hardly conscious of what the emperor was

saying. He smiled, bowed, and bit his lip; he could not trust himself to reply coherently, having other matters in his head.

Sigismund, shrewd enough to see that he was making little progress, suddenly opened an indirect attack. He turned to Henry and pleaded his position as guest of honour in order to ask a boon; could not James be released soon, sent back to his own kingdom? Henry smiled and then pursed his lips, saying guardedly that negotiations to that end were already on foot. Sigismund beamed back at James, making the best of the dubious reply. He dropped his queer, glutinous French, and began to speak Latin, fluent though hazy in its genders. He remembered, with pleasure, how a bishop had once corrected him for making *schisma* feminine, and how, for once, the right repartee had come to him at the right moment. "I am Emperor," he had said, "and Grammar is subject to me." He wished he could think of something as good to set King Henry laughing and attract the attention of this absent-minded young Scot. He talked on in the hope that an idea would come.

"Joan," said James to himself, "Joan, Jane, Joanna, Jean, Jennie, Jehanne. Joan, Joan, Joan."

He did not know why the emperor was talking to him. He did not know why the emperor was sitting there, nor even what had brought him to England. He did not greatly care.

There was, indeed, a good deal of doubt about the last point. It was an open secret that Sigismund was in low water, and that the French, whose hospitality he had lately enjoyed, had promised him a large sum if he could induce King Henry to stay at home instead of leading new swarms of destructive Englishmen across the Channel. But Sigismund must have known that there was no hope of earning that reward: Henry was bent on more war, and not a single *louis d'or* was likely to trickle into Sigismund's empty pockets. No one guessed the truth, except perhaps King Henry and a few clerks at the Exchequer, for no one knew how desperately empty those pockets were. It was difficult to believe that Caesar Augustus had no reason for visiting England—and staying there as long as possible—except the humiliating one that he knew no other place in Europe where he could enjoy such good food and drink, and never pay out a penny. He had been here three pleasant and economical weeks: he was already beginning to wonder what would happen to himself and his dependants when Henry tired of the honour of entertaining them, and packed them off to the Continent again.

The emperor's Latin began to flag. With all the good will in the world, it is not a language that lends itself to jocosity. Henry interposed politely, rising from his chair. The whole room took up the signal. The minstrels, hungry with watching their betters feed, gave the conventional flourish with gratitude and conviction.

"And remember to be thankful to his Majesty's father," said Sigismund to James, "for preventing you from going to France for your education. I've just come from France. I expect they've taught you that all Gaul is divided into three parts. I can tell you their names: Illiberality: Irritability: Inhospitality."

James smiled wanly, wondering how long it had taken Sigismund to think that out. He had heard that the emperor had grossly misbehaved himself in Paris, and that the French had objected to his amorous antics even more than they had objected to his clothes.

Bishop Beaufort put in his oar.

"If you had seen the French whom his Majesty defeated at Agincourt," he said, "you would have said their name was Legion."

Henry frowned at the clumsy compliment. He felt it his duty not to encourage bishops to jest, however mildly, with the language of Scripture. He nodded to James and then beckoned Sigismund to precede him through the little door on the dais.

The company was dissolving into an informal, restless

mob. Lords and ladies laughed and chattered as they grouped and re-grouped themselves, impeding the anxious servants that scurried and ducked between, in their attempts to remove the stools, smaller tables, and so much of the banquet as might be left.

James made his way through the confusion with his eyes darting everywhere. He had seldom been so conscious of his low stature: he was soon regretting that he had left his vantage-ground on the dais. Joan, he remembered, was not wearing one of those high-horned head-dresses that were becoming fashionable. She had had a little golden-threaded net on her head; she would not present a good landmark among all these towering strangers.

He made for the wall, deciding to stand still for a moment and let people flow past him. He struggled through to find himself next to his fellow-prisoner, William Douglas, the heir of Dalkeith. He was leaning against the tapestry, talking half to himself, half to a lanky, middle-aged German, muzzy with wine. Young Dalkeith had probably drunk twice as much as his companion, without losing an atom of his self-possession, nor gaining—to judge by his comments on the passers-by—an atom of good-humour. The foreigner, too far gone to take much in, was listening to his sarcasms with an owlish gravity. James, hoping to learn names, one name especially, ranged himself beside them.

He smiled absently at Dalkeith's sallies. He took the opportunity of a pause in them to ask, with as offhand a manner as he could command, whether Dalkeith knew of a place in the neighbourhood called Woking. Dalkeith had never heard of it, and was not interested.

"Look at Gloucester," he said, "trying to pretend that he hasn't over-eaten himself. He can hardly walk."

James looked, but could see nothing unusual in Duke Humphrey's gait. He was walking slowly; his large melancholy eyes roamed the hall, seeking amusement. A lady of uncertain age hung on his arm, trying in vain to engage his interest.

"He is curiously unlike his brother," James remarked, mainly for want of something better to say.

"Luckily," agreed Dalkeith. "No one wants two Harries."

"Woking!" said the German, unexpectedly coming to life. "We come at Woking yesterday. We hawked there, over the Chobham Heath."

He relapsed into coma, staring stupidly before him like a child with a bad cold.

Dalkeith's face twitched itself into a momentary smile; then he screwed it up to watch the crowd again, with renewed contempt. "Clarence seems to have had enough of it," he said. "He's making for the door. Or perhaps he wants to get out of sight of his duchess with that young madam he's picked up. I expect my lady will be in chase in a minute."

James looked towards the door at the lower end of the hall. A temporary corridor in the crowd enabled them to see that Clarence was indeed making his way out. It was no less certainly Joan that hung on his arm. He was about to start after them, when prudence forbade, suggesting instead what seemed to him a masterpiece of duplicity.

"I wonder who she is," he said. "She looks rather pretty."

Dalkeith fixed ferret's eyes on Joan, loosed off the expected scurrility, and then said he had no notion.

"They ought to be labelled," he went on, "they ought to wear the family arms. Especially the marriageable ones. After all, on this sort of occasion, they're more or less on campaign."

James missed the last words. Prudence or no prudence, he was already making his way towards the door. He tried not to appear hurried, starting off by an oblique route. Young Dalkeith was a prisoner—and ten years of it, as hostage for a powerful kinsman, was some excuse for his malice—but his tongue was free to spread stories.

There was a general movement towards fresh air. James found himself caught in a stream, flowing in the right direction, but with exasperating slowness. By the time he had gained the door and could feel sunlight on his head, the courtyard outside was gay with groups and couples. It was pleasant to escape from the atmosphere of crowded humanity, its perfumes, hot clothes, and wine. But there was no sign of Clarence or Joan, and no means of guessing which way they had gone.

May 1416

VII

He had meant to give them the slip this time, and he had succeeded. He was alone on Chobham Heath.

It had not been difficult. Wintershull, deputy-castellan of Windsor and his temporary tutor, had suggested a day in the tiltyard. James knew how to deal with deputies. By eleven o'clock he was trotting down the Weybridge road with a goshawk on his wrist. He cantered across Runnymede, conscientiously keeping within a few strides of his cantering guards. They were past the abbey before anything was sighted. Then a wild duck rose from the river; James loosed the goshawk and dug in a spur. It was, by all the rules, asking too much of so small a bird: one needed a falcon for wild duck. But a hopeless chase was just what he needed.

The castle grooms had thought him unusually pernickety that morning, in his choice of a mount; but the big black mare he was now riding was justifying his care. She was gaining at every stride. The duck headed due south, keeping a low pitch but plenty of speed. James followed at full gallop till Byfleet came in sight: his attendants, now his pursuers, were well out of view, probably following by means of the hawk above. They could continue to do so; it would be some miles before the bird could stoop, some miles before anyone need draw rein. James, to the mare's surprise, swerved right and began to gallop her due west, towards Chobham Heath.

He was half-way there before he slackened speed. Then the gallop became a trot, the trot jogged down at once into a panting walk. There was no sound of hooves in his wake. For the moment he was a free man.

At a cross-roads ahead, a solitary labourer was digging by the wayside. For a moment James felt inclined to ask him the way to Scotland—or rather to say nothing, turn northwards and see what happened. But he had started in the wrong direction: the very fact that he was only allowed to ride south of the Thames meant that all the bridges would be watched: and beyond the river he had only the haziest notion which roads might lead him on the fortnight's or three weeks' journey home. It would be madness to spoil the negotiations for release when they were so near completion. And there was another goal, considerably more attainable, to which he could ask his way without arousing suspicion.

The man with the spade seemed to have great difficulty in understanding his questions—was evidently giving half a mind only to the stranger's talk: the other half was fixed on his own affairs. It took James some minutes to extort the information that Chobham lay straight ahead, but that one turned to the left for Woking: four miles as the crow flew, bearing left after Danewell, where Bonsey used to have his sheep. But he added, as James thanked him, that she'd killed herself—hanged herself with her own girdle out at Graciouspond farm: that's why they were burying her there at the four-roads: what did James think of that? Her own girdle, over a rafter in the kitchen. James saw that the man had cut a narrow oblong out of the turf, six foot by three.

He trotted off, up and over a slight rise, with only the vaguest idea of what he meant to do. When he had made five or six miles, asked for Woking Manor again, and came in sight of an old-fashioned, rather ramshackle house, he was still as uncertain as ever. He left the lane he was on, and led the mare over some strips of ploughland, to a small spinney of thorn and elder. Here he tethered her and sat down to contemplate the roof which sheltered, unless he was mistaken, the subject of all contemplation.

His seeming-casual enquiries at Windsor Castle had not elicited anything very helpful about Woking. The manor had belonged, for some decades, to the Holland family. The last of them had been made Duke of Surrey by King Richard, and when Henry Bolingbroke deposed and murdered Richard, had tried to raise rebellion against the usurper. He had been mobbed and killed by the townspeople of Cirencester, in loyalty to King Henry the Fourth. Henry had allowed the widow to go on living at Woking. For all James could gather, she might be there still. She was old, and, his informants thought, something of an invalid. Her much younger sister was a far more important person: she had married Beaufort, Earl of Somerset, the bishop's brother. When he died, she became wife to the Duke of Clarence, and was so still. But why, they asked, was James interested in the old lady?

The ill-kept pile across the ploughland did nothing further to satisfy his curiosity. There was little sign of life, and perhaps the family was still at dinner. James was content, for a little, to lie still and watch. He was alone, out of doors and free from surveillance for the first time in many years; when he came to think of it, for the first time in his life. But his pleasure in the situation could not quiet his curiosity; and hunger, too, was beginning to make him restless. He rose, saw that his mare was complacently cropping, and began to cross the deserted field.

If the house was dowdy, its garden was well-fenced: it was also screened from spying by small, close-growing trees. James ranged up and down without finding a gap. Then he came on the back of an arbour, built into the fence. It offered a hand-hold. He swung himself up, felt the stakes sway under his feet, and jumped through a tangle of branches on to a patch of grass. As he landed, he heard a noise behind him and turned to look back into the arbour. There was a small table in it, covered with a cloth of well-darned frieze; on it stood a dish of almonds, some wine, and a little pewter bell. In the chair behind, heavy with food and slumber, sat Bishop Beaufort.

"No," said the bishop, blinking startled eyes. "No, my dear, I was not asleep."

Then he blinked again, saw who it was, and began to struggle up from his seat. His blue jaw sagged, his little eyes strained to their fullest size.

"Your Majesty," he stammered, "I did not know——"

James, almost equally surprised, had the advantage of being fully awake.

"I have lost my way," he said. "We were out with the hawks. Can your lordship tell me the way back to Windsor?"

The bishop moistened his lips, but no sound came from them.

"Unless," James went on, "unless I could ask you first for something to eat. I have had no dinner."

Still bewildered, Beaufort found himself mechanically pushing the dish of almonds across the little table; then he realized their inadequacy and smiled in a shy, almost engaging way. A moment later, he recovered normality.

"But your guards—your attendants?" he said.

"We seem to have lost each other," answered James blandly. "I am hoping they recover my hawk. She was a haggard, but shaping well."

"I fear dinner is finished," said the bishop. "An hour ago. I was just preparing to . . . preparing to . . . I'll see what can be done."

He rang the little bell that stood on the table, and pointed to a second chair.

"Most extraordinary," he murmured, "a most unexpected —ah—pleasure. Would your Majesty care to sit?"

James sat. "It's clouding over," he said. "I believe we shall have rain."

"Yes," said the bishop, "I don't know what has happened to the seasons nowadays. When I was young, we could count——"

A servant appeared and was sent back to fetch food. He was also told to summon Beaufort's sister-in-law, Lady Clarence.

She arrived more quickly than the ordered meal, expressing suitable surprise and satisfaction. She had not seen James come, she said: she had been sitting in the Solar with her daughter and had not noticed anyone coming up the lane. Her eyes seemed to seek a further explanation, sideways, from Bishop Beaufort, but evidently found none. James held his peace until the return of the servant, with wine, bread, and a spiced pasty, interrupted Lady Clarence's flow.

She was fortyish and, thought James, a trifle plump. She talked with an air of worldliness and assurance which did not quite suit her, or ring quite true. She must have been strikingly handsome in her youth; but a life of Courts, two husbands, and children—presumably by the first, the Beaufort—had left her buxom rather than beautiful. She retained a relic only of the ethereal air she might have once possessed. She reminded one, the necessary allowances and deductions once made, she reminded one of Joan. James, chopping his pasty, began to think.

His advent, naturally enough, was beginning to act as a magnet to the household. Servants appeared with unnecessary frequency. Then a boy of thirteen, giving himself the lordliest airs. The bishop introduced him as his nephew, Lady Clarence's son and Earl of Somerset. His mother called him John, but even in her attitude there was a shade of deference. His father being dead, he was technically head of the family, heir of the Beaufort line. James gave a shrewd guess that Lady Clarence's hold upon her children had been greatly weakened by her second marriage, and Somerset soon made it clear that he was the kind of boy to make full use of any such excuse for avoiding control.

"How did you lose your falcon?" he asked, sprawling on a stool and snatching in the air at a hovering gnat.

"It was not a falcon," said James drily. "It was a goshawk. The quarry took a low pitch and I couldn't see for trees."

He almost enjoyed lying to these people. The bishop, at least, lived in an atmosphere where it was recognized that ambition, self-interest, and mere convenience had stronger claims than truth. Lady Clarence was inured, probably acquiescent. And young Somerset, to judge by appearances, would soon enter the same world as his uncle, and take to it as a duckling to muddy pools.

"We'd better send a message to Windsor," he was saying, "to tell 'em you're here."

From the tail of his eye James saw Beaufort make a little gesture, signifying that there was no need: Beaufort had evidently given instructions to a servant—how or when was beyond James's guessing.

"Where's Joan?" said a new voice. "Is Joan here?"

James looked up, to see a thin, pale old lady in a faded dress that reminded him of the fashions of his childhood days. She wore a set expression of gentle, harassed surprise, and her grey hair, like a bird's nest built in too small a hollow, stuck out in wisps from the antique chaperon that was supposed to conceal it. Nobody troubled to introduce her.

"She's not here," said Lady Clarence, "I left her in the Solar." She spoke loudly, as if to the deaf.

"Oh," said the old lady. "Oh. I am sorry. I'll go and see."

She looked towards James, and then suddenly began to cough in a painful fashion. She made as if to retire in confusion, but returned to address Somerset.

"Was it all right?" she asked. "I mean, about the court?"

"Of course it was all right," the boy shouted at her impatiently. "Why shouldn't it be? Go in and find

Joan. . . . Oh, and aunt! why don't you bring her here?"

The lady coughed again, threw a glance of appeal—or was it apology?—in James's direction, and retreated towards the house.

"Been holding court for your aunt?" said Beaufort patronizingly. "That's a good thing. Experience . . . must know about the law."

"It's a devilish nuisance," said the boy, "having to go over to Sutton. That's why I wasn't at dinner. They ought to combine courts for these two manors, make the Sutton people come over here." He reached over to the table and took half a handful of almonds.

"They'd never do that," said Lady Clarence. "They'll never do anything their grandfathers didn't do. And my poor sister encourages them to make trouble. Was that wheelwright creature in court again?"

"He was," said Somerset. "And I made 'em fine him. I told 'em it was time he had a lesson."

"I suppose it's the same everywhere," sighed the bishop. "No gratitude: nothing but grumbling. I find it on my own manors. I wish I knew what's coming over the world."

"Do yours all want to commute?" asked the boy in his most Olympian manner. "Ours do—say they'll pay any rent rather than work it off in labour on the demesne land. What beats me is where they get the money from."

"That's what we all wonder," agreed Beaufort. "And when you try to hire labour to keep demesne land in proper order, you simply cannot get it without paying twice the legal wage. It is time Parliament stopped passing laws about it, and suggested some way of getting them enforced."

"Oh," said James maliciously, "but isn't that the Council's business?"

Beaufort smiled condescendingly, but did not seem to enjoy the comment. "The Council," he said, "is busy with graver matters than the—er—insubordination of the lower orders. That is hardly a matter of high policy—not as yet. And the poor will learn in time what is good for them. This money business is the curse of the country, but it won't last."

"It's certainly that," said Somerset sagely. "They were much happier before they'd seen coin. They'd go back to the old ways if they had any sense."

"I think," said Lady Clarence hesitatingly, "that there are some advantages in the new system. I remember my father grumbling terribly when he was called out on service, instead of paying a money-rent."

"My dear mother!" said Somerset. "That's quite different. You can't compare land-holders——"

"A clove-gilliflower," interrupted a voice behind him, "that's all I pay the king for these two manors. Just a clove-gilliflower on Saint John's Day."

The old lady had returned. She was speaking to Lady Clarence, but her eyes strayed towards James in a rather forlorn fashion.

"It's a good thing," said Beaufort in a low voice, "that the boy's here to help her with the estates. She's getting past it." Then he raised his voice. "Did you not find Joan?" he asked.

"Joan? Oh yes, I found her. She is coming. Just tidying herself."

The old lady smiled at James, a curiously charming smile. "So this," he thought, "is Surrey's widow. King Henry's people lynched her husband at Cirencester, but her sister marries King Henry's son, so as to be Duchess of Clarence. That couldn't happen in Scotland. We hate better than that."

"She's being rather a long time," added Lady Surrey archly—apparently to Somerset's irritation.

"Well, why bother?" he said. "You're always bothering about things that don't matter. I'm tired of it."

"John, that's no way to speak to your aunt," said Lady Clarence, without great conviction.

"I expect the poor boy's tired," began Lady Surrey, in

a weak voice of conciliation. Then another fit of coughing overtook her.

Somerset snorted, rising from his stool. "Your Majesty will excuse me," he said, "I must go down to the mill. I've heard they're cutting down some more willows without permission."

Lady Surrey, hovering behind her family, was heard to murmur that she had granted permission.

"We shan't have a tree left," said Somerset, "if aunt has the management of the place much longer."

It was comic, and yet somehow repugnant to remember that the boy was not yet fourteen.

"Here is your sister," said Beaufort. Before James could turn, he heard Joan's voice behind him.

"Yes. Here I am."

"I'm so glad. This is——" began Lady Surrey, but was not permitted to proceed.

"We wanted to present you, Joan," said Beaufort, with an air of introducing a paradox, "to the King of Scotland."

Joan curtseyed to the ground, rose slowly and smiled at James. He touched Heaven. Lordly as his thoughts of her might be, there was something about her reality that was both a shock and a satisfaction. He even forgot his vague but growing discomfort at realizing that she was connected—and how closely connected—with the people among whom he was sitting.

"I think you saw my daughter on Sunday," said Lady Clarence, quietly. "In Windsor Hall."

Joan seemed to blush a little. "I had that happiness," said James, with complete sincerity.

"I always say," put in Lady Surrey, "that young people ought to go to these festivals. I'm sure Saint George likes to see young faces at his table. And is it true that the emperor brought his heart from Germany? I'm sure it's right for us to have Saint George's heart in England."

There was a pause, no one knowing how to follow up. Joan was looking at the ground; James wondered how long he could gaze at her without attracting attention; but nobody seemed to be watching him except, perhaps, the strange old lady with the bird's-nest hair.

Beaufort was getting sleepy again. Somerset kept glancing at his aunt as if he were wondering how soon she would cough herself into a grave, and leave him to manage the estates unhampered. Lady Clarence was staring at her daughter's hands.

"Joan," she said, "you've been eating oranges."

"No, mother. But I peeled one for Margery Norton's little girl. She's no better today."

Joan looked up at James, as though to apologize for discussing domesticities. "Margery Norton is my old nurse—our old nurse. And her little daughter has caught a fever."

"Oranges?" said Somerset, with the fashionable sneer. "She's not going to have a baby, is she?"

Joan flashed him a look of something akin to hatred. "John!" said Lady Clarence, "please!"

"She isn't eight yet," said Lady Surrey, looking bewildered. "Even younger than you."

James was wondering whether the "even" would goad the boy into further prurience, when Bishop Beaufort roused himself to intervene. "You should try snails boiled in wine," he said majestically. "I was once cured of a fever by that, when all the other remedies had failed. It is a curious thing about fevers. . . ." He launched out on a tide of medical reminiscence, largely personal. Lady Clarence listened politely, her son with a sullen sneer. The old lady was astray in a world of her own. James sat content.

Joan Beaufort: it was a good name. He had been right in assuming that she came of the highest lineage; she was cousin to the king. Not that it mattered—her brother could say as much, young puppy. It did not even matter that the Beauforts had, or could have, so much influence in shaping England's policy. James felt sure of release without their help. It had taken him a little time to assimilate the fact that his Joan was really the niece of Bishop Beaufort. He was glad to think that he would soon be able to claim her as a king without asking assistance from the tubby, ape-faced little bore who was talking about his unimportant illnesses.

He smiled at Joan and she smiled back. This homely, country atmosphere seemed to endow her with a new, if possible a greater fascination. As soon as the bishop had finished, he would find some way of drawing her into the conversation.

There was a sudden thudding of hooves in the dusty lane. James was annoyed to see a familiar face, white with anxiety, bobbing over the hedge before it disappeared round the corner of the house. One of his guards had tracked him down, perhaps by means of the gravedigger at the cross-roads. No matter, he would keep them waiting; he would stay here for supper and ride home to Windsor by twilight.

The man was sufficiently relieved to discover his quarry. He rescued James's mare from the spinney and, though obviously afraid of consequences, acquiesced in James's refusal to mount and ride with him at once: he may have been glad of not setting forth on an exhausted horse, alone with his freshly mounted captive. But long before supper-time a new cavalcade arrived. Beaufort's message had brought Wintershull himself out from Windsor, with an armed retinue. Wintershull was angry as well as frightened; he insisted on an immediate return; he was clearly hoping to pass the matter off by getting James back in good time, and probably omitting to inflict on his guards the punishment they had incurred.

When the time came to say his goodbyes, James was relieved to find that the boy Somerset had disappeared. Beaufort, after exchanging sharp words, in an undertone, with the stupid, peppery Wintershull, was all smiles and compliments to the truant. Joan's curtsey seemed studied and formal: James could think of nothing he wanted to say to her that could be said in public. But, as she rose from the ground, she gave him a single glance that set his heart knocking at his ribs like a battering-ram.

He walked towards the horses in the lane. Wintershull had stayed behind to make a last protest or excuse to the bishop: it was no light matter to lose sight of a prisoner, even for a few hours, when England was bargaining for some thousands in way of ransom. James noticed with amusement that a man-at-arms was now mounted on his black mare: he himself must ride the roan, a handsome horse, but with more looks than speed. 'I'm not likely to feel the black between my knees again,' he thought, 'until it's time to go back to Scotland.'

He had still some yards to go when Lady Surrey caught up with him. He heard her, suddenly, panting at his elbow, and turned to make apology.

"Such an honour," she said nervously. "So seldom nowadays——"

She knelt to kiss his hand and then looked round like a child playing at conspirators.

"Who was it caught you?" she whispered. "Was it that man Bolingbroke? Because you must never trust him, you know. He has no right to call himself king. My poor husband tried to prevent it. And he used to tell me the son would be worse than the father—if ever he comes to the throne. You can't believe a word that either of them says."

She looked at him as if her warning were of deadly urgency. James wondered whether he ought to enlighten her, remind her that it was three years since time had avenged her upon Bolingbroke, and left England to his scapegrace son.

She rose to her feet, the dust clinging to her faded skirt.

"But you'll be kind to *her*," she said, still in furtive tones. "You've chosen well: the best of the family, I always say. She was named after me. My name is Joan, you know. And one day you can take her away from them—all of them. She'll be better away."

Wintershull came stumping down the path. The old lady turned and fled. James was left wondering how he had betrayed his secret to her, and how many of the others had guessed it. As he walked on, he decided that he was tolerably safe from the lot of them. 'Except,' he thought, mounting the roan, 'except perhaps Joan herself.'

Wintershull swung himself up and gave a testy order. The party jangled away towards the Chobham road.

"And then," said Joan to Margery Norton's daughter, "and then he took her away to his palace. And they had a wonderful banquet that lasted for days and days. And——"

"Did they have oranges?" interrupted the little girl, raising her head from the hot pillow.

"Hundreds," said Joan. "There were enough oranges for everybody, and two apiece for the prince and princess. And they kept all the pips, just to remind them what a lovely feast it had been."

"I do like your stories," said the child. She lay back with a tired, contented sigh. "But you never told me," she said, "what the prince looked like. Was he very tall?"

"No-o. He was rather short. But he was very, very strong—and much cleverer than most princes. He was good at riding and tilting, and he could sing songs beautifully. He had dark brown hair, almost black, and great, big bright eyes. And he always seemed so eager about everything, not slow and sleepy like other people."

"And what happened then? I mean, after the feast?"

"Oh, they were married, of course, and had lots and lots of children. Boys mostly. And the prince was king in his own country, and he made wonderful laws to help poor people, and he caught the wicked ones and cut their heads off. And they lived happily ever after, and the princess was never sad again."

"Never?"

"No, never. She had nothing to be sad about. Only sometimes she used to wonder. . . ."

"Yes?"

"She used to wonder whether she ought to tell him how it all happened."

"My mother says she used to tell father all about everything, before he went to heaven."

Joan looked pensive.

"Ye-es," she said. "But she wasn't sure whether she ought to go right back and tell him that it was she who had seen him first, and that she'd gone walking in the garden when she hoped he might be looking. And that she'd dropped her . . . her piece of bread off the table so that he could stop and pick it up for her."

The invalid considered the point for a moment.

"No," she announced gravely. "I don't think she had to tell him that."

May 1416

VIII

A mild surprise awaited James at Windsor: he was told at the gate that a man from Scotland had arrived that morning and was still up in the Devil Tower, hoping for his return. James went to his rooms and found that it was Giffard. He brought letters from Bishop Wardlaw and from the Royal Burgh of Edinburgh. No word from Albany, let alone money.

"But it's something," said James to himself when greetings were over, "to get letters from Scotland that show no sign of being tampered with."

He tore open the bishop's. It was full of details about the progress of St. Andrews' University: no mention of the negotiations with England nor of James's return.

"I hope you found everyone well at home," he said, as he skimmed the pages. "And at Goblin Hall."

Giffard frowned. "They were all well at Yester Castle," he said stiffly. "It is kind of your Majesty to ask." Giffard disliked the nicknames and superstitions that clung round his family home: local legend gave it a diabolical architect and suitable hauntings.

There was a chink of plates outside, and fumblings at the door.

"Well, you can tell me the news after supper," said James. "Have you had any yourself?"

"No, your Majesty."

"Nor dinner either, by the look of you."

James saw that Giffard was eyeing the plates, but he had misinterpreted the look. Giffard was only wishing that it was still his business to lay supper for the king. He secretly resented James having changed so much, with himself not by to watch the process. He could hardly believe that this was the boy he had squired three years ago.

"I hope your Majesty's health has been good," he said, "since I was sent back to Scotland."

James was frowning at his letter. The royal burgh was as disappointing as Bishop Wardlaw.

"It has," he said. "And my studies progress. "Would it shock you, Giffard, to hear I've been writing poetry?"

"Poetry!"

"Yes, Giffard. I knew you'd be shocked."

"I am not. Anything your Majesty writes. . . . Though I must say, the only poems I have tried to read seem to have been written by a poor sort of creatures. They seem to think nothing matters except love—generally for some other man's wife."

Giffard, at any rate, had not changed in three years.

"Your criticism is just, Giffard—but it won't quite apply

to my poem. . . . Hadn't you better go out and get some supper? We can gossip afterwards."

"As your Majesty pleases."

"Oh, and I've just remembered. I thought of something today to add to the poem, and I am short of paper. Ask them to let me have a new quair on your way down."

"A . . . what, your Majesty?"

"A quair, Giffard. Have you forgotten your French? *Cahier*, *quair*, *quire*. A book of clean paper. 'The King's Quair.' That would make a good title for my poem."

"Certainly, your Majesty, I will get you one."

Giffard felt curiously at home, catering for James once more. But nothing could obliterate, even for a moment, the impression that it was not the same James. Something had happened, something more than a few years' growth. Giffard felt suddenly lonely, as though he had lost an anchorage.

James sat down to table. For the moment he wanted Giffard to go. He wanted, still more, to talk, but on a subject that he must mention to no one. Giffard still lingered.

"I've been seeing Bishop Beaufort again," said James, "the one I met at Fulham."

"I thought he had gone abroad. He is going soon, I've heard."

"Oh. Why?"

"They say King Henry wants to be rid of him. His way of gaining influence is to lend the king money, and now, they say, he has overdone it. All the same, if your Majesty can secure his alliance, it might be a good thing. In a year or two's time he may have some influence with King Henry again. They say the king will continue the war, and that means more money."

"In a year or two?" said James, genuinely surprised. "But I shall be free before Christmas."

Giffard, too, looked surprised; but he did not answer.

"But surely you must have heard the news?" said James.

"There's no news these days in Scotland—except of Albany granting away more of your Majesty's land to anyone that threatens trouble. I can tell your Majesty that I am not the only Scot who would lose his right hand to see you back, before Christmas or after it."

James had paused, a slice of meat half-way to his mouth. He put it back, seemed to collect himself, and then spoke in a voice that was only just steady.

"No, Giffard. I meant about my uncle's embassy—his negotiations with England. You must have heard."

"We have that."

"Giffard, they've not failed again? King Henry——."

"No, your Majesty. Succeeded. I never imagined that you had not heard."

"I only hear what suits my gaolers. What do you mean by 'succeeded'?"

"It happened in March. The Earl of Fife came home."

"Say that again!"

Giffard hesitated a moment before letting drive. "Albany did what he set out to do," he said. "He got his son back, his precious Murdoch! They exchanged him for young Henry Percy, Hotspur's son. And we all say that the English had the better of the bargain."

There was a long silence in the little room. The shadows were falling. Outside, a few birds still twittered. James rose slowly from his unfinished meal and walked towards the window. When at last he spoke, his colourless tone struck chiller than any voice of anger or complaint.

"Go and get your supper," he said. "I shall expect you back in an hour. . . . No, tomorrow morning. I feel tired tonight."

Giffard would have given anything to find the right words, the comfort which might soften this blow he had suddenly been forced to inflict. He felt sure that James must not be left alone now. The conventional remedy and the true one was distraction, diversion, new interests.

"If your Majesty desires it, I will bring the quair after supper."

"I shall not be writing tonight."

"I need not tell your Majesty that if there were anything we could do in Scotland——"

"Thank you, Giffard. But if Scotland, even half Scotland, cared whether their king was a prisoner or no, my uncle could never have kept his game going so long as this."

"Perhaps the English——" began Giffard. James waved him into silence, preferring, in his bitterness, the more humiliating alternative.

"Your Majesty does us wrong. And we may do something to prove it yet. Your Majesty must not give up hope."

"No. Not yet. Goodnight, Giffard. You must be hungry by now."

"Your Majesty——!"

"I said 'Good night'."

"Good night, your Majesty."

1416-1420

IX

The festivities were over at Windsor, the last of the guests had departed. Sigismund, plausible and reluctant, had been hustled back to Germany, to resume the weary farce of seedy splendour and impotent dominion. Henry returned to linger at Windsor; but he kept little state, and the place had a desolate, waiting air. He dismissed his prisoners from mind, sending Charles of Orleans to Pontefract Castle, and James back to the Tower. It looked as if the feast of St. George would be their last taste of diversion or society for months or even years.

Strange news was reaching King Henry at Windsor, warning him not to rest upon his laurels. It appeared that there were Frenchmen who were refusing to accept the verdict of

Agincourt. Orleans was a captive in England, but the Orleanists had found a new leader in the Count of Armagnac and were beginning to call themselves by his name. The Armagnacs were attacking Harfleur and its English garrison: they were even sending ships to ravage Portland Bill: they were making up their quarrel with Burgundy, at least until they had given Henry a lesson.

Henry replied by sending a fleet to defeat theirs, and then making proposals for peace. He asked for the hand of Katharine, daughter to their mad old king; he asked for half France as her dowry. When Burgundy and the Armagnacs united to call his terms an impudence, he took ship with Clarence, Gloucester, and sixteen thousand Englishmen, and landed for a second time upon the coasts of Normandy.

Little had been done to guard France against them. They swarmed up the green valleys that slope gently down from the hills of Perche. They encircled ill-garrisoned towns with their entrenchments and surprised little manor-houses where the country squire, with a few retainers round him, sat wondering why Paris sent no help. They behaved, on the whole, as well as armed men can be expected to behave in hostile country. Policy as well as humanity constrained Henry to withhold the worst horrors of war from those whom he claimed as his own subjects. By ordering special forbearance towards priests and monasteries, he increased his reputation for piety, and won support for his claim from local churches. But war is always war : when Clarence stormed a way into Caen, the two thousand Frenchmen who died in arms seemed few beside the unarmed civilians who were butchered. To Caen—or its remnants—came the saint and preacher, Vincent Ferrer, to tell Henry that he was hazarding his soul by the slaughter of so many harmless Christian folk. Henry heard him patiently, and told him, in private, that France had sinned, and that he, Henry, was God's scourge for sinners. And it was true that nothing his men did could match the ferocities which Frenchmen were practising upon Frenchmen in the streets and gaols of Paris.

It was towards Paris that Henry pressed, and still no army opposed him. Only Rouen guarded the Seine. Rouen was too strong to be stormed, but it could be starved. The country people had taken refuge inside its walls, driving in their cows and sheep and chickens through the dust and heat of July. But by September they were eating rats in Rouen, and paying (as we reckon money) two and three pounds for the meal. Rich citizens could be seen grubbing up dock-leaves in hope of nourishment; girls who had held their heads high that spring now sold their bodies for a slice of stale bread. Then those who ate but could not fight —the old, the women and the children—were thrust outside the gates. The English would not let them pass, and they stayed to perish between the lines. Babies were born in No Man's Land, hauled up to the ramparts to be christened, and let down again to die in their mothers' arms. A few survived, perhaps on unauthorized scraps passed to them from the English trenches, and on Christmas Day Henry sent them and the garrison a meal.

A month later Rouen despaired of rescue and surrendered.

The Seine was open now, and all France exposed. It was time that Burgundy and Armagnac made more effective alliance. They met at Montereau bridge, Burgundy coming from one side of the river, the Dauphin, Tanneguy du Chatel, and the rest of the Armagnac lords from the other. They talked of peace and friendship, and wrangled as they talked. Then Tanneguy whirled up an axe and split Burgundy's skull like a water-melon. The man was a murderer himself and deserved his death, but the manner of it was the ruin of France.

The feud was past cure now. The Dauphin held with the murderers, defying England in impotent fashion. For Burgundy's heir was making treaty with King Henry; with him went the old king, disowning his own son. The queen, Isabella the German, even declared that the Dauphin was not her husband's child but the fruit of one of her many debauches. She boasted that Katharine was her only lawful issue and that she was going to marry Katharine to King Henry.

Henry, adopted as heir-at-law to the whore and the lunatic, stormed along the upper Seine to meet his bride. Far south of Paris, English arrows and Burgundian cannon balls began to hum round the towers of such riverside cities as still clung to the Dauphin. The Armagnacs sent everywhere for help, and little help could come. Only a Douglas managed to bring a few hundred Scots. Six thousand followed, later, but the Armagnac knights had nothing but sneers for these new allies, with their uncouth ways and gigantic appetites. They taught their Dauphin to giggle at the wine-bibbers and mutton-guzzlers from the North. The Scots ate and drank no less for their mocking; but they sharpened sword and waited for a chance to prove their mettle in the field.

King Henry, knowing more of their prowess, cast round him for some way to detach them from his enemy. It was little good sending protests to Albany. Albany, having got his Murdoch home, had become an open and active enemy, launching a timorous, ineffective raid across the Border: the *Fool Raid* it was called, until posterity, grown nicer in its grammar, altered the name to the *Foul Raid*. Henry felt he could do better than start useless recriminations with Albany. He wrote home to his deputies, saying that it was time for James, England's prisoner and pupil, to complete his education by seeing service in the field. It was worth trying. There was a chance that some of the Scots in France might refuse to fight against their king.

It was four years since Sigismund had dined in Windsor Hall, four years since James had looked down from his window upon the lady of his ecstasies. He had not seen her since that spring. She had become a memory, a symbol rather than a person, a theme for poems—a mere habit of mind. Then even the symbol began to lose its meaning, the habit grew stale and jaded. He had little left to live for. He hardly knew, hardly cared, whether Joan lived, or died, or was married to another. Albany's incompetent follies on the Border had destroyed, perhaps for ever, the chance of release for Scotland's king. The old ninny would die soon, and the dolt Murdoch succeed him. James must make some life for himself—a perpetual exile. He was at Kenilworth, loitering across the desolate garden that King Henry had planted there, sculling round the boating-pool that King Henry had constructed. There King Henry's summons found him, and the blessed call to action. Within a month he was walking through Southampton streets, choosing a fine grey horse, purchasing tents and such pennons and trappings as a king must take on campaign. It was June, the sun shone brightly on the flickering sea, and the next favourable wind would be speeding him to France.

Hundred Years' War

Ceux qui veulent m'aider me ruinent sans cesse.

COMPLAINTE DE FRANCE (1568).

CHAPTER FOUR

Hundred Years' War

June 1420

I

"HOW LONG SHALL we be now?" James looked at the low Norman coast, pink and gold with evening, and guessed that the answer would be between two and three hours.

He got no answer at all. The shipmaster, a Dutchman from Haarlem, often found it convenient to understand no English. He had been voluble enough in that language on Southampton quay, especially at sight of the loads of baggage he was expected to ship with James: he had contracted with King Henry, he said, to carry cannon to France, not kings. Now he stood dumb and obstinate beside his helmsman, looking towards the western horizon with an anxious air that seemed assumed rather than genuine. Landsmen, his frown implied, must learn that navigation is a highly-skilled mystery, beyond their comprehension. He had discovered that morning that some fool had brought a grey cat on board, inviting the wrath of the dark powers that ruled seamen's destinies: he had had the animal flung promptly overboard, but still pretended to be nervous at the evil omen. The Channel was full of pirates, French or Castillian: he would not feel safe till he had discharged his load and made home again.

Getting no answer, James climbed down into the ship's waist and made his way forward. The whole cf his meagre following was on the forecastle—a chaplain and a Scottish servant called Simpson. Squires and a retinue awaited him at Harfleur, or with King Henry on the Seine. Merton, the priest, sat reading an Office with silent, restless lips. James had not long to wait before he finished and closed his book. Then he picked his way forward, signing to him not to rise.

"Nearly there," he said.

Merton screwed himself round to look landward. "One of the gunners," he said, "was telling me that we must expect the night at sea. He thought there would be no chance of making Harfleur tonight."

"But it's only just round that point," James objected.

The priest smiled patiently. "He's made the voyage twice already," he said. "He seems sure we cannot round the Hève while this wind holds."

James, standing below him, rested his elbows on the forecastle deck. It seemed strange to be at sea again, for the first time since boyhood. He remembered, clearly enough, the preliminaries of that first and fateful voyage—the sea-birds screeching round the Bass, where he waited for the ships: Orkney bringing them round from Leith, boasting that he had done it under the nose of Albany's spies: then the difficult embarkation in the wet March dawn. The actual voyage had faded in memory. He remembered that Giffard had been seasick; he remembered the moment when the Norfolk ships closed round them in the mist, and he first knew himself a captive. Orkney had sworn that they must have had warning, that some traitor had sent news from Scotland. James had been twelve then, and it was fourteen years ago. He had thought of his uncle Albany as a very old man, even in those days: he wondered how many more years must pass before he resigned his Regency for a comfortable grave.

There were sails on the horizon. James, looking up through the spider's web of ropes, saw the boy at the mast-head gesticulating westward. The shipmaster was ordering a new course. Sir William Philips, in charge of the cannon and of King James, clambered out of the poop cabin to start an angry dispute. The Dutchman was obstinate. He was taking no risks, he said, he was turning into Fécamp; he would think about getting round to Harfleur tomorrow or the next day. Sir William could say what he liked: the sea was the sea.

It was still light when they landed. A few ill-conditioned Normans watched them, with grudging interest, as they scrambled up the shingle between clumps of seaweed and lobster baskets. "France," said Merton. "And it has only taken us the two days after all."

"It's taken me fourteen years," answered James. Philips, still smouldering, gave him a look of annoyance: what on earth was the young idiot talking about?

His temper was no better when they reached the inn, a dirty little place called *The Fig-Tree*, half a mile inland. Fécamp, or what there was of it, straggled along a marshy road between the shore and the Benedictine house up the valley.

The landlord was a Folkestone man, and he wanted money in advance. He told them he had been two years in Normandy, ever since King Harry invited English settlers, with a promise of free housing and good trade: and all he'd seen so far was monks and bad debts. Philips stared him into submission and ordered supper. They were given stale bread with half-cooked fish, and paid for it through the nose next morning. As they left, after an equally distasteful breakfast, James was wondering whether the inn-keeper's settlement in France was due to his own patriotism and enterprise—or to Folkestone's determination to be rid of her undesirables.

The shipmaster had his own house of call, nearer the sea: when they had tracked him there, he seemed very loath to leave it. He talked a great deal, in mixed Dutch and English, about the west wind and the danger of pirates. Then he sat down with a grunt and began to discuss midday dinner with a blowsy French girl in wooden shoes, who leant against the ladder which led to the upstair bedroom, and gazed at him as if he had been some kind of demigod, infinitely glamorous.

In the end, Philips stamped out of the house in a fury. "We'll go by road," he said. "We'll ride straight across country to Harfleur, and I'll see to it that Curtis takes the skin off that creature's back when he does get his god-forgotten tub round the point!"

Curtis was the officer in charge of transport at Harfleur, and Philips had a letter made out to him, to be delivered as soon as they arrived. Meanwhile the horses were being got on shore—no easy business at Fécamp. The master-gunner was instructed to stay behind and be as aggressive as possible until he got the Dutch sluggard to move. By noon, Philips, James and their small retinue were trotting past the last hovels of the village, on the road for Goderville and Harfleur.

It was two years since the war had swept over the district and its scars were no longer fresh. But one could not help noticing how many acres of ploughland were now waste and weedy, how many cottages lacked inhabitants or a roof. Where the village of Montvilliers had stood there was a melancholy silence. Soon after Agincourt, the Armagnacs, plucking up their defeated courage, had seized and used it as an outpost for harassing Harfleur. When Henry returned with a new army, the reinforced garrison had sallied out to take a lasting revenge.

From Montvilliers the road began to slope down towards the estuary of the Seine. Soon the lights of Harfleur were twinkling ahead, the silver streak of the river ran leftwards, making for the heart of France. Here was the funnel through which King Henry was pouring England's strength into the Continent: from here the streams of armed men, of waggons and barges, packhorses and cannon, flowed out to deluge the French valleys and seep round the walled towns. Henry himself was on the river, hundreds of miles up its snaky course, beyond Paris, beyond the Armagnac strongholds at Montereau and Melun; he had swept past them to meet Burgundy, take them in the rear, and storm back along the Seine. James, jogging down to Harfleur, knew that he would soon be part of that flowing and returning current. The rights and wrongs of the war were swallowed up in its immensity; there was grandeur in the design that dared to loose these waves of men upon a hostile country of whose very shape they were in ignorance. It was good for a young man to be caught up in so bold and so vast a flood.

The strange thing, next morning, was to hear a Scottish voice in Harfleur. Simpson, drinking with other servants, had discovered that there was a knight from Renfrew in King Henry's garrison, and brought him to pay respects to his king. He proved to be a small, lean creature, more intelligent than attractive. When James remarked that most of the Scots in France were fighting for the Armagnacs, not the English, he replied that he had only come out to clear his estates of a debt and preferred the leader who promised securer pay and easier plunder. The Dauphin and his Armagnacs would be starving soon, as well as defeated in the field. One amassed new debts in their service, instead of diminishing old ones. "And like your Majesty," he said, "I have chosen the winning side."

"I had no choice," answered James, faintly disgusted.

The man changed tack at once, and began to talk about the murder which Tanneguy and the Dauphin had perpetrated on Montereau bridge.

"The Armagnacs will never win after that," he said. "God punishes that kind of thing. There's a curse on them now that only a saint could lift." He had evidently absorbed enough of the talk current among Englishmen to quiet his own conscience. Buchan and the Douglas, he said, fighting on the Armagnac side, were fighting against God: he was sorry that Scotsmen could be such fools.

"King Harry's the man," he insisted, with a slight shiftiness about the eyes that marred his assurance. "Even the French know it now. Their king and queen have joined him and Burgundy. Your Majesty will have heard that they have repudiated the Dauphin, and come to Troyes to marry their daughter to King Harry. What sort of a man will this Dauphin be, when even his parents and sister disown him?"

James said nothing. It was useless—and possibly dangerous—to point out that there is small disgrace in being disowned by a poor old lunatic and an unashamed harlot. The man before him was not likely to listen to any argument that did not assist him in his double task of filling his pockets and quieting his conscience. James, with all the intolerance of the unspoilt, wondered at what street-corner of Ayr—or in what London tavern—he had first decided to call himself a knight. He dismissed him with bare courtesy.

The sooner he left Harfleur the better. Every stroll through its mongrel streets reminded him that the fiery wine of war had merely flowed through them, leaving the dregs behind: here settled, in discreditable ferment, the hucksters and sluggards and sycophants, the women with souls for hire, the men who had already sold theirs for ease and gain. There was a greatness about Henry, whether or no one believed in his cause: it would be easier to fight at his side than remain uncontaminated amidst the slime that lingered where his armies had passed.

It was some days before he had his will, and Philips was ready to ride up the Seine. They put up at Rouen, where broken walls and rickety children told the story of the six-months' siege. James spent the evening watching the English surveyors planning the foundation of a great palace that Henry was building beside the river. Philips had orders to avoid Paris, whose attitude was still dubious—and would remain so until the king swept back upon it with a successful army. From Rouen onward the party was doubled by the addition of twenty archers, riding to rejoin their contingents at Troyes after recovery from wounds or sickness. "And forty men is none too many," said Philips. "The country's stiff with brigands and Armagnacs. The king's doing wonders to clear things up, but some of these folk don't know what is good for them and they hamper his justice at every turn. They won't even give information when we go to smoke rebels out. Maybe they're afraid to."

Signs of war, burnt fields and roofless cottages, grew more frequent as they proceeded. The country people in the fields ran over the crest of a hill or into the nearest woodland at the first sight of armed men on the road. In the village they had the sullen obsequiousness that hoped for money and expected blows.

Their journey was constantly impeded by waggon-trains, reinforcements marching south, wounded returning. Only once did Philips, impatient of delays, leave the main line of the English communications.

They left the river at Meulan to strike across country. The orders were that everyone should ride in full armour, with only the heavy helmet at the saddle. The precaution was soon justified.

They were following a mud track, which summer had caked to iron, through a dense belt of trees. The advanced file came cantering back with news of opposition. James had his helmet buckled on before Philips had issued further orders, and, setting spur to his horse, plunged ahead unaccompanied, followed by angry curses. Philips was an old woman: a knight's business was to ride straight at the enemy. He galloped round a blind corner, came in sight of three men standing, with drawn swords, in the green and broken sunlight, and, charging at the middle one, saw too late that they had stretched a rope, breast-high, across his path. The next moment he was on his back, stunned and bruised. And it was an undeniable relief to hear the thunder of hooves behind him.

The ambush, not expecting so large a party, melted away among the trees. James's grey horse had disappeared with them, and an arrow or two marked the composure of their retreat. James, struggling up, saw Merton wince suddenly and clap his hand to a red furrow on his other wrist. He felt more than ever a fool, and accepted his scolding from Philips with unresentful meekness.

He was still chastened when they put up for the night at Montfort l'Amaury, where the castle was in ruins but the inn unexpectedly comfortable. Waiting for supper, he strolled stiffly to the door and leant there, watching the sun on the motionless trees. A hen pecked inquisitively at the dust of the doorstep. A few paces away, one of the archers was re-bandaging Merton's damaged wrist.

"All the same," he was saying, "I'd rather have half a dozen arrows than another visit from Saint Anthony. That's the thing to tickle you up."

"Oh?" said the priest. "And where did you meet Saint Anthony? I thought he lived in Italy."

"Saint Anthony's Fire," said the archer. "Surely you've heard tell of that. Half of us were down with it in Leche's company. I was lucky not to get it till we were inside Rouen, where I could be looked after proper. You see, father, it begins by . . ."

Embarrassing details followed, partly inaudible. The word "bowels" or its colloquial equivalent seemed to occur with unnecessary frequency.

"Thank you, my son," said Merton, as the operation was finished. "You seem to have learnt quite a deal about the doctor's art. By the way, I don't know your name."

"Page, father. John Page. Not that I ever was one. I was a skinner before the war. Doing quite well, I was. I often wonder what made me throw it up for this game."

"Original sin, I suppose," suggested the priest.

"What's that? . . . Oh yes, maybe that's what it was." The archer grinned. "Well, it hasn't been too bad, and it's not for much longer. They say we'll all be back in London this time next year."

"You think so?" asked Merton.

James saw the man look incredulous, as though no one could dispute so obvious a fact.

"Why, yes," he said, almost irritably. "We've got 'em whacked proper this time. They've had no chance since we took Rouen." From his tone one might have gathered that his own part in the siege, that of Leche's company anyway, was a decisive factor in the war. The thought seemed to restore him to cheerfulness.

"I was making up a rhyme about it," he said, "only the other day. I'm rather a one for rhyming."

The priest smiled. "Did you want to repeat it to me?" he asked.

"Oh, not all of it," said the archer. "It's long."

"I see."

"It began about the Virgin and all that."

"Very proper," said the priest, rising from his bench.

"And then about Burgundy. You know, the one with the eyebrows. Only it's the king that matters." Page looked almost reverent and began to quote, before Merton should escape to supper:

> "*The Dolphin and his Erminacks, Tanny Guy and all,*
> *Our King Harry has caused them all to fall.*"

"Your Majesty!" said Merton, catching sight of the figure in the doorway. "I am glad you are here." He turned back towards Page. "His Majesty writes poems too," he said. "You should ask him for his criticism."

Page looked sulky at the interruption, and James felt called upon to say something.

"I haven't written a poem for years," he said. "But I liked your couplet." Page smiled again, pleased as a child.

"There's some of it's better than that," he said, moistening his lips. "I write 'em quite long."

"I don't know how you find time on campaign," answered James. "I only write them when I've nothing better to do."

The archer was about to say something, perhaps to quote again, when Philips shouted "Supper!" from the window. James led the way and Merton followed; Page was left muttering metrically to himself in the evening sun.

Some days later, when they had put up in the neighbourhood of Nemours, Page knocked on the door of James's quarters.

"Asking your Majesty's pardon," he said, "but if you did happen to be interested in poetry, I thought you might like to see this."

He was tendering, almost defiantly, a thick wad of untidy paper. "My old master in London," he continued, "he told me I ought to keep a journal; so I thought I'd try my hand at writing one in poetry."

James glanced at the handful; it was parchment, not paper—probably scavenged from some deserted monastery. On the first sheet was written, in painstaking capitals:

THE SEIGE OF RONE

By Jhon Page.

"I won't wait now," said the archer, looking down in modesty at his horny finger-tips. "But if you—if your Majesty cared to look through it some time——"

James was already doing so. On the back of some monastic accounts was written a description of the beleaguering of Rouen in what purported to be verse. It had the merit of originality, and also of attention to detail.

They ate dogs, they ate cats,
They ate horses, mice and rats.
A negg was ninepence, a napple was 10*:*
Such were the prices among those men.

"Of course," said Page, retreating towards the door, "I can make it a deal better, write it up a bit, when I get back to London. Maybe your Majesty could help me with a suggestion, if you write poetry yourself." He paused a moment, as if trying to recapture something. "Funny," he said, "but I couldn't help feeling it—what was going on inside, I mean, to say nothing of the women and children between the lines. It doesn't do to think of. There's something wrong with this country. We don't get the like of it in England."

"No," said James, glad to escape from literary criticism.

"You have a king in England, not half a dozen Dauphins and Burgundies and Counts of Armagnac to tear the country in pieces."

"Ah," said the archer, losing interest, "I expect your Majesty knows more of that than I do. I'll wish your Majesty a good night."

James struggled through a fair morsel of the manuscript, and managed to return it next day without committing himself too deeply on its poetic merits.

As the journey proceeded, the country round them began to show more numerous and more recent traces of the war. An unbroken bridge became a rarity and there was hardly a labourer to be seen from the road. Ruined houses were everywhere, and here and there a limewashed wall was spattered with dark brown stains. If there was little else left to tell of those who had died, one could guess that the wolves had had them. It was a great year in the annals of the wolves, who were now sole lords of a hundred manors: their advance-guards and foragers howled in the alleys and graveyards of Paris itself.

James had grown up a prisoner, less accustomed than most men to the signs of death. A true knight, he knew, has no business to be affected by such things, inseparable from war. It was best to ignore them, to concentrate on approaching experience of battle. He looked forward with eagerness to the moment when he would be hacking at a real enemy, and with unblunted sword. He even dallied with a tantalizing fancy, wondering how King Harry meant to prevent him, one day, setting spur to a horse until it carried him into the Armagnac ranks: he could fight at their side with an easier conscience—and at any moment, the way back to Scotland should be clear. And then something happened—something which could not be ignored—which drove all thought from his head.

They were approaching Troyes, where lay Henry and his army. They had picked a curving way between the walled towns which Henry had not yet subdued. They had crossed the Yonne, and slept the last night at Marcilly. Troyes was almost in sight when they started off in the morning.

It was still early when they came to a little wood where a roofless cottage stood in a clearing beside the road. Beside it was an array of tree-stumps that had recently been orchard. The severed trees, the fresh chips of their destruction lay upon the grass. James noticed a child's cart among them, laden with twigs and a broken bottle. As they passed the cottage, one of Philip's men rose in his stirrups and peered over the wall, between charred rafters.

"Look in there," he said, with a half-ashamed grin. "Someone has been foraging."

James imitated his action, took one look inside the ruined cottage, and dropped back into the saddle. An instant had been enough to tell him what had happened. There had been three people in the cottage last night. A man: his wife: a little girl. They were in there now, dead and twisted into attitudes that parodied humanity; and the parents, at least, had not died swiftly or unmocked.

"They cling to their money so," said one of the men, in explanation rather than excuse. "Nothin'll make 'em tell where they've hidden it."

It was half an hour before James spoke. His silence seemed to affect those who rode nearest him, though he did not know—or care much—if they were a little ashamed of their trade of war, or winking to each other at the greenness of the novice.

"Who was it?" he said at last, his sudden voice sounding strangely in his own ears. "Back there, I mean. Who did it?"

"Armagnacs, of course," answered Philips, a little uncomfortably. A minute later, honesty forced him to continue. "No means of telling who did it," he said. "It might be anyone. Not Englishmen, of course. But the rest have all learnt tricks from each other—French, Burgundian, Scots and our Welshmen. Not that the Burgundians had anything to learn. They've been at the game too long."

He rode on, dismissing the matter from mind. When he reined up, it was to peer eastward, and then to point to a saw-edge of roofs and steeples, biting into the sky. "Troyes," he said.

Troyes, when they came to it, was a gay pattern of streamers and garlands and holiday clothes. The bells were pealing, the townspeople cheering and dancing in the street. Even the soldiers, shining with ribboned favours and newly burnished helmets, looked more like actors in a pageant than men equipped to spread death and misery. For King Harry was marrying his princess; her father and mother were there to bless the union, and bequeath their rights in France to the happy pair; Burgundy was with them, smiling assent from his dark, sardonic brows; the Church was bringing out its costliest vestments, its grandest ritual to hallow the triumph of its faithful son. James, hastily decked in new clothes, was brought to see and be seen: all must know that King Harry could command the attendance of a royal guest. Still bewildered, he saw the princess pass to her wedding, bewildered too, and a little scared: the other bystanders saw little but her gorgeous clothes: to them she was a symbol, a prize of victory, whose private feelings were utterly negligible. Besides, what girl could count herself so happy in a bridegroom? Only her father, mumbling mad nothings from frothy lips, cast a slight shadow on the general joy. But he, too, was negligible; he would be dead soon, and Henry king of two kingdoms. He had given his word, for what it was worth: Burgundy had signed the treaty: opposition would soon be ground to dust before the new alliance, and perpetual peace would dawn upon France. No one gave a thought to the discredited, discreditable Dauphin, though but a few miles separated them from the towns and castles and caves where his followers sharpened worn swords and searched empty pockets, swearing that there should be no peace while one Englishman or Burgundian walked abroad with his throat uncut.

July 1420

II

They were beleaguering Melun. James had been kept away from the fighting, kept away, it seemed, from everything and everyone, until the siege was half-done. He had barely seen King Henry, and only from a distance. Henry, apparently, had not yet decided how to use the young King of Scotland. He did not set him against the few Scots in the garrison of Montereau. He had stormed it with Burgundy's help and let Burgundy take vengeance for what had happened on its bridge. The whole business had hardly taken a week. But Melun, where the Armagnacs also had Scottish helpers, looked like offering a longer resistance before it would let Henry sweep downstream towards Paris.

James was quartered on the southern bank, where lay the bulk of the English. Beyond the river, Burgundy's sprawling, ill-kept camp menaced the northern walls. It was linked by a bridge of boats with Henry's more-disciplined cantonments. Here the ground might be indescribably filthy, the men dying of sickness. But the pennons stood in orderly rows, it was easy to find any company one sought, and tents and equipment expected searching inspection. The only dishevelled quarter was next door to James's—occupied by a body of Kilkenny men, under a Butler with the tip-tilted family nose. They looked and talked very like the Highland Scots that James had seen in boyhood. They were not popular in the camp: they went into battle with knives, and their unorthodox methods had a way of succeeding where armoured knights had failed.

For the moment, fighting was restricted. They had given up ladders and scaling parties on the south side: too many men were crushed with stones that way, or scalded to death inside their armour. If the cannon made a breach, the defenders could drive back every assault upon it, killing more than they lost: the Scots, James was told, had been conspicuously damaging in these conflicts. Henry, unaccustomed to such resistance, had swallowed his anger and ordered mines. Barbizon, Melun's Armagnac leader, dug counter-mines to meet them. English and French met underground amid choking showers of earth, and stabbed each other in the darkness. Then they widened the passages and fixed torches and lanterns, so that high-born champions in plate-armour could belabour each other in an infernal tournament. Burgundy crossed the river to take part in the sport and they had erected barriers to fight over, lest he should be felled and dragged senseless into Melun. The precaution became still more necessary when King Henry descended to exchange blows with the redoubtable Barbizon. The encounters gave the men something to talk and bet about, while they did the dull work of standing round Melun until it was starved into despair. Starved it must be, unless the Dauphin collected courage and an army of relief. Frenchmen and Scots gazed southward from the ramparts, tightening their belts; but no Dauphin appeared.

It was at the mouth of the mine that James met King Henry, and that Henry decided to take notice of him. He was burning for an invitation to take his brand-new sword below, but Henry was just emerging and on his way to the royal tent.

"Too late, young man," he said, with patronizing good-humour. "Barbizon's gone to dinner."

He had been sweating inside his armour, and there was a bruise on his forehead.

"May I accompany your Majesty another day?"

"Maybe. We shall see. We must not run any risk of your being captured by these Armagnac scoundrels." He paused, looking at James as though he were trying to remember something. "I have something to tell you," he said. "Tell 'em to bring you round to my tent in two hours' time." He nodded and strode off.

Henry's tent was a magnificent affair, octagonal in shape and big enough to harbour a squadron of horsemen. It was used mainly for business or ceremony: at night-time, Henry rode off to Corbeil, to his bride.

He was signing orders amidst the relics of a meal when James was admitted. "Soldier's fare," he said, "and no time to eat it in. Sit down if you wish. I shall be ready in a moment."

James found himself exchanging guarded greetings with Clarence, and being introduced to a conceited-looking youth of seventeen, who seemed vaguely familiar. It was Somerset, and he had not improved since their last meeting in the garden at Woking. James had to confess to himself that the young puppy was developing a distinct resemblance to his sister Joan. But if something began to stir faintly at the back of his mind, he refused to give it encouragement: Joan was one of the things he must train himself to forget.

"Well," said King Henry, throwing down the pen, "I hear you had an easy journey. The roads are getting safer at last. I'll have put down all brigandage by the autumn. This country will know what it is to be governed."

James said nothing. Henry looked him up and down, as if weighing chances.

"There's a little matter," he said, "in which I require your service. That was why you were sent out here—that and my decision to let you finish your education by seeing real war, before we release you."

"What do you want of me?" said James. Strangely enough, the "release" had lost a little of its magic. He was in the atmosphere of fighting at last, and would be loath to leave it, even for Scotland, until he had learnt to move in it with the ease and familiarity of these Englishmen.

"You know that some of your countrymen are with the rebels?"

"I am told that the Dauphin has some of my subjects in his army."

Clarence moved a step forward, as if to prompt or protest. But Henry checked him with a glance, intimating that he could deal with the matter without a brother's assistance.

"The bulk of them are in the south," he said, "but there is a handful here, inside Melun. What I require of you is a proclamation under the walls, commanding your—er—subjects to surrender to you immediately. I will give them a safe-conduct home, or a place among my men—as part of your contingent."

Glances of approval, a murmur even, went round the company. James made no movement. "Your Majesty forgets," he said, "that I am not a free agent. If I know anything of my Scottish subjects, they would pay little heed to a proclamation signed by a prisoner in the English camp."

Henry's keen eyes did not waver. "That is for me to decide," he said. "I will only remind you that it is in my power to release you. Tonight, if I please. Now, will you obey my instructions?"

James stood silent. Somewhere, at the back of his head, hovered a Latin tag about distrusting Greeks, and their gifts.

"Come, come," said Henry, rising irritably from his seat, "speak up, my lad. If any of these Scots cling to their folly, the guilt is on them, not you. I am only telling you to give them a good excuse to abandon it." He swallowed a moment, and a curious wooden expression settled on his face. "As you know," he said, "I have a mission from God. I must use every means He puts in my power to reduce the number of my opponents."

Again the company murmured its agreement. Silence fell in the tent. Then a slight breeze moved the pole, making its guide-ropes strain and creak. Far away, perhaps inside the starving city, a feeble trumpet was being blown.

"I have passed by this way before," thought James, "or by another very like it. Do they think, this time, that they will get a different answer?"

"Has the boy lost his tongue?" said Clarence suddenly. "Perhaps if he were shown the draft we agreed to——"

James was conscious that Henry's eyes were still on him. Clarence did not matter. One dealt directly with the king.

"If your Majesty wishes for an answer," said James, "I

can give it at once. My Scottish subjects are free to choose which side they will in this war. Placed as I am, I shall make no pretence to fetter their freedom with useless proclamations."

Some three paces lay between him and the king: Henry covered them with aggressive, menacing strides; his hand rose, was poised to strike James across the face. Then suddenly he checked, stood still, and began to smile. It was the famous smile that had almost quieted the Princess Katharine's fears, and nerved men to face death at Agincourt. His hand fell, almost jauntily, on James's shoulder, his eyes, avoiding James's, flashed out at the circle of surprised faces that enclosed them.

"I think the Scots are fortunate," he said, "in possessing such a king. And, since fortune has placed you on our side, we are honoured to have you as a companion in arms."

They were slow to applaud this time, slow to follow the quick turns of Henry's mind. He stood there, patting James's shoulder, and promising to convince him soon of the justice of the English cause. But the delay could not be long. James found himself the centre of a buzz of flattery and congratulation. His Majesty, they told him, had but tested his staunchness: he had borne himself well: they hoped, soon, to have the honour of fighting beside him in the field.

A chattering flood carried him out into the open air, where the prospects of fighting could be discussed without disturbing the king. It appeared that there was nothing on foot that afternoon, unless Barbizon should attempt a sally. But there were invitations to follow various banners next time the alarm sounded; invitations, meanwhile, to dinners, drinking-parties, hunts. There was even the inevitable somebody to catch him up—as he freed himself to return to quarters—and suggest a visit to the north bank that night. Henry, it appeared, was allowing no women in his camp—just riding off to his little Frenchwoman at Corbeil and leaving the rest of them as if they were monks. But Burgundy was allowing anything across the bridge. Burgundy, James was told, believed in the archers' old saying, that no one could call himself a soldier till he'd shot his man and begot his man.

James was as polite as was reasonable; but, for this first evening, he preferred to keep his quarters.

It was still light when a message reached him from King Henry. It was verbal, and as peremptory as the bearer dare make it. James must order his gear to be packed and prepare for a return journey to Harfleur and England, unless he complied immediately with the king's condition—taking an oath, on all the most sacred relics that could be found, that no opportunity should tempt him to escape towards the Armagnac armies. James answered, as proudly as he could, that he would consider the matter and inform his Majesty in the morning. But, even as he dismissed the messenger, he knew that there was no alternative but to comply.

It was about the same time that a bored and hungry Scotsman, pacing the ramparts of Melun, noticed that something was astir in the English lines. He would have given the alarm—for the enemy was up to every trick of war—had he not seen in time that it was only another herald from the besiegers. They were tired of heralds in Melun, having one answer for them all. The man halted below the south tower, and, as soon as Barbizon appeared above him began to read out a paper in the sing-song voice of his profession. He announced, with much circumlocution, that the King of Scots had arrived in the besiegers' camp, and that his subjects were required by King Henry to desert the town, on pain of being held traitors to their sovereign.

He ended with the conventional flourish, and someone threw a pebble at him from the walls. Everyone except the sentinels withdrew to supper, or dreams of supper, and a damp twilight began to shroud Melun.

November 1420

III

"Father, I know what is due to your priestly office——"

"I hope you do, my son."

"And I have some liking for you as a man."

"That is flattering."

"But there are times when I am so angry with you that I can hardly keep my hands from your throat."

James stood over the brazier in his tent, and Merton watched his agitated face with more concern than he thought it wise to betray. "So I have incurred the royal displeasure?" he asked lightly. "Your Majesty will be pleased to remember that it is no part of my office to become a good courtier. I remember"—he was speaking to gain time for thought—"I remember I once preached a sermon in Rome on the text, '*Prophesy unto us smooth things*,' I was young then, but I do not think it was altogether a bad sermon."

"I am not asking you for one now," said James; he paced across the tent and back, balanced a sword in his hand and then threw it down again. "If you had ever been in my position," he said, "you would understand better how I feel."

Merton hardly looked up from the book on his knee. "A priest's task," he said, reflectively, "would be comparatively easy, if he only had to strengthen his flock against hardship and pain. But the Devil is a subtle adversary, and he knows that Doubt is often a more potent instrument."

He paused, looking up at James with a sudden impishness. "I suppose it would be useless for me to suggest," he said, "that you should call Simpson and order supper? There are times when food composes the mind as well as the stomach."

"This is not one of them," said James decisively. "I expect help from you, father, not mockery." He strode irritably to the tent door and pulled aside its curtain. It was November and there was snow on the roofs, slush in the besieging lines. Melun had just surrendered—but it had had the hardihood to delay King Henry for four months. The watery sun of late afternoon shone in James's eyes.

"Besides," he said, in a half conciliatory voice, "I go to the king's tent in an hour's time. There is sure to be food and drink provided for an occasion such as this."

The priest was still following his own line of thought. "Not," he said, "that I will admit any serious difficulty in your position. Your head is naturally filled with doubts and contradictions, born partly of youth and impatience, partly of the sins of others. Such vague troubles afflict us all at times, and we do well to override them. The voice of conscience, which is the voice of God, is never vague. It is generally quiet, sometimes unexpected, and always precise. Oh, yes, always precise. One hears it best, my son, by ignoring the noisy voices that shout Nothing with such insistent emphasis. These are of the Devil and they must not be suffered to drown the more sober instructions of conscience, which leave no room whatever for misapprehension."

"But if I have no instructions?" asked James, turning back into the tent. "If there is nothing, except . . . except. . . ." He broke off, unable to put words to the trouble that oppressed him.

"Then wait. Patience is in itself an act of piety. What else can you do? You have taken an oath not to escape from the army, and you would not have me advise perjury. If you defy the English king and are sent back to prison, no good could come of it. You did not make this war: you did not even choose your side in it. From what I hear of the Dauphin and his Armagnacs, chance has put you on the right side, or the side, shall we say, that is least in the wrong in this devil's business. By fighting for it, you will acquire reputation and experience, advantages which you may one day turn to God's glory and the profit of your kingdom."

"Yes, but, father——"

"Please let me finish! They tell me, though I do not understand these things, that you have done good service at the siege. It is over, and the town is surrendering, but there will be more fighting before God grants peace. Do your part in it, go on with whatever comes to your hand, and do not neglect to pray. You can be sure that opportunities will come for helping in the establishment of Christ's kingdom on earth. That is all I have to say, and my throat is now ready if you still wish to strangle me."

He smiled again, with a little more confidence. "There is something in what you say," answered James reluctantly. "All the same, I . . ."

"It is my business," said Merton, "to see as deeply as I can into other men's difficulties. More deeply, sometimes, than they can see themselves. I have the teaching of the Church to help me. I do not think that I have misrepresented it in what I have said."

"'Then the responsibility is on you," said James moodily. He began to prowl round the tent again. "And the business in hand——?"

"You are invited to the royal quarters."

"To contribute to the pomp and circumstance, when Henry accepts poor Barbizon's surrender."

"Nothing is the worse for being done with ceremony."

"Now I wonder," said James, "if that is true?"

Barbizon's men were to attend in chains. In deference to justice—or as a sop to Burgundy—they were to be held at discretion until they had cleared themselves of complicity of the murder on Montereau bridge. A monk who had forgotten his calling and shot arrows, with unmonastic deadliness, from the walls of the town, was to be hanged out of hand. English deserters and Scottish mercenaries were to be at King Henry's mercy.

There were twenty-one of the latter, and when they paraded before James, stubborn and woebegone, he was glad that he had not added to their burden by signing a proclamation. He spoke shortly to them, since there was little to say, praised the stoutness of the town's resistance, and promised to use his influence with King Henry to get them a safe-conduct for Scotland. He would have liked to offer the journey-money too, but neither his purse nor his captors' generosity was likely to cover the cost. He was mortified to see no spark of hope or recognition in their dull eyes. They stood like so many oxen, staring resentfully at the muddy ground. It seemed as if they could not forgive their king for being brought captive to their enemies' lines. Perhaps, thought James, Albany had begun to poison all Scottish minds against him. He was not sorry when he was summoned to the great tent, to pay his compliments to the ladies.

Queen Katharine lived in camp now, and there was no lack of splendour or elegance in her surroundings. Her guests listened to the best music that two kingdoms could provide, and drank such costly wines as could be brought by sea, or convoyed past the Armagnac raiders of Champagne and the Orléannais. Her parents had come from Corbeil, more splendidly dressed, since the wedding, than they had been able to afford for many a long year. James was presented. It was impossible to judge the mother fairly or look at her with fresh eyes: France was too full of stories about the German harlot, tales of midnight debauch in the Tour de Nesle, and students from Paris University lured there at night, dropped out, next morning, into the Seine. But she was still handsome, and had not forgotten how to be gay; there might be no word of truth in the slanders. It was more chilling to watch the old husband beside her, smiling and frowning at the wrong moments, staring with wide blue eyes at the playthings or bogies that were not there at all. James was glad to escape, to mix with the crowd, to laugh and chatter, to argue whether or no the fall of Melun had opened a clear road to Paris for the Christmas feast.

He was expressing his doubts of it to a lively, pouting girl, when he saw an unexpected face in the crowd. It was his servant Simpson, and Simpson had no right to be there: it was strange that he had got in, without King Henry's livery. In a moment he was plucking his master by the sleeve, urging him to come quickly. He refused to tell his errand, but there was something his Majesty must see at once. The man was in a fever of excitement, and since King Henry was already beginning to dismiss the company, James thought it best to slip away.

The night was luminous with snow, the moonlight clothed everything, even the dirt underfoot, with a grave and melancholy beauty. They sped towards the river. Whatever James must see was, it appeared, at or beyond the bridge. They hurried down wide alleys where tipsy soldiers belaboured each other in cheerful horseplay or sang songs of home. When they reached the river, they found a guard set—the men cursing their luck at being on duty for this night of surrender and rejoicing. But it was not the bridgehead that they were there to watch. It was a gallows, two short uprights, eight feet at most, and a long crossbeam, of new-felled oak. From it hung twenty Scottish corpses, and one man who was still kicking out his feeble strength.

The guests had gone, King Henry's tent was half deserted when James came panting to the door. The musicians, blowing on chilly finger-nails, were wrapping up their instruments for departure. Henry himself stood behind one of the supper-tables, with a bunch of interested attendants round him. He was holding a large silver bowl, turning it over and over in his hands. He raised his head as James burst in, and the two stood eye to eye.

"Well?" said King Henry coldly.

At the back of his mind, James heard a voice telling him that he must try to keep calm, keep calm.

"You know what brings me," he said.

Henry made a motion as if to dismiss his attendants and then checked. James wondered bitterly if it was an audience or a bodyguard that King Henry was retaining. But Henry had little thought of either.

"They were traitors," he said, "traitors to your Majesty as well as to God. The Frenchmen have little excuse, but I shall release such as were not implicated at Montereau. I can have no mercy on foreign hirelings that sell themselves into the Devil's ranks."

James's hand was tight upon his dagger; if it was little better than a toy, fashioned for banquets and balls, a resolute hand might drive home that slenderly tapering blade. But between him and Henry stood a great table and there were armed men around it.

"Fool's errand," whispered the voice within him. "Why did you come, fool? Learn wisdom, fool."

Even so, he could not hold his tongue quiet. "There have been murders since Montereau," he said, "and it is not Frenchmen who are implicated in tonight's!"

Henry turned a blank stare upon him, and then set down the silver bowl upon the table.

"Beautiful work," he said. "I will see the man when we get to Paris. . . . And now, gentlemen, I think it is time we all went to bed."

It was barely three weeks before Henry was riding into Paris, with grinning Burgundy beside him, and cracked old France, and bewildered, rebellious Scotland. A considerable crowd had collected to cheer him and shout "*A bas les Armagnacs!*" The Parisians were hoping that his entry would mean the falling of their famine prices. If Henry did not bring peace, he might push the war southward and drive away the Armagnac hornets who were humming round the adjacent fields, stinging to death all who brought food to Paris.

There were bonfires on the streets that night—a huge one beneath in the square beneath Notre Dame. James, lodged in the Bishop's Palace, leant out of the window to watch its glare on the cathedral towers, chequered with the dancing shadows of the mob. They were singing bibulous triumph as a tailpiece to the *Te Deum* that had been chanted in the chancel.

"Is this the answer to my doubts?" he asked Merton, beside him on the sill. "Am I to imitate King Henry, so as to be sure of success and acclamation?"

"You can always imitate his virtues," said Merton. "He has virtues, you know, quite apart from his devotion to Holy Church. As you have observed, even the French are beginning to admire him."

"Because their own leaders are worse; crueller, meaner—and less successful! It is a choice of evils for poor France."

Someone was throwing gunpowder into the bonfire: it crackled, thundered and flared. The dancers round it sent their hoots and catcalls echoing across the city. They were for the most part French, and the junketings of the French have the demoniac touch that recalls their riots and massacres.

"The world is a sorry place, my son. When we think that we have grasped and digested the full measure of its evil, then something happens to show us that we are only at the beginning. And the evil we can never grasp is the evil in our own heart. The more we denounce or detest the sins of others, the more surely will Time catch us, sooner or later, committing the like ourselves. And for that we must be punished, side by side with them in the same purging fire."

James was still looking towards the red-lit pinnacles of Notre Dame. He was thinking of all he had seen since he had landed at Fécamp—of the dungheaps they had passed that morning where famished children had wriggled themselves into the warmth and now lay dead with hunger.

"I could understand that better," he said, "if it was only the sinner that was punished. But more often, it seems, the retribution is misdirected."

"Beware how you impugn God's justice, my son."

"What had my countrymen done, that were hanged outside Melun?"

"We do not know. And death, if we could see it aright, may be more often a blessing than a punishment. In any case, there are mysteries that only Presumption would seek to plumb. At times we are tempted to ask, as you are asking, why the innocent seem to suffer more sharply than the guilty. We shall not know the answer until we hear it from Him who sinned least and suffered most of all."

It was night. Outside the walls of the city, beyond the cast of those fevered flames, silence and winter brooded upon the tortured plains of France. But in a thousand halls and cottages and cloisters, bewildered minds faced the same mystery, strove for the same Faith, or muffled their doubts in prayer.

April 1421

IV

"So your education has begun at last? I hear you have been in France."

James, standing in the hall of Pontefract Castle and watching the courtiers dance, heard suddenly the well-remembered voice at his shoulder. Charles of Orleans looked older and more worn, but there was still a twinkle in his eye.

"My lord!" said James, and then, rather lamely, "I am glad to see you well."

"You are lucky to see me at all," answered Orleans. "Another winter in Yorkshire will be the end of me."

"Why do the English——?"

"You must not ask me, my friend," interrupted Orleans. "I tried to get them to move me. I even started a rumour that I was plotting here with your uncle Albany to put his fake King Richard on the throne. I thought that might frighten them into moving me south. But it was no good. The English are hardly reasoning animals."

"We are not very near Scotland here," said James, "and anyway my uncle Albany is dead."

"I know, I know. And Duke Murdoch his son reigns in his stead. Over the polar bears, I suppose. If it's much further north than this, I don't envy you your kingdom."

"So Pontefract doesn't agree with you."

"It does not. It freezes everyone's wits, to judge by the inhabitants. They can't even pronounce its name right. Pomfret! What are you doing here?"

"Following the chariot-wheels. The conqueror makes his progress through his own dominions: the captive king is on show."

"I wish the captive duke were. I shall take root here soon, like mildew. Even this visit is a treat for me. The most sensible thing Henry ever did was to marry a French girl. No one else would have the enterprise to insist on a dance in a place like this."

They were standing at one side of the hall, and past them swept the lords and ladies of Queen Katharine's court, bending to the rhythm of a Tourdion. She sat above them on the dais, with Humphrey of Gloucester at her side. She was blossoming now, learning to be queen: but it was a slow process, after a childhood of neglect and suppression, poverty and alarms.

"I am glad," said James, "that she remembered to invite you."

"She would never have dared," answered Orleans, "if Henry had been here. *La belle Catherine* takes pity on the poor prisoner while her husband is away. They tell me he's visiting shrines."

"Yes. He's gone pilgrim to Beverley."

"Oh?" Orleans yawned. "Well, I suppose one excuse is as good as another."

"What do you mean? I don't understand."

"You warriors never hear the news. You don't imagine that Harry would have left his beloved war in the care of that thickhead Clarence, if there'd not been trouble at home?"

"We think a good deal of Clarence out there," said James, and Orleans raised a polite but sceptical eyebrow. "What's the trouble?"

"Ask the stay-at-homes," answered Orleans. "It may be pleasant to know that one's king is taking towns and marrying princesses and bullying foreigners, but it costs money, and labour, and lives. We grow restive in the North. You can be sure of one thing: Henry has not come here to visit saints, but to persuade Yorkshire to go on footing the bill."

"I can be sure of another," said James, with a smile. "That your Grace will always have an entertaining way of turning the news upside down."

"I hope your Majesty will always respond with the same flattering *naïveté*. Or do you grow sophisticated in France?"

"I learn not to expect chivalry in a knight, nor virtue in a woman, nor anything but bad faith from kings."

"Crude. Still very crude. You miss the subtleties. It seems to me that you have not only fallen in love, but fallen out of it again—or think you have. France has a good deal to answer for. I suppose you went to Paris?"

"For one night."

"That is sometimes sufficient."

"I spent most of it talking to a priest."

"You surprise me. Ah, well, *chacun à son gout*. I shall go and talk to the queen. It must be a great privilege to be married to a hero, but I think she deserves a better relaxation than Duke Humphrey while her husband's away."

He swam off towards the dais, through the cross-current of couples: a dance had just finished, and the musicians were being refreshed.

"Curious fellow, that," said a voice beside James. "I can never make these Frenchmen out." It was Northumberland, his contemporary and schoolfellow; Northumberland had been prisoner in Scotland as a boy, and the two were pupils of Bishop Wardlaw at St. Andrews.

"I suppose," he went on, "that he's hoping to be ransomed soon. I don't know where he'll find the money if he goes on spending it at the present rate. Two nobles a day for his food, and Heaven knows what for clothes and dogs and hawking." Northumberland looked wistful. "I suppose they've plenty of money in France," he added.

James never knew how to talk to men like Northumberland. It was better to listen and endure.

"I hope your Majesty's case will be settled soon," he was saying. "We'll be glad on the Border to know that there's a king in Scotland that's on the right side. Albany was hand in glove with the French, and this new man, Murdoch, will probably be as bad. I wanted to come to France, you know, but the king wouldn't hear of it while there was a chance of an attack from the Border."

He looked at James like some large dog demanding sympathy from a stranger. "And what's more," he added irrelevantly, "if this weather goes on, we shan't get a single cartload of hay out of the whole of Northumberland."

James smiled, wondering if it was worth while trying to pick this man's brains—such as they were—about the state of Scotland. "I expect," he said, "that my uncle's death has meant some changes beyond the Border."

"No, I think not," answered Northumberland. "The new man doesn't seem very active. But the Scots like that. It always suits them to have someone who doesn't interfere."

He looked meaningly at James: it was odd to have such

a creature as Northumberland offering one advice, and with such pathetic earnestness, on how to rule one's own kingdom.

"You know," he said, dropping his voice, "there are one or two of us here that think Henry goes too far. We're proud of him, of course, and there's no question of disloyalty. But if you knew how he answers petitions! Justice is one thing, but it's not justice to grant anything and everything a poor man asks—just because he's poor. That kind of thing is dangerous, especially in these days, with all this discontent and heresy among the common people."

The dance was re-forming. James stood silent, digesting Northumberland's words; it seemed as if there was no end to the new lights that could be cast upon the strange complication called King Henry.

Humphrey of Gloucester came wandering past. "The queen was asking for you two," he said, "though I don't suppose she wants to dance with you both." His large, melancholy eyes brightened towards James.

"So tactful, these Frenchwomen," said Northumberland, missing the look. "I'll go to her. You need not trouble."

Humphrey smiled and passed on. James saw him hurry to wrest a likely-looking damsel from her middle-aged companion. The queen was standing up to dance; she had seen Northumberland coming and secured another partner, a dark, handsome creature, hardly older than herself. Orleans stood forgotten on the dais. As the line of dancers began to sway, he came towards James with a glum face. He made as if to pass in silence, but turned back. "I've been telling the queen," he said maliciously, "how wise you've grown in France. She was most interested."

"I saw enough there," said James, "to know what's wrong with your country. It'll be my business, one day, to prevent it happening in Scotland."

"You must have grown very wise," answered Orleans, "if you've discovered that. It's baffled us for twenty years."

He passed on, in no mood for further argument, and made

his way out of the hall. James noticed that an attendant made discreet signs to another and that the second man followed unobtrusively in the wake of Orleans. James wondered which of the bland-faced lackeys had orders to watch himself. England always pretended to be careless, but in secret she took no risks with her valuable property.

He leant against the tapestry, watching the dancers, a line of men and a line of ladies, converging and retreating. He saw them with very different eyes from those which had surveyed the guests in Windsor Hall. He had been in France since then. Now he knew them for what they were, a row of killers jigging towards the mates, whose office was to breed more killers from sleek and perfumed bodies. So it had always been, since the Grecian knights slew Duke Hector and burned his Troy. Perhaps they too had danced, and perhaps their captives had watched them, clear-eyed through suffering, and divined the beast of prey lurking beneath each high-sounding title.

These creatures had souls, perhaps, but once they had said and forgotten Mass, their lives were shaped by appetite, and revolved only round the dowry, the marriage-bed, and the field of slaughter. It was by their appetites that a king must rule them, playing one greed against another; and, if the game grew too tangled and too perilous, then he must remember their other secret—the secret of fear. For with him were axe and rope and the torturer's terrors, and slowness to use them might spell ruin for all alike. Such was the Mystery of Kingship, and those who thought otherwise had no business on a throne.

The dance ended, but the dancer's blood was on fire. There was full-fed laughter and horse-play, over-charged women shrieking in exaggerated alarm. One of them, hot and giggling, caught hold of a burly Yorkshire knight, tied her handkerchief round his eyes and loosed him for the others to prod and pinch, till he rounded on them and sent them flying and squeaking out of reach. One ran full-tilt into Northumberland, crushing her head-dress against his stomach. He held her fast and let out the family war-cry. "Esperancy Percy!" he bellowed and everyone shouted, "A rescue! A rescue!" as he swept her out of the Blindman's path. Humphrey of Gloucester stepped fastidiously aside, as though leaving the children to their silly play. The Yorkshireman tripped over the dais steps and grasped at Queen Katharine's skirt. She pulled it away, looking bewildered and curiously lonely amid the chorus of delighted hoots. And then suddenly, inexplicably, a dead silence fell.

There was a conflict of muffled voices outside the door. Katharine's expression changed to one of guilty fear. The curtains parted, and King Henry strode into the room.

James had not known he could look so old and anxious. There were dark lines beneath his eyes and, if it had been anyone but Henry, one would have said that he had been weeping. He stood looking round as the guests began to kneel and curtsey. Then the blindfolded Yorkshireman spread great arms like an ape's, stumbled forward, and wound them round the king.

"Ee!" he shouted, "caught you this time!"

Henry ripped the covering from his eyes, and threw it angrily to the floor. The man's face was a blank cliff of astonishment.

"You were dancing," said the king. "You had better continue."

He strode up to the frightened Katharine, drew her to a seat and began to talk, rapidly and earnestly. He sat down beside her, taking letters from his belt and summoning first one man, then another, to read or listen. James felt their eyes rest occasionally on himself, and once King Henry nodded in his direction. The news, whatever it was, began to filter round the room. Henry was accustomed to seeing his orders obeyed, but he did not seem to notice that there was little attempt to revive the dancing.

James approached a lady with whom he had taken the floor earlier in the evening. Her father stepped forward from nowhere and bore her off with inadequate excuses.

The guests were gathering in little knots round the walls, whispering or exclaiming in hushed voices. Again and again James felt eyes upon him. A woman broke into sudden tears and was hurried from the room. Then the king beckoned to one of the men who had entered with him and murmured a few words. The man left the dais and came straight to James. "His Majesty's order," he said. "All prisoners to return immediately to their quarters." It was many months since James had been called prisoner to his face.

He walked out, puzzled, but his head high. The last thing that caught his eye was Northumberland's face, stupidly hostile.

He heard part of the truth next morning. It was days before he heard the whole.

It seemed that Clarence, left in command in France, had determined to show that it was not only his brother Henry who could beat the French in battle, and that, under proper leadership, knights could defeat knights without the aid of archery. Easter Eve had found him raiding defiantly towards Anjou, and the Armagnacs closing in upon him. Deaf to all warning, he had hurled himself and his men at an army of them in the woods round Baugé church. It was not Frenchmen that met him, but the Dauphin's hireling Scots. And the wine-bibbers and mutton-guzzlers had earned their keep.

Clarence had been killed in the first five minutes, struck down by a Lennox Highlander. Huntingdon, Fitzwalter and the insufferable young Somerset were prisoners in Scottish hands. Of Clarence's army, only a few hundred men won safe to their garrisons or eluded their pursuers in the woods. The fame of Baugé fight was dancing across France and her cowed champions raising heads again. The Armagnacs were marching upon Chartres, upon Mantes, upon Paris itself. All Henry's conquests were in jeopardy, and it might need a second Agincourt to make them safe again.

July-September 1421

V

"When he has taken Orleans." Humphrey of Gloucester swung his legs over the arm of the great leather-covered chair and rested friendly eyes on James's face. "He said he'd think about it when he had taken Orleans."

"Think about it?" answered James. "He's been doing that for eight years—ever since he was king. But I am still a prisoner."

They were in France again, in the desolate town-hall of captured Dreux. The summer sun, flooding through broken windows, illumined a wilderness of broken furniture and a pile of grey ash where papers had been hastily burnt before the English should break in. Humphrey's voice sounded out-of-place, his elegant limbs sprawled inappropriately in the mayor's great chair. His melancholy, almost womanish face proclaimed him scholar and cynic rather than conquering soldier.

James turned to the window. He could look down upon the fields and vineyards, ruined now, beneath which he had helped Humphrey to drive the slow mines which had left the citadel a tottering peril and Dreux ripe for surrender. Now Henry was come to approve their months of labour, he had hoped for some less dilatory and non-committal answer to the petition that Humphrey carried to his royal brother.

"He means it this time," Humphrey was saying, "and you'll not have long to wait. We march south tomorrow, and we'll be in Orleans before September's out."

The old game of siege and surrender, march and counter-march, had entered on another weary round. There would be no second Agincourt, for the Dauphin, however his Scottish allies might chafe, refused to risk battle for Dreux or any other town. Henry must repair what Clarence had lost at Baugé by slower and more gruelling methods.

James could do nothing but help him, so far as he was allowed, and hope for ransom as his reward. He had even written to Scotland to persuade the Douglas—one-eyed since Shrewsbury fight, limping since Homildon—to throw his weight on the English side for once, and counter-balance his countrymen who fought for the Armagnacs. Douglas had promised, but not come yet; perhaps Regent Murdoch had hindered his departure. If he was going to keep his promise, Henry would have cause for gratitude to James. And James had found a new advocate in Queen Katharine, to plead for him at her coronation feast. Henry had left her behind in England, but her words might bear fruit. Meanwhile, he must be patient and wait for Orleans to fall.

Humphrey had risen from his chair and was turning a mournful eye on the rubbish that littered the abandoned Council Chamber. "Well," he said, "I suppose we should be going. You must help me make out tomorrow's marching-orders. You mustn't tell Henry I said so, but I am beginning to find war an excessively boring business. If I were king, I'd make peace tomorrow, rights or no rights. They're just not worth the trouble."

"You'd release me first, I hope."

"Oh, yes, I'd release you, so long as you promised not to start another war on the Border. Campaigning in France is bad enough: I shudder to think what it must be like in Scotland."

"You'd be safe enough from me. From what I hear of Scotland as Cousin Murdoch's likely to leave it, I'd have my hands full at home."

"And I'd be left to govern England in peace. An excellent scheme." Humphrey yawned. "Have you ever thought," he asked, "how oddly these things are arranged? If the

Almighty was really in favour of peace, He could so easily have made me the eldest son instead of Henry. It would have saved so much unnecessary trouble. Or am I being blasphemous?"

"Probably. But there's no one listening. And you're wrong, you know. You may dislike war, but you wouldn't know how to stop it."

Humphrey looked at him with the far-off eyes of the man to whom imagination is more real than life. "You may be right," he said, "though I don't understand why. But then there are so many things I don't understand. The world always seems to me an unreasonable kind of place. Come and help me make out those orders."

September was half gone before they lay in sight of Orleans, and Henry gave no sign of pressing on the preparations for a siege. James, having nothing else to hope for, told himself, again and again, that the fall of Orleans was to be the signal for his release, that Henry had promised, that Humphrey had seemed sure. Had he been as sure himself, it would not have been necessary to argue so with himself.

The campaign had seemed endless and inglorious so far. Henry had left the great towns unattempted, Tours, Blois and the rest. The Scourge of France fell only on the fields. It was crueller, more searching than ever, sparing little that was unfortified—except churches and monasteries. Henry's men were deteriorating, his own patience was wearing thin; he had once been inspired by the belief in his own cause: he was obsessed by it now. His boasted piety was decaying into superstition.

He halted his army outside Orleans, and left it idle for a day, while he rode off, sparsely attended, to visit a hermit in some unknown village. His most loyal supporters maintained that it was a stratagem of war, whose purpose would soon appear: others winked knowingly at each other, said that "hermit" was as good an excuse as another, and agreed, charitably, that it was a long time since Henry had left his French wife behind in England.

James spent the day hunting. Humphrey started out with him but soon dismounted, sat down against a tree, and announced that he was going to read Plato until the hunters returned. "I suppose you'll come back this way," he said. "And it's too cursedly hot to be running about after animals."

"I suppose we shall have to," James replied. "We can't abandon you there for the robins to cover up with leaves." He rode off, leaving some of the party to doze round the recumbent student of philosophy.

He had brought an old friend, John Page, begging his services for the day from a captain of archers.

"What did your master say," he asked him, "when you showed him your *Siege of Rouen*?"

"Oh, I've not been home, your Majesty," answered Page, "not since I saw you last. I wasn't one of the lucky ones." He seemed to have lost much of his old buoyancy. He used his opportunity to ask James how long the war would last, and, when James professed ignorance, put on the aggrieved air of a man deliberately kept in ignorance by inconsiderate officialdom. "All the same," he said, "I reckon it's not easy to tell while the Kiss-me-tails won't come out and fight."

"The what?"

"Kiss-me-tails, sir. Baisey-me-cues. That's what we call the Frenchmen. And they call us God-dams. I think we've the better of them there. Silly name, God-dams."

They dismounted to shoot, and Page stayed with James while the others were sent over a ridge to beat up game. The archer was very contemptuous of James's bow, with its ivory inlay and peacock-feathered arrows. "You can tell your bowyer," he said, "when next you see him, that he's sold you a pretty piece of trash. English yew, I'll be bound.

We can't grow yew like the Spaniards. You won't find any English wood in Leche's company. You'd better take mine."

The exchange was effected in time for a shot at an old dog-fox—the sole result, apparently, of twelve men beating a couple of acres. It stopped as soon as it came over the rise and stood sniffing. "Get him before he moves," whispered Page. "Then you'll have a brush to put in your helmet like King Harry."

James resisted the temptation of an easy shot, and waited until the animal was trotting again, through a tangle of ferns and brambles. Then he loosed off, and the arrow pierced its hindleg, pinning it to the ground. Page crashed up the slope, pulling out a knife as he went.

"If your Majesty had been born in England," he said, as he returned, "you'd have had him in the head. And I ought to have lent you my quiver as well as my bow." He held out the despised shaft, feathered with peacock.

"I'll get you into trouble with your captain," said James, "if I borrow any more of your gear."

"Kind of your Majesty to think of it, but I could always get arrows back. I don't expect you'd be sending them far!"

He grinned a little, uncertain how his impudence would be accepted.

"I've half a mind," said James, "to empty your quiver and send you picking the lot up, at four hundred yards."

The beaters were reappearing, cautious heads popping up over the skyline, or peering round trees. One of them came running back along the path with a story of men in armour moving along the next valley. It was not thought wise to scatter again, and a signal was given for the return. The last man to rejoin them brought in what he called a prize, a huge, bewildered peasant who stared before him like a cow and seemed incapable of speech. The general opinion was that some soldiers or brigands must have cut out his tongue, until a couple of archers forced open his teeth and found the member intact. He submitted to the investigation with no more resentment than an animal being inspected for market, and relapsed into a dumb stare, expressive of nothing whatever. But when Page opened his wallet and showed a thick slice of bread, he snatched it desperately and vanished with surprising nimbleness into the bushes, while his captors were left laughing on the road.

They rode back to find Duke Humphrey and the way home. Page was expanding a little now, finding that James would allow him scope.

"It's a funny thing," he said, as they walked their horses up a steep hill, "—I mean about the end of this war. There was a fellow in the place where I was quartered, t'other side of Beaugency, that had a wonderful kind of tale he'd picked up somewhere in the south. He said that someone else had said that it couldn't end till a girl came along to lead the men. A maiden, he said. I couldn't make it all out. He talked such a funny kind of French."

"A girl from his own village, I suppose?"

"No, your Majesty, somewhere out east, so he said. Burgundy way. She was there now, he said, waiting for her cue, so to speak. I told him she'd have to get to work quickly—begging your Majesty's pardon—or from what I'd seen of Burgundy men she'd not be a maiden much longer."

James felt it his duty to give a slight frown. "They have queer tales in the country," he said. "I suppose, if she comes from Burgundy, she's going to win the war for your side?"

"That's what I told him. And, anyway, it can't end, can it, till we've won? But this fellow didn't seem to understand that. And, as I say, I couldn't make out all he said."

It was not long before they sighted Duke Humphrey. James saw him wake from sleep at the sound of their horsehooves, and rapidly resume his Plato.

"I don't think much of your quarry," he said, when they had halted by his tree. "Fox—*et praeterea nihil.* I congratulate myself on having spent a more profitable afternoon, with the classics." His drowsy followers stretched themselves and untied the horses. The day was cool again by the time they reached camp.

Henry had returned. He had ridden straight to his tent, speaking to no one and issuing no orders. The men in charge of the siege-train asked their captains whether they ought not to be making ready for the attack on Orleans. They were told to wait, at least till tomorrow.

James, equally mystified and more impatient, sought out Humphrey again as soon as supper was done. They strolled out together to the skirts of the camp. Humphrey was happy to talk, but on every subject except that which was tormenting his companion.

"As far as I can discover," he said at last, "my brother drew just as blank as you did this afternoon."

"Oh? Did he not find his hermit?"

"Oh, yes, he found him—and was treated to another sermon. I wish I understood why Henry lets himself be lectured at by anything with a shaven crown. This one told him that he'd better make peace at once because he had only one more year to live. I suspect that the wish was father to the thought; Henry's not popular hereabouts. But I don't think he'll oblige them by dying just yet; he's not thirty-five and as tough as a stallion. Have you ever seen him catch a deer in Windsor Park? He only needs two men to head it off, and then he runs the beast down himself, on Shanks's mare. Which is more than you could do, my athletic friend."

"We are all in God's hand," said James, sententiously. "Especially on campaign."

"I'd agree with you if there was a Frenchman left with the pluck to try and kill him. But they daren't even risk a battle."

"One might have said the same about your brother Clarence, until last Easter."

Humphrey smiled without a trace of resentment. Old Bolingbroke's sons had never made an affectionate family. "I take it," he said, "that that is a gentle reminder of

Scottish prowess. Come along to my tent. I want to show you a book."

"I've seen all your books."

"Not this one. It's hardly been out of its case yet."

"Tomorrow, then. You haven't told me yet what Henry intends to do."

"Do? March north again, I suppose, or possibly east towards Burgundy. We're doing no good on the Loire, and autumn's coming on."

"But Orleans?"

"Orleans will have to wait till next year—or the year after. There's dysentery in camp, and too many Armagnacs in the offing to risk a siege. Orleans'll be a tough nut, you know."

"But, King Henry said——. I mean, is this because of what he was told today?"

"Oh, no. I've known it some time. We only came here to give them a fright."

James stared at Humphrey, momentarily dazed. It was some weeks since the two had spoken of the matter that lay closest to his heart, but it seemed incredible that Humphrey could have forgotten it, could stand there, with the smile on his face which was so nearly a sneer, thinking only of his books.

"I'm turning in now," said Humphrey. "You'd much better come. We may be packing off tomorrow."

James lingered after he had gone. The last of the sun was turning the shallow breadth of the Loire to a sheet of gold. Half a mile away a dozen of the archers had stripped and were shouting and splashing in the water. Some of them were playing at ball with an apple. Behind them, looking distant in the evening light, rose the towers and steeples of unconquered Orleans.

October-December 1421

VI

One beat them down in one place, but they sprang up in another. One captured Dreux, and raided up to Orleans, but, in one's rear, all Champagne was being wasted by the Armagnac garrisons of Meaux and Compiègne. The Dauphin's men had no Maid to lead them yet, nor any hope of crowning him at Rheims. Many of them thought more of plunder and ravishing than they did of France, and they would have laughed at the notion of taking orders from a saint. But while there was a walled town to be held, a countryside that could be bled for booty and amusement, no English king should call himself lord of the French.

Before Henry had marched fruitlessly towards Orleans, Paris had petitioned him to deal with the devils who held Meaux and flayed the valley of the Marne. Paris was finding its situation intolerable, market-prices a scandal, and the streets crowded with homeless rustics crying, "*Ayez pitié. Je meurs de faim!*" Henry replied that war without ravage was like sausages without mustard. Paris must wait.

It was October before he returned, but he was determined to have Meaux before winter was out. Meaux had the Marne on three sides of it, and new fortifications to supplement those that had been built five centuries before, to baffle the bearded robbers who had sailed their longships from Norway and up the rivers. The English dug their trenches and planted their palisades along the banks. Henry summoned Bretons and Savoyard mercenaries to assist them, though the Burgundians held back. Burgundy himself was a ticklish ally and he had gone to Paris, to shock even Paris with his amours. Henry could take Meaux without his help.

His artillery thundered against the walls, but the defenders' guns did the greater execution. They mended every breach, met mine with countermine, and made sorties where sorties seemed impossible. They had no fear of Henry. They hauled a donkey up to their ramparts, labelled it King of

ENGLAND, and belaboured it till it brayed. This, and some horns they blew daily, with a particularly irritating note, made Henry more angry than became a conquering hero.

His men were deserting and dying of dysentery, the river rose and flooded his siege-works. He fell sick himself, and, though his inhuman energy repaired all losses, he was growing more savage, more reckless, more superstitious. When they brought him the glad news that Katharine had born him a son in Windsor Castle, he said that there was a curse on the place and that Henry of Windsor would lose all that he, Henry of Monmouth, was conquering. He was even forgetting to protect the churches: when his men pillaged the shrine of Fergus, whom the French call St. Fiacre, they went unpunished for the sacrilege. Nothing mattered, except that he must have Meaux.

As if to add fuel to his fire, news came that Normandy, his first conquest, was in danger again. The Armagnacs had broken into it by the back way, along the Breton coast. They captured Dol, and opened a road to Mont St. Michel, whose magnificent rock, with only a hundred men to man it, was still defying England. Then, one biting night in November, they clattered into Avranches and hoisted their white-cross banner above its frosty roofs. Humphrey left the siege of Meaux to help Suffolk and Lord Scales repel the intruders; and when James, hoping to see open warfare, petitioned for leave to accompany him, he was answered, somewhat to his surprise, with a grudging assent.

The threat proved less dangerous than it had appeared. Avranches had been recaptured before they reached it. Scales met them there with the news that Suffolk had gone on ahead, driving the Armagnacs back towards Brittany. "If my lord of Gloucester will stay here and settle things in the town," he said, "I should like to follow on with the reinforcements you have brought."

Humphrey made a wry face. "Your lordship," he said, "is determined that I should do the dull work."

"Your Grace," said Scales, frowning at the note of flippancy, "is brother to King Henry; and King Henry's name, in this district, stands for order and good government. These people are just beginning to know what it is to be properly looked after."

"And that," said Humphrey to James, as soon as Scales had gone to make preparations, "is perfectly true. I know you hate hearing any good of my brother, but you must learn to give the devil his due."

James was to go ahead with the reinforcements. They rode through the foulest of weather, sleet and wind freezing their armour until the touch of it was painful to the bare hand. They had to travel in harness, for they were divided into small and scattered parties, sweeping the country for such Armagnacs as might have escaped Lord Suffolk's net. It was not till they had passed the river at Bault that the sky began to clear a little and a feeble sun struggled out.

They had not gone far along the Pontorson road when their flanking-files came cantering in with news of an enemy. There were dismounted knights at a farm lying behind the ridge on the left, and their pennons showed the white cross. Scales, affecting his calmest and most judicial air, asked about numbers.

"Thirty spears at most," was the answer, "a hundred men all told."

"Archers? Crossbowmen?"

"No sign of either."

"Lead the way."

Squires were shouted for, visors lowered, long spears balanced in hand. It was some minutes before the trotting column achieved the grim orderliness with which an enemy can be met.

It was not known whether the Frenchmen had sighted their scouts: they might be still busy about the farm: a sour smell, drifting in through helmet slits, told that something was being burnt. But it was possible, likely even, that the enemy were already on the run, and would be mere dots in the distance when the Englishmen breasted the rise.

James, gripping his spear, found himself sincerely hoping that they would stand their ground.

The farm-buildings bobbed up into sight. Smoke hung low over the barn, and a sulky fire ate at one of its corner posts. One could see at once that the Frenchmen were neither unaware of their coming, nor on the wing for safety. They were drawn up, in perfect line, at the far end of a long field of stubble. There were the thirty knights, possibly a few more, and the usual complement of squires and men-at-arms. The numbers were about even, the ground level; the Frenchmen had managed that the low sun should be in their adversaries' eyes—a trifling advantage on a dull December day.

The correct method would have been to get one's archers dismounted and shooting as soon as possible, but Scales was unexpectedly adhering to a more ancient and chivalrous orthodoxy. The English wheeled into a rapid line and set spur to their horses.

To an unaccustomed ear, the mere noise—the thunder of so many hooves, the rattle of arms, the throaty shouts of charging men—might be an irresistible terror. And with it came—sharp points ahead, plated bodies behind—such a weight of metal and muscle and horseflesh as no living thing could hope to stand still and survive.

The Frenchmen were not standing still. They were cantering forward to meet momentum with momentum. The horses on both sides, seeing no passage ahead, began to swerve outwards for all the riders' efforts to keep them close. They made little gaps in their own line, and headed for the gaps in their opponents'. James found himself galloping towards a man in a green surcoat. He had hardly picked him out before they were within a few strides of each other. In a second or two the clash would come. Here was exhilaration, the fierce joy that left all other pleasures pale. The man in green was yelling some indistinguishable war-cry. James felt a sharp blow on his head and knew, with sudden glee, that the Frenchman's spear had slithered and glanced from his helmet. At the same instant his own weapon jarred and leapt in his hand: the point was caught, between joints, in his opponent's neck, it was piercing the unseen flesh. Round him the swift rattle of first impacts was swelling to a deafening crescendo of crash and roar and scream, a long half-second of all hell let loose. His spear-shaft cracked and splintered. The green surcoat flashed past, swaying grotesquely in the saddle, with a torrent of hot crimson splashing the horse's mane. This was life: this was ecstasy: this was what he had been born to do.

There was nothing ahead of him now, except a field of wet mud and one plunging horse, in whose empty saddle a friend had sat barely ten seconds ago. James tugged at his near-side rein, reaching across, as he did so, to unsheath his sword. He must turn his horse and have his blade free before he looked round to see what was happening. He had to use all his strength on the bridle before he found himself facing the enemy again.

The charge had carried them further than he could have believed possible in the time. He could see them, at the far end of the long field, wheeling for the second charge. It would be less massive as well as less headlong than the first. There were fewer, far fewer, on both sides. Half-way down the field was a broken line of dark humps upon the earth, some twitching grotesquely, some still for ever.

The lines were approaching again, warily this time. There were few lances left, and sword-blows are difficult at a gallop. Two men were converging on James. One had lost his helmet and carried his blade high, guarding a tangled shock of black and sweat-streaked hair. The other was swinging a mace, with a gentle, menacing motion, on the level of his horse's head.

James rode straight at the bare head, wheeled his sword in a great arc and brought it crashing down. He saw the high parry beaten down, the man wince away as the steel reached and bit into his forehead. Then he felt a crushing pain on his shoulder, saw the sword spin out of his paralysed hand, and was carried, half helpless between and past his adversaries' horses.

He gripped tightly with his knees and put up his left hand to feel the damage. The mace had buckled his shoulder-piece inward, squeezing intolerably on the bruised and powerless muscles. He heard horse-hooves behind him, and, turning in desperation, felt undeniable relief at seeing one of his squires.

"Help me to get this off," he shouted through the helmet-slit. "I can't move my arm, devil take it!"

The man brought his horse alongside, and started to wrench at the twisted fastenings.

"If your Majesty would dismount——" he began.

"Dismount be damned!" said James. "There's still some of the swine to be dealt with." He looked round at the field, which hardly justified his words. Half the Frenchmen were down, the rest had more than one enemy apiece to face, and some were taking to their heels. But he was in no mood for counting. "Quick, man, quick!" he said. "Stop fumbling like that."

As he spoke, he knew that he was being unreasonable. A moment later he had no time for any such thoughts. The man with a mace was galloping towards him. He was escaping from the battle; across his saddle-bow lay his friend, black hair bobbing at every stride. But he was meaning to strike another blow on his way to safety.

Too late, James's squire tried to urge his horse round and interpose. James saw him stretch out an ineffective hand, a yard short of the danger zone. The Frenchmen was rushing past at arm's length, the mace stretched head high. James ducked, knowing as he did so that he was too soon, that the weapon would have time to come down to meet his helmet. Another moment and he knew no more.

December 1421-*May* 1422

VII

They got him to Pontorson before midnight. There was no cause for real apprehension, though mace-wounds, as Scales observed, could be the devil. Not that Scales wanted to make more of the matter than was necessary: he was not eager for King Henry, or even Humphrey, to hear that he had endangered a very valuable prisoner in an unimportant skirmish. James had recovered consciousness on the way, and was fully awake, though somewhat dazed, when judgment was pronounced on his injuries by the medical opinion of Pontorson: this was embodied in an oily little barber with a stomach like a pumpkin, and a thin, yawning priest, who had an air of being too bored and too deeply wronged to be sure whether it was worth while living any longer. They might have been picked for comic contrast by a master of revels. But they contrived to be unanimous in their verdict: a week in bed and no hope of fighting for another two months.

"But your Majesty need not trouble about that," the barber said, "because, as your Majesty knows, there will be no more fighting. Your Majesty has heard the news, I take it. Lord Escailles will have told your Majesty."

"Has Meaux fallen?" asked James confusedly, wondering if he had been unconscious for an hour or two, or for many months. "Have they taken Orleans?"

The barber looked up at the priest as though suspecting delirium.

"My colleague's views," said the priest in a dim and nasal drawl, "are bounded by more local interests. He means, my son, that there has been a victory near Pontorson. Or so they say."

"Yes, indeed. Yes, indeed," said the little man. "And such a battle! Near the Bishop's Park. The Lord of Sudfoulque has beaten these Armagnac ruffians. We are safe again. And we owe it all to your Majesty's English friends. They say there were nearly five hundred men on each side. Think of that. A thousand altogether!"

The priest looked at him along an Olympian nose. "These rumours," he said, "are generally contradicted next day."

The barber countered this, respectfully enough, with a sister-in-law who had talked to a Breton pedlar who had run all the way from the battlefield. The priest withered him by pointing out that no pedlar could have covered the distance in the time. They were soon at it, hammer and tongs, throwing mileages and "as the crow flies," at each other. James was longing for sleep, and afraid that the supercilious priest might start calling him "my son" again. He signed to his squire to pay and dismiss the pair of wranglers. The barber's thanks were lavish and long-winded, but the priest preserved his tired dignity. "Not for myself," he said, lifting black eyebrows as he took the money, "just for the poor of my parish." He gave the squire that look of intensity and conviction which generally accompanies a round lie. Then he sighed, resumed his habitual expression and made for home. The barber ran back to James's bedside, and knelt to slobber kisses on his unguarded hand.

"It is so good of your Majesty," he whined, "to come so far in order to preserve us from our so terrible enemies!"

James flicked him feebly across the nose, and resolutely closed aching eyelids. "And I'll wager," he told himself, already half asleep, "the fellow would have said the same to that black-haired boy I wounded, if the Armagnacs had licked us and come to Pontorson."

He was quicker to recover than they had anticipated, though there was no more fighting to be done on the Breton border. The barber's news had proved correct: Suffolk had beaten the Armagnacs at Parc l'Evesque, and bundled them out of Normandy. Mont St. Michel was beleaguered again, and would be so—though neither garrison nor besiegers could have believed it now—for another twenty years. James rejoined Humphrey at Avranches and then rode eastward, by leisurely stages, wondering whether Meaux would have fallen into Henry's hands by the time he arrived.

He passed a week in Paris, where everyone was talking about Burgundy's outrages on propriety. They spoke as if half the houses in town would soon be noisy with babies exhibiting the famous Burgundy eyebrows. Here too came daily news from Meaux, thirty miles eastward. Henry had taken the town in March, and only the castle defied him. There came a rumour that this too had fallen, that the little nucleus of desperate, and for the most part evil, men, had sent their herald to acknowledge defeat. Paris talked gleefully of a certain elm-tree outside Meaux where they had once tied up their captures, to be tortured through the day and left at night for the wolves to devour. The worst of them, it was said, were to be hanged on it without delay: the others would await King Henry's pleasure.

When the rumour reached him, James was making preparations to ride on at last to Meaux. He had thought of visiting Vincennes on the way, and it now occurred to him that Vincennes would be just the place where he would soonest discover what truth there was in the gossip. Queen Katharine, a young mother now, had just arrived there from England: she was staying in the château with her father and mother, and James would certainly be expected to pay his respects.

It was a clear sunny morning of May, and they had hardly left Paris before the huge tower of Vincennes began to peer at them over the trees. The weather and the prospect of good news combined to make a cheerful party.

They found that Katharine, too, was enjoying the sunshine. She was sitting in the garden with only one waiting-woman beside her. Her mother, Isabella, paced the terrace a short way off, talking in low tones to a foreigner, apparently a fellow-countryman from Bavaria. But her handsome, smouldering eyes were fixed upon her daughter.

Katharine accepted James's congratulations with obvious pleasure. She looked in better health than he had ever seen her, and certainly more at ease. But a shadow seemed to fall upon her face as Isabella approached, her hand resting on the arm of her German squire. The mother's eyes flickered maliciously from her daughter to James, but she was all courtesy, all eagerness to answer his questions.

"Yes, quite true," she said, her old face radiant. "My good son-in-law Henry has them in his power. I hope that by now he will be teaching them their lesson; they have delayed our final victory for six months and more. But the rebellion will soon be crushed now, crushed for ever." She looked imperiously round, pleased with her own rhetoric, and then her voice dropped to a silkier note. "I hear that you," she said, "and that dear young Gloucester have done great things for our cause in Normandy."

James bowed, murmuring that Suffolk and Scales had done all the work. It was obvious that everyone felt uncomfortable except the old queen herself. It was fifty years since she had come to France to spread, not mere discomfort, but ruin and corruption. Whatever kindliness had once been born in her German blood, she had long corroded it with her satanic cruelties, her shameless rape of men younger and better than herself. And fifty years of it had left her with a childlike serenity born of utter callousness, utter self-absorption.

"She is still beautiful," thought James. "She must have been dangerously so when she came to France. I'm almost glad I did not know her then." It was no marvel that her husband was lunatic, her son disowned by his family and half France, discredited by all. James could not take his eyes from her, though she seemed pleased to be so inspected.

He could not help noticing with what care, what snake-like elaboration, the white linen was folded round her face. Habits—some habits—last long.

No one seemed inclined to speak. Katharine's waiting-woman, standing now behind her chair, looked from one to the other, like an inquisitive mouse, and began to flutter the pages of the book from which she had been reading. Her mistress checked her with a gesture of nervous irritation, and even in that tiny movement the mother seemed to take some secret pleasure.

"There is nothing but good news this spring," she said. "Katharine tells me that the babe is in the best of health—and so like his father. The only pity is that she could not bring him to France, so that I and my poor husband could see our grandchild."

The German gentleman grumbled assent, cleared his throat, and looked like saving the company from another painful pause. Then he realized that he had nothing to say, and it was Katharine who came to the rescue. "You may go, Courcy," she said to her attendant. "We shall not be needing you here, and I want the coverlets unpacked and sorted. His Majesty may be here at any time, possibly this evening."

"Indeed he may!" said the old queen. "It is a long time since you were together. If I know my Henry, he will not let many more evenings pass."

Katharine attempted to ignore her, and waved toward the retreating figure of her gentlewoman. "I call her Courcy," she explained to James, "because I have to call them all by their surnames. The other two are Belknop and Troutbeck." She smiled at the names, almost apologetically. "You see, they all have the same Christian name. They are all Joan."

James could afford to smile back, thinking of a long dead self. The name meant nothing to him now. "Courcy," Katharine was saying, "is the youngest of the three."

"And you have dismissed her," said Katharine's mother.

"Is that a hint that we, too, are *de trop*? Friederich! Give me your arm. It is time we went back to our terrace."

She sailed off, her long train rustling on the gravel. "I think my daughter is unusually fortunate," she said as she went. "King Henry the Conqueror for a husband, and the handsome King James for cavalier." She had contrived to leave behind her the maximum of embarrassment.

Katharine was evidently accustomed to such moments: she had had long practice in masking her mother's Parthian retreats.

"It is a long time," she said, dropping suddenly from French to English, "since the sad dance at Pontefract."

"Yes, your Majesty," James answered. "It is a year since we met."

"And that poor Charles d'Orléans! I am afraid he will not soon be happy in England."

"He and I agree in finding English hospitality a trifle—pressing."

Katharine looked up, with sympathy and a tinge of coquettish appeal. "I did all the possible for him," she said, "and more still for your release. You heard me ask his Majesty at Westminster. But you know how they say it happens, when lovers are become husbands."

"I hope," said James, unwilling to let an opportunity slip, "that your Majesty will continue to plead for me."

"I do not see my Harry often. He is away at the wars always."

She smiled prettily. She had her mother's perfect teeth—though James did not want to be reminded, just now, of her mother. He found himself thinking King Harry foolish to be away so often at the wars. But what could one expect of a husband who was so insensitive as to refer to this delicate, slightly exotic creature—James had heard him—as "my Kate."

"They tell me," she said, "that you are musician, that you compose and sing so well. You must ride out here from Paris one evening, and let me judge for myself."

James, looking round the garden, was suddenly aware that Queen Isabella and her German were no longer in sight.

"I am not staying in Paris," he said. "I ride for Meaux this afternoon."

"Oh, but no, no! There is no need. His Majesty comes here at once. There will be—how do you say?—cross-purposes, if you ride to Meaux."

"Then, if I am permitted, I shall be more than happy to sing to your Majesty. It will be a great honour for so poor a musician as myself."

She rose as if to acknowledge the compliment with a curtsey. She had a grace that was all her own, pleasant to watch, and even a little disturbing. "Come in to the château," she said. "I will tell them to bring you wine, and something to eat." She turned to precede him. "Would not your Majesty prefer it," said James, following, "if we talked in French?"

"I speak English for practice," she said primly. "My husband ordered me."

"Your husband is not here now, your Majesty."

She stopped suddenly, turning back on him with a look that was anything but prim. "*Vous avez raison,*" she said. "*Mais pourquoi tant de 'Majestés.' Je m'appelle Catherine, Messire Jacques.*"

"*Lorsque votre mari n'est pas ici, n'est ce pas?*"

"*Oui, lorsque mon mari*——" She broke off suddenly, as if remembering something. "*Allons,*" she said, "*vous devez avoir soif.*"

James followed. He wondered how it was that ladies could persuade one that half an hour on horseback was a sufficient excuse for hunger and thirst; on campaign, one rode through an August day in full armour, and never thought about inns.

She led the way up the shallow steps of the garden entrance and into the cool dimness of the castle. They had crossed a hall and were entering a small ante-room when

Katharine gave a little "Ah!" of surprise. Quite motionless beside a small window, the old queen stood reading a letter. Even James felt a slight shock as if they had come upon something eerie.

"Don't start, child," said the mother, hardly lifting eyes from her paper. "I have more good news for you. Compiègne has surrendered to an English army. This is from my own man, outside Meaux. He sends a list of the Meaux prisoners and what is being done to them. That, too, is good news."

"I am glad, mother," said Katharine. "I mean about Compiègne." Her voice sounded toneless and depressed.

"Send for your Joans, child," said Isabella. "There will be scandal. Or go yourself."

She read on, and Katharine did not move. Suddenly the old woman raised a pair of glittering eyes, and spat out her order again.

"*Va-t-en, bébé!*"

Katharine fled.

Her mother watched her from the tail of an eye and then resumed her reading. She read slowly, one gathered, and with difficulty. All of a sudden she began to laugh softly, insistently, but without mirth. James had sense of a scene being staged for his benefit.

"What is it?" he asked irritably. "Why is your Majesty laughing?"

"At the good news, at the good news! I am getting old, you know, and the old have little to laugh at."

"Is it a jest to you," said James, "that the English should capture the towns of your husband's kingdom?"

She gave him a look of hatred for that: such accusations had no power to hurt her, but the intention was enough. James knew that he had made an enemy, and was glad of it. The old woman had fallen into a deadly calm. "My good son-in-law grows quick-tempered," she said. "He learns that war is trying to the patience, but that it provides opportunities for easing one's discomfort."

James stared, half-fascinated, at the stony face, sepulchrally wrapped in white linen, illumined by the greenish light that struck in through the little window. "I do not understand," he said.

"He is hanging them on their own tree. That is good. He has hanged the men that blew horns at him, and those that beat a donkey on the walls. He has hanged the gunners. That, too, is good; they killed two English earls with their balls, and there should not be cannon in wars. He found an English deserter in the garrison, and has buried him up to the chin, so that he may stay there and starve. And he found some Scots, too. My man does not say how many, but they are all dead. Henry has hanged them."

James stood very still. It was possible, likely even, that the old ghoul was lying to him. She was reading again, watching him with some sixth sense, eyes on her letter. He knew, looking at her, that she had not lied, that the ultimate outrage had been perpetrated again, the unrepeatable been repeated. She ceased to matter; nothing mattered except that boundless, cureless hatred had fallen between him and Henry. He must see him face to face, as soon as horses could bring them together. What he would do was not clear yet, but it must be done swiftly and in anger. He turned and strode out of the room.

"You must not be angry with my son-in-law," Isabella called after him. "They say he is a sick man. And it does not pay anyone to be angry with King Henry!"

James hardly heard. He stopped for no farewells, nor even to leave a message and excuse for Queen Katharine. As soon as he found his escort at the gates, he ordered them to follow him to Meaux, and without delay. The baggage could follow at leisure. There might be no need of baggage.

Before he reached Lagny, it was clear that there would be no need to go as far as Meaux. King Henry was on his way. His troops were in the village by the time James reached its bridge. Proud of hard-earned success, they were in no mood to brook impediment on their road. James's party was hustled aside, his horse forced back into the shady, evil-smelling alley between two houses. Thus wedged, he sat watching the banners and pennons, the haggard faces of the archers, the stern pomp of knights and peers. And behind them, haggard and stern himself, King Henry came riding by.

If James had meditated revenge, even bodily injury, he saw now that he had been anticipated. Death had already stamped a signature across that proud and pallid brow. The king rode in full armour: only the helmet, plumed with a fox's brush, was carried before him. The harness may have been meant to deceive spectators, to cheat himself even, into the delusion that he was not in pain—or the pain not mortal. James was not cheated; he knew that it would not be long before Henry, armoured or no, could not sit a horse at all. He had captured Meaux, in spite of winter and water and disease: but Meaux had taken its revenge.

The procession passed, the press slackened; they were able to extricate themselves.

"And now, your Majesty?" asked one of the men. "Is it right-about-turn and back to Paris? *Deo Gratias*, is what I say. I'm not wanting to leave Paris awhile."

"*Deo Ultionum*," said James to himself, "the God to whom vengeance belongeth." He jogged his horse on to the high road, its head turned towards Paris.

"The king looked poorly," he heard the man say to his comrade. "I hope it's nothing to matter."

"No need to worry," was the answer. "Meaux's a stink-hole: it'd make anyone look yellow. A few weeks with his Kate and he'll be our Harry again."

"Well, I hope you are right," said the first man. "I expect you are." He seemed a little uncertain still.

James was beyond uncertainty. He was remembering a darkened room in Fulham Manor, the sparks that had illumined, momentarily, the death-bed of an elder king. It was only a few minutes ago that he had first seen King Harry resemble his father.

August 1422

VIII

The end did not come at once, not for three months; but James never saw the king again. Henry was, as ever, indomitably busy, and full of fresh projects. He was in bitter pain, but no complaint escaped him. The French doctors told him that he had caught St. Fiacre's fever; St. Fiacre (whose shrine his men had plundered) was a Scot or Irishman, called Fergus in his own barbarous tongue. Henry swore that he must have been a Scot: the Scots had always been his bane: they had killed his brother, their saint was trying to lay a curse on him. But he made no sign of penitence or reparation in the matter of their king. When the midsummer heats assailed him, and even he must acknowledge the end near, he made a few dispensations for the future, mentioning some of his prisoners. He insisted that Charles of Orleans must not be released, certainly not until the baby Henry was of an age to govern England and France. Of James he said nothing, and perhaps had nothing to say.

He roused himself, even in August, on hearing that the Dauphin was advancing from Bourges with an army. But his horse was soon abandoned for a litter, and at Corbeil he had to give up all thought of the journey. They brought him back, by barge, to Vincennes. He had three weeks more to suffer.

He was prodigal of repentance for any wrong he might have done to God or man. The Priests' King was dying as he had lived. He was not neglectful of his worldly responsibilities. He asked old Exeter, brother to Bishop Beaufort and head of that family, to stand guardian to his infant son. Humphrey of Gloucester was to be Protector of England. To Bedford, ablest and most unselfish of the brothers, was given the thankless task of governing France and beating down her Dauphin. For there could be no penitence or renunciation for the one great crime of his life, the crime he left behind him to be two kingdoms' bane. He had long trained and hardened himself in the belief that he had crossed the Channel to enforce just claims, and maintained the war at God's own bidding. It almost seemed as if his ghost would haunt England unless she bled herself white to complete—in the teeth of justice and reason and probable defeat—the terrible mission on which his genius had launched her. One could not guess by what strange casuistry he had cheated his conscience. But he was going to face his Judge without misgivings, apparently untroubled by doubt.

Like his father, he spoke much of a now impossible Crusade. When they read him the Psalms, he interrupted them at "*Aedifica muros Hierusalem.*" "God knows," he said, "that I intended to rebuild the walls of Jerusalem. I would still, if I could live."

His confessor bade him rely on God's mercy and his own good deeds, not on vain deathbed yearnings. "Show him the plans," said Henry, and they brought papers that he had ordered to be drawn up long ago, before he had any thought of sickness: they were carefully and thoroughly prepared, as all work had to be that might meet Henry's eye: they contained a detailed report on the harbours, the roads, and the military defences of Palestine.

He asked the doctors how long he would live. They began with courtly lies, not knowing their man. When he insisted, they told him the truth. "Two hours," they said, "or perhaps less."

He received communion and extreme unction: he lay still, awaiting the end. At one moment he seemed in great agony, but of mind rather than body. "Liar! Liar!!" he cried. "I belong to the Lord Christ!" Then he grew calmer, whispered, "*In manus tuas, Domine,*" and passed away like a child falling asleep.

December 1422

IX

They did not take him to Paris. They did what had to be done to the body and carried it, wrapped in lead, to the monastery at St. Denis. There they made an image of him, a stuffed figure of boiled leather, painting its face, crowning its brows, and putting orb and sceptre in its hands. The varnished idol of King Henry, clad in his own robes, rode on his coffin through the lands he had conquered. It looked with unseeing eyes at Rouen and Abbeville, it rode past Agincourt to Calais and the sea. Archers and spearmen walked before it, trains of priests sang an endless Office for the Dead. Bedford followed, sorrowing for a brother, Humphrey impatient for England. Queen Katharine had something to mourn and much to fear; it was possible that her long future might match her unhappy past. With them came King James, brought to give honour to the gaoler and enemy who had now escaped beyond the bourn of hate.

There were further pomps, larger and more mournful crowds, awaiting them across the Channel. From Dover to Canterbury, from Canterbury to London, the journey was a chain of requiems and masses. It took them ten weeks to bring King Harry to his grave.

Bedford had not come with them to England; he had returned to Paris to attend the funeral of another king: Charles of Valois had followed his son-in-law, rendering his scattered wits into his Maker's keeping. He had died in neglect and even poverty, he was buried without vain expense: it was not splendour that drew the vast crowds of the poor to pay the last homage to the wretchedest and most disastrous of their kings. They lowered him into the vault of St. Denis: there was a short and heavy silence: then the herald at Bedford's side proclaimed a new era in the name of Henry of Lancaster, born at Windsor, sixth of that name to reign in England, second in France.

The war would go on, for the dead king's word was more than ever law: but James would not return to it, except in spirit: he had finished with France. That lesson was learnt, and perhaps over-learnt. He was eager to return home and put the knowledge into practice in his own kingdom. It remained to be seen whether England, now ruled by a ten months' babe, would at last consent to let him go.

He looked to the widowed Katharine for assistance. He did not know that England is often inhospitable to foreign consorts, and will never submit to a queen-mother's rule. Katharine was voted adequate revenues, with some limited rights over her royal son, and then kept as powerless as possible. She was a Frenchwoman, young and extremely prepossessing: England distrusted the combination. But Katharine, her own mistress at last, might discover how the impediments to power could be removed by judicious intrigue. James had hopes of Katharine.

She was, of course, one of many pieces on the board. There might be others whose game would be improved by helping a pawn like James to reach the home-square which involved a crown; he might even bargain with them, promising such alliance as a pawn can offer when it becomes a capital piece. Unfortunately the home-square was occupied and defended. Murdoch, enjoying all the privileges attached to King James's crown, was hardly likely to facilitate his forward movement.

The game was in full swing in England before Henry was in his grave. James attended the final ceremony at Westminster, beside the Confessor's tomb. He watched Duke Humphrey and Bishop Beaufort—already at odds over the Council board—forgetting the solemn chant and the past glory that was being buried, in order to look across the chancel and hate each other. The lion was dead, his cub a helpless emblem: the jackals were already snarling in the deserted den.

England watched in silence. England would have preferred Bedford as her governor, not Humphrey the bookworm. Humphrey must play for her favours, altering his tastes to suit England's demands. He had some success. He was marrying a Dutch heiress, somewhat indiscreetly—for she already had a husband on the Continent. England decided to applaud the indiscretion, if only to annoy the bishops. Humphrey was on his way, by judicious changes of habit, to become a popular hero. His fickleness, his lazy, selfish cynicism, were beyond anyone's power to change.

He needed support, even from the populace. He had much against him. There was stiff old Exeter, head of the Beauforts and veteran of Agincourt, who was official guardian to the infant king. There was his brother, Bishop Beaufort, a painstaking politician, a monument of respectability, industry, and avarice. He was now by far the richest man in England, and—once his official duties were conscientiously discharged—he was busy increasing his riches by a clever manipulation of the wool-market. He was of royal blood, half-way to a Cardinalate, and in alliance, against Humphrey, with most of the great landholders. But England on the whole, London with enthusiasm, was beginning to hope that Humphrey would get the upper hand.

"Father?" said James to Merton, as they sat one day in Westminster Palace, overlooking the Thames. "Father, I want to ask your opinion."

"Yes, my son."

"I am in a difficulty. A matter of right and wrong."

Merton checked an involuntary sigh and began to rub his chilly hands. It was December—a month and more after the funeral—and cold airs blew in from the river. "Is it one that an outside adviser can decide for you?" he asked.

"Perhaps not," said James. "Perhaps I shall not even take the advice you give. But I should like to have it."

The priest blinked a moment and then smiled. "Am I to conclude," he asked, "that you are wanting to do something against your conscience? And that you are cherishing a perfectly vain hope that I may encourage you to do so?"

"No, father, I am serious. And I am not the reprobate you like to think me. I want to do what is right."

"In that case," said Merton, "I may be able to help you. But if my counsel as a priest is sought, I shall expect it to be followed. Disobedience is a sin."

"I do not think that you will be able to instruct me *ex cathedra*," said James. "I believe it is more a question for a Court of Love than a priest."

He looked at Merton wondering whether he could mention such fashionable follies to him without meeting impatience or contempt. But Merton was looking out of window; his mild eye was fixed on the bargemen and the sail they were trying to hoist, stiff and heavy with rime. James resented the distraction.

"Go on, my son, I am listening."

"A young nobleman," began James, "becomes acquainted with a lady of great beauty and high birth——"

"And also—I hope—of unshakable virtue? Otherwise I ought not to listen to your story."

"That is part of his difficulty—that he cannot be quite sure. He meets her in the course of his ordinary duties. He finds himself admiring her greatly for her . . . her outward qualities. He has no deeper interest; only his senses are engaged."

"I take it there is no question of marriage?"

"None at all. As I say, it is only a matter of the senses. And he fears they may lead him into sin."

"He seems to be a very serious-minded young man."

James ignored the imputation, wondering how long it would take him to wear down the priest's gentle mockery.

"He is not so very young," he said. "The question is—are such acquaintanceships necessarily harmful? Ought they to be broken off as soon as their true nature is recognized? I must tell you that, in this case, it would be somewhat damaging to his worldly interests to begin avoiding the lady now."

"She is not married?"

"A widow. But young still."

"And her own feelings?"

"I know little of women—and they are so skilful in disguising what they feel. But I think that she is vexed with desires stronger than those of others. I think she might, if others encouraged her, become very evil. Her mother was very evil."

The priest rubbed his hands, still smiling softly. "One more question," he said. "I am not right, am I, in imagining that you grow tired of a lady's . . . friendship, and wish me to suggest an excuse for deserting her?"

"No!" said James, with almost unnecessary vehemence. "I wish you to tell me the truth." He paused a moment, and then added: "I am certainly not tired of the lady's company. As I told you, I am drawn to her, by certain strings that I despise, with almost dangerous force."

The priest rose, and began to pace the room. His face was solemn now, but James doubted whether he yet considered the matter with sufficient gravity.

"Some of my colleagues in the Church," he said at last, "will tell you that all women are limbs of Satan. The doctrine is certainly cherished in monasteries, where women are—or ought to be—very rarely seen. It is popular, too, in Scotland, if I remember right: but, as you know, I have not been in Scotland since I was a boy. Perhaps I have spent too much time with the rich and worldly-minded to understand the more rigorous views of life. I grow lax, no doubt. But even Scotsmen, even monks, must admit that women have souls to save, and we must sometimes reach them through the channels that please them best. It is dangerous, but I believe it is a dangerous truth, to admit that the Lord created Beauty as well as Virtue, and that there is a right use of the senses as well as a wrong."

"Then you think that by cultivating her society, I . . . I . . ."

"I think that by deliberately avoiding her you might miss a great opportunity of good, for yourself or for her. It seems to me that the Lord must have had some purpose in giving young people such irresistible attractions for each other. Again, I speak with hesitation; you will find plenty of priests to tell you that all such things are unreal and therefore of Satanic, not Divine, creation."

"They seem real enough at the time."

"That is hardly a criterion. Satan is no fool. But, as I say, I do not subscribe to the view. I am sometimes told that I have grown worldly myself."

"I was told by one priest that it was sinful to write poetry."

"Exactly. He may possibly have been right. I expect he was sincere. But we must remember the Apostle's words about 'diversities of gifts' before making up our minds for good."

James thought for a moment before replying. "I am glad," he said, "that I came to you for advice."

Merton was standing near him now, and put a hand on his shoulder. "I hope you will not accept it," he said, "merely because you find it comforting."

"I shall accept it," answered James, "if and when I decide that it is the truth. But, knowing myself, I still think that there is considerable risk in continuing this friendship."

"Risk of what?"

"Of succumbing to temptation. Of allowing my desires to get the better of my judgment."

"They will not do so unless you wish them to. I would

not sanction your seeing your friend again if I thought that you were half hoping for the friendship to end in sin."

He paused and walked a few paces from James's chair. He was quite grave now. "You will find prayer helpful," he said, without turning back. "I do not think that this matter is as important as you would like to make it—though it may, of course, lead to something greater, and in unexpected ways. But it is never safe to venture anywhere without prayer."

James sat silent.

"And now," said Merton, "I hope I have answered your question. Do not sit there too long. It is very cold in here."

He gathered his gown round him, and went out, coughing a little as he did so. James heard him exchange complaints about the weather with the guards outside, and then pass on down the passage.

'He is sincere,' thought James, 'and he is no fool. But I cannot help wishing that it didn't sound so like making the best of both worlds.'

He supped that night with Queen Katharine in Westminster Palace. Before the meal was half finished, he found himself seriously questioning the soundness of Father Merton's advice. Katharine looked remarkably enticing in the soft candlelight. She was in white for mourning, and she knew how to make the best of it. James remembered her in her bridal array at Troyes, and in the low-cut dress she had worn at Vincennes, showing the lovely structure of her firm, white bosom. But on the whole he preferred her as she was now, all the more *piquante* for the nun-like veiling of her form. Her voice, high and clear, had that exciting note that he missed in so many Englishwomen.

'I should not have come,' he told himself. 'Either the father has made a mistake, or he was being indulgent. After all, he must know that I've had far fewer pleasures than most men of my age. And I shan't be young for ever. I am glad I came.' At this point he began to laugh at himself. How many men, he wondered, would have dreamt of consulting a priest before keeping appointments with a pretty girl? He must teach himself, one day, not to be such a prig.

"Courcy!" said Queen Katharine. "Fill up his Majesty's cup. You are growing inattentive, Courcy." The lady-in-waiting obeyed mechanically; her thoughts seemed elsewhere.

"I spoke to Lord Exeter again," said Katharine. "He came to see my little Henry today. And I took the opportunity to tell him that the Council is being ridiculously slow in settling your Majesty's affair. They haven't even appointed any envoys to send to Scotland. 'I know you want to quarrel with Duke Humphrey over everything,' I said, 'but that is no reason why his Majesty's interests should suffer.'"

"It is very kind of your Majesty to take so much trouble for me. I wish I could show my gratitude by doing your Majesty a service." He smiled at her with his eyes. It was amusing to belabour each other like this with titles and formalities, for the benefit of her attendants. Troutbeck, the stout and red-cheeked daughter of a Westmoreland knight—one pictured him only a little stouter, with cheeks of a slightly deeper red—Troutbeck had just left the room, but would be back in a moment. Belknop stood four-square beside the mouselike Courcy, and Belknop, with her large hands and beaky nose, was evidently entering on a middle age that would be the pattern of propriety.

"It is worth much trouble," said Katharine, "to see justice done to your Majesty. Besides, if they know I am working for you, I have a good excuse for seeing you often. Please to remember that, if you are here tonight, it is strictly on the business of the kingdom."

James darted a glance at the unyielding mass of Belknop before smiling acknowledgment. But Katharine did not smile back. Perhaps someone had been lecturing her, Exeter in all probability: it would be like the old hunks to drop clumsy hints about her intimacies. These Englishmen!

He decided to reply with answering gravity. "I am pleased to remember everything," he said, "that your Majesty tells me."

"But you know the sad thing?" asked Katharine. "If I succeed, I fail. If I make them send you back to Scotland, I shall lose your company, lose my cavalier. There are not many young men who like to sit talking with a poor widow."

From the words alone one would have said that she was making advances, inviting indiscretion. Yet he seemed to detect a certain insincerity, almost a mockery, in her manner. He wondered if he had said anything to offend her, but could not remember it. Could something have happened since they last met? He decided, for the moment, that he was imagining difficulties.

"I am sure," he said, "that your Majesty will never lack cavaliers, even in England."

She accepted the compliment, but without enthusiasm. Her eye had gone to the door. Troutbeck was returning and approached her mistress to whisper a message. Katharine listened to it with an impassivity which might or might not disguise eagerness.

"Why do you say 'even in England'?" she asked. "Are the English so dull?"

"Perhaps I am prejudiced. They are my gaolers."

"I have suffered more from my own countrymen," she said pensively, and seemed to fall into languor. "Tell me," she said suddenly, "are the Welshmen English?"

"Yes and no. They speak a tongue of their own."

"You speak the Welsh in Scotland, do you not? I have heard that it is the same language."

"Not the same, though like. It was a tangled story that started at Babel. But it is only the poor in Scotland and the mountain-people who speak the old language; I was taught a little of it, but I never heard it at Court."

"Scotland must be a strange country. It is so interesting to have a Scottish cavalier."

There was no mistaking the mockery this time: it had too sharp an edge. He must have offended her after all; or rather, it seemed—unless his vague instinct misled him—that he had disappointed her, failed to give her something that her inner nature expected of him. He was still puzzling over it when she spoke again. "You have been to Wales?" she said.

"No. Why do you ask?"

"No good reason," she said. "I have had a Welshman suggested to me for my household—as clerk of my wardrobe." James thought he could detect a slight stir among the waiting-women. "He was with my Harry at Agincourt. And he sings beautifully—the songs of his own country. Troutbeck tells me he is here now. Perhaps we could have some music."

"I should be glad to hear him."

"I will match you against each other. Courcy!"

Courcy twittered forward: it was strange that the most aristocratic of the three Joans should also be the most timid.

"See that the harps are uncased and laid ready in the next room."

"Yes, your Majesty." Courcy bobbed and vanished.

"I have been trying a new song since I saw you last," said James.

"You learnt to make songs when you were young, in Scotland?"

"I try to learn everywhere, your Majesty. When I first came here the English music sounded strange to me. I have grown to love it now. My chaplain was showing me, the other day, what the Greeks wrote about music; but, so far, it means nothing to me."

Katharine smiled mechanically. She was hardly listening.

"There is little for me to do, these days," he added in apology, "except study books, and try to write songs."

"Troutbeck!" said Katharine, "we had better go into the other room. We might sing some rounds, so all four of you can come." She turned back to James. "If your Majesty will finish his wine," she said, "we can be going."

Troutbeck, making for the door, encountered the re-entering Courcy. "Your Majesty," said Courcy, with a nervous glance at her companions, "Tudor is waiting outside, and he says he has a message for your Majesty, a private message."

James's eyes were resting, a little puzzled, but pleasurably so, on Katharine's softly-lit face. The candles wavered in a draught from the open door, and at the same moment an extraordinary change came over her features. She suddenly looked round at him, like a guilty thing caught unaware, and with all the hostility of guilt. There was a tiny pause before she spoke.

"Very well, Courcy," she said, "tell him to come in here. If you will show his Majesty into the other room, I will follow him immediately. Belknop, will you please summon Beaufort for the singing?"

James, keeping his counsel, made for the door. Beyond its threshold stood a tall man, with flashing teeth, a fair, smooth skin, a plump and massive jaw. He was not typically Welsh, nor good-looking, as a man reckons good looks. He would make a good steward to a lady's household, one reckoned, hardly a good courtier for their favours: one looked closer at that masculine strength, that mischievous yet haughty smile, and saw that it might be the ladies that did the courting. Here was the assurance, the careless impudence that won them: here was ambition and success. The man might be of low birth and scanty wealth: he might have to sing or intrigue his way into a fortune: but he would have it, he would get there—unless some other man killed him on the road.

Tudor stepped aside. "Your pardon, sir," he said. But he moved with deliberate slowness, and James had almost to brush past him on his way out. A minute later, Courcy had shown him into a long room, tapestried in green, and left him to himself.

There was a large fire, and wine stood on a stool beside it. There were three harps lying uncased and ready on a table. The atmosphere seemed close, with a slightly unpleasing perfume in the air. The tapestry was patterned with woods and forests, hunting-scenes and the energy of outdoor life: but the artist, one would say, had been depicting things of which he had little first-hand knowledge, so that the effect of his handiwork was exotic and almost unhealthy.

James picked up a harp, plucked at the strings a little, and then put it down, in order to walk to the window and pull wide the heavy curtains. The night air was fresh enough.

Below him lay Westminster, the wintry gleam on the river, and London's distant lights. Some years back, a Lord Mayor had insisted on providing London with street-lamps, paid for, it was said, out of his own pocket. His aim had been to hamper thieves and murderers at their work, to put a check, even, upon lechery: a foolish ambition, worthy of a London tradesman. Human nature was a great deal stronger than wicks and oil, or the power of a Lord Mayor's money-bags. If it could not avoid, it braved the light. To judge by what was probably being whispered at this moment beside an abandoned supper-table, it could turn a many-candled palace into the likeness of a brothel.

Let her have her Welshman, for all he cared! It might even make her more eager—supposing she feared shame at all—to get him sent back to Scotland, out of sight and mind. One rid oneself of a king before marrying the servants. She would regret it one day, with nothing to feed her passion on except a rich voice and a pair of glittering, unscrupulous eyes. The man was not even handsome, for all his inches. James stood at the window, looking out over London, and confessed to himself, for the hundredth time, that he did not understand the ways of women.

He could hardly know what strange powers were at work around Owen Tudor. He could not see the man as women saw him; still less could he know what Time had in store. Forty years must go by before the man's story was finished and he was dragged from battle to kneel beneath the headsman's sword. But he would already have begotten, on Katharine's body, a dynasty to unseat York and Lancaster, in whose broils he perished. And even after his death there would be a woman to caress his head—grinning from its rusty spike above Hereford market—to comb the greyed hair for the last time and wash away the blood.

James's thoughts did not range beyond the present, nor escape from the jealous circle of bitterness and disgust. The monks told truth about the world; it stank in one's nostrils. Pent up in their cells, they did well to give thanks to God for preserving them from its snares. He himself could be grateful for his years of imprisonment and thwarted hope, since they had stripped him of all illusion, leaving him clear-sighted to escape corruption. James, with only twenty-eight years of limited experience, stood at the window and despaired of human nature.

And yet, deeply buried at the back of his mind, he was conscious of the very opposite of despair. Something was stirring there, a memory, an atmosphere, a picture that refused to take form. He could not track it down, but it seemed to centre on a word, a name probably, that he had half heard, a few minutes ago, while his mind was on other things. It brought with it the essence of times that he had believed dead, and striven to forget. It reminded him of an immature boy whom the grown man must learn to despise. And yet it was only the past, only childhood and a few bright intervals in later youth, that promised relief from malodorous thoughts. It was worth a little search, if only to assure himself that there had once been other things than the pride of the flesh and the lust of the eyes. He still gazed out into the night, but his mind had begun to race hither and thither on a long-cold scent.

Someone was in the room. Someone had been there for a minute and more, watching him as he stood. He knew now what he had been searching for, and what name it was that had prompted the search. He wheeled round suddenly to face her.

She, too, was in mourning to match the queen's. She, too, was beautiful, but with a beauty that quieted rather than disturbed. He had known her before ever he set eyes on Katharine, known her, it seemed, before ever he was born. There was no sudden rush of emotion, no crash or splintering of long-packed ice. Yet in the space of a few seconds six frozen years were melting away before the sun; the flowers sprang laughing up, the trees budded, the air smelt like morning in Paradise.

"Joan," he said quietly, as if he knew no other word.

She stood solemn for a moment, and then a hint of playfulness on her features grew rapidly into a smile. "We are all Joans here," she said; "I am Joan the Fourth. I only came on Tuesday."

He looked round the room and then back at her. They were alone together. The birds in the tapestry were singing a chorus of joy. "I am glad you came," he said.

Foolish words. Unfathomably inadequate words. But that did not matter.

"It was my uncle's doing," she said. "He wanted one of the family to keep watch on the queen, I suppose. John's furious. He says his sister oughtn't to be waiting on a Frenchwoman." She laughed a little, and her laugh, too, was enchanting.

"Your uncle's a great man now."

Why could he find nothing better to say? What did Bishop Beaufort matter?

"Is that why you're flattering me?" she asked. "Am I to ask uncle to get you your release? When the lion's in the net, the little she-mouse can nibble and help him to get away home."

James hesitated, swallowed, and felt as awkward as a schoolboy. But time was short, for he could hear Queen Katharine's voice in the passage.

"I think," he said, staring hard at his own shoes, "I think I *have* come home."

Open Sesame

. . . By what by-paths and indirect, crook'd ways
I met this Crown.

2 Henry IV. iv. 5.

CHAPTER FIVE

Open Sesame

March 1423

I

"*AND WHEREAS IN this Our Infancy and tender age, it behoves Us to be taught and trained in Courtesy, Learning, and all else that befits a King, We desire (by the advice and assent of Our said Council) that you should diligently watch over and care for Our Royal Person: and by these presents we grant you licence*——"

The secretary's voice droned on through the Council Chamber. Of his audience—the dozen lords, prelates, and gentlemen who ruled England in the name of the infant Henry—the greater part had ceased to listen. He had been at it too long, reading them despatches from France and petitions from home, pardons and instructions and proposed Orders in Council. Only Northumberland roused himself sufficiently to interrupt.

"Who is his Majesty supposed to be addressing?" he asked.

"The new nurse, my lord," answered the patient secretary. "I read out her name at the beginning—Alice Butler."

"Oh, very well. Get on with it, man." Northumberland relapsed into thoughts of supper.

". . . *And by these presents We grant you licence to chastise Our person from time to time, reasonably and as occasion demands, without incurring thereby*——"

Humphrey of Gloucester stirred in the President's chair. "Is all this necessary?" he asked.

The secretary looked more aggrieved than ever. "Quite necessary, your Grace," he said. "The lady refused to accept the position without some such quittance in advance."

"The devil she did! There are plenty of others we can offer it to. Who recommended this Butler woman?"

Bishop Beaufort was seen to look up from a page of calculations. There was an audible stiffening among the half-dozen councillors who owed their seats to his influence or worked for his interests. They were accustomed to Gloucester finding excuses to challenge anything and everything originating from their ranks. They were also prepared to counter the challenge. One of them—Ralph Cromwell, whose lands adjoined the Beaufort manor at Orwell—was about to answer Humphrey, when he saw that Exeter, the bishop's brother, was entering the lists. "I have seen her myself," said Exeter, sitting rigidly upright. "I consider her a most admirable woman."

Beaufort took up his cue. "I, too, saw her," he said. "I hardly think that my Lord Protector will find us a more estimable person." There was a distinct acidity in the way he pronounced Gloucester's new title.

"I was not questioning her morals," said Humphrey. "I merely inquired on what grounds she was considered so suitable to the place. After all, when his Majesty grants someone licence to whip him without committing high treason, we cannot be too careful who that someone is."

He lolled back in his chair, watching his opponents. "Do I gather," he asked, "that she is a dependant of yours, my lord of Winchester?"

The bishop flushed with indignation. But he was too old a hand to reply himself: he had plenty of supporters. "I do not think the recommendation came from my lord," said an insignificant voice.

"No," said another, but from an opposite quarter. "It was my lord of Exeter who proposed her name."

"Ah," said Humphrey, raising polite eyebrows. Exeter sat more upright than ever, trying to look incorruptible and only achieving owlishness. "That is so," he said. "And her Majesty the Queen immediately approved my choice."

"I beg your pardon," said Duke Humphrey. "I did not realize to which branch of the family she was attached."

Exeter refused to be drawn. "She has claims," he said, "distinct claims on our recognition. She is a widow. Her husband was with us at Agincourt, and died in the battle."

"I see," said Humphrey. "That puts her qualifications as a royal nurse beyond the reach of cavil." He yawned, enjoying (since no one else seemed to) the irony of his own remark. Then he flicked a paper in his hand in order to bring the weary secretary back to life. "Go on, man," he said. "Finish it."

The secretary resumed his reading. The document unwound its unnecessary coils before the waiting adversaries, still smouldering at each other across the table. When it was finished, and the seal set, their names were appended at the foot.

"*Le Roi le veult*," said Humphrey, "and I hope his Majesty will not regret his decision when he first feels the birch."

The Beauforts were not amused. "I am certain," said the bishop, "that his Majesty will approve our action when he reaches years of discretion. If your Grace would study Holy Writ, instead of the heathen philosophers, he would know that it is only—er—bastards who escape chastisement in infancy."

"I thank your lordship," replied Gloucester, mimicking the episcopal diction, "but I am acquainted with St. Paul's views on education. My reading is more catholic than you imply."

"I don't understand all this," interrupted Northumberland. "Hadn't we better finish the *agenda*?"

"Very well," said Humphrey with a sigh. "What is the next item?"

The secretary searched among his papers. "A letter," he said, "from the King of Scots. About the question of his ransom and release."

"There's no hurry about that. I think we had better adjourn this session. It has been a long one."

"Her Majesty the Queen-Mother," objected Beaufort, "petitioned us to hasten the matter."

"Not lately, I think. Am I right, my lord of Exeter?"

"No, not lately," conceded Exeter, loath to fail his brother. "Last time I saw her Majesty, she seemed to have lost interest in the matter."

"Well, is it particularly interesting?" asked Humphrey. "We must, of course, release him. But as we have held him for seventeen years, I cannot see that another year or so can make much difference." His voice petered out. He was remembering a past friendship and an eager face clouded with frustration. If only Beaufort did not seem so insistent on securing the release, Humphrey would be glad enough to do the generous thing. It would cost him little, and James deserved a turn of the luck.

His thoughts were scattered by the bishop's harping voice. "The Treasury needs money," persevered Beaufort. "And my lord of Bedford wrote again from France, only last week. May I remind your Highness that there is a French war to be waged—and paid for."

"I am not likely to forget it."

"The Scottish ransom may not solve our difficulties. But it would be an alleviation, a considerable alleviation."

"It might," said Humphrey. "If we could get it."

"I do not know what your Highness means by that observation."

"Then your lordship is not so well-informed as I was led to believe. Where do you suppose that Scotland is going to find such a sum as was suggested? Do you know what the whole revenue of their crown amounts to? Little more than three thousand!" He turned to Northumberland. "Am I right, my lord?" he asked.

"I expect so. Not far wrong." Northumberland, as a Border lord, was supposed to supply the Council with information on all northern affairs; but such brain as he possessed could not grapple with figures.

"I think," said one of Humphrey's supporters, "that his

Highness is undoubtedly right. The Scots may want King James back—though I am doubtful even on that score. They may agree to a proper ransom. But I would wager much against our seeing the colour of their money."

"That's it," said Northumberland, eager to show special knowledge. "That's just it. We've a saying in the North that you can never trust a Scot." Having delivered himself of this gem of wisdom, he turned truculent eyes on Beaufort.

Beaufort was not deterred. "The Scots might raise a special tax for the ransom," he said.

"You cannot squeeze blood from a stone," said Duke Humphrey. "And Scotland, I gather, is principally stones."

"Almost entirely," agreed Northumberland.

"On the contrary," began Beaufort, "the country has considerable wealth. If only——"

"So have my manors," interrupted Humphrey, "if only I knew how to get at it. I should not fancy that this new Albany person is any better than I at fleecing the unwilling. He seems less of a man than his father."

"We were not impressed with Duke Murdoch," said a dutiful ally, "when he was among us as a prisoner."

"It is not a question of Duke Murdoch," persisted the bishop. "King James could be released in exchange for hostages, and could go back to Scotland to raise his own ransom."

"He might try."

"His Majesty has energy, considerable energy, and a will of his own. I believe him capable of overcoming the most formidable obstacles." Beaufort remembered a fence at Woking Manor, and a young man who had climbed it. The bishop had often wondered why he had done so, and was no nearer an answer.

"I think," said Humphrey, "that your lordship underrates the obstacles that Scotsmen can raise when anyone is seeking money from them. And King James, unlike my late brother, will not find prelates in Scotland to lend him money, even at usurious rates of interest."

Beaufort rose, furious. Men had died for saying less of a great servant of the State. "Your Highness!" he began, purpling in the cheeks, "your office gives you no right to——!"

It was his brother Exeter who pulled him down again while Northumberland, in what he thought was a soothing voice, assured him that the Protector had meant nothing personal. "And after all," he added, "it's a matter of '*If the cap fits, put it on.*'"

"Mitre," murmured Humphrey, hoping that Beaufort would hear.

Beaufort was too angry to hear anything. He was looking round the room, tacitly demanding support against the abomination of Duke Humphrey's presidency. Most of the members of Council avoided his eyes, wondering, in an embarrassed way, how the impending scene could be averted. Sir Ralph Cromwell hit on an expedient. "Perhaps," he said, "perhaps their lordships from the Border can tell us more precisely what the Duke of Albany's attitude is likely to be. Is he eager for King James's release?"

The word "Border" suddenly roused Westmoreland. Westmoreland was an old man now, and considered it his privilege to sleep through the few Council meetings he attended. When he spoke, it was always on local matters.

"On my quarter of the Marches," he announced, "they say that Murdoch is frightened to death of the king's return."

"He has negotiated for it more than once," said Cromwell, still trying to support his patron's proposal. "We can only suppose——"

"It's my opinion," pronounced Westmoreland, with quite unnecessary emphasis, "that he will make things just as difficult as he can manage. Even if he were willing to see the king back, his sons would oppose it; they want to succeed him in the regency. And they say he has let them get the upper hand of him in everything."

He glared round, as if defying the whole Council to contradict him. No one, it seemed, had any desire to do so.

Beaufort and Humphrey were still eyeing each other like a couple of jealous tom-cats. Exeter sat stiff as a block. The others were fidgeting, knitting their brows, or simpering in an attempt to look helpful. Westmoreland gave them all a final, warning stare, and decided that he had asserted himself sufficiently to deserve a renewal of his slumbers.

"Most interesting," said one of Humphrey's henchmen. "It almost looks as if we had better postpone the matter for some time—unless your Highness has other views?"

Duke Humphrey did not speak for a moment. With Westmoreland's help he had scored a small but undeniable victory over the Beauforts. He could even afford to be generous, and, now that he need not do so, consent to a motion instructing someone to see if James's release were a possibility. He would like, other things being equal, to do a good turn to a friend. But other things were not equal. There might be something behind Beaufort's advocacy of the business, something that he could not afford to leave unthwarted. And then came the comforting thought that, though James might imagine he wanted to return to Scotland and play the king, James would be much happier in England, much happier in civilization. He would really be doing him a good turn by holding him back.

"No," he said, "I quite agree. Postpone altogether. And I think we had better adjourn now, until tomorrow—if my lord of Winchester will allow us."

The little bishop was staring hard at the table, mastering his anger. It almost made one doubt the wisdom of Providence that this sneering Gloucester should have the power, the hereditary right, to hamper the work of more earnest, more punctilious men, who had a greater stake in the country. But one must keep calm, under whatever provocation. One must consider and decide whether the matter under dispute was sufficiently important to justify a serious quarrel. Beaufort considered, and decided that it was not. He did not quite know why he had allowed that frivolous niece of his to laugh him into a half promise to do something for the young man who had tumbled on to their lawn at Woking. He must, by the way, find Joan a husband soon: she was growing up, and it was time she had a position, responsibilities, dignity. Meanwhile, there was Gloucester to be dealt with.

There was a pause while Beaufort swallowed twice, and recovered his self-possession.

"There are certainly more pressing questions," he said, "than that of the King of Scots. By all means let us postpone it. But I see no excuse for the proposed adjournment until today's *agenda* is finished. What is the next item, secretary?" It was important, he felt, after being worsted by the Protector on one point, to override his wishes on another.

"Letters from Calais," said the secretary, "from my lord of Warwick." He ran a jaded eye up and down his list: there were only two matters outstanding: supper was near—unless Beaufort and Humphrey found something else to jangle about.

"If Warwick's asking for more money," said Humphrey, "tell him we've none to send him. I suppose that is the trouble; it generally is, with captains of Calais."

"Yes, your Highness. Shall I draft a letter to that effect?"

"We can surely wait," suggested Beaufort, "and explain the position to him ourselves. He is coming to England this month."

"Yes, your lordship," said the secretary hurriedly, "and the only other item concerns a Parliament this autumn."

"That's settled," said Gloucester. "I shall call one in October."

"We are hoping," said Exeter solemnly, "that his Majesty will be able to open it in person again."

"In Dame Alice Butler's arms?" asked Humphrey maliciously. Exeter ignored him. "Her Majesty the Queen-Mother should be informed of the date," he said.

"Six months ahead, my lord?" queried the secretary.

"Certainly. Make a note of it."

"My lord of Exeter," said Humphrey, "is thinking of what happened last time."

"What?" asked Westmoreland, unexpectedly awaking. "What was that?"

"Surely you heard the story?"

"Heard? Heard what story? I never hear anything."

"The last opening of Parliament. His Majesty was to leave Windsor on the Saturday and take two days over the journey. They reached Kingston that night, but next day his Majesty refused to be moved—cried and wailed and fought till they had to give in and spend Sunday at Kingston. And next morning he came to London as quiet as a lamb. My lord of Exeter will tell you about it."

Exeter cleared his throat. "An awkward episode," he said. "I do not know what prompts your Highness to recall it. But it suggests, if I may say so, an additional reason for sanctioning the occasional—er—chastisement of his Majesty's person."

"You must not say so in Kingston," answered Humphrey. "The common people there take it as a sign that King Henry the Sixth is going to grow up into a saint. He refuses already to travel on a Sunday."

He rose with a laugh, dismissing the councillors till next day. Beaufort checked their dispersal for a moment. "It is unwise," he said severely, "to mock at the opinions of the common people. They know nothing of government, but in matters of Faith their voice has often proved to be the voice of God."

He returned to supper at Winchester House in a mood of tepid self-satisfaction. He had been thwarted, and even insulted, by the insufferable Gloucester; but he had kept his temper. He had also done his duty as a bishop by administering a small rebuke.

Having no guests, he dictated a letter to King James from table; enjoining secrecy, as between covert allies, he announced that he was pressing the matter of ransom on the Council and, in spite of unconscionable opposition, hoped for a speedy and successful issue. It was wise, he reflected, to keep up connections with anyone who might one day become a reigning monarch; it was a kindly action to feed a young man on hope; and the lie was no worse than the many shifty half-truths with which, in this wicked world, one was forced to build up one's position.

April 1423

II

James lay in bed, an open book at his elbow, and cursed the clangour of the chapel bell. He had had a poor night of it, with sleep endlessly eluding him. He had risen once or twice—though it was April, and chilly—to stand at the window and watch the ruddy twinkle of the stars: when he returned, he was no nearer his object; in the end, he had abandoned the pursuit and settled himself to read. As dawn broke, and he blew out his blanched candle in order to snatch the few hours of slumber that may compensate for a wakeful night, he was suddenly disturbed, and his last hopes scattered, by the hammering of this wretched bell. He cursed it again, longing for it to stop. When it did not, he picked up his book; but his eyes were already smarting from too long a strain, and he had to desist. There was nothing to do except lie and think.

It was Boethius that he had been reading again: he had need of philosophy. The wheel which had seemed to be lifting him, had now twisted down to its lowest compass. If Humphrey had been his friend, Humphrey was doing less for him than his enemy King Henry. If Queen Katharine had seemed a possible ally, she too was lost to him, if indeed she were not becoming a positive danger. She had certainly divined his bond with Joan, and acted in accordance with her nature: she had banished him from her company and, so far as was in her power, broken the intercourse between her unwanted cavalier and her waiting-woman. He had been sent away from London, taken, as in the old days, from one English castle to another, from gaol to hopeless gaol. As in the old days, envoys had come from Scotland to talk about his release. They had reported impending success, and then, as in the old days, returned home with nothing whatever accomplished. The wheel had come full circle.

It had, indeed, been mere folly to hope for anything from Scotland. In Scotland—to judge by the news that trickled through from unofficial friends and well-wishers—everything was going from bad to worse. Old Albany, an unjust steward, had purchased peace at the expense of his master's goods: he had placated trouble-makers, shrewdly and cautiously, by letting them nibble at the wealth and privileges of the crown. But under Murdoch, who had neither shrewdness nor caution, the nibbling became a wholesale banquet; the blackmail was mounting at compound interest, and with it, the greed and insolence of the blackmailers. They did not stop to ask by what right—save that of inertia—he had succeeded his father as regent; they only knew the succession profitable to themselves and hoped that it might prove permanent. Lawless themselves, they flattered and encouraged Murdoch's own sons into lawlessness, until he lived in perpetual dread of the morrow, wondering what crime he would be called on to condone. Such was the news that reached James in prison, and it boded ill for Scotland and for Scotland's chances of seeing her king again. It was certainly depressing matter for a young man to contemplate as he lay in bed on a cold spring morning and waited for the chapel bell to stop its tuneless stroke.

The sound was familiar—and irritating enough—at other times of the day; he had never heard it at dawn before. It must be some sort of feast-day, St. Mark's perhaps, and the chaplain had decided to be conscientious and hold an early Mass. Still, there had already been more than enough bell-ringing to please the Evangelist—if such a noise could please anyone. None of the garrison would come at such an hour, except perhaps that smug little toady who kept the postern and fed the chickens in the West Ward; he was sure to be pious. The rest would be in bed, cursing the bell as heartily as James.

He remembered the last time he had been reading Boethius and fancying himself a philosopher. Within a day he had been raving like a schoolboy, at the sight of a pretty girl, writing poetry, singing, behaving in a way that would have made the least stoical of philosophers smile with tolerant contempt. He had——. No, he was being unfair to himself. He must not blaspheme against that idyll of his youth. Joan was more to him than a pretty girl.

He must write to her again. He had smuggled quite a number of letters to her already, though none in poetry. She had answered, too, though she was no hand at expressing herself on paper. It was hard to picture her mischievous smile behind the formal phrases of her letters. She had hinted once at an attempt to help him by soliciting her uncle's influence. He had discouraged her in his reply; the code of love enjoined fastidiousness about using one's passion for worldly ends. For that matter, with Gloucester in power, a Beaufort connection might be a double-edged weapon, dangerous to the wielder; policy, as well as delicacy, suggested caution. James preferred to write letters to an ideal and unpolitical Joan.

One day, he might write poetry about her again: not directly about her, of course, and certainly not mentioning her name. The poetic lover, whatever his inspiration, wrapped all these things up in a web of allusion and allegory. His lady must be a rose or a dove or a milk-white fawn; he himself must be translated into some humble creature, watching her graceful movements and worshipping her perfection from afar. That was how poets did it, to courtly applause; that was how he had attempted to do it, seven years ago, in his garden room at Windsor. He must try again soon, if only to stop his mind wearing itself out in meaningless activity.

Clang, clang, clang. Would the bell never stop? He remembered suddenly that it was not the Evangelist who was being celebrated; it was St. George, the half-forgotten Cappadocian, whom King Henry had arbitrarily selected to be patron of an aggressive England. King Henry's shadow still lay dark upon the country: his favourite saint must still be remembered with special fervour: probably half the garrison was in chapel, worshipping St. George and King Henry. King Henry's captive would lie in bed and think about poetry.

The bell hastened its beat, as though drawing to a close. It seemed to be saying something, trying to convey some private message. He found himself forced to listen, to wonder sulkily what words were hidden in that harsh clanging. As he did so, they became suddenly clear. "Tell your story. Tell your story," said the bell.

He cursed himself for a fanciful fool. He must put a curb on his imaginings. He would turn over, wait till the racket had ceased, and then try to doze off a little. Since there was nothing for him to do, it was better to lie in bed and do nothing. The last stars were vanishing, the daylight would soon be dazzling to night-weary eyes. Sleep would mean forgetfulness, if nothing else, and there was an hour or two before he need get up.

"Tell your story. Tell your story," said the bell.

He cursed it again, gave up the struggle and heaved himself out of bed. Sloth, after all, was among the deadly sins, and might lead to others, to Wanhope and Despair. He would try and write, if only to stave off madness. He would rummage out the scraps he had written before—poor stuff, probably—and see if he could make anything of them. He might forget his own miseries by imagining the decorative sorrows of some fictitious poet, sighing for a lady of impossibly radiant charms. He opened a long-neglected box, and delved among forgotten letters and the useless petitions that Scotsmen had sent to their hobbled king.

"Tell your story," said the bell. "Tell your——" It

stopped suddenly, with a rattle of rope. He would be able to think now, possibly to write. But he was glad enough to have been tolled out of bed.

He had found the book he was looking for, a trifle musty, with *KING'S QUAIR* scribbled, half in derision, across its cover. There was matter inside, he discovered, of which he had no reason to be ashamed, much to entertain him, a little to admire. The theme was as apt as ever, for he had made his imaginary lover a chained captive, complaining against his lot.

The birds, the beasts, the fishes of the sea,
They live in freedom, each one in his kind,
Yet am I man, and I lack liberty——

He liked, too, the song that the birds were made to sing, announcing to lovers the Kalends of their bliss, and the stanza about the river which flowed beside the palace of Venus, full of the blue-backed fishes with red coral fins. He smiled at himself: he had forgotten how interested he had been in birds and beasts at that time, the *warlike porcupine* and

The little squirrel, full of busy-ness.

He would give Venus a whole menagerie this time. He remembered being taken to see the Royal Bestiary at Woodstock, the caged lions and bears, and the ruins of a huge building, too large for any reasonable creature, in which Henry III had once kept the gem of his collection. 'I'll give her an elephant,' he thought, laughing. 'Why shouldn't Venus have an elephant?'

Seriously, some of the lines were better than he had imagined.

Beauty enough to make a world to dote

still had power to thrill him. He liked, too,

O thou that art my succour, my sweet well
Of remedy, for anxious hearts the cure;
And, when the huge and weltering billows tell
How passions rage, a haven quiet and sure.

The thing was worth finishing and he would finish it. It

lacked shape, and he would have to recast it. He must fit what was good into some comprehensive framework—if only he could think of one. Thinking was not easy, on a cold, depressing morning, with the echo of that wretched bell in one's ears. Thank God, it had stopped at last. He would have forgotten it soon and could write in some more flowing rhythm. "Tell your story. Tell your story." What a silly chant!

And yet—was it so silly? Why should he not accept the advice, and build his verses up round an account of his own experiences? Why, after all, must he follow the fashionable herd, laming good verses by fathering them on gingerbread abstractions? If he wrote his own life into Rhyme Royal, the result might not be what the world recognized as Poetry, but the world's judgment had been known to err. If it was not a method of writing that appealed to some love-poets he had heard of, his aim and inspiration was very different from theirs. One knew the breed—even at King Henry's court—unattached, rather sickly youths who selected other men's wives, preferably rich men's, and used them in order to work up fictitious passions that only became real by being written about, thought over, fostered like hot-house plants. Their only reward, and they knew it, was simple adultery. They might veil the ugly word, but it was the praises of adultery that they sang: love, they preached, was something above and beyond the cramping rules of ordinary life. They were, it seemed, sincere believers in this curious doctrine, contriving to overlook the slime in their own hearts in which its roots were embedded: that they converted their admirers only proved the devil's maxim, *Mundus vult decipi*, The world likes to be deceived. If James were to tell these gentlemen that he was planning a poem to a lady whom, God willing, he desired to marry, they would lift polite and melancholy eyebrows, banishing him from the circle of the elect.

He could accept the sentence calmly. So, though for different reasons, they would have banished Chaucer, if the force of genius had not compelled them to make an exception to their silly rules. He could hardly hope to make another, but he could at least do what nature and originality prompted: he could sit down and write, disdaining allegory, the true story of his life. He could describe his imprisonment and his despairs, even the sea-voyage and capture from which they proceeded; it should be the birds in the garden at Windsor who sang his song—not imaginary denizens of some mystic aviary; and she who walked beneath their song, with a little dog prancing before her, should be Joan, the real Joan (with only her name concealed), the woman he had hoped and was still hoping to make his wife. He would omit his experiences in France, for war as King Henry waged it was hardly a business for a poet's pen. For all else he could find a place, for his secret thoughts, the books that had helped him—Boethius as well as Chaucer—for this restless night of stars and harassed dawn. It would take time, more time than aping his predecessors in their hackneyed postures. But time was the one commodity that he had been granted, in full measure and overflowing, to James of Scotland, the captive, the poet and the king. He took up his pen.

A few yards away, though hidden behind massive walls, a yawning bellringer mumbled his responses to the Mass. He did not know that anything had happened: that posterity would still be reading about his bell five centuries after it had rusted away; that he himself, by a certain twist of the tired forearm, had contributed, in humble fashion, to a considerable revolution in the history of European literature.

April 1423

III

The castle of Doune, recently erected, barely completed yet, looked eastward towards Stirling and the Forth, but west and north at the savage mountains of Menteith. The evening sun, low over the peaks, streamed into a small room, untidy, though expensively appointed, littered with fishing-nets and rods, bird-bolts, hawks' bells, and hunting-tackle. Round the one clear table in the centre, three men sat discussing the future of Scotland, and with it the future of the world.

It was not a kindly chance that had put so great a responsibility upon their shoulders; for none of the three was altogether honest and only one could be called intelligent.

Perhaps Lennox, of the three, approached nearest to honesty, but age, circumstance, and an innate weakness forbade him to make it effective. He had been an oldish man when he visited James at Evesham, and fourteen years had passed over him since that journey. His grey hairs were white now, his forehead was a wilderness of wrinkles. His mind, never very active, was increasingly concentrated on the business of his own estates, increasingly unable to grapple with anything beyond their boundaries. His lands lay westward, almost within sight, between Murdoch's new castle and the mountains: Lennox had only a few miles to ride in order to join these unofficial councils, which were also family gatherings. For Murdoch had married Lennox's daughter, and neither of the two made any distinction in their minds between politics and family matters. It was pleasant for Lennox to have his son-in-law as Regent of Scotland, pleasant to be asked for assistance and advice on affairs of the kingdom. He always gave the same kind of advice; his great desire was to avoid trouble, to see things go smoothly. Since he had turned seventy, he had begun to hope that they would also go smoothly in the next world. But with old age upon him, and death within striking distance, he clung to one worldly vanity. He had always been tall and stalwart: occasional glances at a mirror, and the impression he made on others, assured him that he was a handsome, a really fine-looking old man.

Time had also dealt charitably with his son-in-law.

Murdoch Stewart, Earl of Fife and Duke of Albany, was twenty years younger than Lennox, but his beard was already splashed with grey. He was rather taller, and far more massive. If his eyes were dull and puzzled, they peered out from under a fine broad brow. He was less conscious of good looks, and far less occupied with thoughts of another world: he had hardly grasped, except as a formula, how such a place could exist. Life was sufficiently complicated on this earth, and the satisfaction of worldly desires, however limited, was quite difficult enough, without indulging in ambitions beyond. He, too, wanted peace and quiet before everything, and was puzzled because they so obstinately eluded him.

He had, one would say, all that a man could desire. He was master of vast estates, scattered across the Lowlands: Doune was only one among his many castles, and, for that matter, all the royal strongholds were his, the royal lands and revenues. Even the vague hope towards which his father had worked, the crown of Scotland itself, might one day fall into his lap; for Rothesay was dead, and James an exile, and the house of Albany was their heir. Meanwhile, Murdoch was king in all but name, and, to the outward eye, secure in possession. There was no foreign danger, and no sign of Scotland rising against his mild and muddled rule. It was difficult to see, at first sight, why Murdoch was troubled, miserable even, to the point of despair.

The truth was simple enough. He knew—though he tried to shut his eyes to the knowledge—that for some years he had been sliding down a slope, imperceptibly at first, but lately with increasing rapidity, which must bring him one day to a violent and catastrophic fall. He was beginning to discover that the day was less distant than he had accustomed himself to hope.

He had started his regency by being as friendly as possible with all the great landowners, the powerful families who had permitted him to step quietly into his father's shoes. He had granted them every reasonable request, and, when they trespassed beyond the bounds of reason, had stretched point after point to placate them. So it had gone on for three years, and now their petitions had begun to sound uncomfortably like demands. Nothing seemed to satisfy them, though they grew yearly richer, while crown revenues dwindled and the customs yielded less and less. There was no question of governing them: strange stories reached Murdoch, suggesting that their insolence stretched downward as well as upward, that the common people were suffering as much as the crown from the rapacity of the rich. What happened in the Highlands was hardly his business, for the clans preferred the despotism of their own chiefs to any interference from king or regent: but there was a faint stir in Murdoch's conscience at the tales of oppression among Lowland farmers and townsmen who looked to the crown, not unreasonably, for protection from the great. He could have stifled such discomfort, he could have continued to wink helplessly at the doings of his tormentors, but for a new trouble, the most persistent and nagging of all. His own sons had joined the general conspiracy to thwart and flout him. They obeyed neither regent nor father: they listened impatiently to his admonitions and threats, and then redoubled instead of curbing their misdemeanours. And Murdoch could find no resource, either in his position or himself, for bringing them to heel.

It was not the first time that he had summoned his two relatives to Doune, in the faint hope of gleaning some suggestion of a remedy. He knew, at bottom, that it was futile, and all the more so since he jibbed at confessing the disease. He could only talk generalities, skirt round unpleasant facts, and moan about the difficulty of governing Scotland. This time he had gone so far as to ask them whether he ought to make more exertions for the restoration of King James. What he could not bring himself to discuss with them, what he foolishly told himself they might not know, was the plain fact that he was no longer master in his own house.

It might be possible to deceive old Lennox. Lennox was always ready to ignore anything that was unpleasant to remember. But his folly was contemptible indeed if he imagined he could cheat Athol, the third man who sat with them in the little room at Doune.

Athol was Murdoch's uncle—half-brother to old Albany and to that King Robert who had heard of James's capture and immediately departed, in Dundonald Castle, from a harsh and harassing world. Athol resembled neither. He had none of the family bent for growing old gracefully. He was sixty-five, his skin was blotched and yellow, and he was as bald as an egg. The evening sun, streaming in by a narrow window, shone with pitiless clarity on his pouched and blood-shot eyes, the thin scarlet thread of his lips. But his pointed gaze, the restless mobility of every feature, suggested such intelligence and ability as made his two kinsmen look like a couple of pompous fools.

It was so, indeed, that he regarded them, thinking only how best to soothe and augment their folly. Athol had a great reputation for wisdom, and could give cleverer advice than any man in Scotland. But some who had taken it said long afterwards—if they were still alive—that it was Athol, and not they, that had benefited by its cleverness.

"I cannot see what vexes you," he was saying. "By all we can hear, the lad's well enough cared for in England. And it's as clear as day that the English have no mind to let him loose unless we pay them more silver than we could raise in brass. For that matter, it's more than doubtful if Scotland wants him back, whatever the price. He's been twenty years away and he'll have forgotten our ways altogether."

"Seventeen years," corrected Lennox.

"Seventeen, then. It's more than enough to make an Englishman of him. And from what I remember of him, he was not a bairn that'd grow up into the kind of king we're wanting, any more than young Rothesay."

"Oh, but Jamie," said Lennox deprecatingly, "Jamie is

a very different lad from his brother. I saw him in England, ye'll remember, when I and the bishop went on embassy." He looked at his hands, wrinkled but shapely still, and gave a little chuckle. His brain was slowly focussing backwards. "I mind me," he said, "that he fell off his horse. He sat up all over mud."

"Ah," said Athol, flickering an eye towards Murdoch. "That'll be a sign to us. How long will he stay in the saddle when he has all Scotland to ride?"

Murdoch sat silent but his eyes turned towards Lennox, as though enquiring whether Athol's argument were a sound one.

"Will you tell me this?" pursued Athol. "Do you think the people here will be wanting a king that's more than half an Englishman?"

"No, no!" said Lennox, in a shocked voice. "No, they'll not want that."

"Well, then——!" Athol shrugged thickly-plaided shoulders. He wore the heaviest clothing, even in summer: his little ferret's eyes seemed to peer out of a mass of woven wool.

"I was only thinking . . ." began Lennox, and then petered out. He was waiting to agree with the general opinion, once he knew what it was going to be.

"They ransomed me," said Murdoch, pursuing his own line of thought. "They let me go in the end."

"They did not," contradicted Athol. "There was no question of ransom. They exchanged you for Northumberland. They wanted their Percy back."

"We have no one we could exchange for Jamie," agreed Lennox. "And maybe Athol is right about Scotland not wanting him home. It'd make a big change, going back to one of Robert's branch."

"The English might be glad to ransom him," said Murdoch obstinately, "now that King Henry is dead."

"They'd be glad of our money," said Athol, with a touch of impatience. "That's the way with the English. But I cannot tell where you'll find the silver to pay them. I shall not beggar myself for the pleasure of having Jamie home."

"I've heard," said Murdoch, "that they'd be willing to take hostages, and let him come back to raise his own ransom."

"It'll mean our paying in the end."

"It seems a pity," echoed Lennox. "All's well as it is. If it's a hard life for Jamie, that's their fault, not ours."

Athol tried a new line of attack. "For all we know," he said, "it'd be better for the lad if we leave him where he is. The people here will have heard that he fought on the wrong side in France. They'll not like that. Did you know he signed a paper, trying to get the Douglas to join King Henry against the French?"

"That's true," said Lennox. "That'll count against him."

"It's likely," added Athol, "that he'd try and send us all to fight the Englishmen's battles for them. And hang the Scots who serve in the Dauphin's armies. That's what he and King Henry did in France."

"Ay," said Lennox. "There's a danger of that."

Athol paused. He felt that he was winning, but Murdoch still sat silent and unresponsive. He racked his brain for new arguments.

"There's another danger," he said, "that nobody's talked of yet. If you do have him home, it's as like as not that he'll begin by having the heads off the pair of ye."

"No, no!" said Lennox, considerably startled. "Surely he'd not do that?"

"There's no telling what he'd do. A king is a sore curse to a country—and worst of all to those of us that have land or money."

"But he could not," objected Lennox. "On what charge?"

"Usurpation," suggested Athol. "Or leaving him in prison so long. He could make that treason. He would not mind what the charge was, so long as your land was forfeit."

Murdoch seemed roused at last. His heavy eyes were searching his uncle's face, helplessly trying to gauge his nature. "And you think," he asked, "that we have cause to be feared of that?"

"I do," said Athol. "And, what's more, I'd say you deserved it, if you were such a brace of fools as to bring him home."

Murdoch rose from his seat and walked behind Lennox to the window. In that little room his height seemed overwhelming, like that of some primeval giant. He lumbered into stillness and stood gazing towards the mountains.

Silence fell. Lennox was slowly twisting the heavy gold ring on his finger, waiting for his son-in-law's decision. It was getting late, and he wanted to ride home.

A bee hummed past Murdoch at the window, and so into the room. It hovered a moment above Athol's bald crown and then, flying on to the painted hangings of the wall, began to walk up them, grumbling in quiet indignation.

Athol did not move. He seemed to be gazing at Murdoch's back, but with eyes veiled and thoughts roaming. He had said, he felt, all that was necessary to gain his present point, but it was always as well to estimate other chances, make plans to meet a dozen contingencies.

All should be well if Murdoch accepted his advice and attempted to carry on the present farce of regency. The end was certain, and should be fairly swift. In three years, in five at most, Murdoch's weakness, his sons' insolence, or some new turn from outside, was certain to provoke a crisis and sweep the whole pack of them to destruction. That would leave Athol himself, with his sons and grandson, the next heirs to the throne. Athol did not consciously hanker to be king. He told himself that he was shrewd enough to reject that saddest of illusions. But intrigue must have some goal, some ultimate objective; and life, for Athol, was unthinkable without intrigue.

Murdoch shifted position, kicking away the litter at his

feet. "I'm hunting tomorrow," he said, without turning back from the window. "They say they're plagued with wolves between Crieff and Ben Vorlich. Will either of you sleep the night and come out with me and Walter in the morning?"

Walter was the eldest, and most troublesome, of Murdoch's three sons.

"I'm past it," answered Lennox. "Too old. I stay at home, these days, when it's wolves they're after. I'll be riding home, unless there's more to say. Athol will hunt with you." He rose from table and walked to the door.

"Not this time," said Athol. "I am needed at Methven the morn's morn. I could ride over another day, if I'm not a burden to you—maybe when you're hawking. I'm better with the birds."

"Will you not stay for a sup?" said Murdoch to his father-in-law.

"I'd sooner have it at home," said Lennox, "if you'll excuse me. I'll be telling them to get ready now." He nodded to Athol and passed out of the room.

Murdoch had not moved from the window. He was still staring towards the sun and the distant haze of mountains. Below him, just beyond the moat, a couple of rabbits lolloped out of the bushes, casting long shadows down the slope. With so much that needed thinking out, he had to break off and watch their progress.

"Talking of hawks," said Athol suddenly, "has Walter begged that falcon from you yet? He seemed set on it, last time I came to Doune."

Murdoch swung round with unexpected and unexplained suddenness. "He has not," he said violently. "And he never will! Never!"

Athol could not suppress a quick smile, but immediately composed himself into sympathetic gravity. "You're fond of her?" he asked.

"She's the best bird they've trained for me yet," muttered Murdoch, "and Walter'll not have her till I'm dead."

"Maybe that's why Walter wants her. There's some lads that are only content with the best."

"That's why he'll never have her!" announced Murdoch. Athol thought it best to take no notice of his nephew's vehemence. He stood up, hitching the thick plaid on his shoulders. "Well, well," he said, "I'll be following Lord Lennox to the horses. I shall sleep at Dunblane the night."

"Ay, ay," said Murdoch. "I'll see the pair of you in the courtyard before you go. They'll bring you a sup of wine."

"It'd be welcome!" said Athol with a jocosity that stirred his nephew to dull irritation. He turned to go.

"And you think," asked Murdoch, "that we'd do best to leave things as they are?"

"I do," said Athol from the doorway. "I'm very sure they'd be no better for trying to fetch Jamie home."

A moment later, Murdoch was alone.

He was no nearer a remedy for his troubles. He had been a fool to expect his kinsmen to suggest one. He had asked them the same questions before and received the same answer. Maybe it was the right one: Athol, everyone agreed, had the best brain in Scotland. He had suggested a new and clinching reason for keeping King James at a distance. Murdoch was afraid of his sons, of his own incompetence, of the impending catastrophe of open shame: but, like most men, he was still more afraid of violent death.

Perhaps, on the whole, thought Duke Murdoch, it was better to leave things as they were.

May 1423

IV

"Joan! That is not a proper way for a young girl to talk. Anyone would think that you were the head of the family. I was only wondering the other day, when we said the Mass for your poor father, what he would have said about the way his children have grown up."

Lady Clarence never found it easy to be angry, and it was only a sense of duty that made her try. She had lost two husbands, and was not contemplating a third. If her children were ever to be kept in control, she felt that she must develop a temper of her own.

Joan, more genuinely angry, was struggling with the opposite difficulty—the necessity, for caution's sake, of concealing her temper. She was not very successful. "Well, all I can do, mother," she replied, "is to quote the real head of the family. John was furious when I told him what uncle was suggesting. He says it's dis . . . disparagement."

"My lord the Bishop's suggestions," said Lady Clarence with some pomp, "are a great deal more sensible than your brother's opinions. I am sure there is nothing disparaging in a Beaufort marrying into such a family."

"Well, John thinks there is. He says we are Blood Royal." Joan bent over her work. It was pouring with rain outside, and she sat spinning thread while her mother embroidered a new table-cover. She was on leave from Queen Katharine's household, and had come to the family manor at Orwell—partly because Bishop Beaufort was paying a short visit.

"I dare say we are," grumbled Lady Clarence, "but there are plenty of King Edward's descendants that have made worse matches. Who do you want to marry—the Pope?"

"Which Pope? I can hardly marry all three."

"Joan!! You must not be so blasphemous. You know there was never more than one. The others were just anti-Popes, and, any way, they've been made to resign now."

"I'm sorry, mother."

"So you ought to be. And you ought to be ashamed of yourself, too, for not welcoming your uncle's suggestion at once. If you are too selfish and undutiful to think of the family's interests, you might remember that time is getting on and that good husbands don't grow on gooseberry-bushes. You're twenty-four, you know."

"John thinks we can do better."

"I have no doubt he does! I expect he thinks himself cleverer than your uncle at managing the family affairs. And since when have you begun to take sides with your brother? John this, and John that! You're quick enough to disobey him when it's something you don't fancy."

"Well, mother, when it's a question of marriage, one cannot help having ideas of one's own."

"Ideas!" said Lady Clarence, dropping her hands to her lap. "And what business has a child of your age with ideas? Do you know where you and your brother would be if I'd had ideas of my own when I was young? Believe me or not, you'd never have been born."

"I can easily believe that."

"There you are then! But in those days, children had to do what their parents told them. And I'm sure the world was all the better for it." Lady Clarence resumed her needlework, but her tongue was well under way. "I wish I knew what was coming over young girls," she said. "They seem to think of nothing but pleasure, and late supper-parties, and compliments from young men . . . yes, and those ridiculous high head-dresses that they're beginning to wear now—even girls in their 'teens. When I was young, we used to spend our time spinning and weaving and making ourselves useful."

"You've just reminded me, mother," said Joan quietly, "that I am no longer in my 'teens. And I *am* spinning." She made the wheel revolve with added vigour. At any moment, she felt, her mother would have worked herself up to the familiar crisis, her anger would dissolve, and nothing would be left but the irritating, lovable weakness beneath. Joan hated these exposures.

"I expect," said Lady Clarence, ignoring the repartee, "I expect the truth is that you've taken a fancy to some other young man. I suppose he's Blood Royal, as you call it—and over the left-hand side, as like as not. And not an acre or a penny to bless himself with, I'll be bound."

Joan left her wheel and walked across to the window. The courtyard outside was deserted. The summer rain leapt and danced upon the flagstones, or agitated the silver pools which were forming wherever the paviours had left a depression.

"But of course," said Lady Clarence to her daughter's back, "of course you would never think of telling your own mother about it. That's the last thing you'd think of doing." The wheedling note had begun to creep into her voice. When there was no response, she changed tack.

"The mistake you make," she observed, "is reading too much. It's not healthy in a young girl. There are far too many books in the world, without your wanting to read them."

Joan, watching the courtyard below, saw a figure emerge from the doorway opposite and begin hopping towards her, head lowered, between the puddles. Her brother must have finished his long consultation with the bishop. "There's John," she said. "It looks as if he is coming up here."

"Of course," continued Lady Clarence, "I am not talking of religious books or even histories. I mean poetry and romances and so on. I used to read them, too, and I can't say I've ever had any good from them. They just made me think things were quite different, and much prettier than they really are, and you have to pay for any pleasure you get from them in disappointments afterwards. I sometimes think things were better in the old, old days when no one was taught to read except the priests. I'm sure it would save us all a great deal of unhappiness."

There was a loud clatter on the stair. Joan had barely reached her seat again before her brother entered.

Somerset was twenty now, and looked considerably older. He had seen his step-father Clarence killed at Baugé, been held prisoner himself and reduced to suing to a Scotsman for ransom; but his experiences seemed to have increased rather than softened his arrogance.

He gave the ladies a sulky glance and walked straight to the empty fireplace.

"Oh, is that you, John?" said Lady Clarence. "Have you been with your uncle?"

"Yes, he'll be coming up in a minute. We wanted to talk to you two."

Joan scented danger. There was an uneasiness in her brother's manner that she did not understand. "I hope you persuaded him," she said, as lightly as possible. "I mean about the disparagement."

"Yes, yes," said Somerset. "There's no question of that affair now. It's something else."

Joan felt as if a weight had been suddenly lifted from her mind—to be replaced by a new, and possibly a heavier, one. But she would know more in a minute; she must be patient. Lady Clarence was looking up enquiringly, about to express surprise. Somerset cut her short.

"Why haven't they lighted the fire?" he asked sharply. "It's cold in here. I mean, uncle's coming up and he'd have liked a fire."

"I am sorry," said his mother. "I thought it was so much warmer today. But Joan shall go and tell them to light it. Joan!"

"No, no, no! It doesn't matter now. Do sit still, Joan. You two are always fussing about something." He stood leaning against the fireplace, kicking petulantly at a harmless stool.

"I do hope," said Lady Clarence, "that you have not been disrespectful to your uncle."

"What on earth do you mean, mother? Of course I haven't." Somerset gave the stool a last kick so that it slid out of reach. "As a matter of fact," he said uncomfortably, "I'm beginning to see uncle's point of view. I mean—about getting Joan married. After all, she's no chicken."

Lady Clarence glanced at Joan. "Just what I was telling

her," she said. "But I don't understand; you said just now that there was no question of the match."

"No. That's right. Uncle has a new scheme—since he wrote you that letter. A much better one. He'll tell you when he comes. As he says, it's a magnificent opportunity for us." There was a curious lack of conviction in his tone. Joan knew her brother well enough to guess why he was so lukewarm: the opportunity, whatever it was, was not of his own devising: she only wished she knew better how to take advantage of his dislike for all that originated with others.

"I hope," said Lady Clarence, with a half-hearted attempt at sarcasm, "that it's an alliance with the Blood Royal this time."

Somerset gave her a savage look, stepped away, and hooked the stool towards him. He sat down before speaking. "There's every other advantage," he said, staring between his knees at the floor. "Every possible one. I'd tell you now, before uncle arrives, only I don't want Joan to get obstinate about it."

"You said something yesterday," said Joan, keeping as even a voice as she could manage, "about consulting me before you arranged anything."

Somerset sprang to his feet. "There you are!" he blustered. "You're making your mind up against it before you've even heard his name! You women are the very devil. I tell you one thing, my girl, I'm not going to have an old maid in our family!"

"No indeed!" echoed his mother. "Unless Joan wants to take vows?"

"Take vows?" exclaimed Somerset. "Don't talk nonsense, mother. We haven't the money to put her into the right sort of convent, I mean anywhere that'd give her a chance to get on and make a proper position for herself. That's why I'm agreeing to uncle's scheme. He says it'd be such a good thing for the whole family that he wouldn't mind paying most of the dowry himself. I can't see how else we can manage, with all those mortgages on us, and half my ransom-money still owing. If we don't get uncle's help, we shall have to sell Orwell to marry her properly."

"Not Orwell," wailed Lady Clarence.

"That's what it'd come to. Unless you want us all in the clutches of some damned Lombard."

"But, John dear——" began his mother. Joan cut into her protest. "Would you mind telling me," she asked desperately, "who exactly is being paid to marry me?"

"You'll know soon enough!" Somerset turned angrily upon her. "And I'll thank you not to use that kind of talk when uncle comes up."

"I want to know now," said Joan, rising to face him. "And I want to know what it is that has made you knuckle under like this to uncle's suggestions for my disposal."

The shot went home. She was afraid, for a moment, that it could provoke nothing but a new blaze of anger. But she had found the chink in her brother's armour. "How dare you——?" he began, and then suddenly sat down on his stool. Joan, resuming her own seat, was suddenly reminded of a little boy whose ears she had boxed for tormenting her favourite puppy.

"I mean," he said, speciously reasonable, "that is—I wouldn't let uncle, or anyone else, dictate to me, if I didn't think it was for everyone's good—yours included. I don't know why you're getting into such a way about it, before you even know who it is. It is a wonderful chance for you, really."

"Well, why not tell us?" asked Lady Clarence, a little cowed by her own children's vehemence. "It's foolish to quarrel when one of you doesn't know what she's quarrelling about."

"Uncle told him not to say," put in Joan, following up her advantage.

Somerset managed to ignore her. "As a matter of fact, mother," he said, "it was someone I'd thought of myself. But uncle met him at Council the other day, when he came back from Calais. It's the Earl of Warwick."

Lady Clarence's embroidery slipped unheeded to the floor. "Joan!" she said, in a kind of incredulous ecstasy.

"Oh, come, come, mother," said Somerset impatiently, but she could only murmur "Countess of Warwick," and looked at Joan with eyes of amazement.

"Of course," conceded Somerset, "he has a big position. And he has as much land as anyone in England. Still, it will be quite a step up for him, marrying into a royal family."

"And your uncle will pay the dowry?"

"Most of it. He seems to think Warwick's a coming man, worth winning for his side on Council. I agree. We thought a good deal of Warwick in France."

Joan's spinning-wheel had begun to revolve again, in a listless, preoccupied fashion. Her mother watched her, puzzled and a little disturbed. Then she turned to Somerset. "How old is he?" she asked.

"I don't know. Forty, I suppose. And, by the way, Joan, they say he was a particularly good husband to his first wife."

"She was a Berkeley, wasn't she?"

"Yes. Brought him precious little land—and only gave him daughters. So he'd no reason to be especially kind to her. I expect he'll want an heir now."

"I expect our Joan can manage that." Lady Clarence giggled a little, and she wished she had not spoken.

"I'm only doubtful," went on Somerset, "if uncle's right in thinking it'll be such a good thing, politically. Things are in such a foul muddle since the king died."

"I never understand politics," said Lady Clarence complacently. "I've always left them to my men." She looked round as if for applause. But Joan's eyes were averted, the spinning-wheel was beginning to hum again. "But I feel sure, John," added her mother, "that you'd be wise to trust your uncle. He must hear about everything, on the Council."

"Yes," said Somerset, glad of the normal atmosphere that

seemed to be returning. "And I've just been telling him that it's time I had a seat there. After all, we're the next heirs to the crown, after York and the king's uncles. And he needs all the backing he can get against Duke Humphrey."

"The duke's going abroad, isn't he?"

"Yes. That precious wife of his is taking him to the Netherlands. It'll make things easier for us—especially if she gets him into a mess there—as everyone expects."

The door curtains parted. A tall, absurdly thin servant, dressed in the bishop's livery, peered into the room. Small eyes like a weasel's surveyed the family group.

"Here's your uncle coming," said Lady Clarence. "Joan! You must learn to get up *before* his lordship comes into a room?"

"Please, please! No ceremony for me." Bishop Beaufort looked damp but benignant. He was hoping that there would be no need for anything except benignancy. He had had, on the whole, a successful interview with his nephew, getting his own way with less than the usual friction. Young Somerset was not easy to deal with; in the more secret recesses of his mind Beaufort was afraid of his nephew, and it needed all his advantages of age, wealth and position to disguise and counterbalance that fear. He was correspondingly pleased when he had succeeded in imposing upon him.

"Do not let me disturb your labours," he said, beaming at the ladies. "It is quite edifying, these days, to see such industry. I can congratulate myself on possessing a young niece who does not follow the modern fashion for idleness and—er—worse things." He settled into a chair. He was happier sitting. He felt that it made his small stature less noticeable, hoped, even, that it made him look impressive.

"Shall I tell them to light the fire?" ventured his sister-in-law.

"No, no. Not for me," said the bishop. "I was much too hot in that other room—quite glad to escape into the rain." Lady Clarence could not help glancing at her son. But Somerset's eyes were fixed on the bishop's attendant who stood there, surveying the family from cadaverous eyes. "Get out!" he barked sharply, and the man vanished through the door-curtains. Beaufort smiled indulgently to himself. By bullying the servant, Somerset only acknowledged that the master had had the better of him.

"I trust," said Lady Clarence hurriedly, "that your lordship is enjoying his visit to us—in spite of the weather. It was very good of you to come. I know how busy your lordship must be."

"Cares of State, cares of State," said the bishop, waving a patronizing hand. "I often catch myself wishing that I could have remained a simple priest, with no anxieties outside a country parish. But I certainly do not regret my visit . . . in spite of the weather." He smiled, mopping his wet forehead. "And we must not grumble at a little rain. The pastures benefit, and we must not set our private convenience above the flocks and herds of the poor."

"Your lordship," said Somerset maliciously, "will reap some of the benefit in profits on wool."

The bishop frowned majestically. "My little ventures in wool," he said, "bring me in no profit worth the name, whatever the seasons. I would discontinue them tomorrow if I was not frequently assured that they help the general trade of the kingdom." He ignored Somerset's grimace and looked round with a kind of nervous sanctimony. His eye fell, with relief, on Joan's bent head. "Well, my dear," he asked, "have you heard that we've settled something for you at last?"

"Oh, come, uncle," interposed Somerset. "It's hardly settled yet."

Beaufort's jaw suddenly protruded, if only by a fraction of an inch. He did not turn towards his nephew but stared straight before him at the window. "I do not know," he said, "what obstacles there are to a settlement."

"I hope there can be none," said Lady Clarence.

"None on our side, I trust. And I believe that my lord of Warwick—yes, it is he whom I have in mind—is positively eager to re-marry. I gather that is one of his objects in returning from Calais so frequently. And from the short discussion I had with him, I am sure that my suggestion was more than welcome. It will be quite a love-match. If I were to tell you——" He checked himself and fell silent. There was a point at which pardonable exaggeration became barely pardonable.

"I only meant," said Somerset, with dogged weakness, "that I'd rather it wasn't spoken of yet as quite settled. There's a lot to be thrashed out yet, and it's a mistake to let oneself be rushed into things."

"My dear nephew, I have no intention of letting myself be rushed into anything. I am accustomed to making rapid decisions. I seldom regret them. In this matter, there appears to be no reason for delay—unless you intend to go back on what you said and make trouble."

"No, but——"

"I should hope not. You must realise, my dear nephew, that men who do not know their own minds are not the kind we want on his Majesty's Council."

Joan looked up. The threat was clear enough—and the bargain that had preceded it—though Beaufort still preferred to avoid her brother's eyes. She had only to look at Somerset to realize the certainty of his surrender.

"Of course," he was saying, "if you put it like that. . . . And I suppose it is only details that we've still to discuss."

"Then we *can* take it as settled!" said Lady Clarence. "And the sooner it's announced the better."

"Oh come, mother!" protested Somerset, "there's no hurry about that."

"Well, as your uncle says, there's no reason for delay. We might even have the ceremony this autumn. Joan and I could get everything ready in a month or two, if need be. Why, Joan, where are you going?"

Joan had risen. She was half-way to the door. She stood there, her voice dry in her throat, conscious of all eyes fixed on her. "Where are you going, Joan?" repeated her mother.

"I think," said Joan, after a moment's struggle, "I think I must ask his lordship to excuse me. . . . And I agree with John. I think it would be best to leave the announcement as late as possible." She hesitated, and finished her journey to the door before speaking again. "So many things might happen," she said, made an awkward curtsey, and was gone.

Her mother had risen. She began to follow, but came to a stop as the tapestries of the door swung back into their folds. Something inarticulate, something long-forgotten, was stirring in her heart. Two marriages, the child-births that the first had entailed, a lifetime of impulses crushed behind the dutiful or courtly smile—all this had tamed and shaped Lady Clarence until she fitted unimpeachably into her curious world. But the taming was, it seemed, just lacking in the last completeness.

Neither of the men could see the mother's face, nor guess that it was puzzled and vaguely unhappy. They were thinking of the daughter's abrupt departure.

"She's a queer girl," said Somerset. "It's more than time we married her. I shan't be sorry, for one thing, when she sees the last of that Frenchwoman's Court."

"I see nothing unusual," observed the bishop. "A very natural modesty. We must not forget that girls have their private feelings—into which it may be sacrilegious to peer. Marriage is the one great crisis in a woman's life, and I consider my niece's attitude most becoming—most becoming." He smoothed the robe across his knees and began to inspect his short squat fingers, spreading them fanwise in the air. "I congratulate you, my dear sister-in-law," he said, "on your good fortune in possessing such a daughter. She does you credit."

"Yes," said Lady Clarence, as though half her attention was elsewhere. "I suppose I have been fortunate. All my life." She stood motionless, her eyes still on the door.

"Are you going back to Westminster tomorrow?" asked Somerset. He felt uneasy in the atmosphere of platitude that his uncle exuded.

"Yes, indeed," answered Beaufort. "Council meets again on Friday. There's so much to be done these days, so much to be done."

"And one's fined for non-attendance, isn't one?"

"Fined?" said the Bishop, waking up in irritation. "Certainly not! We arranged that our salaries as councillors should depend on the number of meetings we could attend. That is as it should be, I think. But if I manage to find you a seat—as I may—I hope you will come regularly from a sense of duty, not from a love of the emoluments." He began to get up. It seemed as if nothing could happen to him that had not its ingredient of annoyance.

"I think," said Lady Clarence, in a distant voice, "that I will beg your lordship's pardon. I was wanting to speak to Joan."

"By all means," said the bishop. "Most natural. And pray convey to her my blessing. Great things await her." But when he looked up to give his sister-in-law the appropriate smile, he found that she had already vanished.

May 1423

V

If fortune failed him this time, James swore that he would never trust her and never hope again. He sat in the Tower, reading Queen Katharine's letter, and decided that its arrival, coming on top of so much else, was the best omen he had had for years.

Beaufort had written, months ago, promising support. That might have meant little, had not Joan's letters, too, grown more hopeful in tone. He had thought at the time that she was merely trying to comfort him: but now, for some weeks she had not written at all, and he took that to mean that things were coming to a crisis, and she could not risk endangering them by correspondence. Merton had gone to Scotland and it was more than probable that James's friends, encouraged by his emissary, were forming a party to force Murdoch into action. And now Queen Katharine had written, inviting him to come out to her at Hertford and dine with Duke Humphrey and an army of distinguished guests.

He knew the woman for what she was. At their last meeting she had made it clear that he was personally distasteful, that she wanted to see him huddled away out of her sight. She had once allowed him sufficient intimacy to enable him to guess her secret and Tudor's, and he had paid court to her waiting-woman. The double offence was unpardonable. If she was inviting him to her feast now, it could only mean that she had discovered that he was about to be released, fêted, and lionized, and that she could not afford to have him as an enemy. How pitiably simple these worldlings were! Did she really think that he was deceived?

He would go, of course. He might even pretend to play her game, and be all smiles and gratitude for her patronage. He rode out from the Tower in a mood of pleasant satisfaction with his own cunning. And the pleasure was greatly increased by the thought that, if Queen Katharine held court at Hertford, it was more than likely that Joan would be there.

He had forgotten how beautiful an English summer could be. As he climbed the hills north of London, the sun and the breeze, and the wealth of colours round him, washed his mind of prison sickness, and of the memories of stricken France, ugly with the footprints of camps and armies.

The hay was late this year. They were still cutting it, and the scent made him homesick. He could afford to think of home again, and of the peaceful homecoming that now seemed so near. There would be much to set right, not without jars and maybe blood-letting. But Scotland was not France, and would need no desperate surgery. He would bring her freedom from domestic tyrants. He hoped to bring her an English bride for queen, and a firmer peace with her churlish southern neighbour.

They had started early, in the cool of the morning. He was pleasantly hungry by the time they reached Waltham, ravenous before a turn of the road brought Hertford Castle into sight. However cheerful one's thoughts, a twenty-mile ride made dinner extremely desirable. He sprang from his horse and made for the hall almost too quickly for the ushering servants.

Dinner had started without him, though noon was hardly struck. Humphrey of Gloucester was the guest of honour, and beside him sat Jacqueline, the plump, vivacious little woman whom Humphrey had married in defiance of the proprieties. The company round them was intent on admiring and applauding each other. Katharine gave James a chilly welcome and then resumed interrupted railleries with a young Englishman who seemed to think himself wonderfully daring. There was no sign of Owen Tudor: Katharine's indiscretion had limits. James's immediate neighbours were elaborating some joke unintelligible to a latecomer, and no one troubled to explain it. Only Warwick sat grave and glum amidst the frivolity. Of Joan there was no sign, and James felt immediately certain that she was not at Hertford at all.

It was Friday, and fish was the staple of the feast. James found himself disliking fish. He ate in silence, gradually realizing how much he had built on the hope of seeing Joan.

Dinner ended, and the guests flooded the garden, laughing and hallooing to each other. Some of the younger and more bibulous began to play leap-frog on the grass. James had drunk deeply—to drown rising melancholy and the taste of fish—but he found himself watching their antics with contemptuously sober eyes. The glory was rapidly fading from a day that had promised so much and was performing so little. He began to wonder why he had been invited.

He had caught Humphrey looking at him once or twice,

but as one looks at a child or dog to whom one has done an injustice. He was not going to risk a rebuff by accosting him now, while Humphrey was so engrossed in the charms of his foreign wife. When he joined some of the staider groups, walking between rose-hedges, they received him courteously but without warmth. His most friendly welcome came from one of Katharine's Joans, the apple-cheeked Troutbeck. But he only stayed with her in the hope of extracting news, and when she put him off with vague uncertainties, developing a motherliness of manner that suggested pity, James made puzzled excuses and fled.

The gardens lay inside the castle walls. He sought the angle made by a bastion, where the roof of a small shed, leaning against the masonry, peered over the rose-bushes. Here were gardeners' tools and a rough bench. James sat down. The dry smell of earth and shrivelled leaves was almost comforting. His attendants had probably watched his retreat, and would be coming to remind him that it would soon be time to ride back to prison. Meanwhile, if no one else had marked him, he might have ten minutes to himself.

He was hardly ensconced before he knew that someone had detected him. Queen Katharine was coming down the nearest path, talking to an unseen companion with unnecessary loudness: he felt instinctively that she was manœuvring into earshot and intended him to hear. She was talking the merest trifles at present, and her dupe or accomplice made no audible response. James waited.

"I hear you are to be congratulated," she said at last. "I hope you are not expecting to meet her here. She has left me for good."

"I do not understand. Your Majesty must excuse me if I am stupid today." The man spoke fluent French, but with a stiff home-bred accent. A soldier by his voice, and an elderly one.

"But it is no good trying to deceive me!" said Katharine's voice. "I know everything."

"I wish I could say the same. Your Majesty has the advantage of me."

"I do not think, my lord, that you are as stupid as you say. When I am told that someone is stealing my Beaufort from me, I make it my business to discover who——" Katharine checked suddenly, as though silenced by some unseen gesture. "But what is it?" she asked. "Do you think that I am going to be indiscreet?"

Some whispering followed, in which James could distinguish little except the words "bishop" and "protector." "But, of course," he heard Katharine say, "Humphrey would do everything to prevent it—if only to spite that little Beaufort. I see I must be very careful."

"Your Majesty will oblige me by never referring to the matter again." James knew the voice of Warwick now.

"Until it is concluded?"

"Until it is accomplished. Even if there were no outside difficulties, I should not like the matter discussed at present. I have not yet made my offer in person."

"You are afraid she will reject it?"

"I trust not."

"You have no cause for fear. I am still in her confidence, you know. I am sure she welcomes so certain an offer—and from such a quarter. It is only uncertainty that wearies and disgusts a woman." Katharine's voice seemed particularly far-reaching, particularly emphatic. It seemed to rouse Warwick to a restrained annoyance. "Then I will ask your Majesty," he said, "to respect that confidence."

There was a moment's silence. James could imagine Katharine pouting—that hateful twist of her little French mouth which had once aroused his desires. "I hope," she said, "that your lordship is not hesitating in the matter."

"No. I have no reason for misgivings."

"You will not be disappointed when you see her again. She has grown . . . tolerably handsome, in the last few years. I shall be glad to see her married—and to your lordship. She will learn to mend one or two small faults. Nothing serious—but she needs a husband. I was married before I was nineteen."

"Yes, your Majesty," said Warwick stiffly. "Shall we rejoin the company?"

The voices died away. James was alone.

He had all the news he wanted now, more than Troutbeck could have told him. He even knew why Katharine had brought him out to Hertford. He would not feel, for some hours or days, the full pain of the wound she had inflicted. In the stunned interim, his chief sensation was a dread of the return journey, of those twenty miles—so pleasant-seeming that morning—which separated him from the one place which, for want of a better, he thought of as his home. Anything to escape from the garden, the chatterers, even the open fields and the sight of men. He left without excuse or token, and rode blindly for London.

It was dark by the time they had reached the Tower and its sheltering obscurity. But after an hour or two alone—staring at unopened books and untasted supper, pacing the locked room to deaden thought—he had almost begun to hanker for the road again. The haunted ride had been better than this nightmare of imprisonment. There was no prospect anywhere of rest or peace of mind, only stone walls and the slow stifling of a desperate spirit.

Day followed day without respite. At times he lost all control and, though his body was pent from harm, his mind turned savagely inward, straining and rending its own fabric. He grew violent in self-accusation, suspecting every impulse he had once cultivated. He had never loved Joan: he had loved his own passions and was now caught in a net of his own choice and devising. If she had seemed to respond, it had been for as evil a reason: the empty name of king had tempted her, the vain dreams of worldly grandeur. It had only needed the advent of the secure, the already successful Warwick, to show the whole matter in its true light—a tissue of self-deceptions and scheming lusts. He was fortunate to have escaped from it. If they were to come now, offering Joan as a bride, offering him his crown, he would throw the gifts back in their faces. He was sick and weary of the whole round world, and of all who crawled upon its face. They had elbowed him out of the pack and nothing would induce him to rejoin them in their discreditable antics. He hoped for nothing, believed in nothing: he desired nothing except annihilation.

Merton's return made the smouldering fire blaze up in madness. Merton's news from Scotland—doubtful in purport, tempered to soothe his desperations—only served to feed his contempt and hatred. He despised the priest for kindly meant exaggerations, childish attempts to comfort and to coax. Merton was a fool to think that he could deceive him about Scotland. If ever they persuaded him to go back there himself, Scotland would remember the day with anguish: King James the First would go down to history as the most pitiless of her tyrants. Robbed of his own illusions, he would know how to punish and destroy the creeping and comfortable self-deceptions that defaced her. If there was axe and rope in Scotland, his brother's murder should be avenged a hundredfold, the whole brood of Albany should perish in sacrifice upon young Rothesay's tomb. Then, with ancient reckonings settled, there would be seventeen years of imprisonment to obliterate in blood. There were traitors who had conspired to prolong his exile, cowards and sluggards enough who had not lifted a finger to curtail it. They took their ease, now, in their distant, peaceful homes, pitying him, perhaps, yet grudging the single penny, the one bold word that might bring his liberation nearer. If ever he returned, he would teach them what loyalty a king expects, and it would be centuries before Scotland forgot the manner of that teaching.

Merton listened patiently to the raging, and could do nothing to check its delirious force. Every bond seemed loosed. The devil had taken seisin of a human soul and it was only chance that enabled its good angels to keep the body from deadly and destroying sin. Merton was thankful indeed for the bolts and bars of England's gaol. If he could have released and crowned James now by the signing of a paper, he would have cut off his hand rather than touch a pen.

He did not despair. A priest's experience had taught him patience. It was true that he had never witnessed such a mood before, for he had never ministered to such a man as, for good or evil, King James had grown to be. But he knew what time can do, and what black furies can pass away—provided that the soul they oppress has not violated the unexpressed and inexpressible oath that binds it to its Creator. Of that ultimate treachery there was no sign in James. He was too healthy at the core for his self-inflicted wounds to fester in permanent corruption. But Merton trembled at times to think how long it might be before the injuries could heal.

He tried, once or twice, to stem or divert the torrent. It had not taken him long to discover its source, nor to extract from James some account of what had happened.

"Tell me," he asked. "Is it true that you love this woman?"

"I do not know what love means! It is a trap, a filthy trap."

"My son, I charge you, on your soul's peril, to tell me the truth. Do you love her?"

There was a long silence before James spoke. "I did," he said grudgingly. "Or thought I did. That's done with now."

"Since when?" asked the priest, and could get no answer. "You were sending her messages until a few days ago?" he persisted.

"A fortnight."

"And have had no answer for some time. There might be a dozen good reasons for that. And then?"

Again no answer. "And then," suggested Merton, "you overheard some light talk——"

"I learnt the truth about her! And about myself."

"You mean that you listened to some words from a foolish and spiteful woman—one who had cause to hate you. By giving way to despair, you are merely doing what she wanted you to do, for the sake of her own wounded vanity. Is that not foolish, as well as shameful?"

"It was not what she said," answered James. "It was what that man replied. He did not know that I was overhearing. He is too stupid for such tricks as hers."

"It is many months since you saw your lady?"

"Five or six."

"And before that—six years. Did you ever speak to her of marriage?"

"Never."

"But she understood you to intend it?"

"How should I know? She can marry whom she pleases. I care nothing for her, nothing!"

"You care very deeply, my son. You are lying to me—and to yourself."

"Leave me alone!"

"You once showed me some poetry you wrote of her, I am no judge of such things, but——"

"Poetry!"

"—But it seems to me that when you wrote it, you had not learnt to lie as you are now lying."

"I had not begun to learn the truth! I was in a silly, sickly dream."

"You are much sicker now, and in body as well as spirit."

"So be it! Leave me to rot. Why do you torment me?"

"Because I wish to see you cured—to see you cure yourself."

"There is nothing I can do, nothing worth doing."

"You can face the truth, instead of conjuring up nightmares. Send her one more message. I will see that it reaches her. She will tell you how things stand, for good or evil. And the truth, however hard, is a better medicine than guesses and imaginings. Only you must do it at once, before you have altogether poisoned your mind against her."

James sat silent, staring at nothing. The priest picked up a pen, dipping it in the ink. "At once," he said.

Again there was silence. For a minute and more neither of them moved. Then James began to laugh.

It was soft laughter at first, though bitter enough; then it grew harsh and strident, with more than a hint of delirium. James rose laughing from his seat and staggered towards the door of his inner room. He only paused to turn back upon Merton, yelling at him to go away. He added blasphemies, with the maniac's laughter for refrain. Then as the priest sat unmoved, he stumbled, half-choking, through the door and slammed it behind him. Keys were denied him, but Merton heard him piling furniture on its inner side. Barred from without, self-barricaded from within, he yelled insults through the iron-bound panels, defying the feeble siege of friendship and good intent. Then the voice grew cracked and hoarse, the laughter died to a croaking, and Merton heard him throw his heavy limbs upon the bed. Seventeen years of imprisonment, of treachery and neglect, cruelty and misplaced kindness, had done their work at last. The full force of all that he had suffered, sharpened to a single point, had pierced and laid him prostrate.

It must have been an hour before Merton rose from his seat. It took that time before a man of his particular stamp could bring himself to do wrong, even with the best of intentions. He was an anointed priest: his mind naturally revolted against excuses for practising deception in order that good might result. But he decided, before the hour was out, that for once he would belie his nature and his office. He had argued himself into believing that James, in his right senses, would surely do what was about to be done in his name.

He began to search the room for a book that James had once showed him. He remembered the look of it and had little difficulty in tracking it down. He sat down to read it. The leaves were covered, on the one side, with a blotched network of illegible scribblings; on the opposite side, in a tolerably clear hand, each page showed three or four stanzas of Rhyme Royal.

He studied them carefully, for the choice was wide. No sound came from the inner room. It might be many hours before he would dare to force an entrance and press his services on James, more before he could expect him to come out himself. He had leisure to read and choose.

He could not help smiling a little to himself. James had made such a point of his originality in telling a plain story, avoiding allegory and such hackneyed tricks. He had kept to his purpose, and with interesting results, for some twenty pages. Then dreams and visions, abstractions and goddesses, began to intrude upon the lifelike record of an unhappy youth. Curiously enough, it was here that Merton found what he was looking for, James was picturing himself as taken, in a dream, from Venus's bower to the palace of Patience and the presence of austerer Minerva. Here he was questioned as to the nature of his love, and answered that it did not seek such transient fulfilment as would gratify his passions and dishonour his lady: it craved marriage—the bane of less serious poets,—and unbroken comradeship,

For weal or woe, while yet my life shall last.

Merton raised the leaf up, ran a sharp knife along it, close to the binding, and pulled it free.

He could write a name and superscript later: meanwhile he folded the leaf and hid it in his gown. If messengers could be hired and servants bribed, it should reach its destination. Arriving when it did, it would announce that the sender still hoped, still offered allegiance. He took it out again, read it through, and underscored "*or woe*" in red ink, as if to date the message and suggest that bad news was in the air.

When the mark had dried, he re-folded and re-hid the paper, in no wise regretting his decision.

She could hardly miss the intention. If she was indeed driven into another marriage the message could only cause her pain. There was, perhaps, one chance in a hundred of her escaping—supposing that she wished to—from a betrothal to which the world had appointed her. But, as Merton somewhat sentimentally reckoned, she was presumably a woman after James's heart: he had certainly chosen her in a moment of untrammelled vision, perhaps by divine guidance: it was possible that she was of a kind to seize the hundredth chance, and find means to defeat or outwit the world.

He spent some hours in prayer, as befitted a priest and a sinner. He had short sleep, rising early to make some tiresome enquiries, distribute a little money, and put his missive into what he hoped were the right hands. That done, he returned to James.

He found him risen, and sulky rather than violent, as though grudgingly ashamed of last night's exhibition. But his words seemed wild, his face drawn and white, and his frame shaken with fever. Merton watched him stumble about the room, clutching at the table for support and guidance. Before noon he had collapsed altogether, and allowed himself to be taken to bed. Evening found him in delirium. For some days the doctors looked at their patient with pursed lips, talked of danger, and were clearly saying less than they feared. Merton listened to them gravely, knowing that they would use their utmost skill without any asking from him. Then, one afternoon, he heard them agree, jokingly, that they reckoned to have preserved ten thousand pounds, and would apply to the Exchequer for half, at least, of King James's ransom.

The crisis was past, but James lay dull and senseless. He slept much; when awake, he lay staring at the ceiling with hardly a sign of life. When Merton spoke to him, he gave little sign of having heard, none of understanding.

It was August before he began to recapture the broken rhythm of his life. He still spoke little, and seemed at first to be struggling with some inward perplexity. Whatever it was, it was soon put away, hidden behind a mask of gravity and self-control. He had aged a little, and looked all of his twenty-nine years. A small beard, grown in sickness and allowed to remain, contributed to the impression. To Merton's still anxious eyes, the change in his manner was more remarkable. He seemed more purposeful and yet slower, as though moving to a certain aim in a world that had grown deceptive and unfamiliar. But Merton could not guess, and dared not ask, what was passing in King James's mind.

June 1423

VI

It was summer in Scotland, and her hills shone with green and gold and purple. Nature was repeating once more, in dispassionate majesty, her ancient and unvarying revolution. Only to men's houses came a whisper of some new thing. There was hardly a cottage that had not heard it—from those whose windows peered anxiously at England, to those which fronted the towering cliffs of Orkney and the wastes of Arctic sea. The king, so ran the whisper, the king is coming home again.

It owed nothing to any news from London: it had no foundation in secure knowledge: all probabilities frowned against it. Of those who sped it onward, none could tell whence it had sprung. It seemed to come from those quarters that knew least of England, where no word of English was spoken; for it spread south and east from the mountains or from that wilderness of jagged islands that feel the Atlantic's clear, clean winds. There folk are to be found who boast of seeing glimpses of the future, and many who exalt Vision above plodding Fact. There, it seemed, where the crown's power meant least, some distant seer had felt and proclaimed the return of Scotland's king.

The Highland men, having launched the rumour, might continue to think—untaught as yet by encroaching circumstance—that a king was of less moment than their own clan chiefs, a Stewart no better than themselves. But, through the length and breadth of the Lowlands, there were few indeed who could say that they cared nothing for the news. Some there might be who felt the striking of a sudden chill, as though some huge bird had cast over their homes the shadow of his ill-omened wing. But for one such, there were thousands to rejoice at the tidings, certain that all evil must dwindle, all good take on new life, now that their king was coming home again.

For round that baseless hope there clustered and crystallized the aspirations and yearnings of a whole people, some of them rooted in argument and calculation, the most part wildly and pitiably unreasoned. The poor and oppressed told each other that a champion was on his way, the starving dreamt of an inexplicable plenty. Merchants added a little to their expectations of next year's trafficking, farmers talked to their sons of breaking up new soil. Families and friends smiled at each other in renewed affection: where, in the dungeons beneath men's minds, there lurked ancient and ineradicable hatreds, these were careful to cloak themselves in the guise of lawful resentment or a thirst for thwarted justice. And even those who loved and prayed for all mankind, on lonely rock or in sculptured cloister, had a mystic assurance that God was granting Scotland a new and fairer age. For changes there must be, wide and deep; and they must surely be changes for the better, if it was indeed true that the king was returning home.

Rumour flourished beneath the Border hills, waiting, as expectant witnesses, for the exile's homecoming along the English roads. The hum of Perth and Edinburgh spoke, with rival tongues, of becoming once more the seats of royalty. The great trees that stood round Scone Abbey murmured together of preparations for a crowning. Gossip was busy in the little towns, half marts of trade, half fishing villages, that dotted the eastern coast. Gossip filled the castles and cottages of the cornland from Elgin round to Stirling, from Stirling to Galloway and Dunbar. Wherever men met to traffic or pray, to mourn or drink or make merry, heads nodded and tongues wagged to the tune of the King's Return.

In the very heart of that great expanse of scattered expectation, there was a single place where the rumour could not penetrate except by stealth nor find mention without reprimand. Doune Castle was as near as might be to Scotland's centre: one saw Stirling from its towers, Perth was a long day's ride, and a longer but easier road lay eastward towards Edinburgh. Here Albany had planned and laid the foundations of a home: here Murdoch was Albany and regent in his father's stead. Here, a few months since, he had renewed a decision—so far as it lay in Murdoch to decide anything at all. Faced with collapse and public shame, faced with the contempt and rebellion of his own sons, he had resolved that one remedy at least must be postponed or rejected, that he would not and could not allow the return of Scotland's king.

The little room where his elder kinsmen had confirmed his decision seemed half empty with no tenant of Murdoch's proportions. Nor were the two men there of such a kind as to excite remark. Alan of Otterburn, an elderly formalist, was the regent's secretary. Young Montgomery's official status mattered nothing, for it cloaked rather than explained his real activities. He half stood, half leaned against the table, speaking in a hoarse voice. Otterburn had his back to him, shuffling papers in a massive chest: Otterburn found it easier to deal with Montgomery when one treated him without respect.

"It'll have to come," the younger man was saying. "If

he does not do it himself, I doubt they'll do it behind his back."

Otterburn turned to give him a warning glance. "You forget," he said drily, "that his Grace is Regent of Scotland. It is for him to decide what is expedient for the country." He returned to his papers, wishing he felt as much confidence in his master as duty bade him express. He fidgeted a moment with his hands, and then spoke again, over his shoulder. "Who are 'they'?" he asked.

"The bishops," answered Montgomery, "Aberdeen, Brechin, Angus of the Isles—they all want Jamie back. Old Wardlaw goes without saying."

"Nothing new in all that."

"The Constable. The Ruthvens. The Abbot of Inchcolm."

"He carries no weight. The others we'd a note of already." Otterburn returned a bundle of documents to its place and began to untie the string of another.

"Does the name of Douglas carry no weight?" asked Montgomery, and there was a moment's pause.

"It does that," answered Otterburn, "and on our side."

"These things change. I might bring you proof of it—if you'd think it worth my while."

"I'll believe that when I see it," said the secretary. "We've a bond with the Douglases."

"You've a bond with Archie Tyneman. He's going to France they say, to fight the English, and get captured, unless his luck'll change. Archie's not the only Douglas."

"Most of them signed the bond."

"You know you could never publish it to shame them. It'd smell of high treason against King James."

"Published or no, it's a bond. The Douglases'll not break it. They'll do nothing about King James without our knowledge."

"They're saying it's broken already," answered Montgomery, "and from our side."

Otterburn looked up in enquiry. "Walter?" he asked.

"Ay, Walter. He's been out again, and on Douglas lands: there's a couple of men killed, on a farm near Crawick. The Douglases are saying that if the regent cannot keep his own son off their lands, he can whistle for his bond."

"His Highness'll make amends to them. He might punish Walter."

"He might—if he dared. He's feared of Walter, you know that. Where are they now?"

"Out with the hawks. I told you. Athol's with them."

"That young man," said Montgomery, "ought to be under lock and key—not riding out to hawk with his father and my lord of Athol."

"Hold your tongue," answered the secretary, "unless you're wanting to be under lock and key yourself."

"I'm only telling you what others say. I'm paid, amn't I, to find out what folks are saying? When I'm paid at all!"

Otterburn dropped his papers and faced Montgomery squarely. "Is there any truth," he asked "in this story of the Douglas moving behind our backs? Do you believe it yourself?"

"I do. They, and the bishops."

"Sending to England?"

"They've done that already."

"I doubt the English'll not let him go."

"King Harry's dead," said Montgomery. "By all accounts, there's nothing that mightn't happen. I'm hearing tales."

"We'll not pay you for the clash of the town. We've our own men in London."

Otterburn, as he said it, wished that he had fuller, less confusing, reports from London. The best news would be of the English refusing to let King James go free: little else could save the regency. One could talk of placating the Douglases, but the regent had little left with which to bribe a power that had already swallowed about a quarter of the Lowlands.

"There's something else," said Montgomery, "if you think it worth paying for."

"Making which way?"

"When the west wind blows, all crows fly east."

"Tell me what it is."

Otterburn saw Montgomery open his lips to speak, but he was never to know what tit-bit was on its way. Unmistakable sounds were coming from the stairway. "They must be back," he said, "and I was not expecting them this hour and more. You'd better be away from the room."

Montgomery made for the door, but there were already footsteps on the stairway. He stepped aside. If it was Murdoch or Walter, he might be able to slip out unnoticed as they entered.

It was neither. It was only a falconer, heated with riding. He carried something in his hands, wrapped in a yellow cloth. He looked at Otterburn as if in apology for entering the room and then laid his little burden on the table. "His Highness told me to bring her in here," he said.

He unwrapped the bundle. In the middle of the yellow shroud lay the dead body of a falcon, warm and hardly stiff. The neck had been cruelly wrung, the head almost twisted off the body.

"Who did that?" asked Montgomery.

The falconer turned, startled at the unexpected voice. "There's only one man," he said, "that'd do the like of that."

"My lord Walter?" said Otterburn, and the man nodded assent.

"Is that the bird," asked Montgomery, "that he was trying to beg from his father?"

"That's her," said the falconer. "And he tried again today. All the way to Lanrick and beyond. And when his Highness gets tired of saying 'No' and gives my lord the rough side of his tongue, he snatches her off my wrist and misguggles her like that. I've trained falcons for thirty years, and she was the best I ever handled." He stroked the little body, smoothing its dead plumage.

"What did his Highness do?" asked Otterburn.

"Do?" said the falconer. "He's done nothing as yet. It's not for me to say, but I'm thinking it's over-late to do anything where that young man's concerned."

There was a step outside and Murdoch's great form blocked the door. He came straight in, seeming to notice nothing of Montgomery's escape or the falconer's more dignified withdrawal. He made for a chair by the empty fireplace and threw himself heavily into its seat.

There was silence in the room, a lengthy, insufferable silence. Otterburn stood motionless, listening to the faint sounds from outside, the horses being led to stable, the distant tinkling of sheep-bells by the river. Murdoch stared straight before him with frightened, angry eyes.

The minutes dragged by. Otterburn smoothed out a document and approached his master's chair with a little preparatory cough. Murdoch motioned him aside, imposing new silence. It seemed an interminable time before Murdoch could speak. Even then it was half to himself.

"We'll have to have him home," he said. "We must just have Jamie home."

July 1423

VII

Joan Beaufort had gone back to Orwell. She was helping her mother prepare for the journey to London: she was trying to prepare herself for the momentous meeting with Warwick which should lead, by all the ordinary rules, to a rich and enviable marriage.

She did not allow herself to rest or think. She moved from room to room of the manor-house, sorting, planning, giving orders—trying to escape or ignore the ceaseless flow of Lady Clarence's self-congratulation, which broke out as soon as they were alone. Somewhere at the back of her mind she cherished the obstinate feeling that the ordinary rules might for once be broken, that it might be the unexpected, the wildly unorthodox that was going to happen.

The days passed, and routine impaired her hope. She began to think, rather, of the thousand girls who had been no less sure of last-minute rescue, who had found the dreaded thing come inevitably upon them, and then (as it seemed) grown content to accept it—happy even, remembering earlier fancies with amused contempt. The world was strong, and possibly wiser than one knew. So it had always been, so it would continue to be—so long as there were lords and gentlefolk to live in outward luxury and deny themselves nothing except their hearts' desire.

Two days before the departure, something happened to give a new twist to her thoughts.

She had gone into the garden that morning to find Margery Norton. Since her aunt's death, Margery had left Woking for Orwell, bringing her little girl. They would probably be picking beans together, and she wanted to speak to both. But she had hardly left the door when she saw a man coming from the road; a carrier, by the look of him, but he seemed bent on attracting her attention. "The Lady Joan?" he asked, and, finding that it was, produced a thin-looking letter. "I was told to give you this," he said.

It proved to be a single sheet of paper, on which were written three stanzas of verse; the back was covered with illegible scribblings. The handwriting seemed to be James's, but it was unlike him to be so enigmatic. "Was there no message?" she asked.

"Message?" said the man. "You got it there, haven't you, in your hand? That's what I was told to bring. And only a shilling for coming ten mile out of my way. It never pays, doing things to oblige a priest. Ten miles! And I ought to be in Ipswich by this time. It's Tuesday."

"It's lucky for you you found me," said Joan. "If my brother had been here he'd have had you whipped for disrespect."

"I was told to give it to you, my lady," said the carrier. "I can't do more than I'm told."

She found him a penny and he shambled back towards the main road. She was left with her sheet of poetry.

On second reading, the intent was plainer—as plain, perhaps, as a prisoner could afford to make it. A sudden warmth filled her: the word "marriage" was an inspiration instead of a terror. But James would not have sent, unless he hoped that she could do something to bring about what they both desired. She must tell her brother, tell the bishop, that she could be sure of a better match. She did not know how to bring herself to speak of what must surely be a secret between lovers. She doubted their reception of it: James the king was one thing, James the prisoner another: and possibly England had decided that he must be held perpetual prisoner. She could only pray for more information on how things stood, for the unexpected chance to act—and the courage to seize it.

She folded up the paper into a tiny square and slipped it into her dress.

She was still without a plan when the time came to ride for London. Lady Clarence enlivened the journey by grumbling at the ways Joan had picked up in Queen Katharine's household. She even scolded her daughter for the new-fangled habit of riding side-saddle instead of astride, though secretly she rather admired the fashion: it was certainly elegant and ladylike, but one did not immediately approve anything that the younger generation invented. If Joan had plucked her eyebrows, as so many girls had begun to do, she could have rated her with a more wholehearted conviction. Joan rode on with ears deaf to her mother's voice, worrying at a riddle that seemed to have no answer.

Arrival in London did not bring enlightenment. Its self-absorbed bustle might rouse the spirits, but it discouraged any yearnings for the unconventional. Here Mammon ruled more obviously than over woods and fields, mocking or persecuting all who were reluctant to conform. Rebels against his power begged for bread along the kennels or had already left their blackened heads on the spikes above London Bridge. The whole city preached obedience to established rules.

They had to cross the river to reach Winchester House, where Bishop Beaufort held lordly residence among Southwark slums. He met them himself, cordially enough, but looking anxious and overworked.

"A pleasant journey?" he asked, after perfunctory kisses. "I am glad to see you here. Come in, come in! There's a little collation for you in the winter-room. Supper may be late, and you'll need something after your ride."

He fussed indoors and began to send the servants flying on unnecessary errands. Food and wine awaited them in the misnamed winter-parlour, used impartially at all seasons. The bishop sent for his papers, excusing himself for working while they refreshed themselves.

"Well," said Lady Clarence, as soon as they were seated, "has Somebody arrived from Calais yet?"

"For Heaven's sake——!" began Beaufort, in an agony of discretion. Then he collected himself, glancing at the servants. He talked, uneasily, of mere trifles, until they were dismissed. Then he turned on Lady Clarence with a show of severity.

"The matter you began to mention," he said, "had better wait till your son comes in. I do not wish it discussed more than necessary, especially in company. My enemies—our enemies—have their agents everywhere."

"Not in Winchester House?"

"In Winchester House especially. Loyalty among servants is a thing of the past. Only yesterday I detected——" He paused, and thought better of it. "I will not go into details," he said, "I will only ask you to be doubly careful, now that you are in London. It is of the utmost importance that . . . that certain people should not get wind of our project."

"Do you mean Duke Humphrey?" said Joan, with as blank a face as possible. It was amusing to see Beaufort wince.

"I prefer to name no names," he said, sitting down to his papers, "and I hope you will learn an equal discretion. You are very sweet and innocent, my dear, and it will take you a little time to discover that London is neither sweet nor innocent. All you need know is that there is both the power and the will, in certain high quarters, to prohibit all that we are doing for your happiness—if news of it should get about. So, please, for your own sake, bridle that little tongue!"

He beamed at his niece, a trifle nervously. Then he began to fiddle with his papers.

"Was your lordship wanting this pen?" said Lady Clarence. She had taken it up to scratch something on a torn scrap of paper, nibbling at a meat pasty as she did so. "It doesn't matter," he said rather testily, "I have plenty to read through first." It annoyed him to see a woman using a pen, especially when it was his sister-in-law, whom one did not connect in mind with any such instrument. He soothed himself by continuing his summing-up of the situation. "Not," he announced, "that I wish to alarm you ladies unnecessarily. Our plans are well laid and there is nothing to fear so long as discretion is observed. We can then present the certain person I referred to with a *fait accompli*. He can hardly send tipstaves to interrupt the ceremony."

He settled down to read, with an occasional grunt to mark the importance of the matter. Joan helped herself to more wine, wondering how soon she could make her excuses and depart upstairs. A servant entered, crossed to the bishop, and began to speak in a low, rapid whisper. Beaufort replied loudly and in anger. "Certainly not!" he said. "Tell him not to show his face here again!" and glared the messenger out of the room. Silence fell. Even the scratching of the pen had stopped.

"There, Joan," said Lady Clarence, "that's what I am going to embroider on a coverlet for you. I've impaled the two coats of arms. I believe I'd have made a very good herald." She showed Joan a rough sketch of a shield, badly bulging in the left cheek. It was roughly parted down the centre, as for a marriage, and, in the blots and dashes of each half, the eye of faith could detect the bearings of Beaufort and Warwick.

The bishop was rapt, only frowning and fidgeting with his feet at the half-heard intrusion of his sister-in-law's voice. Joan gave her mother's handiwork a dutiful inspection. "Thank you, mother," she said. "I know you'll do it splendidly in needlework."

"Here is your lordship's pen," said Lady Clarence, rising to brush the crumbs from her dress. "Oh, and when will John be coming?" she said. "Will he be here before supper?"

"What's that?" said the bishop. "Oh—John? I don't know. Probably not."

"Perhaps he's at Council today," said Joan, as naively as she could manage. "When do they finish?"

Her mother took the bait. "Council?" she said. "You haven't found him a seat already?"

"No, no," said the bishop, with embarrassed irritation. "There's been no vacancy . . . and so many other difficulties. Nothing but difficulties. John must have patience."

"Well, it'll do John no harm," said Lady Clarence, "if you can teach him that." She smiled at Joan, rather like a schoolgirl criticizing her teacher behind his back. "Come, Joan," she said, "we must not disturb his lordship any more. I am sure he has plenty of work to do." Joan rose obediently. The scrap of paper slipped from her lap on to the floor.

"Work?" said the bishop, rousing himself to be rid of them politely. "That is the one thing I can never go short of. I can only thank you ladies for sweetening a little of it with your company."

He smiled gallantly, rising from his chair. "Till supper, then," he said.

"Till supper," answered Lady Clarence. She curtseyed and led Joan out.

Beaufort looked down at his papers. England, France, the bishopric, the wool-trade: there was so much to be done, so much to be done. He had better go in to his secretary. They might come back, and one could do nothing with women about. There were compensations in being a priest, and unmarried. One could get ahead with things, most of the time. He sighed, gathered up his papers and made for the door.

Joan was the first to descend, early, for the evening meal. The hour or two of solitude, of changing dresses and nominal rest, had left her as unquiet as ever. In her own heart, she had been walking with James, through a garden from which mothers and uncles were excluded. That fairy-tale, now tawdry from over-use, only served to make oncoming reality less welcome. Love itself would soon be an abandoned folly: she would have, one day, to warn her own daughter against it, if she had daughters; she would have to train them for the market in which she herself had been sold.

She left her room and began to descend the unwindowed staircase. It was dark, and they had forgotten to hang the lamp. Into the pit, she thought, into the pit. I am leaving myself behind in that room, leaving my maidenhead and my faith. I am going to meet John and my uncle again, to hear about interviews and betrothals and convenient dates for the ceremony. There'll be light enough then, fine clothes and the pomp of money. I'd better ask Queen Katharine for advice, pluck my eyebrows and paint my cheeks. Since there's no help, I'll show them I can play the game with the best of them.

"Lady!"

She started and stopped, peering down the slope of the stairs. A man's voice, a common voice, unfamiliar.

"What is it?" she challenged. "What do you want?"

"You, lady. Just a word with you."

She began to make out a tall, scraggy form, standing at the foot of the stairs. "Who are you?" she asked.

"His lordship's servant. Or was . . . till last Tuesday. He's sent me away—to starve. Just a word with you, that's all I'm asking."

She descended a few steps. The man's attitude was respectful enough, slavish even. She remembered him now, though the light was dim. He had attended the bishop's person in the spring, down at Orwell.

"Don't say no, lady," he went on. "It's your charity I'm asking—in the name of the Virgin. Not money. No, no, not money. Just something you could do for me—and wouldn't cost you nothing."

"What is it?" she asked.

The man looked round, saw the open door of the winter-parlour, and peered through. "In there?" he said, returning. "It's empty."

She led the way in, wondering just how foolish she was being. The London twilight filled the room with an eerie atmosphere. The man himself, when she turned on him, looked too tall and thin to be altogether real. He seemed woebegone in face, but not starving, nor particularly ill-clad. "Your ladyship remembers me?" he said.

"Yes. In the country. Why did my uncle dismiss you?"

"That's what I can't tell. No reason, seemingly. He'd been tetchy lately—saving my respect. Then he just turned me away—after ten years' service. And no one'll have me now. I'm not young."

"You're not telling me the truth," she said. "I know his lordship. He would not do a thing like that without a reason." The man said nothing, looking sulkily at the floor. "What is it you want from me?" she asked.

The man hesitated: evidently the interview was not proceeding as he had planned it. "Just to speak a word for me," he said at last. "Ask his lordship to take me back. It's important."

"Important?"

"I mean, that is . . . yes, important to me." He stammered a little and then grew plausible again. "I've no other way to live. Does he want me to turn thief?"

The more he spoke, the less she liked or trusted him. He was evidently keeping something back. "What makes you think," she asked, "that his lordship would listen to me? I know nothing of you."

"He'd do anything you asked," he said earnestly. "Anything. He's often said how fond he is of you. He'd not refuse you anything just now, just when you're going to be . . ." His voice petered out, but there was a queer unpleasant light in his eye.

"Just when I'm going to be——?" she demanded.

"Oh, well, least said, soonest mended. I know it's a secret. Of course, we'd all like to know who it is—just to drink his health and wish you both luck."

"I see. And who are 'we'?"

"Me and the other servants," he said rapidly. "You see, I was hoping, with your ladyship's help, to be taken back again. And maybe I could do something to help you. I know there's difficulties—politics and so on. I can't say I understand much of that, but there's things we hear, back-stair-ways, and things we can do, sometimes, on the quiet. I'd be only too glad if I could help your ladyship over one or two of the difficulties we spoke of. And I wouldn't want money—not if you could do what I was asking."

Joan was beginning to see light. She wondered just how much of a fool the man thought her. If she had any doubts about his purpose, his next remark destroyed them. "Of course," he said, "I'd just have to know who it is. I mean, before I could get to work."

She looked at him again, her eyes more accustomed to the half-light. It was obvious, without a glance, that he was lying, and not very skilfully. Only a desperate gambler would have attempted such a throw. One saw now that he was desperate from fear, not of her or the bishop, not even of starvation. It was something more immediate—torture probably. Some other paymaster was demanding information angrily and with threats. The man, to look at him, might be on the rack already. It was an ugly situation to be mixed up in, but she suddenly saw how she might turn it to account—if only she dared.

"Are you the man," she said, "whom the bishop dismissed for spying?"

It was no good his denying it, after the start he gave. He tried to, volubly at first, then with faltering excuses about a "misunderstanding." He spoke with one eye on the door, already contemplating escape. She checked him with an impatient gesture, wanting time to think. As she turned away, her eye fell on a scrap of paper, gleaming white under the table. She remembered her mother's heraldry.

"I take it," she said, "that you had money from my lord of Gloucester?"

That started him off again, whining that he had never even spoken to Gloucester: what would the likes of him be doing with the Lord Protector? "I didn't suppose," she interrupted, "that he paid you from his own purse."

As she spoke, she heard steps in the passage. She realized suddenly in how dangerous a position she had put herself. But it was anger rather than fear which keyed her, the determination to use, for her own ends, the filthy net that was being spun around her. "Under the table!" she said, in a cold whisper that she could hardly recognize as her own. Then, as she heard the paper rustle in his hand, "Take that where you belong," she said. "Don't say who gave it you, or they'll tell you it's a trap. And go quickly—quickly."

He, too, had heard the step outside. He was already within reach of the door. It was suddenly blocked by the appearance of a man; Joan saw that it was her brother Somerset. He opened his mouth to exclaim; the answering lie, the "Something I left here this afternoon," was on her lips, when the spy, despairing of concealment, hurtled past Somerset for the passage.

He had the advantage of surprise. Somerset, knocked sideways, made an ineffectual grab at him, and then vanished, hallooing, in pursuit. In a minute the whole household was in uproar.

Joan waited in suspense, wishing the man all the wings and cunning that he needed. To be a traitor to her family was enough, to see her treachery detected and frustrated would be the ultimate disaster. But the noise soon spread to the street and lanes outside. The man knew the house, or should know it, after ten years' service and double-dealing. He must have shown them a clean pair of heels, and only a fool would be caught at night, in the mazes of Southwark. It was not long before her brother returned cursing to the door, and stood there, sheathing an unfleshed dagger. His first words freed her from complicity.

"Did he frighten you?" he asked.

She stood frozen a second and more, reckless resolve forming in her mind. Somerset was kicking round the twilit room, still breathing heavily. "Where in hell can he have been hiding?" he said to himself.

Joan nerved herself for the effort. "He was not hiding," she said, with forced calm. "I was giving him instructions."

"Instructions? Are you crazy?"

"No. I have sent him to Duke Humphrey. I saw no other way of preventing this foolish marriage that uncle is imposing upon you for his own purposes."

He stood gaping, unable to take it in. If she had said, "That you are imposing on me," he might have understood at once—and struck her across the face. As it was, he snorted like a puzzled animal, demanding explanation from her.

"Uncle?" he said. "But we were all agreed——" He could get no further, and she pressed her advantage. "John," she said, "why wouldn't you let me discuss it with you? It's not been pleasant, seeing uncle lead you on with promises he can't keep."

"What on earth do you mean?" he said, a world dissolving round him.

"You are not on the Council yet."

"But you don't understand these things! Uncle will tell you——"

"I know quite well what uncle will tell me. Only I'm not so guileless as you, John. And not so hasty."

She had him on the leash now, if only for a few minutes: he was the little boy again, and she the elder sister. She must, at any price, use her opportunity to the end. It might mean exposing her dearest secret, to be pawed by uncomprehending fingers. But it was better to cheapen a vision by sharing, than to lose sight of it altogether. And it was now or never: it might even be easier to speak, here in the half-darkness, to the man who had once been her little brother.

"Yes, but the family——" he was saying, in a curiously deflated manner. He seemed aware that he ought to be storming at her, rating her for unthinkable disloyalties. That, at least, is what the bishop would do when he learnt of it. But John was suddenly conscious that he had no desire to do as the bishop did. "You know quite well," he grumbled, still half-heartedly, "what it'd mean for the family to see you made Countess of Warwick. We can do it, you know; uncle has a tremendous position, whatever you may think of the way he uses it."

"Then make him use it another way," said Joan. "It would mean still more for the family to see me made a queen."

July 1423

VIII

"Humphrey?"

"Yes, my dear. What is it?"

"When are you going to put that candle out?"

"In a minute, in a minute."

Gloucester was sitting up in bed. His plump Flemish wife lay with her back to him, watching his shadow on the wall. It was nearly midnight and time for him to be thinking of her instead of reading.

"What is it tonight?" she asked, with a trace of peevishness. "Not Plato again?"

"No. I've no time for the classics, these days. Just my agents' reports. Nothing you need to bother your little head about."

He re-shuffled a handful of papers, glancing down at his wife. He called her his wife, though she had another husband on the Continent, and the Pope had quashed her second marriage—much to Humphrey's annoyance. Jacqueline was heiress to a rich province, besides being a lady of considerable attractions. To do Humphrey justice, it had not yet occurred to him that his Holiness's interference might one day provide him with good excuses—when her charms were eclipsed by another woman's and her rights in Hainault had proved impossible to enforce. He was certainly not tired of her yet. The warmth of her body, so close to his, was almost sufficient to make him scamp his reading and blow out the candle.

"I've nearly finished," he said. "But there's one I can't make out."

"Something about Hainault?" she asked. "Something I can help with?"

"Oh, no. London."

"Oh." A sulky yawn followed.

"Well, we can't go off and conquer Hainault for you if it means leaving a set of misbegotten Jacks-in-Office to ruin England as soon as my back's turned."

"No. I suppose not."

Silence again. The rustle of papers had ceased. Jacqueline rolled over to see Humphrey knitting his brows over a torn scrap, well scribbled over.

"What is it?" she asked.

"I wish I knew. I can't make head or tail of it."

"Who brought it?"

"I don't know. Some numskull. They say it came from Winchester House. There's a wedding in the air, and I told them to find out who it was that old Bishop Pug-nose is loosing on his niece. And all I get is this."

"Let me see." Jacqueline sat up and peered at the paper. It bore a few lines of writing, apparently kitchen accounts, and above them a round-edged pyramid, covered with what looked like carelessly drawn centipedes.

"Is it a mitre?" said Humphrey.

"No, it's a coat of arms. You're holding it the wrong way up."

"But the writing——"

"Never mind about the writing. You don't pay your men, do you, to find out how much ginger the Beauforts bought last month? Turn it the other way up."

Humphrey obeyed, rather reluctantly; it was humiliating to be less intelligent than a woman.

"That's it," said Jacqueline promptly. "A shield—and impaled. One side for the Beaufort wench, t' other for her intended."

"I believe you're right."

"I know I am. And may I remind you that it's midnight." Jacqueline slipped down among the sheets again, darting him a glance. Humphrey, unconscious of the challenge, was still staring at the scribbled device.

"But they'd never dare!" he said softly. "They couldn't without my licence. This is a State matter."

"Would you grant them licence?"

"I'd see 'em in hell first."

"Then they'll probably do it without asking you. And anyway, you can't stop them tonight. Do blow out that candle."

"It *is* Warwick," said the impervious Humphrey. "The fool can't draw, but I swear that's Beauchamp and that's the Newburgh chevron."

"Does it matter?"

"Matter? Good God, Beauchamp and Beaufort? He owns half England, and the bishop's got more than half the money. Not while I'm protector! They could put me on the rubbish heap in six months. Warwick could choose a new king if he wanted to—their son could, anyway, if they have one!"

"She'll manage that for him."

"She's not going to have a chance. He's a crown tenant and I can stop the whole game."

"Dear, dear. I hope the poor man's not in love with her."

"At his age?"

"Why not? Most men like strawberries and cream in their forties." Jacqueline sighed. "I must ask her one day," she said, "what she does for that complexion."

"You're talking rubbish. Warwick's in love with nothing except money—and power. That is, if he's been consulted yet. It'd be like Beaufort to fix it all up, and then spring it on him. Not that he's likely to refuse, if Beaufort promised to do all the dirty work, bamboozling me and so on. I tell you, it's just a conspiracy, to play the devil while I'm abroad. Well, I shan't come to Hainault with you till I've scotched it."

"Will it take long?" Jacqueline yawned audibly.

"No. . . . As a matter of fact, I can leave instructions."

"Good. Make sure they're obeyed."

"Of course they'll be obeyed."

"Dear Humphrey! Or should I say, 'My dread lord'?"

"Why do you say that?"

"Because you're so easy to tease. It's your chief charm."

Humphrey frowned, turning to give Jacqueline the benefit of his disapproval. She lay looking up at him, quite unabashed—and abominably enticing. He frowned again, but with less conviction. He had enjoyed frivolity in the old days: his brother Henry had reprimanded him for it, more than once; when one had a kingdom to rule oneself, one began to understand Henry.

"I shall have to do something," he said. "And at once. I'll have to do something tomorrow."

"Oh, yes. Tomorrow."

"Why do you say tomorrow in that voice? I can't understand you."

Jacqueline did not reply. Her eyes twinkled up at Humphrey, blinked sleepily, and then twinkled again. She made sure of him, and turned away, facing the wall and waiting for him to make the next move. She had sufficient confidence in herself to guess that she would not have long to wait.

Humphrey's papers slipped to the floor. To maintain his dignity, he had to lie still a little, staring at the ceiling and trying to think about politics. But it was only a minute or so before he blew out the candle.

December 24th, 1423

IX

Bishop Beaufort sat at ease in Winchester House and sipped his Christmas wine. He felt that he had deserved his rest.

All was well at last, but it had been a harassing autumn. It had looked at times as though the Scottish treaty would never take form. But now it was settled, and a draft of it lay on the table before him; it gave England the promise of a considerable sum of money, and the prospect of peace on the Border; it gave James his freedom and a wife. Everything was there, in black and white, except the name of the bride: James, it was stipulated, could choose any English lady, even one of royal stock. That blank had had to be left while Humphrey of Gloucester was in England; it could be filled in now, for he had departed, with his paramour, on a wild-cat expedition into Hainault.

The tricking of Duke Humphrey had been, on the whole, the most gratifying part of the whole business. He had got wind of their first scheme—Beaufort had never discovered how—and sent forth orders to put a stop to the marriage between Joan and the over-powerful Warwick. He had left England pluming himself on having put a fine spoke in the Beaufort wheels, with never a suspicion that the Beauforts had changed direction and were stealing a good march on him.

They had kept him so completely in the dark about the Scottish treaty that he had even acquiesced when the bishop had put up his brother Exeter to propose that, when James had chosen his bride, her dowry should be paid out of public funds. This was only fair, of course, since the marriage, and the peace it entailed, would save the English Treasury large sums for the military defence of the Border. Still it had been amusing to get it past Humphrey's unsuspecting nose. And when he had murmured something about mentioning the lady's name, they had put him off with a good excuse, which had even found place in the clauses of the treaty—that "ladies of the Realm of England are not wont to offer themselves in marriage unasked."

Yes, the bishop told himself, he certainly deserved his rest after so satisfactory a piece of work. There had been a few features in the business that he had not quite understood, and one interview that he was doing his best to forget, had almost succeeded in forgetting. But all else reflected great credit on his own patience and ingenuity, on his sense of duty to his family and his country.

Bishop Beaufort nursed the cup of wine in his fat little hands, and reflected that, however baffling things might seem at times, perseverance and attention to detail made all come plain in the end . . . or almost all; and what was still inexplicable could be safely ignored as of no great importance.

He was right: the central mystery in the affair was of no

great importance, as he was accustomed to reckon things. His well-trained mind was hardly the right one to judge of it at all; such love as had brought James and Joan together defied the kind of calculation on which his career was built. He had been in the room when they had first met as covert but acknowledged lovers, and had caught no inkling of the glory that encompassed them. The strange union of boundless pride and utter humility, the glimpses of the eternal purpose for mankind, the power to see, in a fellow-creature's eyes, the lamp of an abiding home—all these things had been there before him, and yet beyond his ken.

He had his compensations. There was the wine at his lips. There was comfort and rest from labour. James and Joan were spending Christmas at Hertford, under Queen Katharine's reluctant roof; they would not be back in Southwark until the wedding, in a month's time. Meanwhile he could enjoy his well-earned holiday, cosseting his stomach and his self-esteem. It was a gruelling business to govern England while England's official governor was thwarting one's every move. And the task was unworthy of his great abilities; they deserved a wider, a less cramping scope.

King Henry had done him an ill turn, forbidding him to accept the Cardinalate that Rome had offered him; years might pass before the offer was repeated, and it was more than time he took that first step towards his ultimate, his more than justified ambition. An English Pope was just what Europe needed—a man of integrity, of course, a rich man for preference, industrious and experienced in government. Such a man could best deal with the many difficulties, the aftermath of the barely-healed schism, the trouble with the Czechs, the heresy and discontent throughout Christendom. Having dealt with them, he could reign in splendour and unbroken ease. Beaufort's imagination was well launched now, the walls of Winchester House were receding, dissolving, transforming themselves into the marbles of a Roman palace, built new to house the greatest and most successful Pope of the century.

A knock on the door. No peace for the conscientious. A servant announcing my lord of Somerset.

The name alone was sufficient to irritate Beaufort. It reminded him, unpleasantly, of the one recent incident he had contrived to forget—of the young bully storming and ranting against the Warwick match, shouting the extraordinary news of his sister's secret conquest. When Beaufort had hedged and promised to think it over, his nephew had pounded on the table in the most disrespectful way, demanding instant action and bludgeoning the bishop into reluctant consent. One was not afraid of the young hothead, of course; the idea was ridiculous; but there had been a certain relief in seeing him take his departure. Beaufort had been left to his own reflections, and it was these that had really decided the matter; he had remembered that a change of front would baffle Duke Humphrey, already suspecting and preparing to oppose the Warwick match: that to have a queen for niece—even a queen of petty Scotland—might be an asset to a Papal candidate: that his bargain with Somerset himself (Beaufort almost chuckled) could be considered as null, and with it the promise to find him a seat on Council: finally, and not least, that there would be no call to fulfil his other promise and pay Joan's dowry, because the English treasury would do that for him.

All the same, it was pleasanter not to remember the original interview. A petty matter, but galling to a mind revolving the destinies of all Christendom.

The servant was waiting for an answer. "Tell his lordship," said the bishop irritably, "that I am unable to see him at present. Give him the compliments of the season and tell him that I shall hope to see him at my Christmas Mass."

"Very well, my lord."

"Tell him that I am busy . . . no, that I am at my devotions—praying for a blessing on his sister's marriage. Advise him to do the same."

"Very well, my lord." There was something like irony

in the fellow's tone, and an unmistakable grin on his face. Beaufort was in half a mind to call him back as he walked to the door. Then some odd impulse suggested another, an honester reprimand. He could hardly believe that it was himself that was doing it. He had upset the dregs of his wine in the process. He was slipping on to his knees beside the table, as if it was his stall in Winchester Cathedral. He was burying his tired, harassed face in a pair of short and stubby hands.

March 1424

X

They were riding northward; they were riding towards the Border. Tomorrow—perhaps at noon, perhaps even earlier—they would be in sight of the Scottish hills. The wheel of Fortune was spinning its fastest now, sweeping James upward: nothing could happen to deflect or hinder his ascent. Tomorrow the prison gates would swing open at last: tomorrow the pawn would be a king.

James rode towards his heritage with his bride beside him and an obsequious escort of knights and lords and prelates trotting and chattering in their wake: his late gaolers were coming with him to pay the farewell compliment at the Border, his subjects-to-be had hurried southward in the hope of being first to greet the rising sun. All was as he had pictured it, a thousand times over, through eighteen years of unfulfilment. It was happening with the exact smoothness of a well-rehearsed ceremony. Even the weather was kind—as he had always imagined it—with the sun smiling on the little sea of cheerful, bobbing faces, on the moving patchwork of costly clothes and coloured pennons. Only one thing was quite different from what he had foreseen, and that was himself. He sat his horse in a dream, unable to glory in the wave that swept him on. Something must be dead inside him: how else could he be missing the savour of his triple triumph—of an exile's homecoming, a lover's union, the accession of a king?

For months now, things seemed to have rushed past him in a dream. He had done all that was required of him, bargained and issued orders, greeted and dismissed, signed or refused to sign. The English, expecting to do business with an artless, eager dupe, had been obviously astonished at his caution and precision. And yet he could hardly believe that it was he who was so dealing with them: some machine inside him seemed to move his tongue and hand, while his real self looked on in detachment, a trifle bewildered. Zest and reality must return soon, perhaps—so he told himself—when he touched Scottish soil. Meanwhile, the machine could do the work for him, while he himself, in a dull, sober acceptance, rode onward to his kingdom.

Even in the wedding there had been the same tincture of unreality. He had been a mere puppet at the princely ceremony in Southwark Church: he had sat dazed in the great hall of Winchester House, watching the large crowd that ate and drank and danced in his honour. He remembered the bishop's face, swollen like a ripe gooseberry, the childish triumph that radiated from Lady Clarence, and Joan gazing at her husband with happy, incredulous eyes. He had watched her with pride as she received the hollow congratulations of the many, the few heart-felt good wishes. He had been alone with her at last, shut away from formalities and the world's impertinent intrusion. All this had happened to him a month or so back, and he felt as if it had happened to some indifferent stranger.

He had come nearer to grasping at reality, a week ago, at Durham. It was there that the last step in the negotiations had been taken, and the Scottish hostages delivered into captivity. England's polite hypocrisies, maintained to the last, had kept alive his angry contempt. The English had renounced any claim to a ransom—and then demanded a fantastic sum of money for their "expenses" in holding him prisoner for eighteen years, for his bed and board and education. He knew that they had the whiphand, and, though he fought every inch, he had had to agree in the end. His final signature had just been affixed at Durham, in that vast Norman nave, built, one would say, to give room for an empire's business to be transacted. There he had pledged Scotland to pay a yearly sum far greater than her whole revenues, leaving Scotsmen in prison until the debt was paid. And of all the vast concourse that stood round to witness the deed, hardly one, except James himself, imagined that the oaths could ever be kept or that England would ever see the money.

It was from Durham onwards that the sensation of dreaming became strongest of all. So many youthful memories assailed him, so many half-forgotten faces came swimming back into his ken. Mar's was among them, ogreish and yellow of tooth: he had saved Scotland at Harlaw fight since James had sat with him by the fire at Evesham: his opinion of his own importance was not diminished. Master Robert Lanyne's eyes had lost some of their hunger; he brought compliments from a now flourishing university. Lanyne came in the train of Bishop Wardlaw, James's old tutor, and Wardlaw seemed far smaller and less imposing than he had in the old days. Lennox was as much of an old sheep as ever: he brought advance greetings from his son-in-law Murdoch and delivered them with the usual solemnity. Athol came with him, bald, bland and cunning, prodigal of congratulation, yet contriving to suggest that he had many secrets to tell the king, when time should serve, and a few, perhaps, that he would never tell to any man. There were Border lords in plenty, a Campbell from Lorne, island chieftains even, as well as grave burghers from Edinburgh and Perth. Their faces, the tang of their Scottish speech, brought back the long dead years of childhood. At any moment, James felt, he might be seeing his mother's tired frown, reckless, bright-eyed Rothesay, or the silvered grandeur of his father's brow. But the dream retained life's sober logic, and no ghosts came trooping southward to escort the exile home.

Giffard was one of the last to appear, slower in manner, more cautious than ever, incurably middle-aged. "It has happened at last," James said to him. "But we would never have believed, in the old days, that it would take eighteen years."

"Your Majesty says 'we'," answered Giffard, rather stiffly, "but I hope I cannot be accused of encouraging your Majesty in unjustifiable hopes."

"No," said James, "no one could have discouraged me more thoroughly. Even now, I suppose, you are thinking of all the accidents that might happen between here and Perth."

"We shall do our best," said Giffard, without a ghost of a smile, "to guard your Majesty from all harm. But I once ventured to remind your Majesty, when we were in England, that no one is safely king until he has been crowned at Scone."

James took Giffard's croaking lightly, though some of those that heard wondered at the presumption. Joan, who knew little of Scotsmen, was the most surprised. "What is that man thinking of?" she asked Athol, who rode beside her.

Athol seemed to hood his eyes. "Maybe he's thinking," he said, "that there's one or two in Scotland that'd be glad if his Majesty never reached Scone at all. There have been mice playing while the cat was away, and maybe they'll not relish their game being interrupted now."

"You talk in riddles, my lord."

"I find it safest, your Majesty."

"If you know of mischief, it is your duty to speak plainly."

"I know nothing; I only suspect. I'll warn his Majesty when I'm surer. And maybe I'm just an old woman, finding trouble where there is none. We shall see, we shall see."

They had ridden past the belt of the great English castles and entered the No-man's-land of loop-holed farmsteads and lonely peel-towers. The Border had been unusually peaceful for some years now, yet no one dared to build for comfort or unbattlemented ease. Poor men's eyes, half-hostile, peered at them from little hovels, humble enough to be spared by a raider or, unspared, to be rebuilt in an evening, when the raid had passed. They had not reached the Scottish frontier but it lay abreast of them, towards the west. There lay Roxburgh, with its Scottish castle still in English hands: there lay Otterburn, where a Douglas had beaten the Percies and died himself, in the hour of victory, beneath a midsummer moon. They passed Homildon Hill, which had seen so many Scots butchered by the arrows, so many more—with Murdoch among them—carried into captivity. When the Cheviot lay behind them, there was but one hill between them and the Tweed; James asked what it was called, and they told him, "Flodden Edge." The name meant nothing to him or to those that rode in his train. A century must pass before his great-grandson was to lead their descendants, and all that quaint, ruffianly pageant which we call Mediaeval Scotland, to perish in an evening beneath that forbidding hill.

It had been arranged to ride northward through Berwick, but Scotland was too near now to be resisted. James ordered a change of direction; wheeling leftward, he led his cavalcade through Crookham to the ford at Coldstream.

It was afternoon. The harbingers, pressing ahead to demand lodgings for the night, roused the little township as they passed, with the news that the king was at hand. Farmers and cowgirls, priest and blacksmith and beggar came flocking towards the Tweed. A new age was coming to Scotland, and they watched it ride in with the gay lords and ladies who came splashing through the ford. Their wondering eyes were fixed upon the young man at the head —short of stature, but with a proud carriage, and bright, thoughtful eyes.

James saw the dumb welcome in the faces of the little crowd. He heard them break into scattered shouting as he breasted the bank and drew rein in Scotland. A woman ran forward and stooped to kiss his stirrup. He did not regret the formal rejoicings that would have awaited him beyond Berwick: he was glad to have entered his kingdom by surprise, among these homespun, weatherworn folk. Their welcome might help him to awake from his dream, to dissipate the muffling mists of unreality.

He swung himself off his horse, knelt down and kissed the ground, as if to draw new strength from the touch of home. The country people, still eating him with their eyes, seemed content to accept whatever strange action he might perform. His own escort were less at ease, Mar sneering openly, the bishops hardly comprehending a sacrament unknown to Holy Kirk. And Giffard, sitting his horse in rigid disapproval, seemed to repeat his warning that they were not yet at Scone.

April 1424

XI

They had pitched a great tent in the garden of Melrose Abbey. James and Joan sat on an impromptu dais at one end of it, with the great lords who had come to welcome and bring them home. Murdoch himself lingered at Doune or Stirling, but had sent his sons, young James and Alexander and wild Walter, who was still unpunished for the strangling of his father's hawk. Walter came to ask for knighthoods for all three, and Walter's askings had the tone of a demand. King James had postponed his answer. He was determined to commit himself to nothing, especially where the house of Albany was concerned. He gathered that other demands were in the air, conditions, even, upon which they would allow him to go to Scone for the crowning. They were strong enough for it, and might be relying still on Douglas's help—though Douglas himself, the great

Earl Archibald, was fighting in France. James must look round him before he either granted or denied what was demanded by so great a power.

The Abbot of Melrose was doing the honours, introducing the succession of lesser men who came to welcome or petition their king. The petitions were oddly varied—burghers of Fife complaining that the Highland chiefs were robbing their peaceful fishing-fleets in the Sutherland sea-lochs; minor barons from Angus talking of a plague of starlings, very destructive to the crops; Edinburgh merchants describing the growth of immorality in their city, insufficiently repressed by the Burgh Council. These last (James was slily informed from elsewhere) had little to grumble about, considering the number of illegitimate children they were supporting (or not supporting) in outlying farms. The monks had further tales of growing wickedness, holy men maltreated, monastic dues withheld. Pluscarden and Lindores had sent their almoners, Iona its own abbot—bringing with him a breath of Iona's half-legendary sanctity. There was even a deaf old monk from Scar-Inch in the outer Hebrides, who could tell tales of Atlantic whales and pirates from Orkney and Trondhjem Fjord.

The churchmen were at it now. Joan, unable to understand their queer Latin, gazed beyond them at the crowd of bonnet-lairds and townsmen. They were mostly in middle age, and she wondered why Scotland, so full of eager young faces, could show so few elder ones that were not stiff and guarded. Perhaps life was harder here, and those that began with more openness and generosity than Englishmen, were sooner chilled into dour and watchful greybeards, with a grievance against things in general. She must ask James if they could not attract the younger men to Court and teach them to grow old more gracefully. Her gaze wandered unhappily over the rows of solemn worthies that waited and stiffened themselves to meet their king. And then suddenly, with something of a shock, her eyes came to rest on a single face.

A man was looking at her—or at James—with a curious and alarming intensity. His thatch of flame-coloured hair should have drawn her attention earlier. Beneath it was one of the most striking faces she had ever seen, seamed like a mountain crag, set with cold grey eyes. The man himself was tall, raw-boned and powerful, but there was no mistaking the intelligence that accompanied his physical strength. If he, too, cherished some secret grudge against life, it would be a reasoned one, and, unless his looks belied him, he would maintain it against God and Devil alike—or go down defying their omnipotence. She should have realized at once that it was James he was looking at, not her. He would not be a man to whom women were of the slightest importance. But she had a curious feeling that James ought to be warned.

She must pull herself together, and not allow fancy to run riot. The man did not matter, and the chances were that, when once some question of a few acres or shillings was settled, neither she nor James would ever see him again. It was mere imagination that pictured him pursuing, in petty matters as well as great, an abstract and impossible justice. She had picked out an interesting face among a crowd of dullards, that was all. She must look at him again in a minute and persuade herself that he was indeed negligible.

The last of the monks was finishing his peroration, beseeching James to establish peace and justice and to defend Holy Kirk: he included, one might suppose, Holy Kirk's vast share of the wealth and land of Scotland. He adjured the king to foster learning and piety, crushing the heresy that Satan had begun to spread. He came to an abrupt finish. James, for the twentieth time, promised to do all these things, and then the Abbot of Melrose consulted his secretary and sent a message to the lay suitors. James leant across to Lennox.

"I hope your lordship will tell me," he said, "if I give offence anywhere without meaning to. I am still a stranger in my own kingdom."

"I am sure," answered Lennox, "quite sure, that your Majesty's graciousness exceeds expectation. A most gratifying afternoon." He looked a trifle uneasy, in spite of his words, and glanced towards Athol.

"Your Majesty'll not hope to rule Scotland," said Athol, "without giving offence. There's some evils that grow fatter on fair words."

James frowned slightly, and seemed inclined to change the subject. "Who is the tall man," he asked, "the one with red hair?"

Joan looked up. "So you noticed him too?" she said.

"Graham," said Lennox, "Sir Robert Graham. A strange man, your Majesty. Kinsman to my lord of Athol."

"By marriage, only by marriage," said Athol. "He is uncle to the Earl of Strathearn, young Malise, and cares more for him than he does for his own sons."

"Is that what makes him so glum?" asked James, laughing.

"I think he looks dangerous," said Joan, lightly. There was a strange, cold feeling at her heart. "Perhaps he's been crossed in love!" she added, and regretted it at once: she felt as if she were behaving like a schoolgirl.

"He owns little land himself," Lennox was saying, with a slight tone of discomfort. "Not an important personage."

"Maybe no," said Athol, shaking his bald head. "But his Majesty might do well to remember him."

James was looking at Graham again. "I am not likely to forget him," he said. Then he fell silent and the whole group on the dais stiffened into formality as the next deputation approached.

It was some time before Graham was beckoned forward. He stood with eyes on the floor, as though he had already looked his fill and taken the king's measure. His petitions, if trifling, were numerous. It appeared that he had lost much, here a little and there a little, while the house of Albany ruled. When he raised his face, it was to look towards Lennox—and Lennox fidgeted a little under the scrutiny. He spoke with reserve at first, but as one who knew the law and his own rights. He hoped, rather pointedly, that the new king would see justice done. Then he warmed to it a little, hinting at scandals such as no one had mentioned yet. The waiting audience seemed to come to life, associating themselves, by murmur or gesture, with this champion bolder than themselves. Then he checked his flow, ending soberly and within the limits of his private pleas. He seemed to leave his backers a little disconcerted, as though they would have welcomed further vehemence.

James answered favourably but without committing himself. He promised that Graham's petitions should be examined and justly dealt with. He was conscious, all the time, that Joan sat ill at ease beside him, watching Graham; he was glad for her sake to dismiss the man. Graham made his bow and marched out of the tent, a little alley forming among the crowd as he went. One gathered that, unlike his fellows, he was not meaning to stay and sample the abbey's outdoor hospitality.

The sun was low before business was finished and James emerged from the tent, to be greeted with music and the sight of loaded tables. Weary of ceremony and its long delays, the company soon dissolved into informal good-fellowship. The prelates, deprecatory at first, ended by drinking and laughing with the rest. James was only too glad to unbend a little, strolling from one chattering group to another, and only annoyed when his approach provoked a sudden hush. The incident of Graham's speech was not the only hint that he had not heard all that his petitioners would have liked to tell him. He was hoping for more enlightenment, now that he no longer sat on a dais with great lords standing round.

His path had already diverged from Joan's when a shout of merriment attracted his attention to a knot at whose centre stood the deaf old monk from Scar-Inch. Murdoch's son, Walter, was leading the laughter, and when it dwindled, as if ashamed, at the king's approach, Walter laughed louder and more insolently than ever.

"Your Majesty!" he spluttered, "d'you know what the old fool's asking? He's wanting us to tell him if it's true that the English are born with tails! That's the story, where he comes from. I told him to ask your Majesty, because you, . . . because. . . ." Walter's voice suddenly dropped. He had seen James's face. Even so, he was tempted to finish as he had intended "—because you have married an Englishwoman." James could guess quite well what the jest had been, but even Walter would hardly dare to repeat it to him. "Because," he said lamely, "your Majesty was so long in England."

"We all believe strange things," said James sententiously, "about distant places." He turned away, glad that Joan was not hearing. He stood a moment apart with only a small following behind him.

He would have to deal with Walter yet—and for worse crimes than an impudent, even a treasonable, jest. Rumour had it that Murdoch had found Walter beyond control. But Murdoch, as James was beginning to realize more clearly than ever, had found most of Scotland beyond control. That very morning, the Abbot of Melrose had told him tales of this peaceful-seeming country round the abbey, less peaceful when the Haigs of Bemersyde were riding out to plunder. It seemed as if all Scotland might be suffering from like disturbers of her peace, laughing at regents and their feeble protests.

"Your Majesty must be thinking us a horde of savages. I fear your Majesty'll not be far wrong."

It was Athol at his elbow again, Athol, as often, uncannily plumbing one's thoughts. James felt a sudden unaccountable anger, a sudden impulse to strike him across the bald pate. "I said nothing, my lord," he answered coldly.

"Maybe no," said Athol, "but your Majesty was looking a peck of things." He turned to smile back at Lennox beside him. The two old men made the strongest of contrasts, Athol breathing intelligence, suspicion and cynicism, handsome Lennox a monument of stupid conventionality.

"Your lordship," said Lennox, "has no right to give his Majesty an ill opinion of his own subjects. I am sure that everything in Scotland . . . that most things . . ." He seemed to have difficulty in finishing his sentence. He turned, ill-advisedly, to the Abbot of Iona. "I was just telling his Majesty," he said, "that he must not judge Scotland by the opinions of the discontented grievances, of course, such as we have been hearing all day, but . . . My son-in-law's regency. . . ." He found it harder than ever to proceed, with Iona's grave eyes resting on him.

"I am thinking," said the abbot, "that his Majesty will do well to judge for himself. This is hardly the time to speak of such things, but your lordship will be doing the devil's work if you try to persuade him that there is not a great deal amiss in Scotland, a great deal that will have to be set right."

Athol was grinning in the background, glad to find this unexpected ally, glad to see Lennox entangling himself to no purpose. Lennox, annoyed at contradiction, was summoning up an irritating heartiness. "If it is killing and thieving you mean," he retorted to the abbot, "I've heard you've a pretty set of robbers in the Isles. I've heard——"

His opponent cut him short. "I was not speaking of the Isles," he said. "Your lordship will know the text about the beam and the mote. There are evil men on our coasts—but in your lands, too, and my lord Athol's, God's poor are plundered and His Kirk defrauded."

Heads were turning now, listeners approaching. A ring had begun to form. No one was sorry to see old Lennox routed. "As your lordship remarked," he answered lamely, "this is hardly the time to be talking of such things."

"I can only ask his Majesty's pardon," said the abbot, "if I have said too much." He turned away, but they made no avenue for him, unwilling to see him depart. "Say on," someone called out, "his Majesty is listening!" James added his own voice. "I hope there is no time," he said, "when I am not ready to hear of wrongs I can redress." There was no doubt which way the tide was setting. More than one voice cried out, "God bless the king!"

Lennox flushed in embarrassment. The beard wagged on his hesitating jaw. "Of course, of course," he said, "but it's no time—— I mean, it's a dog's life his Majesty can look for, if you listen to every grievance that anyone'll put."

There was an angry murmur at that, and the abbot gave it sanction. "If I may speak for his Majesty," he said, "he does not come among us to be idle."

The crowd was pressing in, their intent growing articulate. Lennox wore a look of discomfort and alarm. The onlookers had begun to cry shame upon him. What right had great lords to speak so lightly of their miseries? They were sick from years of frustration, furious that anyone should confuse or mislead their new-found champion. They had spent the long day whispering to each other of their wrongs, laying them, as much as they dared, before the listening king. Now wine and excitement were loosing the clamour of their unguarded tongues, and they pressed round James with all doubts forgotten.

"If we could but tell your Majesty——"

"Our fields bare, our trees cut down——"

"No trade these seven years——"

"Not a bridge on the Clyde a man dare use——"

"It needs twenty men, in arms, to take a wagon to Dundee——"

"We've a saying in our part that it needs a squadron to guard your cow, and an army to keep your castle."

"It's a hard thing we're asking——"

"It's war we want, war on tyrants and robbers!"

James caught their ardour. "By God," he shouted, half at Lennox, half at his opponents, "dog's life for me or no, I'll not rest till the key keeps the castle for you, and the bracken-bush the cow!"

He looked round him at the flushed faces, at hope and

fierce longing and patience at last discarded. They were shouldering him on to a chair, a king's sanctity forgotten in the joy of finding a leader. They cheered him to the echo, fell silent for him to speak, and broke in upon his speech with new applause. They were packed close around him and the garden beyond was empty, except where Joan stood among a knot of tonsured heads. She was looking across at James, proud and loving and a little frightened. He smiled back over the shouting; he must let her know that there was nothing to fear, that Scotsmen, well-led, could teach the world a lesson in loyalty and achievement.

One of the wilder spirits, careless of distances, started crying, "To Scone! To Scone!" The whole crowd took it up, insistent that they must crown him king. They would bring him on the way, their swords should guard his progress. They would have rushed out, there and then, to saddle their horses, if he had not quieted them a little and imposed some semblance of common sense. Darkness had fallen upon Melrose before he could get them to disperse, and he had pledged himself to start early on the morrow.

It was evident, when he rose next morning, that they had spent the night in action. Many new faces were gathered to greet him in the dawn twilight and accompany him northward. Some must have ridden ahead, spreading news which brought reinforcements in as the march proceeded; before Edinburgh was reached, James found himself at the head of a little army of farmers and small squires.

Opposition, if opposition had indeed been plotted, was taken by surprise. Lennox had disappeared, presumably to his own estates. Walter, fleeing ahead to Edinburgh, was arrested there, and placed, for safety's sake, under lock and key. Murdoch made no protest against his son's imprisonment: he observed every formality, meeting James near Stirling to surrender his regency. The great lords who had not come to Melrose were all riding in now, obeying the summons to attend a coronation. There was no check to the triumphal progress. On a bright morning in May, James and his following rode into Perth, and knew that Scone was three short miles beyond.

There was no Stone of Destiny at Scone. Edward of England had carried it away to Westminster, in the old days of Scotland's humiliation. Scone Abbey had seen no king crowned for a generation: its buildings seemed impoverished and decayed. But the little mound was still green beneath the vast and solemn trees: the Tay still hurried past, babbling of Highland forests. Here the great ones of Scotland, masters of half her soil, were gathered to set James and Joan upon their thrones. They came armed and spurred, as custom demanded: it was so that a small band of desperate men, fleeing from Edward's soldiers, had set the crown upon the Bruce's head: it was so that their earlier ancestors had consecrated Malcolm Canmore, when the fitful fever of Macbeth's life was over and he slept in a royal tomb beside the Duncan he had murdered.

By a strange irony, it was Murdoch, as Earl of Fife, who must lead his cousin up the mound and buckle on him the kingly sword. His fingers fumbled a little, perhaps from clumsiness, perhaps from reluctance to seal the frustration of his own royal hopes. He rose from his knees, and shambled down to rejoin his peers and kinsmen. Further off, silent and watchful, stood a great ring of lesser men, still greedily expectant of a new and better age. As Bishop Wardlaw pronounced the last blessing, a wild-haired man was seen to run forward, trailing a Highland claymore. He knelt on the grass and began to chant, in an eerie sing-song, the names of the royal line. "*Benach*," he began, "*Benach de Re Sheamus Mac-Ian, Mac-Robert, Mac-Walter*——" and would have made his way backward to Trojan princes and judges of Israel; but a great roar of Lowland cheering drowned his voice—earls and bishops, knights and commoners uniting to hail their king. All Scotland had gathered to grace the primeval sacrament, all Scotland was shouting among the trees.

James looked up to their branches, nodding indifferently above him. More than ever did he feel that nothing about him was real, that he was surrounded and encompassed by a dream. But he was on the brink of understanding: he knew, at least, that if he had indeed fallen to dreaming, he must not expect to awaken on this side of the grave. For he was a man full-grown, knowing now what illimitable mysteries beset us, and unable to recapture the easily-answered questings of a youth. If he had come home, it was to a land of strangers: their difference from himself must add its contribution to the essential loneliness that vexes every human soul. And, to crown all, he had been chosen, by birth and consent alike, to be their figurehead and high-priest, the reigning demigod of their tribe. Through him must pass and round him linger all the yearnings and aspirations and hatreds that consumed them. He had become a king, and no king, however unworthy, could be quite as other men.

Reprisal

Between the acting of a dreadful thing
And the first motion, all the interim is
Like a phantasma or a hideous dream.

Julius Cæsar, II. i. 4.

CHAPTER SIX

Reprisal

June 1424

I

"WILL YOU HAVE this here, your Majesty?"

"What is it?" Joan turned to see Margery Norton holding a small square of tapestry against the bare stone wall. She was growing accustomed to being called "Majesty" by her new subjects, but the title still came oddly from her old nurse. "I suppose so," she said, in a disheartened voice, "though nothing will make this room look much better than a dungeon."

They were at Perth, and—since Perth's ramshackle castle was still under repair—guests of the Black Friars. Joan had heard of people, and not merely heretics, who spent their time denouncing the luxury and corruption of the monasteries. She often wished, these days, that the Black Friars of Perth lived a little more luxuriously than they did.

The old woman was mounting a stool and reaching up to a row of rusty nails. "Cobwebs," she grumbled to herself. "Does nobody ever sweep cobwebs in this country?"

"They are probably afraid of killing the spiders," said Joan, smiling. "That's bad luck, here, especially in the king's family. His Majesty is kin to the Bruce."

"Oh," said Margery, grunting as she stretched up, "and who may the Bruce be? Does he live at Perth?"

"Hush, Margery, you must not ask these things. We're in Scotland."

"Don't I know it?" said Margery. "And how am I to learn, your Majesty, if I ask no questions? I'm doing my best." She looked pathetically English and out of place, perched on a stool in that gaunt and gloomy room. It would not be luxuries that Margery lacked: a damp and draughty cottage would probably suffice her—but with wattle-and-daub walls, and neighbours who spoke in her own soft accents. She climbed down, looking for something new to occupy her. "There's a tear in that tablecloth," she said. "I'd better mend it now."

"Well, be quick with it," said Joan. "His Majesty will be back from Parliament at any moment."

Margery dived into the unseen recesses of her attire and brought needle and thread to the surface. "It won't take me long," she said, "if your Majesty will let me sit down to it." Margery had been undergoing lessons in etiquette.

"Of course I will." Joan picked up her own needlework —almost her first since the wedding. She had taken to it a few days ago, mainly in order to disabuse her new subjects of any notions they might have about the fecklessness of Englishwomen. "And I had better tell you about Bruce," she added, "while there are no Scots folk in hearing."

"Yes," said Margery, with obvious distaste. "Thanking your Majesty for the trouble."

"Well, he was King of Scotland long ago. One of the greatest—so far. They say he freed the country when no one else could have done so."

"Freed it from what, your Majesty?"

"Well, from us. From the English."

"Oh." Margery was not impressed: she seemed about to add some comment and then, thinking it disrespectful, desisted. She darned in silence for a time. "And did he kill spiders?" she asked at last.

"No. Never. They brought him luck—at least, one did. He was sleeping in a cave or somewhere, one night——"

"In a cave, your Majesty? I thought he was a king."

"Yes. King of Scotland."

"Then I've been all wrong, thinking the Black Friars

was no fit place for his Majesty. Maybe I should have been thankful it's no worse."

"We're only here, you know, till the castle is repaired." Joan crushed an impulse to share grievances with her servant. "And it's a fine building in its way," she said, "even if it's not what we're accustomed to."

"Yes, your Majesty," said the old woman, finishing off her darning. "Your Majesty knows best." She patted the table-cover back into position, and stuck the needle into the bosom of her dress. "I suppose it's safe, anyway," she said, looking towards the window. "Should be, with all these bolts and bars—and a moat to keep 'em out."

"Keep who out? Who are you talking about?"

"I don't know, your Majesty. Just anyone."

A timid knock drew Margery to the door. She opened it, listened a moment, and then bobbed into the room again. "One of the Brothers, your Majesty, to say that the king's on his way back."

"Very well, Margery. You can go. And ask them to hurry dinner, will you? They were not expecting his Majesty so soon."

She sat sewing still, awaiting James. She wondered if she would ever learn to accept Scotland and Scottish life. She had done her best so far, for his sake. It was a pity that he had cherished such rosy memories through his years of captivity: she had half believed his praises of Edinburgh, "finer," he had insisted, "than any English city"; she could remember her incredulous disappointment when she first saw its single ragged street climbing up towards the cruel rock. Stirling was no better, though by Stirling she had learnt to expect less. Perth was pleasantly situated, but hardly the capital city that James talked of making it. To eyes accustomed to the south, a spirit of savagery seemed to brood over the whole country. She could not imagine, yet, how men could think of it as home, though she herself must learn to do so. Yet there was no self-pity in her reflections. Whatever her grievances, she had to admit that she was happy, happier than she had believed possible. Nothing really mattered except James. Even the Black Friars was enchanted when she could hear, as she now heard, the sound of his step on the stairs, running up to meet her with most unkingly leaps. She rose in excitement and, a moment later, was safely in his arms.

She was still insatiable for love; she could not help feeling disconcerted that his boyish mood could not last, nor his preoccupation with herself remain unmixed. She had married a king, and of no fairy-tale kingdom. She had hoped to forget it for an hour at least, but it was not long before he was striding up and down the room with furrowed brows, looking older instead of younger than his years. She tried to laugh off her disappointment.

"James," she said, "I wouldn't have thought it possible. You remind me of my uncle."

"Your uncle? Not the bishop?"

"Yes—when he'd come back from a Parliament. I suppose it has the same effect on all men."

"I wish I had something like an English Parliament to deal with. They talk, at any rate."

"Uncle used to say that was just the trouble."

"Well, I'd rather they did that, than sit there hugging their swords, like a row of statues in a church. One can't begin to guess what they're thinking of. It's more like a tournament than a Parliament—even the clerks look like heralds. Half the Commons won't come at all—sending one proxy to represent half-a-dozen of them. I can't blame them, either. It saves money and trouble. Why should burghers and knights come? They can't presume to discuss anything when the barons and bishops only sit and frown."

"Doesn't that make it easier for you? I mean, can't you get things passed more quickly?"

"Passed? There's no trouble there. I've been putting things through that the English peers would not stomach for an instant. It's uncanny, the way no one has a word to say."

"Perhaps they like your laws."

"They couldn't—some of them. They'll pass them all right. They'd vote away their own lands and pass sentence on their own brothers. And all the time they'd be wondering how many men they can count on when they go home to raise rebellion."

"Rebellion?"

"Yes, and it might come before I even know whose toes I've been treading on. Some of them need a good hard stamping on, for that matter. But I wish I knew how far it's safe to go."

Joan sighed, picking up her work again. "I wish I could help you," she said.

"You can, my dearest. You will be able to—when we know more where we are. They've forgotten what it means to have a Court in this country, a place where there's a little civilization, a little talk that isn't about oats, or wolfhunts or brawling with your neighbour."

"A court? Where?" said Joan mischievously, looking round the room. James did not stop in his pacing. "I can build," he said, "when I get the money. I must find some money."

"Where?" said Joan again.

He came to a halt, looking at her. "There's enough in Scotland," he said, "enough that belongs to me. Only it's slipped into other people's pockets during the last twenty years."

"Can you make it slip back?" she said.

He stood looking at her for some seconds more, and then walked to the window. It looked southward over Perth. A shower was threatening. The sun was hidden. Only the river gleamed silver in the middle of a grey picture. He turned back, as if dissatisfied, and threw himself into a chair. "I must be king," he said. "It's time that I was king!"

She was too wise to ask for explanation. She waited, quietly drawing the thread through her work, once, twice, a third time. Then her hands fell to her lap and she sat motionless. His eyes strayed up to her, almost reluctantly.

It would be so easy to do what would best please her and most comfort him—to go and sit beside her, forgetting everything except their love. She promised refuge from all that was ugly and intolerable and yet had to be faced. But it was a coward's refuge, a drug that must be increased with each indulgence. He did not really crave for it, if it clouded other things in his mind. He must get them clear first, and ready shaped for action.

"Joan?"

"Yes?"

"I may have to do something—an evil thing, that will earn me much blame and hatred. I cannot tell others, nor even you, why it is necessary. When it is done, it may be possible to reign—and reign without harshness or bloodshed, as my poor father dreamt that one might do. Until it is done, I am not myself, and this country is ungoverned, whatever laws are passed."

She was silent a moment before speaking. "Is it anything I can help you with?" she asked.

"No. I am only telling you of it to clear my own mind. No one can help me to decide."

"Is it anything to do with the money?"

"Oh, yes. Money buys anything: swords, and men to swing them. I saw enough in France——"

He rose, walked a step or two, and halted again. The light from the window fell full upon his face. "And they deserve it," he said. "By God, but they deserve it!"

Joan felt a sudden chill at her heart. He was talking to himself, but not so much to clear his mind as to convince himself: to convince himself of something against which conscience, or some part of it, was still protesting. She was deeply in love with this man: she knew him brave, believed him wise and just: but there was a glint in his eyes as he stood there, a shadow round his mouth that disturbed and even repelled her. She rose, half-frightened, whispering his name.

In a moment, the evil had vanished. She could forget,

or almost forget, its warning. He was smiling at her in pure love, holding out his hands. She glided to him, buried herself in his embrace. The shower had broken outside and the rain was descending. But they were alone together, young and incredibly happy. There was nothing else she need think of, not even the crown that had been clamped upon his brow. Their passion for each other, with all its intensity and purity, could make any burden bearable, purge both of them from any creeping evil. She was lost in him and he in her, so that nothing else mattered. If evil encroached, it should destroy them both, but drive no wedge between them. And how could she fear any evil that they could face together?

But even as she clung to him, she felt, in her deepest heart, the sudden seed of fear that had fallen. She tried to assure herself that it would not, could not, take root. She wished she was not hearing, through his whispered love, the splashing of rain-drops on the window: it was a foolish fancy, of course, but they reminded her at one moment of tears, at another of dropping blood.

June 1424

II

"They'll never stand it. I tell you, uncle, they'll never stand it!" Malise Graham was barely seventeen, but he felt that his peerage gave him the right to pass judgment upon matters of State. The Earldom of Strathearn was not a large one, but its position gave it some importance. Malise had only ridden a few miles out of Perth, but he was already upon his own land: from where he lay, on a bank above the rough road, he could look up the long valley that gave him his title and his money. His thoughts were not upon it, but upon the city behind it and the Parliament that had met there.

He looked towards his uncle and combed the heather beside him with spread-eagled fingers. "He's over-hasty," he said. "He'll have to walk a deal more cannily if he's wanting a long reign."

Sir Robert Graham smiled a little smile, and ran a knotted hand over his red hair. He still had food in his lap for, unlike his nephew, he was taking his wayside meal with slow deliberation.

"There's leeway to make up," he said. "It's a hundred years since we had a king with a will of his own." He paused to pick a piece of gristle out of his teeth and flip it into a gorse-bush. "You'd not remember King Robert," he said. "And they say the grandfather was almost as weak. It's a long time since this country was governed at all. I'm not surprised they're misliking the experience at first."

"Nor at last, either," answered Malise. "James is not the Bruce, and folk'll not let him walk over them. Laws for the salmon, laws about our retinues, laws to turn us all into archers——"

"He's been to France," said Graham. "He's seen the English shoot."

His nephew snorted. "Do the English have sheriffs nosing into their houses," he demanded, "asking for papers and title-deeds when everyone knows whose the land is? There's talk enough about justice and crown rights, but I'm thinking it's just money that Jamie is wanting. Aren't the new customs enough, and the tax he's raising to pay his English friends? Even the Albanies never raised a tax, and they were paying out all the little pensions that Jamie's put a stop to. How is he meaning to spend it all—on stockings for his London lassie?"

"Wheesht, man, wheesht!" Graham pointed towards the servants who sat at a respectful distance, but hardly out of earshot of an over-excited boy.

"They're not listening," grumbled Malise. "And they'd not tell if they were."

"Anyone'll tell if he's paid for it."

"D'you think King James has his spies out already?"

"He'd be a fool if he hadn't. He's king. It'll not be difficult to find men for the work, now that Murdoch is drawing in his horns and dismissing his agents."

Silence fell for a minute. Graham finished eating, and picked the shreds of his meal from his knees. "Where'll the dogs have gone?" he said, looking up the hill-side. "Did they start a hare or something?"

Malise was not listening. "He's not even good-looking," he said, half to himself, "like Albany's kin. He's half a head shorter than me, and I've not finished growing. I wonder how long it'll be before Murdoch is sorry he brought him back."

Graham, smiling at his nephew, grew grave before he spoke. "I take it," he said, "that it'll be useless telling you to check that tongue of yours."

"He's riding for a fall, uncle," protested Malise, but without raising his voice. "We've all sent our kin to England, as pledges for his ransom. And instead of thanking us, he's challenging our titles to our lands."

"Maybe he's wishful to be king. He cannot be that without land and money."

"He'll take my head before he has mine!"

"Maybe he'll have both, if you talk to others as you're talking now."

"Did you hear," insisted Malise, "that he's meaning to forfeit Lennox?" Graham looked up in surprise. "Who's been telling you that blethers?" he asked.

"Lennox expects it himself. He's buying in arms."

"Lennox is an old sheep. He'd buy arms to fight his own shadow—and even then he'd run away. And I would not blame James for robbing that nest, nor Murdoch's either. They've been feathering them this long while with James's goods."

He rose, picked up his sword, and buckled it on. "Time we were going," he said. "The light will be gone by the time you reach home."

"I'm not for home tonight," answered Malise. "I'm sleeping at Methven."

"Methven? Is it Athol you'd be supping with?"

"It is that. And why not?"

"Listen, Malise. I've a warning for ye."

"You always have plenty of them. Sir Robert the Grim."

"This is no joke. You can say what you like to me, here on the heather, and you'll maybe take no harm. But if you so much as hint to that old snake at Methven that King James is too fond of the silver, or too fat for your taste, or what not, you can count on one thing—King James will hear of it, with maybe a little added, just as soon as it suits Athol that he should. Neither you nor any man knows what may be going on inside that lump of baldness, and most of us think it's wiser to put no more ideas into it than are there already."

Malise had turned uphill, scanning the skyline. He gave no sign of having heard his uncle's words.

"There they are," he said.

"Who do you mean?"

"The dogs. They've lost us." He gave a piercing whistle and watched the little dots in the distance as they hesitated, turned, and came rushing back towards the road.

"Maybe you're right," he said carelessly. "I'll mind what I say at Methven." His manner did not inspire confidence in his discretion.

He slid down the bank, swung himself on to one of the horses that the servants were bringing, and waved a farewell from the saddle. A moment later he was rattling down the road, the dogs prancing and yelping beside him.

Graham stood on the edge of the bank, his red hair brighter for the evening sun. He was troubled, and not only for Malise: there was a Providence that watched over foolish boys or taught them, by some minor mishap, how to hold their tongues. His other anxiety was wider and vaguer, embracing a nation's fate. He had endured Albany's rule and Murdoch's, and welcomed their supplanter: he would not be sorry to see him work their ruin, if only in revenge; but there was a suspicion at the back of his mind that there might be something behind what Malise said, and that James, having ruined Graham's enemies, might put in jeopardy all that Graham most loved.

August 1424

III

"Are you a Highland man, Master Cameron?" James shot the question at his new secretary across a large table, now a wilderness of parchment and tape.

Cameron looked up from his writing. "No, your Majesty," he said, "I was born at Cameron, near St. Andrews."

"Oh; Fife." James's eyes had not left the papers he was studying. "Were you brought up there?"

"I was not, your Majesty. I . . . I grew up in the towns—Falkland mostly, and Stirling. I was an orphan. Cameron is a small village, and few of the people have enough for their own children."

"But you went to the University?"

"I am not the only poor man that has cause to be grateful for your Majesty's foundation."

James grunted, acknowledging the flattery. There was silence for a moment; Cameron's pen was at rest, while his mind travelled backward in time. He was in a fair way now to attaining his considerable ambitions, but he had not yet attempted to forget his origin. It was said that he had kept himself from starvation, for several years, by "holding horses" in the streets of Stirling. The phrase covered a multitude of less savoury duties—dubious errands for the rich and the outwardly respectable. Now that he had climbed from a small post in the Kirk to that of king's secretary, he looked forward to meeting those who had hired and degraded him on more equal terms. Few of them would recognize him, fewer still would remember how much he knew. They themselves had perhaps contrived to forget it—how certain men, once inconvenient to them, had disappeared among the hills on dark nights of winter: why such and such a girl, comely ten years ago, was now plucking at men's sleeves in Dunfermline market, and generally plucking in vain. But Cameron had forgotten none of these things: some day, he felt, his memories might be of use. Meanwhile, there was work to do.

"Does your Majesty need advice about the Highlands?"

"What's that?" asked James, rousing himself from his paper. "No. That must wait, I think." He looked at Cameron as though trying to recover a thread of thought lost among a tangle of matters to be considered. Then he gave it up. "Who is summoned for this afternoon?" he asked.

"The Abbot of Cambuskenneth. My lord of Athol. The Provost of Dundee. . . ."

"Tell them," interrupted James, "to admit Athol as soon as he arrives."

Cameron rose from his stool. "His lordship will be glad to advise your Majesty," he said, "on the question we were discussing this morning."

"Is there any question," said James, half to himself, "on which he would not be glad to advise me?"

"His lordship has a great reputation for wisdom."

"I have noticed that you are all afraid of him," said James. Cameron, finding no answer, began to move towards the door. "Do you think I was right," said James, "letting him persuade me to arrest the Graham?"

Cameron hesitated. "The Graham is a dangerous man," he said. "The Albanies found him troublesome. I think his lordship's advice was sound."

"I'd have preferred something more definite."

"That is not easy, your Majesty, in such cases. My lord of Athol spoke of the Graham talking treason to the young

Earl of Strathearn. Treason is careful to leave as few traces of itself as possible."

Cameron waited for a reply and, getting none, continued on his errand. James picked up the papers again. Now and then he felt for a pen, to initial a document or scrawl a short note. A light breeze from the window stirred the hair upon his head. It brought with it the faint fragrance of autumn cornfields, of pastures and distant forest. Cornfield, pasture and forest—such was the theme of the documents that littered the table. But here their spaciousness was reduced to inky scrawls: here were listed their rents and purchase-prices, lying reports of their annual yield: here, in letters and petitions, indignant owners struggled for their possession with querulous claimants. No mention was made of their unpurchasable fragrance, their golden beauty beneath a summer sun. Man, it seemed, cared little for such things. Man only desired them, only bound himself to them with paper bonds, in order that he might fill his belly or feed his pride.

Cameron spoke a word or two through the door and returned to his place. The scratch and rustle of his pen resumed its regular rhythm. James had sat back in his chair and was gazing out of window. He was not thinking of the cornfields nor of anything his eye could see. His mind was half upon the work before him, with all its irritating detail, half upon the greater problem that loomed behind it, simpler, daily more insistent and yet defying solution. It was partly a matter of money, partly of less ponderable things. It was not laws, such as Parliament or committees of Parliament passed for him so glibly—though they could not tell him how to get them obeyed. It was not signatures to petitions, the royal seal upon charters. These things made up the routine of kingship; they were here beneath his hand. The reality lay behind, still in the balance.

He had wished, at times, that it would come to rebellion and civil war; there would be a clear issue then, treason to denounce, loyalties to invoke. As it was, he felt hemmed in by something that professed loyalty and yet thwarted his every intention. By the time he came to grips with it, opposition had always entrenched itself behind specious barricades of privilege and ancient custom. The steel might be bared, tentatively, behind his back; before he could round upon it, it was in its sheath again. With each month that passed he felt himself losing ground, betraying the high hopes on whose crest he had ridden to the throne. The tide might ebb soon, leaving him as powerless and despicable as his father had been. Whoever was master of Scotland, it would not be the King of Scots.

"Your Majesty has finished with the Treasurer's report?"

"What's that? . . . Oh, yes. You can do what you like with it. It makes cheerless reading."

"The money for your Majesty's ransom comes in more quickly than we expected. The first instalment, at least."

"Yes. The first instalment."

"The English are lucky if they get that, your Majesty. Scotland is not accustomed to being taxed."

"It'll have to get used to it."

Cameron pursed his lips. "The English," he said, "captured your Majesty's person in time of truce. They held you unjustly for eighteen years. We owe them nothing."

"And my oath?" said James.

Cameron shrugged his shoulders and took up the report again. "The customs are increasing," he said.

"And half the increase goes to Albany!" answered James. "I wonder that Murdoch did not pawn the crown to himself and charge me interest. There's little else that he and his father left unmortgaged. I only wish I knew the remedy."

James was twisting a pen in his hands, crushing the feathered stem. Cameron watched him in hesitation. There was so much one might suggest, but nothing without danger. He decided to venture along a hackneyed line.

"If the Douglas came back from France," he said, "there'd be more of a counterweight to Albany. They say he is winning great battles against the English there. That'll be a strength to him. If your Majesty could recall him, tempt him back to Scotland——"

"I could have two masters instead of one! Is that it?"

"Two might cancel out. There's little love lost between them, these days, and one could be played off against the other."

"That's a coward's game, Cameron—and a fool's game in the long run. I mean to be king."

"But, your Majesty——"

"Get on with those papers." James rose and began to pace the room. Cameron subsided, but without resenting the rebuke. Sooner or later, James would have to listen to those that knew Scotland best. He watched him reseat himself and return to his reading with moody, abstracted gaze.

It was so that Athol found them, and one could have sworn that in the instant of entering, before he melted into obsequiousness, his little bloodshot eyes had taken in the whole situation, his cunning brain had guessed what theme occupied the king and his secretary.

"Were you wanting an old man's advice?" he asked, as soon as James had given him leave to sit. "It's little I can do these days except talk."

James handed him a petition. "Will you give us your opinion on that?" he said. It was a trivial matter—a couple of Tayside villages pleading inability to pay the tax. Athol began to read, slowly disengaging the heavy cloak from his shoulders. "They're in your homage," said James curtly. "You'll know if they are telling us the truth."

Athol skimmed through the petition. It was amusing to see his nephew occupied with such details: it was amusing to see him so clerkishly busy at the work-laden table. "It'll not last long," he reflected. "He'll soon be preferring horses, or the ladies, to Master Cameron's company." Athol stroked his flimsy beard. "And anyway," he told himself, "they're just chasing their own tails. There's little they can do with their papers that'll make any difference."

Athol was feeling well, vigorous even; he enjoyed good health for his age. He felt ripe for new undertakings—new mischief as his enemies would call it. Not that he had many open enemies; some were dead, and the few that survived had long lost power to harm him. He had seen to that, less from vindictiveness than as an exercise of skill. He liked to believe, he had almost persuaded himself, that he was devoid of real malice; he had worked dispassionately, though in tortuous fashion, towards good ends; there'd be little against him on the Judgment Day, except, maybe, that he had sometimes played with fire. Athol, a known master at deceiving others, was also successful in deceiving himself.

He returned the petition to the table. "Was that all?" he asked.

"What is your advice on it?" countered James, ignoring the question.

"Oh, grant it. Grant them their exemption. They've had their troubles, this year and more. The oats were all burnt in June."

"Burnt? Who by? Highlandmen?"

There was a pause. Athol's eyelids flickered. Then he decided to lie. "Not this time," he said.

"Then who sent them?"

"They wore no man's badge."

"Where did they come from?"

"I cannot tell. They did not pass me at Methven."

"But you can guess who led them?"

"I might that." Athol licked his thin lips, wondering how far he could safely go.

"I want to know."

"It'd be no more than a guess."

"So be it."

"A year ago, I'd have said cousin Walter. Murdoch's Walter."

"He's in prison."

"He has two brothers. Wee James, and Alexander, that your Majesty knighted to please Murdoch. We're a fruitful family, we Stewarts. We swarm and multiply, like the caterpillars in the Bible tale."

"And this outrage——? You say that one of these two——?"

"I say nothing, your Majesty. I'm safer so." He smiled knowingly, sure of success. There was only one small factor he had overlooked: Cameron was reading the petition. "There's nothing here," said the secretary, "about the plundering my lord speaks of."

Athol was hardly an instant in replying. "Would it be wise of them to speak of it," he said, "with the plunderers still free to strike again? Would it be wise to complain to his Majesty if it was his Majesty's own kinsmen that had done it?"

"Do you suggest——?" began James.

"I do not. I'm not thinking you'd protect the house of Albany from justice. But poor folk might: they know little yet what manner of king they have. They might be thinking of Albany's sons as your Majesty's next of kin. Heirs to the Crown." He paused, running a gnarled hand over his baldness. "Things'll be better," he said, "when we hear news of another little Jamie to inherit from your Majesty."

He smiled, with an unpleasing attempt to look benignant. James looked at his leering face with something of a shudder. It was one thing to make Joan a queen, another to expose her, even in thought, to the calculations of such creatures as Athol.

Cameron scented the need for some distraction.

"Since there's no mention of the matter here," he said, "would it not be wiser to ignore it?"

James, looking at his secretary, missed the tiny flash of anger in Athol's eyes. "Maybe it would," said the old man quickly. "There'll be more of the like you may have to ignore. All over the country."

"I do not think," said James, coldly, "that the state of the country calls for your lordship's comment."

Athol's eyes hardly flickered. "I'm glad of that," he said.

"Then maybe it'll not be long before the key is keeping the castle, and the bracken-bush the cow."

James sprang to his feet. Athol, rising more slowly, was quick enough with his tongue. "And there's no need," he said, "to be giving way to anger because your old uncle tells you what you know already."

"What do you mean?"

"Well, I thought that you had come from England with some very particular notions of what a king should be. Supposing now, that I agreed with those notions—supposing I had some idea how your Majesty could teach them to Scotland? There's many of us know how sore she's needing the lesson."

James stood silent, staring at Athol and beyond him. The man was of his own blood, yet in no sense a rival. He was old, past the ambitions and hatreds of middle age. He had given his son for the king, sending the Master of Athol to England as hostage for the ransom-money. He was no fool: whether one liked or disliked Athol, the man had brains. And James knew that, from one quarter or another, he was desperately in need of counsel.

He was not long in reaching a decision. "You may sit down," he said. His eyes searched Athol's face for the slightest hint of triumph, but found nothing. "Have you come to tell me," he asked, "that I'd be wise to use the Douglas against Albany?"

"I'd tell you no such thing," said Athol. "If the Douglas is winning battles in France, and getting his reward from the Dauphin, he'll come back twice as strong as he went. De'il knows that was enough already. I think your Majesty'll need to do something about Albany before the Douglas is here to double all your difficulties."

"Do something?" said James. "When I've neither cause nor means?"

"I'd say you had cause enough. The means'll come if you look for them."

"If you knew where my revenue stood——!"

"I can guess. And is that not cause? If a poor man had done what Murdoch and his father did, twenty years together, you'd have him hanged for robbing you."

Athol gazed straight at his nephew. For once he kept his eyes steady, candid almost. "And when you'd done it," he said, "the money would be yours again."

The shaft seemed to strike home: Athol seldom drew a bow until he was sure of his quarry. James walked slowly to his chair, sat down and stared in front of him. "It'd mean war," he said.

"It might," said Athol, "and it might not. There are ways these things can be managed. It'd not be difficult to catch Murdoch unawares, and bring him to book before the Albany men could muster."

"I caught Lennox, as you call it. He's in prison now. But I can get no evidence to try him on."

"Lennox is kin to Murdoch. Imprison both and there'll be evidence and to spare, when folk see that you've a mind to ruin all Albany. And your judges'll not need evidence against either, once you've made your will clear."

"I came to Scotland to do justice, not to intimidate my own judges."

"Then you'd best release Lennox. They'll not condemn him until you give the word."

"I shall hold him until I know how he comes to be so rich."

"You know that already: he was a regent's father-in-law. And you'll not hold him once the house of Albany puts the screw on."

"I can resist pressure."

"You've not felt it yet." Athol, sure that James was weakening, had begun to warm to his work. He leant forward, his eyes beleaguering his nephew. "If you'd known Scotland," he said, "you'd never have clapped doors on Lennox alone. You must strike at them all, or at none of them, and you must strike to kill. That's the only thing that's understood in this country. We kill to get: we kill to keep: and we do not let go again till we're killed ourselves. That's Scotland, God forgive her! Am I right, Master Cameron?"

He stared at the secretary, defying him to contradict. He was annoyed to see hesitation, perhaps a shade of repugnance, on Cameron's face. Cameron turned away, looking down at his papers; they represented his duty, the little circle in which a king's secretary could move without blame and without immediate danger. He knew well enough that James was hovering on the edge of greater, more perilous things. Athol was probably right, whatever his motives: but it was no part of Cameron's business to help him spur James towards heroic decisions of dubious morality. If it came to that, there was a chance of things improving without catastrophe. Murdoch might fritter away the strength of Albany, his sons might ruin it by some rash folly. The Douglas might remain in France. Even if no such thing happened, James might sit in some security on his impoverished throne, using what power was left to him with a little more wisdom, a little greater effect than his old father had done. And Cameron could look forward to many years of usefulness and dignity, privileges and perquisites, the certain and comforting prospect of a bishopric to come.

"I hope," he said, "that things are less serious than your lordship represents them. It might be possible to replenish the royal revenues without resorting to bloodshed."

"You can ask a wolf," said Athol, "to cough out the yearlings he's swallowed. But I'm doubting if he'd humour you."

He looked to James, as if demanding agreement. James sat inscrutable. His uncle's words hammered at his ears, demanding acceptance. They were echoed from within: dark thoughts, locked in through years of imprisonment, were stirring to life.

"When all's said," began Athol's voice again, "it's with them that the killing began."

James turned his head slowly. "I do not understand that," he said.

"I had two nephews," said Athol, "when Albany was first regent. It's a long time back since the other died, but it'll be as long again before I forget young Rothesay." He paused, letting the name sink in. "There's another thing to learn about Scotsmen," he said. "They'll not respect a lad that will not revenge his own brother's murder."

The silence was long this time, intolerably long. The room seemed to grow darker, though there was no change in the outside light. James felt his thoughts grind again in the old harsh circle of suspicion, anger and recurring doubt. The whirl was faster now, the jar more painful—urging him to the remedy that was at last within his power. For what remedy was there but to strike out and drown his doubts in blood?

"Your lordship goes a long way back," he heard Cameron saying. "Maybe an old tale like that is best forgotten. The men that made it are in their graves."

"Are they?" said Athol. "I'm thinking they're not." He was sitting back in his chair—magnificently at ease, while Cameron fidgeted at the table. "Can you tell me now," he asked, "what were the names of the two turnkeys at Falkland that had charge of my lord Rothesay?"

"How should I remember?" began Cameron, and then seemed to check. "There was a man called Wright," he said more slowly. "A Falkland man."

"There was that. And another called Selkirk. Albany brought him from the South."

"Your lordship has a good memory," said Cameron, grudgingly.

"I need it sometimes," replied Athol. "And now, Master Cameron, you have been looking into the Treasurer's rolls. Will you tell his Majesty the name of the man that's collecting royal dues at Kinghorn, and no doubt pocketing a deal of money by the way."

"Wright."

"It's the man, Master Cameron. You know that. And Selkirk's on the same work in Haddington. Albany gave them the place as soon as they'd done what he wanted done at Falkland. Twenty years they've been there. Murdoch paid them when Albany died. These last few months, it's King James's money they've been handling. That's a fine jest. His brother's murderers."

"We cannot be sure," said Cameron, unsteadily, "that they are the same men."

"You know it. You're of the Kirk, Master Cameron. Would you tell his Majesty a lie? Half Fife was in the secret. Half Scotland by now. Laughing."

Cameron sat helpless and abashed: the man's essential weakness, masked by the hardening processes of his youth, was laid bare under Athol's pitiless search. He could only stammer himself into silence.

James, eyes shut, fists clenched, heard them through a mist. His mind flew back to childhood. He did not know Falkland well, but he remembered stopping there once, a year before his brother's death; it had been his uncle Albany's favourite home then, though later he had avoided it, preferring Stirling and Doune. James remembered a little garden, grey battlements, his uncle's face watching him from a window. He had seen, too, by a chance, the dungeon where the thing was to happen; inside the door was a few feet of stone ledge, and then a drop, down which one thrust the prisoner, so that he lay bruised while one turned the key upon him. There would be no need to do more: the door could stay locked, no food or water need enter: it did not take long for a man, a prince even, to die of hunger. There were tales of a woman coming by night to feed the prisoner through a grating, with the milk from her own breasts; Rothesay had always had a way with the women. Such interference could be quickly ended, by a knife-thrust, if necessary, and a hasty grave under the court-yard stones. Other tales—and more probable ones—told of the prisoner raving in anguish, tearing at the flesh of his own fingers in despair of food. A little patience would be needed, a little shutting of ears to the cries from under ground: it would not be long before the two gaolers could claim their reward from Albany. What was left in the dungeon could be carried to Lindores Abbey, for the monks to bury with mourning pomp. Scotland could be told that her heir had died of a wasting fever: one could say, hiding the mangled fingers, that the body showed no marks of violence. Old King Robert might rage at his son's murder, but Albany was stronger than the king. Albany had a bond with Douglas in those days, and no one would dare to gainsay what Albany and the Douglas said.

James opened his eyes. He saw Athol, leaning forward at him, goatishly intent. So he sat, his case proved, demanding blood. It was all the more revolting in that Athol had no personal grievance against Albany or Murdoch. Whatever horrors might haunt the past, here was actual and present evil—evil personified in a bald skull and gloating, red-rimmed eyes.

James rose to his feet. At all costs, he must prevent Athol casting his evil spell upon him. He must have time to think—and alone. He must dismiss Athol, and Cameron too. Better still, he must go away himself. Go into the open air. Go anywhere.

"My lord," said James, "if our cousin must be brought to trial, it will not be for what his father did twenty years ago."

He made for the door, Cameron preceding him to open it. He paused there. "I would rather play your game, Master Cameron," he said, "and call back the Douglas." A moment later he was gone.

Cameron came back into the room. It angered him to see Athol sitting there, a smile still on his lips, showing no sign that he had incurred rebuke. And, thought Cameron, a just rebuke.

"I take it," he said drily, "that your lordship will not call on me again to confirm such ancient tales. His Majesty may not listen so patiently another time."

Athol gave no sign of having heard. He sat staring at the floor, a faint smile haunting his thin lips. He did not move while Cameron returned to the table, and resettled himself to work. But when the secretary was still he spoke quietly, half to himself. "There'll be no need of a second time," he said. "The work's done. We'll have only a wee while to wait."

He rose, straightening stiff knees, and gathered his heavy homespun cloak round him. He paused, on his way out, to speak again. "And you, Master Cameron," he said, "were a fool not to back me better. When the wheel is rolling down the slope, it's wiser to be on the uphill side."

He turned and was gone, seeking his horses. As he rode home to Methven, he was still thinking of Murdoch's death. The country would be the better for it, no one could deny that. Jamie would be stronger, with most of the Albany lands reverting to the crown. There would be pickings for everybody, for those who gave evidence and those who sat in judgment. It would be a big clearance, for if Murdoch went to the block, his three sons would have to accompany him, and maybe the old fool Lennox. It was never safe, in Scotland, to do things by halves.

When the house of Albany was destroyed, Athol himself, half-brother to old King Robert, would be next heir to the crown. King James had no son yet, and might die without one. Maybe it was folly for an old man to dream of inheriting, but it was pleasant to look forward to a son or grandson on the throne. It would be something to think about through the lonely, the rather terrifying, evenings, in the gaunt rooms of Methven.

August 17th 1424

IV

Archibald, Earl of Douglas, looked out on the French fields—his one sound eye straining through the helmet-slit —and swore that his luck had changed at last.

He could see, quite plainly in the dusty sunlight, the doomed army of Englishmen beyond the river. There might be a few veterans of Agincourt among them, but the majority were young levies, jaded with long marching. Bedford, their leader, was King Henry's brother; but King Henry himself was dead. They were separated from their Burgundian allies. Bedford could not save them from the army of Scots and Frenchmen that waited with Douglas to cross the water and destroy them. Douglas, with his son and kinsmen, would be known for all time as the men who had reversed the verdict of Agincourt.

It was time, and more than time. He had been fighting, against one enemy or another, for a matter of thirty-five years, and had never yet managed to be on the winning side. He had fought the Percies on the Border, and been captured in an inglorious skirmish. He had joined them against old Henry, and been captured again at Shrewsbury, losing an eye in the battle. He had marched with Albany against Roxburgh, and the enterprise had petered out as the contemptible Fool Raid. They had nicknamed him Archie Tyneman, the Loser, Archibald the Unlucky. The whisper had gone round that there was a curse upon him, and men made excuses for not following him to war. All that would be over now.

The Dauphin at least had had faith in him. Since Baugé, the Dauphin had not grudged Scotsmen their wine and mutton; he had made Douglas Duke of Touraine, sent him, along with his own Armagnacs, to chase Bedford out of Maine. They had chased him into Normandy, cornered him here outside Verneuil. They had only to cross the shallow stream and finish the work. The Tyneman would know, at last, what it felt like to win a battle.

What lay beyond, he could decide later; probably a return to Scotland. One might use new-forged strength and reputation to break Albany—if one was sure that King James would be properly grateful, and rule Scotland as the Douglas directed. But, meanwhile, there was a victory to be won.

The Frenchmen were inexcusably dilatory. They had stood in their ranks the whole morning, staring across the water at Bedford's men. Douglas and his son clamoured for instant attack, before the English could slip away into the hills of La Perche. But the sun had begun to stoop over Verneuil before they could get their way.

The Armagnac host began at last to move forward. The mounted knights trotted impatiently ahead, splashed into the water, and bobbed up the farther bank. They began to canter towards the enemy, braving the arrows. When they reached the line of archers, they were galled but unbroken by the volleys; they scattered their tormentors and crashed into the English men-at-arms. Two more lines of cavalry followed; the foot-soldiers, wading through the ford, would soon be at their back. Some horsemen were already circling round their enemies' rear, plundering his baggage. Bedford was being driven in from the front, and his retreat was already cut off.

He was putting up a stiffer fight than they expected. Henry's war-machine was still formidable. Douglas had ordered no quarter, and men fought for their lives, not for chivalry or ransoms. Bedford rode from one squadron to the other, urging desperation. The English gave way more slowly, breaking the momentum of the assault. In a few minutes they had brought it to a standstill: the fight swayed this way and that: they began, here and there, to hack their way again on to the ground they had abandoned.

Slowly, incredibly, the Scots and Armagnacs felt themselves edged backward, pressed and jammed against their oncoming infantry. Still stronger in numbers, they were being struck down in hundreds, dragged from their horses, trampled to impotence and death. Backwards, still backwards, went the struggling, cursing mass. They would have given no quarter in victory, and they asked none in defeat. Boys from the lonely glens of Galloway died side by side with the olive-skinned aristocrats of Perigord and Provence. Soon the survivors, still battling against the relentless pressure, would feel the soft mud under their feet, the water soaking into steel-plated leggings. The retreat would not be a rout, but it would soon become mere slaughter. The verdict of Agincourt would be ratified once more, sealed with new torrents of blood.

They buried Archibald the Unlucky in Tours Cathedral, in the heart of the Duchy he had not lived to rule. They buried his son beside him. The French wasted little time on his obsequies, having dead lords of their own to honour. There were few Scots to mourn him, for two thousand of them had obeyed orders and lay dead beside Verneuil. It was Scotland herself, when the news came, that saw the greater lamentation. Some wept for a son, a husband or a brother. Others, untouched by private loss, felt the blight that had fallen on the country's hopes.

There was only the young king to look to now. He would have no ally against opposition at home: men doubted if he could find strength and courage to be master. But wiser heads nodded more cheerfully. There is no loss without gain. It was something to be sure that, for another generation at least, no Douglas could challenge or overawe the crown.

December 1424

V

"So we are to spend our Christmas at Linlithgow?" Joan looked up from the letters which the Abbot of Melrose had brought her. "I hope," she said, "that it is a little warmer in Linlithgow than it is here in Edinburgh."

She smiled at James's letter-bearer. When one got used to his name—Abbot Fogo, by all that was barbaric—one found him friendly and comforting. It was good news that James had chosen him for his confessor.

"It is that," he answered. "Your Majesty will find that there's nothing so cold as this rock between Berwick and Orkney. I wonder that your Majesty does not ask my colleague of Holyrood for shelter in his abbey."

Joan was amused to see that he was hardly looking at her, for fear that she might find inspection embarrassing. It was common knowledge that she had not followed James on his progress along the Border because an heir to the throne was expected in a month or two.

"His Majesty wished me to remain up here," she said, "while the new building is being completed. I am his viceroy over the joiners and masons."

"I have no doubt that his Majesty is well represented," he answered, with only a trace of a smile. "I wish he had such good officers in every quarter. He has given us many excellent laws, but we cannot always give him the men to enforce them."

Joan glanced at her letters again. She had heard much of James's new laws—so many of them on matters she had imagined to be beneath a king's notice. Scotsmen were being commanded to abstain from football in order to practise their archery. Innkeepers were forbidden to overcharge customers, for good inns brought travellers, trade, civilization. And there seemed no end to James's queer interest in regulations about close seasons for the salmon, about heather-burning and the keeping down of rooks. She remembered one thing about them that might serve to tease the abbot.

"At least people can understand them," she said, "now that he's had them put into Scots instead of those Latin rigmaroles."

The abbot was not to be drawn. "A wise move, for the moment," he answered. "Of course, with his Majesty's assistance, Holy Kirk will soon be able to establish more schools and teach everyone that matters to speak in her own tongue. We still need more money, but . . ."

"We all need that," said Joan. "His Majesty especially. They say our cousin Murdoch has it all."

A shade crossed Abbot Fogo's face. "There are many," he said, "to speak ill of the duke. One cannot govern without making enemies. And to have ruled—to retire from government—that loosens and sharpens their tongues."

Joan was silent. She felt, as often, on the brink of things beyond her present comprehension. "His Majesty," she said, consulting the letters, "hopes to meet at Linlithgow on Friday."

"Yes, your Majesty. We have only an hour or two's journey, but he thought it safer that we should not make it till he was there himself."

"Safer?" Joan sighed and leant back. What sort of a country had she come to, where one could not move from one palace to another—if palaces they could be called—without thinking in terms of safety?

"Your Majesty is unwell?"

"No. But I will ask you to leave me now, abbot. I have these letters to read."

He bowed and withdrew. The interview was ended. Some other time, perhaps, she would get him to tell her more exactly what shadow it was that seemed to descend when Murdoch's name was named.

She had more news from James before the week was out. He spoke of staying some time at Linlithgow. He had no doubt chosen it for her sake—the one royal seat that was not nine-tenths a fortress. They could hear their Christmas Mass in St. Michael's Kirk, and make merry in the long rooms overlooking the little loch. Christmas meant more to her, since she was English, than the half-pagan Hogmanay. She would be glad to have him with her afterwards, for she could not help feeling a little fear. Reading between the lines of his letter, she gathered that he would stay at Linlithgow until his son was born.

James himself, working northward from Melrose to Ayr, from Ayr to Stirling, had enough that was present to occupy his thoughts. He had taken Cameron and the business part of the Court on a visitation of the West. They had inspected such royal lands as twenty years' regency had not lost to the crown; many were in sad condition—though James would not go to Dundonald, likely to be most neglected of all, since his father died there. He passed through counties where he had no possessions, upbraiding slothful or stubborn officials and trying to keep his temper. Most of them did not owe their position to his, or even to the Albanies' appointment, but to heredity or inertia. Duties and dignities had become attached to some corner of Scottish soil, which their fathers had left to them. One did the duties, in the king's name, so long as his demands on energy were not unreasonable. If one neglected them sometimes, that was no ground for deprivation of office, still less of estates: a king must learn the limits of his power and the soundness of lazy old customs. James fumed inwardly, biding his time. King Stork must accept the officials that King Log had left in place. Something would have to be done soon to bring Scotland to heel behind the crown. It was early days yet, with his first Christmas not yet come.

Joan left Edinburgh to meet him on the day he had appointed for her. If all went well, he would be able to ride out from Linlithgow to bring her back. She was bringing with her a few packhorses, laden with unexpected luxuries, modest enough for a royal festival: a ship from Flanders had made Leith roads at the end of October, bound homeward from Stavanger. She was glad enough to say good-bye for a time to the windswept castle of Edinburgh, dismantled by Bruce lest it harbour English garrisons, still in ruin when King James came home.

There was no sign of James on the road, and by the time they reached Kirkliston it became clear that something was amiss. There was a dull red glow on the skyline ahead. Abbot Fogo was for turning back, but Joan, in discomfort and some pain, told the litter-bearers to proceed. "His Majesty would send warning," she said, "if he did not want us at Linlithgow." It was foolish, perhaps, but it would not do for the king's English wife to be suspected of cowardice.

Her decision was soon justified. A few miles on, they learnt that there was no danger. But Linlithgow Palace, by some accident, had been set ablaze. They finished the journey, to find James, with blackened face and hands, directing such salvage as was possible. He was happier than he had been for months; he preferred this to signing papers or browbeating reluctant sheriffs. He had the whole town at work, rescuing what could be rescued, fighting the flames which had already reached the roof of St. Michael's. The palace was beyond hope, but Linlithgow would not hear of king or queen returning to Edinburgh for the night. The best house—a stone-built one of which the owners were inordinately proud—was turned inside out to make room for them. Bedcovers, curtains and clean rush-bundles were seen trotting along the street, burghers and burghers' wives wheezing under the loads. James, still in schoolboy mood, stood directing operations from the doorstep. Soon after nightfall, king and queen were dining in impromptu state with the principal freemen of the town—who sat and stared at them with bulging eyes. James had them plied with strange wines and Flemish sweetmeats until they began to laugh back at his sallies, thinking themselves—and him—the finest fellows in the world. When Joan escaped to bed, they were uproariously electing him a member of the Town

Council, Deacon of the new Guild of Fire-dowsers and Water-carriers. She reckoned that half of them would be under the table before James followed her upstairs.

Margery Norton helped her to bed, scolding her as if she were still thirteen. Joan found herself suddenly far wearier than she realized, and had fallen into a light sleep before the old woman left the room.

It seemed hours later when she awoke, though she saw that the candles had barely burnt an inch. The room was unfamiliar: she wondered where she was, and why so cold a breeze was blowing. Then she saw James standing at the unglazed window, with the heavy curtains held back in his hands. He was looking up at the frosty stars.

He saw her stir, smiled back over his shoulder, and looked out of window again. "*High in the rounded orb of Heaven's face*," he said.

"What's that?" she asked drowsily.

"A new first line for *The King's Quair*. Do you like it?"

"Not so much as the other one you showed me. Nor will you, when you are sober."

"You misjudge me; I am sober now. I am sorry you prefer the old one. I was thinking of finishing the whole poem by repeating the first line."

"Finishing? *The King's Quair* will never be finished. It's like Penelope's web."

"You're wrong again. I shall finish it in Edinburgh, next month. You know we shall have to go back to Edinburgh now?"

Joan shivered. "I was afraid so," she said.

"But I'll rebuild Linlithgow for you before next Christmas. It won't take long. They're good fellows in Linlithgow."

"I said you were tipsy."

"No, no. Only happy. Happier than I've been lately."

"Will it last?"

"Maybe. It'll come again, when I'm rid of . . . certain

worries." He closed the curtains, and came to sit beside her, holding her hand. "You can help," he said. "Being with you makes a difference. And, soon, you'll be making me happier still."

Joan closed sleepy eyes and opened them again to look up at him. "Can I call him James?" she said. "He won't be born on St. James's day, like you. But I should like to call him James, all the same."

"I'd like it, too," said James.

For a minute or two they held hands in silence. "You are not regretting it?" he asked. "I mean, you are liking Scots folk better now, aren't you?"

"I never said I disliked them."

"You've looked it sometimes."

"I tried not to. And I am liking them better now."

"Things like tonight help?"

"Oh, yes. I like your townsmen better than some of the others. Murdoch, and that old bald horror."

"I know. But Athol's too useful to be kept away from Court—for the present. We can't choose our company."

"No." Joan was almost asleep.

He was silent for a moment, and then she felt him disengage his hand. He tiptoed back to the window. "Listen," he said.

She could hear nothing at first, nothing except the lowing of an ox in the cold fields outside the little town: the noise came dully, muffled by thick curtains. Then, unexpectedly, she heard the sound of a single quavering voice, attempting song. It gained confidence, and was joined by others, swelling into a ragged chorus. There was something pitifully brave in the sound.

"Listen," he said again. "It's '*Late, late on Evenings*'."

It was a thin, ghostly little tune, fashioned for poor hovels that cowered low on windswept moors. James peeped through the slit of the curtains. Outside, in the moonlight, the street was dotted with dark figures: pinched, ragged figures, barefooted on the frostbound earth. The free burghers slept by warm fires, in fur-covered beds. The poor of the town had come to make their midnight offering to the king.

January 1425

VI

It was still winter. If a first false promise had reached the Lowlands, there was no sign of spring among the western mountains. Brief sun looked down on snow-strewn glens, and was quickly blotted out by new storm-clouds. Through day and night, grey weather or foul, the great winds piped and thundered across the upper crags.

In the village, the few cottages, of Inverarnan, men had bidden each other good-night and taken early refuge in their homes. The peat fires were banked up, warming the feet of sleeping families. Only here and there was a man awake. One might sit up, mending broken gear for the morrow, while opposite him crouched an old woman to whom sleep came less easily with passing years. There was rain falling outside; as the wind changed, they could hear it patter on the cowhide that was stretched across the door. Once the old woman turned her head, as if some other sound had reached her. Footsteps perhaps. No one but her would have heard them. No one, hearing, would care to be peeping out. She returned to her memories, her thoughts of next day's meal. If anything walked abroad on such a night, it would not be good for human eyes to see.

Yet footsteps there had been, and it was a man that had passed, pressing on through darkness and rain. He should, by rights, have skirted the village, leaving the track for a little; one could not tell whether the Highland folk would speed or obstruct the passage of a stranger under the king's ban, escaping from the king's prison; he had risked it. fearing to lose his way. He was—or had been—Sir Robert

Graham: it might be wiser, for a short time, to take some other name. He had broken from gaol some fifteen hours ago, and had ridden twelve of them, until his horse—a poor creature, but the best a fugitive could come by—foundered near Inveruglas, beside the loch. He was making for Loch Awe and the Campbell country; he had friends in Lorne. If he was alive by morning, he should have reached Crianlarich, whence one began to turn westward for Glen Awe.

He was still at odds with himself about his imprisonment. No charge had been laid against him, and his gaolers, knowing nothing themselves, had bid him wait: the king's pleasure would be signified in time. He had written to his kinsman, Athol, asking for assistance or, at least, enlightenment. He could not have guessed that it was Athol, following some tortuous scheme, that had recommended King James to lay him by the heels. Athol had answered his letter, with considerable obscurity. He too had preached patience: Graham gathered that he might expect release by Easter, when great things would be happening in Scotland. Graham had had experience of Athol's hints: he preferred not to wait. He had friends, money, and more agility in his tough body than most men of forty. He had made his escape.

The rain beat in his face, the wind was against him. Sodden wisps of red hair escaped from under his bonnet, lashed at his brow and temples. He did not doubt that he would reach his destination: he had weathered worse nights than this. He had a plaid, a sword of sorts, and long, tireless legs. Pursuit was unlikely, now that he was past Inverarnan. He had only to keep his wits about him, and he would be in Lorne within the week.

He might have to stay there a year and more, while his son cared for the estates in Kincardine and sent him such money as could be spared. A shilling went a long way in the Highlands and he would not be a burden to his hosts. He would have time to think, to speculate on his own ill-luck and search for a remedy.

He had brains as well as muscle. He had read much, dabbling in theology, and training himself thoroughly in the law. He loved the law: the contrast between abstract justice and his own frustrations pleased while it angered him. He had a new wrong to contemplate now, an unjust, unreasoning arrest. He had known much injustice, and imagined more. He had grievances against Albany, against the Kirk, against most of his own kinsmen—except Malise. Behind them all lay another, half-conscious, quite unformulated, a grievance against life itself. Its root lay, perhaps, in the man's own ability and the insufficient scope it had always found. The plethora sealed him as one of the unquiet spirits, by turns self-righteous and desperately self-accusing. Now he was tramping Glen Falloch, with nothing before him but a year's obscurity among Highland herdsmen or Highland reivers.

Dawn came late, and found him still striding on. He had tried to rest occasionally, until the cold goaded him into motion again. He had missed the path more than once. He was still a mile or two from Crianlarich, where he hoped for food and perhaps wine. The rain had stopped. Daylight, seeping into the glen, showed no sign of life round him, except a scurry, far up Ben Lui, which might be an eagle seeking the upper mists. Then a wintry sunshine began to paint the rocks and the rain-pitted snow-drifts. He would be dry by the time he reached the village.

All the same, he was glad of a fire when he got there. He sat close to it, wolfing the bannocks and salt mutton that they gave him. His spirit began to thaw a little, as he stretched and turned his legs to the blaze. He talked to his hosts, but no one asked his name.

They spoke their own Gaelic, differing a little from the language of Graham's poorer neighbours. But he had no difficulty in understanding them. They had news from Edinburgh, and were surprised to learn that he had not heard it: it was strange how news travelled in the Highlands. Edinburgh meant little to these people, King James was a distant rumour. But they told him that King James's queen had been brought to bed on Christmas Day, and given birth to a daughter. She was to be christened Margaret, so they had heard. The king must have been wanting a son: maybe the Englishwoman would give him one next time. Meanwhile, Murdoch of Albany remained the heir to Scotland. They hoped it would not come to that.

Graham rose, thanked them for the food and struck out for Tyndrum. They did not expect payment, and would have refused an offer of it. They wished him a good journey and watched him out of sight. A strange man, they told each other; maybe he was after killing a man, and had need to hide from the dead man's kin. There must be some secret he carried with him: Lowland lairds did not walk alone in the mountains for the sake of pleasure. One of them suggested that he might have incurred the king's ban: he had sat glum enough when they were talking of King James.

There was one thing they could not guess, for Graham himself was not yet aware of it. They could not know that he carried with him, hidden deeply in the mind, a tiny seed which would one day blossom to be King James's bane.

March 1425

VII

Athol had spoken, and, as usual, it looked as if Athol would prove right. Secretary Cameron—as March approached and summonses were issued for a new Parliament at Perth—grew daily surer that James was meaning to try a fall with Albany.

Cameron slept close to the king's chamber in the castle of Edinburgh which James had begun to rebuild. Comfort and regular work were both difficult, since the masons and joiners, presumably for lack of money, had been ordered to suspend their half-finished task. Cameron, trotting after the king with an armful of papers for discussion, was as likely as not to run against an abandoned trestle or find himself playing catch-as-catch-can with the wind at some unfilled gap in the walls.

There was plenty that needed discussing. James had ordered drafts for a dozen new statutes. There was to be a law against poachers and beggars, laws to establish new hospitals and discourage heresy. An attack was to be made on Highland robbery, and, if possible, on the Lowland lairds who abetted the robbers and shared their booty. An enactment was contemplated—hardest of all to frame, and harder to enforce—against the bonds of alliance between great nobles, and the private wars they engendered. All this needed thrashing out and James was seldom there to do it. Cameron would discover that he had ridden without warning to Leith, or to visit his wife and baby with the monks of Holyrood Abbey: that he had gone—or had said that he was going—to hunt deer on the Pentlands: that he was closeted with some stranger, questioning him on a new project that would be forgotten next day. Cameron knew the signs only too well, and could draw his own conclusions.

He was quite dispassionate about it. He had seen many men, young or of tender conscience, hovering on the edge of drastic and violent plans. James asked no advice, but was clearly battling with indecision, wondering how far Athol's counsel was prompted by malignancy, how far by wisdom. It was, perhaps, a crime that Athol had recommended, but it was doubtful whether anything short of a crime could make James master in Scotland. It was possible that James was going to shrink back at the last moment. It remained possible, so far as Cameron could calculate, until a certain morning in February when he knocked at the king's door and, entering unanswered, found an unexpected visitor in the room.

They knew each other at once, though they had never spoken. Cameron was a public figure now, and, in his humbler days, had known better than most people who Montgomery was and how he earned his money.

"Why are you here?" he asked.

Montgomery gave him an arrogant stare. "Not at your bidding," he said, "nor, it seems, by your advice."

"His Majesty has many advisers. I do not pretend to assist him in all his many affairs."

"There are some affairs," said Montgomery, "to which his Majesty admits no advisers. Or only one." He puffed out his chest, walking away from Cameron. One could guess that he had had little work of late, since Murdoch had need of fewer agents, and was making the most of a new promise of employment.

"In that case," answered Cameron, determined to remain unruffled, "I had better not intrude. But perhaps you would remind his Majesty, since he has found a trustworthy messenger, that we have letters for the north. I take it you go to Methven nowadays, not Doune."

Montgomery was too old a hand to show surprise, but he was at a loss for an answer. As he stood hesitating, Cameron turned to find that James was at the door.

He saw a shadow of annoyance cross the king's face at seeing them together. He made his bow, asked for a later appointment, and departed. There was a time, he reflected, when he would have been tempted to listen at the keyhole. He had good cause, nowadays, for not thinking of such things. Bishops—and Cameron had a notion that his bishopric would soon be within his grasp—should not be found in undignified postures. And, a more clinching reason, he hardly needed to overhear. One of two things was being transacted behind that door, and probably both. Montgomery was repeating messages from Athol to the king, suggestions for the arrest of Murdoch and his sons. Montgomery was promising to give evidence, from his private store, which would justify the arrest of Murdoch, and more than an arrest.

It became clear, before they left for Perth, why Athol had not come to Edinburgh himself. Athol lingered at Methven, but visited Stirling and even Doune in transparent secrecy. Tongues were soon wagging. It was said that the old serpent, meeting Murdoch at Stirling or riding out to hawk with him along Allan Water, was starting plots to thwart King James, perhaps to bring him down. Those who talked in that way had not begun to plumb the depths of the old serpent's subtlety. For Athol, having decided that King James must ruin Albany, was luring Murdoch on, to the edge of treason, in order that King James might have every excuse.

He was at Perth when Parliament opened, but there was no sign of Murdoch there. A week went by, and King James's laws about poachers and hospitals were dutifully passed. Murdoch sent a letter, full of unconvincing excuses for his absence: when it was read before the assembled lords, Athol pursed dubious lips and looked unfathomable. Next day, he rode southward, visited Doune and returned as far as Dunblane to sleep. Murdoch sent off a second letter, promising belated obedience to King James's summons. Next day, early in the morning, he set out from Doune. He was attended, inexplicably enough, by a bare half-dozen of his spearmen.

There is a place on the road between Dunblane and Doune which is known to this day as Murdoch's Ford. In Murdoch's time the track ran muddily down to meet the water beside a little, half-ruined house. No one knew how it came to be built, nor who had last lived there, apart from thieves and fugitives. The roof had long vanished: nettles and chickweed sprouted through the floor. Along the adjacent bank, stunted willows leant over the water. It was the centre of the kingdom—so learned clerks reckoned—equidistant from sea to sea: as it were, the heart of Scotland. It was perhaps appropriate that there should be a certain mystery about the place.

Murdoch would have to pass the place, riding to Dunblane and on to Perth. He had passed it before, a thousand times. It held no special significance for him.

He was far from an old man, but, on the morning of his departure, he seemed almost senile; he was full of anxious, inconsistent orders and querulous reprimand. His squire, Christopher Chalmers, upon whom the burden of it fell, was at last goaded into retaliation. "If your Grace does not know his mind better," he answered, "maybe it'd be wiser not to go at all."

"I have no choice, man," answered Murdoch. "Would you have me loiter at Doune till I'm dead?"

"You might be better here," said Chalmers, "than riding to Perth. It'd be safer, if tales are true."

"Tales?" said Murdoch. "What tales, man, what tales?"

"Nothing new. But I've had another letter from my young brother Thomas, that's a Perth merchant these days. He says that King James has only called a Parliament in order to put the house of Albany where he'd have us." He looked at Murdoch in annoyance, not without a tinge of affection. Chalmers was an orphan: he and his brother had been brought up in old Albany's household and taught to regard him as a king of men, and almost as a father. Murdoch, a poor substitute for the dead, still carried a little of the old glamour about with him.

"That may be," Murdoch was saying, "but how can you be sure that it's Perth I'll go to?" He tried to look cunning, and the attempt sat ill upon his solemn, handsome face.

"You should know," said Chalmers, irritated again.

"Your Grace should know." As he spoke, he realized, suddenly and incredulously, that Murdoch did not know. Encompassed by danger and rumours of danger, he was setting out on a journey with a mind not quite made up yet. The man deserved whatever ruin awaited him. "And I," asked Chalmers, "am to stay and guard Doune? Is that what your Grace was meaning?" On that point, at least, he would compel Murdoch to make up his mind.

"Ay," said Murdoch, still hesitant. "I was wondering, Chris——. But maybe you'd be better here."

Chalmers, watching him depart, felt a slight pang of conscience: it was perhaps foolish not to have insisted on accompanying him, to whatever destination. But the horse-hooves were already sounding fainter, and it was too late for second thoughts. He turned back from the battlements, wondering what provisions, and even what store of weapons, had been left in his charge at Doune.

The small escort that rode with Murdoch were glad to be moving at last. As they neared the ford, they saw him rise in his stirrups, peering doubtfully ahead as though something or someone awaited him beside the stream. They, too, expected reinforcement, Albany men from Fife and Kinross, or possibly—though their master was still a prisoner—retainers of Lennox. The laws made at last year's Parliament had forbidden lords to travel with long retinues, but even Murdoch would not be so foolish as to abide by the law, while the whole country was alive with threatening rumours.

Some hundred yards before the road dipped down to the willows, Murdoch called a purposeless halt. He seemed half inclined to turn back. Twice he kicked his horse round with a heel, scolding at it with an embarrassing petulance. The men waited, chafing. They were accustomed to his irresolutions, his fits of doubt or lethargy on the verge of action.

He mastered his indecision at last, wrenching his horse round till it faced Dunblane and the road to Perth. He looked at his men's faces, as if seeking counsel, and found no comfort on them. "We must go on," he said. "We must just go on." A cloud passed over the sun's face and dulled the daylight as he jogged down the slope.

They were waiting for him by the ford—not Athol, nor men of Albany and Lennox: they came from Stirling Castle and wore King James's badge. There were a score and more sitting their horses beside the stream, and others were issuing from the ruined house as they heard his party approach. There was no question of resistance. Their leader rode up to him and said something in a low voice. Murdoch's men were told roughly to go home. They saw Murdoch deprived of his sword. He gave no sign of resistance, hardly of resentment. One would have said that he had ridden out that morning expecting, if not inviting, capture. The creeping paralysis that had blighted his life, robbed it of usefulness and dignity and honour, was now reaching its final and strangling stage.

He rode into Stirling like a man dazed. He rode through silent streets, where women whispered to each other in the doorways. He climbed the steep, cobbled hill, and saw the castle gates. They opened to receive him and then swung fast again.

March 1425

VIII

"So we meet again in two months' time?"

King James was proroguing Parliament, and the members were saying a temporary farewell to each other as most of them dispersed for home. They had plenty of matter for discussion and speculation, though many were in doubt whether it was quite safe to speculate openly.

"I'll see your lordship in Stirling in two months?"

"Ay. May. There'll be great doings then, I'm thinking."

"Ay. Best say no more till the time comes."

They would have liked to discuss Murdoch's capture and the news that had followed it. There had been other arrests—Otterburn the late Chancellor and Montgomery his agent: it was an open secret that Montgomery had arranged for his own, so that he could more plausibly turn King's Evidence. Lennox was already in prison, and wild Walter had been chained at Edinburgh since the king's march to Scone. His brother Alexander had been seized at Falkirk, but the youngest of them, called James after his cousin and king, had escaped and taken refuge in the Highlands. "And maybe he's wishing now," said the gossips, "that his house had treated the Graham more fairly in the past. He and the Graham could be plotting fine treason together among the Highland men."

Once free of Perth, tongues wagged a little more freely. Some said that cunning old Athol had helped James to save Scotland from a civil war which the Albany faction had been preparing. Murdoch was a dullard, but his kinsmen might have been pushing him to anything. Others argued that the king was merely taking a belated vengeance for his brother Rothesay's murder—and no blame either. A few, tight-lipped and sure of their own wisdom, said it'd be just the land and the silver that Jamie would be wanting. All took it for granted that Murdoch, his two sons, and possibly Lennox, would be dead before midsummer.

Secretary Cameron was less certain. He knew men, and he knew King James, more complex and less calculable than most. James would say nothing of his intentions, except that he was aiming at justice and security. Cameron, accustomed to regarding such words as so much wind, was not quite sure. But he had to admit that a queer incident, happening shortly after the prorogation, was likely to influence James in the direction of severity. If it had no direct bearing on the trial that was impending, threatening the extinction of the house of Albany, it was certainly an untimely reminder of the bankruptcy to which justice and order had been reduced after twenty years of the Albanies' regencies.

It had happened in the north, where Mar was justiciar, and the news of it came to Perth, in strange enough fashion, while Mar was present. He had come south for the Parliament, and decided to remain there, during the prorogation, until the lords reassembled to sit in judgment on Murdoch and his kin. He enjoyed playing the great man in Perth; he enjoyed seeing men point at him, as they still did, as the man who had broken the Highland hordes on the slopes of Harlaw. His uncouth features and tombstone teeth became familiar in the streets, and not less by candlelight, with such maids of Perth as were maids no more. They endured his face for the sake of his money, his fame, and the glamour which even he could acquire by travels and campaigns on the Continent. By day he could drink and boast of his horses and go hunting with King James.

They were riding back, one evening, from a long day on the Ochil Hills. As they clattered past the Greyfriars, what seemed like a child or dwarf rose from a bush by the roadside and swayed forward, with a curious stumbling movement, to catch at the king's stirrup leather. James saw at once that it was a woman, a poor woman, not remarkable except for her tiny, stumpy figure. His men, on tenterhooks for his safety these days, were round him in a moment. Even when they saw what it was, they would have beaten her off with whips; but she clung there with such courage, and with such desperate appeal on her weatherworn face, that James called them off, and ordered one of them to hoist her on to his crupper and bring her along with them. He was growing accustomed to unusual methods of presenting a petition.

Joan was waiting for him in the castle by the bridgehead. She was always anxious at his absences and correspondingly relieved at his return. She stood with Cameron at the doorway, on a balustraded platform from which two sets of six steps ran down, to left and right, to the courtyard level. James rode alongside, and kissed her hand over the parapet.

"A good day," he said, "and plenty of meat for your kitchen."

"A good day," echoed Mar. "Five bucks, a boar, and a Highland witch." He pointed to the woman, who had just been pushed off, to slide into a squatting position beside the carcase of a deer.

"You can count her as part of *your* quarry," said James, "if she comes from the north." He stood up in his stirrups and suddenly jerked himself, sitting, on to the stone balustrade. He gave the horse a gentle kick with his boot, sending him towards the grooms, and then sat dangling his legs over the courtyard. Mar was dismounting in more orthodox fashion, grunting as he did so.

"How do you know she's Highland?" asked Joan, looking at the woman as if she came from Polar regions or the realms of Prester John.

"By the weave of the clothes," answered Mar, "I'll even make a guess at her clan. Is it Clan Choinnich?"

The woman, hearing a word she understood, nodded assent, and began to talk in soft, quick Gaelic.

"Supper is almost ready," said Joan, as James took her hand under his arm. "Business first," he said. "You must assist me. The power behind the Bench." It pleased Joan to be spoken to, occasionally, in phrases that meant little outside England.

A man came forward as interpreter, a cross-eyed fellow from Caithness, who had spent twenty years wandering round Scotland. James was recovering what little Gaelic he had picked up as a child, but it did not see him far. He had to wait while the woman poured out an unintelligible story, apparently of suffering and wrong. She was speaking fiercely into the man's ear, glancing occasionally towards the king and queen. Mar climbed the steps and stood beside Cameron. He could understand the tale without difficulty, and seemed to be amused, if a little ashamed to smile outwardly. The woman, for some strange reason, had begun to untie the thongs of her shapeless deerskin brogues.

The man, bending over her, gave a last nod, and stood up to face the king. He began to repeat what he had heard in halting language, referring back to her, now and then, by an exchange of gibberish.

The story enforced conviction. It conjured up a series of pictures, all the more vivid for being mirrored in two simple minds—pictures that were humble, pathetic and then suddenly of unbearable horror. One saw the little cabin by the ford, almost leaning against the blacksmith's stone cottage: the man and woman who contrived to live there, not unhappily, in bitter poverty: then came the day when the woman was left a widow and her husband's body must be carried away in haste, because it was plague-time: she was alone and helpless, hardly able to reach the gear which he, almost twice her height, had hung for the last time upon his smoky walls. The little gnome, it seemed, had set her teeth and lived: soft-hearted neighbours had found her a couple of cows, and the clachan had plenty of common pasture. All had been well, as well as the poor could hope, until the raiders came. They had ridden over the hill at daybreak, searched the cottages for anything worth carrying off, and begun to drive away the cattle, splashing through the ford. The villagers watched in dumb anger, only the widow lashing the robbers with desperate words; for her one chance to live was wading away across the river. Twice the leader of the plunderers, waiting till all were past, told her to keep back her tongue; once he bruised her, brutally, with a swing of his spear-shaft. Still she screamed at him that she would have justice on him, the new king's justice, if she had to walk to Edinburgh itself. He turned on her at last, in a cold fury, telling her that she should be well-shod for the journey. He jerked his chin to his men, and in a minute they had her on her back beside the forge, knees in air, bare feet held down upon the anvil. The fire was blown up, the horse-shoes were hammered into a new shape and nailed, red-hot, into the shrinking flesh. Then the men cracked whips again, and drove on with the cattle, stifling such qualms as they might feel with the dull jests of stupid demons. "And you'll have something more now," their leader had shouted back, "that you can be telling your king!"

Last autumn, said the squinting interpreter, that was when it had happened. Wounds like hers took some months to heal. His Majesty, if it so pleased him, could see the scars. But she had heard that the king would be in Perth for Easter and had walked from Dornoch Firth: a priest in Tain had given her money for the journey.

He fell silent. The group in the sunny courtyard seemed frozen into stillness. The woman's dumb eyes searched the king's face. Mar, gross and ruddy in the doorway, began to fidget uncomfortably, thinking of dinner.

James felt Joan's hand, unconsciously gripping his wrist like a vice. He loosened it, and slid off the balustrade on to the flagstones below. He walked towards the woman and she knelt clumsily. He looked at her in silence. There was little he could say. Kingship had failed, not for the first time: the king must take up the ceaseless task of trying to catch up with failures.

The woman took his hand and began to kiss it, almost greedily. He represented her one hope and desire in life, the yearning for vengeance. She should have it in full measure.

"She knows the man's name?" he asked.

Yes, she knew the man's name. She would remember it when all else was forgotten. It was Donald of Ross—Donaill Abradhdubh they called him. He came of a black race, and was the blackest of them all.

James looked back at the steps, at Joan and Cameron, at Mar, hatefully smiling.

"My lord," he said, "you will send letters to the Sheriff of Ross—and tonight. You will tell him to come and seek me, at Perth or elsewhere, bringing the man Donald and all who were art and part with him. They shall be shod with iron before they are hanged."

Mar pursed his lips, affecting a dignity that despised hustling. "Tonight?" he said.

"Tonight!" James mounted the steps, and stood beside Mar's ample form. "If he is not here by Assumption, he ceases to be sheriff, and you to be justiciar for the north."

He took Joan's hand and led her in, Mar grimacing a little as he stood aside for them. The last few words had been spoken low, too low to be overheard in the courtyard. "And that was wise," said Mar truculently. "When a challenge like that is given me in public, I've a way of taking it up."

He glared after the king, and then down towards the lamed woman, sitting patiently while the men hauled the dead bucks past her towards the kitchen quarters. He reluctantly admitted to himself that James was probably right. She would go caterwauling all over the Highlands if they did not give her what she wanted. And the old women of Perth would enjoy seeing Donaill Abradh'dubh dealt with in the market-place. It was only the king's manner that Mar felt a right to resent. He asserted it by sending an additional oath after the king.

Cameron heard it, and decided that he would be risking nothing by pouring a little oil on ruffled waters. "His Majesty speaks abruptly," he said, "but we must remember that he has a great deal weighing on his mind."

"Less than he had a month ago," answered Mar. "He has little to worry over now that he's got the Albanies to the knackers. There's only the killing to be done."

"Your lordship," said Cameron primly, "has no right to assume that there is any bloodshed in contemplation. We must await the trial."

Mar was too irritated to know whether he should laugh or show anger. "Is your Secretaryship telling me," he asked, "that you do not know his Majesty's intentions?"

"I doubt," answered Cameron, "whether his Majesty's

intentions are formed yet." He motioned Mar to precede him in the direction of supper. "The Albany lords were arrested for fear they were about to stir up civil war. We cannot be certain yet that such was their intention. I fancy we may know more about the subject in the course of the next few weeks."

May 3rd, 1425

IX

Before Man had learnt skill in the art of slaughtering his fellows, Nature herself had shaped a fortress at Dumbarton. Its rock rose steeply from the Clyde, unscalable in the face of opposition. When Scotland grew to be Scotland, Dumbarton became one of the kingdom's keys, guarding the Lowlands from such wild folk as might dwell round Loch Lomond or sail the western firth. Like many strongholds that are reputed impregnable, it had often fallen to escalade. Its very strength, the sheer drop of the basalt cliff, tempted its possessors to leave the castle half-garrisoned, and tempted the garrison to relax precaution, even when nights were darkest.

It was not long since Dumbarton—like so much else in Scotland—had belonged to the house of Albany. But Murdoch had been forced to surrender it to his son Walter, and Walter had forfeited it to the king. King James's own uncle, the Red Stewart of Dundonald, was now sitting in its rough-hewn hall. He had finished supper. He had drunk enough ale to raise his already high opinion of himself. He was talking to a priest.

His connection with the king sprang from a union unrecognized by the Church. Nor was there anything red about him, these days. His face was wrinkled and parchment-pale: it was framed in grey and even white: there was no sign of the auburn hair he had inherited from his mother—

an Ayrshire lass, long dead, who had once slept the night beside a long-dead king of Scotland.

He was of middle height, blear-eyed and bony. One of his hands helped to prop his head, while the other crumbled the scraps of bread on the table. His tongue had been active, despite half-hearted interruptions from the priest, for a matter of two hours. He always found it easy to ignore or override those he talked with, for he was more than half deaf.

"Dun-Breton! Dun-Breton!" he was saying in scornful accents. "Believe it or not, the man tried to persuade me that Dumbarton took its name from the Britons of King Arthur's time. So I just looked at him and said, 'Did you never learn Latin, Master Prior?' And then I looked at him again, stared at him in silence, to show my contempt for his Gaelic notions."

"In silence?" asked the priest impishly. "Did you say in silence?" He was a smallish man, or at least one of those that look small when seated. The chin of his wise, patient little face seemed a very short way above the edge of the table.

Sir John Stewart did not seem to realize that he had spoken. "Would you believe it?" he went on. "Would you believe that I had to enlighten him in the end? '*Domus barathri*,' I said, 'the dwelling by the gulf.' '*Dom-baraton*,' 'Dumbarton.' Clyde mouth is certainly a gulf. People have certainly dwelt here since Roman times. Could anything be simpler? I expect the place got its name when Julius Caesar led his cohorts into Scotland."

"Oh," said the priest. "But did he?"

"Agree?" said Sir John, mishearing. "Of course you agree. You are an intelligent person, a man of learning. Not like my friend the prior. It is a pleasure to have an educated man to talk to, especially in these uncultivated regions. When my nephew, the king, commissioned me to come here, I told him at once how it would be. 'I shall be like the poet Ovid among the Vandals,' I said. 'There's no learning west of Glasgow.'"

He reached for a jug and poured out all that was left of the ale.

"I met a man in Paisley," said the priest, "who had been to Italy." His voice sounded a little wistful.

"Just what I say," answered Stewart. "It is a university that we need here in the west. I was always an advocate for Scottish universities: indeed, St. Andrews owes more to me than posterity will ever know. But the Highlands will never be safe until we establish some outpost of learning at their gates. Why, twenty miles from where we are sitting, the greatest landholders talk in Gaelic—like any common hind. They don't know a hundred words of Scottish—and some of them have hardly heard of Latin." He paused, swallowing his indignation and his ale. "I drew up a scheme once," he continued, "for establishing colleges in the Highlands. The Regent Albany professed himself deeply interested in it. I have sent a copy to my nephew for consideration, and I have hopes, high hopes, that he may adopt it. If he can find the money."

"I have never seen his Majesty," said the priest, by way of distraction. "You were at Scone, were you not, for the coronation?"

"What's that?" said Sir John, and waited for the priest to repeat himself. "Yes, yes," he said, "almost a year ago. He is of small stature, like yourself. My cousin Murdoch seemed to tower over him at the ceremony—like a giant in the Greek fables. But he is said to be unusually strong and active for his size. Of his learning I can speak myself—without feeling ashamed of my relationship. He writes poems, though he seemed reluctant to submit any to my judgment. He has studied music thoroughly, even the Grecian theoric: in Aristophanes, you know. As he grows older, he will no doubt perfect himself in more important branches of learning."

The priest still hoped to head Sir John off on to less rarefied topics. "I wonder," he said, "what his Majesty's intentions are with regard to his cousin Murdoch. They say that the whole family is under arrest, except the youngest son. James, is it not?"

If Stewart heard, he was not interested enough to pursue the subject. He was soon launched upon a genealogical discourse: it wandered through inaccurate Latin into ridiculous guesses at Hebrew, tracing the line of Stewart, by way of Nero (an undervalued musician), back to the Psalmist King David.

The priest smiled and nodded. It was time for bed. His thoughts were far away. He wondered, for a moment, how this fantastic old pedant had come to be in charge of Dumbarton Castle in such dangerous times. Then he remembered that Colquhoun of Luss, a hard-bitten scamp of a fighting man, was the real warden: Colquhoun was away for the night, leaving only the figure-head. The priest himself would be gone next morning, before Colquhoun returned. He would be on his way to Lanarkshire, to the parish that awaited him. A pleasant place, he had been informed, among simple country folk—folk who might stare blankly at the mention of the Trinity, but were at least untouched by discontents and heresies. Of such, he told himself, was the Kingdom of Heaven. By all accounts they paid their teinds without too much grumbling. He had been lucky to get the benefice, just in time; his brother, a Glasgow clothier, had influence with the bishop. Bishop Lauder, they said, was dying and could not last the summer; there was no knowing if his successor would accept recommendations from honest clothiers to whom he might or might not owe money. A priest's life was a chancy business. He must remember to say more prayers to God, in gratitude for his new benefice.

He suddenly awoke from his reverie to find that Sir John was rising from his chair.

"I will show it you," the old man was saying. "I think I have it in the east room. That is, if you are interested in such matters."

"Oh. I am," said the bewildered priest.

"A most curious document," continued Stewart, "well worth perusal. It was sold to me as a saintly relic, but it is not that. I cannot boast that I have altogether solved its mystery, but I am quite sure that it must have come down to us from a very early time, probably from the ancients."

"Who gave it to you?" asked the priest at a venture.

"Why, I was just telling you. This English traveller. He had it from an Italian merchant in London. I will fetch it you. I always keep it locked up. —Unless you care to accompany me to my room?"

He looked doubtfully at the priest and seemed relieved when the invitation was declined; one felt he preferred nobody to know where his treasure was hidden.

"I will return immediately," he said, and departed happily, smiling—as the priest had to admit to himself—a curiously winning smile.

He did not return for the better part of half an hour. It took him that time to find his private keys in the pocket of a night-gown, unlock an iron-bound chest and then, discovering that the document was not there, cast about for some other hiding-place. He had not been many weeks at Dumbarton, but his room was already a labyrinth of forgotten treasure-holes. He was an old man, deliberate by habit and beginning nowadays to fumble with his hands. He remembered the place at last, in the window jamb: he had pried out a loose stone there and scooped a little hollow behind it.

He stopped once or twice to listen to sounds from below. He was far too deaf to hear much through stone walls and floors, but he suspected some disturbance. Perhaps the men-at-arms were making merry. Perhaps some woman was creating a hubbub, as was the way of women. The world would be better without such irrational, ignorant creatures.

He began to descend the stairs. As he passed each arrow-slit, he had to shade his taper to prevent it guttering out in the draught. He was unsure of tread, and the steps had been worn uneven.

He kept tight hold of a scrap of paper, covered with crabbed scrawls in some dialect of Spanish. It had been sold to a credulous Englishman as a letter from St. Elizabeth to Our Lady. It had actually started its career, some ten years back, as a tavern-reckoning in Barcelona.

As Sir John reached the last step, his taper flared up and then went suddenly out. He groped for the doorway and began to make cautious progress along the passage to the hall. He halted a moment, vaguely disquieted. The noise, which he could neither locate nor explain, seemed to be increasing and approaching him. He was an old man and naturally fretful. He was in total darkness.

The next moment he had stumbled and fallen full length. It felt as though he had tripped over some drunkard, lying asleep in the passage. He tried to raise himself on a bruised elbow, but it slithered in a pool of moisture. Groping along the floor, he came on something soft and round. It seemed warm. A man's head: tonsured: a priest's head. It was attached to nothing, had been severed at the neck. He felt the moisture trickle through his fingers.

As he struggled up in terror, the light of torches flared along the passage. There were men approaching, armed men in Highland garb. He saw their chequered plaids, their war-shirts dipped in saffron. The mountaineers had scaled Dumbarton rock.

They had seen him before he could think of escape, and were laying rough hands on his shoulders. They dragged him into the buttery, where a man had more room to swing a claymore. They stood round him, shouting their excitement. In the last moments of his life, his ears were afflicted with the barbarous jargon of the Gael.

In the deserted hall, among empty ale-jugs and crumbled

bread, James, son of Murdoch, was counting the money from the castle's rifled treasury. There would be little enough of it, when he had shared part of it out among his triumphant Highlandmen. He must keep back all he could, for rebellion could not prosper without money. The king, arresting the leaders of Albany, had bottled up most of their wealth and could use it against them. But the night's work promised well; Dumbarton had proved an easy prey and, if the Lennox men had had the same luck at Inchmurrin, if Bishop Finlay of the Isles could rouse the seaward clans to rebellion, then the king's crown might be in jeopardy before the summer was out.

The men had begun to drag the bodies into the hall. They were counting their quarry. They reckoned thirty-two men slain and, laughing at their own jest, added half a man for the priest.

James, their leader, insisted on a proper burial, a mass if it could be managed, for Sir John the Red. The man had been his great-uncle, and, if a bastard, yet of royal blood. When they laid out his corpse for the funeral, they found a small paper—some talisman or cantrip, they imagined—tightly clutched in the dead man's hand.

May 24th-25th, 1425

X

Parliament had reassembled. It was sitting at Stirling town. There was a long list of statutes for which the king would demand its sanction, but no one was much interested in them at the moment. The half-warlike aspect of the conclave, the tournament ceremonies that had impressed James when he was fresh from England, these seemed more appropriate now to the business that weighed upon every mind. Tomorrow the assembly would appoint its men for a court martial; it would shrink in numbers and become a tribal gathering for human sacrifice, a small group of the elder wolves asserting the blood-right of the pack. And it was King James that had given the word.

Secretary Cameron sat at his table, watching the ranks and tiers of the assembled lords.

He knew now that he had lost an opportunity last autumn. He ought to have supported Athol more whole-heartedly or, better still, anticipated Athol in recommending ruthlessness to King James. Now that it was happening, he could see that the thing had been inevitable from the first. He should have seen it earlier, gained favour and position by urging it on the king before the demands of circumstance grew unmistakable. Men born to power could maybe take things as they came: men who must climb to it out of obscurity had need to foresee their coming. So Joseph, foreseeing famine, had risen from slavery to a palace, to lordship over all save Pharaoh: so poor men in every generation had risen through warfare or commerce or the Church, until they forced open the gates of power and wealth. Cameron was determined to be one of them: he craved money, importance and the opportunity to patronize all that deserved patronage. But, if he was ever to be a power in Scotland, with money to patronize anything more than street-music, he must learn to be quicker in reading the signs of the times, in recommending the destruction of those whom Time had condemned.

The doom of Albany was plain enough now, written, if nowhere else, on the faces of the great lords who sat pretending to listen to the trivial first day's business. Some, like Mar, were wooden and callous. Some seemed to be chewing their own self-righteousness, reminding themselves that they had disliked or even opposed the house of Albany. A few betrayed slight uneasiness, as though fearing, at the last moment, to be implicated: but from these least of all could Murdoch expect mercy—unless it were mercy to be hurried more swiftly to the grave.

There, too, sat the king, calmer than usual, his brow

knitted over the passing routine of legislation. Cameron was not deceived; he knew James too well. The struggle might be over, the die cast, but conscience would be still at work, asking if it was indeed justice and necessity that had decided the matter, or love of power and gold. James had something of his old father in him, and would never listen in complete serenity to that flattering courtier whom kings call Reason of State. He might be doubting now whether mercy did not mean more than power, whether successful kingship was worth the wrong that it demands. Cameron was thankful that he was not in Murdoch's shoes: but he was glad, too, that he was not in the king's.

Before Parliament was dispersed for the night, the news from the west country was read aloud. Dumbarton had been retaken; of its captors, the Highlandmen who had slain the king's uncle, five had been taken prisoner and were awaiting a savage punishment; James, son of Murdoch, had escaped; he and Bishop Finlay were thought to have fled to Ireland. Lennox's men still held out in Inchmurrin Castle, but the king's promptness had isolated their rising, and averted the general war they had hoped to wake; they had accomplished nothing, except assure that Lennox should share Murdoch's fate.

The trial lasted two days. The verdicts were in no doubt, nor the sentence that must follow. The king had spoken; the twenty-one lords who had been chosen as judges, had only to fulfil his intention. Murdoch's own servants had turned against him: Otterburn gave an account of his stewardship to his master's enemies: Montgomery, having opened secret stores of information, was proving his new loyalty by helping the king's men to force Inchmurrin Castle. The Court, for that matter, had no need of witnesses. The judges themselves knew what Murdoch and Lennox had been doing while James was in exile: some of them had even shared in the proceeds, but that was beside the point. They had only to record their verdict that both men had quietly committed robbery upon the king's goods, and permitted young Walter to commit it violently upon the poor and defenceless.

The younger man was the first to suffer. He was taken to death at the close of the first day. On the next, sentence was passed at noon on Lennox, on Murdoch and on Murdoch's second son. It was to be carried out at sunset.

They were led away, young Alexander in proud defiance, Lennox dazed and incredulous of violent death: Murdoch, for any sign he gave, might have been dead already. No sentence could rob the three of their comeliness and commanding stature. They dwarfed King James as they passed out to death. He could, no doubt, have beaten all three in fight, by courage, training and muscle, as he was now destroying them by force of law. But his small, thick-set figure, sitting tense on the throne, was no match for Alexander's towering youth, Murdoch's massive and uncomplaining dignity or the silver beauty of Lennox's age.

Stirling town climbs steeply up its rock: the castle, at the head of the single street, looks out upon precipice beyond. It is easy for a man there to feel as if he trod a platform hung from heaven by invisible chains: easier still for a woman that has been bred in English midlands. Queen Joan sat at a window on the northern side. She looked out, conscious only of height, unconscious of the rock beneath: one had to crane far out to see it at all: the distance to flat earth was more apparent, the minuteness of those who walked upon it. There seemed to be an unusual number of them, small streams of people all making eastward. She could guess their purpose and what they went to see. It was better not to think of it. It was better to think of baby Margaret in the room behind her, asleep in her gilded cradle. For the rest, she could not hope to understand Scotland's politics, its feuds and hatreds and alarms. It was enough that James, with whatever hesitations, had taken his decision.

She looked to the Ochil hills, black with forest, across five miles of plain. She looked westward of them, where, far more remote, the whole huge line of the Highlands ran athwart the sky. Dwarfed by distance, their peaks seemed hardly higher than the airy palace in which she sat. But they spoke to her of mystery, wildness and horror. She knew that folk lived in their very shadow, and wondered what barbarians could think of such places as their home. Even from this distance thought sickened at their savage challenge. It was better to turn back from the window, to be a wife and mother instead of the enchanted princess in the sky.

As she turned, she saw that there was a servant at the door. He had come to announce Abbot Fogo: as James's confessor, the abbot had lodging in the castle.

He seemed grave, hag-ridden almost. He had nothing to say, except that the Court had risen and that his Majesty would be returning soon. After some minutes of embarrassing silence, Joan asked him whether he would be with them for dinner.

"No, your Majesty," he said, "I . . . I think not. Unless——." He hesitated, clearly wanting to say more than he dared. He gave it up at last. "If his Majesty wants me," he said, "I shall be in the Chapel. Perhaps you would let him know."

He looked at the baby with a strange fixed stare, standing for a minute or more above the cradle. Then he glanced at old Margery Norton, sitting on guard beside it, vacillated a moment, and was gone.

Joan took up a piece of embroidery. There was a strange hush throughout the castle. A dog barking in the hayfields, hundreds of feet down, seemed only to stress the silence aloft. Joan bent over her work.

She hardly heard James enter, he came with so quiet a tread. He crossed the room like a cat, glancing towards the cradle. Joan felt that his sleeping baby was only an excuse for a quietness prompted by other feelings. She signed to Margery to be gone.

James was looking down from the window and did not turn back to her when they were alone. "We must have a garden down there," he said suddenly. "The soil's good, and it's crown land. The tenant can be shifted elsewhere."

"If it's ready in time," said Joan, "I can take Margaret there and teach her to walk."

James did not seem to hear. He paced to the door and back again. He looked towards the distant mountains, still flecked with white. "The summer's begun," he said, "we shall have hot weather soon."

She wondered why he found it necessary to make conversation. She was content to sit in silence, near him and near their child.

"Did the abbot come in here?" he asked.

"Yes. He went to the chapel. Did you want him?"

"No. Not especially."

"He could not keep his eyes from Margaret. I thought he was going to give her his blessing or something."

"We all need blessing," said James sententiously. "Kings and queens especially." Joan looked at him with puzzled eyes, but he was entirely grave.

"So Margaret is to be a queen?" she said.

"Probably. God help her!"

"Have you arranged the marriage yet? Is it to be France or baby Henry? We'll have to decide soon: she's five months old."

The flippancy seemed hardly to penetrate to James. He began to fidget round the room again.

"I hope," said Joan, more seriously, "that she will have as good fortune as I. Or are you going to use her for your politics and alliances? We owe her something better than that, don't you think, considering how happy we are ourselves?"

James turned away. "You may be right," he said. "We shall see."

He went back to the door, and opened it this time. He paused on the threshold. "I shall dine alone," he said. "In the South Tower. Entertain the company for me." The next moment he was gone.

There was little rest for him, in the South Tower or elsewhere. He dined, he attempted to read, he began to roam the castle again. At one time he seemed drawn towards the chapel, but, as soon as he entered, the sight of his confessor, bent in prayer before the altar, drove him away again. He could only return to a private room again, glance through more books, and await supper.

He had told himself, a hundred times, that the thing was just, as well as necessary. The death of Murdoch and Lennox was the fitting end to a long story, stretching back over twenty years: a story of incompetence and disloyalty, oppression and theft. The argument seemed unanswerable —and yet powerless to keep out the creeping doubts that tormented him. He could not trace them to their source, for he had contrived to forget those other threads in the story's web that had no connection with necessity or justice. He was not thinking of the day when he, a child of eight, had come suddenly upon his old father, weeping for Rothesay's death: the day—still less reasonable—when he had sat up in an English field, with his face covered in mud, and seen Lennox smiling at his plight: the day when he had first heard that Murdoch had been ransomed and himself left prisoner: the long years of confinement, poverty, and neglect. These things had not been, could not be, cited to twenty-one lords, sitting as officers of justice, but they had played their part in bringing four men to the block.

The sun was setting as he sat down to his evening meal. He had little taste for food. Only the wine gleamed temptingly, and the first draught of it promised respite from self-torture. He could drink deep. The thing was done now, past recall. It was wisest to forget, to welcome every instrument of oblivion. He drained the cup again and again, and made his man refill it without stint. He did not hear the hinges creak as the castle-gate swung open. He did not know when the mournful procession began its appointed journey.

A little to the east of Stirling Castle, the plain that surrounds it is broken by a few hillocks, fragments, as it were, from the one enormous rock. On the last of these, rounded and grass-grown, stood a low hunk of granite whose cold touch had been, to many men, the last they knew of Scotland. No one could tell the story of its more ancient bloodstains, but there was now a fresh one on it, hardly a day old. Murdoch, climbing the slope of the Heading Hill, saw, between the shoulders of his escort, the spot where his son had died last night.

He reached it himself. He did not look up to the castle, nor across to the distant mountains. His gaze strayed up the river valley, over humped trees golden in the sunset. He could see, or almost see, the distant towers of Doune. There his father had built proudly, lived proudly; there he himself had reigned. It would be Jamie's now. Everything was Jamie's. The tale of Albany was told.

A man, stripped to the waist, was balancing a long sword in his two hands: a squat man, hardly reaching to Murdoch's chest, but with the shoulders of an ox. Murdoch stared, fascinated by the red gleam of the sunset along the blade.

His whole desire, the prayers and appetites of fifty years, shrunk suddenly to one overmastering wish. One of the others must be the first to go. That would give him another minute, more than another minute of life. If they began with the eldest, it would be Lennox: if with youth, then Alexander. He was safe for a little space. He could watch the birds in the evening sky or look across trees towards Doune. He could even do as the priest bade, remember his sins, and God's unending mercy. Something else must happen before he, Murdoch of Albany, was called to kneel at the stone.

They were holding the crowd back in a ring, but at no great distance. He recognized a number of faces: Christopher Chalmers, his squire—with his brother Thomas, the Perth merchant; his falconer, clad in green; a woman that had once nursed him when he lay sick at Doune. Most were from Stirling, but Stirling had been within his lordship, and these folk his tenants; they watched with friendly and pitying eyes. One old man was weeping already.

He felt a hand laid on his forearm. The broad-shouldered, half-naked man was standing beside him, about to speak. In his eyes was neither friendship nor pity.

"You first, my lord," he said.

The Yellow Shirts

What are these men doing in our mountains?

THE SONG OF ROLAND.

CHAPTER SEVEN

The Yellow Shirts

June 1427

I

In the ramshackle old house which still served St. Andrews University as headquarters, Master Laurence of Lindores sat opposite a frightened minor cleric and looked at him as though he were some unimportant insect. Their interview had been a harsh one from the first, for it is astonishing what one priest can say to another when no laymen are in hearing, and Master Laurence was not a man to mince matters. But the worst was over: the more serious delinquencies had been catalogued and the appropriate penances fixed: nor, to judge by the look of the culprit, was he likely to omit the smallest detail of his self-punishment. Lesser matters were now in question.

"It has come to my ears," Master Laurence was saying, "that you neglected to read the prayer for the king, queen, and princesses last Sunday. This must not occur again. I know quite well what you will tell me. You will say——"

The object of reprimand, stirred to faint protest, tried to indicate that he had no intention of saying anything. But the hard voice went on.

"You will say that no ecclesiastical rule obliges you to pray for their Majesties—merely an Act of Parliament. I would remind you that the statute was passed at the same Parliament as the recent and much-needed law against heresy. So long as secular princes assist us in our war against the powers of Evil, we are under an obligation to assist them by obedience and prayer. . . ."

Master Laurence believed in mixing instruction with reproof: he was soon deep in an exposition of the correct relations between Church and State.

It was not his position as rector of the university that made him a terror to his subordinates: it was not even his Papal commission as Inquisitor for the kingdom: it was the man himself. He was of a type rare in Scotland, impossible among the English. Outwardly, he was sallow, sharp of nose, and with piercing eyes set beneath high arched brows. Behind them lay a brain remarkable for its limitations, more remarkable for the concentrated power which those limitations only intensified. Such a mind is commoner in Spain or Italy, but even there it would have been hard to match its superb freedom from sentiment, vagueness or compromise. It had one function—to enable its possessor to despatch, with no hint of fumbling, the business he had chosen for his life-work, and to go on despatching it long after most men would have turned aside for rest, amusement or observation. Such men as Lindores, by all the logic of religion, should be assured of salvation in the next world as a reward for their undeviating persistence in this. But it is a little difficult to see what position and what employment will be found for them in Paradise.

The man he was addressing was long past any such speculation. He sat under the rector's cold eye like a fascinated rabbit, only listening in the faint hope of picking out some sentence he could understand.

"Temporal powers come and go," concluded Laurence. "Holy Kirk is by no means dependent on their support. But so long as the king is her zealous servant, we must give him all our countenance against opposition or detraction. Have I made myself clear?"

"Oh, yes," began his victim. "His Holiness the Pope——"

"I know what you are going to tell me. You are thinking of the misunderstanding that has recently arisen between King James and his Holiness, the dispute over the Glasgow bishopric. Such affairs are inevitable, but temporary, and you can leave their settlement to your superiors. Until his Holiness launches excommunication or interdict—and there is no question of either in this case—the lower clergy need take no cognizance. You may . . . you may——"

For a moment the rector felt put out. The man before him had risen and was staring past him towards the door, presumably at someone else who had entered. It was probably the bishop.

"You may go now," said Laurence, without turning round. "And do not let me see you here again on similar business."

To his annoyance, the man hesitated, awaiting a confirmation of his dismissal. He received it apparently by nod or gesture, and made his departure. Master Laurence rose to make a stiff bow to Bishop Wardlaw. "Good morning to your lordship," he said.

"And to you," answered the bishop. "I am glad to find that you are keeping them up to the mark. To judge by the news, my old pupil may soon need all the prayers we can give him."

"Does your lordship consider this unhappy dispute——?"

Wardlaw waved a hand. "Rome!" he said, with a charitable smile. "We all know Rome by now." He was not surprised to find his smile unreturned. He seated himself in the rector's chair.

"No," he continued, "I was thinking of our own country. I was talking, last month, to the subject of this dispute you mentioned—Bishop Cameron, if the Pope will allow me to give him the title. He tells me that his Majesty intends to take some measures against Highland disorder. One cannot stir that hornet's nest without danger. And, nearer home, some very drastic steps are in contemplation. We all understood about Albany, but the other earls and barons have not incurred a similar guilt."

"Are others to be killed?"

"Oh, no, no! I trust we shall see no more executions.

It is only a question of titles to land. Have you heard that he is depriving that young Malise of the Earldom of Strathearn?"

"No." The rector seemed to lose interest. He had picked up a paper from the table. He disliked Wardlaw's attitude to secular affairs, just as he disliked his extravagance in money matters, his occasional levity, his strange popularity among the students.

"Of course, we all know that half the land-holders are rogues and potential rebels. But it may be unwise to confiscate and redistribute their lands without a more legal excuse."

"I do not study secular politics," said Laurence, slightly contemptuous. "But I consider that a king has every right to redistribute earldoms and baronies. Land, to them, is merely office. Holy Kirk has no hesitation in dismissing or transferring her unsatisfactory officials."

"Has she none?" said the bishop, with a twinkle. "Is that really so? I only wish you were correct, my dear rector." He stroked his beard. He had a forty years' experience of Holy Church, and his views of her were based on observation rather than theory.

"But I was not thinking of Right," he said. "The king is king. I was more concerned with the dangers he may run into by asserting it. We're an ill race to rule, in Scotland."

"All government is dangerous," replied the rector. "Power corrupts. It corrupts kings and barons alike. When one thinks of the roots from which secular power has sprung, one can hardly wonder at the robbery and murder that accompany it. One is sometimes astonished that any country enjoys peace for two consecutive years."

He returned to his paper, having, as he imagined, said all that could be said on the subject.

"I do not think," said the bishop, "that his Majesty is as yet corrupted by his opportunities—or by his successful use of them in the past. I trust not; I trust he is aware of the possible contagion. I wonder, now, whether I could discuss the matter with him, next time we meet—in the light of your admirable exposition."

Whether Wardlaw intended flattery or satire, the rector was impervious to both. "Our colleague of Melrose," he said, "is his Majesty's confessor."

"I accept the rebuke," answered the bishop, "but I was thinking of a less formal discussion. I have known his Majesty since childhood." He rose and strolled to the window, peering out with short-sighted eyes. There seemed to be some bustle in the streets, unusual at such an early hour.

"I wonder," he said over his shoulder, "what makes you take so unfriendly a view of the secular power today. I suppose you have been hearing this rumour among the students. You need not fear, you know. I am sure it will come to nothing."

Laurence looked up from his reading in some irritation. "I do not know," he said, "to what your lordship refers. I am not in the habit of listening to rumours among the students."

"They say there is talk at Perth of his Majesty transferring this university—your university—to that city. An unwise scheme, I consider it. As I say, I do not think it will come to anything."

"Transfer the——? But the thing's impossible. We have a Bull from Rome."

"Bulls can be bought," said Wardlaw absent-mindedly. "His Majesty has money now to purchase a new one." He did not see his companion stiffen in resentment at the words. His attention was arrested by what was happening outside the window.

"Someone is arriving," he said. "Quite a cavalcade. Now I wonder——"

Lindores also had heard the bustle. "I have had no notice," he said, "of any important visitor. Possibly my Lord Abbot from Balmerino——"

"Balmerino does not bring so many men-at-arms. Nor make them ride so hard. That outrider's horse is in a lather of sweat. I must go and see."

He had almost reached the door when an excited student rushed in, hardly avoiding collision with the bishop's stomach. He pulled up short and was about to laugh it off when he caught the eye of the rector beyond. He collected himself, made sober apology, and delivered his news.

"I thought so," said Wardlaw. "My old eyes are better than I feared. It is more than time that his Majesty paid us a visit. Be off with you, and tell your friends to cheer louder."

The student grinned and disappeared.

"They need no encouragement to be noisy," commented the rector. "Such a visit as this, entirely unannounced, is a sufficient interruption to their studies, without our countenancing their demonstrations."

He looked at the bishop, who was standing with a rapt expression by the door. He wondered if he had overstepped the limits of due respect. "Your lordship will pardon my words," he said, "but I must remind you that I am rector of this university."

"I am not likely to forget it," said the bishop quietly. His thoughts were elsewhere, and a trifle anxious. He was remembering the conversation of some minutes ago; Lindores had formulated, in his dry, academic fashion, certain thoughts that he himself had been entertaining of late. It might be a good thing, it might even be a duty, to lay them before King James. Age and old acquaintance gave one certain privileges. He could not exactly presume to question, or even discuss, James's intentions with regard to the earldoms—the transfer of land and power from one hand to another. But it might be possible to suggest that one success could whet a king's appetite while it blinded his judgment, and even his conscience. James had seized the lands of Albany and Lennox—justly, perhaps—was using them for his own ends or had distributed them among his supporters. The temptation to repeat the manœuvre, without bloodshed but with less justification, must be overwhelmingly strong. One could, perhaps, put in some friendly word, suggesting that precipitancy might be dangerous, might wake opposition in some unforeseen quarter.

There was also the matter of the university. He had made light of the rumour, but he had reason to think that James was indeed contemplating a change. St. Andrews was remote, and James was apparently wanting to concentrate everything at Perth, to make it Scotland's capital in all senses. He must be dissuaded. The university was, in some sort, King James's own creation: he must not be allowed to spoil it by transplanting it just as it was beginning to strike root and flourish.

Wardlaw could hardly attack the king at two points. He stood to lose at both, incurring reproof for overmuch meddling. He had better concentrate on the second, which was already within his province. King James's policy for the earldoms—his conscience, too—were as clearly outside it.

The rector was grumbling again. "It is very inconsiderate of his Majesty," he was saying, "to give me no notice of his coming. I hope your lordship will remonstrate with him."

"I shall do nothing of the sort," answered the bishop, "except, possibly, on this question of robbing us of our university. I am old enough to be grateful for occasional pleasures, and unorthodox enough to prefer them when they come unexpectedly. And it is always a pleasure to welcome an old pupil."

August 1427

II

It was not often that Sir Robert Graham found himself thinking of a woman. But idleness and a hot summer's day can tempt the sternest mind to uncommon relaxation. Graham lay couched in the bracken beside Loch Earn; the sun was comforting, the flies that had accompanied his morning's walk had now ceased to tease him. If he was never quite at peace with the world, he was at least enjoying a truce.

He had not chosen the spot for comfort, but for safety. Behind him lay the little village of Ardvorlich and, above it, the short pass that led past Dubh Choirein to Callander and the Lowlands. He had come to await a messenger who was bringing letters from home and an instalment of money. It was not safe for him to go to his own estates, except quietly, occasionally, and for a day or two at most. King James's men showed little sign of molesting him and had perhaps been instructed to forget about the prisoner who had escaped from them more than two years ago: but Graham had no wish to remind them or their master of his existence, and he felt it wiser to remain in hiding behind the wall of the mountains. His son and his stewards were caring well enough for his farms in Kincardine. He was passably contented with his Highland friends—so far as one of his unquiet spirit could know content. There were even hours of comparative happiness, such as the one he was now idling away, staring at the loch's blue waters and recalling tender, half-buried memories.

There had only been two women in his life, the one who had given him birth, the other whom he had hoped to marry. Both were long dead—his mother when he was barely a lad: the shock of that loss had left him, for all his self-reliance, curiously baffled and astray. Later, when the time came for mating, Fortune had seemed to smile. Like King James, he had come to love, and love deeply, the woman whom Worldly Prudence and Policy suggested to him for wife. And then suddenly Worldly Policy, embodied in the elders of the two families, had decreed that she must be given up to his elder brother. Nothing he said or did could alter the decision. Greybeards lectured him on the importance of her dowry, the greater convenience of the new arrangements; they had spoken as if no other considerations could conceivably exist. Outwardly resentful, secretly humiliated, he had been forced to step aside; he had hardly dared to speak of the one thing that mattered most to him. He had surrendered unimaginable joys to a brother who seemed as indifferent towards the bride as he himself was desperate to possess her. He was too proud to show a wound, and, by the time he had reached full manhood, those who knew him best would have sworn that he was one to whom women had never meant anything. His own turn came to marry, and he hardly cared who was to share his bed and bear his children: their coming did not seem to stir his heart for an instant. He neglected them—perversely, as others thought—to lavish a wealth of hoarded affection upon his brother's son, Malise. Yet in truth there was no hint of perversity in the man's soul. If he differed from his fellows it was by virtue of an almost inhuman integrity, which drove him onward to conclusions logical enough, but beyond the conception of easier-going men. If there was perversity, it lay in his fortunes rather than his nature: circumstances seemed to delight in driving him, unwillingly, towards dark and crooked ways.

He had certainly not prospered as his abilities deserved. His powers had little outlet. His unusual knowledge of the law, painstakingly acquired, was allowed to rust in idleness. His capacity for leading men, for inspiring loyalty, if not affection, was turning sour for lack of employment. He was close on fifty, but he had held no office, exercised no trust. Albany had suspected and impoverished him, King James, for once, had followed Albany's lead. If Graham had a task to perform in this life, he must seek it out soon—and not from the house of Stewart.

It had occurred to him, more than once, to wonder whether God might have put him into the world, given him his love of justice and ancient custom, in order to create a makeweight, a rebel if necessary, against the greed and pride of the crown. He had put the notion aside, but it had come back to him, time and again, with each new turn in Scotland's fortunes and his own. He had thought of it much during his short unjust imprisonment. He had listened to the widespread indignation at James's high-handed justice and dubious taxation. He had not loved Albany, but he loved still less the structure that James was raising on Albany's ruins, the deliberate ousting of the nobility from all positions of trust except the merely ornamental, and the employment of lowly-born quill-drivers, who would not dare to oppose his will. James had even got himself into trouble with the Pope, conferring a bishopric on that smug little upstart Cameron, and maintaining him there after a Papal court had issued a sentence of deprivation. One could only hope that Rome might inspire the Scottish Kirk to take up the quarrel and form a party against the king. Graham himself, had he been a priest, would have known how to denounce royal aggression in the name of Christ: he would not have played Cameron's game, picking other men's brains and toadying to the king for preferment. Perhaps, once he had lost his true mate to his brother, he could have found a mission and heart's ease in the Kirk. It was too late to think of that now. He could only wonder whether, as a small man on the fringes of a great family, he could strike any blow for his injured country.

Perhaps he deceived himself imagining that any mission awaited him. Perhaps he was intended to live and die a country laird, untried and unmeddling in higher matters. It might be mere pride that prevented him from making his submissive peace with the king and returning to Kincardine and his estates. The future would show. There was no certainty or completeness in the chain of the things that seemed, at times, to lead him to more than an honourable obscurity. He must wait and be sure. Meanwhile the sun shone warmly, the bracken was soft and green, and it was pleasant to lie and think of a past in which politics had seemed dull and unnecessary, when youth and love had made the world a glorious venture—more glorious than he had since come to think it.

His golden memories were soon disturbed. A rustle and crackling up the glen proclaimed that someone was coming down to Ardvorlich and the loch-side. Graham was on his feet in a moment, stooping for the unbuckled sword that lay beside him. He had hardly gripped it when he was smiling at his own fears. The king's men would hardly penetrate to Loch Earn, and Highlandmen, however eager for raids on their neighbour's cattle, were not given to attacking solitary strangers. He was awaiting a messenger from Kincardine, from his son Robin: this was probably the man now, crackling down the glen.

It proved to be no messenger, but Robin himself. Greetings were constrained: the younger man seemed glad to hand over two letters and a small purse, without comment. His eyes avoided his father's, and without difficulty; it would have been hard to say which was the shier of the two.

The son had inherited little of his father's craggy and imposing mien. A fresh complexion, slow, good-natured eyes, no sign of inward fire. He lacked the resolute energy that would have attracted Sir Robert's attention and respect. But he also lacked Malise's innocent, half-womanish grace. Father and son were neither alike enough nor different enough to make an affectionate pair.

The younger man vanished into the bracken, seeking a burn from which to quench his overdue thirst: it had been hot in the pass beneath Ben Vorlich. The letters, to judge by their bulk, would take his father twenty minutes to read.

After some mouthfuls of delicious coolness he strolled back to the Ardvorlich hovels and exchanged a word or two, in broken Gaelic, with an old man that sat sunning himself in his doorway of roughly-piled stone. Then he turned down the slope again. His father was sitting as motionless as a statue, letters in hand, eyes fixed staringly on the mountainside across the water.

"Robin?" he said, nothing moving but his lips. "Why did you not tell me?"

Robin hesitated, wondering what had frozen his father. Then the hard voice broke out again.

"What does he think of us?" said Graham, with cold ferocity. "Does he think Scotsmen are so many sheep—that there's no law or right in the country? Does he think he can play at loggats with our lands and lives?"

"Who?" asked Robin, and immediately wished he had not spoken. But his father seemed too intent to have heard.

"And if he's thinking," said Graham, "that we'll suffer from him what the English suffer from their kings, he'll be wiser before the year's out. He and his butter-faced English wench!"

"He's not touched *our* land yet," said Robin, feeling, as ever, that he was failing his father.

"He's wronged a Graham. And your own cousin at that! Have ye not heard, man, what King James has done to your uncle's son, Malise? He's stripped him of Strathearn, taken the earldom away! D'ye want more than that?"

"No," said Robin, "maybe not," and fell silent for a minute, gathering courage to speak again.

"They say," he ventured, "that Malise has been talking foolishly—treasonably. That young man could never learn to keep his mouth shut."

Graham rose angrily from the bracken.

"Is it the time," he asked, "for a son of mine to be thinking of that? If you care nothing for law and justice, you might take notice when the earldom of Strathearn leaves our hands to feed King James's lackeys."

"It's worth little enough," said Robin resentfully. "It'll not be for greed he's taken it. It's gone to Athol, and Athol knows better how to manage Strathearn. They say Malise is to have Menteith in its place."

"They say!" snorted Graham. "I'll believe what they

say when I see it done! And what kind of good will it do Malise to be Earl of Menteith—or anywhere else—once Jamie has him locked up in an English prison?"

"What's that?"

"It's written here." Graham thrust out his hand, clenched round the crumpled letter. "Malise is sent hostage to London, in place of one that's dead. And in London he'll stay till King James sees fit to pay the English what he owes them—which'll be never."

Robin turned aside, looking up towards Ben Vorlich. He did not wish his father to detect the slight pleasure he could not help feeling at Malise's removal from the scene. But Graham was angry enough at the news he had read to misinterpret his son's movement.

"Ay," he said, "'I will look up to the hills, from whence cometh my help.' God! we shall need it! Murdoch did himself a fool's turn when he sent the best men in the kingdom as hostages to get James back; but I'm thinking he did Scotland a worse one, one that'll ruin her yet. Where is the man now?"

"Who?" asked Robin.

"King James."

"I'm not sure. Maybe in Edinburgh."

"We cannot touch him there."

"Touch him?"

"We must do something—and quickly," said Graham meaningly. "But maybe not that. Not for a wee while."

He began to kick nervously at a tussock of grass. It was obstinate, but yielded at last, rolling a yard or two down the slope.

"Maybe we can do something in Parliament," ventured Robin. He felt that his father was on the verge of unnamed dangers.

"Parliament?"

"You were talking of law and custom a while back."

Graham looked gravely at his son, sobered by the appeal to his honesty.

"Maybe you're right," he said. "We ought to try that first. Is there talk of another Parliament soon?"

"Not that I've heard. Only a Court for the Highlands. They say he'll be holding it at Inverness, this summer or next."

"This summer's half gone: it'll be next. And he'll learn a lesson or two from the Highlandmen. If he tries his tricks on the chieftains and their lands, we'll have Harlaw over again—and worse. There'll be a number of Lowlands lords that would help them this time, against King James."

Robin glanced at his father in alarm. Harlaw was a mere name to him, a boyhood memory, but it was an ugly one. Nobody knew what hordes the mountains might spew forth. And Robin, being of the younger generation, thought of them as the permanent enemy, hardly as possible allies.

"I doubt," he said, "whether they'd have much help from the Lowlands."

"They'd have mine," said Graham, "and yours too, my lad. We could count on what's left of Albany's men and maybe what's left of the Douglas."

His eye seemed to kindle at the thought of such a combination against the crown.

Robin watched him, momentarily undecided. But, if there was a conflict of loyalties, there could be little doubt which was paramount. It would be a chance to let his father know that he was a Graham first and last, and a better one than Malise.

"He could keep old Athol to advise him," Sir Robert was saying. "He could keep all the fools he's bribed with other men's lands. Much good may it do him!"

"He'd not keep Athol," said Robin, "nor that grandson of his, if they thought it was we that would win."

Graham looked puzzled and then began to chuckle. He met his son's gaze with something like affection.

"You're right, Robin," he said. "You're beginning to

know your map of Scotland. I'll make a politician of you yet."

Robin pressed the advantage that his trite sarcasm had won. "Is it politics you'd be teaching me?" he said, "or is it high treason?"

"King James might call it that."

"You said you'd try Parliament first."

"Maybe I will. Next year. We can find out how things lie this winter; it's little use talking, until you know who'll be on your side when you stop talking and get out the spears."

"You'll need plenty of them when the time comes," said Robin.

"I shall that." Graham buckled his sword into its hanger. "Come with me to Craggan," he said. "Unless you are afraid to be seen walking with a traitor!" He began to jog downhill to the lochside path with long, resolute strides. Robin trotted in his wake. The mountains above them were bright with summer. The sun had begun to stoop but its strength had hardly dwindled.

"The Bruce was proclaimed traitor once," said Robin, "and Wallace was killed for treason."

"Ay. Scotland's seen some wonders in her time."

"She has that," answered Robin, with the sentimentality of youth. "But it'll be a longer time before she sees me afraid to be found walking with my father."

July 1428

III

"So his Majesty goes to chastise the savages? I hope that we can get him to attend to our business before he leaves Edinburgh."

Regnault of Chartres, Peer of France, Duke-Archbishop of Rheims, looked across the breakfast-table at his two fellow-ambassadors, and wondered at the strange chance that had brought him with them—and for the second time in his life—to this out-of-the-way corner of the earth.

"Not much doubt of that," said Stuart of Darnley. "He's postponed his visitation to the Highlands for a year already. He can postpone it another week or two to settle with France."

"I hope you are right," answered Regnault. "He seems unduly preoccupied with these domestic matters."

It was humiliating, he felt, to come to Scotland for assistance. No doubt the country was in the ascendant; James had done wonders for her since Regnault's last visit, back in Albany's time. But it was not Scotland's progress that had brought Regnault so much as his own government's desperate plight. France had not even a king; Regnault's own cathedral of Rheims—her Scone, so to speak—was in English hands; her uncrowned Dauphin was incredibly in debt, and tied to the aristocratic creditors who mismanaged for him so much of his kingdom as was not in England's or Burgundy's power; the Dauphin was a poor-spirited creature, always talking of abandoning the struggle altogether; he had even written to James, a year or two ago, asking if Scotland could provide an asylum for a fugitive Dauphin of France.

Regnault himself never dreamt of surrender; he had too long an account to settle. His father had been murdered in Paris, in the days when the Butchers' Guild ruled it, bloodily, with Burgundy's approval; his three brothers had been killed by English arrows at Agincourt. He was a priest and believed in a divine justice. He was a gentleman, and gentlemen did not allow disasters to diminish their courage. England and Burgundy might seem to be rooted for ever on French soil, twin trees of evil that shattered every instrument one used against them. "All the same," he told his master, in the idiom of France, "one does not throw the handle after the axe."

The two men with him saw the common purpose from

different angles. Stuart of Darnley, born a Scot, had long learnt to spell his name in French fashion. He had helped to win Baugé, and become Count of Évreux, Seigneur of Aubigny-sur-Nère on the strength of it. His whole career was built on the alliance between France and Scotland, and might collapse with its breach. Évreux itself was in English hands, and he was a mere shadow of a count until Frenchmen, possibly with Scottish help, should send Bedford packing out of Normandy. He sat beside Alan Chartier, soldier beside scholar, and swilled Scottish ale that reminded him of his childhood.

Chartier's motives were also professional. He was a diplomatist by career, and preferred to be a successful one. After acquitting himself well in embassies to Pope Martin and the Emperor Sigismund, he had a reputation to maintain. He was also, and more by inclination, a writer and orator, a poet of sorts: he had collected vast stores of erudition and potential rhetoric on the subject of the "Auld Alliance," and he was determined not to waste them. He had traced its history back to Charlemagne and compared it to the eternal covenants of Holy Writ. Lest any demand written evidence, he had maintained that it was not a matter of ink and sheepskin but a living compact written on men's hearts, in the blood of the French and Scots who died in battle at each other's sides. The moment was approaching for him to show a similar eloquence on the project which was to seal a renewal of the alliance—the glorious betrothal of a Scottish princess to the Dauphin's son and heir. Chartier licked his lips at the promise of so fruitful a theme.

"We have not seen the Lady Margaret yet," said Regnault. "Let me see: how old is she exactly?"

Darnley knitted his brows, attempting arithmetic. But Chartier had every fact at his finger-tips.

"Three," he said. "Her sister is not two yet, but the Princess Margaret is three years and seven months. She was born at Noel." His mind began to revolve the possibilities of that birthday: one could hardly compare the infant bride to Our Lord, but some use might be made of the coincidence, if only as a passing ornament to a paragraph.

"And his Highness is five," said Regnault, "or nearly five. He was born before that dreadful business at Verneuil. It will be some ten years before the marriage can take place."

"The betrothal will be enough," said Darnley tersely. He disliked references to the battle of Verneuil.

"Then we had better make it unusually binding," answered the archbishop. "Much may happen in ten years. That is, if we are really determined that it shall lead to a marriage."

He sighed a little, sipping some water. Early in youth, after escaping from the Parisian mob that had butchered his father, he had taken a lifelong vow to drink nothing but water for breakfast on two mornings of the week. Times had changed since then. He had kept alive, by one shift or another, and grown to be a prelate and statesman, hardened to the ways of Courts. But it still seemed to him a pity that princes could not form their leagues without such misuses of the Sacrament of Marriage.

Chartier was looking at him as if there were some misunderstanding: Darnley was clearly nettled. "Determined?" he said, "of course we are determined! The prospective wedding is the foundation of the whole treaty. It's the only thing the common people understand. When they marry their children into a neighbour's family, it means a bond of friendship, the right to call on each other for assistance. When princes do the same, great alliances are cemented."

"The common people?" Regnault raised a polite eyebrow. "I did not know," he said, "that it was necessary to conform to their views."

"That is the mistake," persisted Darnley, "that all you Frenchmen make. You despise your commons. Henry of England knew better; he used his to shoot down your nobles. You will never beat the English until you take a leaf out of Henry's book."

Regnault smiled a faint smile. "I must defer to your opinion," he said, "in matters of war. You may be right. But I would recommend you, when you start raising your legion of commoners with the news of the betrothal, to conceal the fact that the princess is only three."

"We need say nothing about it," said Darnley, rising irritably from the table. "We can just announce that her dowry will be four thousand Scottish spearmen—paid in advance. That is enough to put heart into them." He turned contemptuously away from the smiling archbishop. "Master Chartier," he said, "wait on his Majesty and ask him to grant another audience to our embassy today."

Chartier bowed and withdrew. Regnault also rose from table, preparing to follow him out of the room. "It is possible," he said, "that I underestimate the military importance of the common people. But I cannot help thinking that you, my lord, underestimate their intelligence. You may find that they are not so easily gulled into taking heart. I sometimes wonder if anything will rouse them—short of a miracle. And such diplomacy as ours can hardly result in miracles."

He sighed, cast a glance at Darnley's rigid, sunburnt face, and walked musingly from the room.

They did not leave Scotland until they had achieved, outwardly at least, the object of their mission. James pledged himself to revive the spirit of the old alliance, dormant since the treaty that had released him from England. He went so far as to sign an agreement, acknowledging baby Margaret's betrothal to baby Louis and promising active assistance to the Dauphin. It was liberally punctuated with "Ifs" and "Whens," so that an experienced statesman might well doubt whether it had much binding value. It certainly did not seem worth the painstaking skill, worthy of an inalterable covenant, which Master Chartier had lavished on its phrasing.

James was too busy and anxious to give the matter the thought it deserved. Scotland was occupying his whole mind. He had tried to raise taxes and was failing: the attempt had helped to alienate the merchants and farmers on whose shoulders he had been borne to sovereignty. He had paid England one-third of the promised ransom, and England would have to whistle for the rest. He needed money to teach the nobles that the crown was their master, and that the crown must decide on what terms they took service and money from the poor. They were resenting his redistribution of their lands, and his agents brought him hints of underground activities that they had scented rather than fathomed. A false step might destroy him and his wife and children altogether, whatever foreign marriage treaties he might have signed.

He would have to tell Joan, and at once, of the agreement with the Frenchmen. He did not relish the task, but he chose, boldly, what seemed the most difficult moment. He waited till night-time, when she had led him, a candle in her hand, into the children's bedroom, to see little Margaret sleeping beside her sister. There, in low tones, he told Joan what he had that day signed.

She stood motionless. Her utter silence began to frighten him, then made him wonder if she had understood. It was a minute and more before she spoke.

"I thought," she said, "that I came to Scotland because we loved each other. I did not know you wanted me to breed children that you could sell to any country that needs your help against England."

He had almost forgotten it: he had almost forgotten that, for her, the bitterest of the business would be that it was aimed against her own country.

"That means nothing," he said. "It's a mere flourish, the promise to send help. I doubt if the French will even ask for it. I'm told the Dauphin has to go sponging on the Chinon innkeepers before he can get a sheep's tail for supper. Do you think he can really take four thousand new men into his pay? And if he can't have them, I can call the whole bargain off, even the betrothal. There's always a way out of these things."

There was silence again, except for the light breathing of the children. James felt that he had made a sufficient answer. He even grew pleased with himself again. Now he came to think of it, the most amusing part of the whole business would be seeing how England took it, and what kind of protest came rolling over the Border. Bishop Beaufort would be blamed: Gloucester would accuse him, again, of letting a King of Scots out of prison to make friends with England's enemy. Bishop Beaufort must deal with his own troubles.

"If it means nothing," said Joan in a toneless whisper, "why must you do it at all?"

He grew hot at that, telling himself that he was not ashamed of what he had done, only angry at her interference. "I cannot have my policy weakened," he said, "by women's fancies. Margaret will be grateful, one day, if we succeed in making her Queen of France."

"Would I be grateful now," she answered, "if my family had married me as they planned?"

"We were fortunate—exceptionally fortunate," he answered, still angrily. "Our children cannot expect the same good chance. And, for all we know, this boy Louis may grow up into a paladin of love."

"May," said Joan. "And may not. I thought, since we were fortunate, as you call it, we might be able to teach others that love is not always such a blind guide as worldly people would like one to think."

James walked a step or two away, unable to reply for the moment. Margaret turned over in her sleep, frowning a tiny frown. She nosed down among the bedclothes and began to breathe regularly again.

Joan raised her head to look at James as he leant against the mantelshelf. It was summer, and there was no fire: the only light came from the candle in her hand.

She saw him as he was—or as he had become. The gallant, headstrong boy was a middle-aged husband now, a creature that had to be flattered and obeyed. She must even acquiesce in and admire the loss of generous impulse, the growth of wary, half-selfish calculation. He was fonder than ever of his own way, less scrupulous in his methods of gaining it. He had changed outwardly too, as youth dwindled away in him. He had grown burly, almost fat. He reminded her a little of her uncle. She had once pictured herself as helping a fairy-tale prince from prison, inspiring him to do battle with a crass and shabby world. It seemed, now, as if he had gone over to the enemy: all that was spiritual or rebellious in her would soon be left widowed and alone. She looked at him with distaste. Her eyes did not soften until they had left his face for that of the child—the child who was already being exposed to the world's heartless clawings.

"You must trust me," he said, "to do the best for her and for everyone. You don't understand politics. No woman can."

"Perhaps," she said, without looking up, "we are all the better for that."

He smiled in uneasy contempt, and came back to the head of the bed. Still she ignored him. "You once told me of your father," she said. "I wonder what he would have said about this business."

She expected reproof, counter-accusation. It did not come. It was a minute or more before he spoke, and his voice was curiously gentle.

"My father," he said, "knew nothing of government. They'd crowned him king, but he left the burden of it on other men's shoulders. It was easy for him to blame them when they staggered."

Silence again. Then, unexpectedly, his hand sought hers.

There was no pathos in the gesture, no appeal to sentiment. The grasp was too firm for that. It meant and demanded courage, courage to go on loving what the world had corrupted and must continue to corrupt: courage to accept what no woman—no man, for that matter—can fully understand.

The wonder was, not that he had changed since marriage and kingship, but that so much of him was unchanged. He still saw clearly, acted bravely on what he saw. The pressure of his hand was reassuring, almost inspiring. He was not, could never be gross, in spirit or body. What was waste and luxury in her uncle was muscle and energy in him. If it came to that, she too must have changed, lost her freshness for him. She must be content to trust him as he asked, to believe without understanding. Nothing mattered, so long as they moved, to whatever end, together.

The envoys, returning to France to report success, found nothing the better for their absence. The Dauphin was helpless, between his friends and his enemies. Burgundy was irreconcilable. Bedford's armies were closing on Orleans.

The Court at Chinon made the most of their treaty, spreading tales of an approaching marriage and of new allies from the North. Puzzled captains, at their wits' end for argument, used the rumours to quiet their discontented men, whose pay was months and years in arrear. Peasants heavy with misery and hatred felt a faint twinge of hope. They did not know where Scotland was, but they gathered that the Dauphin had borrowed some new help against Burgundy and the Goddams. The war might be over a little more quickly, possibly in one's own lifetime: one might know yet what it was to sleep quietly at night and have a chicken in the pot. It was time that something happened; name of God, but it was time!

Far away in Lorraine, in the castle of Vaucouleurs, a

country girl was being interrogated: did she think that France could be saved and, if so, by what means? "No one in the world," she answered, "neither kings, nor dukes, nor the daughter of Scotland, can restore the kingdom of France. In me alone is help." There were many girls in those haunted and hysterical days, who boasted as wildly; but this visionary was Joan from Domrémy, and God had indeed shown her what was hidden from the kings.

August 1428

IV

"There is the town, your Majesty. There's Inverness, devil take it."

Mar's portly voice roused James from a traveller's day-dream. He reined up his horse on the ill-kept track they were following. It had brought them to the top of a broken ridge: below, on the near side of a meandering river, lay a few houses of dressed stone, churches, a priory, and a huddle of roughly-piled huts: here was Inverness, the chief, the only thing that could be called a town beyond the Highland line.

James had hardly pictured so peaceful a setting. There were mountains enough in the distance, and one could only guess what lurked beneath them: kelpies and demons, perhaps, such as country-folk dreaded, outlaws and robbers whom it was a king's business to destroy. But on the near-by slopes, sheep and cattle grazed quietly, and in a hundred little patches, fenced from their nibblings, the rye and oats waved a ripening harvest. On the river foreshore beside the Black Friars, fishermen were singing as they spread their nets in the sun. The ruins near the track he was riding, marking the stronghold where Macbeth had murdered King Duncan, seemed only to emphasize the peacefulness of the life that had succeeded a savage age. On this side of the river there was nothing—except the newly re-fortified castle from which Mar must have ridden out to greet him—which confirmed the ceaseless tales of violence and disorder in the Highlands.

Mar was taciturn for once: no boasting of past campaigns, no grumbling at the sad difficulties that beset a justiciar of the north. He was labouring, perhaps, under the double anxiety that kept all Scotland in suspense—the uncertainty about the king's purpose at Inverness, the greater and more lasting uncertainty about the feeling among the clans.

One had to look westward, and beyond the river, for a reminder of that menace: one knew then why so much cattle had been brought to graze on the safe side of the water. On the flat heath and deserted meadows beyond, shifting clumps of bright colour, green and red and warm brown flesh, showed where the Highlandmen camped. It was noon, and they were busy round their brushwood fires, roasting their fish and venison. Their activity, at this distance, looked like the capering of painted pygmies. They were out of earshot, but one could imagine the chattering of their outlandish tongues.

Their chieftains had been summoned to meet the king at Inverness, and with the chieftains had come men from a hundred glens and islands of the north and west—climbing passes that had never known a road, wading through rivers that disdained a bridge. They brought fear with them, the fear of the unknown. Tales of their feuds, tales, especially from blood-soaked Strathnaver, made one forget that they, like most men, must spend most of their time wrenching a peaceful livelihood from soil or sea. The Lowlands remembered only their raids, the terrible downrush of alien devils from the mountains to the cornland. For each passing year now was making the Highland line into something more like a frontier between two stranger races—dividing language from language, Celtic custom from a half-Roman, half-English law, an elder way of life from one more like that of changing Christendom. And since Harlaw fight, it was not merely raiding-parties that might come sweeping over that frontier.

James's eye wandered over the flat-lands. No skill or experience could enable a man to number an enemy so scattered with any approach to accuracy: but it was clear that the chiefs had brought little more than a bodyguard each, leaving their clans, unmartialled, to reap their harvest at home. And he himself had an army at his back.

That he would meet them as enemies he did not doubt. He alone knew his own purpose—to bring justice and king's law into the Highlands. It was a lifetime and more since David Bruce had done the same, and the Highlands had forgotten the feel of an overlord's hand. It was not likely that they would lie tame beneath the grip.

He took a last look westward. He had been sighted already: the pygmies were beginning to scramble up from their fires, pointing, gesticulating, peering up at the distant figures that surrounded their king. James gave the bridle a shake and set the horse in motion. Behind him, banners spread, harness buckled for battle, his host came clattering downhill towards the town.

The Highlandmen watched the hill-crest in something akin to dismay, as file after file of king's men came into sight and then dipped downward into Inverness. They were not afraid of the bowmen; they had heard of the marvels of English archery but laughed at the notion of James reproducing it, by statute or byelaw, among Lowland clowns. They were not impressed by the full plate-armour of the knights: these new-fangled extravagances were nothing to the ancient sweep of the two-handed claymore. It was the numbers that astonished them, the bare fact that the king had brought an army at all. There had been rumours in plenty, ever since James had left Aberdeen. There was the thing itself, no longer to be scoffed away, marching into Inverness before their eyes.

They were still, they reflected, on the right side of the river. They could go home. If the king had challenged them to war, the clans would have come in force. He had only summoned the chiefs to a Court—a Parliament, as some called it. If he came in fighting trim, he could have no complaint if they declined the challenge.

The men clustered round their chiefs, mutely anticipating the order to go home, a few bold enough to pour out their own advice in risk of rebuff. They were frozen into silence. Here was no matter of clan politics, to be discussed with the elders. The chiefs would talk with each other—where no feud forbade. A few would decide with no man's help. The men must go on with their cooking.

Before sunset, the matter was settled. They would do what they had come for. Even those most conscious of crimes—as kings and Lowlanders counted crime—refused to turn tail now. The king would not dare to provoke rebellion in the mountains. He had enough troubles already, with Albany barely crushed and half the nobility alienated by his doings. They had imagined that he would find it impossible to collect an army from his grumbling kingdom. They had been wrong, to judge by the look of things on the hill-crest. But he must know that he could not extend his notions from the discontented Lowlands to the ungoverned west, the ungovernable north. By crossing the river to meet him next day, they would be challenging him to bring them to book. They would wager a hundred head of cattle that he would not dare to accept their challenge.

James supped in the castle that night. He smiled in turn on his loyal visitors—the prior of the Dominicans, the little deputation of burghers, the grammar-school dominie who had brought two promising pupils to lisp Latin verses at their king. There was no question of anyone asking him what was intended on the morrow. He could keep his counsel.

As he went bedward, he stopped on the stairway, and beckoned Mar to catch up with him. "I wanted to ask you," he said, "if nettles grow up in the mountains?"

Mar, as fuddled as he generally was by bedtime, was taken

at a loss. "Why not?" he said. "Only they'll maybe grow bigger than they do in Lothian."

"They probably need grasping just the same," said James. "I hope you have plenty of dungeons in your castle."

Next morning saw the chieftains, one after the other, come across the wooden bridge into the town. None of them was allowed to bring a retinue—not even young Alasdair Macdonald, that called himself Lord of the Isles and boasted, at home on Islay, of independent sovereignty. Alasdair came with his mother and half a dozen servants. Of the fifty other chieftains, none brought more across the water. They came at short intervals, fearing clan-quarrels. One by one, they reached the castle gates, and were admitted.

The clansmen, their misgivings redoubled, crowded the further bank and thrust an advance-guard along the bridge. Morning became afternoon, and afternoon wore on to evening, but no sign came from the castle. Its blank tower stared inscrutably down at them. They grew restless enough, easing swords in their scabbards, stringing and unstringing their bows. They shouted to the king's men who lined the far bank or guarded the bridge—jovially at first, but, as the hot day lengthened, with increasing insult. They knew that assault was hopeless. The bridge was narrow and the men beyond had torches burning all day to fire it, if need be, in an instant. If they tried to swim and wade, the rush of their charge would be lacking, and only a charge could have bent their adversaries for an instant. Even so, some were for attacking: death or disablement was preferable to abandoning their leaders in the jaws of the king's trap. But the Macdonalds would not move without more certainty of treacherous dealing, and the Camerons counselled patience, reliance on the king's good faith.

The barrier of armed men cut them off from Inverness,

where many of their kinsmen had come to dwell, forgetting the mountain air: it also guarded them from the ebb and flow of rumour that was vexing the town. By noon, there was no doubt that the king had ordered the chiefs to be massacred without trial: he had seized them as they entered, one after another, and hurried them away to be strangled in separate dungeons. An old man whose cottage was in the Doomsdale had heard screams inside the northern wall. A fish-wife, returning from the main-gate with her unsold burden, had been told that the king, glorying in his triumphant treachery, had whispered an impromptu verse to his shocked attendants.

Behind the strength of our castle wall
Let us cannily spread the net.
By Christ on the cross, I know them all
To deserve the death they shall get!

So circumstantial a story must convince the most sceptical. The king was known to make verses: he had probably picked up habits of blasphemy among the godless English: Our Lord on his cross figured on the arms of Inverness. The chain of evidence seemed complete.

An hour later, the tide had set in an opposite direction. It was first reported that trials were actually in progress and that one or two of the chieftains were acquitted and might be released. Before dusk, it was said that the king had only pretended to make arrests: it was a mere joke: he was feasting the chieftains now and making high revel. He had bought their loyalty by innumerable concessions—among others the right for their clansmen to trade free of tolls with this royal burgh of Inverness. The royal burgh was properly indignant at this wanton attack on its pockets. A crowd in the market-place hustled one of the friars to the Clachnacuddin Stone and insisted on his drawing up an angry petition in which his Majesty was respectfully but firmly reminded that he was infringing the municipal charter. It required all the scolding of the soberer graybeards before the people would disperse and wait until the truth were known.

The truth, when it slowly emerged, was as disappointing as usual to those who throve on sensation. The king had certainly arrested the chieftains and heard witness against them from every quarter of the Highlands. A pretty tale it made, for it was years since a king had attempted to push his justice up into the mountains. The Macrurie and the Macarthur were beheaded. A Campbell who had tried to win favour by acting as king's agent in the Isles, and so far exceeded instructions as to murder a Macdonald, was taken out to be hanged. Most of the other captives were to be released as soon as it was safe to do so, half of them within the month.

Mar was dubious about the whole business. Arguments about the crown's rights and the unity of the kingdom were so much wind to him, and sleeping dogs were best let lie. The final leniency set the cap on the whole folly: if the king really felt it necessary to provoke cattle-thieves by putting them in irons, then he should have finished the business by slitting their throats. What, for instance, did James imagine he was doing by letting loose young Alasdair Macdonald to rouse the Isles to rebellion? Come to that, Alasdair's mother, Donald of Harlaw's widow, would probably rouse them to release him if he were held in prison. The only thing was to keep the old bitch under lock and key, and find some charge or other on which to behead the son.

"And would the Isles take that tamely?" asked James.

"They'd start fighting among themselves," Mar answered, "to decide who is to be next lord and next Macdonald. The pup's unmarried and there's no heir—though I'll wager he's been helping to people Islay with a bastard or two."

Mar appeared to think this witty. He invited an answering smile by baring his hideous teeth.

"Then there's only one way," said James, studiedly unresponsive. "I shall take Alasdair to Court and teach him manners. The queen is always asking me to bring some younger men to Court."

Mar grinned again. "Why did you not bring her on here," he asked, "to take her pick of the Highland lads? She'll be having a dull time at Aberdeen with all those cod-faced Dutchmen."

Mar had returned from Flanders with no great opinion of its inhabitants, and he extended his dislike to the Flemings that had settled so numerously in Aberdeen.

"Her Majesty is following me here," said James stiffly, "in a day or two's time. I did not wish her to come until I was sure there would be no need of fighting."

"We'll have our bellyful of that," replied Mar, "before the winter. I know these vermin. There's only one way to govern them—if you want to govern them, God help you. Find out which are stoats and which are weasels, and then find out how to set them at each other's throats. The only remedy for a Macdonald is a Mackenzie or a Campbell. And, talking of Campbells, it was a fool's move to hang that man for doing your work for you."

"I came to do justice," said James, drily. "I will try your methods, my lord, when all others have failed."

"That may be sooner than you think."

"Possibly. Time will show. But now we had both better go to bed. It is nearly midnight."

Mar had a right to speak freely. As justiciar for the north, he had suffered the consequences of Albany's folly in the Highlands: if James, too, was making mistakes, Mar would have to bear the brunt of retrieving them. One must allow his tongue a deal of licence—within limits.

He overstepped those limits as he lighted the king to his bedroom, waving the servants away as if he wished to show special attention himself. But when he halted at the bedroom door, he was leering again in a particularly distasteful way. His first question was whether James was not now regretting that he had left Queen Joan behind.

"Would you care for a stop-gap?" he asked. "There are

some pretty bits of Highland lamb at Inverness. Stiff at first, you know, but you'd have no difficulty. A king's a king."

James stared for a moment, genuinely at a loss. As Mar's meaning reached him, he was still wondering whether to be angry or laugh in the man's face. He suddenly felt the hopelessness of the barrier separating them. Early in life, each of them had made a choice—or had it thrust upon him. The passage of years had only taken them further apart, until certain things became unthinkable to James which to the elder man were matters of course. It was useless to show anger, useless to laugh. He took the candle from Mar's hand and passed into his room without a word, closing the door behind him.

"These poets!" said Mar to himself, left suddenly in pitch darkness. "They write God knows what about women, but when it comes to the point they haven't the guts of a rabbit." And he stumbled downstairs to drown his contempt—and his anxiety about the clans—in another cup or two of Highland ale.

August 1428

V

James had gone hunting from Inverness, somewhat against advice. They had begged him to take a large escort, and every precaution; they had insisted that, whatever direction he took, it must not be beyond the river. It was true that the bands of clansmen had disappeared: some, no doubt, had gone home and left their chieftains in prison. But others might be lurking among nearby hills, watching their opportunity: they might well have sent back for reinforcement to avenge the insult put upon their leaders. Joan, who had now reached Inverness, added her entreaties to the general warning: even Mar agreed that there was no need to crown folly with lunacy.

James acquiesced, promising to hunt the eastward country, towards the Findhorn. He went so far as to borrow a huntsman's livery, in order to make a more dubious mark for a distant bowman: its colour reminded him, suddenly, of Giffard's superstitions, twenty years ago. Even so, his men seemed unusually careful to prevent him riding more than a few paces ahead of them, and they kept an anxious eye on every gorse-clump and thicket: James felt a little as if he was still a prisoner of England, hunting under guard. It was all the odder, therefore, an hour or two after the start, to find himself suddenly alone.

He could not imagine how it had happened. They had passed Daviot in cavalcade. They had climbed the track to Moy, casting round for a quarry. Then, a few minutes later, Martin had bayed and streamed off, apparently on the scent of a deer. James had cantered after him, and not a single huntsman had followed.

Martin was a wolf-hound, a recent present from Abbot Fogo, whose knowledge of hounds was defective. James had christened him after the reigning Pope, whom Martin resembled, he said, in never listening to reason. Still, he did not wish to lose him. James saw him careering up an unexpected track, chasing a hare. James shouted and cursed, but Martin took no notice. They reached the saddle of a small glen and dipped down beyond, out of earshot of voice or hunting-horn. It was all a little eerie.

James rode on, puzzled, but half-hoping for an adventure. The glen they had now entered seemed to grow narrower and more shut-in as they descended it. Granite cliffs peered down upon it, over the heads of the birch-trees. The track twisted and diminished, the ground grew stonier. There was no question of cantering: soon the horse fell from a trot to a cautious jog. Martin had vanished, and the track looked like petering out. James drew rein, whistled several times, and was on the point of deciding to lose his hound for good. Then a sudden yelp on his left drew attention to a possible path through the trees. It seemed to lead straight into the cliff, but James, forcing his way through, came suddenly on a little grass-grown clearing, overhung with rocks like three sides of a cauldron. It might once have been a quarry, scooped by human labour. High up on the mossy granite was one of the most curious carvings he had ever seen: a serpent, apparently, cut Pictish-fashion, doubled back upon itself. Directly below that heathen symbol, James saw a dwelling, half cave, half cottage; in the wall of rough stones that closed its front there was a doorway, screened with an untanned bull's hide. Facing it, alarmed and suspicious, Martin was crouching on his haunches, sniffing the air with an occasional whine. If the hare had indeed chosen so unlikely an asylum, the dog seemed curiously unwilling to follow.

James was about to whistle him off and rejoin the hunt—if he could find it—when he heard a noise from the hut, a kind of crooning song, unlike any he had heard before. If the place was inhabited, it seemed stranger still that a hare should have taken refuge there. Then the sound ceased, and, hardly seeming to move her leather curtain, a woman stood in the doorway.

She was dressed in Highland fashion: she was neither young nor old: she was certainly unkempt and dirty. But for a pair of bright black eyes she would not have attracted a second glance. She was talking to herself, or more probably, to the dog: Martin cowered, whined again, and crawled back behind his master's horse. The woman raised her voice a little, and James began to make out something of what she was saying. He had not imagined he knew so much Gaelic; much escaped him, but the main trend was clear, if a trifle mad. She was saying, over and over, that a man should not ride out hunting dressed in green. The Little People wore green themselves, and it was never wise to be making them jealous. Only a fool and a Sassunach would despise the Little People's anger.

James wheeled his horse round, to return to the main path. He hoped there would be no difficulty in finding his party again. The woman behind him was still talking, her voice rising and falling with no reference to the sense, or nonsense, of what she was saying. Martin slunk ahead, apparently eager to be gone.

James had lifted his hand to part the boughs of the first trees when a sudden phrase arrested his attention. The woman was still blaming the folly of those that rode the glens without heeding the ancient cautions. It was not a thing a man should do, she said, unless he had protection: and how could anyone expect protection that had killed his uncle's son?

James reined up and sat suddenly still. The woman could hardly know him, especially in disguise; had the Devil prompted her words? If she had indeed recognized him, how dare she speak such words in the ears of the king? Everyone knew, or ought to know, that Murdoch had been judged by his peers, condemned on ample evidence. There was no question of cousin killing cousin. It was treason to suggest it.

He knew, all the same, that he was powerless to punish. He sat limply on his fidgeting horse. He had no will left, except what compelled him to wheel back until he faced her again, to sit listening without protest or stir.

It was not for that killing, she was saying, that he ought to fear: there had been reason in it, as well as thirst for the silver. The danger lay elsewhere. It would not come yet, not till after the sun had been darkened at midday.

There was a man with red hair, and another, a kinsman, with no hair at all. The first of them he had seen once, and had wronged, and must see again. But a third meeting, unless it were prevented, would mean death for both, and for one, maybe, damnation. All this she had from Huthart, and, of all the spirits, Huthart had never tricked her yet.

James listened still. Maybe she would warn him again, she said, nearer the time. Maybe she'd seek him out, not wait for him to come riding down the Glen of the Snake again. He'd not remember her, even when she came. It'd be an ill thing if she could not prevent it, an ill thing for Scotland. It was fortunate, today, that the dog had followed her, bringing his master after him. *Cha d'thainig so g'un abhair*, she said, it had not happened without good reason.

James was recovering movement. The woman had begun to talk at random. He must be gone.

He had heard, often enough, of witches and warlocks in the mountains: half these Highland folk might be worshipping Odin or Nuada for all that the Kirk knew of them. This woman seemed harmless enough, in spite of her lucky hits; an Eastcheap fortune-teller could probably do as well, without risking his soul. She was growing quite unintelligible now, swinging her body to the senseless rhythm. James wheeled and spurred his horse, felt the birch-twigs whip his cheeks, and crackled through to the main path. He was soon trotting again, and had reached the head of the glen. It would not take him five minutes to regain his party.

They seemed to have made no progress in the longish time he had been absent. The hounds were still scuttling round the same thickets, the huntsmen still heading them back from the same distractions. It was stranger still that, after the jealous anxiety that his guards had shown all morning, they did not seem particularly relieved at his return from absence. For any sign that they gave one would have said that they were unaware of having lost sight of him for a moment.

October 1428

VI

"Well, man, what did his Majesty say to you?" Athol leant back in his chair.

"Little enough. But I can have the place."

"You can? I'm glad to hear that, now. Though I did not think he could refuse us." The old man looked at his grandson with something like affection. Robert Stewart was good-looking enough, with crisp black hair and fine, strapping shoulders. His dark eyes were a trifle small, his chin too heavy for perfection. But a strong chin meant perseverance, a determination to realize ambitions instead of dreaming about them. And Robert had plenty of ambitions.

"Well," said Athol, "King James'll have a sonsy cup-bearer. Maybe the queen spoke to him. She has an eye for a fine-looking lad."

"It's chamberlain, not cup-bearer," said Robert. He disliked picturesque archaisms. "I'm only to take the cup," he said, "at the great feasts."

"Well, well," said Athol, "and maybe that's a good omen. A Chamberlain's a kind of Steward, and it's Stewards our forebears were, mine and his. And they rose from the stewardship to the throne itself."

"Ay," said Robert, "his side of the family. Bessie Muir's bairns."

"Our side might inherit yet," said Athol, watching him with a curious intensity. "Jamie has daughters, but these are no times to be taking a lassie to Scone."

"They are not," said Robert, with a slight frown of discomfort. He leant against the edge of the table at which his grandfather sat, and stared out of the window at the dark fir-trees that grew close round Methven's walls. "We'd need a man," he said.

"You're not forgetting, are you," asked Athol, "that it's you that's heir? Your uncle in England has no sons: your father's dead, and I'll not be on my legs much longer."

"I'd not be a man," said Robert, "nor your grandson, if I forgot that." Athol tittered a little, and fell silent. "I used to think of it once," he said, "when I was your age. But there were so many in the way then, Rothesay, Jamie and all the Albanies. There's only Jamie now."

"Ay," said Robert, "there's only Jamie." Their eyes met for a moment, but avoided each other again. "But it's no good thinking of that now," said Athol.

"No," said his grandson, "not just now."

They were silent again, old Athol drumming lightly on the table with gouty fingers. Then he rose stiffly from his chair, shivering a little, and wrapping his cloak around him. "Did he say anything about the land?" he asked. "A king's chamberlain needs land."

"Oh, ay. There's a wee parcel round Crieff and a larger one in Fife. Albany land. King James has something to give away, these days. You should know that."

"I do. I'm looking after some of it for him, till I die. I helped him, you know, against the House of Albany."

"Ay. Maybe he's grateful."

"I do what I can for Scotland. The Lord has given me a brain that's not so thick as most in this country. And I've kept my eyes open. I've always kept my eyes open."

Robert did not look at his grandfather, standing at the doorway. He was looking out of the window. "You should have those trees thinned," he said. "They'd hide too much, if you were besieged here."

"Besieged?" Athol smiled contemptuously. "I've lived through worse times than these and had what I wanted without fighting. You can do the same, if you'll keep half your wits about you." He pulled aside the homespun curtain. "I'm getting old," he said, "and my work's done. You'll not be seeing me at Court much. Maybe when it's at Perth you'll be riding out to Methven to tell your old grandfather the news."

"Maybe," answered Robert. "But I'll be busy."

"You will that. The Highlands today, the Border tomorrow. If you ride everywhere with Jamie, you'll be growing hard skin where you're softest."

"He wants me tonight. We're leaving Perth early the morn."

"Tonight?" There was a trace of disappointment in Athol's voice, as though he were hoping to see a little more of this irresponsive grandson of his. "Well, well," he said, "you'll be back in a wee while."

He paused, took a step through the doorway and then turned back. "Since you've spoken her name," he said, "did you ever hear tell that Bessie Muir was not married to her king—not until after the bairns had been born?"

"No, I'd not heard of it. It'd be going a long way back."

"Long or short, it'd mean they'd no right to wear a crown—nor their bairns after them."

"It'd mean that, and more."

"Ay. If it were true. It'd make me King of Scotland these many years, and Jamie just nobody at all." Athol had hardly turned back. He was still avoiding his grandson's eye.

"It'd make me your heir," said Robert. "Maybe we should be finding out if it happened to be true."

"Ay. But not just now."

"No," said Robert. "Best look around first."

"Best say nothing. Jamie's a good lad. He'll not make a bad king, now I've helped him to the silver. You'll give him my compliments?"

"I will."

"Will you sup with me before you ride back? It's lonely supping by myself every night, with nothing to think about but the past."

Robert never erred on the side of being over-affectionate, and he was not greatly drawn to his grandfather. But there was something now that he wanted to discuss.

"I can sup with you and ride back late," he said. "I'd be glad of some more talk. Better talk about the future than sit thinking of ghosts."

February-April 1429

VII

Berwick-on-Tweed was having a surprise. In the whole course of its history the town had never seen such a procession as came lumbering through its streets in the February that followed King James's ride to Inverness. Berwick was used to armies, had had its bellyful of them since Edward of England inaugurated a century of war by inflicting pillage and massacre on the town he had come, among others, to annex. Berwick knew something of wealth, too, for it had once led Scotland in commerce, and had now risen from its ashes to be a market for rich England's trade. But the combination of warlike display and costly luxury that Bishop Beaufort was pouring into its midst left the citizens gaping with open mouths. Bishop Beaufort—Cardinal Beaufort as he had recently become—was always a believer in display. He took a low view of human nature, and had long ago decided that the best way to govern is to dazzle and appal. He had been leading Crusades against the Bohemian heretics, and saw no reason why the Church Militant should be ashamed to parade its destructive power. He was, he calculated, one of the richest men in Europe—and he was certainly fond of his well-earned comforts: he liked these two facts to be plainly understood wherever duty or ambition made him a traveller.

The aggressively warlike part of his escort had to stay behind when he crossed the Border. He was, in some sort, an ambassador of peace. One imposed peace, of course: only a fool would ask for it unarmed. But there were certain conventions to be observed in crossing frontiers, and, for that matter, a distant threat was often better than the immediate flourish. But while the knights and archers quartered themselves on Berwick, the waggons could go forward. He could take with him the carpets and tapestries and bedding, the gold and silver plate, the well-drilled cooks and caterers, the jester with his pet monkey, the needless swarms of secretaries. If Cardinal Beaufort deigned to accept the hospitality of threadbare Scottish monks, he could at least give them a taste of what they missed by not being successful Englishmen.

James heard of his arrival at Coldingham Priory, and of the extent and nature of his baggage. "There are two ways of meeting that kind of thing," he said to Joan. "The first is to out-Herod Herod, and I cannot afford it. I shall try the second."

He collected half a dozen bonnet-lairds to attend him, one secretary, and a small escort of spearmen; he rode out from Linlithgow in his soberest, most workmanlike clothes. He reached Coldingham unharbingered, and properly splashed with mud. He asked to see the prior first, without mentioning any guests from England.

The method of approach was all the more thorough for Joan's last-minute decision to stay behind. Everyone took it for granted that she would accompany the king, and she herself had some curiosity to see what manner of man her uncle had become. But instinct, the instinct to stay away, proved stronger, and she begged James to excuse her from the meeting.

"He'll bring too many things with him," she said.

"He's certainly doing that—by all accounts."

"No, I meant too many things, or reminders of them, that I would rather forget."

James wondered whether she still hankered for the flesh-pots of England. Not that he particularly wanted her to come. In any case, one never knew whether a woman's reasons for doing things were mere excuses. Then an idea struck him.

"Did the doctors say——?" he began.

"Oh, no. Not yet. . . . But you can make that the excuse if you need one."

"I certainly shall," answered James. "Your uncle is a great champion of family affection."

"Yes," she said gravely. "That's part of the reason."

Then she shook her head in a way that reminded him of days long dead. "I am afraid I cannot explain," she said.

"I'll do the explaining. I've things to discuss with him that will take more getting round than that." He smiled like a mischievous child, and kissed her on the forehead. "Make it a boy this time," he whispered, and was gone to make his preparations for departure.

It was the first of April when he rode into Coldingham: a good omen, he thought, for what he hoped to do to Beaufort. Not that it would be easy: the bishop, for all his faults, was tolerably shrewd. The English had sent five other envoys as assistants, but not from any doubt of his unaided ability. Some, including two northern bishops, would be coming to discuss local Border matters; one, and perhaps more, came in Duke Humphrey's interest, to keep jealous watch; the feud between Gloucester and Beaufort had not slackened, would probably grow ranker till one or both were dead. As Warden of the Marches, Northumberland accompanied the embassy. James had not seen him since the dance at Pontefract: he had aged a good deal in appearance, but did not seem to have learnt much from the passing years: the overgrown schoolboy was a little more overgrown. He gave James a stiff bow and then fastened on him the familiar, obstinate stare.

Beaufort's greetings were more elaborate, and comically patronizing. If James had ascended a throne since last they met, Beaufort wanted to make it clear that he himself had become a Cardinal. Certain nervous twitchings of the hand suggested that ambition was still unsatisfied, still resentful at the slowness of just progress; Beaufort would not die happy unless he died a Pope. Meanwhile, he was plainly resolved to be master of the interview.

"We shall hardly get beyond the preliminaries today," he observed, as soon as the group was seated round the priory table. "Your Majesty will no doubt wish to wait for the arrival of his household before discussing the graver issues. I am sure that we are all flattered to see him riding ahead to meet us with such informal—dare I say, such affectionate haste? I can only hope that it is not only my family connection with your Majesty that inspires the compliment. I trust that it is also a desire to remove all misunderstandings between the rulers of two neighbouring kingdoms and bestow upon their peoples the blessing of a stable and an equitable peace."

James waited for him to finish. He even paused a little, to make sure the spate was exhausted. Then he spoke quietly.

"I have nothing to wait for," he said. "I have brought with me all the household I need. And I have little leisure. I should prefer to discuss the important points—whatever they may be—here and now."

"Just so, just so!" said Beaufort, attempting to cover his confusion. "We all, er . . . No time to waste. Cares of State." He smiled sideways at his colleagues, as if to apologize for his nephew's eccentricity. He was thinking that Scotland must be even more uncivilized than was reported: after five years of reigning over it, James seemed to be reverting to barbarism. 'My poor niece,' he thought, 'my poor niece: no wonder she is ashamed to come and meet her old uncle. . . .'

James interrupted the train of reflection. "Well?" he asked, "what are they, these graver issues?"

"Really, your Majesty," began Beaufort, wincing under the second shock, "this is hardly the way to get our business done. Such abruptness can only lead to misapprehensions, misleading statements that we should inevitably regret. There is a decency in things, and a reason for it. Let me remind you that I have had a long experience of such negotiations as these, longer than your Majesty's; and it teaches me that divergences from the usual procedure are seldom profitable and generally mischievous. I remember that at Constance, in the course of the great council there——"

This time James cut in before the flood was finished.

"I apologise to your Eminence," he said, "for my lack of experience. But I have a kingdom to govern, and my time is precious. May I know the object of your mission?"

Beaufort's face was redder than his hat. He sat back and looked at his companions, as though leaving them to find some way of dealing with a refractory child. But if they felt any sympathy—which was doubtful—they were certainly careful not to show it. Most remained expressionless, Northumberland gazing at King James with a crass intensity.

"Our main object was to felicitate your Majesty . . ." began one of the bishops, and then suddenly wondered what he was going to say.

It was Northumberland that came to the point. "Scotland and England are at peace," he said.

"That is certainly a matter for felicitation," said James, enjoying his own irony. "The truce has some years yet to run. It is a little early to talk of a renewal, but you will not find me unwilling."

"We can hardly talk of that," said Northumberland bluntly, "while Scotland is in negotiation with France."

"With the rebels," corrected Beaufort, "with the rebel party in France. Since my lord has mentioned it, that is certainly one object of our mission. We are authorized to ask your Majesty for an explanation."

There was a moment's silence, while James considered. Holding, as he calculated, most of the trumps, the best play was to show his hand.

"I owe you no explanation," he said. "My envoys are at Chinon. I see no need to send a copy of their instructions to Westminster."

"They say," answered Northumberland, "that there's a betrothal being concocted between the Princess Margaret and the son of the—er—the French pretender. We do not know if the story is true."

"If it were," said James, "it would be my business, not England's."

"Not England's business!" said Northumberland angrily, "everything in France——"

The cardinal cut him short. "We should regard any such bargain," he said, "as a breach of treaty, an infringement of the truce with England. We should be glad of your Majesty's assurance that no betrothal is contemplated. It would be a direct attack on our king's undeniable right to the crown of France."

"I would remind your lordship," said James, "that I am under no obligation to recognize that right. I would also remind you that I have had no communication with Chinon without considering carefully what its effect would be elsewhere."

"Your Majesty must have been misinformed about England. We are forced to take a most serious view of the matter at Westminster."

"I was not misinformed at all. I thought you would take a most serious view of it. And I was not deterred."

Beaufort gasped, unable to believe his ears. Northumberland, more than ever like a schoolboy, decided to meet defeat with recrimination.

"And your ransom?" he asked. "When will that be paid?"

James was expecting this, though he hardly knew how to answer it. These men were quite aware that they would never see their money. They knew, or ought to know, that the promise had been extracted from him under duress. For that matter, they could blame themselves if, by demanding far more than Scotland could ever pay, they had given him an excuse for stopping payment altogether. In any case, no king—except Robert the Third of unhappy memory—could go on bleeding his country and strengthening her inveterate enemy for the mere luxury of keeping a pledge. But they knew, too, that the whole sorry business must put him in a disparaging position, and they had come apparently to watch his discomfort, make capital from it if they could. He sat silent, smiling a slightly contemptuous smile, but with little conviction in it. If he felt contempt, it was partly for himself.

Northumberland blundered on. "Negotiating with Frenchmen," he said, with childish sarcasm, "may have given your Majesty low standards of good faith." He looked round his colleagues, asking for unanimity. "Englishmen," he said solemnly, "demand to be treated with the same honesty as they invariably show to others."

James almost laughed. He had seen enough, at King Henry's Court, to sharpen the bitter jest. A certain jingle came into his head, an old, old rhyme that an indignant Scotsman had put on paper, in the days when Balliol had relied on England's promises, and Bruce had been less trustful.

It is of English nation
The common-kenned condition,
Of Truth the nature to forget,
When they will them for winning set:
And reckless of good faith to be,
When they can their advantage see.
There can no bond be made so firm,
But they will make their will its term!

"Common-kenned." It was certainly a matter of common knowledge among England's immediate neighbours, though it had hardly penetrated to the English themselves—perhaps would never do so.

"I trust I make myself clear?" said Northumberland.

Yes, thought James, abundantly clear. He was still thinking of his rhyme. He remembered how he had once read it to Joan, and how she had flared up at him, asking him if he really believed that of her country. "Oh, yes," he had said, "and it would be easy to prove it to you." Then he had softened the blow by adding, "And of all other countries, too." The English only differed in being a little more sincere in refusing to confess or even face the truth. Their King Edward, against whom old Barbour had written his rhyme, had carried the motto, *Pactum serva*—"Keep your word"—through a lifetime of transparent perjuries, against Welshmen, Scotsmen, his own subjects even. He would have liked to quote the verses into the solemn sheep-faces in front of him. But it would be quite useless. It would merely make them angry, tempt them to build new buttresses round the unshakable walls of their own self-righteousness.

"Your Majesty is amused?" Beaufort was looking at him as a schoolmaster at an inattentive pupil. James decided to hedge.

"No," he said, "but I must challenge imputations on my good faith. I have been unpunctual in my payments, but not dishonest. I have found it quite impossible, since coming to Scotland, to keep to the suggested times and seasons."

"And we may expect payment soon?" asked Northumberland.

"I have hopes," lied James.

"We should prefer," said a grave bishop, "something more substantial than your Majesty's hopes."

"You have our hostages."

Beaufort snorted. "It is no profit to us," he said, "to keep so many of the Scottish nobility under restraint."

"Then why not release them?" James had decided to be provocative: only a crisis could show how far these men had been instructed to go.

"I must ask your Majesty to cease jesting. There is no occasion for a jest!"

No, indeed, thought James. He was already coping with all the Scottish nobles he could manage, without having another twenty-five let loose on him, embittered by exile. But that was hardly the point at issue.

"I can offer no further security. I would not if I could. My captivity was a breach of honour to begin with. The large sum you saddled me with, on my release, will always be the least and last obligation that I can lay on my people."

He had done what he wanted, apparently. Even the

bishops were angry. Northumberland was half on his feet, leaning across the table. Only Beaufort seemed to realize the danger of discomposure.

"All I can say," Northumberland was spluttering, "is that there are more ways than one of enforcing payment! A truce is a truce, but it only lasts till someone is goaded into breaking it!"

At the back of his slow mind he knew that he had no business to say such things. He had half an eye on Beaufort; James, watching like a cat, saw the sudden flick of Beaufort's hand, and the momentary consternation on several English faces. James knew that he was safe. He knew what he had suspected from the beginning, that every soldier whom England could afford to pay, every gun and arrow she could collect, would soon be needed round beleaguered Orleans. Westminster had instructed its envoys to bluff, avoiding the ultimate threat that might mean war on the Border: the more fools they must be at Westminster to let Northumberland accompany the embassy.

"I observed at the beginning," said Beaufort, with pompous haste, "that we should make little progress if we started in this inexcusably irregular fashion. The observation, if I may say so, has been entirely justified. I think we had better adjourn until tomorrow, when a more normal procedure—which I must demand of your Majesty—should produce better fruits."

His eye was still on Northumberland, warning and repressive. James suddenly saw an opportunity.

"I must ask pardon," he said, "for the unfruitfulness of my methods. I can easily change them if your lordships wish."

"We should be most grateful," said Beaufort, still a little uneasy.

"As your Eminence observed, my experience of diplomatic matters is a limited one."

"I did not intend——" began Beaufort, generous at the apparent prospect of success.

"Your Eminence was right," interrupted James with a polite smile. "I hoped I was conscious of my own limitations. I certainly know them now. I can best make amends by appointing representatives to negotiate for me. I can leave all those questions to men more experienced than myself, and with ampler leisure."

A shadow crossed Beaufort's face. "Yes, but your Majesty——" he said.

James waved him into silence. "You shall have your wish," he said, "as soon as I can grant it. I shall naturally have to consult others, discover the most suitable persons to negotiate with your Eminence. I assure you I will not be over-hasty. Indeed, mere circumstances forbid it. Travel is a difficult matter in my poor kingdom—especially in February. This country——"

Beaufort made a last effort to interrupt, but an unsuccessful one. James was making gestures implying snow-bound Alps and Pyrenees between Edinburgh and the Border. "This country," he concluded, "is not England. Your Eminence may have to wait here a few weeks, a few months even. But since your Eminence wishes, quite rightly, to prolong negotiations rather than impair them by precipitation, I am willing to comply."

He was enjoying himself now. He was pleased with his own parody of Beaufort's eloquence, pleased with the sight of Beaufort's face. It told him that he had won. In order to come north at all, the cardinal must have left in the balance his rivalry with Duke Humphrey, his intricate machinery for making more money, his pursuit of European position and the Triple Crown beyond. He would have allowed himself a fortnight across the Border, three weeks at most: Scotland might be worth that to him. But more might spell incurable damage to weightier interests; and it was hardly a question of weeks, for James could keep him dallying till the summer in this obscure corner of an unimportant kingdom. It would not be long before Beaufort would have to make his excuses and trundle himself back to

London, with his cargo of purple and fine linen and nothing whatever accomplished.

"These representatives," said Northumberland, clearing his throat, "I take it that your Majesty will grant them full powers? I mean—to stop the intrigue with France and arrange for our money to be paid."

James could not help smiling. If it were a mere contest of undiplomatic bluntness, Northumberland could beat him unstretched.

"I cannot," he answered, "grant them greater powers than I have myself. My envoys are already at Chinon, and there is no means of recalling them. And I have no money, at present, to satisfy your lordships' demands."

He rose and left them bowing goodnight to him, with sideway glances at each other. He would have given a good price to overhear the recriminations that would follow his departure.

The prior was waiting for him with a letter from Joan. She must have sent a courier after him within a few hours. In the packet were some overdue reports from the north for which he had not been able to wait at Linlithgow. Joan wrote to say that Margaret seemed to be recovering from the slight chill which had kept her in bed: that a wreck was reported from Dundee, apparently a foreign ship: and that young Alasdair Macdonald had vanished from Court the night before James set out and was now said to have been seen riding, at a desperate pace, on the road to Glasgow and the west. Joan hoped that her *protégé* had not been driven away by any trick played on him by her other young men.

'Now I wonder,' thought James, 'what that young limb is doing. I suppose it means trouble in the Isles. It may even mean that my English friends have been combining embassies of peace with mischief-making among my subjects.

It would not be the first time that rebellion in the Isles started with a word from Westminster.'

Then the northern reports engaged his attention. There were enough of them. He would have to sit up late to finish them. And it was no good anticipating trouble with Macdonald.

It was late, too, before Cardinal-Bishop Beaufort sought the curtained bed that he had brought from England. Before he reached that haven, he had come to an important decision.

He must acknowledge a serious mistake. James was naturally worried by the difficulties of governing his rude and disordered kingdom. He had expected sympathy and friendliness from his uncle, and, meeting only formality, had given way to his irritation. He was probably regretting it now, looking forward to their next interview as an opportunity to make amends. His uncle would give him every facility, waiving his right to scold.

He might, indeed, drop a few hints about common courtesy, and what is due to a cardinal. But he would follow them by an appeal to James's common sense, his gratitude to the man who had released him from prison, his duty to the family into which he had married. "I must remind your Majesty," he pictured himself saying, "I must remind your Majesty how seriously I compromised my own position by insisting on your Majesty's enfranchisement and coronation. Your Majesty's present policy, your intrigues with French rebels and dilatoriness in paying England her just debts, will be, so to speak, debited to my account. I can assure your Majesty that my difficulties are just as great as yours: Duke Humphrey is worse than many Highlandmen. And your Majesty's present attitude is turning my position from an arduous into an insufferable one."

He spent the next hour or so persuading himself that James

would see reason. James was a good lad at heart, if slightly difficult to manage. It was a pity that Joan had not come with him. He must write to Joan tomorrow, asking her to use all her influence on the side of her uncle and of common sense. Beaufort was, by this time, too sleepy to remember that James was a middle-aged man, ruling a kingdom, upon whom the term 'good lad' sat somewhat foolishly.

He slept late next morning, dressed, prayed and breakfasted with dignified deliberation, and sent to request an interview from his nephew.

He was told that King James had ridden away soon after dawn, leaving somewhat meagre apologies. He had had to leave for Edinburgh on business connected with his kingdom: he was unlikely to return for a week or more: his secretary would answer any questions, while the king was deciding on the choice of the promised plenipotentiaries: he commended his uncle and the English lords to the cordial hospitality of the Coldingham monks.

Berwick-on-Tweed saw Beaufort's caravan repassing its streets with unexpected promptitude. There was no explanation, certainly no hint that the mission had been anything but a success. The cardinal rode in a magnificent litter, with such dignity as befitted a prince of the Church, an uncle of a crowned king, a diplomatist returning from a skilfully managed triumph. Such outward trappings might disguise a lacerated self-importance, but for his private comfort he could do nothing except repeat, with sickly iteration, "My poor niece! My poor little Joan!"

March 1429

VIII

It was raining on Islay. The sodden turf squelched underfoot, Loch Finlaggan was alive with a million dancing pinpoints, and Ben Bhan loomed vaguely through a veil of silvery grey. Most of the neighbouring islands had vanished: Jura was an uncertain ghost. It had begun raining, for no observable reason, an hour or two after dawn: and there seemed no reason for it to stop that day, or even that week.

At times like these, a mainland stranger visiting these western isles—bastions, as it were, pushed out from Scotland to break the first strength of the Atlantic—might well conclude that spring here was merely a matter of softer but more insistent rain. Not that Islay welcomed strangers. Her poorest herds and fishermen felt that she needed all the mystery that they could wrap round her, to shield her dubious claims to sovereignty from the chill winds, impatient of anachronism, that betoken a new age.

For Islay boasted a Court, a seat of government. In the castle on Loch Finlaggan the Lord of the Isles sealed his charters and issued orders for the whole nook-shotten coast and intricate archipelago of the west. No one attempted to justify the conservatism. Skye would have been more convenient, Ardnamurchan more central. But it was on Islay that Fergus Mor had first landed, bringing Jacob's stone from Ireland, and with it, also from Ireland, the very name of Scot. The stone had soon been carried to Dunadd, then to Dunstaffnage, and then across Scotland to Scone: the symbol of power had followed the reality, quitting the Atlantic inlets for the Lowland seaboard of the east. The Macdonalds were left behind to struggle or bargain with the Viking power, and feed their pride on an insubstantial tradition. When Norway, beaten at Largs, retreated to the Orkneys, they still remembered that Islay had a royal past. Within a century a head of the clan, Alasdair's grandfather, had dubbed himself *Dominus Insularum* and begun to play the petty king in somewhat tentative fashion. He paid grudging homage at Scone while he exchanged secret embassies with Irish chiefs—and with Scotland's enemies at Westminster. His son had roused the whole Highlands and poured their manhood in arms upon the eastern coast, until Mar met and checked him at the red Harlaw. And now the third Lord of the Isles, Alasdair, a young man of doubtful mind, had returned home to Finlaggan after a year in Lowland prisons and at King James's Court. He had arrived, jaded and irritable, on a golden April evening, gone to bed in brooding silence, and woken next day to find Islay tinkling with miniature rivulets and the unceasing downpour of the rain.

For some minutes he wondered where he was. He could not recognize his room in Dun Finlaggan, the positions of bed and window, nor the stag's antlers on the opposite wall. Then the smell of a peat fire and the lowing of Highland cattle reminded him that he had left behind him the few weeks of prison, the many months of humiliating kindness, that lay between him and the day when he had set out from Islay to answer King James's summons to Inverness.

He had held a council before going there. They would make him call another one today: his mother had collected most of his councillors on the beach last night, to receive their young lord at his homecoming. They had said nothing that mattered, only wagging their beards to express congratulations on his safe return from among the Sassunach. They must have been reserving their fire for today. Old Macgee of the Rhinns had been most vehement last summer in advising him to defy King James's summons; he would no doubt remind Alasdair of the fact now, over and over. Macgillivray, and the other two chiefs from Mull, had probably sailed across in order to say biting words about the faith of the Sassunach. Colonsay, Keeper of the Records, would pull a wry mouth and ask how he was to prevent posterity knowing that the Lord of the Isles had spent a year in chains.

None of them would believe that, after the first few weeks, his stay had been voluntary. They could never understand what glamour a young man might find in the English-speaking Court, with its silks and cedar-wood, its spiced foods and sleek, fragrant ladies. By their island standards he should despise all this, as foreign and corrupting: he should prefer the straw beds and noisy cows of Islay. No good Gael could have lived a year in the Lowlands, except under compulsion. It would be hopeless to try and explain.

He was glad it was raining. It gave him an excuse to put off the formal meeting. The traditional council-table was a block of stone on an islet in Loch Finlaggan, reached by a dozen stepping-stones. They might take it as evidence of effeminacy if he refused to splash across and sit there in damp clothes, but he could ignore their prejudices. He would invite them to a feast and a *ceilidh* in the hall of Finlaggan. He would make them drunk enough to forget their ancestral grumblings. He needed drink himself to clear the headache he had acquired by too much ale last night. The island ale was stronger than he had remembered.

He put his head out of the window, glad of the refreshing raindrops. In the courtyard below a girl was gathering in some sodden linen that had been left out on the stones. She was hooded and muffled in a woollen plaid, but when she turned to call back towards the house Alasdair saw her face. She had raven-black hair, a pleasing contrast with the scarlet of her sleeves. Her eyes, too, were black, with that sharp light in them that can draw a man more surely than any softness. Her voice, still strange to him after a year of Lowland Scots, gave an unquestionable thrill. He wondered why she was bothering about the linen; it was soaked already and might as well stay there till the rain chose to stop. He would have liked to call out and tell her so, with some jest in Gaelic. He noticed that she had no coif on her head under the plaid. A maiden. Before he could think of his jest, she had left her task unfinished and darted back into shelter. Alasdair turned back from the window.

He encountered his mother. She must have been standing close behind him, seeing what he saw. She was smiling now, in a way that he had disliked since early childhood.

"So you are waking at last?" she said. Her greeting seemed to imply an intention to cure him, soon, of recently-acquired habits, such as sleeping late after the Dun was astir.

"I am," he said drily. "What would you be wanting in here?"

"I was coming to see my son."

"You have seen him now. Are you pleased?"

"I am. May I ask what it is you'll be doing today? It's foul weather, and likely to be."

"I was thinking we ought to feast the men you have brought here," said Alasdair.

His mother's eye lighted up a little. "I was thinking the same," she said.

"Shall we be calling up the steward?"

"No need," she answered. "He has had his orders. While you were sleeping."

Alasdair had to acknowledge, when the time came, that his mother had given excellent orders. Food and drink, fuel and music, there was no stint in her hospitality. The guests were seated before noon, staid and watchful. It took an hour and more to melt their gravity. Alasdair had them plied with unceasing wine, and few of them held back: only the old man from the Rhinns took nothing but ale, and little enough of that. Alasdair's own cup, with no reminder from him, was refilled before it was empty: once he saw his mother beckoning a servant towards it.

All was going better than he had planned. He was certainly getting more enjoyment than he had expected from this politic banquet. He found himself unaccountably glad to be home again. He was remembering year-old happenings far more clearly than last month. King James's Court was receding into dimness, slightly distasteful. The king himself was a vague memory and Queen Joanna's beauty was forgotten. He could only recall the sneer on the face of one of her waiting-women, Bishop Cameron's hostility, and the barely-veiled insults of young men who found island habits boorish and an island prince a laughing-stock. In another minute he was remembering the trick that had been played on him at Inverness, the weeks of impotent fury in which he had paced his dungeon and cursed King James's name.

He did not notice how closely Macgee of the Rhinns was watching him. He did not see the glances that the old man exchanged with his mother, nor the gesture made to MacMhurrich, hereditary minstrel of his house. He only saw MacMhurrich rise quickly to his feet, run his fingers across the harp, and pour out his voice in song. The hall was soon ringing with the mighty deeds of Somerled and Ragnald, with the praises of Donaill and of the clan that he had sired and named. From Antrim to Cape Wrath, there was no spot where the Macdonalds were not famous and obeyed. They had peopled Skye and Benbecula, Uist and Eriskay and Glengarry. They were lords of all the seas, and every island paid them tribute. When the lord of Islay went forth to war, then such glory followed as the world had not seen since Alasdair the Great, Lord of Macedon, led his swordsmen against the Babylonian king. No man, no monarch even, could insult or imprison a Macdonald and escape without paying the price. And if the insult were deadly, then only the blood of thousands could redeem it.

It was not long before they had their chieftain at their mercy. He was younger than they, and twice as drunk. He was home again, lord in his own castle—not courtier to a patronizing queen. Everything conspired to help their cunning. Even the rain ceased to fall, and the sun blazed on Islay with intoxicating splendour. They carried him, shouting with excitement, across the stepping-stones to the islet in the loch. There was no question of a council, but they told him that he had forfeited lordship by imprisonment, and must be crowned again with the crown of the Isles. They set him on the ancestral stone, his feet in the carved footprints, and waved their swords round him in the rain-washed air. All Islay, mysteriously summoned, seemed to be gathered at Loch Finlaggan. No man had seen a fiery cross carried past his croft, yet many had already donned their saffron-dyed shirts. A few trailed long, two-handed claymores. For the saffron shirt meant war.

Alasdair was given no respite, no time to think, between noon and nightfall. He was early in bed, but not alone. In the far corner of his room, under the stag's antlers, lay the huddled heap of a red-sleeved gown. As he sighed and snorted himself to sleep, the boats were already gliding out from Askaig and Ardmore. They bore messages to Ardnamurchan, to Skye and the outer Hebrides. Nor was it only the Macdonald lands that they sought. The summons was going to Macleans and Mackinnons, to Clan Chattan and Clan Cameron. All were warned to meet at Inverlochy at the gate of the Great Glen, ready to march northwards upon Inverness: for at Inverness, in the person of its chieftains, a whole race had been outwitted and dishonoured with prisoners' chains.

April-June 1429

IX

A Highland army could gather and march with astonishing swiftness. The clans brought few provisions with them, and no baggage. They ate what the country provided—or could be forced to provide at the sword's point: they slept tentless, if necessary in the snow, with no covering but their plaids. Barefoot, or in rough bag-shaped brogues, they could march thirty miles a day without noticing the absence of roads and bridges. There was nothing to check their pace but their own wilfulness, or a chance of cattle-lifting, or victory and the heavy booty that victory might entail.

Alasdair kept his host together, on the northward march, without much difficulty. His summons to arms had met with no opposition, and but little reluctance. The Camerons and Clan Chattan were the slowest to move, but even they reached the *rendezvous* at Inverlochy before April was out. The screen of mountains, the concerted silence of half a nation, forbade any news of the gathering to reach Perth or Edinburgh. In a few days after leaving Inverlochy, the long yellow snake had wriggled its way up the Great Glen, skirted the lochs, and emerged viciously into the little plain which fed the town of Inverness.

As the smoke from ruined fields smudged the sky, the few score merchants, the many cottagers, fled through the streets towards the castle, where Mar sat cursing King James's folly in letting Alasdair escape. He opened his gate to such as brought food, cattle, or money to bribe him: the poorer were told to find shelter in the hills, or swim for it to Kessock and the Black Isle. So much was routine-work, dictated by Mar's experience of war at home and on the Continent: he did not expect a long siege, knowing too much of Highland ways: but it was as well to take every precaution. The clansmen might try to carry the castle by assault; some of them might plan to clamber in by night and open the way for the waiting host. If they did neither, he was tolerably safe; they would stay round the town until they were tired of replundering its ruins, and then go home—long before an army of vengeance could come northward from the Lowlands.

Inverness had already vanished, and in a single evening. The burghers looked down from the castle on the skeletons of a few stone-built houses standing forlorn in an acre or two of blackened ash: here and there fragments of a human body showed where some fool had been late in taking refuge

—or had attempted to stay and defend his possessions. Mar, still cursing, sent messengers to King James—wary men who knew the hill-paths—to tell him that Inverness was destroyed, but that it was too late to do anything. Then he waited for the Highlandmen to go, sleeping little and taking care that his watchmen did not sleep at all.

Alasdair and his men made merry round the shores of the Firth, venturing to Dingwall and eastwards to Cawdor Castle in their search for cattle and booty. The more they found, the less they talked of staying out the summer, to meet King James if he came north with his armoured knights. Prudent old men remembered Harlaw: even the youngest felt that the blotting-out of a royal burgh was sufficient vengeance for the dishonour done there to their chieftain. If a Lowland army was on its way, it would be better to go home first and stow the booty in lonely glens or island pastures; then, if they felt inclined, they could return and give battle. But there was plenty of time in any case. King James would take a month or two to gather an army, and several weeks to get it to the north.

James knew that only speed could enable him to teach the marauders a lesson. As soon as Mar's message had confirmed the ugly rumours from the north, he had Alasdair proclaimed rebel: the clans were ordered—for what the order was worth—to desert him and go home. A summons to arms went through the Lowlands, from Perth to Galloway and Berwick. The more remote did not all obey, but when young Douglas smilingly ignored the missive, young Douglas found himself a prisoner—and remained so till the campaign was over. The merchants of Aberdeen and Dundee were ordered to put their ships at the king's disposal: the eastern counties were ransacked for chargers and baggage-horses. Those who knew Scotland smiled at the king's panoply and asked each other if he imagined he could fight an Agincourt or a Baugé on the broken slopes of Cairn Meol.

It was not long before he stopped their smiling by listening to their advice. Once past Dunkeld, there was less heraldry about the army, and less talk of cavalry manœuvres. The mountains closed round their road as they approached Pitlochry: the Clan Donnchaidh men, hating Macdonalds, joined them from the glens on each side. But beyond their country, and athwart the road north, lay the lands of Clan Chattan, which had joined, however unwillingly, with the Lord of the Isles. James was taking risks.

Clan Chattan, its fighters away in the north, its loyalty to the Macdonald doubtful, allowed King James to pass. He dealt sternly with the fools that wanted to revenge the sack of Inverness on the defenceless clachans. The men must pay for everything, show every courtesy—unless they wanted to swing from the nearest tree. James himself summoned a meeting of the old men, whose sons were with Alasdair, and listened patiently, through an interpreter, to their long-winded excuses. The women began to bring food and fuel to the roadside, and sell them without exorbitant profit. They stared round-eyed at the overdressed Sassunach, at the piles of plate-armour strapped to their baggage-horses, at the sticks and canvas wherewith these strange beings, prodigal of needless labour, built themselves a town to sleep in each night. Secure from opposition, James passed Dalwhinnie before June was ten days old, and dropped down into the valley of the Spey.

The old campaigners were reduced to grumbling that he could never have done it but for perfect weather and tracks as smooth and dry as a carpet. No leader, they said, had any right to count on that. If James attempted further follies, they would go home.

The effect on the enemy was more immediate. When Alasdair, dallying at Inverness, heard that King James was in Glen Spey, he flew into such a rage with Clan Chattan, that Clan Chattan's chief left his presence vowing vengeance for the words that had been put upon him that day. Alasdair, meanwhile, was giving the signal for rally and retreat. Encumbered with spoil and cattle, restless with jealousies and recriminations, the Highland host sprawled past the lower end of Loch Ness and jostled itself into the Great Glen again, bound for home.

Mar opened his castle-gates, sent word to King James, and then went to his bed to sleep the clock round twice. Mar was ageing rapidly, more from self-indulgence than any weight of years. And now that the summer's campaign was finished, there was no point in being indecently active.

James thought otherwise: the campaign had barely begun. His advisers told him that it was useless to proceed; they pointed out that there would be nothing he could do at Inverness, except watch the burghers rebuilding the *débris* of their town. They had scared Alasdair into scurrying home, and that was all that could be hoped for. He would not be able to get the clans out again for a year, or maybe two. What more could James hope for? "I want to be king in Scotland," he said. "I want to make it twenty and fifty years before my towns are burnt."

He marched his men to Kingussie and made them encamp there with all fuss and circumstance. He kept them two days, and rose early in the third night, long before dawn. He sniffed the air for good weather and then began to issue orders to a yawning retinue. The army was to march as soon as it was day. It was to breakfast first, but carry, at most, four days' provisions. Tents and banners, casks and bedding, everything except the armour was to be left behind.

The surprise and misgiving grew when it was announced that the march was to take them west, up the Spey instead of down it. James left his more active captains to keep the column moving and rode ahead with the doubters. They found hard dry turf up the valley, a track to lead them to easy fords, a cloudless sky overhead. On the heights to their right scattered men of Clan Donnchaidh ran and clambered abreast of them, armed with bows to shoot down any other runners, who might be carrying tales to Macdonald. Only one man, dressed in deer-skins, was to be allowed to outstrip them: it was understood that he bore some secret message to the chieftain of Clan Chattan.

It took some time before the full boldness of James's plan was grasped. He was heading for the Corriearrack Mountains and the high track, which some called a pass, leading down to Abertarff and Loch Ness. If he got the men over it, he would cut into the middle of the Great Glen, arriving close on Alasdair's heels or even—if the Highlandmen had dawdled—across his front, barring him from Inverlochy and the Isles.

The Highlandmen had certainly dawdled. They had driven their cattle a few leisurely miles a day. The younger men were constantly diverging, in the hope of rejoining the march with an increase of booty; their relatives refused to budge until they returned, successful or empty-handed. Everyone overate at nights, slightly reducing the huge herds that retarded the march, but waking next day disinclined for effort, and ripe only for bickering with men from rival clans. Alasdair, content with his success and plunder, presided over the ungoverned array, glad that he had removed it from Inverness and the possibility of Lowland attack.

They had not left the thirty-mile length of Loch Ness when James had first glimpse of them. He had brought his men, by hook or crook, three-quarters of the way up the Corriearrack Pass: he had left them sleeping on the grass, enemy-fashion, while he pressed ahead with a small escort, crested the pass, and rode downhill until Alasdair's watch-fires were in sight. They were dotted along the loch-side, mile after mile. They seemed all the more numerous since so many burnt doubly, reflected in the water. The extent of country they covered at night might well appal the leader of a small army: but it was reasonable to guess that it did not signify numbers so much as indiscipline and careless security. James sat gazing for long minutes at the panorama; he could picture what darkness and the distance hid—the tipsy men round the fires, the red glow catching the patiently reproachful faces of hobbled cattle: the sackfuls of gear from houses that were now grey ash.

At last he raised his eyes to the captains at his side. "I think we have them," he said.

They wheeled their horses round and rode back, over the crest, to snatch some hours of sleep among the men.

It was dawn when he led them over to the spot he had visited last night. He was not prepared for what daylight revealed. Before their eyes, glittering in the summer sun, rose range after range of massive peaks: Cairn Eige towering over Tigh Mor, Ben Screel half masking the distant mountains of Skye. It was an appalling sight for men bred among fruitful valleys and wooded hills. Man had not yet learnt to find grandeur in the barren savagery of high peaks. Some nerve in James's mind, the poet's perhaps, tingled with a pain that was more than half pleasure. Most of the men round him were muttering and crossing themselves in dismay at the barbaric spectacle. Many fell to the ground as a swooping shadow seemed momentarily to blot out the sun. An eagle was rising, fleeing from this incredible intrusion upon his lonely kingdom. But the omen was good—even in a place fit only for demons, lunatics or Highland men. And, whatever its terrors, the tracks led downwards now, to valleys where a Christian could feel comparatively safe. They needed no order to begin the descent.

Alasdair had heard news of their coming, but far too late. It was hours before he could rouse his clans, or make them believe that a Sassunach army was indeed marching down into Lochaber. It was within striking distance before evening, and his plans were still confused and contradictory. He had listened to those who counselled him to climb the foothills and attack before the Lowlanders could debouch upon the flat ground round the head of the loch; he had tried to muster sufficient force to meet them above Cullachy.

Then, seized with misgiving, and hoping for a night's respite and preparation, he had suddenly ordered a retirement to the plain. The majority of his men complied, cursing his indecision. As they fell back, they saw that Clan Chattan and Clan Cameron had stayed behind, to welcome and cheer King James.

The desertion turned an already wavering scale. The king's men doubled the pace of their descent, their steel plate glittering in the red sun of the late afternoon. Clan Chattan and Clan Cameron, as if to prove their new-found loyalty, swept down upon their late allies with fierce intensity, backed by a solid mass of armoured knights. The spectacle of disunion and treachery, the folly of leaders who asked a Highland army to retreat and fight on the defensive, the utter unexpectedness of any battle on such ill-chosen ground, all this completed the ruin of Alasdair's helpless host. The king's men were soon pouring down on a chaos of flying clansmen and stampeded cattle.

Night closed upon moors red with slaughter. From the rocks of Cairn Dubh, broken men peered down upon them, in terror of pursuit. There, hundreds of feet below, the king's men were lighting fires, singing of victory. But outside the protecting circles of light and company, in lonely hollows, and on open moorland, wounded men rolled over in search of sword or dagger before the wolves should leave the forests to seek their midnight meal.

August 1429

X

The great bell of Holyrood Abbey fell suddenly quiet. The lay brother, sitting nervously at the keyboard of the new organ, summoned up his courage and struck the first notes. For all was ready and everyone assembled: Bishop Wardlaw, who had come from St. Andrews to sing the Office: the king, queen and Court: the two unofficial envoys—the indignant Benedictine from Rome, the courtly gentleman from French Chinon: Mar, no longer tied to Inverness by threatened onslaughts: the Provost of Edinburgh and his merchant friends, cheerful in their hopes of returning prosperity. The chapel was filled to overflowing: the thanksgiving Mass could begin.

It was the king himself who had insisted that the Holyrood monks must purchase or build themselves an organ: he had sworn that, sooner or later, he would teach his countrymen, musical as they were, that music can be more than a pastime. The lay brother at the organ had been chosen to begin the innovation.

James had had little leisure yet to teach Scotland anything, except obedience and submission to a long-neglected crown. It seemed as though he had hardly once rested since he had crossed the Tweed to Melrose, five years back. He had ridden the length and breadth of the Lowlands, humbling the proud and defeating their combinations against him, hanging thieves and dismissing unfaithful stewards of his prerogative. Maybe the worst was over now: the hurrying footsteps behind him, that had seemed to threaten the destruction of himself, his family and his appointed task, were dying away, outdistanced at last: he would be able to slacken pace, look round him and be king.

Bishop Wardlaw, the *introit* ended, listened while the canons broke out into chanting. Good voices, good material for King James's experiments. Wardlaw was a judge, or had been in youth: he had heard the chanting in Notre Dame. He wished his old pupil luck. He wished him luck, too, with all that he was trying to do for Scottish schools. There was no more talk of shifting the university from St. Andrews: there was talk, rather, of making it the leader in a new and general system for bringing learning within the reach of more Scotsmen. One could think of such things, after beheading nobles and winning battles. Wardlaw was officially celebrating a thanksgiving for the queen's delivery from childbirth, but he knew of a dozen other reasons for gratitude to Heaven.

Near him stood Bishop Cameron, silent too. Cameron had no voice for singing. He was thanking God for his bishopric, for James's refusal to let the Pope oust him from it, for the blossoming of all his long-desperate hopes. He was secure now, if he played the game carefully, as secure as the king himself: no combination of the high-born and jealous could force James to dismiss the once landless orphan from the niche he had carved for himself, high up on the wall of Scotland.

They dared not voice their discontents now, they had been driven, it seemed, to pitifully underground movements. One had only to maintain the watchful eye, the ever-open ear. The king's laws, mere laughing-stocks once, were beginning to be obeyed. He had just ventured on one of the boldest, against Cameron's advice: he was trying to prevent the great land-holders from evicting their tenants without good cause shown. Scotsmen who had watered their patch of soil with labour and patience and a little love were not to be expelled from it by mere caprice. James wanted to be remembered as one who had used the day of victory to remember God's poor. A dangerous ambition, thought Cameron; if it grows on him, the watchful eye will be more than ever needed.

The *Gloria* was finished, the congregation knelt.

Sir Robert Stewart, Chamberlain to the Court, was on his knees behind his royal master. He could give more heartfelt thanks than any present for the queen's delivery: for it was only another daughter that she had given James, and Sir Robert might still think of himself, secretly, as Scotland's heir. He had come to think of himself as more than that, as rightful king in James's place. What did succession mean, and the sanctity of kingship, if doubtful marriages were to infect the royal line? His grandfather Athol should have been king, not Bessie Muir's unlawful brood. But he knew that this was no time for such thoughts.

He must wait, cherishing his own lineage, until some outside thing shook King James's security. There was no sign yet, no hope for another claimant; but one could not tell what the future might hold.

Mar, close beside Stewart, disliked thinking of the future. He was getting old more quickly than he thought reasonable. He no longer enjoyed women as he had done a few years ago. He had been ill lately, and hated being ill. He had thought of making a disordered stomach, this morning, an excuse for not coming to hear shaven-pates caterwauling in the chapel: then he had remembered the feast that was to follow, and decided to go down to Holyrood after all. He was anxious, too, about the next few years. James's way of playing with fire was hardly fair on the justiciar who had to govern the north all the year round, not merely on summer campaigns. He had pulled James out of a nasty situation, by defending Inverness Castle while the royal army scaled the Corriearrack and gave the Highland men a beating. That bold stroke had been followed up, the broken clans hustled westward through their glens, pursued, even, into the Hebrides. James's officers had taken ship: they reported that their siege-engines were pounding, even now, at Finlaggan and Dun Tulm. Alasdair, by their account, could be little better than a hunted fugitive. Mar was sceptical. Everyone exaggerated his own successes, believed what he wanted to believe. The Macdonald power was tremendous, even the lordship of the Isles meant something still. In the Highlands, it was always the unexpected that happened. Mar would be happier, would know he was safe for a year or two of ease and pleasure when he saw Alasdair—and that mother of his—in chains and a dungeon.

The French envoy, too, was thinking of war, and more confidently. In his country, the tide seemed at last to have turned. The miracle had happened: a country girl from Lorraine had bundled the Englishmen back from Orleans, beaten them in pitched battle at Patay. As he knelt in

Holyrood Chapel, she might, even now, be kneeling in recaptured Rheims, watching Regnault crown the Dauphin as Charles VII. Charles had sent him to Scotland with letters about Margaret's betrothal—but no longer letters from a desperate suppliant. England's protests against the match were feeble and negligible: she had not dared to back them by war on the Border. England was principally occupied in blaming Bishop Beaufort for letting King James go. Beaufort was in temporary eclipse at Westminster, England's sun might soon be setting in Normandy. The new dawn would be brighter to French and Scottish eyes.

Joan knelt with her ladies—as custom prescribed—on the opposite side of the aisle from her husband and his lords. If James looked across at her, it was to see her still beautiful, still the woman of his choice. She had attempted the hard task that his destinies set her. She was beginning to accept Scotland, rude and foreign as she must find it; she had penetrated, here and there, below the forbidding surface, finding something to admire and even love. Time would assist her, and she was brave.

Joan, intent on the prayer, did not see James glancing across at her. Prayer was answered sometimes: one was encouraged to be importunate. She had secretly asked the monks of Holyrood to join their prayers to her own, to ask Heaven for one more favour: she wanted a son.

She was glad to be at Holyrood; the place had a fascination for her, in spite of the wild country that crept so close, the savage hump of Arthur's Seat. She would ask James, one day, to stop tinkering with Bruce's ruins on the windswept rock and build a palace, for herself and the children, beside Holyrood Abbey. Now that there was no war nearer than the Isles, one need not live perpetually on the brink of fortified cliffs.

Someone or something was coming down the aisle. She could hear shuffling, slow but unmistakable, like that of some clumsy animal. It could hardly be a dog, though dogs in church were common enough in Scotland, and no one seemed to mind. But the tread was too heavy and rhythmic. She resisted the temptation to turn round.

It was a man, advancing, creeping almost, towards the altar-steps. A beggar, only half clothed, tousled and unshorn. A young man. Why had they let him in?

She felt that everyone was watching him. Even Wardlaw, his back towards the congregation, must be feeling the distraction; his voice wavered a little in the Office. The intruder paused beside her in his strange progress, looking towards the king. James gave no sign. When a precentor moved out of his seat, as though to ask for instructions, he bade him, by a single gesture, to return. The man in his shirt turned to continue his journey to the altar. Joan saw that he had a naked sword in his hand, but held it by the point in token of surrender.

She saw who it was now. Alasdair Macdonald, once her courtier and *protégé*: Alexander *Dominus Insularum*, no longer lord of a single isle. He must crawl to the altar, a beaten man, and await the end of Mass to know what punishment or mercy was in store.

Joan wondered, with a sudden enlightenment, how far the scene had been prearranged. Alasdair would hardly plan it, but his friends might have advised him to make the desperate gesture. A man whose life is forfeit will play strange tricks to redeem it. James might even have insisted. James knew the value of ceremony to anyone that must rule others. Certainly the witnesses were well chosen. Christendom, as well as all Scotland, would soon know what might otherwise have been in doubt. James Stewart, exile and prisoner, had not only returned to his kingdom, but had now made himself its master—plain and mountain, Lowlands and Highlands, the isles and the circumambient sea.

Summer's Lease

And summer's lease hath all too short a date.

SHAKESPEARE. Sonnet XVIII.

I think you are
All things except success ; all honesty
Except the ultimate honesty of the earth ;
All talents but the genius of the Sun.
And yet I would not have you otherwise.

John Brown's Body. STEPHEN VINCENT BENET.

CHAPTER EIGHT

Summer's Lease

June 17th, 1432

I

"*WHERE ARE THE MEN, and what will be their names,*
That are not feared to fight against King James?"

"That's not so bad. I'm getting the trick of it."

"Stop rhyming, my friend, and finish your works."

"I can do both, mynheer, I can do both:

The Highlandmen and English faster run,
Now that our king has bought a gun, a gun."

The young man from Perth was rubbing oil over the king's great cannon. Beside it, his back to the cliff, the old Flemish gunner sat on the parapet: the wall was narrow and his ample posterior bulged over, a curious sight from the street far below him.

"He has had mine gun for two year," he said. "Why do you make poetry now?"

"I just felt that way. Two years? I could make something of that, too. The prince is two years old." The young man was silent a moment, rubbing the carved work round the touch-hole. "Tell me," he said at last, "are there storks in your country?"

"Storks? *Ja.* Why do you ask?"

The man from Perth did not answer: he was too busy thinking.

"It is getting dark," said the Fleming. "Does it get dark at noon in Scotland?"

"*Only two things*——" began his companion, and then

glanced up at the vast expanse of sky. "Ay, it is getting dark," he said, in a puzzled way, and shrugged his shoulders, as though leaving nature to explain her own behaviour. "*There will be but two things*," he recited, "*that a king can want. And one year brought 'em both out of Brabant.* I'll wager you cannot tell what that means."

"I can be happy, my friend, without that knowing. Is the rust gone?"

"Nearly. . . . It means that a king needs cannon, which you brought him, and an heir, which the storks brought him the same month. And both of them here for us to see." He pointed along the ramparts to where the little Prince James was rolling pebbles over his nurse's shoes.

"You are bad poet," said his companion. "My gun, she come from Flanders, not Brabant. Is there no rhyme for Flanders in your language?" He screwed his large body round, twisting from the hips, and spat thirty feet down the rock. "And will you tell me," he asked, "why it get dark in Edinburg at this time of day? And in June."

"June—noon. Noon—June," said the young man from Perth. "That should be easy."

Others were taking notice, too. Doors were opening in the street below, tiny figures emerging to stare upwards at the sky. The white patches of their faces showed unnaturally, even at this distance, in the gathering gloom. The young man glanced downward and then up again at the sky. The shadow that was falling upon Edinburgh town, on Leith and the sea beyond, drove the thought of rhyming from his head. "It'll pass," he said, "anything'll pass if you give it time." His voice sounded less confident than his words.

The nurse had caught Prince James up in her arms; she was coming towards them, making for indoors. Of the four people on the rampart, the child alone seemed undisturbed by the darkening day.

"Hey, Janet," said the young man with forced heartiness, "are you coming to give the bairn a ride on our gun? It's slippery enough with the grease—but that's good practice for sitting a throne."

"Hold your wheesht!" said Janet. "I am taking his Highness in. This is not canny, with the sun setting at midday. We're for the house."

The Fleming had risen, inadvertently blocking her path. She stepped aside, almost into the gun, hoping to squeeze between his girth and the parapet. The babe, touching the greasy metal, suddenly began to scream.

"*Ach, neen, mein kind,*" said the gunner, "*moet niet vreezen het kanon.*"

"Give over," shouted the nurse, above the child's screams, "would you be putting evil words on him as well?"

"No, no; not evil," protested the Fleming. "It was to say he must not fear a gun."

"It'd be nothing strange if he did fear your noisy, stinking devil's work. Have you let the thing off when he's by?"

"We have not," said the young man from Perth. "Get in with you, nurse." He was afraid of the clamour attracting the queen or someone who might tell the queen. He also thought, with Janet, that the heir of Scotland was better indoors while the sun was playing such tricks.

The object of their anxiety was still giving lusty tongue. His blue eyes were fixed in terror on the oily monster before him, his little face was quite scarlet, except where the great birthmark that disfigured it showed a deeper, angrier colour. Janet pushed the foreigner aside and hurried towards shelter, half-scolding, half-crooning to her charge. His squalling ceased with an almost magical suddenness. He was smiling again before she had him indoors.

"That's strange now," said the young man, "he'll have to learn, one day, that it's only another man's gun you need to fear, never your own."

"I see one burst one day," objected the Fleming. "When we was shooting at Duke Homfrey's Englishmen in Hainault. And there was little what had been the crew."

"Badly served? Too much powder?"

"May-happen. It was too late to find out."

The gloom was like a summer-night now, the sun in almost total eclipse. "I've a mind to go in too," said the young man. "I've plenty to see to indoors."

"It will be darker indoor. I stay here."

His companion lingered. "It is a bad omen," he said. "Maybe the plague's coming to Edinburgh again. Or maybe it's the king's life that's pointed at, God save him. But I've heard no tell of war."

"Omen?" grunted the Fleming. "You think of nothing but omen here." He stirred uneasily on his feet, kicking the toe of a heavy boot against the stone wall. "Dark is bad," he conceded, "for the gunner, most bad. He cannot see to shoot."

They stood in silence, loath to acknowledge the strength of their unreasoning fear. It was five minutes before either spoke.

"I am not sure," said the young man at last, "that it's not getting lighter now. But it's an ill thing to have happened."

"It is. Your king, he pay me to take my gun and shoot her at his enemies' houses. But I cannot shoot her in the dark—if they come to where he is at night. Was that why you fear the omen for his life?"

"Not here. I wish he was living here always, instead of at Perth."

"But you are from Perth, mine friend. Do you so hate your home?" The Fleming, glancing up at the lightening sky, began to re-settle himself on his stone perch.

"I do not. But the king'd be safer here. The castle at Perth is little more than a ruin. And it's ower near the mountains."

"Mountains?" The Fleming looked round him at the panorama of Pentlands and Lammermuirs, the Ochils on the skyline and the nearby crags behind Holyrood. He thought of his own home by the Scheldt. "Is Edinburg in your plains?" he said, laughing.

"It's not the hills that matter," said the younger man. "It's the folk that live in them. There's plenty within a day's journey of Perth that'll sell themselves and their swords. And there'll be purchasers, too, especially if the king tries again what he has tried already. A day's journey."

He looked at his companion who was still thinking of Flemish flats and chuckling half-heartedly at his own jest. The eclipse had depressed both of them, suggesting gloomy thoughts. The man from Perth was also remembering his home.

"Or maybe a night's journey," he said. "They could be half-way back to their mountains before it was dawn."

September 1432

II

The king sat in Dunfermline town, feasting his nobles. There was red wine, French, Spanish and Greek, to stand beside the home-brewed ale: there were sugar-plums and cinnamon cakes to give a fashionable finish to the banquet. The king's guests sat on birch-wood chairs: wax candles shone down on the white linen from Tournai, glittered above on the gold and vermilion of the repainted rafters.

The splendour had provoked grumbling enough to begin with: Bishop Wardlaw had been blamed for extravagance, back in Albany's time, but his palace was primitive beside the lavishness and elegance of the Court. Queen Joan's ideas of housekeeping had been denounced as English and sinful: the king had been held womanish for giving her scope. There was little of such talk now. Some of the Scottish nobles were already beginning to look askance at their own homes, where the hens wandered into the dining-hall and the master, occupying the only chair, offered rough benches to his women and his guests. They had begun to spend their silver—shamefacedly at first—on the continental luxuries that were borne yearly, with increasing abundance, into Leith and Inverkeithing and Dundee. The more enterprising of them might begin to bully the burghs, as King James had bullied Edinburgh, into training Scots lads to make as good joiners and limners as the foreigner. That would be a better use for their money than overeating themselves on ill-cooked mutton, swilling too much ale, and buying such hordes of weapons as tempted them to fight each other without further motive.

Mar was at the feast. He had come south again, after some years of further trouble: it had been his own fault this time, for he had tried to use Alasdair's defeat as an opportunity for mopping up Macdonald lands: he had a good beating at Inverlochy from Alasdair's nephew, spent rheumatic nights in the heather and had his disaster retrieved by royal armies while he was in bed at Lochindorb. He was hardly less boastful. He was telling the Abbot Fogo long stories of his Hungarian stallions, with embarrassing details about their prowess in breeding progeny. Athol sat on the other side of him, older, uglier, a little more bald. He, too, came seldom to Court these days: he mouldered at Methven, getting Court news, one supposed, and no little gossip, from his handsome grandson, who was even now carrying the cup round at the feast.

The older men were all sinking into insignificance. James was entertaining their sons more often or advancing new men, less highly born, in the teeth of aristocratic growlings. Crichton, who was barely thirty but in the running to be Chancellor, was holding forth now, to a crowd of his contemporaries, with stories of his embassy to Norway and of the diverting habits of the Norwegians. Queen Joan, surrounded by munching clerics, leant forward to listen to him.

James had let her attract young men to her Court, apart from those he wanted for officials. He smiled at the resultant jealousies. The only dangerous ones centred round her English friends, and for them a watchful eye was needed. There was one she had brought, Andrew Gray, who had married a Scottish heiress, displacing Scotsmen in her family's favour. The Scots liked him none the better for that. Young Douglas had delighted the discontented by being conspicuously rude to the Englishman a few days ago. Young Douglas had fought in France, and, though he had escaped the slaughter at Verneuil, he did not forget that his father and brother had been hacked down there by English swords. He sat now two places from Gray, muttering to his young friend Hay of Errol. Errol looked the worse for drink. Robert Stewart the cup-bearer stopped to whisper something in their ears: they laughed, but without recovering good-humour. They looked surly enough when Joan laughed towards them, amused at Crichton's wit.

Beside her, seemingly above them all, King James sat in silence. It was only eight years since he had been crowned at Scone, but there was already something legendary about that squat and powerful figure. The superstitious spoke of unseen powers helping him on: he could hardly have done so much unassisted, starting from so little. A country that had forgotten kingship, had seen him make the crown, for good or ill, her ubiquitous and unshakable master: those who had once derided its powers, those who had misused them for private ends, were now converted to loyalty or cowed into impotence. There had been little bloodshed, since the first year—but that little had been sudden, sharp and unhesitating. The Lowlands had needed no second lesson, since Murdoch and his kin died on the Heading Hill. Half a dozen executions, a single battle in Lochaber, had served to tame the Highlands. Mar's greed had provoked a second campaign, but it was soon over. The stars in their courses seemed to fight for King James.

James himself had no thought of unseen powers at work. He had observed, calculated, and acted on his conclusions. If any single force secured his present position, it was the force of money. He was rich now. In the byways of Fife and Menteith, the broken men of Albany might mutter that it was blood money on which the king grew great: they had forgotten that it was their dead masters who had first robbed the crown.

He had a European position. He had defied the Pope successfully, cancelled the tribute his predecessors had paid to Norway, betrothed his daughter, for the first time in Scottish history, to an heir-apparent of France. He had an heir himself. Joan, praying for a son, had been granted twins. They had christened the first Alexander, asking the pardoned Alasdair to stand godfather, in Holyrood Chapel, a year after he had crept there in his penitential shirt. Alexander had not lived six months. But little James was strong and healthy. Joan wanted to call him Rosy-face, because of the birth-mark: Fiery-face, said James, would become a king better. He promised well. King James, if fate were kind, would live another thirty years, and train a son to continue his name and work. The house of Stewart would root itself upon the throne. Douglas might glower and Athol sit weaving endless spiders' webs. The crown was their master, and James could take his ease, smiling at his prelates and barons, at the young men who chattered round his board and glanced towards their king with awe-struck eyes.

He listened to the graver conversation of those near. The Abbot of Melrose had emancipated himself from Mar's stable-anecdotes, and was defending his opinions against an attack from Walter Bower, the young Abbot of Inchcolm: the theme was a hackneyed one—how much Scotland's Kirk owed to St. Columba and its Gaelic founders, how much to Rome. Bower was a patriot and planning to write a history of his country: he was all for native products, and was making slighting references even to King David, who had done so much to Romanize the Kirk. Abbot Fogo was up in arms: it was an outrage, he said, for a young man to speak ill of King David in his own town of Dunfermline. He challenged Bower to go out and look again at the abbey buildings, so largely David's work. "King David was a saint," he said, "if ever there was one."

"He left broad lands to your Melrose Abbey," interposed James, unable to resist the temptation. "Is that what your lordship means?"

"To the whole Kirk, your Majesty!" said Fogo hotly. It was curious to see the lamb-like old man become such a lion in controversy. "King David's saintliness has left memorials everywhere."

"It has indeed," said James. "He was a sore Saint for the Crown. I should have been twice as rich if King David had been less pious."

Fogo looked put out. He was saved from having to answer by a sudden clamour in the body of the hall. Young Hay of Errol had risen from his seat beside Douglas: he had hurled himself in fury at Andrew Gray. Men tried to thrust themselves between them, even Douglas was quick to restrain his friend's folly. Errol's eyes were flashing madly and there was a drawn dagger in his hand, a long, heavy hunting-knife. Crichton caught the wrist behind it, wrenching Errol into immobility: the others had seized his left shoulder. So they stood, suddenly frozen, nothing audible but Errol's gasping breath. Slowly, inevitably, all eyes turned towards the king. It was no light matter to draw steel at the royal board.

The whole company had risen, mutely dissociating itself from the scandal. Errol's hand opened limply, his weapon clattered on to the stone floor; they freed his arms and he stood upright, sufficiently sobered. James sat unmoved, his eyes on the culprit. Mar was whispering something, grinning, into Fogo's unwilling ear.

"Stretch that hand upon the table," said James.

Errol looked at Douglas a moment and then obeyed the king. Even Mar had fallen silent, and there was a hush like death.

"Sir William Crichton, pick up that knife. Give it to Sir Andrew Gray."

Errol's eyelids hardly flickered, his hand rested motionless on the cloth. Douglas took half a step forward, as though about to protest. But no words came, and he stood looking defeatedly at the floor. Crichton stooped to retrieve the weapon, held it out to where Gray stood, pale and reluctant.

"Take it, Sir Andrew, and do me justice. Strike off that man's hand."

Gray's fingers closed slowly on the hilt, but his hand, grasping it, fell back to his side. He looked round the company, as though asking them to witness that he acted, if he must act, under compulsion.

The Abbot of Melrose broke silence, the others following. They begged for a pardon. They reminded James that Errol was his kinsman: that drink and anger may betray the wariest: that the king, being all-powerful, could afford to be merciful. Bishop Cameron, adding prose to their poetry, urged that no blow had been struck.

"A weapon was drawn," said James.

Errol's face had not altered, his hand rested unmoved upon the table. Round him stood his friends, his rivals and enemies, all willing for him to escape the penalty. Behind them were clumps of frightened servants, half fearing, half hoping for the worst. It would be something to tell Dunfermline that great lords could be maimed like common folk.

Still Gray held back. "Your Majesty," he said, "if my voice is needed for this man's pardon, I will gladly give it. I may have angered and provoked him. Whatever offence he did me, I will forget it."

"He has not offended you," said James. "He has offended the king."

Douglas raised his head. "He will not offend again," he said. "If I were to go surety for the future, your Majesty——"

"I am not concerned with the future. I am concerned with what has already happened—and at my board."

The prelates began to speak again, one after the other, urging leniency, promising God's blessing: kings grew great by justice, they said, but sublime by mercy. They knelt in supplication, as if to the altar. Only Mar was still standing, showing his teeth in a faint smile of scorn. To him, a tablecloth was none the worse for a splash of scarlet; and a man whose life was forfeit might count himself lucky if he only lost a hand. The priestly voices rose and fell round him, like healing waters round a defiant rock. James smote on the table, commanding silence. "Sir Andrew Gray!" he said. "Obey my order."

Gray raised his hand. Errol faced him, eyes steady, hand rooted to the table.

"Wait!"

It was Joan's voice. She was standing beside the king, waiting to speak. James rose.

"This is no place for you," he said.

"It is not. This is my dining hall, not a scaffold."

"You need not be present," said James, avoiding her eye. "Your Majesty may withdraw."

"I will not go unless you pardon him," she answered. "He is young. He does not understand the ways of Court."

"He is about to learn them."

"He is our guest."

"And has abused our hospitality!"

"I demand the queen's grace. I have never asked it before. Grace for your Majesty as well as for this man. Your Majesty will repent the judgment tomorrow, cursing your own deed. And you cannot undo it. The man goes crippled for life."

"The crown brooks no repentance. Its Majesty demands justice."

"There are some things more important than a crown!" Her tone was almost defiant.

James looked at her, for the first time, straight in the eyes. She softened a little, began to plead earnestly and passionately. There was nothing unexpected in what she said, nothing compelling: but her manner seemed to imply an obscure warning, a secret, hidden from him and for some reason incommunicable, which made a pardon urgent and imperative. That, too, he felt, could be discounted. Women had strange fancies, and one could not rule a kingdom by their whims.

He was about to turn away, but his eyes sought hers again. He had forgotten how beautiful she was, how much he loved her. She was very near him, warm and fragrant. For a moment he felt tempted to make her stay and witness the bloody compass of his power. Love demanded a sacrifice to mark its triumph, and chance had given him Errol for a victim. Then, obscurely, he knew the impulse for what it was, and expelled it, glad to escape.

He found himself wondering, in slightly shamed fashion, whether she might not be speaking the truth, whether she might not have access to some wisdom he could not share. By the creed he had learnt and made his own, women, for all their outward folly, were in mystical touch with the Divine. In the ultimate matters, birth and death and bloodshed, they might have glimpses denied to men. He saw that she was not pleading for Errol: it was not his victim's hand that she believed to be in peril, so much as his own honour, his prospect of happiness, here or hereafter, the welfare of his soul.

He silenced her with a gesture, and stood thinking, in that hall full of dumb statues, through an intolerable minute.

"You may sheathe the knife," he said. "I will bid the company good night."

Before the obsequious clamour could arise, the flatteries and gratitude, he strode to the dais door, and himself held back the curtains. It pleased him that Joan gave no sign of triumph, had no side-glance for anyone but him. She sailed towards him, the perfect queen, and bowed her head a little as she preceded him through the door.

July 22nd 1433

III

"So you regard the case as a hopeless one, Master Laurence?"

"Quite hopeless. I saw the man privately, between the second and third sessions of the court. I detected no symptoms of repentance." Laurence of Lindores sat grasping the arms of his chair, the throne from which, as Inquisitor General, he had been presiding over a long day's proceedings.

Bishop Wardlaw paced the empty court-room in some agitation. "I hoped," he said, "I have always hoped that Scotland could be kept free of this curse. It is thirty years since we had to—since a heretic suffered. And even then it was not in this diocese."

"Twenty-six," said Laurence, "if you are referring to the man Resby. And may I point out to your lordship that the only way of keeping Scotland free from heresy is to send those who propagate it to the fire. One may indulge in leniency to ignorant men who entertain erroneous opinions. But leniency to those who wilfully teach them is a crime."

"Those, too," said a third voice, "who come here from other countries to infect good Scotsmen with foreign poisons."

It was Walter Bower, the young abbot who had come to represent Inchcolm at the trial. He enjoyed a considerable reputation in his own monastery for scholarship and theological skill; finding it at a discount in St. Andrews, he was all the more inclined to assert himself.

The inquisitor turned on him unmercifully. "The man's origins," he said, "have nothing to do with the matter. If he were a Scotsman, he would still be a heresiarch."

"Oh, certainly," agreed Wardlaw. "It would not alter the case if he were a subject of the Grand Cham. But I cannot help wishing——" He resumed his anxious walk, deciding to keep his wishes to himself.

"I agree, of course," said the persistent Bower. "But I

still think it argues greater guilt for the man to leave Bohemia, which is a nest of heresy in any case, in order to infect such a country as ours. Scotland is famous, among other things, for its strict adherence to the Catholic Faith."

Wardlaw paused, smiling in spite of himself. "You are helping, are you not," he asked, "to write a chronicle of Scotland?"

"I have thought of it, my lord. There seems need of someone to continue Fordun's work into more modern times."

"Then we can be sure," said the bishop, stroking his beard, "that posterity will be left in no doubt about the virtues of Scotland."

Bower suspected ridicule. "Nor," he said hotly, "of the evils of heresy. I have just written——"

The inquisitor cut in sharply upon them.

"We do not wish," he said, "to hear what you may have written. We wish to hear what objections his lordship may have to the sentence of the court being executed tomorrow."

"Tomorrow?" Wardlaw looked up in surprise.

"Certainly. As I have just told you, there is not the slightest chance of getting the man to repent, or even acknowledge his guilt. The sooner he is . . . eradicated, the better for everybody."

"I suppose so, I suppose so. All the same . . ." Again Wardlaw found it impossible to give expression to the vague doubt that hovered at the back of his mind. Laurence of Lindores was not a man in whose company one found it easy to put formless hesitations into words.

"In which case," said Lindores, after a barely respectful pause, "I must request your lordship to put the matter to his Majesty tonight. The condemned is already in the hands of the civil officers, but they will want his Majesty's confirmation, since he happens to be at St. Andrews."

"Yes, I suppose so," said the bishop. "Do you know, Master Rector, I almost wish that he were not?"

"If you think he is likely to show any weakness——"

"Oh, no. Oh, no. Far from it." Wardlaw waved a deprecating hand. "But the very fact that Holy Kirk hands her excommunicated children over to be punished by temporal power, seems to me to imply that there must be some offence, some slight taint in the shedding of blood—even heretic blood. It certainly excites odium in weak and discontented spirits. I feel it would be more honest if we could bear that odium by executing our own sentences ourselves."

"It is mainly a question of custom," answered the inquisitor, "and of avoiding conflict with the temporal power. In any case, since the odium you speak of is clearly unjustified, there seems no reason why Holy Kirk should not place the burden on other shoulders than her own. I do not think it is a very crushing one."

"Unless my observation is at fault," put in Bower, "the name of heresy is so detested in this country that more people would ask why Holy Kirk declines the glory of stamping it out with her own hand."

"She does so in effect," said the inquisitor, and rose from his chair. He waited a moment, until Bower also was on his feet. "And now, my lord," he said to Wardlaw, "may I assume that you will confer with his Majesty as soon as possible? You have told us that this will be the first execution for heresy ever held in your diocese. May I remind you that there will be . . . arrangements to be made, wood to be purchased and so forth? These things cannot be done by merely thinking about them."

Seeing Wardlaw silent, he presumed assent, and made his way, past empty benches, towards the door. Then he thought of something and turned back.

"It is curious," he said, "that you should mention the question of his Majesty's personal views. The accused asked me, when I saw him in private, whether he could appeal to the crown."

"On what ground?"

"On no valid one. He seemed to think that all foreigners were, in some special sense, under royal protection. I suppose he hoped to make an impression on his Majesty, so as to prejudice the proceedings in his favour. I told him, of course, that Canon Law takes no cognizance of nationality in cases of heresy."

"You were right, I suppose," answered Wardlaw. "All the same, I may as well mention the matter, when I speak to his Majesty."

"You think that wise?"

"I think it might be unwise not to do so. After all, we do not wish any loophole to be left for complaints against our procedure."

"Well, so long as you can guarantee us," said the inquisitor, "against unwarranted interference!" There was a faint, a very faint glint in his eye, such as one might see in a cat's when she suspects that some arbitrary human may deprive her of the captured prey beneath her paw. It was unexpected in one so passionless, so utterly logical, as Master Laurence of Lindores. It roused again in Bishop Wardlaw the vague uneasiness that he had contrived to forget. But they were almost at the door, Wardlaw leading, before he found words again.

"Do you know, my dear rector," he said, half turning back, "what my difficulty is about heresy? No one could detest it more than I do, and there certainly seems no method of preventing its spread except the rather extreme one that we are now using. But . . ."

He paused, looking back at his companions. There was an almost comic consternation beginning to appear on Bower's face, as though he feared some scandalous indiscretion from the bishop and was prepared to mistrust his ears. Laurence of Lindores was perfectly self-possessed. He raised a thin eyebrow.

"But——?" he said.

"Well," faltered Wardlaw, "I know that our Lord drove the sinners out of the Temple with a whip, in righteous indignation. His Apostle even commanded anger—'Be angry and sin not.' But I always find it hard to picture Him, in cold blood, putting His hand to a faggot or the handle of a rack. And I find it even harder to picture Him consigning a sinner into the hands of the temporal power—shall we say Pontius Pilate's?—to be burnt at the stake."

He fell silent, watching their faces harden. The inquisitor's was almost dangerous.

"But I suppose I am getting old," continued Wardlaw, weakly, "one loses one's grip of practical matters as one approaches the eternal ones. I certainly do not wish to face my Creator in the consciousness that I had said anything to deter you from your duty."

He left them standing in the doorway, and passed on to his palace, wondering how soon King James could spare time for an audience. Bower waited in silence, awed for once by what he had heard. This was an occasion, he felt, when the inquisitor for Scotland should be the first to speak. The inquisitor's opening observation was not very helpful.

"You overheard?" he asked.

Bower had heard or overheard, put it as one liked. He could hardly help it, at a distance of two yards.

"You will be pleased to remember," said Laurence drily, "what his lordship said about being an old man. Human frailty grows with age, particularly intellectual frailty. I think the correct course would be to forget his lordship's words."

"Certainly. If you wish it."

"I do not wish. I order." The inquisitor's eyes searched Bower, as though for signs of contumacy. They appeared to be satisfied at last, finding only submission. It looked almost as if Master Laurence of Lindores was about to smile, perhaps for the first time in several years. He did not go quite so far, but the tone of his next words suggested that he was deciding, if only for the avoidance of scandal, to treat the incident as lightly as his nature permitted.

"And I hope," he said, "if you ever come to write this chronicle you are planning, that there will be no reference to his lordship's lapse. It might lead posterity to make false deductions about the Kirk in Scotland."

"Your Reverence can rest assured," answered Bower, "that posterity shall hear nothing of the matter."

James was staying with the bishop—his usual practice when he visited St. Andrews without Joan. Wardlaw's extravagance might be considered a slight scandal among his colleagues, but it at least made his palace a pleasant house to visit.

James heard the bishop's report in silence, and with a certain reluctance. One was always glad to do Holy Church a service, if only to repay her—or her Scottish branch—for years of loyal support. But, with so many scoundrels and murderers to put to death, there was no pleasure in adding heretics to the number, folk who were generally admitted (but for their infectious opinions) to be rather better than their neighbours.

"I shall not be able to attend myself," he said. "I must be in Dundee tomorrow night, and the tide never waits for a king's convenience."

"No, your Majesty." Wardlaw looked, if anything, relieved. "I see no advantage in your Majesty's attendance."

"Well, I'll sign anything they want signed." James turned to Sir Robert Stewart, waiting at his elbow. "Get a message sent to the Provost," he said. "I can see him in two hours' time."

He watched the young man depart, and began to fidget with the ring on his finger. "I am sorry I cannot be your lordship's guest for longer," he said. "This place is full of pleasant memories for me."

"I am glad they are pleasant," said Wardlaw. He seemed relieved to pass to any other subject than the one they had been discussing. "I also look back on the old days as happy ones."

"Your other pupil does you little credit," said James. "Young Percy is Earl of Northumberland now, but his brain is thicker than ever. He gave the whole game into my hands at Coldingham."

Wardlaw stroked his soft beard. "I have noticed," he said, "that the English often choose their less intelligent countrymen for missions that demand delicate handling." He smiled at his own irony, and was disappointed to see that James seemed hardly to have heard. The king had gone grave again, fiddling with his ring.

"What is the man's name again?" he asked. "Master Laurence's quarry?"

"Crawar, your Majesty, Paul Crawar—as far as we could make it out: Bohemian is a strange tongue. He came here to practise medicine, presumably as a blind to his heretical mission. He had some small successes as a doctor, and they increased his influence with ignorant townspeople."

"Naturally, naturally. And did you say he appealed to the crown?"

"So the rector tells me."

"Curious. I wonder if I ought to see him."

"Surely that would be most unwise, your Majesty?" Wardlaw looked positively uncomfortable.

"I see no harm," said James. "I can promise you that he shall not convert me!"

"Oh, no. I was not imagining——"

"If it's assassination you are thinking of, I fancy I can protect myself against a saw-bones from Prague. Or shall I have Robbie Stewart here with a drawn sword?"

Wardlaw looked a little hurt. "As it happens," he said, "this man's heresy does not incite him against temporal princes. Rather the reverse."

"I see," said James, more soberly. "But I think I had better speak to him, in any case. I dislike leaving appeals to the crown unanswered, from whatever quarter."

It was a strange, rather repellent atmosphere that seemed to hang round Paul Crawar. It was not merely the fear of an imminent and terrible death that he brought into the room with him, inevitably affecting its occupants. He was foreign, speaking in ugly, grating accents: sallow and ill-favoured, like many of his race; dressed in fusty clothes like those of a petty Edinburgh tradesman. But apart from this, there was a feeling that he moved in some other and unintelligible world, where the laws that govern most men's lives are repudiated or reversed, where unnamed possibilities threaten unnamed dangers. The harsh, pedantic voice, dry in the throat, seemed familiar with ideas that sane men ignore, abstractions that rob life of its colour and the comforting limitations that shield it from despair.

He was tired as well as woebegone. They had not tortured him, but he had had no respite from unequal argument through a week and more: the recurrent circle of accusation and defence seemed to have bitten an inescapable channel in his brain. James could picture Laurence of Lindores, trained and self-trained to the game, driving him point by point from every position, and yet never, perhaps, understanding the secret of the man's obstinacy, nor making his own motive understood. As James listened to Crawar now, feverishly attempting to justify himself at the last moment, he could hardly believe that the man could be a danger, so out of touch did he seem with other minds. Poor people, of course, artisans and merchants had different ways of looking at life, and might feel the contagion. For their sake, the Church had to condemn the most extravagant views. One had heard of heretics that had tried to abolish marriage, called property un-Christian, run naked through the streets. John Hus, whom Crawar no doubt reverenced, had thought it sinful to play chess. Holy Church had her faults, but she was certainly a bulwark against some crushing absurdities.

Master Laurence had insisted on being present at the interview. Every time he interrupted with some relentless comment, Crawar fell dumb, as if knowing the uselessness of answer. One saw why he had attempted to appeal to the king.

He should have known by now that nothing on earth could save him from the fire, hardly even a rescript from the Pope—whose authority he had impugned. He clearly knew all the details of James's quarrel with Rome, and would have made capital out of it if he could. There was no warrant in Scripture, he said, for papal tyranny: he had his own interpretation of Christ's charge to Peter.

"Your Majesty observes," said the inquisitor, "what use can be made of the Bible when it is put into the hands of every Jock and Jenny."

"What authority *does* he accept?" asked James. "Who is to govern us?"

"Himself and his like," said the inquisitor contemptuously. "Their own inner enlightenment, which the Devil plants in them."

Crawar was looking at the king. "The Church himself," he said, "condemn one Pope in rape and sodomy. Must we obey such man?"

"He is thinking of the anti-Pope John," said Bishop Wardlaw.

"Does it matter?" objected Laurence, "No man is free from sin. If sin is to invalidate a man's powers, in Church or State, there is an end of all obedience. Your Majesty would give cause for treason every time you swore an oath in anger."

"We do not counsel rebellion against princes," said Crawar. "Some of us think that, in each nation, the prince should rule the Church."

"Is that what your Wicliffe meant," asked Laurence, "when he spoke of God obeying the Devil?"

"Perhaps," said Crawar sullenly.

"And you really believe," asked James, "that such a teacher spoke the truth?"

"I believe he spoke more truthful than the bishops who burnt his books. And I am to die for that faith—unless your Majesty will save me."

"I cannot save you," said James. "The most I could do"—he saw the inquisitor stir uneasily—"is to persuade you to recant and save yourself."

"He has been given every opportunity——" began Master Laurence. Wardlaw, moving unexpectedly, waved him into silence. It was a long one, Crawar standing motionless, inconceivably lonely, in their midst. When at last he spoke, it was without raising his face from the ground.

"I cannot do that," he said.

Laurence of Lindores sat back in his chair. The other two were still leaning forward, watching.

"Can you tell us why?" asked James.

There was no answer this time, and James felt bound, at whatever cost, to persevere.

"The inquisitor will have told you," he said, "that I have no power to save you. We are all subject to Holy Kirk—and you do not tempt me with your schemes for putting her beneath my feet. But if you will save yourself by recantation, I can see that you do not suffer tomorrow. I ask you again, what reason can you have for rejecting this mercy? If you think yourself wiser than Holy Church, wiser than the whole human family, you should at least be able to tell us your reason."

Again there was a long and heavy silence. Crawar looked round at the three faces, and then down to the floor again, shifting on his feet. He had reached the end at last, and the final, flimsiest hope was torn from him. The king would not and could not save him from tomorrow's blinding terror. Conscience forbade him to save himself. He stood more upright now, the tired look seemed to fall from his hunted face. He was transfigured—the certain prospect of death working upon him as death itself on other men. When he began to speak, the harshness, the pedantry, were no longer noticeable.

Half of what he said was barely intelligible, much of it fantastic. His aims, so far as one could understand, presupposed impossibilities. Yet one had to listen, one had to try and understand. The inquisitor would have silenced him, but James forbade it with a gesture. James's mind seemed to be groping, past the man's absurdities, for some strange vision that lay behind—something forgotten or maybe yet unborn: a world, if it could have been realized, where Christ's words had become the immediate stuff of ordinary life and all the ugliness of the channels whereby the Church diffuses them had vanished like a nightmare.

The glimpse was as fleeting as it was fanciful. The next minute he could see nothing but an obstinate foreigner in seedy clothes, preaching formulas that had long been refuted.

The man himself saw that he was losing his audience. Laurence had closed his eyes some time ago, and Wardlaw stared patiently at his folded hands. Crawar spoke only to James, and now with the insistence of conscious failure.

"You tell to me," he said, "that I think myself wiser than all other. No, I know myself ignorant man. The Apostles were ignorant men. I am not worthy as them, but I believe. And now if you kill me, I know more than you. Master Hus, he said, 'Who is killed, he is conqueror.' I think, too, that what I believed yesterday, I *know* now—because I die. What Master Inquisitor and my lord here will never know, unless someone kill them for the Faith. What your Majesty will never know in this world."

He ceased speaking, and without waiting for dismissal, made for the door. But he reached it with faltering steps, as though doubt were already returning.

"I would say no more to you," said James. "You have chosen. God must judge us all."

The phrase seemed trite. It perhaps invited the inquisitor's comment, which came as soon as Crawar had departed.

"I would remind your Majesty," he said, "that God, in the person of His Church, has already judged. I told your Majesty that no good could come of tampering with her decision."

"I am not sure of that," said Wardlaw. "We may at least have shown his Majesty that the danger of heresy is a real one. As you know, my dear rector, I am reluctant to admit the necessity of extreme measures: but I must confess, after what we have just heard——! My hair stood on end at some of the things he said."

"Fortunately," said Master Laurence, "most people feel the same in this country. As Bower of Inchcolm assures us, Scotland is not a promising field for those who would sow heresy."

James raised an eyebrow, wondering if Bower and Master Laurence knew Scotland as well as they imagined.

"Scotsmen are certainly unlikely," said Wardlaw, "to listen to those who are so obviously under diabolical influence."

"Did you notice," said Laurence, almost eagerly, "how the Devil is gaining on him now that Holy Kirk has pronounced excommunication? He seemed to think that his approaching punishment was in itself a sign that he was wiser than us."

"Wiser," said Wardlaw, "than we will ever be. That is what he said."

"I think," said James slowly, "that he was wrong there. There is a Calvary awaiting all of us—kings and prelates as well as heretics."

He was glad to see that, though the inquisitor was looking at him with searching indignation, old Wardlaw seemed hardly to grasp the implication of his words.

January 1435

IV

A windowless room, draughty and yet stuffy, smelling of wool, hides, and worse. A warehouse. Not what Sir Richard Whittington or his London aldermen would call a warehouse, but handy enough by the standards of Perth. Handier still—since it stood in a back street like the Water Vennel—for activities more questionable than commerce. For one purpose or the other, it served its owners well.

They were considered, in Perth, to cherish notions above their present station—especially Christopher, the elder brother. Both had been born gentlefolk, but Thomas had taken to trade early, while Christopher was playing squire to Albany, warden, at need, of Doune Castle: all that was over since Murdoch died. Christopher and Thomas Chalmers had climbed the Heading Hill and stood among the weeping crowd, saying farewell to the house of Albany and to their own hopes of being more than petty merchants. Thomas had wept with the rest, when the three magnificent creatures, Murdoch, Lennox, and young Alexander, were transformed, by stroke of sword, to twitching bundles on the grass. Christopher had not wept. But neither of the brothers, since that day, had been loyal subjects of King James.

They must earn a living, and could not even hint to others at the secret enmity. But they could keep friendship with those who misliked the king's ways, harbour them from time to time, as they were now harbouring one in their evil-smelling warehouse. In a corner, hidden from the street door, Robin Graham was dozing on some empty sacks, recouping himself for several sleepless nights.

They came to rouse him at nightfall, when the South Street shop was closed. Thomas had the key of the Water Vennel warehouse, for Thomas was accounted leader in the partnership. But he talked to Robin of indifferent matters, handing him food and ale from under his gown, until Christopher pushed his way in from the street.

Even then there was little to say. All arrangements had been made; Robin could bring his father from the Highlands as soon as he liked to come. There was a fortnight yet before Parliament opened at Perth; a mild January made travelling easy, even by night. Sir Robert would be able to talk to the lords of Parliament, at their lodgings or elsewhere, during the early sessions. Whether or no he could get them to listen and form a party to thwart the king's will—that was another matter.

"We have had letters," Robin told his shelterers, "promises of assistance. Father says that King James has tripped himself up at last, robbing the Earl of March. They'll not stand much more of his forfeitures."

"It'll be seven years since the last," said Thomas cautiously, "seven years since he deprived Malise. You cannot just call it a habit."

"He'll make it a habit," said Robin, up in arms at once, "if he's successful this time!"

"He'll not be successful," said Christopher, "if your father can get the other earls to stand firm."

"If!" said Thomas. He took the ale-bottle from Robin: politics were politics, but there was no need to see good liquor wasted. "I'm thinking the earls are like other folk," he said. "They'll get angry when a man takes what does not belong to him, but they'll *do* little till it's their own gear he's after."

"When it's too late?" asked Robin.

"When it's too late," said Thomas. "Folk are silly cattle, most of them." He looked at the bottle in his hand. "Will you be wanting any more?" he asked.

Robin ignored the question. He was looking at Thomas in some distaste. His father would do little if he had to rely on such slow, money-minded assistance. Luckily, Christopher, so like his brother in some ways, was poles apart in others. They had the same eyes, the same dark hair. But Christopher's cheeks had stayed spare and almost haggard while his brother's were rounding into portliness. His voice too was sharp and high, his movements exact and decisive: Thomas rumbled and fumbled. It was hard to believe that Thomas was indeed the younger.

"When is the king coming?" asked Robin. "Will he be here before the opening?"

He looked at Christopher, but it was Thomas that replied. "Tuesday week," he said. "I saw Sir Robert Stewart the chamberlain yesterday, about the hangings up at the castle. He won't let me supply new ones, though the ones he has were woven before King Robert died."

"Maybe he's wanting to buy elsewhere," said Christopher, remembering trade for once.

"He'll not dare!" answered his brother. "The king owes me too much money—unpaid yet. He could not take his custom from us."

"I doubt he'll not keep to the castle much longer," said Christopher. "It's three parts ruin. He'll build himself a new one out of the customs money. He's building everywhere." He sat down on a bale of wool, nursing his hatred of King James.

"Is Sir Robert Stewart in Perth now?" asked Robin.

"No. Rode away to Methven last night, to see his grandfather. And starting back for Linlithgow today. So he said."

"Why do you ask?" said Christopher.

"No reason. My father spoke of him. He might join us, for all he's a king's officer. You can never tell—with Athol's house."

"They might be useful," said Christopher, "so long as you don't trust 'em too far. I've a notion that Duke Murdoch, God rest his soul, trusted old Athol too far."

"My brother," said Thomas, "has a deal of notions about Duke Murdoch—most of them fancies. I keep telling him you can't afford fancies when you're in trade."

"Nor in politics," said Robin, looking older than his age.

"You may be right about the chamberlain, even about old Athol. They're a power in Scotland. I'll have another talk about it to my father."

He rose, stretching cramped limbs. "And the horses?" he asked.

"What horses?" said Thomas.

"Well; whatever we come on will have to be sent back to the Highlands. We'll want something here, ready any day, in case things go wrong and my father has to leave Perth with King James's men at his heels."

"If it's horses," said Thomas, "you'll be better to ask Chris." He looked at the ale-bottle in his hand. It was far from empty and certainly enticing. But maybe it would look better if he waited till he were home. He put back the stopper and concealed the bottle under his gown again.

"That'll be arranged for," his brother was saying. "If things begin to look dangerous, we can bring 'em round and hide 'em in here." He looked at the available space, calculating what sacks might have to be moved.

"I'll not have them soiling my linen," said Thomas, patting a bale. "Look at that now, Master Robin. That's Dornewyk, that is. Came in the *Lion* from Campveer to Dundee. And what I had to pay for it there in customs would buy King James another set of hangings, curse him, if he'd only buy as he ought."

Robin was not interested. He was already following Christopher to the door.

"And you think," asked Christopher in a low voice, "that your father can do the trick in Parliament?"

Robin paused before answering. "We must try that first," he said.

"Will you let him know one thing?" said Christopher. "Will you tell him that if it fails, Chris Chalmers is still with him—and to the end." And he made a gesture—in a manner surprisingly expert for a merchant—that boded no good to King James.

January 1435

V

James was riding out to Kinnoul. He had been thinking for a long time of visiting the old lady of Kinnoul. Now at last he had leisure and a spell of fine weather.

He had reached Perth earlier than necessary, for Parliament had been postponed for a day or two. His preparations for it were completed. There was likelihood of trouble, but he could do little to guard against it until he knew from what quarter it threatened. His agents were puzzled and could only guess at what was in the wind. Young Stewart the chamberlain, who should have known most of the doings of the nobility, refused even to guess: he merely put a sullen expression on his handsome features, and implied that it was not his business to act as King James's spy.

It was presumably the nobility that would make trouble. James had decided to repeat the turn he had played on Malise, successfully, seven years ago. He was forfeiting the Earldom of March.

The crown needed more land and wealth before it could be secure. The reviving power of the Douglas was only one of many that might soon be able to challenge it—in his son's reign, if not his own. And the March earldom was not only wealthy, it was exceedingly dangerous in any hands but the king's. It lay, as its name implied, at the gateway of the country: old Dunbar, holding the earldom for King Robert, had played Scotland false and brought in English armies that captured Edinburgh and Leith. Albany had pardoned the old fool, as he pardoned most traitors: he had allowed his son, young George Dunbar, to inherit the earldom. James had recently declared the pardon invalid, the land forfeit to the crown. He had a poor case, legally, but the crown must be above law or perish. Dunbar had been arrested before he could make trouble, and was being compensated with another earldom, up in Buchan. The trouble would come from his friends.

It was no good anticipating it. It was better to enjoy a fine winter day, to ride beside Joan across Tay and up the hill of Kinnoul: to speculate, not without laughter, on Lady Erskine's age. She could hardly be as old as they made her out, unless she had Methuselah among her ancestors; but she was long past attending Courts, and had been blind for many years now. She would be able to remember the days of David Bruce, the great Bruce's son. If she was the staunch old lady they reported her, she would remember them with distaste: David had been a poor creature, always hankering for the fleshpots of England; he would have sold the crown —if they had let him—to Edward of Westminster. James hoped for the old lady's blessing and approval, if only by contrast with the King David of her youth. "And I shall remind her," he told Joan gaily, "that we Stewarts inherited from the lass—Bruce's daughter, not his scapegrace son."

"Will she need reminding? They say she knows everyone's great-grandparents."

"Then you had better not tell her who you are. There's a King Edward among yours!"

It did not take them long to reach a little-used track, branching leftward from the Dundee road. It led uphill, through thick belts of trees, where tradition said that Tay had once made a vast loch, dragon-infested, before reaching the sea at Lunan Bay. At the top of a long avenue stood Kinnoul Castle, old-fashioned but in better repair than they expected, trimmer, as Joan ruefully observed, than their own castle at Perth bridgehead.

They rode into the courtyard to find tables spread for their reception and a host of gaily dressed Erskines, ladies for the most part, curtseying on the flagstones. The entrance to the living rooms had once been a matter of a ladder, removable in time of assaults, but a stairway had been built to reach the ledge of the door. Half-way up it stood an old lady, surveying what, one imagined, was largely a company of her own descendants—girls of eighteen and matrons of forty or more. Joan saw at once that she could hardly be within years of the miraculous age with which gossip credited her: eighty, she judged, at most. She did not even seem blind. Her eyes followed them as she rose from her stiff obeisance. But neither Joan nor James was prepared for her first words.

"We are more than honoured by your Majesties' visit," she said. "I will tell my grandmother that your Majesties are come."

One stood paralysed, glad that no answer was called for. To judge by the way the younger girls were watching, the same comedy had been played on guests before—if not for a king's benefit. James preserved the utmost gravity.

"We shall be happy to receive her," he said. "Or to come up to her room, if we can spare her the discomfort of descending."

Lady Erskine, it appeared, was in no mind to spare herself. She emerged from the door and climbed down, past her granddaughter, feeling before her with a stick. There was little other sign of decrepitude, and even the blindness was not self-evident, while she was moving on ground that a century had made familiar. There seemed to be a certain life in the white film of her eyes as she was led lightly to the king. He would not let her stoop to kiss his hand, and insisted on a chair for her at once. "So kind," she said, "so kind," and asked if she might put a hand on his shoulder before they sat. James guessed that she had heard tales of his lack of inches. She concealed any disappointment she might feel at finding them confirmed. But when she was presented to Joan, she seemed uninterested to the point of discourtesy.

"Kinnoul is honoured indeed," she said, peering back in James's direction. "I get few visitors, and these children of mine only come to see me when I have guests to receive. It takes a king to bring so many of them together."

"They make a fine sight," said James gallantly. "You must tell me how many are unmarried, and I will see if I can find husbands for them when the lords meet for Parliament next week."

The old lady expressed her thanks and was then understood to mutter something about the baggages being quick enough to find husbands for themselves. Maidenly modesty, one gathered, had died out in Scotland, during Lady Erskine's lifetime.

The presentations, lengthy enough, were enlivened by her somewhat tart comments on the many members of her family whose conduct had fallen beneath her own standards. One, a widow of fifty, had once allowed herself to be betrothed to an English lord. "We soon put a stop to that," said Lady Erskine, but implied that the lapse left a certain stain.

She was eager for news, hearing little, she said, since her daughter had died: her servants were mostly numskulls, reporting things that no one in his senses would believe. She seemed doubtful about several things that James told her, pursing thin lips and suspending judgment. Her family generally managed to cover the resultant pauses with some change of subject, and once Joan stepped into the breach.

"His Majesty was hoping," she said, "to hear news from you. He was saying that you would be able to tell us about King David's Court."

A flutter of suppressed dismay was followed by awkward silence, before Lady Erskine spoke.

"There are plenty who could tell his Majesty of that," she said. "It is not a pleasant subject. I would rather speak of my girlhood. Few of my contemporaries can be living now, and those times should certainly be kept in memory as long as possible. My grandfather used to talk as though Scotland reached her highest glory in King Alexander's time. But I am sure that Largs was a small affair compared with Bannockburn. I can remember how we all felt when we heard the news of that."

There was a pause before James could collect himself. "Is it discourteous," he said, "to ask your ladyship's age?"

"No, no. But I fear that I am never quite sure. They

tell me I was born while Edward was besieging Stirling, before he murdered Sir William Wallace. But he besieged it more than once." She grew inaudible, and then said with sudden clearness: "But he never took it, of course!"

James did some rapid calculations; most of them ended by giving him a figure in the region of a hundred and thirty. It did not seem impossible; nothing seemed impossible today.

"My wife should have asked you," he said, "for your memories of the Bruce."

"Perhaps," said the old lady grimly, "your wife finds him an unwelcome topic. Many of her countrymen used to do so, in the old days."

Joan tried to pass it off lightly. "We have no reminders of such ancient disagreements in England," she said; "few of us contrive to live so long as your ladyship."

Lady Erskine said nothing.

"The queen," said James, "has only one grudge against the Bruce, and I share it. He hardly left us a single royal castle to live in, and my father and grandfather did little to build up what he had dismantled."

"The Bruce was right," said the old lady with sudden energy. "Castles harbour English thieves. They take them with those cowardly engines of theirs, and it costs good Scottish blood to get them back. It is better to rely on knights and spearmen than silly stones. How many of them do the English hold now?"

"Only Roxburgh and Berwick," said James. "Close upon the Border. The Bruce has done his work, and there is peace."

"But of course," said Lady Erskine, pursuing her own thoughts. "Men were men in those days. The Bruce was taller than any man since him, and twice as strong. And Wallace, they say, was half a head above the Bruce."

She sat staring fiercely before her, clutching the top of her stick as if it had been a sword-pommel.

"Perhaps," she said, after a moment, "her Majesty would

like to see the garden. They tell me they have built a garden under the west wall, and Englishwomen, I believe, are interested in such things. Children!"

Several middle-aged ladies hastened forward to conduct Joan to the despised garden. There seemed to be a general agreement that the manœuvre might avoid further and more awkward embarrassments.

"And now," said Lady Erskine, as soon as they were gone, "I must ask your Majesty's leave to retire. I find the wind trying. I am not so young as I was."

James offered her his arm, and she accepted it with dignity. At the top of the steps, she stood, panting a little, before taking final leave.

"They tell me," she said, as she recovered breath, "that your Majesty has had troubles in the kingdom. Among the Highlandmen, and elsewhere."

"They are right, your ladyship. I am glad to say that I have got the better of them now."

He wondered, as he said it, how far it was true, and what troubles awaited him still—in Parliament for instance. But one would not wish to vex this old spirit with tales of disquiet.

"I was told that you had done so," she said. "Scotsmen are so foolish, fighting one another. We are a small nation, if a strong one. We need to remain united."

"Your ladyship speaks truth. I have spent the ten years of my reign preaching the same doctrine, at times by force of arms. As I was saying, I believe that I have converted all who count."

"I am glad to hear you say so," answered Lady Erskine, laying a hand upon his shoulder. "Your Majesty will now be free to prosecute the war. I take it that the present truce need not last much longer?"

There was a pause before James spoke. "And I," he said stiffly, "trust that the truce will soon be changed into a lasting peace. This country needs peace, and we have no quarrel with England."

Lady Erskine seemed to consider this a moment, but to no purpose. "I do not understand that," she said.

"Times change, your ladyship."

"There are things that never change."

"The world would be a sorry place if old hatreds did not die."

She had no answer to that, or none that she thought worth giving. James saw that she had shut her mind against any attempt to understand it. She stood blinking resentfully in the wintry sun. The thousand wrinkles of her face cast a thousand etched shadows, like the ridged terraces of some Highland glen. He suddenly felt an immense pity for her, not unmixed with reverence: it seemed terrible that such force and loyalty as hers should be hardened and sharpened towards the one narrow issue, that a century of life could do nothing to give the soul larger wings.

"I will trouble your Majesty no further," she said. "I can make my own way, now that I am on the level."

She left James standing on the top step. She tapped her way into the shadow of the doorway and down the cold passage. She muttered to herself and scolded at servants who came forward to assist her. She reached her own room. Long after James had rejoined Joan and cantered back through the checkered sunlight of her avenue, she sat rigid on her hard stool, refusing comfort.

"With his own mouth," she repeated, "with his own mouth he told me that they were still in Roxburgh and Berwick!"

January 1435

VI

In the Charterhouse of Perth, King James's own foundation, young Lord Orkney sat by a comfortable fire and listened, not without protests, to the Graham's opinion of King James.

"You talk dangerously," he was objecting. "We want no Highland feuds in Parliament. And my house, Sir Robert, has always held with the king."

"And been ill-rewarded for it!" Graham flashed back the unthinking answer. "Your lordship will pardon me," he continued, "but I cannot think that the name of Sinclair stands as high under King James as its services deserve. Your lordship's father did all he could to ransom him from England. He——"

"He could do no less," answered Orkney. "He was in charge of Prince James's ship when it was captured, eighteen years before. He was glad to make his somewhat belated amends."

"But, your lordship——"

Graham had halted in his restless stride. His mind did not right itself quickly after checks to his eloquence. He had been living too long in rough places, with no intellectual equal to interrupt—or even understand—his diatribes.

Orkney, with hardly so profound a mind, had managed to pull him up short more than once: he was barely thirty, but accustomed to make his objections tell. His father had died of the plague, and left him earl in boyhood, heir to Norwegian jarls, master of Caithness, and indisputably the most powerful man in the far north. It was almost by courtesy, one felt, that he accepted the summons to come to Perth for a Parliament. It was certainly a concession to grant Sir Robert Graham, though twice his age, a private interview by evening, in his handsomely furnished lodgings in the Charterhouse. Few men in Graham's position would have asked such a thing, fewer still demanded that it be kept secret from the king. And Orkney, the indulgence accorded, was not the kind of young man to let Graham put faulty argument upon him, with whatever rhetoric.

"You had better come to more recent times," he said. "We were discussing tomorrow's business."

"Tomorrow's business," answered Graham, "is of a piece with all business in this poor country. The king takes what he pleases and gives as little as he can contrive. The nobility, and your lordship among them, has spared neither gold nor service to put him where he is, almost above opposition, far above legality. Yet he treats you as dogs. He keeps your sons and kinsmen in English prisons, hostages for his unpaid ransom. He——"

"We could ransom them ourselves," said Orkney, "if we would spare the money. You need not tell me that old Athol could not buy his son back if he cared to pinch himself a little at Methven. For that matter, if the lot of us combined to raise a tax, we could finish up the whole business."

"Your lordships would have to take care," said Graham, "to manage it yourselves. If the money passed through the royal coffers, it would go to building King James a new castle."

"He needs one, at Perth," said Orkney flippantly. "I can hardly listen to denunciations of his building work, sitting in the Charterhouse he founded." Despite his words, he felt there was some truth in what Graham had said. He sipped a cup of wine, wondering whether he could express his agreement; he decided that there was little point in encouraging an already inflamed discontent.

"I consider it most unselfish of his Majesty," he said in the same light tone, "to bring over Carthusians. Being married, he has to lodge in that mouldy ruin by the bridge. Bachelors like me can enjoy the hospitality of his new foundation."

He took another sip of wine. The Charterhouse monks might not allow themselves ladies for guests, but their cellar was some compensation.

Graham watched the young man drink. He refused to accept diversion from his purpose, let alone defeat. Orkney should be promising-enough material. A personable creature, but no trifler at bottom. Dark and rather sallow, wiry in limb, like the Highlandmen: taller than most Highlandmen, as much a Norwegian, or maybe Norman, as a Scot. But Graham disliked the little moustache above the smiling mouth, the gold rings gleaming in the candle-light.

"I would beg your lordship," he said, "to listen seriously to serious matters. Our time is short, and I am in some danger."

"You have been trying to raise opposition, in Parliament, to his Majesty's decision about the March earldom?"

"I have been hoping your lordships would do so, now that he is condescending to acquaint you, formally, with the injustice he has already done."

"Some of us," said Orkney, "may have known of it at the time. Angus enforced the forfeiture and arrested Dunbar."

"With a Crichton and a Livingston to assist him!" Graham's grey eyes besieged Orkney's face, demanding an answer to their indignation from within. "My lord of Angus," he said, "may work beside King James's jumped-up foundlings. The other earls are asking why all offices are kept for bonnet-lairds and poor scholars from Wardlaw's college!"

"Sir Robert Stewart holds the chamberlainship. The Stewarts, I believe, boast of good blood." A Sinclair could talk that way, and no one know how far he jested. Orkney reckoned Odin and Thor among his forebears and a less questionable pedigree, hung on his walls at Freswick, was longer than the king's.

"Sir Robert Stewart," countered Graham, "has little more than the name of chamberlain. He tells me himself that he is elbowed away from all that matters: he is powerless against Crichton and Cameron and the rest."

Orkney stirred slightly. So this fanatic, he thought, has been talking to Stewart too? It was not surprising to hear what he had gleaned. The whole Athol family had been born discontented. It was almost a relief to hear that young Robert was content to grumble to Graham—when his old grandfather, in the days before he was bald and discredited, would have been intriguing for his low-born rivals' deaths.

Orkney rose from his chair.

"Well, Sir Robert," he said, "I will weigh what you have said. I think there is sense in it, as well as exaggeration. But I must wait to see how matters shape—and particularly what the other lords of Parliament are doing. How many have you seen?"

Graham hesitated before speaking. Then he glanced round, approached the table, and spoke in a low voice. He had a formidable list to present, for half Scotland's soil was represented at Perth, and Graham had not been idle. He tried to give the impression that all were pledged to peremptory, unyielding action. He had some justification where the kinsmen of Dunbar were concerned, and the wreckage of the Albany confederation. The other lords had been more non-committal, though none defended King James's outrage. It had been left to this young man from the far north to remain so coldly poised.

"Will you have some wine before you go?" said Orkney, when Graham had finished. "Pour yourself out a cup."

Graham did as he was bid. At the first taste, he found that his throat was drier than he had known.

"I have heard," said Orkney, "that you make it your business to know everything. Can you tell me if there is any news of the French ships setting out for Dumbarton?"

"I have heard nothing," answered Graham, and gulped a second draught. Then, as he set down the cup, a new thought struck him, making him look up at Orkney's averted profile. The Frenchmen were coming, this year or next, to take the Princess Margaret away, and marry her to their king's son: an escort, and a large one, would be needed, if she was to escape the same fate as her father. Orkney was hoping for the command of it, hoping to be created Lord Admiral for all Scotland. He would sail into La Rochelle with pomp befitting the guardian of a queen. He would prink it among the Frenchmen, angle for French lordships with Darnley and the rest. Now that King Eric of Norway was confirming his Jarldom of Orkney, he would have foundations in three countries for a European position. But he needed his commission from King James, and would do nothing to hamper its sealing. Graham, embittered and self-blinkered, suddenly told himself that he had been a fool to attempt Orkney: doubly fool to trust him with schemes and names, that King James would give his right hand to know.

"What is it?" said Orkney, turning back to him. "Do you not approve the abbot's taste in wine?"

"No, your lordship. It is not that. But I must be going. As I said, my position is a dangerous one. It is fortunate for me that I am not known at the Charterhouse."

"It is. But I am not going to ask what position you will sleep in tonight. It's too cold for a bed on the heather." Orkney had never heard of the Chalmers brothers, merchants of Perth, nor had he noticed the flecks of greasy wool that hung on Graham's cloak.

"And no word to the king?" Graham felt it best to make the direct challenge. Few men, especially young men, could avoid betraying themselves, if only by a flicker, under Graham's close scrutiny.

"No word to the king," repeated Orkney, his face candid and even serious. He had no intention of playing the informer on a man he could not help respecting.

Graham turned away, making for the door. Orkney, as the distance between them lengthened, recovered his lighter tone.

"Unless," he said, stroking his little moustache, "unless you are planning to murder his Majesty tomorrow."

Graham was far from the candle, and had already pulled the bonnet over his eyes. His rugged face was in shadow and half disguised. Orkney, even if he had meant anything by the jest, could hardly have seen whether or not his words had had any effect upon the Graham.

January 1435

VII

Parliament had opened at last; it had been sitting three days, and the pack was already in full cry. There was no question now of mute defiance, of lords sitting silent, in martial array, and then going home to plot opposition in the country. They were at it here and now, articulately rebellious. James's attempt to recreate Parliament on the English model had at least produced an active opposition.

The rafters of the old Assembly House were ringing with grievances and accusations. No one had yet dared to attack King James, but there was hardly a royal officer on whom they were not thundering anger. The ministers of the king's household, pale and tight-lipped, clung to their places like sailors to the helmsman's seat, though tempests make the tiller useless. Only Robert the Chamberlain seemed calm. Cameron was not there: Cameron had gone to Rome to settle the quarrel about his bishopric. He would probably return to find a new secretary in his place, one more acceptable to angry nobles. Even James would not be able to resist such pressure. Cameron would be lucky if he returned at all: he might find it healthier to forget about Glasgow and beg himself some position in Italy. His colleagues, facing the storm in Parliament, were wishing that Cameron had never gone abroad. For the last month or two they had been groping in the dark. They knew that resistance was hatching, though they had not guessed that it would burst out in Parliament. They knew it must have some nucleus, some shifting centre round which it was crystallizing. Cameron, with his knowledge of Scotland's more dubious byways, might have been able to detect and expose it. They were telling themselves that his presence might have saved not only his post and bishopric, but ten years of back-breaking effort to rebuild a ruined throne.

James himself, sitting above the turmoil, did not think the danger quite so sweeping. Still, it was serious enough.

It came, of course, from the Lords. Of the other two Estates, the prelates took no part, and most wished the king's cause well. The Commons were negligible: James's attempt to get the shires represented and induce the members to choose themselves a Speaker, like the English, had broken down upon their laziness, their grudging of expense, or their fear of local lords. A few burghers, holding proxies for all the towns in Scotland, were all that Scotland's Third Estate saw fit to send to Perth. They crouched timidly on obscure benches and watched their betters assault the ministers of the royal household.

Money, as usual, was the apparent grievance, the symbol, if not the essence, of the struggle. The great landholders were denouncing the dues that the Treasury pillaged from their estates—wardship dues while they were minors, marriage imposts when they came to mate, death-duties when their course was run. Such things had been unheard of in Scotland these eighty years and more. By what right did Court lackeys bring in their foreign tallages? A man's land was his own. He earned his right to it by fighting when the kingdom was at war. Why should he pay, pay, pay, in time of peace? There could be no right or justice again until the king dismissed the foxes that were nibbling away the law that guarded men's property.

Stewart had tried to meet their arguments, quite ineffectively, and had soon given way. Crichton was howled down before he could speak. The treasurer, spinning technicalities, was laughed into silence. Then as the clamour for their dismissal broke out once more, James smote suddenly on the arm of his throne, commanding quiet. He must stem the torrent himself.

They had left him a spacious loophole, but he would not take it. It looked too like a trap. He had only to change his officers, and all, for a time, would be well. They knew, and he knew, that it would mean a change of policy, a surrender that amounted to collapse. They imagined that he was about to make it, and prepared their triumphant applause.

"My lords," he said quietly, "I am sorry that a misunderstanding has arisen. It can be quickly set straight. You accuse my servants of taking your money unjustly, and demand their dismissal. I must tell you, once and for all, that they acted, and shall continue to act, by my orders. Do I make myself clear?"

He had certainly made himself clear. These men respected boldness, even if they were determined to oppose it. They were silent now, waiting for what he would say. He turned to Stewart, asking for some document he had no need of. He needed a moment or two of silence. Then he spoke again.

"Your lordships ask," he said, "by what right I make levies on your wealth, and I answer, by ancient custom. You say that this custom has lapsed for eighty years and more. Again I answer you, this lapse was a disaster, a wound in Scotland's heart. Regents, and before them a crippled king, forgave you all your debts. And to what depths did Scotland fall beneath their rule? Our country was impoverished, our corn and traffic destroyed. Loyalty and honest toil became the laughing-stocks of successful robbery. Our name was forgotten in Christendom, or remembered only for contempt. By God's grace, the crown has changed all this, and by God's grace the crown shall continue its work. I have given you peace, within doors and without—not the peace of slow decay, but the peace of promise and fruition. I could not do this without money. I cannot now. You say you would pay to prosecute a war, with your blood and gear. Will you not pay to prosecute justice and prosperity? These things, my lords, are bought at a price: the crown must pay that price: it is for you to give freely, strengthening the crown. Those who sat on this throne before me, those who usurped it from me, preferred your murmurings to the voice of duty. There are some of you that would have such rulers again if they were able, but I cannot think that the best of you, the most of you, are of that persuasion. I tell myself that there are enough men in Scotland who would rather see her what Bruce and Wallace made her, than reap their petty harvest of sloth and blackmail and pride. It is for you, my lords, to tell me if I have been mistaken."

There was silence in the hall, difficult to interpret: perhaps a dangerous silence. Douglas half rose from his seat and then subsided again. Orkney was smiling inscrutably. It was the bishops that made the first movement, Wardlaw bending forward to nod and whisper appreciation to a colleague. Even the burghers had begun to fidget before an earl or baron moved again. The king had won.

"And now," said James, "if your lordships consent, we will proceed to the business of the day."

He leant back, leaving the word to his officers. He knew that his victory could be only a temporary one. He must think soon how it could be made the successful skirmish that leads to a full campaign of triumph. He knew that he had hoodwinked them; not for their own good, though perhaps for Scotland's. The Scotland he envisaged was one that had little room for them, save as occasional captains, Court ornaments in peace. He must crush their pride and power into the mere dust of its ancestral self before his efforts could attain their logical end. He must blindfold them while he laid the foundations of his despotism. For he had persuaded himself, rightly or wrongly, that only a despot could save Scotland from misery and frustration, and that Heaven had appointed him and his heirs to fulfil that destiny.

He was curiously tired, from long anxiety and its sudden relief. The quiet was grateful, the droning voices of the ministers and their clerks, the reluctant silence from the nobles' benches. James did not realize that the catastrophe was preparing, the inexplicable, inexcusable mistake was being made.

Sir Robert Stewart had risen. He was already reading out the sentence of forfeiture on the Earl of March.

James had assigned the task to Stewart, the only minister to whose high birth no exception could be taken. It had been arranged provisionally that he should seize an opportunity early in the proceedings, before opposition gathered and became self-conscious. But only a fool or traitor could fail to see that opposition was already gathered, was lurking, only half beaten, in hope to spring up again. Was the man mad, to scatter gunpowder on a sulky fire?

Stewart got small way with his reading. Before one half of the lords realized what was being announced to them, the other half were already on their feet. In a few minutes the clamour was redoubled, and, if it died down, it was only to give some spokesman an alley of assault. James, exonerating his ministers, had swept away the only breastwork between him and his enemies: he, and he alone, must answer for what the crown was doing to Dunbar. He would have a hard task. They were asking why he spoke of living on their dues and tallages? He was demanding those and then taking their earldoms too. His security and justice was a trick to rob them of their lands. If Dunbar's father had turned traitor once, he had been amply pardoned by the crown. If King James deprived him now, King James would find excuse tomorrow to rob every lord in the land, every poor man even, whose property might enrich a royal estate. Behind the speakers' arguments rose voices crying that March must be reinstated, crying of Malise and the pillaged earldom of Strathearn. In another moment, someone would remember Albany and call on the crown to disgorge Doune and Falkland, Menteith and Fife.

James sat unmoved, still royal in bearing, but empty of resource. He had ceased to curse Stewart for his blunder, his folly in not waiting for another day. Spilt milk was spilt. He could only search his mind, feverishly, for some new expedient, some excuse, however hollow, to stop the rebellious mouths. Guardedly his eyes peered out at the faces, flushed or pale, the strained brows and waving hands. And then, with a shock like cold water, he came to a sudden stop.

There was a face beside the burghers, a face he had not

seen for ten years: but he had said, in the tent at Melrose, that he was not likely to forget it. How it came to be there was past guessing at. Sir Robert Graham had not sat down with the rest that morning: he had not been there, at least not visibly, while James was speaking. Someone must have smuggled him in, been prevailed upon to find him entrance, by that piercing glance that was now fixed on James. And it would not be long now before he revealed to what end he had come.

For Graham was rising—had risen, to his full height. He was advancing upon the king. For an instant James felt the soldier's instinct to draw sword and fall on guard against danger; then he put it aside, smiling at himself. The others had seen Graham now, and were watching him stride slowly through their midst. His grey eyes still burnt at James; the red hair flamed as he passed each patch of sunlight from the high barred windows. From sun-shaft to shadow he passed, from shadow to dusty light. He approached the throne, began to climb its steps. James sat still, more in bewilderment than policy. Graham's outstretched hand fell upon his shoulder: Graham's voice spoke the incredible words.

"James Stewart," he said, "I arrest you in the name of Scotland's Three Estates, who are no more bound to obey you than you to serve the Law. I declare the Law broken and by you. I declare our allegiance ended."

The challenge was issued now, the long battle joined. One of the minor angels who work under the Recorder's direction opened a clean book and wrote the heading on its first page. Perth: January: Thirty-sixth year, Fifteenth Century of Grace. He looked down to see what the little puppets would be doing—the king on his throne, the rebel straddling its steps. His pen began to move. He would need to write small if his tale were not to overflow its appointed volume. For its end lay three hundred years ahead. Three nations must be shaken to their roots, many homes burnt and hearts broken, before the quarrel could be laid to rest between Parliaments and the house of Stewart.

The Earl of Orkney leant forward on his bench among the lords, watching the two figures on the dais. He knew at once, and with amusement, that Graham had thrown away the game. It was a good thing that he, for one, had given his nocturnal visitor so little encouragement. The others should have realized that the man, turned inward upon himself through years of wandering, was bound to make some such false move as this. King James needed only to sit still. King James, having a head on his shoulders, would probably sit extremely still. And what, Orkney wondered, did Graham imagine he could do then?

He saw Graham turn back, calling for the support that had been promised him. Did the man think that Hamilton, or Dalkeith, or the Douglas himself, was going to spring up, at the orders of a crazy Kincardine laird, and march the king off to the Perth Tolbooth? These men might admit him to their lodgings by night, listen to his arguments and even consult him on points of law: there was much sense in his arguments, and he certainly knew his law. But they would hardly be grateful to him for standing up in open Parliament to announce that they were art and part in sedition with so obscure a malcontent. It was always dangerous, thought Orkney, for men with brains to meddle in politics, unless their brains had been well rinsed in floods of common sense. Graham, uncle to disinherited Strathearn, might picture himself as leader to a wavering nobility; but he would soon find them wavering in the wrong direction when he tried to put the picture into action.

Graham was haranguing the lords now, scolding them almost. None of them moved, except in resentment. If that stony figure on the throne should come to life, rising to order the arrest of Graham, then they might have done something to protect their self-appointed champion. But there was no movement on the dais, except in Graham's tormented face. Orkney leant back, smiling at the inevitable collapse of headstrong gestures.

And then suddenly, surprising himself, he felt a pang of shame at his own facile amusement. There was nothing laughable in Graham: there was folly perhaps, but grandeur too, and not a little pathos. That rugged figure, towering impotently over the king, did indeed stand for Scotland, the Scotland of which James knew little, the Scotland that defeated King Edward's attempt to enslave her, and remains for ever suspicious of like attempts: the soul that is so quick to believe herself wronged and will attempt all heroisms, stain herself with all sins, in the effort to right that wrong.

Graham had turned now, knowing at last that he had leant upon a broken reed: it hardly detracted from the tragedy that the reed was largely of his own imagining. He was saying something, bitterly enough, about the instability of human allies: even at that moment the law-court phrase came most readily to his lips. "Who serves man," he said, "serves by short process." Then he marched slowly through the hall, with long strides, not deigning to look at those who had refused him aid. He passed out into Parliament Close, into the sunny High Street; he sought byways, where his son waited with friends and hired horses; and no one followed to tell the folk in the streets what had passed in Parliament, or to seize the rebel before he sought Highland sanctuary.

Behind his heels was silence, discomfort, and a certain emptiness. Something very strong and quelling had left the assembly, passing into obscurity and probable destruction. Even the king seemed grave and hesitant, having looked more closely than the others into the Graham's eyes. It was a minute or more before he made a little gesture to a clerk, and the man rose, to read out, in a parched voice, the long-winded preliminaries of some petty charter.

October 1435

VIII

Queen Joan sat in Saint Margaret's little chapel, perched high on the rock of Edinburgh. She often came there nowadays, leaving her women to imagine that it was to say her prayers. She seldom knelt, or even prayed sitting. She had brought a book in, though she had read little today. She was no saint, as Queen Margaret had been; but she felt kinship, across four centuries, with that other Englishwoman who had come to be Scotland's queen. The country had been wilder then, certainly more foreign: even the Court spoke Gaelic, until Margaret came. Margaret—if one could trust the chroniclers—had set herself gallantly to her task of bringing Scotland a new civilization and a new Christianity: Latin had ousted Gaelic from the Mass, in sign that Scotland was launching, urged by her queen, into the full stream of Europe's fellowship. The whole country was, in a sense, a monument to what one woman can achieve; but here, in the little Norman chapel, something more intimate and personal had survived from the wrack of wars and hatreds. Joan who had been ten years a queen, and felt that she had achieved nothing, could sit here and draw comfort from the unrecriminating dead.

She needed comfort. She was alone and afraid. James had ridden west, leaving her and the children behind and would hardly be back until the New Year. The Court was scattered: he had taken Robert Stewart with him—to keep an eye on him, he said—and was visiting the royal farms and castles in Renfrew, Ayrshire and Galloway. He had made her anxious, ever since the Parliament at Perth, with his sudden activities and uncharacteristic suspicions. He seemed to have lost his hard-won serenity in these last months, rushing feverishly from one thing to another as if in fear of pursuit—as if Time were his pursuer and his working day already dwindling to some destined end. Yet, so far as she understood these things, there was no cloud on his horizon, no sign of such opposition as could thwart the development of his schemes for Scotland. He was richer by the forfeiture of Dunbar's earldom, and had stifled the discontent it had provoked. He would be richer still when old Mar had drunk himself into the grave and left his heirless estates to the crown. Cameron had gone to Rome, Rome was sending an envoy here to settle the weary quarrel. England seemed too busy to protest against little Margaret's betrothal by war. James could surely look forward to many years of peaceful mastery.

There had been, of course, the letter from Graham—surely the strangest message ever sent from a subject to a king. It reached Perth soon after Graham had been proclaimed outlaw—from some unknown glen or fastness in the Highlands. He had upbraided James with ruining his life, had renounced all allegiance, and proclaimed that if they met again, it would be as man to man—and sword against sword. In any country except Scotland, the whole thing would have seemed a misplaced jest, and even at Perth it had caused some laughter. But James himself had been grave, and seemed unable to dismiss Graham from his mind. He had taken an unusual step, which vexed Joan while it pleased her. He had taken her into the Parliament House, little Fiery-face in her arms, and made the lords and prelates, even the embarrassed burghers, take an oath of fealty to his queen. It was astonishing, if he really feared assassination, that he did not take better precautions, instead of riding round Scotland with so small an escort, accepting hospitality in a dozen ill-fortified monasteries. Perhaps he cherished—in that side of him she had never understood, the deeply Scottish side—some of the stoic fatalism that haunts the race. Perhaps, too, he trusted the strength that God had given him: Joan told herself, still with pride, that there were few men in Scotland who would care to meet their king sword to sword.

She shivered a little, drawing her cloak round her. The wind had begun to moan round the chapel, muttering at the little jewelled windows and the worn threshold of the door. The autumn gales would be here soon. She must tell her women to get out the winter mantles, she must order two or three chests up from Linlithgow Palace. She wished that James were home.

There was one consolation about winter. It would delay little Margaret's departure from home. They had expected Girard the Frenchman to bring his ships to Ayr or Dumbarton any time during the summer: James had spoken of meeting them there while he was in the west. But even if they had arrived already, it would be too late in the season to send them back with their prize—their capture, as one might say. For little Margaret could hardly go willingly to a foreign country and a husband she had never seen. She was pitiably young, and seemed to have inherited more of her father's sensitiveness and poetry than his ruthless devotion. Joan sighed, hoping that the winter would prove a long one, even that Girard's fleet might be shattered by its tempests—or captured by English ships.

There was a knocking on the chapel door; Joan rose, putting her book under her cloak, and told the newcomer to enter. She had not imagined that a woman would knock so sturdily, but it was one of her ladies that came in: she had forgotten that it might be Katharine, the strapping, fair-haired lass that had arms like a labourer's. Katharine was so taciturn that one hardly knew whether one liked her or not. When she did speak, it was generally to make some gloomy comment on misfortunes that others avoided by ignoring them. Everybody had found it appropriate when she had attached herself, with a kind of sullen loyalty, to the king's third daughter: for poor little Joanna had spoken no word in her five years of life, and the doctors said that she would grow up dumb.

Katharine stood there now, saying nothing, and Joan had to ask her whether dinner was ready. "It is that, your Majesty," she answered, standing aside for her with a hand upon the massive bolt of the chapel door.

The sky was overcast, outside, and they looked down on a sea mist creeping up from the Firth. "It is cold," said Joan, "I wish we could winter in Perth again."

She passed on to the ramparts, not waiting for a reply; but Katharine followed her with unexpected comment. "I was speaking yesterday," she said, "to the lad that's guarding that gun. And we were both of a mind that his Majesty is safer in Edinburgh Castle than in Perth."

"You may be right," said Joan, not troubling to think out what Katharine might imply. "But it's cold work waiting for him here."

"It's not so cold here," said Katharine, "as it'll be in our graves." Katharine knew, and resented, her reputation as a skeleton at the feast, but she could not prevent herself playing up to it all the more. Then she saw Joan's smile, and hastened to fall into her usual glum silence, swinging her strong arms as she walked.

October 1435

IX

"And it was here that my father died?"

James stood, with Sir Robert the chamberlain, in the courtyard of Dundonald Castle and gazed round him at the ill-kept walls. There was grass growing in the chinks—ferns even. The battlements tottered. The courtyard, to judge by the droppings, was principally a shelter ground in which the village-folk of Dundonald could leave their sheep and cows when they did not want to stay and mind them.

By the guard-room door stood a large clumsy fellow, some ten or twelve years younger than the king, swinging a cluster of old-fashioned keys. One would not have thought about the man's age, nor troubled to look twice at him, but for a pair of soft brown eyes, liquid as a woman's, that sorted ill with his heavy shoulders and large, stupid face.

"Ay," he was saying, "I've heard that. My mother could tell you more, down at Auchans. She was here at the time."

He scratched himself on the thigh. He was evidently unaccustomed to the presence of kings, though he was a royal officer, Doorward of Dundonald and son to a Doorward. They kept the old title in this out-of-the-way place. His father had been ten years dead, and since then there had been nothing and nobody to give check to his will. He had ruled the castle, an unintelligent autocrat, with little interference from the world beyond the hills. It did not occur to him that the king's visit might imperil this satisfactory state of affairs.

He shambled upstairs, escorting James to the western rooms. Stewart was left below, to kick his heels in annoyance: the king was frugal of time, these days, and did not generally waste it on things no longer significant. To Stewart's way of thinking, Dundonald should never have been significant. Old King Robert, Bessie Muir's son, had had no business on the throne at all, no right to transmit it to James. Stewart had thought a great deal about the matter lately. It might soon be time to do more than think.

James followed the Doorward into a spacious room, with wide windows commanding Arran and the Firth of Clyde. Autumn clouds darkened Goat Fell. James pictured his father lying there—for it would be to this room that they would be likely to bring a dying king—and looking his last upon Scottish mountains. Twenty-five years had passed since then, and walls and floor had been open to the unthwarted busyness of mildew and spiders.

The Doorward could tell him nothing, had a notion, even,

that the thing had not happened there, but in some narrow room, loopholed for arrows, over the main gate. There was no tradition of King Robert at Dundonald: he had left as little mark upon it as upon his kingdom. The castle had opened her gates to him, and then opened them again to speed his bones on their last journey, to rest among the monks of Paisley. It was easy to forget such a man as John Stewart, even though he had been crowned as King Robert the Third.

James turned from the window and began his descent to the courtyard. The men would be waiting: neither they nor the chamberlain had any instructions about the next move. James had said nothing of his vague intention to stop a night at Dundonald: he had been half ashamed at this homesick hankering for the past. He had justified it, to himself, as a tentative hope that, by sleeping here, he might intercept some message, some counsel from long-dead wisdom, whose follies would have been winnowed by time. He felt in need of counsel, and trusted no living man's perception. But one could not tell others of such a fancy. If he gave the order now to ride on for Ayr, no one would guess that he had changed his mind.

He paused on the steps. The Doorward was still shuffling about in the room above, kicking against anything that lay on the dusty floor. James looked out of the little staircase window, at the autumn hills that brought back memories of childhood. A great wave of homesickness swept over him, a yearning for some of the things that he had made it his business to destroy. He was a king, a great king, successful and renowned, and he suddenly felt himself a little boy, afraid of everything he had since learnt to conquer, afraid even of his father and his father's face. The memory of that long-dead majesty was mingled with that of others. Graham's face as he had seen it in the Parliament, baffled, betrayed, and noble, seemed suddenly crowned with his father's snowy locks. In another moment, he seemed to be kneeling to his father only, giving account of his stewardship: his father was kind, as always, trying to help him out: but he could find nothing to say, nothing to boast of, that did not seem tainted with selfishness and blood. He knew suddenly what Joan had meant when she said at Dunfermline that there were things more important than a crown: he knew, for the first time in life, what the priests meant, about the meek inheriting the earth.

It took him a minute and more to recover his balance, to remember that every man has a different part to play, between the cradle and the grave, and none can afford to hanker for another's virtues. He must be content if his own had made it possible for others to practise meekness unharmed. He raised himself from the window-sill. The footsteps above him had begun to descend. He must brace himself to meet the only life that he was fitted to understand. He must leave Dundonald. The dead were dead.

It was not the ruinous state of the castle that was making him do so, nor the utter lack of any fit lodging for a king. The day was far from spent, and it would do this laggardly lout of a Doorward no harm to bestir himself and put his castle into some semblance of order. For that matter, whether the king slept there or not, the whole place would have to be overhauled soon: an overseer must be sent to see that the neglected stone-work was rebuilt, the rotting timber replaced. A royal castle so dilapidated as this was the kind of scandal that King James was not disposed to tolerate. But, meanwhile, it was not the lack of comfort or dignity that was urging him to ride on. It was a distaste, a fear almost, of the influence he had thought of courting. If the dead had any message for him, it might weaken the purpose on which he was set: if a warning, it might be one that he must disregard. It was not only in flattery that men told him he was making a new epoch in Scotland. He was at war with the past: he could not afford to listen to its midnight whisperings.

He regained the courtyard. Robert Stewart came forward to meet him, the men rose from lounging and chattering: they stood to their horses, awaiting his order.

"Saddle!" he said. "Send men ahead to Ayr. We will want quarters there tonight."

There was a sudden gust as they mounted, stirring the faded leaves on the cobbles and sending new ones to join their company from the trees outside the main gate. James swung himself up, with half an eye on the clumsy creature in the doorway, still fumbling at the lock with his keys. James waited. Like all who lack height, he knew that sitting on horseback gave him a better chance to inspire the requisite terror into this self-satisfied custodian who had spent ten years contentedly neglecting his charge. The man should learn from what origin he drew his petty powers, and what responsibility they entailed.

At the same time, he reflected, Dundonald was barely worth the repairing. It might be unwise, too, to start re-fortifying royal castles in this quarter, provoking the Kennedies and Cunninghams who lorded it over the western shires. He had enough opponents in districts that mattered, without raising suspicions elsewhere. The place was hopelessly old-fashioned: it had been built too close to the wooded hill behind: a few cannon there would soon make it untenable: archers even, as archers went nowadays, could clear the walls of defenders while sappers crept up, unhindered, to pick away their stones from below. Was it worth while raising the sound of hammer and trowel here, to frighten Dundonald's ghosts from their now familiar decay? Dundonald had done its work, centuries ago, against wild Cumbrians and Norwegian pirates from the Isles. It had earned its rest, and he could leave it to moulder in peace.

The Doorward turned, jingling his muddle of keys. He blinked at the horsemen, as if surprised to see them already mounted. He was certainly unconscious of any impending reprimand.

James shook his bridle, and his horse started forward.

Angry at his own weakness, he dug sharp spurs into its side. In a moment he had clattered away through the gate, and silence surged back into the castle of Dundonald.

January 1436

X

Aeneas Silvius Piccolomini was having the tossing of his life. Every time the ship descended into the yawning gullies of the sea, his eyes bulged and his stomach felt as though it was not there. Every time she began to labour up the opposing slope, he became unpleasantly conscious that he had a stomach, and a rebellious one. He could think of nothing except his own misery and his yearning for stable ground. He could do nothing except pray to the Virgin and promise her that if she landed him safe in Scotland, he would walk barefoot through the streets and buy her a candle at her nearest shrine. Aeneas was a classical scholar, a cosmopolitan and a wit, but he carried with him, from his dusty home on the Tuscan farm, a truly Italian confidence in the saints.

Like many priests, he was experienced in sea-voyages, tempests even—as the Mediterranean reckoned tempests. He had always tried to live up to his first name and its adventurous traditions, just as he always remembered his second, and felt poetical, whenever he saw a wood. The real trouble with him was that he was intensely interested in everything and wanted to go everywhere. Like many of his contemporaries and countrymen, he found life absurdly short for all that there was to see and do. He had stuffed himself with learning at Siena University, with such avidity as to endanger his health. He had left to act as secretary to any Cardinal that was likely to travel the world and give him a chance to see men and their cities. He had found himself in Albergata's train at the Conference of Arras, and when Albergata wanted someone to go on to Scotland and talk to King James about the stale old quarrel with the Papacy, Aeneas immediately volunteered for the voyage. Each time the North Sea hit his ship, Aeneas wondered how he had come to be such a fool.

He saw that the tempest was beginning to die down at last, that there was land, possibly Scottish land, on the horizon. The Virgin wanted her candle.

He had had to travel by sea, for anyone coming from Arras was extremely unpopular in England. The Arras conference was engaged in picking away the foundation-stone of England's position in France, persuading Burgundy to desert his English allies and fight for the king whom Joan of Arc had crowned. The attempt was already succeeding when Aeneas left: the Hundred Years' War was likely to end in a humbling of England. To Aeneas, France, England and Burgundy meant less than Cicero's style or a rediscovered Pheidias, but the scholar who mixes in politics must take the consequences of other men's hatreds. The English had arrested him in Calais and only released him at the insistence of their fat, uneducated little Cardinal—the one that wanted to be Pope. Aeneas had blessed Beaufort's forlorn ambitions, and taken ship from Sluys to Leith. If fortune was kind, the dismal coast-line he could now see might be that on which Leith stood.

No, said the captain, hardly yet. He was running for Dunbar at present; they could shelter there and make Leith in a day or two. Aeneas had no intention of making Leith by sea. He was for dry land here and now. He swore he would not mind walking into Edinburgh barefoot, so long as he could get off the still heaving deck.

Barefoot he went, for a respectable proportion of the way. As soon as he had landed, he piously removed his shoes and asked which turning would take him to the nearest altar of Our Lady; the people of Dunbar told him that there was none nearer than Whitekirk, ten miles away. He set out gallantly, with snow on the ground. His servants had to support or carry him most of the way, and he contracted such gout in the soles as was to accompany him throughout his long journey to the Papal throne and the classic tomb in St. Peter's. Aeneas Silvius Piccolomini, landing seasick to struggle along treeless paths, was not entirely to blame if he saw Scotland in the worst of tempers.

Even his scientific researches were baulked. When he asked to see one of the Scottish barnacle-trees, which bear wild geese instead of fruits, he was told that they certainly existed, but "a little further north." Aeneas had come quite far enough north already. He hazarded a sceptical guess that the same phrase would meet the seeker at each stage of his journey, till he reached the Shetlands or *Ultima Thule*.

But there would be compensation, he told himself, in meeting the king. James must be something quite unique, worthy of a chapter in one of the innumerable books that Aeneas meant one day to write. Here was a king who could not patronize art and music and literature, as did the Italian princes, for Scotland had none to patronize. But he had improved on their example, writing poems himself and composing music of which an Italian *maestro*, even, had written with approval. James must have made a great sacrifice to duty when he left nominal captivity in England—where some culture had penetrated—to govern tribes of savages. His reign, they said, had been a troubled one: what else could be expected when a sensitive poet is put in such a position? Aeneas looked forward to meeting a kindred spirit, isolated and probably longing for such refreshment as his visit might provide. King James would be glad to discuss poetry with a lover of it, might even sing some Sapphics or Alcaics of his own, set to his own music. The tinkling of a lute would be grateful after the incessant screeching of the sea-birds that swooped and yelled along the Lothian coast. It would be a queer experience, something to make his friends stare, when they read his letters or welcomed him home to Siena.

When he reached Dalkeith, he discovered that he was not the only emissary from civilization. A man called Girard, they said, had been in Edinburgh for a long time, with a pack of Frenchmen, waiting to take the king's Meg away with them: yes, the princess too—so they'd heard—had begun writing songs like her father, only in French instead of good Scots: oh, yes, King James wrote in Scots, not Latin or any of your fancy languages. Aeneas sighed, but was glad that Margaret could look forward to happiness in France, where poetesses were trained and appreciated.

King James's statute for helping innkeepers had not prompted the host at Dalkeith to make his establishment much better than a pigsty. Aeneas, accustomed of late to the spacious hostelries of Germany and Flanders, preferred a chair by the fire to the bed he was invited to share with fellow travellers and lice.

He had been lucky to find someone to talk to, for the first hour or so. Two brothers called Hall, crossing from Fife, had been driven out of their way by storms, and, like him, were finishing their journey on land. The elder, John, was by way of calling himself a knight. His brother had once thought of entering the Church, and had acquired more than a smattering of Latin at St. Andrews. When he heard that Aeneas was going to the king, he said something, in a low voice, to his drowsy brother. Sir John seemed to agree, and it was then suggested that they must all meet again in Edinburgh, and hear the foreigner's impressions of James and the castle. Perhaps if Aeneas was lodging there, he could take them to his rooms: they had always wondered what kind of a place the king was building for himself up there. It would be different, no doubt, to the foreign palaces—if Aeneas had moved in palaces. But they would be interested to see it.

Aeneas expanded reminiscently. He was vain, and it was not everyone that could say he had served the great Filippo Maria of Milan. They should see Filippo's *palazza*! He had been a strange master, but very liberal, very generous. One gathered from Hall's sneer that the same could not be said of James: according to him, half Scotland was indignant at James's way of soaking up money, and at the new tax he was trying to raise. One gathered, from guarded phrases, that Hall had no great opinion of his king: he excused himself by saying that he had been born a vassal of the great Count of Lennox, whom the king had unjustly put to death. Filippo too, said Aeneas, had had to do so much killing: it haunted him, apparently, so that he went about stabbing at his bedroom hangings, in terror of assassins.

The word had the oddest effect on Hall. He stared at Aeneas as if he were a dangerous magician. He nudged and whispered to his brother. Then he seemed to conclude that whatever had startled him may only have been a coincidence. But it was not long before he made brief excuses and rolled into bed. The two left early next morning, and no appointment had been made for a meeting in Edinburgh.

The town, to Italian eyes, matched its cheerless country. Siena was proud of its brick-paved streets, and the bylaws which compelled its citizens to sweep them once a week. Edinburgh had only one thing that could be called a street: its citizens also used it as a sewer and had not swept it once in all its ill-smelling history. The castle was clean enough when one reached it, but abominably cold and windy: hardly a good spot for a sufferer from incipient gout.

Aeneas made himself as comfortable as possible. It might be tomorrow or the next day, he was told, before his Majesty could see him. He was shown the old chapel, the much-prized gun, and the room where his Majesty's books were kept. He was invited to borrow one, and left browsing round the scanty shelves: he was disappointed to find so many of the books were in English and so few of the rest were off the beaten track of old-fashioned libraries. Boethius, in a poor crabbed hand, was not of great interest to an Italian of the New Learning: and he could not translate the comments that were scribbled, in boyish lettering, on the margins and fly-leaf. The room seemed even draughtier than the one that had been assigned him as sleeping-quarters, and there was little temptation to stay.

He was still searching, as a last chance, for something less ordinary, when he became conscious of a strange sound, proceeding from some adjoining place—a moaning sadder, if possible, than that of the gale outside. Agog with curiosity, Aeneas limped out into the passage. The noise came from the room opposite, and he put up a tentative hand to see if the door were quite latched.

As his fingers touched its panel, things began to happen with fantastic suddenness. His ears were abruptly assailed by the most horrible shriek he had ever heard in his life, followed by another and another. He was no coward, but he felt a curious weakness at the knees. He could think of nothing like it since his boyhood at Corsignano, when they were killing pigs on the farm. Could Scottish pigs have louder lungs? Could even Scotsmen put the castle's butchery next door to its library? The questions had hardly flashed up in his mind when a new gust of wind swept the passage and swung open the door on which his hand was resting. And the sight that was revealed was more inexplicable than the noise.

An old man with white, wildly tousled hair was standing in the middle of the room, rhythmically waving the bare arm that he had thrust out from the homespun blanket on his shoulders. He seemed to be in the position of instructor to another man, short, burly, and the better dressed of the two, who sat nursing a kind of bladder under his arm: this was connected to some wooden pipes, one of which was applied to his mouth: it was from these, it seemed, that the appalling screeches were proceeding. And the man who fingered them, instead of trying to silence or pacify the contrivance, was apparently increasing the volume of its clamour with all the strength of puffed cheeks and labouring lips.

Aeneas Silvius Piccolomini stood paralysed with astonishment, doubting the evidence of his senses. It was some time before he could recognize the thing for a barbarous reproduction of the barbarous instruments which he had seen shepherds carrying in his own country—presumably to scare away wolves. It was many minutes before he could be convinced that his inquisitiveness had led him, forestalling diplomatic punctilio, into the presence of the king.

He had to admit, afterwards, that the king had treated him well enough when it came to a formal interview. He condoled with him on his injured feet and promised to give him two horses as well as journey money. The business was successfully if summarily despatched: James, the bagpipes laid aside, seemed haunted by some anxiety that made him eager to get foreign questions settled and out of the way. He ended with a present of a fine pearl, which Aeneas, like a good Italian, kept for his mother at Corsignano. But the visitor was barely mollified. From student days to Popedom, he would always be a man of strong preconceptions, successful and happy when he found them justified. But the upsetting of them wounded him like an injustice.

He was accustomed to work off his annoyances with his pen. And the eve of his return journey found him sitting in a crowded inn-room at Linlithgow, writing a letter to his friend, Gregorio Lolli. He told Gregorio that he was coming home by land, preferring Englishmen to waves. The letter could go by the ship that had offered to take him. "*I myself, my dear Goro, am trusting to God and a good disguise.*"

He wrote that he was hoping to see more trees in England. "*There are few or none here, which hardly pleases your Silvius. They say there are forests in the other half of Scotland which is inhabited by a second tribe, speaking another language. Here they buy their timber from Norway, and use little in their houses, which are principally of mud. In their fires—believe it or not—they burn a kind of black, lustrous rock which they pick out of their soil. I suppose it contains sulphur. There is nothing to make a man wish to remain here except the oysters, which are excellent, and some of the Scottish maidens, who are unusually handsome. Of the latter I will tell you more when we meet.*

"*You need not believe anything you hear of their king. He is square, fat and unprepossessing: our friend Bernadino, who loves painting kings, would not take him for model. In spite of the rumours that reach Italy, he does not know what music is. I shall not reveal how I learnt this, nor must you ask me to speak of it. His own subjects consider him brave, but cruel, very vindictive and eaten up with avarice. He has very bright eyes.*

"*I return by the west road to Luguvallum, and then cross England to the New Castle. Only so, they tell me, can I be sure to avoid English armies who may be advancing as I write. For they fear a new war between the two nations. There is one way to please all Scotsmen and that is to abuse the English.*"

He looked up from his paper at the faces round the coal fire; they were watching him as though he were some Turk or wanderer from Cathay, instead of an ordinary Papal envoy. They chafed against the Papacy in this country: Clement, he remembered, had once excommunicated their beloved Bruce for stabbing someone in a church, and they cherished long memories, having nothing better to think of: it was lucky that heresy had no attractions for them, or Scotland might prove a pretty kettle of fish. No good thinking of that: he must finish his letter and sleep: a journey awaited him.

He handed the letter to the shipmaster next morning and went to seek his new horses. Within a few days, shipmaster, ship and letter were on the floor of the North Sea, likely to remain there till Doomsday. But the substance of what was written at the inn was not lost to posterity. It can still be found, buried under mountains of close-printed Latin, in the *Commentarii*, the *Historia*, and the *De Viris Claris* of Aeneas Silvius Piccolomini, better known to Europe as Pope Pius the Second.

Spring 1436

XI

"He has chosen the Spanish ship, father. He says she sails faster than the *Marie*, and his daughter must go on her."

"The Spaniard! Name of God, does he want a mutiny? Anything to delay us, anything to waste more time. Are we never to get this cursèd princess away from her cursèd family? One would imagine——!"

Girard cut short his own tirade by rising from his seat and hitting his head painfully on a beam of the *Marie*'s sterncastle. Girard had been on board for a fortnight, lying in Dumbarton roads, but he still forgot, whenever anything happened to annoy him, that the cabins of converted whalers are not designed to accommodate the display of indignation.

He glared angrily at his son Joachim in the curved doorway, and Joachim shrugged his shoulders as if to disclaim responsibility for the hard edges of beams as well as for King James's choice of ships.

"It may be his English queen," he said, "who makes difficulties. One cannot blame her for not wanting to lose a daughter to her country's enemies."

"No, one cannot," said Girard, sobered by his accident. "And the king is right about the ships. Only we cannot tell our fellows that something built at Bilbao sails faster than a good French ship. But will you suggest, my son, what we are to tell them?" He sat down again and began to brush his head lightly with the feather of a pen.

Joachim sympathized with his father. It was eighteen months since Girard had come to Scotland, and all that time he had been trying to fix a compromise between two kings, so far apart that letters took many months to exchange, both of them standing on dignity and each trying to get the other to pay as much of the expenses as possible: and the Scottish one, it seemed, was half looking for an excuse to call the whole bargain off. When the kings had been finally jockeyed into agreement, Girard had had the sailors to settle: "*seafaring folk,*" as he had to report to his government, "*are marvellous to deal with, and there is but little reason among them.*" Joachim had always admired his father's ability, though the conscious display of it was sometimes irritating: this Scottish affair was perhaps his masterpiece.

"I have found it!" said Girard suddenly, with the air of a Charlemagne. "Listen. The princess embarks on the Spanish ship: the king is satisfied. As soon as we are out of sight of this crag, Chepye will have orders to bring her to, the *Marie* runs alongside, and the princess is transferred: the sailors are satisfied. The voyage continues in peace. But they must be told now, before we start. That is the only way in which we can reach La Rochelle without trouble, and I am the only man who would have thought of it. You understand?"

"I understand."

"Then go at once and arrange it."

Joachim obeyed. The matter was settled. The sailors were pleased, in their childish fashion, to be conspirators in circumventing a king's whims. He had been difficult, that king, in spite of the presents. Matters had been facilitated by the presents, arriving in a French ship that had unexpectedly made Dumbarton a few days ago: a mule—a rarity in Scotland—for King James: special gifts for Queen Joan, who needed more placating, wine, apples and three barrels of chestnuts: the queen, one understood, *tenait bonne table.* The fleet could sail.

Scotland was insisting that it must be a large one: twelve hundred men had been raised to escort Margaret past England. The truce with the English was expiring and they would have some excuse for attempting to capture a princess who personified the Franco-Scottish alliance. For that matter, they had already renewed their aggression, without excuse. They had welcomed the fugitive Patrick Dunbar, son of the dispossessed Earl of March, and sent him back across the Border with a small army of English raiders. It had had a good beating at Piperden and slunk home with tails trailing. But it had shown that England, being squeezed out of France by daily defeats, was seeking opportunities for spite against France's ally.

Orkney had been created admiral to command the convoy. He had some of the greatest names in Scotland under him—Stewarts, Maxwells, Gordons, Campbells, Kennedies, Cunninghams. Andrew Gray, the Englishman who had married a Scottish heiress, was accompanying them—his wife was dead, but he was still disliked by Scotsmen, and glad to be away from their jealousies for a time. It was only for a time. The Scotsmen would have to return soon after the wedding. Few even of the servants and gentlemen could stay in France. Margaret, by treaty, must be surrounded by Frenchmen and Frenchwomen, so that she might learn more quickly to think of herself as French.

Tragedy, or the spectre of it, always seems to overshadow the first parting in a family of children. Dumbarton Castle had seen bloodier sights, but few more moving. Prince James cried much, partly at seeing his mother's tears: he was too young to know what was happening, and would hardly miss one out of his many sisters. But dumb Joanna, nearly ten now, clung desperately to Margaret, as if to express what she could not say in words; the waiting-woman Katharine, ashamed to be weeping herself, had to come forward and part them, taking Joanna away to some secret comfort or distraction that only those two silent creatures could share. Joan was still struggling with remorse as well as grief: she still felt that, having herself escaped the usual fate of princesses and found love, she should have done more to protect her child from the evil-minded goblin who sits chuckling in most royal bedchambers. The splendour and circumstance that rode the water outside, waiting for the twelve-year-old bride, was as hateful as the pomp that leads a victim to the scaffold. How could James allow those gaily-gilded ships to sail away with her child and leave her a bribe of chestnuts? James himself, all excuses and delays expended, was facing the reality he had sought eight years ago and had only now begun to fear. As they went down to the quay, he was wondering in obscure fashion, whether it was not his own fortunes that were sailing away, never to smile on him again..

The anchors rose gurgling from the water, the Frenchmen sang of home. Orkney leading, the whole fleet began to slide past the streets, bright with pennons and garlands, past the battlemented rock. Joan climbed to the ramparts to watch the ships dwindling towards the west. The March sun was already stooping, the glare on the water would hide them before they wheeled southward to creep past the Cumbraes or under the shadow of Goat Fell. Margaret would go to rest soon, crying herself to sleep in her strange and undulating bed. She would remember that she was a king's daughter and be brave. She would be comforting herself, perhaps, with the thought that France was a fine country and Frenchmen—some Frenchmen—made gallant and handsome husbands.

Some months later a jaded steward was standing in a room of the Tower of London, presenting Charles of Orleans with the accounts of his vast French estates. He had to do much explanation, for the captive duke had not seen France for twenty-one years. He had to ask pardon, too, for delays in his journey. "The English made me go to Calais," he said, "to get a safe-conduct from their captain."

"Ah, yes. They still hold Calais." Charles yawned.

"They hold little else, your Grace. Calais, Harfleur, Bordeaux. The Maid from Lorraine spoke truth."

"Yes, and was burnt for her pains. I am inclined to attribute more importance to the fact that my cousin of Burgundy has at last remembered that he is a Frenchman.

I wonder how his Majesty liked welcoming that cut-throat back into the fold."

The steward looked embarrassed. Feuds could not last for ever.

"His Majesty," he said stiffly, "is at Tours for the wedding of the Dauphin and the Scottish princess."

"Ah, yes. I hear that Regnault is to officiate, and no doubt Alan Chartier will celebrate the occasion with odes and panegyrics. They must be glad to think that their visit to the North Pole has borne fruit."

"They say the princess is very beautiful, your Grace."

"Do they? Most unusual! But I fear that they will not have the face to pay a similar compliment to our Louis. I saw a portrait of him, not long ago. And, from what one hears, even Chartier will have difficulty in eulogizing his moral qualities."

The steward was more embarrassed than ever. His Grace, he reflected, had been so long away from Court that one must overlook the vagaries of his tongue.

"Your Grace," he said, "was acquainted with the King of Scots when he was in England."

"Oh, yes. We were fellow . . . guests at Windsor. It is a curious thing, that these young men with their heads in air end by becoming the most ordinary, and even cynical of parents. But I am sorry for *la belle Marguerite*."

He stared into the fire. Twenty years of captivity—possibly another twenty ahead. Nothing to do except learn English—he could write rhymes in English now—to eat and sleep and go through accounts of lands he must never see. The ways of the Almighty were very strange. James had been free for ten years, and by all accounts was making just those mistakes, running his head into just those dangers that a man of Orleans's perception would have known how to avoid. London expected news, any day, of rebellion in Scotland. London was no doubt prejudiced, but, still, one remembered that young man at Windsor.

"I remember," he said, more to the fire than to his

steward, "I remember saying something that I thought rather funny at the time—something about his not knowing on which side his bannocks were buttered. I wish I felt like being funny now."

Margaret had made a swift voyage. She was not transferred from the Spaniard to the *Marie*: it had not been King James, but his own son and the sailors that Girard was deceiving. They were too busy with storms to bother about the slight put on good French ships—and too thankful to escape the attempt that England made to capture them. They were glad to see again the two grim towers that guard La Rochelle, and to glide between them into the little square harbour.

It was a very different France that Margaret entered from any that Charles of Orleans had known. There was laughter and poetry and splendour in the towns, rising from the wrack of ancient treacheries. It was fourteen years since the leathern idol of Henry of Monmouth had ridden across the plains that he had conquered at Agincourt: Henry of Windsor, or the jarring lords that governed in his infant name, had lost all that his father had bequeathed. As war's tide receded to the coasts, Knowledge and Beauty flowed back into France from the Italian cities that had given them shelter and new life.

The Scottish princess had a rousing welcome, from La Rochelle to Tours. Her new father-in-law and his queen did their kindest to make her feel at home. But the hook-nosed misshapen boy whom they had begotten to succeed them as Louis the Eleventh, looked sourly at his foreign bride. It would not be long before he would be encouraging his evil-minded friends to laugh at her behind her back. It would not be many years—nor she quite twenty—before he had killed her with his neglect and abuse and open ear to all who slandered her. She took to sitting up all night, since he refused to share a bed with her, writing endless poems as an anodyne for despair: dawn would find her still at her desk, searching for the elegant rhyme, the inevitable epithet. A young girl needs sleep; the lack of it, and the lack of love, left her too weak to resist illness, too willing to quit a miserable world. When she lay dying in the cloister-house of Chalons, her husband paid no visit to her bedside. And when all was over, he gave swift orders that the whole pack of her silly poems should be burnt.

Autumn 1436

XII

King James's fortunes might or might not have sailed to France with his daughter. They certainly seemed to be deserting him in Scotland.

He had raised a tax, the second in ten years, to pay for her voyage and dowry. It spared the poor, but the great landholders and more prosperous towns had a new grievance against the crown, and used it, among other things, to stint payment. The English had tried, though without success, to intercept the fleet, to cage Margaret in their prisons as they had once caged King James. That and the inroad that had ended at Piperden, made him so angry that he swore to teach England a lesson. The truce would expire in May; by June he would be besieging Roxburgh. All Scotland was summoned to retrieve this last corner of her soil from the hereditary enemy. If the lords would not pay for their lands, they must fight for them. The levies were martialled from the royal estates, the Fleming trundled his great gun down from Edinburgh's ramparts. Joan heard it thunder past her windows as she took her leave of James: she was to spend the summer at Perth. "You must ride out to Kinnoul again," he told her. "You must tell Lady Erskine—if she's still alive."

He could be gay still, though it was a somewhat feverish gaiety. Joan felt again the impression of a man whose time grows short. The war itself was a gambler's throw. A king could often harness a people's wavering loyalties by pointing them outward, against a foreign enemy. But there had been kings who had played that game and lost.

It was August before he could form the siege, and the guns begin to lob their balls across the Tweed. He wrote home sparingly, speaking of great difficulties and even disaffections that he had to overcome. Joan could glean from other sources how great they were, and how little the king had overcome them. There were men enough round Roxburgh, siege engines, and stores of arrows. But, for all James's statutes, there was little skill in archery, and, for all his driving power, there was no heart in the siege. The few English laughed in their castle: no one liked to think what might happen if Northumberland or Duke Humphrey marched north with an army. Such were the echoes that reached Joan from the Border.

She heard other echoes too, subterranean sounds from nearer home. Cameron came and went, leaving disquieting news. The spies told of movements among the great families, movements in the Highlands. They talked of plots, whose threads reached from Perth to the Border, whose object was to threaten the king with the armed men that he himself had gathered for the war. Their information was of the vaguest, and they themselves confessed that someone seemed to be putting up a screen of exaggerated rumours, perhaps to hide some quite minor manœuvre.

Joan would not risk it. When James wrote that he might have to abandon the siege, for this season at least, she decided that he must be induced to abandon it at once. She left the children, travelled post-haste to Melrose, and asked Abbot Fogo to ride over to the camp and bring back the king. When James came, she pleaded, argued, insisted, and then pleaded again. James gave way, sent orders to disband, and rode ahead to Edinburgh, clear of his own army.

He held a Council-General there, a kind of attenuated Parliament—"packed," his opponents would rather call it: it certainly passed laws that took some of the powers of justice from the rich and the landholding, concentrating them in the crown. It also forbade men to carry gold and silver out of the kingdom, and this—a mere commonplace of law-making—could be represented as another sign of the king's rapacity and greed. He dismissed the council after six weeks of overwork, and a kind of calm seemed to descend upon him. He talked cheerfully of Christmas and Hogmanay. They would go to Perth, he said, to join the children: they would forget about business for a month or two, play games, make music and be merry. They would leave Edinburgh at once, cross over to Fife, and send Robert Stewart ahead to make arrangements. Stewart seemed unusually pleased: he was generally contemptuous of mere pastimes and always complaining, as chamberlain, of the dilapidation of Perth Castle. This time he maintained that it was reaching a stage beyond repair or habitation: would his Majesty not stay with the Black Friars, just outside the city walls? Joan, newly come from Perth, reluctantly confirmed his opinion: she had been talking to Chalmers and his brother, she said, about new hangings: when they had come to take the old ones down, Thomas Chalmers had told her that the walls and floors were actually unsafe.

"Very well," said James, "the Black Friars was where we first set up house in Scotland. I'll write to the prior and tell him to buy plenty of Christmas geese. And we can start for Perth tomorrow."

One crossed the Forth by the ferry. One rode past Dalmeny to reach it, along a shore that was curiously wild and desolate, considering that it was so frequented: no one with a few pence to spare would think of going north by any other route.

The grey sea slapped and sprayed against sharp, limpet-grown rocks. The sea-gulls wheeled, poised themselves, and sailed rigid down the wind. Here and there, scraps of driftwood peered out from bundles of mildewed seaweed. The air was blusterous here, though beyond the water there was dead mist—Fife shrouded and Inchgarvie blurred. Every now and then a scurry of rain smote their cold cheeks as they rode.

She rose up from beside the path, scaring the horses. James knew her, though he could not recall where he had seen her before. No one else seemed to recognize her or take her for anything but a crazy beggar in a Highland plaid. Her voice, too, seemed familiar, though again he found it impossible to place. He connected her, obscurely, with woods and summer, not with this December-haunted shore. She might have come back from some recent time, or from childhood, before ever the sea and the English had entrapped him and warped his heart: she might have come back to him from a dream. He would have ridden straight past her, despite her words, but he had to stop—possibly suspecting treason—and send back to ask who had put them into her mouth. And when she followed up, saying that Huthart had told her, he struggled in vain to remember where he had heard Huthart's name. She could give no precise warning, nor tell him, this time, of what men he must beware: she did not say that one of them was riding at his side, had so ridden for close on ten years. Only she repeated, over and over, that if King James crossed the water, he would never come back alive.

They did not let her delay them long. She tried to run after them to the rough stone wharf, but no one was looking back as they embarked. Joan had not understood her Gaelic, and Robert Stewart voiced the general opinion—though with unnecessary vehemence—when he dismissed her as a drunken fool. But when the boat had pushed out and was heading towards Inchgarvie, she was standing on the wharf with the water lapping at her bare feet and the sea-birds screaming over her head. And still she cried that, unless they turned back now, no power on earth could save the King of Scots.

The Felling

For it is a jeopardous thing in the night, if men of war enter into our lodging.

FROISSART III. 138 (trans. BERNERS).

CHAPTER NINE

The Felling

January 1437

I

SIR DAVID DUNBAR leant out of his window and watched the tennis-balls sail up and disappear again over the wall of the Black Friars' courtyard. He wondered if it was the king himself that was playing or some of his household. It interested him to remember that he had not seen James at tennis since they were both prisoners in the Tower of London.

Sir David lodged in a house built into the north-west wall of Perth; his friends had told him that he was inviting arrest by staying there, now that the king was at the monastery, only a few hundred yards outside. He was a marked man, they said; his father had been stripped of his Earldom of March, and the king, having done them that wrong, would keep the whole family in suspicion. David's brother had committed treason already, bringing in the English army that was defeated at Piperden. The king was careless enough, in all conscience, about those who had no cause to love him, but he could hardly stomach being overlooked daily by a traitor's brother, a man whose father he had injured. "But he knows," said David, "that I have great cause to love him. He is, first, my king. Secondly, we were fellow-prisoners, and when the English set him free, he insisted that they must release me too."

They objected that all that was thirteen years ago, and he answered simply, "Then the king has saved me from thirteen years of prison. If I know my father and brother, they would not have spared the silver yet to buy me back."

"He'll put you in prison again," they told him, "if you don't find a lodging t'other side of St. Johnston's Kirk—or away from Perth altogether." David looked at them stolidly, and said that he believed the king to be just.

They gave it up at last, telling Sir David that he should have lived in the days of Roland or King Arthur, when heroics paid. He smiled and kept his counsel. He had not told them one of his motives for staying where he was—that his rooms were reasonably convenient and surprisingly cheap, and that even so his rent was in arrears. He had, too, a faint idea that being near the Black Friars' might give him an opportunity of doing the king some service; but he could not have said whether he wanted it in order to repay him for thirteen years of freedom, or to heap coals of fire on his head for his treatment of the family.

It was the king himself that had been playing tennis, taking advantage of the first fine day in an immoderately foul January. The Black Friars' yard made a possible court, though chases and penthouse would hardly have satisfied the precisians of London or Paris, and the balls were for ever losing themselves in odd holes and corners.

James was glad to find himself in better condition than he had expected: neither his forty-two years nor his increasing weight prevented him from beating Sir Andrew Gray in a couple of sets. Sir Andrew needed humbling: he had come back from France with a cargo of fine new clothes and was obviously looking for a new wife. He was still young, and Queen Joan was not the only woman to consider him extremely handsome. The Court had once nicknamed him "the King of Love," and James had chaffed him last night, when they were playing chess, because there was talk of a prophecy about a king's death in the new year: James said that there were plenty of rivals, and even husbands, waiting their chance to kill the King of Love.

He left Gray accepting Orkney's challenge to a further set on the improvised court. He watched the first few services, and then went upstairs, through the great room to the smaller one—the best the monastery could afford him—which he used for dressing and changing. An hour or more passed, and he did not emerge. Joan followed him there, wandering in when she came up to get ready for supper.

"The prior has been looking for you," she said.

"I know. I sent for him. Am I so difficult to find?"

Joan pouted. "They'd hardly expect to find you here," she said. "What have you been doing?"

"Writing poetry."

"In here?"

"Well, it was quiet. The children were out there in the big room, playing Roxburgh. Katharine and Joanna had my riding boots for cannon, but they couldn't get Jamie or any of the other girls to be the English. I came in here to finish this."

He pointed to the open book on his knee. He was sitting on a bench with his ink on a stool in front of him. "I have felt lately as if I wanted to finish things. It's twenty years since I began this."

"If it's *The King's Quair*," said Joan, smiling, "that'll never be finished."

"It is finished. I've started another poem, a short one. Curious thing about the *Quair*; I found there'd been a page cut out. I wonder when that happened."

Joan said nothing: men had strangely short memories, even for things that one would have imagined to be as important as anything in their lives. They only remembered about laws, and when old battles had been fought.

She moved to the door. "Shall I send Elizabeth for the prior?" she said, "she's just across in the bedroom." Elizabeth was the new lady-in-waiting, a pretty, ineffectual creature, with auburn hair and no common sense.

James grunted assent, and Joan went to despatch Elizabeth. It was more than likely that she would bring the wrong person. Joan returned to sit beside her husband in his untidy room.

"Were you meaning to speak to him about the children?" she asked.

"No. Why?"

"Well, the prior is a long-suffering man, and I suppose it's an honour to have us two in his house again. But we're not two now—we're eight."

'Nine,' James was about to say. Then, through his preoccupation with his poem, he remembered that one of the children had sailed away in the ships. The lords had brought back good news of her—if one could take it at face value: she wrote cheerfully—if one did not read between the lines. But he was glad that he had not reminded Joan of the absentee.

"So we are a burden on the house?" he said. "Has the old man complained?"

"Not to me. But I am sure he would be glad to see our numbers reduced. Could I not take the children to the Carmelites—or up the river to Scone?"

James was scribbling again. "No," he said. "I want you with me. Send the children to Stirling if you like."

Joan sighed; her life was becoming increasingly a matter of the children. Little James and his sisters seemed to be her one satisfactory contribution to her husband's kingdom. All else she did was clumsy—or immediately misinterpreted.

"I would rather not be away from them," she said, "I should like to give more time to them than I could to Margaret when she was their age."

Joan, it seemed, needed no reminder of Margaret. James buried himself in his verses. "I shall tell the prior," he said, "we may not be here more than another week or two. I shall certainly not let you go away from me."

She must talk to him some other time, she reflected—if only for the prior's sake. Meanwhile it was pleasant to be wanted. She had many things to be thankful for. It was even pleasant to sit beside him like this, watching him write. The book on his knees was a reminder of certain gracious things, such as few women could treasure—of a sunlit garden where the birds sang in triumph, and a little dog that pranced before her down the path.

He, too, she told herself, had been true to their vision. He had kept faith, making her wife and mother—queen of one of the few Courts ever gathered in which there had never been a whisper of royal mistresses or an unlawful prince. One forgot what other women suffered.

"I found it too difficult," he said, "trying to write as I did then. Twenty years make a difference." He turned over, to a page near the end. "Listen to this," he said. "This is where I am supposed to be talking to my own self.

Ah, busy ghost, still flickering to and fro,
That never art in quiet nor in rest
Till thou returnest where thou camest fro'
Back to thy first, thy own and proper nest. . . ."

"Yes," said Joan, rather doubtfully. "I like that."

"But it hardly sounds, does it," he asked, "as though it belonged to the same poem as '*Away, winter, away!*' I was in two minds about it, but it went in, in the end, because, as I say, I must finish. But then I found myself writing another stanza that I shall have to make into a separate poem. In Rhyme Royal, but I think I could give it two more stanzas and an Envoy, to make a ballade of it. The last line would make a good refrain." He searched among the leaves of the worn book and took out a loose sheet of paper.

"Read it to me," she said, knowing that he wanted to be asked. She took the book from his knee, glancing through it as she listened.

"It's a little solemn," he said, looking at her with an

almost boyish apology. "That's one of the reasons that it can hardly go into my *Quair*. It goes like this—

Be not too proud in your prosperity,
For as it comes, so shall it pass away.
You have short time to reckon on—for see
How soon the green grass turns to yellowing hay.
Trust most in God, Who is best guide to Man,
And for each inch, He will repay a span."

"Yes," said Joan, "it certainly is solemn. I see what you mean." She had ceased to turn over the pages, and was looking at one of the stanzas towards the end of the book. It was her book, written because of her. One could not blame her, he thought smiling, if she preferred it to better, maturer work.

"James," she said, "why do you say I have saved your life?" She showed him the book—pointing. "*And even from Death my life she has defended,*" he read.

"Poetic exaggeration." He smiled. "You would, too, if need be. Anyway, imprisonment was a kind of death, and you saved me from that." He returned to the paper in his hand, reaching out for a pen.

There was a knock on the door. Joan had done Elizabeth an injustice, for she had found the prior. James went out to speak to him in the doorway.

"I am very sorry, father," he said, "I did not really mean to trouble you. It was a question of that great square hole over the courtyard where we are playing tennis now. The balls are always going in there and it spoils the game."

"I see," said the prior. "Of course your Majesty knows that this building was not designed——"

"No, no, of course not! All the same, as we are playing there—— By the way, what is that hole?"

The prior glanced doubtfully past James towards the queen. "As a matter of fact," he said, "it leads to a vault under the great room that your Majesty is using, where your Majesty's children are now. And the vault is connected with the privy."

"I see. I might have guessed that, I suppose, every time I went near it. Well, will you have it blocked up? I'll bear the cost, of course."

"Yes, your Majesty. As soon as possible. I doubt if we have any timber at present, but——"

"Well, use stone, father. Take those spare blocks that are outside the chapel. Get the men to do it tomorrow morning, if it's another fine day. I should like to play again in the afternoon. It'll not take them more than a couple of hours."

"Very well, your Majesty." The prior turned to go, and then hesitated. In another moment, James guessed, he would summon up his courage to say something about the house being overburdened with children. James felt disinclined to tackle the subject just now, and he wanted to finish his *Ballade*.

"Thank you, father," he said, "you can talk to Sir Robert Stewart about the men's wages."

He returned to the room, leaving the old man standing. He was soon dipping his pen again, with a second stanza forming. '*Since words*,' he wrote—

'*Since words are slaves and only Thought is free,*
Keep thy tongue still, knowing what tongues can do,
Shut up thine eyes from this world's vanity—'

He was engrossed. He had forgotten Joan and her waiting-woman. He had quite forgotten the few words he had exchanged with the prior. He did not know that he had just destroyed his best chance of escaping from a terrible and rapidly nearing death.

January 1437

II

Old Athol crouched unhappily over the dying fire, listening to the night wind that piped a dreary song round Methven's roofs. He felt cold. He always felt cold these days. The fire would be out soon, unless he called someone to bring fresh logs. But he sat on unmoved, staring at the dull glow with bloodshot eyes.

He was lonely. He had never had a friend, but it was only lately that he had begun to know loneliness as a thing to be feared. He had once found sufficient company in his own busy brain; he had been almost happy, watching the huge, hopeless tangle of men's hatreds and appetites and fears, and occasionally, by a deft fingerstroke, adding another knot of his own devising. But now gradually, invincibly, this grey shadow was descending on him: what had once meant so much to him now meant nothing at all: life had turned itself inside out, as it were, revealing the ghastly simplicity of its unchangeable mechanism. He had heard men say that they did not believe in Hell and might once have agreed with them. He could not now, having been there.

He had sacrificed his eldest son to ambition, sending him to England, in order to win King James's favour, as a hostage for the irredeemable ransom. He would have given much now to have the Master of Athol sitting with him, chatting of the world's folly, sharing his contempt for all except the disillusioned. His grandson Robert was not contemptible; that young man knew what he wanted and had few illusions. But once he had accepted Athol's help to become king's chamberlain, he had gone his way. He came to Methven occasionally when the Court was at Perth, a few miles away: but he kept back the best of the news and merely talked, fleeringly, of things that Athol could easily discover for himself. He met all attempts to probe his own activities with a blank wall of irritable silence. His position was an honour, a source of influence to the family:

King James was said to be very fond of him. But he was no companion for an old man by a dying fire.

Athol had done well for his family, except in the matter of its one supreme ambition. He had been too young to prevent the crown passing to his half-brother, the lame old driveller who had wept himself to death at Dundonald. Robert III and Albany had ruled—possibly illegitimate—while Athol, undoubted son of an undoubted queen, had been left to plot and undermine and watch their branch of the line ruin itself. The ruin was all but complete now—Albany, Rothesay, Murdoch and Murdoch's sons. But King James had fixed himself securely, taming the nobles and winning the foolish Commons' hearts. His English wife had given him a bairn to succeed him, and Athol's long dream would never be more than dreaming. Soon Athol would be dead, and no one would even know that he had dreamt.

He cocked his head, listening. He wondered if it was voices below that he had heard, or only the wind in the fir-trees. The wind, most likely. There would be snow and the slush of snow on the roads. No one was likely to come to Methven so late. He would sit where he was a little longer, drink another cup in the hope of warmth and comfort, and creep away to bed. Another day ended, another step towards the grave he half dreaded, half desired.

He began to chafe his thighs with puffed hands. He was cold: my lord the king—the rightful king of Scotland—was cold in the hams, and had not sufficient spirit to call a man and have the fire mended. He smiled in self-contempt. He remembered a morning at Kindrochit, long, long ago, when one of the Clan Cameron women had told him that he would not die until he had worn a crown. Highland folk were always saying such things—if only to keep Lowlanders gaping: they hit the mark occasionally and were remembered while the thousand misfires were forgotten. The Cameron woman may have had some instinct, common enough everywhere, for divining a stranger's suppressed desires: her guess might even have created, or helped to create, that wish. But she would not have been able to tell him how he could realize it—with Jamie standing four-square in his way, and now Jamie's bairn. He must just be content to have done what he had done for Scotland, without having worn her crown—cleared her of much folly and incompetence, played the part for which the Lord had designed him. It had been a good game while it lasted, and one must expect a little weariness and depression at the end, especially if one had been too busy to plan for an old age of ease and facile popularity. It was wisest not to think too much, to have another dram, and then go to bed. He laid his hands on his knees in order to hoist himself up, and then paused, listening again.

He had been right after all. Someone must have come to Methven: someone was on the stairs. Athol, watching the door, saw it swing suddenly open; his grandson Robert entered.

Greetings were strained. Athol, still sitting, made some poor jest about thinking of a dram and then finding a king's cupbearer walk in. Robert filled him a cup at the long table, brought it over to the fireside. "You can be drinking it," he said, "while the others come up."

"Others?" asked Athol. "What others will that be?"

Robert did not answer. A little clammy fear was beginning to stir in Athol's heart.

"The fire needs mending," said Robert. "We may sit late."

"I'll ring a bell for more wood," said Athol, trying to rise. "There's little enough in the basket."

"No!" The young man laid a firm hand on his shoulder. "Better without servants," he said. "I'd as soon do it myself." He took up the basket and went out with it.

Athol gripped his knees, steadying himself. He should be welcoming this visit, any visit. It should be good news that there were still folk who wanted to consult old Athol, sitting late on a January night. Why then was his throat so dry, why such weakness in his knees? Robert would be bringing them in soon. Athol craned over the fire, his gaze averted from the door. He would not even look up when they entered.

It was so that they found him, with his back resolutely turned. He knew most of them, though not all. The Tintsmuir men, old Fifeshire retainers of Albany, were strangers to Athol, but not Sir John Hall, nor the half-trained priest, his brother. He knew the two Chalmers well, plump Thomas, and Christopher that had once been a squire and a gentleman. Robert Stewart led them in, pushing open the door with his basket of logs, and jerked his head to the stools and benches round the table. He came to the fire and poured half his load on to the greying pile. The business and clatter dislodged Athol so that he turned at last, looking round to the open door. He could not help seeing who the last-comers were—Robin Graham, and Robin's father.

Sir Robert Graham was gaunter than ever, and tanned with exposure. One would say that he had gone hungry of late, from impatience if not necessity. But there was a steady fire in his eye, not quite the fire of madness. The fear that had gripped Athol became a terror. He burrowed down towards the fire, as if to shield himself behind his grandson. "I'll not speak with them. Tell them I'm sick," he said, and saw the young man's lip curling in contempt.

They had begun to talk behind his back, quietly, as if Death were already among them. Thomas Chalmers was telling them how he had persuaded the Englishwoman to abandon the Castle at Perth, not to take the king there for Christmas. He, too, sounded husky and frightened, covering his fear with boasts. He told them what he had found out about the Black Friars', outside the walls, and which rooms the king was occupying. The Black Friars' had a little moat of its own, he said, but Chris was arranging to have hurdles there so that they could throw them in and make a causeway. And then, he said, there'd be only the locks and bolts.

"I'll be seeing to those," said Robert Stewart from the fireplace.

John Hall was heard to remark that the king was a great man with a sword, and that they'd not have much time for their work. Stewart cut him short, promising that, on whatever night they fixed, the king's sword should be missing.

"How many men'll you bring?" Athol recognized John Hall again, speaking, apparently, to Graham. Certainly Graham answered.

"I could maybe bring a hundred and more," he said. "I have some already, and my lord of Athol's name'll help me to raise some more on Tayside. I'd not planned to bring them inside the Black Friars'—only to spread them round, so that we're not disturbed till we're finished."

Hall was heard to ask whether the Highlandmen would know what it was that was being done.

"They will not," said Graham. "I am telling them that it's a matter of fetching off a lass—a lass promised to Robin here, and then denied him. They'll have had such work before. They'll hardly see what house we are at, in the dark, and they'll not know the king's there till we've killed him."

The word moved Athol at last. He had known all along what their purpose was, but he had had to hear it spoken. He turned, stammering incoherently, and met Graham's puzzled gaze.

"Did you not tell his lordship yet?" asked Graham of Robert Stewart. "You promised us his help and countenance."

"Not yet. But I can still promise."

Athol rose unsteadily. "You'll promise nothing in my name!" he protested. "I'll not join you. I'll never join you!"

"You will," said his grandson, and Athol knew that he spoke the truth.

"I'll sooner warn the king," he cried, battling against the inevitable. "I'll tell him you put it to me and I'd have none of it!" It was a pleasure, even at such a moment, to see the sudden scare in the faces round the table. Only Stewart's and Graham's were unchanged.

"I thought," said Graham gravely, "that if there was one thing we could be sure of, it was that my lord of Athol would not play Scotland false."

Stewart knew his grandfather better and spoke to better purpose. "The king would not believe you," he said. "You'll have played that game once too often. King James knows now that you denounce and inform to help yourself, not him."

"Do you tell me," asked Athol, "that he'd rather trust you?"

"He would that," answered Stewart. "I'd have his ear first. I am his chamberlain."

"You seem very sure, my lad!" said Athol, weakly blustering. "Would you have me try it? I know the names." He looked round the circle, hoping to scare them again.

The young man shrugged his shoulders. "Try it, then," he said. "The most that the king'd do would be to take a little more care for a week or two, a month maybe. He'd not arrest a sheep-dog on your word." Athol tried to interrupt, but Stewart looked him between the eyes, quelling resistance. "We'd have him in the end," he said, "and then we'd have you too."

There was some stir at this, but Stewart was master of the smaller men. Only Graham voiced the uneasiness. "I did not think," he said, "that we should be needing to fall to threats. And against our own kin."

"Maybe we'll not," said Stewart, "when my lord remembers that he'll be king next month."

They had him in the end, between threats and promises. He said a little about the dangers, about the wisdom of leaving things as they were, but he knew, all the time, that he was helpless in their hands. Too much of their planning was rooted in his own, too many of their words tugged at his own desire. At the supreme turn of a life of scheming, he could find no trick to disengage himself from this net. Each time they spoke—Graham for Scotland and the Law, Stewart for ancestral claims, the Albany and Lennox men for vengeance—Athol could see strands of his own past cunning twisted into the cords that had drawn these men together, and now bound them to a common purpose.

As he listened, grasping the scope of their design, he began to wonder whether he indeed desired to escape them. It dawned on him that they might succeed: it dawned on him that—with such diverse forethought and resolution as was gathered round his table—it was almost impossible that they should fail. They had not looked far beyond their first task, that of murdering the king. Once that was accomplished, Athol would be their guide. They would need his counsel, and, if only to make Robert Stewart king, must put him first upon the throne. Old passions began to stir in him, old pleasure in a plot afoot.

It augured well that there was so much harmony among them. The Tintsmuir men—hardened cut-throats with ten years of homeless outlawry to avenge—were perhaps the most unruly. But when Graham rebuked one of them for saying that the Englishwoman should be despatched after her husband, Athol noticed that they accepted the rebuke without grumbling. All waited on Graham to fix the night for action.

"I'll be bringing the men down Glen Almond," he said, "and I could get them to Methven by the nineteenth, the Tuesday. They'll be hidden by his lordship's trees through the day, and the rest of you could meet us here by dusk. The thing could be done on the Wednesday night."

A week after Ash Wednesday, calculated the younger Hall. The Tintsmuir men said the moon would suit, the Chalmers brothers agreed that they could find a pretext for closing their shop without exciting suspicion. But when Thomas spoke the only word that hinted at possible miscarriage, Graham came down on him like thunder.

"We knew, months back," he said, "what it was we'd laid hand to. We are to rid this poor country of a tyrant; and there's little that has been done yet in Scotland without men that would risk the worst. There's a saying I have read of, about men that make a covenant with death."

Athol was glad now to be a partner with them, glad, at least, to see them working with such devotion towards an end that he had sought for sixty years. He would have preferred to be the leader from the first; his ancient cunning might have been a safer guide than Graham's smoky grandeur. Already he was seeing something they had maybe overlooked. He would nurse it till the moment came.

He should have seen far more that they overlooked, far more than that paltry detail. He should have looked a few weeks ahead, and seen Scotland aghast at what they were plotting so glibly under his roof. Athol, of all men, should have known that rumours are only rumours: that the fears of rebellion which had brought the queen to Melrose, James from Roxburgh, had little or nothing to justify them: that the great lords, though resentful at the king's unchartered aggression, were far from ripe for treason, very far from acclaiming his murderer in his stead. It would have been well for Athol if he had not blinded himself to these things.

It would have been well for all of them, for they were to meet again. Not in secret, but with thousands watching from the slopes above Edinburgh Grassmarket. Not in suspense, but helpless and hopeless, suffering every torture that a brutal age could devise. Graham would last longest—the red hair streaked with white, the grey eyes staring bloodshot to the unanswering sky—crying out that he could bear no more, and that, if he cursed God in his agony, he would bring his tormentors' souls to damnation as well as his own: and yet with his next breath he would be repeating that he had done nothing except free Scotland from a monster and a tyrant. Athol himself would long ago have denied his accomplices and begged mercy, though to no purpose: and before they had their will on him, they were going to crown his bald head, in mockery of Highland prophets, with a ring of red-hot steel.

He saw none of this. He saw only the crown of Scotland, and the little thing whose neglect might keep him from winning it. He was hugging the secret to himself now, watching the doomed men mutter to each other in Methven hall. When they rose from conclave, his moment had come. As they filed out, Graham and Robin leading, he contrived to pluck at the elbow of one of the Tintsmuir men.

"You're not forgetting the bairn?" he whispered. "There'll be many to say I'm no king while he's living. There's silver at Methven for the man that remembers the bairn."

February 20th 1437

III

"He'll see you the morn. He'll not see you at this hour of night."

Katharine the waiting-woman blocked the wicket-gate with her sturdy person. It almost looked as if the other woman, the wild creature on the swing-bridge outside, would refuse to accept dismissal and try to rush her way in. You could never tell with Highland folk.

"Were they giving him my message?" she asked, seeing no hope of entry. "Did they tell him that it was I who met him by the ferry and have walked round the waters of Forth, to see him again before it is too late?"

"It's too late tonight," said Katharine intolerantly. "And Sir Robert the chamberlain said that he'll have you whipped if we hear more of you before the morning."

She began to close the gate. She was in ill-temper, and for several reasons. It never improved her temper when she was parted from Joanna; the prior had made complaint and the king had had little James and his sisters sent away to Stirling, saying that the Court would follow soon. That was two days ago, but the Court showed no signs of moving south.

"Is it gaming they are?" said the woman outside. "Is it singing and harping? They'll not be singing tomorrow if you shut me out. And you'll be sorry for it yourself, my fine lass. You'll curse the hour you barred a door against me."

Katharine was already shooting the bolts. It was useless talking to some folk. Come to that, there was a deal too much talking in the world. It was always better for a body to do something, and be finished with it. She turned back and climbed the stairs towards the great room.

They had finished their games and music: they should never have started, in Katharine's opinion, with Lent a week old. Elizabeth was collecting the harps and chess-boards in her feckless, irritating fashion. The company were round the fire when Katharine entered, at the far end of the room. The king and queen were saying good-night to Orkney and Crichton and that dressed-up English popinjay. It was late, and the visitors would have a muddy walk up Black Friars' Wynd, and then, maybe, delay and trouble with the guard at the Town Gate. It'd be after midnight, Katharine reckoned, before some of them were in their lodgings and abed. She'd better help Elizabeth meanwhile, or the room would never be cleared up. She'd better blow out a few of the candles; there'd be no need now to have so many wasting themselves.

None of the lords slept in the Black Friars', not even Sir Robert Stewart, though he would be the last to go; it was his business, as chamberlain, to see that all the doors were properly barred for the night. He was handing round the cups now for the farewell drink—the *voidée* as the Court had learnt to call it since the Frenchmen's visit. It would not be long before the great room was empty.

She saw that the king was laughing over some joke with Orkney; he had laughed a good deal these last few days. Katharine, so far as she thought of the matter, had no great opinion of the king. He was a man, to begin with: he was a talkative body: he was always busy with his own notions, too busy to take proper notice of his children. If he must listen to an old dodderer's complaints and send them away, he should have sent the queen with them—and her ladies-in-waiting. The king was the king, of course, but Katharine despised her companions in service who were always goggling at the man.

Elizabeth was approaching him now, going to pick up a chessman that had rolled towards the fireplace. One could trust Elizabeth to notice anything like that, when it gave her an excuse for going near his Majesty. One could trust her, too, to knock against the standing fire-irons—as she was doing now—and send the tongs clattering. A young man beside the king stooped to pick them up, smiling at the clumsy girl. The king suddenly stopped laughing, gazing at the tongs in the young man's hand.

James was conscious of Katharine's eyes upon him, conscious of attracting general attention by breaking the merriment with his sudden silence. He felt a strong wave of that black depression that had dogged him of late, though company and music had made him forget it these many hours. It was not unmixed with fear, fear of something unseen and forgotten. He must trace it down immediately, he must remember. His mind raced up and down, like a hound seeking a scent. Then suddenly he discovered what had escaped him, and at the same time felt a sharp disappointment, knowing that the discovery increased rather than cured his uneasiness. His eyes rested, unseeing, on Elizabeth's hair, auburn in the candlelight, and on the young man who simpered at her, twisting the tongs in his hands.

"I had a dream last night," he said slowly. "I dreamt

I was fighting a snake—no, I think it was a kind of giant toad. And I had nothing to defend myself with except those fire-tongs."

"I had a dream too," began the young man, with sudden eagerness; James knew, irritably, that he was seizing an opportunity to recount to the king some experience at which half the Court had already yawned. "I dreamt," he said, "that your Majesty and the Graham were——"

James saw, from the tail of his eye, that Orkney had flicked the young fool into silence with a sudden gesture; he had an obscure feeling that he ought to cancel that order and hear the end of the story so greedily begun. But Orkney was already speaking himself. "Will your Majesty not tell us," he said, "how the combat ended? I trust that Sir King vanquished Sir Toad."

"That," said James slowly, "is what I cannot remember."

He looked round to see that Joan was already dismissing the company and preparing to retire. Even those immediately round him were breaking away to say their good-nights to her. It would be best, he decided, to be rid of them all quickly and follow Joan into her room as soon as the waiting-woman had finished untiring her for bed. He slipped his hand into Sir Robert Stewart's arm, and began walking him to the door.

"I shall make it part of my chamberlain's duties," he announced, in an effort to recapture the lost gaiety, "to expel all nightmares from the Black Friars' before I go to bed."

"Your Majesty," said Andrew Gray, following behind him, "your Majesty would sleep better if you did not sit up so late to write poetry. I hope the ballade you were telling us of is finished."

"The three stanzas were finished days ago," said James. "I haven't managed the *Envoi* yet, but I shan't sit up over that."

He said good-night to the company and watched Stewart shepherd them out of the room. When he turned back, it was to find the ladies already departed, and himself alone.

It was curious, he thought, the way that black mood had so suddenly swooped back upon him. It was not merely the remembering of the dream. It was something older, reaching farther back. It linked tonight, vaguely, with the days of his boyhood in England. Imprisonment, that was it. The shadow of his many prisons had lain too long upon his mind to be exorcised by his dozen years of freedom. Something about the Black Friars' had recalled unconscious memories of his cooped-up sufferings. He must think of quitting the place in a day or two, going to Edinburgh or Linlithgow. Meanwhile there was bed. He crossed the great hall, and went into the room where he changed clothes.

He was always ready long before the queen, having no maids to make ceremonies out of combs and the folding of petticoats. He would often come into her room before they were finished, in his nightgown and furred slippers, in order to chaff them while Katharine glowered her disapproval. Of all the king's unaccountable habits, this was the one that angered Katharine most.

He did not come in that night. When they had finished their work and emerged from the queen's room, they found him by the fire of the great room. He was leaning his forehead against the stone mantelshelf; he had shuffled off a slipper and was warming his foot over the dying embers. They curtseyed him a good-night, and Elizabeth presumed so far as to add a word or two, wishing him dreamless sleep. He frowned slightly at her, but replied gently, and then walked to the bedroom door, humming to himself.

Half-way there he stopped dead, listening. The girls, making for the main door, had halted on its threshold. For a long half-minute they stood motionless, ears and fancies strained, while unbroken silence held the great room. But there could be little doubt about the sounds outside.

They saw the king run suddenly to one of the barred

windows, and peer out, over the courtyard and its wall, over the snowy field beyond. He did not look long. A moment later, he was in among them, a hand on each doorpost, listening in silence down the dark well of the stairway outside. From below came the sound of a door swung open, the tread of heavy feet. They remembered that there was no other way out of the great room except to the bedrooms. As Elizabeth turned instinctively in their direction, she remembered, with growing fear, that there was no escape from the dead-end of those two rooms. She could not tell why the king was already rushing towards his, until she heard him crying from within to Sir Robert Stewart, crying for his missing sword.

A moment later she saw the queen appear, white-gowned and wraith-like, in the doorway. She heard her cry, "Bar the door, fools!" and turned back to see that the implied reproof was only half justified: Katharine was already swinging the massive timber into place.

The king was back in the room. He was running from window to window, wrenching at the bars. He was a strong man, but they had been socketed into the stone with molten lead, an unshakable barrier. He ran to the fireplace, snatched up the tongs, and began to lever up a plank in the middle of the floor. He had remembered the vault below, running from the privy to the courtyard wall, right beneath the breadth of the great room. The plank was giving; its nails creaked as they left their cross-beams. He would need to get up a second, perhaps a third, before he could get through.

Katharine, thrusting the door into position, noticed with a sudden leap of the heart that the great square bolt was missing: there was nothing with which to fasten it, nothing she could drive through the wide, empty staples. Already there were torches flaming up the stairs, dark shapes of men outlined against the glare—armed men with naked swords. She swung the door home, and thrust her arm through the staples.

The planks had yielded quickly. Joan was soon helping the king to lower himself into the evil-smelling darkness. As he leapt down, he remembered the opening that had looked out on his tennis-court, and remembered, also, that it was now blocked with mortared stones. He could just see a glint of snow through the tiny airholes that the workmen had left. Even so, if Joan and the girls had time to replace the planks and smooth the rushes over them, he might lie hid until help came. His enemies, whoever they were, were not likely to know of the vault. Nothing mattered except time. The vault was deeper than he had expected—or himself shorter. He could not reach up to help them replace the flooring. But he saw the gap close, heard the rushes rustled into place. The thunder of entering footsteps seemed almost simultaneous, but it passed over him, and no hand tore at the boards. They were making for the bedchamber, searching the great room. For the moment he was safe.

It was Katharine who had made the time, Katharine and Joan. The girl was young and strong. She could hold the weight of a man, two or three men perhaps, though her arm was cracking. But there were more than three, there were many: the door was coming open, if only by an inch or two. Joan turned to see it, to see a sword blade thrust through the crack, high up. As it came sliding down, she left her women, rushed forward to mask their work and distract attention. She saw the blade descend, and, instead of stopping at Katharine's arm, shear clean through it and grate upon the floor. The door flew open and the girl was hurled, maimed and bleeding, into the corner beside it. Only Joan stood between the murderers and the barely-concealed refuge.

She tried to grapple with them but one of the Tintsmuir men swung a sword at her side. Robin Graham caught his arm, crying shame on him. He broke the force of the blow, so that it bit into her, but not mortally. He put an arm round her, dragged her out of the room and half led, half pushed her down the stairs. Then he ran back to join the hunt, to see if the king had been found in the bedchambers.

It was useless for her to follow him back. There was only one hope now. Clutching her wound, she staggered to the wicket gate and out into the night. The plank-bridge had been swung back, but someone had filled the narrow moat with beams and hurdles. She crossed, splashing in a few inches of icy water. Beyond rose the walls of Perth, and, peering over them a single lighted window. She began to run across the snow.

Dark figures were converging upon her, springing up from every side. Highlandmen, and armed. They would catch her before she could run another yard. She stopped, swayed, and put all her strength into a cry for help, her eyes straining towards the lamp in the window. She shouted once, twice and again. Then the flat of a claymore-blade descended on her head and she fell unconscious.

They stood round her, puzzled. This was too old a woman to be Robin's lass, they said, the lass they had come to carry off. Maybe it was the mother. Let her lie there, she would recover her senses in a minute or two. They scattered to their posts.

Sir David Dunbar, sitting up late to read an old romance, heard a faint cry from outside the city. He peered out, extinguished the lamp that marred his vision into the dark, and then peered again. He saw dark figures moving on the snow-peppered fields. He saw torches racing and tossing in the Black Friars'. He snatched up his sword and ran down into the street.

It took him a little time to find the watch, and longer to rouse the sleepy guard at the Town Gate. But others, too, had seen that something was amiss outside: the general voice roused someone to find the key, throw open the gate to the considerable crowd that had gathered, weapons in hand. Perth was too near the Highlands for its citizens to sleep over-sound at night, or out of reach of their broadswords. They burst out, Dunbar leading. He soon outdistanced them. There seemed to be men in every field, but they were all making west, away from the city, and singly. Only on the Methven road could he come up with a numerous party, and he went for them unaided. He was the only man that night to strike a blow for King James. It was a good blow, though it cost him his left hand, maimed in retaliation by the sweep of a Highland claymore. He was hurled back on to the slush, and the murderers melted into darkness and the mountains. They were to scatter to many different refuges, but in none could they find a Scotsman willing to shelter or tolerate any that had had a hand in the plot to murder the king.

James had stood rigid in the darkness and the stink. He heard the thunder pass over his head, roll towards each of the smaller rooms, and then pass back again, seeking the door and the stairs. The Black Friars' was a labyrinth, and they would need to search. Silence fell, and he waited through minutes that seemed like long hours. He heard, as if muffled, the distant clock of St. Johnston's Kirk, striking a half-hour. He waited again, and then softly, disastrously, he began to call to Joan.

It was not Joan that answered him but her maid Elizabeth. Katharine was lying unconscious by the door, and the others were trying to staunch her wound, save her from bleeding to death. They hardly noticed what Elizabeth was doing. She was sweeping away the rushes, lifting first one loose board and then another. She craned down into the darkness. "They are gone," she said.

They were not gone. The two Halls were coming quietly up the stairs, were already on the threshold. They had seen all that they needed to see.

James had watched the gap reappear above him, looked up to the candlelight on the rafters of the great room. He saw the girl bending down to call to him in the darkness. The next moment she seemed to lurch forward and pitch down beside him upon the stone floor of the vault. A man stood where she had knelt, another behind him. They were leaping down now, with long knives in their hands.

He was too much for them, though they were two against one, armed against a defenceless man. In a minute or two they were lying where he had hurled them, Sir John stunned against the stone wall, his brother, half-strangled, under the king's feet. The lion was not going to die tamely. His assailants were not dead; they had a few months more in this world; but they would carry to the scaffold the marks where the king's hands had gripped them.

They had been the death of him none the less; his hands were so gashed and mangled, parrying their thrusts, that he could hardly hold the knife he had wrenched from them. Now there was another figure above him, standing where they had stood. He saw the glint of red hair as Graham peered down into the vault, peered at the prostrate girl, the two felled brothers, the king with bleeding palms. And Graham had a sword.

He stooped and swung himself down. There were others pressing into sight above, Robin and Chris and white-faced, miserable Thomas. James saw only the poised sword, heard only the hurrying beat of the wings of Death. He cried out for another minute's respite, for a priest to shrive his soul.

They wondered how he could think them so simple. In another minute the watch might be upon them, all Perth might be upon them. They could not imagine that his thoughts were not on Perth or Scotland or anything of this world's fashion. He was thinking of the Presence for which he was bound, and of certain things that might cloud his welcome. Of Murdoch on the Heading Hill, of old Lennox that was more fool than traitor, perhaps of Margaret, pining to death amid meaningless pomp. But even these were fading into insignificance as he reached out to the great splendour,—the light that had once shone in pin-points from his children's eyes, or glimmered distantly from Highland peaks. It was not distant now. The glory and the terror of it were rushing upon him with the speed of a single sword-stroke. Graham was no bungler.

They had brought Joan back to the great room, empty now of retreating enemies. She made them carry her to the dark gash in the floor, support her on the brink of the uptorn planks. She could see little beneath, with her head still swimming and the candles guttering in a hundred draughts. She could hear nothing except the sobbing of a frightened girl. "Jamie!" she called, "are you still there, Jamie?"

His body was still there, stretched stiff on that fetid floor. Already the calm was descending upon his features, the wisdom that seems to know all secrets, to have solved every riddle that still baffles the living. But the spirit that had earned wisdom was not there, nor the courage undaunted by riddles. The king that had led Scotland for twelve brief years in a leaderless century: the lawgiver, the warrior, the sweet singer: the lad that had seen her from a prison window and loved her for a lifetime: none of these was lying in the dark pit, nor would ever come again within the compass of her voice.

THE END

Postscript for Pedants

In the Author's note which precedes this book, it was stated that an attempt would be made to observe a certain rule about the major actions of the more important characters. In practice, I have found it impossible to write a novel without one large and several small infringements of this rule. I record them here for those interested in the authenticity of the story.

The large lapse is in Chapter Five. The whole story of Joan's projected betrothal to the Earl of Warwick is fictitious. Warwick was a widower and remarried a year later. But there is no record of any *rapprochement* with the Beauforts.

The Document empowering Alice Butler to smack King Henry VI is historical (and extant), but I have antedated its signature in Council by about a year.

I have also ventured to place James's letters (p. 67) in the less probable of two possible Januaries (see Balfour-Melville in *Scot. Hist. Rev.* 1922).

Somerset was not Somerset in the summer of 1416: the title was held by an elder brother, who did not die till the following winter, and is only used here to save a possible confusion in the reader's mind. On the other hand, his aunt did hold the twin manors of Woking and Sutton, and did pay a clove-gilliflower to the king as her rent.

Graham was betrothed to the lady who subsequently married his brother, but it was his second brother, not (as here implied) the Earl of Strathearn.

For James's Highland campaign, there are no details known: the chronicles say that Alasdair Macdonald sacked Inverness, met James "on a certain moor in Lochaber," and was there deserted by Clan Chattan and Clan Cameron, and completely routed. All else is guesswork, based on a walking-knowledge of the terrain. (I have very rarely presumed to write of any places in England, Scotland or France that I have not visited myself.)

There is a contemporary witness for the Highland woman who came to the ferry and the Black Friars' to warn James of his danger—and even for her "familiar" Huthart—but her previous meeting with him in the forest of Moy is quite imaginary. The other warnings, including the dream about the toad and the tongs, are mentioned in a contemporary pamphlet.

The rather surprising account of the Perth Parliament (pp. 509-517) is an attempt to reconcile the same pamphlet with the narrative of Hector Boece a hundred years later.

Those who have argued against James's authorship of *The King's Quair* seem to me to have conclusively refuted each other without seriously shaking the orthodox view. Some of the linguistic arguments, especially, are models of self-defeating ingenuity. I have therefore assumed that James wrote this exceedingly beautiful poem, beginning to give it its present shape (for such long works grow slowly) in the year 1423. I see no reason to accept the note scribbled, in a different hand, on the cover of a later MS. as evidence that he finished it while still in England.

The quotation on p. 169 is my own pastiche. That on p. 170 is from *The Seige of Rone*, by John Page, archer in Leche's company.

I hope modernists will not quarrel with my spelling of proper names. The fifteenth century took wide licence in such matters, and I have sometimes followed its lead—generally for a reason. "Athol," for instance, is spelt with one "l" in order to make it clear that the Earldom held by the "old serpent" (as Bower calls him) has no connection with the modern Dukedom of Atholl.

Apart from these matters, I have attempted to draw the most probable deductions from the State Papers and chronicles of the fifteenth and early sixteenth centuries. I have tried to harmonize these with the many interesting traditions that James has left behind him among the Scottish people. The method will enrage professional historians, to whom probability and tradition are inadmissible; they will no doubt be able to take their revenge by detecting me in demonstrable error. I can only say that the error is unconscious, and committed in spite of considerable labour among meagre and often contradictory sources. My task was greatly lightened, half-way through, by the publication of Mr. Balfour-Melville's erudite *James I, King of Scots*; and I have been saved from many mistakes by the careful revision of Mr. P. J. W. Kilpatrick of the University Press, Edinburgh.

One other apology seems due. In spite of a Welsh-sounding name, I am an Englishman and a great admirer of the English race. But it has proved impossible to write truthfully about the early fifteenth century, from a Franco-Scottish point of view, without exposing some extremely damaging flaws in the old tradition of English excellence and honesty. I can only say that I am as puzzled as anyone can be at the spectacle of the most kindly and trustworthy of peoples committing so many of those acts of cruelty and bad faith which generally disfigure the relations of a strong nation with weaker neighbours. I can see no solution of the implied problem, and do not think it is likely to be solved until the day of judgment, when moral problems (one imagines) will not be argued in terms of race.